The Original Fire and New Flames

History of the Catholic Church in Orissa: 1850-1922

The Original Fire and New Flames

History of the Catholic Church in Orissa: 1850-1922

Jesuraj Rayappan, SVD

ISPCK

2018

The Original Fire and New Flames *History of the Catholic Church in Orissa: 1850-1922* — Published by the Rev. Dr. Ashish Amos of the Indian Society for Promoting Christian Knowledge (ISPCK), Post Box 1585, 1654, Madarsa Road, Kashmere Gate, Delhi-110006.

Online Order: http://ispck.org.in/book.php

Also available on amazon.in

ISBN: 978-81-8465-669-5

Laser typeset by

ISPCK, Post Box 1585, 1654, Madarsa Road, Kashmere Gate, Delhi-110006
• *Tel:* 23866323/22

e-mail: ashish@ispck.org.in • ella@ispck.org.in
website: www.ispck.org.in

Dedicated
to
My parents

Mr. Manuel Rayappan
and
Mrs. Cecily Rayappan

For guiding me to

Appreciate and

Learn from History

Contents

Acknowledgements

It is my pleasure and duty to express gratitude to Professor **Rev. Fr. Jesús Lopéz-Gay, SJ** who took personal interest in directing this dissertation. My sincere thanks are due to the Professors of the faculty of Ecclesiastical History of the Pontifical Gregorian University, Rome.

I am indebted to many others who helped me in one way or the other to complete this thesis.

My special thanks go to Prof. Dr. John J. Paul, Department of Social Sciences, The Leadership College, Fitchburg, for the valuable suggestions and his readiness to accompany me during my research. I am indebted to Mr. Jeevan Nair, senior journalist and editor for going through the text and offering some valuable suggestions.

Sincere thanks are due to my confreres, in Rome and in India, for their friendship and support that I availed throughout my stay in Rome. My special thanks go to Fr. Josef Alt SVD, the former official historian of SVD who helped me during my licentiate and doctoral studies.

To my parents Late Mr. Manuel Rayappan and Mrs. Cecily Rayappan for instilling in me a sense of discipline and love for poor, I am ever grateful. To my brothers Mr. R. Antonyraj, Fr. R. M. Jeyaseelan, SVD and Mr. R. Singarayan and my sisters Mrs. Arockiamary and Mrs. Alphonsa, whose constant encouragement and prayers accompanied throughout my stay in Rome and my service in Odisha, I owe my gratitude and appreciation.

The list of well-wishers will be long if I am to mention all of them. Finally, I would like to thank my provincials and the confreres who granted me the opportunity to pursue my studies and carry out this project.

List of Abbreviations

AA	Analecta Augustiniana
ASS	Acta Sanctae Sedia
AMSFS	Archives of the Missionaries of St. Francis de Sales
APBS	Archivum Provincae Belgicae Septentrionalis
APF	Archivum Congregationis de Propaganda Fide
ARSI	Archivum Romanum Societatis Iesu
BM	Bibliotheca Missionum
Cf.	Confer
Civ. Catt	La Civiltà Cattolica
CM	The Clergy Monthly
DIP	Dizionario degli Istituti di Perfezione
Ed./eds	Editor/Editors
GEL	Gossner Evangelical Lutherans
IMR	Indian Missiological Review
NZM	Neue Zeitschrift fur Missionswissenschaft
IES	Indian Ecclesiastical Studies
ICHR	Indian Church History Review

LMC	Les Missions Catholiques
MB	Missions Belges de la Compangnie de Jesus
PUU	Pontificia Università Urbaniana
Rs.	Rupees
VJTR	Vidya Jyoti Journal of Theology
ZMRW	Zeitschrift fur Missionswissenschaft (und Religonswissenschaft)

Glossary

Avatar	An incarnation of Vishnu.
Bandi	Bullock cart (Telugu word).
Begari	Voluntary commutation of services.
Bethbegari	Compulsory labor without payment, which the tenants render to the landlords or Zamindars.
Bhoji (bodji)	A general dinner to mark a completion of an event in which all those present and invited will take part.
Bhuinar	An Oraon term for the original settlers.
Bhuinari Survey	The register of all Bhuinary lands.
Bissoyees	Hill chiefs (among the Kondhs)
Bonga	A Munadri term for a spirit.
Chaprasi	An orderly or messenger. A church leader in the village, who conducts prayers and arranges for the visit of the missionary.
Chowkidar	A night watchman, the lowest-grade in the British Indian police.
Chundi	Tuft of hair worn at the crown of the head.

Collector	The administrative head of a district in Regulation Provinces, corresponding to the Deputy-Commissioner in non-regulation areas.
Dal	A generic term applied to various pulses.
Daroga	A police officer or the title of officials in various departments, especially in police and jail departments.
Dewan (Diwan)	The chief executive officer, next to the ruler in a feudatory state or semi-independent state. A vizier or other First Minister to an Indian Chief or feudal Rajas. He is generally a representative of the British Government.
Dhan	Paddy, or rice with husks.
Dhan Gola	Paddy Store.
Dharam	A variant term of a Sanskrit word Dharm or Dharma, means religion.
Diku	Literally, a foreigner; term used by the Mundas for the men who came from elsewhere as landlords. The pejorative association of the term is looter, deceiver, exploiter and troublemaker who is responsible for their present wretched condition.
Djani	Priest
Farmen (firman)	An imperial (Mughal) order or grant.
Guru	A Hindu religious preceptor. In some areas it could refer to a schoolmaster.
Hanria	Local rice-beer in Chotanagpur.
Ind	A Hindu festival imitated in some villages by the Mundas (tribes) and consisting essentially in a sacrifice followed by dancing that might continue throughout the night.
Jagir	Revenue Freeland or village in lieu of payment for service. A lease granted by the chief of Chota Nagpur to his foreign agents for services rendered.

Jagirdars — Holder of service tenure. Later they considered themselves landlords.

Kalu — liquor produced from Palmyra trees

Karnam — A village accountant.

Khuntkatti — Pertaining to the original settlers of a village. A Munda term used in conjunction with others as in the next two words.

Khuntkattidar — A descendant of the original settler.

Khuntkattihatu — A village of the original settler.

Mahato — The civil head in an Oraon village.

Mahua or Mohul — A tree, *Bassia latifolia*, producing flowers used (when tried) as food or for distilling liquor, and seeds furnish oil.

Manki — The head of a group of Munda villages.

Mardum Sumari — A yearly account of the progress of the mission that every missionary had to render the superior in August.

Munda — The civil head of a Munda village; any one of the Munda tribe.

Mutha — A group of villages.

Padhan — A village headman; a class of proprietary tenure-holders or sub-proprietors.

Pahan — The religious head of a Munda village. Formerly he was also a civil head.

Pakhal — Boiled rice soaked in cold water.

Panchayat — A village council of elders. Literally, council of five; the managing committee a village Cooperative society.

Pargana — Region, a fiscal unit of administration.

Parha (Patti) — A group of villages. Both terms used for the confederation of villages by the Mundas and the Oraons.

Parja	The tenants in a traditional Munda village.
Patro	An officer equivalent to Dewan or Manager of any state.
Puja	An Offering, Worship or a Sacrifice (bloody) to the gods.
Raja	Literally, King, but in Chota Nagpur it is also used for the chief of chiefs who did not receive the honors of kingship nor special property rights.
Rayat (Ryot)	A tenant, farmer or peasant. Sometimes he also called *Ganju* or *Ganjhu*.
Sal	A useful timber tree in Northern India, *Shorea robusta*.
Sanad	Firman, a grant, a written order signed and sealed by a king or Government.
Sardar	A leader. Term used of the leaders of the Sardar Movement and later for those who took part in the movement.
Sarna	A plot of land kept aside for the spirits by the Mundas. Hence called the sacred grove for the spirits to dwell in. There they offer the sacrifices, in return the spirits are believed to protect their territory from any harm. Among the Oraons it was called *Jaher*. This term also refers to the religion of the tribals of Chotanagpur.
Thana	A police station, and hence the circle attached to it.
Thika	A lease in payment for goods.
Thikadar	A holder of the lease. Later acted as proprietor and claimed the land.
Zamindar	a landlord; proprietor of land directly responsible to the Government for payment of rent. Originally a revenue collector; the British regarded him as a landlord or a landholder; hence term was used for landlord.

Introduction

The eastern state of Orissa has always had an important place in India's history. It is a land known for its glorious past, particularly its religious and cultural heritage. It is the land where Emperor Ashoka renounced bloodshed and embraced Buddhism, which converted him from 'Ashoka the Terrible' to 'Ashoka the Merciful'. It was here that Mahatma Gandhi is said to have taken his vow of poverty. Orissa is also a land ravaged by frequent famine, starvation, illiteracy and abject poverty.[1] To this land of apparent contradictions came the Christian missionaries to teach the love of God and fraternity.

The Christian missionaries in Orissa launched their arduous drive to Christianise a territory that proved to be fatal to the newcomers, particularly Europeans.[2] Their activities began following the Goomsur rebellion,[3] when British troops went on an expedition to quell the rebellion, where they found the horrendous *Meriah* sacrifices and female infanticide prevalent among the Kondhs. As a rehabilitative measure, the British government sought the missionaries' help in protecting and educating the freed *Meriahs*. The Baptist missionaries responded immediately with the establishment of orphanages for orphans and *Meriahs*.[4] The Missionaries of St. Francis de Sales[5] sought a mission where the Europeans were little known and caste practices less in vigour. They found the place of their desire in Ganjam, particularly in the Kondh mountains.

After the first response of the Panos at Montacallau in 1853, the Catholic missionaries began with the conversion of 'native' people. From then onwards, the Church that appeared to be an elite body or that belong to the Europeans, Goans and *Madrasis* or people from the South, became a Church of poor Dalits and Tribals.

Songs and catch phrases in honour of the missionaries still echo in the jungles of Chotanagpur and in the Kondh mountains: *Chote-mote Hoffmann duniya karal sin injot re: Chote-mote Hoffmann sahib* (Dear humble Hoffmann sahib brought light into our world, dear humble Hoffmann sahib),[6] and *Pitile Pito, Marile Maro,* (strike us if you wish, beat us if you wish).[7] These phrases expressed the confidence and willingness of the locals to submit to the guidance of the missionary, even if it meant receiving any punishment he might give in the process. This was indeed a great step for the people, who lived in freedom and in seclusion. Once they accepted the terms both the parties kept their word (e.g., the missionaries provided protection and help, and the people accepted baptism). However, the Hindu literati and the people who subjugated the tribals and dalits in India for centuries, view the work of the missionaries with suspicion and contempt.

Catholics in Orissa are greatly indebted to the French Fransalians and the Flemish Jesuits for their untiring zeal in establishing the kingdom of God in the remotest corners of Orissa. Ignored for centuries by their Hindu neighbours and even by the British administration, the dalits and tribals lived a life of contentment and happiness, though in ignorance and illiteracy.

Living in the inaccessible mountains, hence deprived of basic amenities, the Kondhs and Panos believed that their well-being depended on the goodwill of the spirits. Nature and the spirits, both malignant and benevolent, controlled their rhythm of life; their aim was to live in peace with everyone and to experience prosperity. Since the spirits and gods controlled their world, they believed that they had to offer sacrifices in order to appease them when they were angry. They did this in spite of their abject poverty and frequent misery.

One hundred years ago the inhabitants of Chotanagpur, that is, the Mundas, Oraons and Kharias, were abhorred by their wealthy Hindu neighbours. Adding insult to injury, their powerful neighbours often snatched away the little property that they had. They were degraded to slavery and forced to work in the fields of the landlords. They were oppressed and alienated, as their land gradually drifted into the hands of usurious zamindars. They were reduced to the status of 'non-people'. They were despised and cried out to God, their only hope. Their mourning was turned into joy with the arrival of a Flemish Jesuit, Fr. Constant Lievens, S.J. (1856-1893), in 1885.

In spite of a shortage of personnel and resources, Fr. Lievens, the great apostle of Chotanagpur, had an ambitious plan when he set out to work for liberation of the aborigines. Countless people waited at his *dera* or hut to obtain his *darshan* or vision and to get a chance to meet him to present their case, which probably encouraged Fr. Lievens to draft a plan and light a fire that would go on blazing. Given the difficulties of providing personnel and resources, the idea to spread south until they met the French MSFS who were heading towards the north, appeared to be unrealistic at the time. His dream of developing a community of active and vibrant Christians in all these territories seemed impractical.[8]

Under his leadership the Flemish Jesuits 'lit the fire' in Chotanagpur, which blazed initially in the present Jharkhand state but later spread to the neighbouring states like a wildfire. The growth of the mission was so quick that the Belgian Province of the Society of Jesus could not provide personnel for the growing requests. At present the Catholic population of Rourkela Diocese alone counts 215,329 that constitutes 10.41 percent of its total population of 1,624,000.[9]

Nomenclature

"History of the Catholic Church in Orissa: 1850– 1922" is an attempt to study the spread of Catholicism in Orissa. Begun in the middle of the nineteenth century, Catholicism made inroads in the mountains where fever and poverty reigned supreme. Therefore, the study attempts to investigate some of the important issues such as the work of the missionaries and their methods. Hence, a clarification of some of the terms is in order.

Orissa: Though the word 'Orissa' is used generically to indicate the present eastern state of India, which is now called Odisha, 19th century Orissa was geographically limited – the tract extending from Chilika Lake to the Subarnarekha river, which administratively equalled the present civil districts of Cuttack, Puri and Balasore. The unity of Orissa was realised only in 1936, when various Oriya-speaking tracts were added to the original territory. The present area became the state of Orissa in 1949.

This study is done in the hope of tracing the origins of the Catholic Church in this area. This would place the present Church in the right perspective and draw inspiration from the dedication of the missionaries and laity in establishing God's kingdom in Orissa.

Catholic Church: An inter-denominational approach perhaps would have been more appropriate for fostering the unity that has begun to develop after the recent religious persecutions that claimed the lives of a few Christian missionaries in Orissa. However, considering the vastness of the topic, the study limits itself to the Catholic Church (Roman).

This study seeks to find the general direction that the history of the Catholic Church in Orissa took in the second part of the nineteenth and the early twentieth centuries, when the MSFS and the Jesuits brought the gospel to the people of lower origin. In order to highlight the 'turns' and 'bends' that this history took, the thematic presentation focuses on some leading persons who guided the course of action. Such a study is necessary for the understating of the Church, particularly when it attempts to liberate the people.

Reasons and Results

The portrait of Fr. Jean Marie Dupont, MSFS (1816-1887) is printed on the cover page of the controversial work of Arun Shourie, *Christian Missionaries in India* with a crucifix in hand and surrounded by a few children, obviously from the orphanage of Surada. This work presented the missionaries as aggressors, as collaborators of the British colonial regime, as people with vested interests in continuing the British Raj in India, and as perpetrators of violence against the culture and religions of the native population. More questions were raised on the picture than on the content of the book. This motivated me to find out to what extent Fr. Dupont, or for that matter all Christian missionaries, went beyond the limits in their effort to establish the kingdom of God among the Panos, Kondhs, Oraons, Kharias and Mundas.

Two important considerations guided me in the choice of this topic: Firstly, until now the history of the Catholic Church has never been the subject of any scientific investigation. Secondly, in what way were the European missionaries, who left everything to follow the Lord and assumed India as their second home, manipulators of the ignorance and poverty of the people and opportunists of British colonialism? Thus, I consider it appropriate for me to investigate the history of a territory where I am assigned as a missionary.

The present study is an attempt to describe the History of the Catholic Church in Orissa. The missionaries who started the Church were not aware of today's missiological developments. Rather, they responded to the suffering of the people. In fact, they too suffered with them by sharing their condition in the remotest places. The missionaries proclaimed God's message in a tangible way, in a way that the poor, illiterate people could understand and follow. In this, the two religious congregations (MSFS and Jesuits) left an indelible mark on the mission they served. It was not just their spontaneous and immediate response to the dehumanising conditions of the dalits and tribals that brought the people close to them and to the Catholic Church. It was also their presence and their willingness to contribute to the overall development of the people, which sprang from the charisma of their religious institutes that brought tens of thousands to the flock of Christ.

Methodology

In an effort to make the study intelligible and scientific, the method followed is chronological, thematic and analytical. Care has been taken to exclude all unnecessary details, which would deviate the reader from the flow of thought. The exposition of the work is almost totally based on archival sources, namely, the correspondence of contemporary missionaries, the reports of the vicars apostolic, bishops and religious superiors of the mission. The footnotes will supplement the basic facts with explanations and sometimes the content of the original documents when considered important. Secondary sources were consulted only in the absence of primary sources. Published sources are used when considered necessary and authoritative.

However, this study as the title might suggest is not the mere conglomeration of chronicles that describes the activities of the missionaries. Its focal point is to situate the mission in its historical perspective and to analyse and evaluate the work of the missionaries, particularly the trends operative in bringing the people to the knowledge of truth. The study is undertaken with the fond hope that, in revealing the light and shadows of the missionaries' activities, it will reinvigorate the Church in Orissa, which is still in its infancy, and which often falls victim to calumnious attacks of religious fanatics.

Why investigate two religious congregations with missionaries representing different nations, different peoples, and different languages? Beyond their differences was a unity of approach and dedication. The missionaries' proverbial availability and readiness to undertake even hazardous journeys to help the people were motivating factors in recognising the patterns in evangelisation in both missions.

The well-ordered Jesuit Archives (ARSI) in Rome and the Provincial Archives of the Belgian Jesuits (APBS) in Heverlée, Belgium, made the work easy for consultation. However, the other important archives, viz., the General Archives of the Missionaries of St. François de Sales, Annecy (AMSFS) and the Archives of the *Propaganda Fide* (APF) presented problems. Some of the sources in the APF, particularly between 1919 and 1922, are not available due to technical difficulties – they were not bound. Although the MSFS archives claim to follow a loose classification, the researcher is led to confusion when a document is not found in its proper place. This is primarily due to the fact that not every document is classified. Hence, there exists the possibility of misplacing it any time it is taken for consultation. Some of the letters of the missionaries who were economical by using tracing-paper on both sides or by writing both horizontally and vertically, are fragmented or have gaping holes in them. This made it difficult to decipher the message of the document. Therefore, one has no choice but to have recourse to Maurice Domenge's *La Mission du Vizagapatam* and Jean Rey's *Les Missionnaires de Saint François de Sales d'Annecy*. It is unfortunate that the Archives of the Province of Visakhapatnam do not conserve any of the documents relating to the mission in question, nor do the Diocesan (now Archdiocesan) Archives of Visakhapatnam.

Limits of the Study

Due to the vastness of the territory and the involvement of two religious congregations, both the territory and the period of study had to be limited.

Territory: The study restricts itself to the founding of the first stations in Ganjam and Gangpur missions. Even though Balasore is part of Orissa, the study does not include the territory for two reasons: (1) an extensive territory would not do justice to the topic; and (2) although established in 1865, Balasore remained stagnant and missionary activities were limited to orphanages and schools.

The establishment of the Catholic Church among the *Savaras* in southern Orissa and *Kisans* in western Orissa, two leading tribal communities, has been excluded from this study by reason of their numbers, i.e., they are negligible.

Period: It was about the year 1850 when two veteran Fransalian missionaries set out to explore the possibilities of starting the mission in the Kondh mountains (Ganjam District). Since they found a favourable situation, the mission was begun. In 1922, the Ganjam mission was finally handed over to the Vincentians (Congregation of the Mission). Though the Gangpur mission began at a later period, i.e., 1891, the Jesuit mission reached its zenith in 1922, when Gaibira was established as a new parish, the third one in Gangpur.

This study to a large extent represents the missionary perspective, which could sometimes be apologetic and absolutist. Seldom did the missionaries highlight the defects of the mission and the missionaries, except when it was obvious and required immediate action. Therefore, the perspective of the history is seen mostly from the missionary point of view and not from the perspective of the laity, which would have helped to verify or contest the claims of the missionaries. In the absence of documentary evidence, no consideration could be given to the viewpoint of the laity.

Although serious effort was made to consult all the documents available for the period embraced by the study, one cannot rule out the possibility that certain documents escaped the attention of the investigator.

Subject Matter

The work is divided into five chapters with two parts in each chapter: the first part dealing with the Ganjam mission and the second with the Gangpur mission. Though the two missions do not coincide in their foundation – Ganjam was founded in 1850 and Gangpur in 1891, an attempt is made to group them under various themes.[10]

The **first chapter** seeks to elucidate certain historical and cultural factors that propose a background to this paper. A true comprehension of the dalit and tribal problems lies in their historical background, which contains inseparable realities of their socio-economic, socio-political and religious systems. Without this it is impossible to understand their unwillingness to depart from even an unproductive plot of land and from inaccessible mountains infested by malaria and far from all basic amenities. The missionaries (MSFS) themselves had neither prior experience in mission work nor any specific knowledge about the people and their culture.

The **second chapter** inquires into the mass conversion and analyses the charisma and work of some of the leading personalities of the mission. The general history of the Catholic Church in India provides the setting, which will be developed with the founding of the mission in Visakhapatnam and Ranchi. Even though establishing a link between the church in the Portuguese settlements in Orissa and the nineteenth-century mission is probably impossible, the establishment of different centres at some of the commercial stations is considered in order to show that Catholicism is not new to the people of Orissa.

Some of the dominant features of nineteenth-century Catholicism in India are also discussed. In taking over the Visakhapatnam mission the MSFS inherited three stations (Ganjam, Berhampur and Cuttack) that were founded by the Jesuits and later visited by the Theatines. Fr. Constant Lievens lit the fire that spread to and even went beyond the neighbouring states. The conversion *en masse* appeared like a revolution, when some of the neophytes refused to do *bethbegari*, forced labour and to pay the excessive tax. The missionaries considered it a 'crisis'.

The **third chapter** proposes a study on the difficulties and hardships of missionaries and their efforts to establish mission stations at Surada, Koussipanga (Ganjam) and Kesramal (Gangpur). The quest to move to interior places brought them to Surada, where the MSFS established their first station. The plans to christianise Surada and its vicinity were often frustrated. Initial struggles and fear paved the way to the founding of centres in Montacallau and Koussipanga. Efforts to expand in the vicinity are considered. The missionaries did their best to obtain a strong foothold in the Kondh mountains, i.e., in Koussipanga. In spite of their efforts, the response of the people was not satisfactory. The missionaries used all the resources they had and all the methods they knew, but the result was far from being satisfactory. However, the Great Famine of Orissa in 1866 provided an opportunity to exhibit their Christian charity and forced them to remain in Orissa.

In western Orissa, the mission encountered a different obstacle. The 'crisis'[11] was not limited to the civil boundary of Chotanagpur but went beyond it to inflame Gangpur. But from the beginning the mission experienced strong resistance from the feudatory chief of Gangpur. Further, the movement was controlled by the consolidation policy of Msgr. Goethals, the Archbishop of Calcutta. But the dedicated and persistent missionaries persevered until there was a change of heart.

The **fourth chapter** looks into the spread of Christianity and the foundation of some mission stations. Having strengthened Surada, the first station in Ganjam, the missionaries directed their attention to *extra muros*. They began to accept new requests and improve the existing mission. Msgr. Zaleski, the Apostolic Delegate in India, once told Msgr. Clerc, Bishop of Visakhapatnam: "If you are able to obtain the resources and men of which you are in need, your Kondh mission would become in time a small Chotanagpur (prospering mission of the Jesuits of Ranchi)."[12] They brought in new personnel with the intention of extending the existing stations and establishing new ones where it was suitable. Though there were variations in their approaches, they were unified under the Superior of the mission. With the ever-increasing number of requests and village deputations, the missionaries had no choice but to move into the frontier to spearhead a movement of grace. How could a single mission station, situated more or less at the centre of the state, cater to the pastoral needs of about 22,252 (1914) Christians spread in an area of 2,492 square miles? The establishment of Hamirpur in Eastern Gangpur and Gaibira in Western Gangpur is considered.

The **fifth chapter** investigates the missionary methods of the MSFS and the Jesuits, in order to discover the lineaments and the trends of the Catholic mission. Though the traditional missionary methods (schools, hospitals, development projects, etc.) were used, they were adapted to the local needs. Since the stations were far away from the centres of the mission (Visakhapatnam and Calcutta), the missionaries were sometimes deprived of basic amenities. In some cases, the mission stations in Orissa were considered to be a cursed land or a place of punishment. An attempt is also made to evaluate the outlook of the missionaries and their impact on the people. Thus, by presenting the merits and shadows of the missionaries one can get a rather clear picture, wherefrom one can draw conclusions for the future.

In the evaluation and general conclusion, issues are identified which have an impact on the present Catholic Church in Orissa. It is hoped that a return to the original spirit of the Catholic Church in Orissa would not only help the people to identify with their humble origins but would also invite today's Christians (both ordained and laity) to rededicate themselves to the service of the people.

Endnotes

[1] J. RAMANATHAN, "Orissa Background", in S.V. ALBERT (ed.), *Orissa: Church and People Groups*, Madras 1992, p. 13.

[2] Here are some of the denominations that established their stations in Orissa in the 19th century: The Particular Baptists, the General Baptists, the American Freewill Baptists, the Evangelical Missionary Society and the Roman Catholic Church. Cf. D. SWARO, *The Christian Missionaries in Orissa. Their Impact on Nineteenth Century Society*, Calcutta 1990, p. 1.

[3] Unable to pay the arrears to the British by 1836, the Zamindar of Goomsur went into hiding in the Kondh mountains, where the Kondh chiefs gave him hospitality and protection.

[4] During the organised suppression of the *Meriah* sacrifice, government officers rescued many boy and girl victims from death. These children were placed in the care of the Orissa Baptist mission (part of the General Baptist Missionary Society) in its 'orphan asylums' in Berhampur and Cuttack. Cf. B.M. BOAL, "The Church in the Kond Hills", in VICTOR E. W. HAYWARD (ed.), *An Encounter with Animism in the Church as Christian Community. Three Studies of North Indian Churches*, London 1966, p. 268; Neyret to Mermier, Visakhapatnam, September 6, 1850, in *Lettres des Missionnaires 1845 – 1857*, AMSFS 7Z/5H5; The stations established by the General Baptist Missions in the Oriya-speaking area of Madras Presidency were Berhampur (1836), Ganjam (1840), Padri-Palli, Russellkonda (1861) and Aska (1899). Cf. D. SWARO, *The Christian Missionaries in Orissa*, p. 2.

[5] Missionaries of St. Francis de Sales (MSFS) are also called 'Fransalians' in India. Both MSFS and Fransalians are used in this study.

[6] C. BECK, "Three Great Missionaries of Chotanagpur", in C. SRAMBICAL (ed.), *Lead me to Light. Divine Word Missionaries 1875-1975*, (1975), p. 94.

[7] F. MOGET, *Early Days of the Visakhapatnam Mission 1846 – 1920*, Bangalore 1997, p. 251.

[8] Fr. Lievens' plan was to bring together "all the aboriginal tribes of Chotanagpur, then penetrate into the independent states of Sirguja, Jashpur, Udaipur, Raigarh, Gangpur and Bonai and convert all the aboriginals in these states, making one vast Christianity of them all. This would bring us to the extreme boundary of our mission, but the plan of Father Lievens did not stop there. There our Belgian mission would link up with the mission of Central India, entrusted to the French

Salesian fathers (MSFS), who would take up the work with the aboriginals beyond our borders, and the combined efforts of the two set of workers would form all the aboriginal tribes of this part of India, to the number of several millions, into one vast and compact Christianity. This was not an idle dream; this was the set of plan of Father Lievens and of his great chief, Fr. Grosjean, the superior of the Bengal mission in India." VAN DER SCHUEREN, *The Belgian Mission of Bengal*, vol. I, Calcutta 1922, p. 22.

[9] Rourkela Diocese (Orissa, India) consists of the former feudal states of Gangpur and Bonai. But most of the Christians are from the former Gangpur State. Cf. *Annuario Pontificio per l'anno 2002*, Libreria Editrice Vaticana, Città del Vaticano 2002, p. 509.

[10] The years 1850 and 1891 refer to the time when the missionaries established contact with the people and when the latter began to receive baptism.

[11] The mass movement in Chotanagpur was seen as a revolution and the missionaries were blamed for the state of affairs, particularly when the Christians refused to pay excessive taxes and to render other services to the zamindars and others, whom the tribals served. The Christians' self-assertion and refusal to do *bethbegari*, forced labour, irritated the zamindars and others.

[12] JEAN REY, *Les Missionnaires de Saint-François de Sales d'Annecy*, SIPE, Thonon-les-Bains 1956, p. 439.

Chapter - 1

Socio-Historical Background

In order to get a clear perspective on the topic under discussion one has to understand and analyse the context in which the said topic is to be studied. This is imperative for any critical analysis of the past, because it helps to sift the evidence from any form of prejudice to which the writer might have been exposed. An objective background would help in the appreciation of the problems that surround the area and the people who live there. An analysis of historical, religious, socio-cultural, economical and political aspects would help us to comprehend a reality that might even seem incredible to any contemporary person. In order to understand the political background of 19th century Orissa, a scanty historical sketch is provided not to glorify its historical, cultural and spiritual heritage but to grasp the development of the state. This in turn helps us to understand the background of the dispersed people, the focal point of our study. Besides explaining the geographical setting, an attempt is made to clarify the terms and usages that are special to the people in the region.

In order to achieve this goal, the chapter is divided into three sections. Section I deals with the common topography and history of Orissa. Section II deals with the history of Southern Orissa, especially Ganjam District, where the Kondh Hill Tracts are situated. This section also discusses the social, political, economical and religious aspects of Kondhs and Panos, who responded positively to the force of grace. Section III gives the historical sketch of Western Orissa, which centres upon the erstwhile Gangpur state, and analyses the social, political, economic and religious aspects of Chotanagpur tribals: the Mundas, the Oraons and the Kharias.

1. Orissa in General

Orissa, as a region, is ancient and rich in spiritual and cultural heritage. The word 'Orissa' derives probably from a Greek word *Oretes*, the Sanskrit equivalent of which may be *Odras* or *Odràshtra* or land of the *Ods* or *Uriyas*.[1] The term refers to rice, which has been the main crop and staple food of the country; hence, it could mean either the rice-eating or the rice-growing people.[2] Orissa today consists of parts of three ancient regions: Kalinga, Utkal or Odra and Kosala, which under political and economic pressure in the course of the centuries joined together in the 12th century A.D. to form Oriya society as a distinct entity in India. Of all the regions, Kalinga was best known and more advanced in all respects.[3]

Topography

Orissa is situated between 17°49'N. and 22°34'N. latitude and between 81°29'E. and 87°29'E. longitude. It has an area of about 155,707 sq. km., according to the census of 1981. It is bounded by the states of Bengal on the northeast, Bihar on the north, Madhya Pradesh on the west, Andhra Pradesh on the south and the Bay of Bengal on the east.[4] Geographically Orissa can be divided into two major zones: the coastal plains and the mountainous regions mostly inhabited by the tribal people.[5] The mountainous portions cover about three-fourths of the entire state as per the present configuration and hence determine the economic conditions of the state.[6]

Orissa, basically an agricultural state, depends largely on irrigation for a successful harvest. As all the rivers are rain-fed, most of them dry up during the summer. The construction of reservoirs for irrigation purposes is a relatively recent phenomenon,[7] thus leaving agriculture at the mercy of the often-erratic rain.

The climatic conditions also vary in respect to the type of land. In general, Orissa enjoys a tropical monsoonic type of climate like most other parts of India. During the winter, excepting northern Orissa, most of the state remains dry. The winter in the Ganjam forests can be bad, as sometimes one can notice a thin layer of ice on the rooftops.[8] However, this is not a normal occurrence. The heat wave in Orissa can be very severe in May and June, namely till the arrival of the monsoon. Many a time the missionaries were advised not to visit people during the day, as it could be fatal.[9]

Orissa is known for devastating cyclones and droughts, resulting in frequent famines. During the monsoon, the cyclonic storms that originate in the Bay of Bengal often cross the east coast and make a north-westward journey. As a result, the coastal areas are frequently affected by inundation while the rest of the state experiences a climatic depression that often brings relief to otherwise disillusioned farmers. There are two cyclonic peaks: one during May-July and the other during October and November.

Early History

In the absence of any historical chronicle of the ancient period, the history of Orissa is reconstructed on the basis of historical information contained in inscriptions, coins, literary works and archaeological findings.[10]

The early history of Orissa is intertwined with the great Mauryan Emperor Ashoka (272 - 237 B.C.), the illustrious son of Vindusara, who invaded Kalinga in 262 B.C., a feat that could not be achieved by his predecessors, Chandragupta Maurya and Vindusara. Ashoka's conversion to Buddhism is attributed to the horrors of the Kalinga war,[11] that led to much bloodshed and untold suffering of the people. This turning point in his life changed him into a benevolent king and a great missionary of Buddhism.[12]

The next great ruler of Orissa is Kharavela.[13] He is well known for the Hathigumpha inscription (1st cent. B.C.) found at Udaygiri hill at Bhubaneswar. The inscription speaks about the achievements of Kharavela, the third ruler of the *Mahameghavahan* dynasty and one of the great rulers of ancient Kalinga. Although a Jain by faith, he conducted extensive military campaigns and his influence was felt from the eastern coast to the western coast and from Mathura in the north to the Pandya kingdom in the south.[14]

Later History

The rulers following these great men are grouped under different dynasties. There were a few rulers who were known for their benevolence and building activity. The history of *Bhaumakaras*[15] is reconstructed on the basis of a number of copper plates issued by the rulers of this dynasty. We know that out of eighteen rulers of this dynasty, as many as six were women, which is unique in Indian history.[16]

The *Somavamsis*, also known as *Panduvamsis*, were the next important rulers of Orissa. Their rule extended from the middle of the ninth century till the early part of the eleventh century.[17] Then came the *Gangas*,[18] who ruled an extensive territory with the help of a powerful army. They themselves were great warriors. They attempted to bring about harmony between *Vaishnavism* and *Shaivism*.[19] The art and architecture of Orissa reached its moment of glory during the reign of Chodagangadeva (1077-1147), Anangabhimadeva III (1211-1238) and Narasimhadeva I (1238–1264). Chodagangadeva was a great warrior and builder, who "besides the Jagannath temple at Puri[20] and numerous forts, constructed the temples of Vishnu at Mukhalingam and at Simachalam".[21] Both are found in the present State of Andhra Pradesh. It is widely known from inscriptions that Narasimhadeva I built the Sun temple at Konark.[22]

In the 15th century, *Gajapati*[23] kings of Orissa ruled over a vast kingdom extending from the Ganges in the north to Kaveri in the south. But in the following century they ceded a great portion of it to Vijayanagar and Golkonda rulers.

The political history following this period is one of dismemberment and annexation. In 1568,[24] Orissa lost her 'independence' and suffered from Afghan invasion (1568-78), followed by Mughal domination (1578-1751), Maratha control (1751-1803),[25] and finally British rule (1803-1947): the British East India Company from 1803 to 1858 and British Administration under the Empire from 1858 to 1947.[26] The British annexed Orissa in three different phases – southern Orissa in 1768, coastal and northern Orissa proper in 1803, and the western hilly tracts, namely, Sambalpur in 1849—and administered the areas under different administrative units, i.e., Madras, Bengal and Central Provinces, respectively. Besides, there were twenty-four tributary *mahals*, most of which were essentially raised to the status of princely states that maintained their semi-independent nature. A *dewan*, or prime minister, was appointed as a representative of the British Administration. At the close of the 19th century, more than half of the area of the present state was under the control of the 24 feudatory chiefs.[27]

Having seen a general political sketch of Orissa, a short description of the places or the centres of activity, where Catholicism spread during the period under survey will elucidate the missionary efforts.

Ganjam District

Ganjam[28] was the most northern district of Madras Presidency, which was earlier called the Northern Circars. It had an area of about 8,313 sq. miles with the population of circa 1,520,088, according to the census of 1871.[29] With its thickly wooded hills and fertile plains, Ganjam district was one of the most beautiful districts in the Presidency. The district was divided into plains and *maliahs*. The plains were the country below the *ghats*.[30] The summer lasts for three months (March, April and May), while the winter is pleasant. The hill climate is extreme in comparison to the plains of Orissa. "In May the shade temperature may rise to 105° - 110°F or 40° – 43° C yet may approach freezing point in the coldest nights of December and January, with ground frost in the early hours. The cold season ends in February, after which it is increasingly hot until the arrival of the heavy south-west monsoon."[31] During the monsoon, which lasts from June to November, the climate is oppressive because of the proximity of the sea. However, due to the occasional shower the heat is tempered.[32] Ganjam town was notorious for malaria, and for this reason it ceased to be the headquarters of the district.[33] Commenting on the inclement weather, Barbara M. Boal writes: "climate of *kondhistan* (the habitat of Kondhs) is so notorious for its insalubrity and the baneful effects it has on the health and constitution of strangers".[34] Otherwise, the climate is pleasant and some of the plateaus and slopes are being considered as potential holiday resorts for Orissa.[35]

A Historical Summary of Ganjam District

Historically, Ganjam was part of the ancient Kalinga kingdom. Like the rock edicts of Dhauli, near Bhubaneswar, Emperor Ashoka has left a rock edict in Jaugada. Ganjam area shared the fate of Kalinga except for occasional encroachment on its southern border, i.e., the Vengi kingdom. The Chola conquest of Vengi and Kalinga, which took place at the end of the 10th century and the beginning of the 11th century, had its impact on Ganjam.[36] Narrating the origin of the Gajapatis' rule in Orissa, the Imperial Gazetteer recorded: "The power of the Gajapatis of Orissa, whose descendants still hold considerable portions of the District, was founded in the fifteenth century by a minister of the former dynasty."[37] As internal strife mounted among the Gajapati kings, their power also waned. About 1571, Ibrahim, one of the Muslim rulers of Hyderabad, took advantage of the uncertain rule in Orissa and made himself master of Godavari and other districts as far north as Chicacole. For about 180 years, Ganjam district was part of the Chicacole *Circar*, controlled by the Muslim rulers from Hyderabad.[38]

In 1752, the struggle between the French and the English for pre-eminence in India was at its height. Out of gratitude for the services rendered by the French, Salabat Jung conferred all the honours and privileges on Monsieur Dupleix, the distinguished Governor of Pondicherry. He also assigned to the French, along with other districts of the Northern Circars, the Chicacole *Circar* for the equipment of the French auxiliaries. The French accordingly established themselves at Masulipatnam.[39] But their advancement towards north Ganjam did not make any impact on the territory. Ganjam had numerous zamindars who were frequently annexing villages that were under the government of British East India Company and who were also quarrelling with one another. Some of them declined to pay tribute until compelled to by force. Disturbances occurred with regular intervals and in an open manner between 1813 and 1832, caused mostly by a faction of eleven hill chiefs. "By 1832 the Bissoyis'[40] doings became so intolerable that Mr. George Russell, first member of the Board of Revenue and name-father of Russellkonda, was sent to stop them. He proclaimed martial law, captured the Bissoyis and their forts one after the other, hanged some and transported others, and gave the district a spell of quiet. In 1836 he followed a similar policy in Goomsur, and since then there have been no disturbances of importance."[41]

The hill tract attracted the 'white man's'[42] attention after the war in 1836, when the ruler of Goomsur, refusing to pay tribute to the English, took refuge among the Kondhs.[43] It was then that the British came to know of the horrendous human sacrifices. Thinking it to be a turbulent area, the British Government "considered it necessary for the prevention of further disturbances that the administration of criminal and civil justice in the hill *zamindaries* would be removed from the ordinary courts and placed under the collector, and Act XXIV of 1839 was passed giving the collector as the Agent to the Governor, Fort St. George, the necessary powers".[44]

Thus, "in 1845 the Government of India created a special agency for the suppression of *Meriah*[45] sacrifices and female infanticide throughout the hill tracts of Orissa, and appointed Captain Macpherson, Agent under Act XI of 1845. All the Ganjam Maliahs, then under the Collector and Agent, were therefore transferred to him".[46] After prolonged difficulties and persuasion that claimed to have arrested the heinous crimes to some extent, the agency itself was done away with in 1862. This resulted in the retransfer of the jurisdiction to the Collector.

The people of the district may be divided into four broad categories: Uriyas (Oriyas, those who speak the language of Oriya but non-tribals and non-dalits), Telugus (those who speak Telugu as their mother tongue), Kondhs and Savaras. The Kondhs and Savaras, who are for the most part cultivators, inhabit the hills. They are described as being "miserably poor".[47] While the Savaras do not enter the purview of the survey, socio-economic and political aspects of Kondhs are in order.

People under Study

a. Kondhs

Kondhs, also called Khonds or Kandhs, a term given by their Oriya neighbours, are a Dravidian tribe inhabiting the south-eastern part of Orissa, particularly on the Ganjam mountains.[48] Their mother tongue is *Kui*, a Dravidian language that has some similarity with other Dravidian languages, such as Tamil, Telugu and Kannada in grammar.[49] Aryan literature has portrayed them as *Rakshasas*, the black-faced demons, who accompanied Lord Ram in the conquest of Ceylon. They were under the command of Hanuman, the monkey god.[50] This needs to be attested by the standards of critical history as this could possibly be a result of some prevailing prejudices, since they were placed under some Aryan kings who took away the tribal autonomy or independence.

They prefer to call their habitat *Kui Dina* (*Kui* county), while the nineteenth century British romanticists referred to the area as *Kondisthan* (place of Kondhs). More recently, some Indian writers have called it *Kondhland*.[51] Most of the present mixed forests contain valuable hardwoods such as *Sal* (*Shorea robusta*), as well as strong creepers, useful herbs, edible roots, leaves and berries. The lives of the inhabitants depend largely on the forest produce when there is scanty rain and persistent famine.

Origin of Kondhs

Their own traditions concerning their origin are of little value, but they were almost certainly at one time the rulers of the country in which they lived.[52] Most probably they lived originally in the plains, but the arrival of Aryans, as in other places, pushed them into the hills and mountains.[53] Their love for the mountains and the jungles and their desire to live freely and fearlessly motivated them to move into new terrain. Their main occupation was hunting, but sometimes a Kondh family may clear a small patch of land in the forest, set fire to it and sow the seed in the ashes. They raised few food crops yet cultivated a lot of turmeric for sale. They regarded themselves as owners and proprietors of the land that they cultivated.[54] Barbara M. Boal commented: "Their social, cultural, economic and religious life is built on the belief that they are the traditional owners of the land. Also, in Kondh language, the spoken word in the presence of one's fellowmen and the creator are binding, needing no documentary proof of sale."[55]

Belief System of Kondhs

The Kondh pantheon consists of 84 gods of whom *Bura Penu*,[56] the Great Earth God, is the chief. He is the god of light, creator and sustainer.[57] The Great Bura God created a consort for himself, *Tari (Tani) Penu*, the earth goddess.[58] To her human sacrifices were offered.[59] Bahadur wrote: "It was incumbent on the Kandhs to purchase victims. Unless bought with a price, they were not deemed acceptable to the goddess, and, as a rule, victims from their own tribe were not thus procurable; but sometimes the Kandhs sold their children because of the economic hardships, and they might then be purchased as Meriahs."[60] Thus the Kondhs are divided in their acceptance and worship of their supreme deity: those who worship Bura Penu as the supreme god and those who worship Tari Penu as the supreme god. The positive cult of the earth as practised in the olden days has declined. But individuals continue to propitiate the earth[61] in their own fields at the time of planting the rice seedlings and at the time of harvest, and the hamlet priests (*Janis*) make offerings when the first seed is sown and when the flowers are first gathered from the *Mahua* (*Bassia latifolia*) tree.

Every Kondh village has a place of worship, the centre of Kondh habitat, which is often identified with a heap of *darni* stones.[62] Among the Kondhs, when a child is born the first thing they try to find out is whose soul has entered into him/her. When a child cries a lot, then they are sure that they have not yet found out the soul. A sorcerer is then called to resolve the question.[63] The tribes believe that the souls of the departed are reborn as children,[64] and boys have on occasion been named *Majhilan Budhi* or the old head-woman, whom they believe to have been born again with a change of sex.[65] Besides these cases, "Kondhs don't believe in an inevitable cycle of life, death and rebirth. Some fresh lives are born into families in addition to the reborn ancestors – hence the need for divination".[66] They do not eat the meat of tigers because they consider them to be an incarnation of a divinity or a demon, which will confound those who devour such animals. For similar reason they cannot eat even the animals killed by a tiger.[67] They believe in spirits, particularly the ones that are harmful. Such spirits have to be propitiated. Those who die of violent death are thought to be roaming around in the form of spirits harming persons.[68]

The dead are normally buried, but the practice of cremating the bodies of adults is increasing. This could be due to the influence of Hindu culture, to which they are exposed. When a body is buried, a rupee or a copper coin is tied in the sheet so that the deceased may not go penniless to the other world. Sometimes the dead man's clothes as well as his bows and arrows are buried with him. Kondhs identify a variety of situations that cause pollution and prescribe many purification ceremonies. At the village level, the most common pollution is caused by *Sidi Saki* or unripe death, such as tiger-mauling, death in childbirth, suicide, falling from a tree, drowning, etc. In such circumstances they consider the entire village as polluted until the traditional purification is performed.[69] The Kondh worships his bows and arrows before going out to hunt, and he believes that every hill and valley has its separate deity, who must be propitiated.[70] Regarding the belief system of Kondhs, Barbara M. Boal observed: "The Kondhs have always considered their spiritual beliefs, customs and practices to be rooted and grounded in the values practiced by their ancestors before them".[71]

Meriah Sacrifice

Here is an account of the infamous *Meriah* or the human sacrifice of the Kondhs.[72] Our knowledge of it is derived from the accounts written by British officers in the middle of the 19th century.[73] The sacrifices were offered to the earth goddess, Tari Penu, and were believed to ensure good crops and immunity from all disease and accidents.[74] The mode of putting him/her to death varied in different places. One of the most common modes seems to have been strangulation or squeezing to death. Sometimes the victim was cut while alive. After the symbolic wounding of the victim by the officiating priest, people cut the flesh of the victim with a knife. The persons who had been deputed by each village instantly took the flesh cut from the victim home.[75] In each village all who stayed at home fasted rigidly until the flesh arrived. The bearer deposited it in the place of public assembly, where the priest and the heads of families received it. The priest divided it into two portions, one of which he offered to the earth – goddess by burying it in a hole in the ground with his back turned, and without looking. Then each man added a little earth to bury it, and the priest poured water on the spot from a hill gourd. The other portion of the flesh he divided into as many shares as there were heads of houses present. They buried the morsel in the field where they expected a bumper crop. The remains of the human victim (namely, the head, bowels and bones) were watched by strong parties the night after the sacrifice, and the next morning they were burned along with a whole sheep on a funeral pile. The ashes were scattered over the fields, laid as paste over the houses and granaries, or mixed with the new corn to preserve it from insects. On the day following the sacrifice, the Kondhs brought a buffalo calf, cut off its forefeet, and left it there until the following day. This was followed by women disguising themselves, armed liked men who drank, danced and sang around the spot. The calf was killed, cooked and eaten.[76] It was a Herculean task for the British to extirpate these practices. Using a friendly approach (particularly with the chiefs), admonitions, and proposals to substitute buffaloes in place of humans, they gradually helped them to abandon the tradition of human sacrifice.[77]

Female Infanticide

Female infanticide[78] was a prevailing practice in areas such as the *zamindaries* of Surada, Korada and the borders of Chinna Kimedy. This was not considered to be a sin or moral evil, because the Kondhs understood that the newborn infants were not ratified members of the kin-group and thus they were not full persons.[79] The clans practising female infanticide did not offer human sacrifice to *Tari Penu*, because they believed that *Tari* is subordinate to *Bura Penu* and the Supreme Being would protect them.

Some of the reasons given to justify the practice were: First, they believed that *Bura Penu* saw evil in the first feminine creation and therefore they want to avoid bringing evil to society. Explaining the situation Barbara M. Boal cited Macpherson, who reported that "throughout the Kondh country two-thirds of the feuds and clan warfare were the result of unresolved marriage disputes, and the average must have been even higher in the clans practising infanticide".[80] Second, the bride price and its payment after desertion, plus payments for new marriages, led to innumerable misunderstandings and conflicts. Therefore, fathers very often looked upon their girl babies as 'trouble-makers' and found female infanticide the lesser of two evils. As the British officers and other outsiders realised, tradition, myth and folklore held great influence on Kondh society, but so did the socio-economic factors underlying the traditions. Prejudices against women had a link with endless quarrels over property in the contracting and dissolution of marriage, since Kondh women had the right to change husbands at will.[81]

Socio-cultural Aspects of their Life

Kondh is a generic term that stands for various groups and subgroups. The Kondhs are divided into different groups mainly on the basis of geography and socio-cultural dispositions. Kondhs could be divided into five broad categories: *Kutia* Kondhs, *Dongoria* Kondhs, *Malia* Kondhs, *Kuvi* Kondhs and *Desia* Kondhs. The inhabitants of the Ganjam Mountains in general are shy, timid and hesitant to associate with people of the plain.[82] Exogamy is strictly observed among the Kondhs. Major Macpherson says that among the Kondhs, intermarriage between persons of the same tribe, however large or scattered, is considered incestuous and punishable by death.[83] Kondhs are faithful to their friends and devoted to their chiefs;[84] they are resolute, brave, hospitable and industrious,[85] but these qualities met with little recognition among the Oriya Hindus.[86] Speaking about the virtues of Kondhs, T. J. Maltby commented: "They are too simple-minded to tell a lie, and prefer the truth. Death is preferred to transportation for lie."[87] Kondhs are known for the love of their race and territory, because of which they experience independence. No Kondh can imagine migrating to other places no matter what the situation may be, for only infidels migrate.[88] This is due to the strong bond that exists for both the living and the dead, between an individual and the community. The Kondhs are poor but they live with the hope that one day all their sufferings will disappear and that there will be a feast. Barbara M. Boal observed: "Man in Kui society has meaning primarily as a member of a group. His loyalty to, and place within, the kinship group goes without question, and governs the life of traditional Kondh or Christian alike. His secondary involvement is in the village community where similarly prescribed patterns are laid down for him. These regulate both his community commitments and his personal behaviour."[89]

A distinctive mark of Kondh women is facial tattooing; far from representing beauty, it portrays a period of vulnerability and aggression. The facial tattooing of Kondh women began when Kobi Upendro became a Raja. He came from the original lineage of the peacock, or *medarabonjo*, literally the one hatched from the peahen's egg. He was a knowledgeable man but an evil one. It was from his time onwards that *Kui* women's faces were tattooed (to make them unattractive to him) – for he used to come up and take away the attractive women.[90]

Socio-economic Life

The Kondhs are strictly agricultural people, and the salient features of their religious belief bear references to the fertilisation of the earth.[91] The lifestyle of Kondhs is simple. Their houses are made up of wooden logs, planks and a thatched-grass roof. They are a close-knit group. They practise patriarchy. At the death of the father, the eldest son assumes the leadership and becomes the head of the family. Kondhs are intimately connected with the forest and land. They cultivate *kandulo* (haricots, a kind of bean), turmeric, mustard, ginger, sesame, etc.[92] Their cultivation is dependent on rain. When the rainfall is scanty, they turn to the forest for its products: fruits, roots, etc. They are poor even though they are known as hard workers. Since they are a shy group they depend on Pano neighbours for the sale of their products. Using the simplicity and vulnerability of Kondhs, the Panos often exploited them. *Mohulo* or *Mahua* (*Bassia latifolia*) is very much linked with the life of Kondhs.[93] It is not an exaggeration to say that this tree with its flower has saved the entire population during famine.

Though agriculture is the main occupation, it is not very developed. Every village has a number of paddy fields to cultivate and a forest tract to make into arable fields. The villagers set fire to the area, as a preparation, and cultivate it for three years. They raise *kueri* (millet) in the first year and *kandulo* (bean) in the following two years. In the fifth year they allow the land to lie fallow. Then they once again begin with the cultivation of *kueri*.[94] The cleared land has to be distributed equally to all those who live in the village. Then it depends on the family members to develop the land for cultivation. The Kondhs were in a semi-savage stage and they sowed very little. The forest offered them three-fourths of their food: fruits, herbs, leaves, roots and game.[95]

Socio-political Life of Kondhs

Kondhs had a definite political system that was later influenced by outsiders. Formerly, some Kondhs were under the dominion of the kings of Khurda and others were under the *Patros*. In their political hierarchy, after the Rajas and *Patros* came the *Moliko*, *Digalo* and *Podhano*.[96] In every district there was a *Moliko*, and he was assisted by a *Digalo*. A *Moliko* was always a Kondh, but as he was uneducated and unable to understand Oriya he was assisted by a *Digalo*, who as a rule was a *Pano* (panam). The *Moliko* and *Digalo* presided over the meetings and judged certain cases. Every individual gave some amount of rice as payment for their service. In every village there was a *Podhano*, which was a hereditary title. In order to obtain this position, one had to be from the family of the chief and to be capable of exercising the office. The traditional Kondh leadership was strong and respected by the members. The village headman was considered to be the symbol of the group's well being.[97]

Jani, the high priest, was also an important person in the traditional Kondh hierarchy. His chief function was to celebrate the community sacrifices to *Bura* God or Tari Penu. This office was inherited. Next in line were the priests who were considered divine. They had some practical knowledge of herbal medicine. Then came the *Darni* keeper, who represented the community in performing necessary rituals and sacrifices at the *Darni* stones. He was chosen by the deity and ratified by the community. The Kondhs were born cooperators. They lived in a community and died in a community. Individualism was traditionally non-existent and even today, despite the onslaughts of modern influence, it is only slowly encroaching upon the Kondh community. Their villages may be scattered, but their clan bonds are still very tight.[98]

b. Panos

The Panos, a Dravidian caste,[99] form one of the largest groups of *dalits*[100] in Orissa. There are myths and traditions that flood around the Pano community regarding the name itself.[101] Very little is known regarding the origin of the Panos[102] and the purpose of their migration to the hills from the plains.[103] One of the probable reasons for their migration to the hills is that they belonged to an untouchable caste and wanted to avoid the caste stigma. So, they did not mind living a life of hardship in the hills.[104] R. K. Nayak is of the opinion that the Panos were once considered as tribals but after 1950 they were included in the list of Scheduled Castes.[105] This could be an added reason why they chose to live in the mountains. The Panos are considered to be of lower status in the caste hierarchy and are landless agricultural workers, often renting fields from the Kondhs. Some of them are petty traders. Many Panos are cattle dealers or hawkers. They buy herds of old animals in the Orissa plains and sell them to the Kondh villages. Some of them are petty merchants, for they buy salt and snuff tobacco at Surada or other centres in the plains and sell it from door to door in the mountain villages. When their goods are sold, 'they bring home part of their earnings and drink the rest'.[106] Kondhs found the Panos to be indispensable neighbours from time immemorial for providing certain necessities of daily life. One could speak here of a symbiotic relationship between the two.

The Panos have their own language, but they quickly learn the dominant language in their vicinity. "Thus, in Phulbani, a large number of Panos call themselves *kui Panos*, since they speak *Kui* (Kondh language) at home."[107] Though the origin of the Panos lies in obscurity,[108] they have been part of the *Kui*-speaking community and have been influenced by the beliefs and practices of the Kondhs. They are so flexible that they speak *Kui* like their mother tongue and their life style and religion is firmly rooted in Kondh culture.[109] "In Koraput district the Panos live with the *Kuvi* Kondhs, *Dongria* Kondhs, and *Konda Doras*; in Ganjam district, with the Saoras and Kondhs; in Phulbani district, with the *Maliah* Kondhs and *Kutia* Kondhs".[110] But the Kondhs consider them socially inferior.[111]

Pano Belief System

The Panos' belief system does not conform to the Hindu pattern, but rather to the dominant cultural and religious practices of the place. Like their tribal neighbours: Panos believe in a world of spirits. In general, there are two kinds of spirits: benevolent and malevolent. Benevolent spirits do good and protect human beings. If offended, they withdraw their protection and allow the person to be vulnerable to the attacks of malevolent spirits. There are some spirits that are by nature malevolent. They roam around the area looking for victims and they dwell in odd places, like "steep cliffs, high trees, dense vegetation, deep ravines, waterfalls, caves, deserted houses, burial grounds, cremation sites and so on".[112] Unnatural deaths are caused by the malevolent spirits. Panos believe that *gramdevta*, the village deity, protects the village. She is propitiated regularly with offerings. The village priest is responsible for keeping the deity happy.[113] Panos believe that harm can be inflicted on a person, including taking the person's life away, through a magic spell or black magic, which the Panos call spiritual means. They also believe in witchcraft. Witches are not respected but feared, as their sight might bring evil to any one. The concept of evil eye is also deep-rooted among the Panos. Though a witch can cause disease or bring other serious disorders to the family or to individuals, the spell can be removed or rectified by another, more powerful witchdoctor.[114] Some of the tribal priests are invited to perform certain rituals of the Panos.[115] They believe in the ancestral spirits that protect them.

> The ancestral spirits protect their household from possible dangers and provide it with good bounty. The family must always apportion a share for them during feasts and festivals. Ancestral spirits can also be erratic, just like living human beings. If they do not receive due attention, they might make their displeasure known by way of sending diseases, or effecting a crop failure, sickness to the domestic animals and so on. Persons dying unnatural or violent deaths turn into malevolent spirits. They are not accepted among the ancestral community, and hence ceaselessly roam around looking for company. No death ritual is performed for such spirits.[116]

Like the tribals, the Panos consider the family in which a child is born impure for 21 days. This period ends after the *ekoisia* ceremony[117] is performed, in which the mother takes a purificatory bath and washes her clothes. The baby is also given a purificatory bath. The relatives, neighbours and village elders are invited for the occasion, which concludes with a feast.[118]

Deaths can be natural – old age, sickness, etc. – or unnatural. Persons dying a normal death are given a normal farewell. On the third day following the death of the person the relatives gather at his home for the purificatory rites. Some cooked food is taken to the grave for the deceased.[119] Besides the ceremonies following the death of the family member there is also a common ceremony that is performed annually. "On *Kartika amavasya* (new moon of November), the Panos perform a collective community ceremony for the ancestral souls. All the ancestors are remembered on that day. The households also perform rituals in their houses. The village priest officiates at the community sacrifice, which is followed by a community feast."[120]

Socio-economic Life of Panos

The Panos are skilful basket makers. Their baskets with different designs are sold easily in the tribal market. The tribals need the baskets for various storage purposes. Traditionally, the Panos were also known as weavers. They wove their own clothing and that of the Kondhs, who, not being mobile, found it difficult to obtain clothes from outside.[121] Panos are talented musicians. They provide musical services for the many non-tribal families in the area, on the occasion of marriages, initiation ceremonies, death ceremonies, and various other ceremonies.[122] Besides providing victims for the sacrifice (animals have now replaced human victims), they carry messages, such as the summons to councils or field-work.[123] The Panos are richly rewarded for their musical services by the non-tribals. This trade provided seasonal employment to quite a number of Pano families in the area.[124] However, being the servants of the Kondhs, the Panos had no right to own forests or to undertake any agricultural activities without their approval. They were landless for several generations. With the changing times, and in the course of land settlement, some Panos have managed to obtain land in their own name.[125] Many 'well-to-do' Kondhs have employed Panos in their hill plots for agricultural labour.

The Pano traders move from house to house, collecting agricultural surpluses and forest products from Kondhs and paying them in cash or with other items the latter need. Though they do not get a good price for their produce, the Kondhs are happy to obtain them at their doorstep. With an extensive amount of produce and an inability to market them, the Kondhs are happy to be relieved of their marketing responsibility. The Panos also understand the Kondh economic cycle well and know their seasonal necessities. This way the Kondhs can devote more time to agricultural activities and to social interaction.[126] In speaking about the occupations of Panos, the outsiders mirror existing prejudices: "weaving, trading and theft". However, there is at least one group of Panos that has taken to thieving as their main profession.[127] Outsiders might see the Panos as parasites who exploit the poor tribals. But the reality is different. They help the tribals during the lean months by bringing provisions to their doorsteps. They advance credit and provide the basic necessities of the tribals. They exchange old and infirm animals.[128] Describing the Panos, Col. E. T. Dalton, who is known for his contribution to the ethnography of Eastern India, wrote:

> The low bastard Hindu people called Pans [Panos], already noticed as procurers for the Meriah sacrifices, are numerous in Boad [Baud] . . . The Kandhs associate with them on a more equal footing, allowing them to hold land and share in the village festivals. They also ply their trades as weavers, and the poorest of them work as farm labourers, cultivating land belonging to Kandhs and making over to their landlords half the produces as rent.[129]

The forest also offers the Panos some income through leaf plates, brooms, ropes and mats. The Panos' economic wretchedness is described in the following words: "During the months of March to May food is in short supply. All agricultural produce would have been consumed by this time and the people solely depended upon the availability of food from the jungle. Some forest flowers and roots are still available in the jungle. These are collected, processed and eaten. Mangoes are available from April."[130]

Political System of Panos

There is a *Panchayat* in all the areas where the Panos live. Elucidating the purpose of Panchayat, the Society for Evaluation states: "It is an assembly of people which is constituted to settle disputes or to rectify a social transgression or wrongdoing within a community, according to its code of conduct."[131] Besides acting as a guardian of the community and settling inter-caste disputes, the *Panchayat* played a pivotal role in the social, economic and religious development of Panos. The village headman is called *Bada Nayak,* senior head. He is responsible for the well-being of the community and his word is final in village meetings. He is assisted by the *Sana Nayak,* the assistant head.[132] The Panos are widely scattered, although their larger concentration is in the districts of Phulbani, Koraput and Ganjam.[133]

Symbiotic Relationship between Panos and Kondhs

The tribals and Panos have been living a symbiotic life for generations. There have been cultural exchanges, socio-economic reciprocity and sharing of modern objectives as well.[134] Their relationship is mutually beneficial.[135] Since Panos are considered culturally inferior, no intermarriage normally takes place and inter-dining as a rule is avoided.[136] It is believed that the tribals brought Panos to perform certain roles, both economic and social. Traditionally every Kondh village designated three Panos for specific functions. One such role was the *Barik*. Describing the role of the *Barik*, Barbara M. Boal wrote: "The role of barik was of a social nature. He assisted the village headman in organising village meetings and carrying messages to different villages and also liaising between the tribals and outsiders. He assisted them in interacting with different government offices whenever necessity arose."[137] The second was the role of the *goudia* or herdsman, an important one for economic development. The Kondhs, who preoccupied themselves with the cultivation of their hill plots, could not tend their cattle. Hence, they required the service of the Panos as *goudia* or herdsman, for which they were given a just remuneration in kind (usually daily portions of cooked food). An annual grant of paddy rights and other items needed by the Panos were also provided.[138] Women from *goudia* families assisted their husbands in tending the cattle. Finally, the Panos were employed as *Jhatenis* (sweepers). Very often women were employed for this role. The remuneration was mostly in kind.[139] Panos also sometimes performed the funeral ceremonies of Kondhs.[140]

Panos and Meriah Sacrifice

Generally, the Panos are considered inferior to Kondhs. But those who supply sacrificial buffalo were considered equal.[141] One of the important functions of Panos was to provide sacrificial offering for the Meriah sacrifice. Before the British visited the hill tracts, the Meriah sacrifice involved human victims. Speaking about the Panos, Bannerman, Magistrate of Ganjam District in the 1840s, described "a set of infamous wretches who carry on a trade in the blood of their fellow-men".[142] In distinguishing the two groups, Kondhs and Panos, Macpherson had this to say about the latter: they were "excluded from the property in land and from power to practice the only honourable art (farming); and depressed by a sense of social inferiority; a mean, false, mercenary and thievish race, who live chiefly upon the ignorance, the superstition, and the industry of the primitive (Kondhs) as low priests, brokers, pedlars, sycophants and cheats".[143]

Living in remote jungles inhabited by fierce animals and impenetrable to outsiders, and surviving in a malaria-infested terrain, the Kondhs led a simple life, but one filled with ignorance and superstition. They attributed their 'backwardness' to the anger of God and to the spirits. How long must they still live this secluded and withdrawn life? How long have the Kondhs to wait for the dawn? Oppressed in every corner of life, marginalized and despised by outsiders, the Panos looked for a time of plenty and prosperity. Will their dreams be a reality one day?

Gangpur

The three major aboriginal tribes of Gangpur State among whom Christianity took a deep root are also included in the study. They are the Austric-speaking Mundas, their kinsmen, the Kharias, and the Dravidian-speaking Oraons. A better understanding of their acceptance of Catholicism would obviously require a thorough investigation of their social, economic, political and religious background. Even though they came under different political administrative units, most of the tribal inhabitants of Gangpur share a common heritage with their kinsmen of Chotanagpur and still maintain their roots in Chotanagpur. In fact, Gangpur State itself was part of Chotanagpur division until 1905 when it became part of Orissa division.

The Topography of Gangpur State

Gangpur,[144] at the beginning of the 20th century, was a tributary state of Orissa, in the British Bengal Province, lying between 21" 47' and 22" 32' N. and 83" 33' and 85" 11' E., with an area of 2,492 square miles. It is bounded on the north by the erstwhile state of Jashpur and Ranchi District; on the east by Singhbhum; on the south by the former states of Bonai, Sambalpur, and Bamra; and on the west by the state of Raigarh in the central provinces. Gangpur consisted of a long undulating tableland about 700 feet above the sea, dotted here and there with hill ranges and isolated peaks which rise to a height of 2,240 feet.[145]

The plateau is enriched by rivers, which pose a threat to the inhabitants with their seasonal floods, causing enormous destruction. The principal rivers are the Ib, which enters the state from Jashpur and passes through from the north to the south to join the Mahanadi in Sambalpur, the Sankh, and the south Koel. The latter two meet in eastern Gangpur, and the united streams, under the name of Brahmani, flow south into the plains of Orissa.[146] The confluence of the Koel and the Sankh is said to be one of the most beautiful spots in Gangpur. According to a local tradition, the sage Parasara is said to have become infatuated with the fisherman's daughter Matsya Gandha here. The offspring of the two was Vyasa, the reputed compiler of the *Vedas* and *Mahabharat*. As with most Indian rivers, these too run dry during the summer months. Hence, the adjacent forest offers food to the hungry tribes whenever they were unable to cultivate their land, as well as refuge to various wild beasts.[147]

The Historical Situation of Gangpur State

The prehistory of Gangpur awaits a clear solution to several problems. Since the state did not enjoy total independence, its political history is limited to that of its neighbouring states. The documentary evidence needed to construct a historical background is scanty.

It was probably during the time of the Gangas (1038-1435) that Bonai and Gangpur were consolidated as separate political units, and regarded as feudal states.[148] In his efforts to trace the origin of Gangpur kingdom, C. W. E. Connolly wrote: "The earliest chiefs of Gangpur that there is any information of belonged to the Kishori Bans, and were descendants of the famous Kishori Bans of Puri, who after their defeat by the Mahrattas fled in all directions, one line settling here."[149] Gangpur continued to be under the control of the Chauhan rulers of Sambalpur till 1818, which itself belonged to the Maharajahs of Nagpur. In the meanwhile, the British invaded Orissa in 1803 and soon after tried to expand their power to other parts of the territory. Major Broughton conquered Sambalpur in January 1804. Though in the Treaty of Deogaon of December 17, 1803, Raghuji Bhonsla ceded the territory of Cuttack to the East India Company, he was unwilling to part with the territory of Sambalpur, but the chieftains and Zamindars were unwilling to return to the Maratha authority and "voluntarily surrendered to the British Government". They declared their willingness to pay the tribute that the British Government would fix.[150] Thus, Gangpur was also ceded in 1803 to the British East India Company by the Treaty of Deogaon but was restored to the Maharajah in 1806. It reverted to a provisional engagement with Madhuji Bhonsla in 1818 and was finally ceded in 1826. In 1821 the federal supremacy of Sambalpur over Gangpur was cancelled by the government, and a fresh *Sanad*[151] was granted to the chief. In 1827, after the permanent cessation, another *Sanad* was granted for a period of five years, but this was allowed to run until 1875 before it was renewed. The last *Sanad* was granted to the chief in 1899. The state was transferred from Chotanagpur to the Orissa Division in 1905. At the turn of the century the recorded population had increased from 191,440 in 1891 to 238,896 in 1901. With the establishment of the Bengal-Nagpur Railway, which runs through the south-eastern corner for about 70 miles, Gangpur had the potential to develop trade and commerce. About the same time when the actual parish at Kesramal in Gangpur was established, the inhabitants of Gangpur numbered around 260,000, of which the Oraons alone constituted 60,000.[152]

Villages in Gangpur are held either on feudal tenures or on farming leases. The feudal tenures date back to early times when the vassals received land grants for rendering military service. The other villages are leased to small farmers, called *Gaontias* or *Ganjhus*, who pay a fixed annual rent and are remunerated by lands, called *Bogra*, which are held rent-free.

After the *Kol* insurrection of 1831–1833, a new province called 'South Western Frontier Agency' was created under Regulation XIII of 1833, which later (in 1864) was called *Chutia Nagpur* (Chotanagpur) with a commissioner acting in the name of the governor-general. Gangpur was transferred to the Agency. In 1891 fresh *Sanads* were granted to Gangpur and Bonai which regulated their relationship with the British government.[153] On October 16, 1905, Bonai and Gangpur were transferred from the control of Chotanagpur to that of the Commissioner of Orissa. In the following year, the Office of a Political Agent was created for the Orissa states under the commissioner. In 1912, Bihar and Orissa were constituted as a separate province,[154] and "the Orissa states continued to be under the Orissa Division till 1922, when the Political Agent was designated as Political Agent and Commissioner, Orissa Feudatory States, and placed directly under the Governor of Bihar and Orissa".[155]

The People under Study

a. Oraons

The word *Oraon* is probably derived from *horo*, man, a Mundari word, and a similar word *Koro* is found in *Kurukh*, the language of the *Kurukhs*, another name for the Oraons.[156] The *Kurukhs* are said to have migrated from the Karnatic region. They split into two groups: one following the Ganges, occupied the Rajmahal jungles; the other, much larger, occupied the north-western corner of Chotanagpur. Their language, akin to Kanarese, indicates that they must have originally come from the south and gradually displaced the Mundas from many of the areas in the Ranchi plateau, which they now inhabit.[157] It may be also mentioned that, according to the Oraon traditions, the tribe had a long and happy stay on the banks of the Sone River, in what is today the Shahabad district.[158]

The Oraons are perhaps best known as *Dhangars*,[159] not only in the Chotanagpur region but also among their kinsmen in other parts of the country. Their language is also called *Dhangar*. The name Oraon is given to them by their Hindu neighbours.[160] For some unknown reason there seems to have occurred a split in the tribe: the *Nagpurias*, the *Kisans* and the *Dhankas*. "Many thousands of Nagpuri Oraons are found in Gangpur, their villages studding the country side by side with *Dhanka* and *Kisan* villages. The bulk of the Oraon population of Gangpur, however, is made of *Kisans* (in Hindi it means farmers) or *Gangpuria Oraons*".[161] The *Dhanka* Oraons are rather numerous in Gangpur. Their tribal language does not seem, any more than that of the *Kisans*, to offer important points of difference from the Nagpuria, or standard, Oraon. A few words may be peculiar to them.[162]

Religious Practices of Oraons

In religion, the attitude of Oraons is one of reverential fear towards the spirits, and this expressed itself in a dependence on, a propitiation of, and a prayerful submission to these spirits.[163] The beneficent spirits were arranged in a hierarchical order with Dharmes at the top, who saw all that men and spirits did and thought.[164] The sacrificial offering to him must be white (either fowl or goat), and it must be made facing east. This particular rubric is not observed for the rest of the spirits. Dharmes, the supreme god of light and life, is the creator god of Oraons. He is both good and powerful. The desire of the righteous is to live with him after death; yet homage and sacrifices to him are meaningless, precisely because he is so good.[165] The *Dandakatta*[166] (crossing the stick) is one of their most important ceremonies, for it is performed at every venture of social consequence, at feasts and festivals, and at the commencement of every important event in the life of Oraons. A white fowl is sacrificed to appease him. Oraons believe also in evil spirits, which are to be propitiated with sacrifices during sickness and times of calamities.[167] L. Cardon observes that "other spirits, of a distinctly malignant character, do not live among us as a rule, they are tied up in some unknown place, whence however they can be occasionally released at the call of a sorcerer or a witch; then they play a havoc on the lives of men and beasts, cause illness, spread epidemic, etc."[168] The worst superstitious practices are those connected with the hereafter.[169]

Socio-cultural Background

The child receives its name from its grandparents or from one of the ancestors.[170] People of non-Oraon caste are naturally outside of the community, and food, as a rule, is not taken with them. But, apart from this, they are treated with consideration and even kindness. The fact that the Oraons of Gangpur eat with the Mundas is remarkable, but incontestable. It is one instance of their many departures form the customs extant in the rest of the tribe.[171] Oraons believe that the mother is defiled from the day of her delivery. She is debarred from entering the kitchen for fear of defiling the cooking utensils. She is expected to stay in a corner of the house where her food is handed to her. On the ninth day, when the *Chathi* ceremony takes place, she purifies herself in the river and the infant's fluffy hair is cut, for it is considered to be unclean.

The Oraons generally regard their deceased as part of their family. Oraons cremate their dead like their Hindu neighbours. This may take place either immediately or after the bodies have been laid in a village grave for six or eight months. In either case, the ashes are collected in an earthen vessel and buried close to their house. Later the ashes are ceremonially carried on a particular day, when the river has practically no water, to the riverbed where they are deposited in the family *kunddis* (deep round holes).[172]

The Oraons are divided into many exogamous clans, called *gotras*. Very often the name of the clan is taken from a fish, bird, animal, vegetable, etc. They respect their totemic animal or bird, and its killing or harming is prohibited. Traditionally the *Dhumkuria*, or youth dormitory, played an important role in instructing the youngsters in their way of life in the community. It was a school where the youth were initiated into the multifaceted reality of life. It is in front of the *Dhumkuria*, in the *Akhra*, that youngsters learn to sing and dance.

Economic and Political Conditions

The descendants of the Oraon village founders were known as *Bhuinars.*[173] Although there was no joint ownership of land, they were the owners of the *Bhuinari* village lands. The *Mahto* (the village headman) and the *Pahans* or *Naigas* (the village priests) must belong to the *Bhuinari Khunt* (the lineage of the village founders), and they alone were entitled to enjoy the fruit of the village service lands.[174] The political organization of Oraons is similar to that of their tribal neighbours, the Mundas. The Oraons have a confederation of several villages, called *Parha.* A *Parha* normally consists of either 7, 9, 12, 21, or 22 villages. An annual meeting of *Parha* is called *Parha Jatra*, when the communities of a *Parha* settle all their disputes and confirm their tribal solidarity by means of a big feast.[175] The Oraon is one of the largest agricultural tribal communities. Due to depletion of the land-man ratio, rough topography, uneconomic land holdings, poor quality of soil, lack of irrigation facilities, lack of job opportunities in the industries, and a lack of specialisation, a large number of Oraons migrated to the neighbouring states of Madhya Pradesh, Orissa, West Bengal as well as other parts of the country.[176]

Just as the Mundas, so too the Oraons have a value-system enshrined in their traditions and socio-religious practices. The Oraons are guided concretely by their cultural, social and religious values which provide the basis for Oraon morality. Oraons believe that God has given human beings the command to be honest, truthful and generous and that he rewards them for their good deeds and punishes them for evil ones.[177] Next to God, Dharmes, the village *Panchayat* is considered to be the supreme authority among the Oraons. The *Panchayat* settles all disputes within the tribe, and the *Panchayat*'s decisions are binding. Panchayat counsellors delight to feast on the produce of a fine or of the fees exacted when a case has been judged.[178]

Every Oraon is expected to abide by the norms of the tribe. Any breach of behavioural norm is frowned upon and sanctions are incurred against the offender.[179] Oraon dances, besides being a source of entertainment, also have a magical significance attached to them.[180].

b. Mundas

The Mundas,[181] one of the tribes of the central zone, are found on the plateaus and mountain belts north of the Krishna River and south of the

Indo-Gangetic Basin. Sarat Chandra Roy, one of the authorities on the tribes of Chotanagpur, was of the opinion that before the arrival of the Aryan tribes in northern India, there were traces of the Mundari dialect in the Gangetic Plain.[182] Most authors apply linguistic analysis in their efforts to determine the prehistory of the Mundas.[183] The tribe is divided into many clans or *kili*, which are endogamous in nature.

Religious Beliefs of Mundas

The Mundas have their own myths of the creation of the world and of the origin of man. At the head of a multitude of spirits is *Singbonga*, also called *Haram*, the Creator God. He is the Supreme Being, literally the *One* or more exactly, the *Old One*. He is eternal, omniscient, omnipotent and omnipresent.[184] *Singbonga* is neither the sun nor dwells in the sun, though he is in heaven. He is identical with the *Haram* of creation. In other words, in primordial times the creator was called *Haram*.[185]

Mundas believe in spirits (*bongas*).[186] There are hosts of them, such as *Burubonga* (spirit that dwells on hilltops), *Ikirbonga* (spirit of the deep waters), *Nagebonga* (spirit in the ravines), *Dasaulibonga* (spirit in wooded spots), *Condor Ikirbonga* (spirit in groves near a pool of water) and *Candibonga* (spirit in rocky places).[187] These *bongas* (spirits) are invoked and propitiated either to ward off impending harm or danger or to appease their displeasure caused by their living relatives' negligence in offering them their timely dues (food and drink). P. Ponette is of the opinion that the spirits do not have any divine status and hence one could very well conclude that the Mundas are monotheists.[188] The village god who takes his abode in the *sarna* (sacred grove) is propitiated by sacrifices offered by a *Pahan* (the village priest). It is fear, not love that prompts them to offer sacrifices to the many *bongas* or spirits.

Affirming the influence of the annual agricultural cycle on the festivals of Mundas, Susan Chand writes: "The religious aspects of Mundas are closely related with the annual agriculture cycle and the recurring rites of passage. The main festivals include *Mage, Phagu, Sarhul, Hon-ba, Batuli, Dasai,* and *Sohrai.* The folksongs are accompanied by folk dances. The celebrations accompanying these festivals, songs and dances provide occasions for collective action and build up social solidarity."[189]

Socio-cultural Background

The ethics of the Mundas are rooted in their religious faith and in the communal structures of their society, the tribe. A Munda finds salvation in and through his tribe. And it is through the tribe that he preserves his life and remains linked with the *Singbonga*. Therefore, the state of an outcaste is akin to death. By an infraction of the code of conduct established by the community, one voluntarily severs the connection with the origin to which one owes the preservation of life.[190] In this context, it could very well be said that any offence committed against the tribe is also committed against the Supreme Being, the *Singbonga*, and that whatever offends him also hurts the tribe.[191] The dead are buried in a north-south direction with the head turned towards the east to remind them of their true home which is said to be in the north, somewhere in the Gangetic valley. The head turned towards the East would mean the orientation towards God (sun).[192]

Economic and Political Situation

The Mundas organised themselves into independent village communities, and each community is said to be the proprietary body owning all the land outside the village boundary. The Mundas have a democratic form of government. They did not allow their own rajas to interfere in the village administration, which was considered a family matter. The administration of justice was carried out by a village chief who was a direct male descendant of the original founder of the village. It is generally understood to mean that *Singbonga* exercises much of his authority on earth through the *Panchayat* or the village elders and that the authority of the *Panchayat* derives from *Singbonga*. The *Panchayat* interprets the tradition, which is a special gift from *Singbonga* through which he voices his commands.[193] Mundas are agriculturists who transformed the forest into arable land. Hence the forest tract of Chotanagpur belonged to them. Like other Chotanagpur tribes, Mundas too depend on the forest for their subsistence, i.e., for their fuel, timber, honey, *lac*, *Mahua* flowers, medicinal herbs and oils, etc.[194]

Inheritance among the Mundas passes only to sons. Failing these, the property goes to the brothers of the deceased (if any). In the world of the Mundas, the daughters do not belong to the family and as such have no rights to family property. Women have an exclusive right over their ornaments. However, they do not inherit any share of the family property. It is a custom with the Munda to raise stone-monuments over their dead. And if the Mundas move away from a place, these monuments remain to indicate their former presence.

Dancing is the inevitable accompaniment of every gathering, and it is one of the primary elements of their socialisation. Dancing and singing by both men and women in the village *akhra* signifies a feeling of mutual cooperation amongst the Mundas. They have a variety of dances suitable for special times and seasons. There are specific songs and dances associated with the annual cycle of tribal festivals, *Jatras*, socio-religious functions and life cycle events. The motion is slow and graceful with a monotonous singsong being kept up throughout the dance. The steps are in perfect time and the action wonderful.[195]

c. Kharias

It is said that the original occupation of the Kharias was to carry *Dhoolies* or litters, and the name itself seemed to have been derived from *Kharkharia*, a palanquin or a litter.[196] They are also cultivators and collect forest produce.[197] The Kharias, who are said to have had their home originally somewhere in Central Asia, came to India together with the proto-Australoid group, via China and Burma.[198] The movement of peoples brought the tribe to the regions of Ayodhya, where they settled down for some time, and then later to Rohtosgarh. The Kharias are divided into three groups; the *Paharia*, the *Dhelki* and the *Dudh* Kharias. Among the three groups, the Hill Kharias are shy by nature, for the presence or intrusion of a foreigner would impel them to move to a new forest. The Dhelki Kharias are mostly found in the Gangpur and Jashpur regions. The ancestors of the Dudh Kharia marched to the plateau of Chotanagpur and settled down along the southern Koel and the Biru region.[199]

Religious Beliefs of Kharias

The Kharias believe in a Supreme God, the creator and ruler of everything. They call him *Maha Ishwar*– the great God, or *Sakhi Gosain* – the all-seeing Deity or *Ponomeshor* – living rock, names possibly borrowed from Hinduism.[200] They worship the sun (Bero), but it is not identical with *Maha Ishwar*. Pious Kharias, with hands joined and touching the inclined forehead, salute the sun every morning before brushing their teeth. The head of each family offers sacrifice, but on solemn occasions, the village sacrificer performs the rituals. The Kharias believe that since *Ponomeshor*, the Supreme God creates *Dubos,* the world of spirits, they are subject to him. Commenting on *dubos*, Marianus Kujur observed: "They find the presence of *dubos* everywhere. The belief in *dubos* among Kharias is so manifesting that some people call their religion 'animism'. The Kharias believe in three types of *dubos* 'namely' ancestral *dubos*, benevolent *dubos* and malevolent *dubos*."[201] They also propitiate evil spirits or *Bhuts* by means of sacrifices. It is fear, not love, which prompts them to worship these spirits.[202] The Kharias believe in witches who are deemed to be wicked women who have power to harm others.

The Kharias make a clear distinction between the soul of man *'jiu'* and his shade *'chain'*. These are kept united as long as a man is alive, and though his shade may sometimes become visible, never so his soul. The shade is hardly of any use to him.[203] The ethical behaviour of the Kharias is inherent in their religious beliefs. Misconduct in their behaviour would cost them degradation in the hierarchy of status.[204]

Socio-cultural Background

Kharias have a variety of folksongs and dances. They vary according to the season. Every season has a typical song, which must not be sung outside the season. In the same way, dances are limited to a particular season.[205]

The simplicity and gentleness of the Kharias won them many friends even among the European missionaries. Their generosity and docility were very much lauded. Some of the missionaries even went to the extent of comparing them with their kinsmen. "The fickleness of the Oraons and the self-conceit of the Mundas, make no part of their character; and all the missionaries that have come into familiar contact with them acknowledge that their feelings are refined and nearer to our standard".[206]

Economic and Political Situation

The father as the head of the family has authority over its members. He alone may dispose of the family's property, and everybody in the house is expected to obey his commands.[207] The office of the *Pahan* is hereditary among the Kharias. In return for his services he holds, free of rent, a certain amount of paddy fields. Kharias do not generally marry off their children before they reach the age of 18 or 19. It is the parents' duty to find a suitable partner for their children. It is generally believed that children who marry on their own bring disgrace to the dignity of the family. *Panchayats* among the Kharias function, with a few exceptions, along the same lines as those of the Oraons.

History of Economic Oppression Leading to 'Bethbegari', Forced Labour

This short analysis of the Oraons, the Mundas and the Kharias does not portray the historical background that led to the state of *Beth-begari*, forced labour.[208] In an attempt to explain their degrading condition, M. Vanden Bogaert proposes four distinct periods that developed in the life of tribals up to the present day. However, this study will limit itself to just three periods: 1) the Original or Tribal Society, existing in the plateau since prehistoric times, 2) Feudal Society, imposed during the Moghul period and 3) Capitalist Society, imposed during the British colonial period.[209]

The Original or Tribal Society

The peace-loving tribals of Chotanagpur knew no alienation from their property until the emergence of their 'Raja', or chieftain, about 500 A.D.[210] These chieftains were probably natural leaders whose function became hereditary. The Raja was considered to be at the service of the tribal community -- especially during the threat of foreign invasion, when the tribals would gather under the leadership of their Raja, to defend their territory. The tribals felt an urge to contribute regularly to his upkeep. The Raja possessed or claimed no sovereignty over the land, exercised no particular authority over the village administration, and levied no taxes. The land belonged to the villages; the Mundas, on certain occasions, redistributed it according to each one's needs. Thus, one could say that the Raja was truly a servant of the community. The *adivasis* (the original settlers or tribals) proudly declared that they were the true Rajas of the land.

Feudal Society

In 1585, Akbar, the Moghul Emperor, sent a force under Shahabaz to subdue the Raja of Chotanagpur. In 1616, Akbar's successor, Jahangir, demanded a tribute of Rs. 15,000 from Raja Durgan Sal. As he was unable to pay this exorbitant amount, he was imprisoned at Gwalior between 1616 and 1628.[211] This was the first prolonged contact of the Chotanagpur Raja with other rulers and their imperial splendour. On his release, he began to introduce many new ideas and practices into his territory. He introduced Brahmin priests, Rajput courtiers and warriors, and other caste Hindus brought from outside. He even went to the extent of contracting marriage alliances with the neighbouring Hindu Rajas.[212] The new officials were given rights to supplies from the villagers who used to pay rent as well as offer their services to the king. The new system of service grants or *jagir* and its new beneficiaries or *jagirdars* were a burden on the people. The newcomers were used to a landlordism that the tribals were ignorant of.

Gradually the rights to service grants were interpreted as property rights, and through the cleverness of their officers, many villages were reduced to rent-paying tenants. Thus, the hereditary lands of the *adivasis* were slowly slipping away from their hands. To add to this, the Raja also introduced temporary leaseholders or *thikedars* into the area. They too joined the *jagirdars* in exploiting the people. This was the beginning of the landlord system and of a systematic robbing of the ancestral property of the *adivasis*. The people became restless, as a result. There were even some recorded tribal insurrections. Not satisfied with their nominal possession of the villages, the leaseholders or *jagirdars* pleaded with the Raja to grant them rights over the land.[213] The loss of land had its adverse effects on the socio-political and economic conditions of the people, whose freedom to relish both the produce of the land and the land itself was snatched away from them.

Capitalist Society

In 1765, grants of the Diwani (the office of Prime Minister) of Bengal, Bihar and Orissa were made over to the East India Company by the Moghul Emperor Shah Alam II. This affected the tribal population to a large extent. Although Chotanagpur passed into British hands, an effective administration was not established before 1834.[214]

On June 4, 1809, the zamindari police system was introduced when the Raja was ordered to establish police stations. The new police system exacerbated the displeasure of the peace-loving tribes, giving an upper hand to the zamindars, who maintained an organised body to execute their well-planned drive towards the elimination of the proprietary rights of the tribes. To make matters worse, the petty officials of the new police system were brought in from Bengal and Bihar. This infuriated the tribals of Chotanagpur as a whole and the Mundas in particular. Consequently, there was a series of uprisings of both the Mundas and the Oraons. After the uprising of 1811, Chotanagpur was brought under the direct administration of the East India Company (in 1817), depriving the Raja of his position and thereby reducing his standing to that of a tributary chief.[215]

Tribal Insurrections

From 1789 onwards, the villagers revolted repeatedly but they could no longer avail themselves of the leadership of the Raja. The British, interested in peace and revenue, subdued the tribals and at the same time tried to legislate in their favour. Thus in 1809 they introduced the judiciary system. The law of proscription convalidated all usurpations and also opened the door to more impudent outrage. To add insult to injury, the court was situated at Chatra, a day's journey away for the poor tribal (who would thus lose a day's wage). Besides, the lawyers generally belonged to the class of exploiters and did not know the local language of the tribals who usually produced no document to support their claims.

In 1820, a great insurrection occurred against the *jagirdars* (those who held leases) and the *thikedars* (those who oppressed the tribals). Besides these, the tribals also hated the Hindus and the Muslims, because they were normally the moneylenders and made enormous profits. The tribals were hardly able to bear their heavy load, which degraded them and led to inhuman conditions.[216]

Messianic Movements

Between 1895 and 1900, and again at the beginning of World War I, various prophets (*Bhagat*) arose among the tribals. The *Birsa movement* among the Mundas between 1895 and 1900 and the *Tana Bhagat movement* among the Oraons during World War I were millenarian and messianic and prophetic in character.[217] At this time Birsa Bhagawan[218] became prominent among the Mundas with his movement to exterminate all that was anti-tribal and hence foreign.[219] The Oraon leaders and the followers of the Messianic Movement call theirs the *Kurukh Dharam*, or the real and original religion of the *Kurukhs* or Oraons.[220]

In discussing the tribals, A. Van Exem observes that "their social organisation, their well-balanced laws of marriage and inheritance, their pre-democratic form of leadership according to which community decisions are taken with unanimity, their innate sense of justice, all point to a highly civilised past".[221] They led a hard life close to nature, following the seasons on which their economy depended. Their cultural and moral richness was obliterated when in their distress they found no one to cling on to except the magicians and sorcerers who assured them of a brighter, bounteous future.

Conclusion

Reduced to miserable conditions, the illiterate and ignorant tribals longed for a saviour from within, but their prayers and sacrifices to different *bongas* or *bhuts* or spirits did not alleviate the misery inflicted upon them. It would be unfair to accuse the spirits of failure, despite the many sacrifices offered, to mitigate the suffering caused by the pernicious human avarice. Their *Dharam* or religion offered neither temporary relief nor a permanent solution to their problems, which eventually reduced them to a nomadic state. In their distress they longed for a messiah who would not just give them economic assistance but would also restore them to their former status, a status stemming from control of their ancestral land. The loss of their traditional lands led to an identity crisis. It is significant to note that the desire for liberation from their oppressors was not totally absent. Certain illustrious men had the courage to oppose the oppressive power structures. Yet the insurrection did not succeed because of the lack of dedicated leadership. One wonders how long they will have to wait for their Lost Paradise!

Endnotes

[1] In fact, the word orua has been widely used in Orissa since early times, which is said to be the same as the Greek word oruza, meaning rice. The Oxford Dictionary states that oruza is a borrowed word possibly from some oriental source. The oretes or the or or odra means people, which may, therefore, mean the 'rice-eating' or the 'rice-growing' people. In Persian and Arabic, Orissa is represented as Urshin or Ursfin as found in the writings of the geographer Ibn Khurdabhi and also Hadud-al-Alam belonging respectively to the 9th and 10th centuries A.D. Alberoni in his famous work on 'India' refers to Orissa as Urdavisau which is a derivative of the Sanskrit phrase Odra Vishaya. It was in the early 15th century that names like odisa, odisa rashtra and odisa rajya came to be known and used in both public and private records. , the extent of its territory was indeterminate till the 7th century A.D. Cf. N.K. SAHU et al., History of Orissa, Cuttack 1989, pp. 15-16; T.J. MALTBY, The Ganjam District Manual, Madras 1882, p. 95.

[2] However, the geographical boundaries of the state of Orissa were not fixed until the 7th century. It was only during the 12th century that the territories of erstwhile Kalinga and Utkal were united. Subsequently the Oriya script originated and the famous Jagannath and Sun temples were constructed. J. PATHY, Ethnic Minorities in the Process of Development, Jaipur 1988, p. 67.

[3] Traditionally one can speak of Kalinga, Utkala and Kosala as the forerunners of present-day Orissa which became an administrative unit on April 1, 1936. Sardar Ballabhbhai Patel, the then Union Home Minister, left no stone unturned to amalgamate all princely states with Orissa, popularly known as Mughal Bandi and Garjats. His efforts continued till the merger of Mayurbhanj, last of the princely states, with Orissa on January 1, 1949. Cf. N.C. BEHURIA (ed.), Orissa State Gazetteer. Orissa State, vol. II, Cuttack 1991, pp. 8 – 9.

[4] N. C. BEHURIA (ed.), Orissa State Gazetteer: Orissa State, vol. I, Cuttack 1990, p. 10

[5] Ibid., p. 30; A.C. PRADHAN, A Study of History of Orissa, Bhubaneswar 1988, p.1.

[6] N. C. BEHURIA (ed.), Orissa State Gazetteer: Orissa State, vol. I, p. 33.

[7] In spite of the construction of reservoirs for irrigation there is drought and scarcity of water during summer. Ibid., p. 54.

[8] Ibid., p. 118; Bro. Piccot described the climatic conditions of the mission: "Il y a environ un mois qu'ici deux ou trois matins le thermomètre descendit jusqu'à 5 degrés en dessus de zéro." Piccot to Clavel, Surada, February 23, 1857, AMSFS, 7Z/5H5; However, Msgr. Rossillon sees the climate differently: "Le thermomètre descend parfois jusqu'à 15°, 10° et même plus bas, sans jamais passer 0° cependant, et c'est alors pour nous un froid de Sibérie." P. ROSSILLON, "Cent Kilomètres sur des épaules Kondes", in LMC 44 (1912), p. 340.

[9] Here is a vivid description of the heat by one veteran missionary from Ganjam, Fr. Dupont : "Une heure après le coucher du soleil le thermomètre anglais Farenheit marquait 95° de chaleur dans une grande vérandah, soit corridor, exposée de tous côtés à la fraicheur de la nuit. À Aska, dans un grand bureau, le même thermomètre marquait, ces jour-là, 115°. Mais sans thermomètre, quand je fus de retour à Berhampore, je reconnnus bien que les jours prècédents avaient été d'une chaleur exceptionnelle, car les feuilles de quelques arbres plantés vis-à-vis de notre église et déjà bien grands, se trouvaient en grande partie brûlées comme si one y eut fait un grand feu à côté." Dupont to Superior, Berhampur, August 10, 1882, AMSFS 5H5-2/2.

[10] N. C. BEHURIA (ed.), Orissa State Gazetteer: Orissa State, vol. I, p. 137.

[11] A. C. Pradhan commented: "The Kalinga War of 261 B.C. is the sheet of anchor of Orissan history. With it begins the dated history of Orissa, even though the history of the land can be traced to a period as early as the sixth century B.C.". A. C. PRADHAN, A Study of History of Orissa, p. 9.

[12] Emperor Ashoka pursued the path of benevolence and justice. Buddhism spread in Kalinga under his patronage, and later became the state religion. Under royal patronage the art of stone masonry developed to a great extent. Edicts were engraved on the Dhauli rocks (near Bhubaneswar) and the Jaugada rocks (Ganjam district) to announce his administrative and religious principles to the people. The rock inscriptions of Ashoka date back to the 3rd century B.C. "One of the remarkable Rock Edicts gives details of that terrible campaign: 150,000 became captives, 100,000 were slain and many times that number died in the consequent famine and pestilence". B. M. BOAL, The Kondhs: Human Sacrifice and Religious Change, New Delhi 1993, p. 322; N. C. BEHURIA (ed.), Orissa State Gazetteer: Orissa State, vol. I, pp. 183-184; J. MURRAY, A Handbook for Travellers in India, London, 1929 lxxvii –lxxxiv.

[13] There is no unanimity among historians with regard to the duration of the reign of Kharavela. However, with all probability one can conclude that he "could not be earlier than second century B.C. and later than first century B.C. Most probably he belonged to first century B.C. Kharavela was undoubtedly a benevolent monarch. He was concerned with the well being of his people. That's why he remitted taxes, dug canals and organised festivals and musical performances". A.C. PRADHAN, A Study of History of Orissa, pp. 18, 23.

[14] N. C. BEHURIA (ed.), Orissa State Gazetteer: Orissa State, vol. I, pp. 138, 184-185.

[15] From 736 A.D., when the first Bhaumakara king Sivakaradeva I ascended to the throne, till the death of the last of Bhaumakara ruler Dharma Mahadevi and the occupation of the kingdom by a Somavasi King Dharmaratna (960 - 995), the Bhaumakaras ruled Orissa, which was known by the name of Tosali. Cf. Ibid., pp. 191–194; A. C. PRADHAN, A Study of History of Orissa, pp. 41 - 49.

[16] N. C. BEHURIA (ed.), Orissa State Gazetteer: Orissa State, vol. I, p. 139.

[17] The Somavamsis left their legacy in art and architecture. The Orissan temple architecture, which began with in the Sailodbhava period, reached its perfection in this period. Though they were ardent shaivites they pursued the path set by the Bhaumakaras in granting religious tolerance. "The absolutism of Somavamsi rulers (they were absolute monarchs) was tempered by the kings' respect for Dharma (religion), the protection and welfare of the subjects, the wise counsel of ministers, and the injunctions of the scriptures." Ibid., pp. 199 – 202; A. C. PRADHAN, A Study of History of Orissa, pp. 56 – 69.

[18] The Gangas, distinguished as later or imperial Gangas from the early or eastern Gangas who ruled Kalinga about the 5th century A.D., ruled from 1038 with the enthronement of Vajrahasta V till the capture of Bhanudeva IV, a weak and imbecile ruler in 1435. Cf. N.C. BEHURIA (ed.), Orissa State Gazetteer: Orissa State, vol. I, pp. 202 – 207; A. C. PRADHAN, A Study of History of Orissa, pp. 79-104.

[19] Vaishnavism is a belief that centres on Lord Vishnu as the supreme deity in Hinduism, whereas Shaivism upholds Lord Shiva as the supreme deity.

[20] Jagannath, Lord of the Universe, is really a name of Krishna, one of the avataras or manifestations of Vishnu. (The doctrine of Jagannath is all-enveloping, so that he could be considered as appearing in the form of Brahma and even Buddha) The immense popularity of the temple town is due to the doctrine preached that before God all are equal, both high castes and low castes. There are three deities worshipped in the magnificent temple: Jagannath, Balabhadra, his brother and Subhadra, his sister. The three images are annually drawn in procession at the Rathajatra, the car festival, which attracts devotees from all over the country. In times past there were devotees who would immolate themselves under the wheels of Lord Jagannath with the hope of obtaining salvation. Cf. J. MURRAY, A Handbook for Travellers in India, p. 511.

[21] A. C. PRADHAN, A Study of History of Orissa, p. 85.

[22] Sir John Marshal, then Director General of Archaeology, stated that there is no monument of Hinduism that is at once so stupendous and so perfectly proportioned as the Black Pagoda, another name for the Sun Temple at Konark. The temple is carved in the form of a chariot of the Sun God to whom it was dedicated. There are a number of very fine carved figures of green chlorite on the walls, often erotic in posture. The temple is called black in contrast to the white washed pagoda at Puri. Cf. N.C. BEHURIA (ed.), Orissa State Gazetteer: Orissa State, vol. I, pp. 139 –140; T. J. MALTBY, The Ganjam District Manual, p. 97; J. MURRAY, A Handbook for Travellers in India, p. 514.

[23] Even the present king of Puri is considered to be a descendant of this dynasty. The office of the king of Puri is limited to some spiritual services to Lord Jagannath, the most famous of which is Chhera Pahamara, sweeping the chariot of the three deities during the great Car Festival in Puri. This shows the boundless devotion of the king to the worship of Lord Jagannath. Kapilendradeva's (1435 - 1468) accession to the throne, which established the rule of Suryavamsi Gajapatis (Gajapatis means the lords of elephants), opened a new era in the history of Orissa. Cf. A C. PRADHAN, A Study of History of Orissa, pp. 105 – 139; N. K. SAHU et al, History of Orissa, pp. 237 - 238.

[24] In 1568, the area of present Ganjam district was conquered by Golkonda (Sultans) and in the early 17th century the districts north of the river Subarnarekha were annexed to the Bengal Subah of the Mughal Empires. However, "the fate of Orissa was determined when in 1751 the Marathas conquered the central and western Orissa whereas southern and northern Orissa remained under the rule of the Nizam of Hyderabad and the Nawab of Bengal respectively". N. C. BEHURIA (ed.), Orissa State Gazetteer: Orissa State, vol. I, p.3.

[25] During the Maratha reign, Orissa was under two administrative blocks: 1) the Mughalbandi area, the coastal areas (Cuttack, Puri, Balasore, etc.) and 2) the Garhjats, the tributary states, that were about 24 in number. The tributary chiefs paid an annual tribute in order to retain their independence. When the British took over the administration, the Mughalbandi areas came under their direct rule,

whereas the Garhjats obtained their semi-independence. Cf. M. DHALL, The British Rule: Missionary Activities in Orissa 1822 – 1947, New Delhi 1997, p. 42.

[26] The East India Company took control of Orissa in 1803. Even the East India Company did not unite the Oriya-speaking territory; on the contrary it was administered by five political authorities or units, i.e., Bengal and its Orissa division, Chotanagpur, the Central Provinces, Madras and the Garhjat Mahals of feudatory states of Orissa. Ganjam and other Oriya-speaking areas south of Chilika Lake remained linked to Madras; Midnapore to Bengal; Singhbhum, Seraikela and Kharsawan to Chotanagpur Division; Sambalpur and the Chhatisgarh feudatory states to the Central Provinces. Cf. N. C. BEHURIA (ed.), Orissa State Gazetteer: Orissa State, vol. I, p. 3.

[27] J. PATHY, Ethnic Minorities in the Process of Development, p. 68.

[28] Ganjam lies between 18° 12' and 20° 26' N. and 83° 30' and 85 12' E. with an area of 8, 372 miles. It was once the headquarters of the district, but the derivation of the name (Ganjam) is unknown. Some would find the etymology in Ganji – am (store house of the world). But this is not a satisfactory answer. With its mountains, forests and valleys, it was one of the most beautiful districts of the Madras presidency, winning the affection of almost every officer who served in the district. Cf. The Imperial Gazetteer of India, vol. XII, Oxford 1908, p. 143.

[29] T. J. MALTBY, The Ganjam District Manual, p. 1.

[30] The Imperial Gazetteer of India, Vol. XII, Clarendon Press, Oxford 1908, p. 143.

[31] B. M. BOAL, The Kondhs: Human Sacrifice and Religious Change, p. 35.

[32] T. J. MALTBY, The Ganjam District Manual, p. 2.

[33] Ibid., p. 3; The Imperial Gazetteer of India, Vol. XI, p. 144.

[34] B. M. BOAL, The Kondhs: Human Sacrifice and Religious Change, p. 92.

[35] R. K. NAYAK et al., Kondhs, p. 4.

[36] The Great King Rajendra Cholan left the record of his victories on Mohendragiri, which is situated in Ganjam District. Cf. The Imperial Gazetteer of India, Vol. XI, p. 145.

[37] Ibid.

[38] T. J. MALTBY, The Ganjam District Manual, p. 99.

[39] Ibid., pp. 101-102; The Imperial Gazetteer of India, Vol. XI, pp. 145 – 146.

[40] Bissoy or Bisaye, although an Oriya Hindu, was regarded as hereditary patriarch of a loose federation of Kondh clans and was agent for Kondh affairs to the Rajah of Goomsur. Cf. B.M. BOAL, The Kondhs: Human Sacrifice and Religious Change, p. 76.

[41] The Imperial Gazetteer of India, Vol. XI, p. 145.

[42] It's a local name given to British officers. People were generally frightened of them.

[43] In 1835, Raja Dananjia of Goomsur failed to pay the heavy arrears that had in fact accumulated from his father's time, who already had fled in 1832. Since conciliatory efforts had failed, Mr. Stevenson, the Collector for Ganjam, issued an arrest warrant for the Raja. Open rebellion broke out and martial law was proclaimed. The Raja and his followers fled to the fever-ridden foothills. Traditional Kondh hospitality was offered to the fugitive Raja. The British troops found it difficult to penetrate into the fever-ridden jungles. It was at this time that Mr. Russell arrived as the special commissioner with greater powers over the area. Cf. B. M. BOAL, The Kondhs: Human Sacrifice and Religious Change, pp. 73 –74.

[44] T. J. MALTBY, The Ganjam District Manual, p. 13.

[45] The victims of human sacrifice were called Meriah by Oriyas. The Kondhs called them tokki or keddi. A person of any race or age and of either sex was acceptable, if purchased, as were the children of the purchased Meriahs. Male and female Meriahs were encouraged to cohabit so that the children born out of this union could become Meriah. Cf. M.S. CHATERS, An Account of the Religion of the Khonds, London 1852, p. 36; K. P. BAHADUR, Castes, Tribes and Culture of India. Bengal, Bihar and Orissa, vol. III, pp. 21– 22.

[46] Russelkonda (Russell's Hill), now called Bhanjanagar, was the headquarters of the Maliah tracts. Ibid., p. 14; J. MURRAY, A Handbook for Travellers in India, p. 516.

[47] T. J. MALTBY, The Ganjam District Manual, p. 10.

[48] The origin of Kondhs and even the derivation of the word 'Kondh' is obscure. 'Kondh' is a word given to the tribe by outsiders. 'Kondh' probably is a Telugu word, meaning hill or mountain. Given a chance, the community prefers to call itself Kuiloka or Kuienju, which derives from the word Kui, the language they speak. Some scholars, such as Barbara M. Boal, prefer to call them Kui people, which may possibly be derived from ko or ku, a Telugu word for 'mountain'. These people occupy a vast territory filled with mountains and valleys that cannot be penetrated by either Indians or Europeans without contracting the fatal mountain fever. Some scholars are of the opinion that the word might have been derived from the Tamil word khand, a hill, or from kandra, an arrow. Others think that it is identifiable with the Oriya word khanda meaning an area of land calculated by the quantity of seed sown in it. This, they say, is because the Kondhs are believed to be a race of peaceful cultivators who once lived in the plains of Orissa. There is another theory that explains the origin of the Kondhs. The tribe got its name from the Oriya word for a sword, which is khanda. The khand (sword) is the totem of the tribe. This explanation appears to be most plausible. The Oriya spelling for kondh is kandh. Cf. K. P. BAHADUR, Castes, Tribes and Culture of India. Bengal, Bihar and Orissa, vol. III, pp. 18 – 19; T. J. MALTBY, The Ganjam District Manual, p. 65; R. CUGNET, "Lettre de M. Richard Cugnet, vicaire général de la mission de Vizagapatam, à MM. les Membres des Conseils centraux de l'Œuvre de la Propagation de la Foi", in Annales de la Propagation de la Foi 52 (1880), p. 103; B.M. BOAL, The Kondhs: Human Sacrifice and

Religious Change, p. 21; R.V. RUSSELL, The Tribes and Castes of the Central Provinces of India, vol. III, London 1916, pp. 464 - 465.

[49] B. M. BOAL, The Kondhs: Human Sacrifice and Religious Change, p. 27.

[50] P. ROSSILLON, "Moeurs et Coutumes du peuple Kui. Indes Anglaises", in Anthropos 6 (1911), p. 998.

[51] R. K. NAYAK et al., Kondhs, p. 3. Living in scattered settlements, the Kondhs were politically under three separate authorities. M. Dhall writes: "The Kondhmals sub-division in the north was administered by Angul, the Balliguda sub-division was controlled by an Indian civilian collector and a portion of Ghumsur which was in the hill tracts was administered by an Indian Deputy Collector. The last two areas were within the Ganjam District and therefore were a part of Madras Presidency. The whole of Kondh region however was known as the Hill – Tracts Agency and these Collectors had special powers as Agents to the Governors." M. DHALL, The British Rule, p. 74.

[52] It was a custom until recently for the Raja of Kalahandi to sit on the lap of a Kondh on his accession while he received the oaths of fealty. The tribal chiefs were also present for the coronation that took place in a village to which all the chiefs repaired. The Raja was also accustomed to marry a Kondh girl as one of his wives, though later she was not allowed to live in the palace. These customs indicate that the Rajas of Kalahandi derived their rights from Kondhs. They also signify that at one time the Kondhs were the masters of the forest. It was later that the royal families acquired mastery over the land. This would also mean that the Kondhs were not subjugated by the Hindu states. It is said that they were also credited with driving away the Muslim invaders again and again from their territory. Cf. R.V. RUSSELL, Tribes and Castes of Central Provinces, vol. II, p.465; J. PATHY, "Colonial Ethnography of the Kandha 'White Man's Burden' or Political Expediency?", in Economic and Political Weekly 30/4 (1995), p. 226.

[53] Commenting on the origin of Kondhs, Barbara M. Boal wrote: "No mythology or legend yet discovered furnishes any clue to their origin or place of descent. They believe themselves to have existed in Orissa from the beginning". B. M. BOAL, The Kondhs: Human Sacrifice and Religious Change, p. 21.

[54] K. P. BAHADUR, Castes, Tribes and Culture of India. Bengal, Bihar and Orissa, vol. III, p. 18.

[55] B. M. BOAL, The Kondhs: Human Sacrifice and Religious Change, p. 360.

[56] Barbara M. Boal wrote: "Great Bura God is the Supreme Being. He is self-existing, source of all Good, Creator of the Universe, Creator of Man, Creator of the inferior gods." Ibid., pp. 94 & 274.

[57] Barbara M. Boal remarked: "Bura decided that he must create inferior deities whose functions would be to regulate the powers of nature for the use of man; to instruct man in the arts necessary to life; to protect man against every form of evil; and in return, man must seek their favour through worshipping them

with food offerings they desire. But Bura also made it understood that these inferior deities were only worshipped by the sanction of Bura and Tari – for worship was due to Bura and Tari alone, and therefore these two must continue to be the first names involved in ceremonial." So, three classes of inferior gods were created corresponding to the needs of man. To list a few important ones: Dondo Penu – the god of punishment; Loha Penu – the god of war (iron); Darni Penu – the god of the household who guards every home; Danderi Penu – this is also a kind of household god who guards the rear side of the house; Karang Penu – the god of illness; Djodi Penu – the god of rivers; Oda Penu – the god of paddy fields and the tiger god. Cf. Ibid., p. 96; P. ROSSILLON, Moeurs et Coutumes du peuple Kui. Indes Anglaises, in Anthropos 7 (1912), pp. 650 – 651.

[58] Tari is also invoked by other names: Darni goddess, the earth goddess; Jakeri (founder) goddess; so that the central Darni shrine-stones may also be called Jakeri or founder-stones and the shrine-keepers the Jakeri or founder. "Bura God found that Tari wanting in wifely attentions and affectionate compliance, so Bura God created man from the earth's substance, to give him really devoted service… Tari's jealousy led her to open rebellion against Bura. Therefore, she introduced every form of moral and physical evil. She introduced diseases, deadly poisons and every kind of disorder." B.M. BOAL, The Kondhs: Human Sacrifice and Religious Change, pp. 94-95, 182.

[59] Tari Penu, the earth goddess, by shedding her own blood, manifested to her votaries that it had beneficial effects and persuaded them that this process of fertilisation must be continued by periodical human sacrifice in her honour. The sacrifices were offered to the earth goddess, Tari Penu or Bera Penu, and were believed to ensure good crops and immunity from all diseases and accidents. In particular, they were considered necessary for the cultivation of turmeric. The Kondhs argue that turmeric could not have a deep red colour without the shedding of blood. The victims could be of any race or caste, young or old, male or female, though naturally strangers were preferred. Commenting on the Meriah, Rossillon observed, "D'autres victimes humaines devenaient nécessaries en temps d'épidémie, ou autres clamités publiques. Elles étaient aussi offertes à titre privé dans certains cas de maladie ou d'infortune dans les familles". P. ROSSILLON, "Moeurs et Coutumes du peuple Kui. Indes Anglaises", in Anthropos 7 (1912), p. 652; K. P. BAHADUR, Castes, Tribes and Culture of India. Bengal, Bihar and Orissa, vol. III, Delhi 1977, p. 21; R.V. RUSSELL, Tribes and Castes of Central Provinces, vol. II, p. 497; B. M. BOAL, The Kondhs: Human Sacrifice and Religious Change, p. 8; A detailed report regarding the practice of Meriah is given to the Propaganda by Mgr. Neyret, Vicar Apostolic of Vizagapatam. Cf. Msgr. Neyret to Cardinal Fransoni, Vizagapatam, November 5, 1850, APF Indie Orientali: Scritture Riferite nei Congressi, vol. 12, ff. 1107-1109.

[60] K. P. BAHADUR, Castes, Tribes and Culture of India. Bengal, Bihar and Orissa, vol. III, pp. 21– 22.

[61] The earth, say the Kondhs, was originally a formless mass unsuitable for cultivation and human habitation. But when Bura Penu [Tari Penu] said that human blood had to be cast in front of him, they sacrificed a child and immediately the earth received its form and became productive. However, this situation would continue only if they continued to offer sacrifices time and again. Cf. P. ROSSILLON, "Moeurs et Coutumes du peuple Kui. Indes Anglaises", in Anthropos 7 (1912), p. 652.

[62] The number of darni stones varies between three and twelve, but three stones always remain at the head of the heap. These represent the family: two for the married couple, pondri riari (this is an ancient word meaning married couple) and a flat one for the child, ronde mila. Cf. B. M. BOAL, The Kondhs: Human Sacrifice and Religious Change, p. 365.

[63] There is a rite to find out the name through the dropping of uncooked rice. If the rice floats on the water, then the child should not be called by that name, but if it sinks, then that is the name of the child. P. ROSSILLON, "Un baptême d'enfants au pays des Khondes", in Annales de la Propagation de la Foi 89 (1917), pp. 144 – 145.

[64] Barbara M. Boal observed: "Ancestors do not suffer human limitations of mobility, though in order to return to the fuller and more desirable state of the living they may seek rebirth into their kin group. When a baby begins to show decided personality characteristics (probably about six months), he arouses speculation as to whose spirit may have re-entered the living world at his birth, either temperament or physical features being the guide". B.M. BOAL, The Kondhs: Human Sacrifice and Religious Change, p. 258.

[65] R. V. RUSSELL, Tribes and Castes of Central Provinces, vol. II, p. 469.

[66] B. M. BOAL, The Kondhs: Human Sacrifice and Religious Change, p. 364.

[67] P. ROSSILLON, "Moeurs et Coutumes du peuple Kui. Indes Anglaises", in Anthropos 6 (1911), pp. 1001 – 1002.

[68] Ibid., pp. 649 – 650.

[69] Purification ceremonies require a little uncooked rice, chicken's blood, an egg, etc., with the celebrant's fasting (not only abstaining from food but also from sexual intercourse for two or three days prior to the ceremony), and a ritual bath. Cf. B. M. BOAL, The Kondhs: Human Sacrifice and Religious Change, pp. 246 – 248, 267 and 350.

[70] Otherwise the deity may hide the animal and allow the wounded prey to escape. Cf. R.V. RUSSELL, Tribes and Castes of Central Provinces, vol. II, p. 474.

[71] B. M. BOAL, The Kondhs: Human Sacrifice and Religious Change, p. 378.

[72] The mode of performing the sacrifice is as follows: ten or twelve days before the sacrifice, the victim was denoted by cutting off his hair, which, until then, had been kept unshorn. Crowds of men and women assemble to witness the sacrifice. Since the sacrifice is declared to be for all mankind, they wish that

no one be excluded. The sacrifice is preceded by several days of wild revelry and gross debauchery. On the day before the sacrifice the victim, dressed in a new garment, was led forth from the village in solemn procession, with music and dancing, to the Meriah grove, a clump of high forest trees standing a little way from the village and untouched by the axe. Here they tie him/her to a post. He was then anointed with oil, ghee and turmeric. People continue to pay their homage to him throughout the day. They love to get a smallest of relic, a particle of the turmeric paste with which he was smeared, or a drop of his spittle, etc., because these were esteemed of sovereign virtue, especially by the women. The crowd danced round the post to music, and addressing the Earth said, 'O God, we offer this sacrifice to you; give us good crops, seasons, and health'. Cf. R.V. RUSSELL, Tribes and Castes of Central Provinces, vol. II, p. 474; R. CUGNET, "Lettre de M. Richard Cugnet, vicaire general de la mission de Vizagapatam, à MM. les Membres des Conseils centraux de l'Œuvre de la Propagation de la Foi", in Annales de la Propagation de la Foi 52 (1880), pp. 105 – 108; Msgr. Neyret presents a moving account of the infamous belief of the Kondhs in his letter to Monsieur Mermier, founder and superior of the congregation on September 6, 1850. Cf. Archives MSFS 7 Z / 5 H 5; For a detailed study of Meriah sacrifice and the prayers attached to it see the third chapter of B. M. BOAL, The Kondhs: Human Sacrifice and Religious Change, New Delhi 1993.

[73] The first observations were made by Mr. Russell during the Goomsur wars from 1835 to 1837. The earliest account of human sacrifice was submitted on May 11, 1837 to the Madras Government by Mr. Russell of the Madras Civil Service. Later, on November 24, 1837, additions were made by Mr. Arbuthnot, Acting Collector of Visagapatnam. Variations in the precise manner in which the Meriah was put to death were also noted by Capt. John Campbell and Capt. S.C. Macpherson, officers under whom the expedition to the Kondhmals took place (1837 – 1845). In June 1841, a full report was presented to the Supreme Court of India; later it was given as an address to the Royal Asiatic Society, London. In June 1841, Capt. Macpherson collected the prayers used at the Meriah sacrifice. Cf. B. M. BOAL, The Kondhs: Human Sacrifice and Religious Change, p. 185.

[74] To quote Barbara M. Boal: "All available versions of the myths of origin of the sacrifice are similar on this one point: that it began through the Earth Goddess' insistent demand for human flesh-food and her refusal to accept any animal substitute; and that she first 'taught' them exactly how to procure and kill the victim and offer the flesh. Only then would she keep her side of the bargain". Ibid., p. 241.

[75] In times past, in order to secure its rapid arrival, they used to have a relay of men, so that they may receive it in the village as soon as possible and bury it in their places before sunset.

[76] Extracts from the earliest description reported to the Madras Government in 1837 by Mr. Russell of the Madras Civil Service. Cf. B. M. BOAL, The Kondhs: Human Sacrifice and Religious Change, p. 189.

[77] The purpose of the Meriah, as a rule, was to increase fertility of the soil. They hoped to obtain this by burying bits of the flesh of the victims in the fields. The British officers did not fail to point out the failures or the inefficacy of the sacrifice. They were even willing to take the blame on themselves. They tried to cure common sickness by posting a doctor in the hill tract. Though between 1837 and 1854 no fewer than 1506 victims were rescued, the economic status of the people remained the same. The Kondh people gradually became convinced that their fields produced crops as good as formerly, and that sickness was no more prevalent. Animals were substituted for human victims, and it is believed that the Meriah horrors have finally been suppressed. Cf. V. A. SMITH, The Oxford History of India. From the Earliest Times to the end of 1911, Oxford 1928, p. 690; R. V. RUSSELL, Tribes and Castes of Central Provinces, vol. II, p. 479.

[78] As far as the origin of female infanticide is concerned, Kanchanmoy has the following to say: "The Kondh tradition had it that in ancient times two sisters, having failed to get husbands, got involved in incestuous relations with their first cousins – uncle's sons – and the resultant social disgrace drove them to suicide by drowning. The men blamed the girls for the social opprobrium suffered by the two families and decided to destroy their female children at birth itself as a precaution against the occurrence of such scandals in future." M. KANCHANMOY, Changing Tribal Life in British Orissa, New Delhi 1998, p. 47.

[79] B. M. BOAL, The Kondhs: Human Sacrifice and Religious Change, p. 121.

[80] Ibid., p. 122

[81] The entire chapter of M. Kanchannoy on "Female Infanticide in the Hill Tracts of Ganjam" is well documented with convincing arguments. Cf. M. KANCHANNOY, Changing Tribal Life in British Orissa, pp. 45 – 58.

[82] R. K. NAYAK et al., Kondhs, pp. 7 - 8.

[83] K. P. BAHADUR, Castes, Tribes and Culture of India. Bengal, Bihar and Orissa, vol. III, p. 19.

[84] The faithfulness of Kondhs to their chief is proverbial. Probably this induced the British to stop interfering in the internal affairs of Kondh. The principle of authority is very strong among the Kondhs. The clan chief has all the power over the clan, the chief of the village over the village and the head of the family over the family. They are like kings in their respective areas. Cf. P. ROSSILLON, "Moeurs et Coutumes du people kui, Indes Anglaises", in Anthropos 6 (1911), p. 999.

[85] Similar comments were made by Macpherson, a government officer who spent long years among the Kondhs and who had a good acquaintance with them. Kondhs are strong, intelligent and good-natured. In times of peace they are jolly companions and in times of war dangerous enemies. Cf. Ibid., p. 998.

[86] R.V. RUSSELL, Tribes and Castes of Central Provinces, vol. II, p. 470.

[87] T. J. MALTBY, The Ganjam District Manual, p. 68.

[88] P. ROSSILLON, "Moeurs et Coutumes du People Kui, Indes Anglaises", in Anthropos 6 (1911), p. 1000.

[89] B. M. BOAL, The Kondhs: Human Sacrifice and Religious Change, p. 54.

[90] Ibid., p. 137.

[91] The professions found honourable for Kondhs are agriculture, hunting and war. It is probably for this reason that Kondhs were unable to procure victims for the Meriah sacrifice and sought the help of Panos. Ibid., p. 100.

[92] Msgr. Rossillon observed : "Les principales céréales cultivées chez eux sont : kudinga le riz, kanga les lentilles, ioelaka le mais, kueri le millet; à ces céréales ajoutons les haricots (kandulo) de plusieurs espèces". P. ROSSILLON, "Moeurs et Coutumes du People Kui, Indes Anglaises", in Anthropos 6 (1911), p. 1001.

[93] Everything in the tree is useful: oil produced from the fruit mixed with clarified butter possesses medicinal effect, the flower is used as food (they dry and preserve them for the monsoon when they are unable to procure food), and to make liquor. Cf. Ibid., p. 1002.

[94] Ibid., p. 1008.

[95] NEYRET, "Extrait d'une lettre de Msgr. Neyret, évêque d'Olène et Vicaire Apostolic de Visagapatam, à MM. les Directeurs de l'Œuvre de la Propagation de la Foi", in Annales de la Propagation de la Foi 27 (1855), p.361.

[96] Patros are the representatives of the kings. They generally belong to the Brahmin community. Moliko is the recognised head of the Kondh community who takes the service of a Pano with a title Digalo. Digalo is the spokesman of Moliko who is shy and uneducated.

[97] Some of the functions of village headman are "to preside over the traditional village council; to receive important guests; to perform certain duties for the community on ritual occasions; to be ultimately responsible for ensuring that festivals are rightly fixed, the right sacrifices and offerings arranged, duties rightly allocated, invitations to the right guests from neighbouring villages, and, if the need arises, to meet with the headman of other villages on some wider issue, one of them being elected leader for that specific occasion, and simply as 'first among equals'". R. K. NAYAK et al., Kondhs, p. 31.

[98] Ibid., p. 117.

[99] Society for Evaluation, The Panos. Study of a Scheduled Caste Community in Orissa, Social Services, Research and Training, Delhi, and National Institute of Social Work and Social Sciences, Bhubaneswar, 1995 – 1996, p. 2.

[100] The term dalits denotes people who are considered to be low in the caste hierarchy. They were formally known as Harijans, a term given by M.K. Gandhi, or 'Scheduled Castes', a term now in use in the Constitution of India. They are socially outcaste who live economically in misery, and religiously seemed to be polluting. However, given a chance they prefer to call themselves Dalits, because it conveys what they are. "The term dalit derived from the Sanskrit root dal which

means to crack, open, split, etc. when used as a noun or adjective it means burst, split, broken or torn asunder, downtrodden, scattered, crushed, destroyed, etc." This expresses the state in which they are found. Dr. Bhimrao Ramji Ambedkar (1891 - 1956) coined the term dalit to portray the "oppressed and broken victims of the caste-ridden society". L. STANISLAUS, The Liberative Mission of the Church among Dalit Christians, Delhi 1999, pp. 2 -3

[101] Panams, Pans, Panas and Panos are the words used to refer to the group. The word Pano is probably derived from the word Pani, which means water. This could be a functional name as their ancestors used to carry water to the kings. As the years went by, the people were identified with what they brought, hence they got the name Pano. There is yet another explanation found in the Rig Veda 6.37,74. It speaks of a group called Pani. This was one of the important groups, namely Rakshasa, Asura and Pani. It is common belief that the present Panos are the descendants of that group. However, these are popular understandings that are prevalent among the Panos themselves. Sociologists and anthropologists are yet to discover the hidden and forgotten origin and history of the Panos. Cf. Reported from an interview conducted by S. SINGH, A Critical Study on Socio-Religious dimension of Pano Marriage, Khristo Jyoti, Sason, 1998 (unpublished).

[102] Nothing is known regarding the origin of Panos. They are thought to have been Hindus but have accepted the beliefs and rituals of their hosts. For example, in the Kondh hills they adopted the beliefs of Kondhs. Cf. B. M. BOAL, The Kondhs: Human Sacrifice and Religious Change, p. 22.

[103] Regarding the migration of Panos to the Kondh Mountains, J. Pathy wrote: "All accounts suggest that the Kondh purchased Meriah through the Hindu low caste Panas (Panos), who lived in and around the Kondh villages. Existing evidence points to the immigration of this caste to Kandhland less than 200 years ago. They came after being exiled from some of the neighbouring Hindu kingdoms for their alleged involvement in thefts and robbery. The Kandhas (Kondhs) gave them shelter in their villages, and they in turn acted as mediators between the Kandhas and Oriyas, and worked as weavers and traders. In other words, if the Panas were the sole procurers of the victims, the tradition of the human sacrifice by purchase of victims can at best be traced to the end of the 18th or beginning of the 19th century, which almost coincides with the East India Company's attempts to annex the territory." J. PATHY, "Colonial Ethnography of the Kandha. White Man's Burden or Political Expediency?", in Economic and Political Weekly 30/4 (1995), p. 224.

[104] However, the real reason needs to be unearthed. Cf. Society for Evaluation, The Panos: Study of a Scheduled Caste Community in Orissa, pp. 1, 12.

[105] Panos are one of the 93 Scheduled Caste communities in Orissa. R. K. NAYAK et al., Kondhs, p. 10.

[106] They are presented as the laziest race in the country. Otto Waack in his work on 'Church and Mission in India', cites D. N. Majumdar that "An entire

tribe cannot be criminal, nor even can a large section be so... Many members of criminal tribes do not commit any crime, neither do they have any ambivalence towards crime". These are some of the 'white man's' prejudices concerning Panos. This possibly mirrors the existing prejudices, particularly when they are compared with the shy, introvert and community-bound Kondhs. O. WAACK, Church and Mission in India. The History of Jeypore Church and the Breklum Mission (1876 - 1914), Delhi 1997, pp. 36 – 40; F. MOGET, Early Days of the Visakhapatnam Mission 1846 – 1920, Bangalore 1997, p. 246.

[107] Ibid., p 8.

[108] The whole question centres on whether one considers their origin as tribals or dalits. Some like R. K. Nayak and Bailey are of the opinion that at one point they were considered as tribals but later were included in the list of scheduled castes – and so they are considered untouchables. But if one assumes that the Panos were once tribals, then they are not Hindus. Anthropologists in general are of the opinion that the tribes, who have their traditional religion, do not come under the fold of Hinduism. Cf. Society for Evaluation, The Panos: Study of a Scheduled Caste Community in Orissa, p.9; R. K. NAYAK et al., Kondhs, p. 10.

[109] Ibid.

[110] Society for Evaluation, The Panos: Study of a Scheduled Caste Community in Orissa, p. 8.

[111] The Kondhs consider the Panos inferior not because they procured human victims for the sacrifice nor because they brought the victims through abduction or fraudulent means, "but because they did it for purposes that were deep-rooted not in their own religious values but in Kondh". B. M. BOAL, The Kondhs: Human Sacrifice and Religious Change, p. 292.

[112] "A person killed by a tiger turns into a dangerous spirit, which roams around in the jungle in search of victims. The family of the victim is temporarily excommunicated till the stipulated sacrifices are made to rectify the relationship resulted in the death of the person. A person dead by this kind of unnatural death is either buried or cremated far from the village, mostly in the jungle. This site is normally avoided for fear of being attacked by the tiger. The site itself is sealed by a gunia doctor." Society for Evaluation, The Panos: Study of a Scheduled Caste Community in Orissa, p. 45.

[113] Ibid., p. 43.

[114] Ibid., p. 49.

[115] "Kondh beju and bejuni in Bissam Cuttack area, and dissaris in South Koraput, are hired by Panos, to perform reparatory rituals in times of sickness, death and impurity." Ibid., p.55.

[116] Ibid., p. 59.

[117] Ekoisia is a purificatory ceremony performed on the 21st day of the birth of a child. Till then, not only are the mother and child considered to be impure, but

also the entire family. After this purificatory ceremony the mother is allowed to enter the kitchen and to cook food. After this ceremony, the child is also accepted as a member of the community.

[118] Ibid., p. 51.

[119] Ibid., p. 54.

[120] Ibid., p. 58.

[121] The demand for the clothes woven by the Panos could also be another reason why Panos migrated to the hill tracts. Traditionally they were the major suppliers of clothes to the tribals. Cf. Ibid., pp. 39, 63.

[122] Their musical instruments consist of mahuri (pipe), dhola and badya (drums). They were paid for their musical service in kind. They are not only good instrumentalists, but also good singers and dancers. Ibid., p. 38.

[123] B. M. BOAL, The Kondhs: Human Sacrifice and Religious Change, p. 23.

[124] Society for Evaluation, The Panos: Study of a Scheduled Caste Community in Orissa, p. 64.

[125] Ibid., p. 66.

[126] Ibid., p. 68.

[127] One can't generalise and apply this to Panos as a group. There are some villages that have taken to robbery, one such a group is "Jayantira Panos" of Jajpur area in Orissa. They have some prescribed rituals to be followed before they set out for their work. They have their reasons for such practices. For a detailed study on the Jayantira Panos see M. BEHERA, The Jayantira Pano: A Scheduled Caste Community of Orissa, K. K. MOHANTY (ed.), Bhubaneswar 1991; B. M. BOAL, The Kondhs: Human Sacrifice and Religious Change, p. 23.

[128] Society for Evaluation, The Panos: Study of a Scheduled Caste Community in Orissa, p. 13.

[129] E. T. DALTON, Descriptive Ethnology of Bengal: Tribal History of Eastern India, Calcutta 1872, p. 299.

[130] Society for Evaluation, The Panos: Study of a Scheduled Caste Community in Orissa, p. 81.

[131] Ibid., p. 27.

[132] Ibid., p. 32.

[133] Ibid., pp. 95 - 96.

[134] Ibid., p. 102.

[135] R. K. Nayak is of the opinion that their mutually beneficial relationship goes back to the pre-history times. Cf. R. K. NAYAK et al., Kondhs, p. 10.

[136] If it occurred the entire family has to undergo a ritual cleansing. B. M. BOAL, The Kondhs: Human Sacrifice and Religious Change, p. 23.

[137] "When the headman tells him to call a village meeting or to give any information to the villagers, he gives the message in a loud shout either in the evening or early morning, when all are in their homes". Ibid., p. 11; Society for Evaluation, The Panos: Study of a Scheduled Caste Community in Orissa, p. 61.

[138] Ibid., p. 62.

[139] Ibid., p. 70.

[140] P. ROSSILLON, "Moeurs et Coutumes du people kui, Indes Anglaises", in Anthropos 7 (1912), p. 656.

[141] As a sign of their acceptance as equals, those Panos who provide victims for the sacrifice were given a turmeric bath, along with the elders of the village. Society for Evaluation, The Panos: Study of a Scheduled Caste Community in Orissa, p. 56.

[142] B. M. BOAL, The Kondhs: Human Sacrifice and Religious Change, p. 24.

[143] This is yet another example of an outsider's prejudice against a group, which scored low in terms of character or submission, especially when compared with the Kondh neighbours. Such condemnation today would be erroneous and offensive as many groups of Panos are highly responsible and are attracted to the welfare of those around them. Cf. Ibid.

[144] Gangpur comprises a major part of the present civil district of Sundargarh in the state of Orissa. Although the State was under the Orissa division, it enjoyed its semi-independent character until the independence of India and later became part of the Sundargarh civil district of Orissa State.

[145] The Imperial Gazetteer of India. Vol. XII, Oxford 1908, p. 140.

[146] Ibid., p. 140.

[147] Ibid.

[148] N. SENAPATI (ed.), Orissa District Gazetteers: Sundargarh, Cuttack 1992, p. 54.

[149] However, "the local traditions of Gangpur mention the existence of a Kesari line with sixteen kings who ruled over Gangpur. It is said they had their headquarters variously at Belsaragarh, Junagarh, Masabiragarh, etc." Ibid.

[150] Ibid., p. 59.

[151] A Sanad is a (i) charter or grant, giving its name to a class of states in Central India held under a Sanad, (ii) any kind of deed grants. Under the Sanad the chief was formally recognized and permitted to administer his territory subject to prescribed conditions, and the tribute was fixed for a period of 20 years, at the end of which it was liable to revision. Cf. Indian Year Book, Bombay 1930, p. 11.

[152] F. J. BOWEN, Father Constant Lievens: The Apostle of Chotanagpur, London 1936, p. 155.

[153] A Sanad was granted to the then Raja Raghunath Sekhar Deo, in order to show his power and position vis-à-vis the British. Cf. N. SENAPATI (ed.), Orissa District Gazetteers: Sundargarh, p. 61.

¹⁵⁴ Ibid.

¹⁵⁵ Ibid.

¹⁵⁶ The Oraon tribe today prefers to call themselves the Kurukh people and their language Kurukh. For the sake of uniformity and to avoid confusion, Oraon is used in this work.

¹⁵⁷ There are various theories relating to the origin and migration of Oraons. S. C. Roy locates their original home in Deccan, whereas Col. E. Dalton assigns their origin to the western coast of India, but their own legends and folk tales narrate the Deccan or Konkan as their original home. From there they migrated to the Chotanagpur plateau via Shahabad and Rohtas. Cf. S. FUCHS, The Aboriginal Tribes of India, New Delhi 1973, p. 177; C. SAHU, "Oraon Dances of Bihar", in R. D. TRIBHUWAN et al. (eds.), Tribal Dances of India, New Delhi 1999, p. 245.

¹⁵⁸ L. CARDON, On the Oraon Tribe, APBS, India 1 –General, p. 1; F. A. GRIGNARD, "The Oraons and Mundas: From the time of their settlement in India", in Anthropos 6 (1909), p. 7.

¹⁵⁹ The official and recognised name of Oraons is kurukhs, but strangers call them Dhangars, which means "slaves". Cf. Ibid., p. 9.

¹⁶⁰ P. TETE, The Kharias and the History of the Catholic Church in Biru, Ranchi 1990, p. 40.

¹⁶¹ L. CARDON, On the Oraon Tribe, p. 1.

¹⁶² Sometimes the Gangpuria Oraons are referred to as Berga Oroaons, which stands for Belkha Oraons, i.e., Oraons of the kingdom. Ibid., pp. 1-2.

¹⁶³ F. DE SA, Crisis in Chota Nagpur, p. 30.

¹⁶⁴ Besides Dharmes (Sun God), the Oraons worship other village deities like Deasuli, Sarna, Burhia, Darka, Deswali and Gairahi Khunt. Cf. N. DUARY, "Oraon Dances in Chotanagpur: An Impact Study", in R. D. TRIBHUWAN et al. (eds.), Tribal Dances of India, New Delhi 1999, p. 255; F. DE SA, Crisis in Chota Nagpur, p. 31.

¹⁶⁵ L. CARDON, On the Oraon Tribe, p. 24.

¹⁶⁶ Dandakatta, is a ritual act of thanking the Supreme God, Dharmes, for all the blessings received such as good crops, numerous head of cattle, healthy children; at the same time, it is also an intercession for happiness and prosperity. The purpose of this ceremony is to obtain protection from evil and misfortune caused by natural calamities and sickness. Cf. B. TIRKEY, "Oraon Approaches to God and Spirits", in Sevartham 7 (1982), pp. 26-27.

¹⁶⁷ P. TETE, A Missionary Social Worker in India: J. B. Hoffmann, The Chota Nagpur Tenancy Act and the Catholic Co-operatives 1893-1928, Roma 1984, p. 4; "Strange as it may seem, the chief duty of the Naiga, the heathen priest is not sacrifice; praeternatural healing comes first. When a man falls sick, when epidemics break out, his it is to discover to which kind of harmful spirits the visitation is due. Once the harmful spirit is discovered propitiatory sacrifice is performed according

to the prescribed ritual. It is the naiga, the heathen priest to determine whether a goat, a cock, a cow or a buffalo is offered for the sacrifice". L. CARDON, On the Oraon Tribe, p. 8.

[168] Ibid., pp. 24-25.

[169] As soon as a dead body has been taken out to be carried to the funeral pile on the masra, a stop is made: and the mourners strew the house floor with fine wood ashes; then, before starting themselves, they lock the door carefully. As soon as the home is reached after the ceremony, those ashes are scrutinized for footprints of fowls, snakes or cats, or for marks left by a thread. From these signs a judgement is made whether the deceased has been taken to the bosom of Dharmes or swallowed up by the devils. Ibid., p. 27.

[170] The desiccated umbilical chord of the infant is buried in one of the common rooms where the cattle spend the night. This often reminds them of their native place. "A paddà nù enghai kuddà gararkì ra'ì; in that village my naval-string lies buried". Ibid., p. 14.

[171] Ibid., pp. 3 - 4.

[172] Ibid., pp. 14-15.

[173] "A small presence of Oraon tenants claim to be addiyar, i.e. to have sprung from the original settlers who cleared the primeval jungles and first put into value the fields still today in the possession of posterity. It is in this particularised sense that the word addyas, or rather its Hindi equivalent bhuinari has found its way into the CN tenancy Act". In common Oraon parlance, the word addi (ancestral) has a much wider application. Every Oraon styles himself in his heart an addyas by reference to some settler of the first hour. Every Oraon treasures up the name of his ancestral village and cherishes the memory of his ancestral fields. People residing out of their ancestral villages are particular, when they afford it, in carrying the remains of their dead to the Kùnddi of that village. Ibid., pp. 2-3.

[174] The Mahto is the secular head of the village. He is responsible for the protection of the village from any external threats. He is respected by every member of the society. The Pahan is the religious head of the village. He is responsible for the sacrifices and offerings made to gods and the spirits. He acts as a mediator between people and the mystical powers. These two offices are important, and they are responsible for the well-being of the community. P. EKKA, "Messianic Movements among the Chota Nagpur Tribes", in Sevartham 4 (1979), p. 22; C. SAHU, "Oraon Dances of Bihar", in R. D. TRIBHUWAN et al. (eds.), Tribal Dances of India, New Delhi 1999, pp. 246 – 247.

[175] S. FUCHS, The Aboriginal Tribes of India, pp. 152-153.

[176] The life of Oraons is centred around agriculture. Therefore, land plays an important role in the life of the people. F. A. Grignard is of the opinion that in times past, in order to fecundate the earth, more particularly when there was drought they spilled human blood. Cf. F.A. GRIGNARD, "The Oraons and Mundas", p. 11; N. DUARY, "Oraon Dances in Chotanagpur: An Impact Study", p. 254.

[177] D. BARA, "Oraon Marriages: Socio-cultural Context", in Sevartham 14 (1989), p. 64.

[178] L. CARDON, On the Oraon Tribe, p. 19.

[179] P. PONETTE, "Oraon Ethical Values", in Sevartham 9 (1984), p. 57.

[180] D. BARA, "Oraon Marriages: Socio-cultural Context", p. 64.

[181] "The name 'Munda' is a Sanskrit word and means 'Headman'. It is an honorific title given by the Hindus and hence became a tribal name". S. CHAND and P. BHINGRA, "Folk Dances of the Mundas", in R.D. TRIBHUWAN et al. (eds.), Tribal Dances of India, New Delhi 1999, p. 186.

[182] P. TETE, A Missionary Social Worker in India, p. 1.

[183] Commenting on the origin of the Mundas, P. Ponette refers to the migration theory proposed by W. Schmidt; namely, the Mundas could have reached India along a south-eastern route, hopping from island to island where traces of rare agglunative language can still be found all along the route. Stephen Fuchs has sometime back proposed with some cogency an alternative route, by the north, over the Himalayas, that led them into India through the Himalayan passes in Himachal Pradesh and Nepal, a theory which recent linguistic research would seem to favour. The whole hypothesis of the Munda migration based on linguistic analysis is inconclusive, as language affinity does not necessarily imply their identity. There is no documentary evidence, or at most very little, to support this hypothesis. Cf. P. PONETTE, "The Evolution of the Munda Tribe", in Sevartham 7 (1982), p. 3.

[184] "He (Singbonga) is the one whose 'arm is like a load of poles' (who is omnipotent), whose 'ears are like the flapping ears of an elephant'. Who 'sees with twelve eyes and hears with thirteen ears' (is all knowing) the one who 'on a blue thread eyes on winding rope, climbs and descends, winding and unwinding' (whose presence extends to every place), the one who is 'from the very beginning and from all eras', and whose 'chest like a stone' (permanent, unchangeable)." Cf. A. VAN EXEM, "Tribal Religion at the Crossroads", in IMR 3/2 (1982), p. 87; P. TETE, A Missionary Social Worker in India, p. 2.

[185] Ibid., p. 3.

[186] The original meaning of the word 'bonga' as found in the writings of Hoffmann, was moon. "Thus Singbonga meant 'moon of the day', just as 'nida bonga'meant 'moon of the night'. The word 'bonga' meaning 'spirits' is only a modern, derived meaning". M. TOPNO, "Spirits in the Life and Belief of the Mundas", in Sevartham 3 (1978), p. 6.

[187] Ibid., p. 7.

[188] P. PONETTE, "Ethics of the Mundas", in Sevartham 4 (1979), p. 114.

[189] S. CHAND and P. BHINGRA, "Folk Dances of the Mundas", in R.D. TRIBHUWAN et al. (eds.), Tribal Dances of India, New Delhi 1999, p. 188.

[190] Ibid., p. 108.

[191] Regarding the ethical life of Mundas, Philip Barjo comments: "The greatest offense to Singbonga is the breaking of the more important of these regulations, unwritten and handed down by ancestors. These include exogamy, endogamy and monogamy in marriage and conjugal fidelity. Not only the offenders themselves but the entire community is appropriately punished by Singbonga for the non-observance of these great ethical values." P. BARJO, "The Religious Life of the Sarna Tribes", in IMR 19/2 (1997), p. 46.

[192] J. M. KUJUR, "The Kharias and their Dances", in R. D. TRIBHUWAN et al. (eds.), Tribal Dances of India, p. 132.

[193] Ibid., p. 106.

[194] S. CHAND and P. BHINGRA, "Folk Dances of the Mundas", p. 187.

[195] R. V. RUSSEL, The Tribes and Castes of the Central Provinces of India, vol. III, p. 516.

[196] J. M. KUJUR, "The Kharias and their Dances", p. 128; R. V. RUSSELL, The Tribes and Castes of the Central Provinces of India, vol. III, p. 452.

[197] Kharias are basically agriculturist and their implements of cultivation are very similar to those of their agriculturist neighbours. J. M. KUJUR, "The Kharias and their Dances", p. 128.

[198] P. TETE, A Missionary Social Worker in India, p. 4.

[199] Fr. Kujur remarked: "The three endogamous groups (Paharia, Delki and Dudh) of the Kharias are further divided into exogamous clans like Dundung (eel), Kiro, Kerketta, Soreng, Kullu, Tete, etc." J.M. KUJUR, "The Kharias and their Dances", p. 129.

[200] In explaining the names of God, Paulus Kullu wrote: "The Kharias call God by the name Ponomeshor, which some non-Kharias consider a borrowed form of the Hindi word Parameshwar (All powerful supreme being). For the Kharias the name Ponomeshor is not a personal or proper name, it is a qualitative or attributive word. This word literally means a stone, rock which is alive, strong, immovable, impenetrable, etc." Cf. P. KULLU, "Figures of Christ in Kharia Religion", in Sevartham 10 (1985), p. 100. When sacrifice is exclusively offered to God, the term Sakhi Gosain is addressed, which is translated as all-seeing-God by some, but according to P. Kullu, it actually means 'God as Friend'.

[201] Enumerating the world of spirits, J. Kujur wrote: "The Kharias believe in the existence of soul, which after death remains as a spirit. The Kharias personify and deify the dead ancestors. The ancestral spirits are known as Burha – Burhi (old man and old woman). They are benevolent and look after the family… The Raksa Dub literally means protecting spirit. They believe that Ponomeshor has created Raksa Dubo in order to protect the village from enemies. It signifies that Ponomeshor is the protector of the whole humanity. The Raksa Dubo is believed to have a fierce look so that evil spirits are afraid to enter the village… They offer sacrifices to evil spirits not out of love but out of fear. They think

that by offering sacrifices to them they can pacify them and thus avert illness and calamities. Among many spirits considered to be evil witches, Chordevan, baghia, churil, mua, etc some people call these evil spirits as bhuts (spirits)." J.M. KUJUR, "The Kharias and their Dances", pp. 130 - 131.

[202] P. TETE, A Missionary Social Worker in India, pp. 4 - 5.

[203] L. CARDON, The Kharias and their Customs, Louvain 1923, p. 4.

[204] The Kharias believe in an endless transmigration of the soul or Jiu into men and beasts, and even into plants; for according to them, animals and plants have, like human beings, their own souls that are bound to be born again. They have no hell or heaven. As punishment, the soul of a wicked man after death reincarnates into some lower beasts, a pig or a dog for instance, while the soul of a good man, as a reward, revives into a human being, but always a man of the same tribe. They consider adultery, incest, theft, false testimony, calumny, neglect of parents when old, insulting or striking them, as morally wrong and very bad. Cf. Ibid., p. 13.

[205] J.M. KUJUR, "The Kharias and their Dances", p. 133.

[206] L. CARDON, The Kharias and their Customs, p. 2.

[207] Ibid., p. 6.

[208] Here is a copy of a Kamia bond which a man had to sign for the interest on the loan of a paltry sum of Rupees 2. "I do hereby agree that in lieu of the interest on the principal amount advanced by the above-named creditor to me I will serve under the said creditor as a kamiyan, tilling land, digging ground, cutting wood, going abroad tending cattle, going to the jungle, etc., and doing such other works. I do further agree that I will not claim any pay or remuneration for my services besides the usual allowance of coarse grain for food, etc., as prevalent in the neighbouring villages and that I will be entitled to discontinue my services under the said creditor from the date on which I shall pay up the full amount advanced without any interest to the said creditor... In case I discontinue my services without paying off the debt or fly away to some other place the said creditor shall be entitled to realise the amount advanced by him with interest from my person, and in case I die before the debt is paid up, my heirs shall be liable for the payment of the said debt under the above-mentioned terms". A. NADER, The Ignatian Land, Calcutta 1925, pp. 24-27.

[209] Vanden Bogaert proposes four periods that are like solidified layers, superimposed on each other. They are 1) the Socialistic Society, introduced after Independence; 2) the Capitalistic Society, imposed during the British Colonial period; 3) the Feudal Society, imposed through the Moghul conquest, and 4) the Original or Tribal Society, existing in the plateau since prehistoric times. Cf. M. VANDEN BOGAERT, "Social Transformation of a Tribal Society. Fall-out of Evangelization in Chota Nagpur", in Sevartham 11 (1986), pp. 19-35.

[210] The Nagbansi line of Rajas seems to have taken charge around 500 A. D. "The Oraons declare that they were in Chutia Nagpur (in Kurukh it is called

Kurkha, Oraon land) before the birth of Phani Mukuta Rai, the first Nagbansi Raja; and the present Raja claims to be the 52nd in descent from Phani Mutuka". F. A. GRIGNARD, "The Oraons and Mundas", p. 17.

[211] The 41st Raja Bairi had submitted to Mughal Emperors in Delhi, but his successor the 43rd Raja Madhu Singh initially resisted the yoke of Mughal dominance but later yielded to the pressure and assisted them in conquering Orissa. Since Durgan Sal was unable to pay the tribute he was taken prisoner. Ibid., p. 18.

[212] A. KANJAMALA, Religion and Modernization of India. A Case Study of Northern Orissa, Indore 1981, p. 56.

[213] P. TETE, A Missionary Social Worker in India, p. 6.

[214] Ibid., p. 7.

[215] Ibid., p. 8.

[216] Ibid., p. 10.

[217] Van Exem wrote that the Tana Bhagat movement, started by Jatra Oraon at the time of the First World War, was not only a refusal to pay rent, but also a drive against the spirits. The very name, Tana Bhagat, is derived from the cry of Jatra's followers, Tana, Baba, tana butanike tana' – 'pull them out, pull them out, pull the spirits out'. Cf. A. VAN EXEM, "Early Evangelization of Chotanagpur", in IMR I/4 (1979), p. 358; P. EKKA, "Messianic Movements among the Chota Nagpur Tribes", in Sevartham 4 (1979), p. 21.

[218] Birsa Bhagwan, also called Birsa Munda, a former Protestant, preached a message of liberation from the slavery of the dikus, the foreigners. He considered himself the saviour of the Mundas. His teachings were a strange mixture of religion and politics. He propagated Hindu ideals of ritual purity and asceticism, while at the same time encouraging his followers to defy the government by disobeying the officials. He forbade the worship of idols and taught his followers to worship the one God. Influenced obviously by Christianity, he preached a millenarian message promising that the final kingdom was reserved for those who followed him. He claimed to possess certain magical powers that would turn even the bullets of enemies into water. Birsa found it easy to incite his followers to revolt. On Christmas Eve of 1899, he ordered a general massacre of the rajas, the zamindars and the Christians, who had left him on the advice of the missionaries. His anticipated pardon from jail was interpreted as the result of his magical powers. However, he later died in jail. Cf. S. FUCHS, Rebellious Prophets: A Study of the Messianic Movements in Indian Religions, Bombay 1965, pp. 21-46; P. EKKA, "Messianic Movements among the Chota Nagpur Tribes", pp. 21-33.

[219]The term 'foreign' is not restricted to non-Indians but applies to all those who are non-tribal and in particular to those who deprived them of their hereditary right over the land.

[220] S. FUCHS, Rebellious Prophets, p. 35.

[221] A. VAN EXEM, "Tribal Religion at the Crossroads", in IMR 3/2 (1982), p. 85.

Chapter - 2

First Strides of Catholicism in Orissa

The arrival of Christian missionaries, who came to live among the tribals and dalits with no other motive than to serve God and his people, brought these oppressed groups a ray of hope. This chapter, after providing meagre information available about the beginnings of Christianity in India, will describe the first mission stations established in Orissa during the Portuguese period as well as the 19th-century missionary activities, which vitalised the dormant missionary efforts in India.

Due to the vastness and complexity of the topic, this study limits itself to some of the salient features of the nineteenth-century Catholic Church. It will consider those Apostolic Briefs and Exhortations, which shaped the missionary character of the Catholic Church in India and are relevant to the missionary activity in Orissa. This chapter will also investigate the despatches of missionaries from newly founded congregations, which not only established 'frontier missions' but also provided old ones with renewed vigour. It is also appropriate to consider the internal organisations relating to the missionary efforts of the two major congregations studied here – the Society of Jesus and the Missionaries of St. Francis de Sales. This will form a background for the Ranchi (Chotanagpur) and Visakhapatnam[1] Missions. In conclusion, this chapter will recall the initial efforts of the missionaries in exploring the *terra incognita*.

Christianity in Orissa up to the 19th Century

According to the time-honoured traditions of South India, the Christian presence in India is almost as old as Christianity itself. Tradition holds that the Apostle St. Thomas landed at Malinkara, a village near Cranganore in Kerala about the year 52 A. D.[2] There he established seven churches, whose members were commonly known as 'St. Thomas Christians'.[3] Then St. Thomas proceeded to the neighbouring country where he achieved the crown of martyrdom.[4] For unknown reasons, early Christianity in India did not spread to other parts of the country. The diffusion of Christianity in India was largely the work of the later *Portuguese Padroado*.

Maritime Evangelisation

The great age of conversion[5] dawned with the exploration and discovery of distant lands. A desire for lucrative business, inquisitiveness and a spirit of adventure brought the European merchants to the shores of Malabar and even beyond. Once they became familiar with the sea route to distant isles, the Portuguese explorers were convinced of the need to spread Christianity. They thought that if the conquered peoples became Christians they would be loyal to a Christian king. This would logically mean that missionaries accompanied all the expedition groups that went to the East. They could proudly proclaim that they had come in search of 'Christians and Spices'.[6] This is attested to by the fact that Christianity under the Portuguese flourished along the coast. One of the original dreams of the Portuguese was to establish Christianity in the entire territory that they thought was under their control. They tried to achieve this in many ways but not without much struggle and resistance on the part of native Hindus.[7]

Having established themselves in Goa by 1510,[8] missionaries, approved and supported by the Portuguese authorities (as representatives of the King of Portugal), were sent to Bengal with the hope of establishing Christianity there and subjugating the territory to *Padroado*. Their plans to subjugate the territory worked well for Goa, but the situation was different in Bengal. Although (Portuguese) missionaries had established some mission centres that coincided with Portuguese mercantile stations along the Bay of Bengal, the missionaries were busy in administering the sacraments to the Europeans who lived there for trade and commerce. For this reason, the missionaries did not take the initiative to convert the native population. It was probably for this reason that these centres disappeared like 'sandy constructions on a sea-beach'. The Jesuits[9] and Augustinians[10] were the early evangelisers in Bengal.

The Orissa coast held a strategic position on the map for the Portuguese, since its waters were less rough than other coasts in India. During the first quarter of the 16th century, the Portuguese founded a few settlements along the coast. Initially they obtained a royal sanction for their trade. Commenting on the Portuguese merchants' supremacy on the Orissa coast, Ganesh Chandra Rath observed:

> Portuguese merchants established their commercial supremacy and by 1599 A.D. the Portuguese trade in Orissa was already in a very prosperous condition. Thus, the people of Orissa can be said to have had an uninterrupted commercial and maritime trade from the 16th century B.C. to the end of 16th century A.D. At that time the Orissa coast was known as *Kalinga* coast and the merchants of Orissa earned the reputation of being *Sadhabas*, rich and prosperous. During the 16th century A.D. ships, great and small, adorned the ports of Orissa.[11]

The maritime importance of ports like Pipli, Balasore and Ganjam, known for "the facility for reconstruction of ships and the availability of export commodities, encouraged multinational European companies to establish their factories in different port towns of Orissa".[12]

Christian Presence in Orissa: The Portuguese Period

J. J. A. Campos thought: "The earliest European settlements in the Gulf of Bengal were established in Orissa. It was the same with the Portuguese as with the English and the Dutch".[13] It was natural for missionaries to follow Portuguese Christians, wherever their work took them, to provide for their spiritual needs. Thus, one might conclude that the expansion of the mission work occurred, at least initially, wherever they found Portuguese traders and their servants, particularly in some of the coastal settlements that were situated in Orissa. As mentioned earlier, in comparison with the ports in Bengal, the ports in Orissa were ideal for navigation. These are some of the stations.[14]

a. Hijili

This coastal station was situated on the border between Orissa and Bengal. J. J. A. Campos observed: "It was formerly an island now united to the mainland and was a district of Orissa under native rulers. At the time of the Portuguese occupation, it had its own chiefs but in 1505 according to local traditions the Muhammadans under Taj Khan and his brother, took possession of it."[15] Hijili may have been the first European settlement in the Bengal region and the Portuguese merchants carried on a brisk trade there. Because of this the Christian community was also large. Two churches were successively built there, which grew into parishes, owing to the increased number of Christians.

A. Hartmann records: "In 1622 Fr. Manoel de Esperança had gone to Orissa to establish a new Christian community near Hijili, because he heard that many Portuguese lived there whose faith had grown cold. When the Moslems heard of his intention, they tied him to a tree and whipped him. They also threatened to kill him, if he should continue his efforts".[16] He therefore transferred the people to a new location only to discover that it was infested with tigers. The second church was erected because of a persecution, which resulted in the destruction of Hoogly in 1632. Many Christians took refuge in Hijili. This exodus also affected Banja, another settlement in the vicinity. As trade declined, so did the Christian community. By the beginning of the 19th century the Christian community disappeared, and the two churches were destroyed.[17] Hijili was later called *Feringhi* or *Feringhee Desh* (a term applied to the Portuguese).[18]

b. Balasore

Balasore was situated on the coast of Orissa,[19] that is, on the Bay of Bengal. J. J. A. Campos remarked that, "the Portuguese had a small settlement in Balasore of which no vestige now remains".[20] There was the Church of Our Lady of the Rosary, which existed till 1730. It was a parochial church having, probably, a resident friar. It formerly had several thousand Christians, but by the year 1720 it counted only about 1,000. One can argue that it was the decline in trade that contributed to or even resulted in the poverty of the people.[21] The revival of Christianity began with the arrival of the Belgian Jesuits in 1865 when Fr. Sapart[22] came to stay in Balasore. The mission began to produce results, particularly during the time of the Great Famine. In any case, the number of adherents was so negligible that it never made any big news in the mission.[23] In August 1672, Balasore received a distinguished guest, Msgr. Francis Pallu, Vicar Apostolic of Tonkin, who was on his way to his mission. Due to inclement weather, he had to remain in Balasore for some time. He spoke of the deplorable condition of Christianity in that region. It was from here that the missionaries took care of Cuttack where there were some Christians in the service of Nawab, the governor of the country.[24]

c. Pipli

Pipli was a maritime town situated on the Bay of Bengal,[25] in the kingdom of Cuttack (*Cateca*), where the Portuguese also had a settlement.[26] The Portuguese seem to have settled in Pipli by 1514.[27] During the first decades of the 17th century there was a parish there with about 300 Christians.[28] There was also a Dutch factory there, but it is asserted that the vicar of the place, Francis de Piedade, managed to get the local Muslim governor to chase them away in 1622. The Augustinians built a residence, and a priest visited regularly whenever there was a need, like baptism, marriage, etc.[29] Most of these Christians were either Portuguese or Indian soldiers in the service of the Muslim chieftains. When the military unit was disbanded later in the century, the Christians dispersed and the parish itself was closed down.[30] The priest of Balasore looked after the few that remained at Pipli.[31] However, it is not certain when the mission was closed, since some sources indicate that the church was destroyed by a cyclone in 1832.[32]

d. Tumlok

Probably called by other names, like Tamboly or Tamluk, this was yet another coastal settlement where there was the Church of Our Lady of Hope. According to Campos, "Tamluk is situated on the southern bank of the *Rupanayan* and was an important seaport in ancient times mentioned as *Tamalites* in Ptolemy's geography".[33] The settlement was meant for the few Christians who were dependents of the Portuguese who had commercial dealings there. The church was built under the influence of the famous Augustinian traveller and official visitor, Fr. Manrique, who obtained a *firman* to this end from the Muslim Governor of Cuttack.[34] This privilege was received either in 1635 (according to Campos) or in 1640 (according to Hosten). By the beginning of the 19th century, the church and station had completely disappeared,   i. e., when the trade ceased, the community also disappeared.[35]

e. Banja

Though situated in the vicinity of Tamluk, Banja seems to have been a much more important centre for Christians. There were a *casa misericordia*, a hospice, a hospital and an alms-house, typical establishments found in almost all the important Portuguese centres in India and the Far East. There was also the Church of Our Lady of Salvation. The number of

Christians was large, and they were considered wealthy, generous and helpful. However, the settlement reverted to the jungle by the beginning of the 19th century because of the bad climate, which had disrupted trading possibilities.[36]

Towards the end of the 18th century there was a general decline of the mission stations in Orissa due to the declining importance of the ports along the coast and to the internal struggles and misunderstandings among the missionaries of different congregations. The missionaries themselves were discouraged by the meagre results.[37] As noted earlier, the Christian community consisted mainly of the Portuguese who settled there for the purpose of trade and commerce and the Indian soldiers who were stationed there as soldiers for the local chieftains. These groups subsequently left the place because of changing fortunes and opportunities for military service. Referring to the work of the Augustinians, A. Hartmann wrote: "In (the) whole province of Orissa the Augustinians walked from settlement to settlement taking care of the Portuguese and taught in between also the pagan natives."[38] However, the number of conversions of the native people probably was so meagre that it never found a place in any of the important works of the place.

Nineteenth Century Christianity in India: Some Features

The nineteenth century is generally considered as the century of missionary enterprise. The century witnessed the establishment of new missionary congregations, the revival of older congregations with a reinvigorated missionary zeal, and an inspiring leadership provided by the Congregation for the Propagation of the Faith. These factors affected the history of the Catholic Church in India, which experienced a rejuvenation of missionary efforts and a vast expansion of mission.

The spring of this new missionary activity took place during the pontificate of Gregory XVI (1831 - 1846), the former Prefect of the Sacred Congregation for the Propagation of the Faith (commonly known as *Propaganda Fide*).[39] Unlike preceding centuries of missionary endeavour, when countries such as Portugal and Spain were the patrons of mission, the *Propaganda* became directly involved in the affairs of mission. This involvement of the Holy See was necessitated by the degenerating conditions of the mission under the Portuguese *Padroado*. The situation of the Catholic Church in India was far from satisfactory. Convinced of its special mandate, the *Propaganda* despatched missionaries there despite its encroachment on the privileges granted to the Portuguese Royal Patronage. That the *Propaganda* from the beginning had "insightful ideas as to how missionary activities were to be conducted is evident in the fact that it recognised two fundamental principles on which missionary activity was to be based: the bringing up of an indigenous clergy; and (the) accommodation and adaptation to the cultures and traditions of the people".[40]

However, in reality, the *Propaganda* found it difficult to discharge its duties due to inherent rivalry among various religious congregations, diocesan clergy and political powers. On the one hand, the Catholic mission tried to win adherents by eradicating numerous social evils that enslaved the masses, particularly superstitious beliefs such as Meriah, female infanticide, etc.; on the other hand, it presented a community hampered by dissension, lack of evangelical zeal and paucity of personnel. These limitations will affect the Catholic Mission in India.

The salient features of nineteenth century Catholic Mission need to be considered because of their importance to the history of the Catholic Church in India, and for their impact upon the missions in Orissa, so vast a field. Thus, this essay will offer a brief description of some important issues during this period.

Padroado – Propaganda Conflict

The spread of Christianity, as found in India today, owes a great deal to Portugal, which under the royal patronage (*Padroado* in Portuguese)[41] tried to spearhead the challenging task of evangelising India, whose civilisation was based on religions that are older than Christianity itself. However, the Portuguese did not know much about India. Undeterred by the innate religious outlook of the Indians, the Portuguese proceeded to realise their two-fold goal of 'evangelisation and commerce'. J. Comby writes: "We can not isolate the apostolic zeal of the evangelizers from the lure of profit for the navigators. We need to consider the global motives of the discoverers, as they must have been perceived by those whom they discovered."[42] This was generally also the pattern of evangelisation in almost all the newly acquired territories.

However, as K. S. Latourette recorded:

The flourishing missions of the sixteenth and seventeenth centuries which had planted Christianity firmly in the Portuguese enclaves and had brought into being small Roman Catholic communities in several parts of the country, notably in the south, had declined. Roman Catholic Christianity was suffering from an ebb tide that was not to be halted until well along in the situation were being circulated in Europe.[43]

Commenting on the negative impact that *Padroado* produced, J. J. A. Campos wrote:

After spreading her influence over two worlds, Portugal had exhausted herself. The task undertaken was too great for a small nation. The energy soon spent itself out... Pampered by wealth, the Portuguese in India had grown indolent. Luxury bred vice and profligacy. The civic virtues of the earlier rulers had given place to venality and corruption. Concealed beneath the pomp and splendour of the Portuguese in India lay the seeds of decay and dissolution.[44]

In his work *Disputed Mission*, Ines G. Zupanov writes that the general situation of the mission in India was affected by the prevailing outlook of the time:

From the beginning of 17th century, the Roman Church authorities tried to assert direct control over the overseas missions and circumvent, in many respects, the dwindling Portuguese jurisdiction. In 1622, a special Sacred Congregation for the Propagation of the Faith (*Sacra Congregatio de Propaganda Fide*) was established, claiming as its aim the proselytism of the non-Christian world, which the Padroado was unable to reach.[45]

A careful observer could note at the close of the eighteenth century that the Roman Catholic Church in India was in decay. But, "when the 19th century dawned, the Roman Catholic missions in India had reached a point of weakness almost amounting to extinction."[46] The suppression of the Society of Jesus had a disastrous impact on the missions, as few were willing to continue the magnitude of their work.[47]

One of the main concerns for the Pope was to increase mission personnel, whose recruitment had been paralysed by anti-Catholic movements in Spain and Portugal, which traditionally provided personnel for the mission. So the Holy See implemented a strategy to promote a resurgence of the decadent mission by "the division of missionary areas and their transfer to the various orders and congregations".[48] Efforts to ameliorate the situation increased during the pontificate of Gregory XVI (1831 - 1846), a former Prefect of the Congregation of the Propagation of Faith who was well acquainted with the local conditions of the mission territories. "The Pope himself undertook the reorganisation of ecclesiastical affairs in Asia, beginning first in India."[49]

Multa Praeclare **and its Effects**

Adding confusion to chaos, one can note, was the absence of shepherds in the more important dioceses. Since the death of the Archbishop of Goa in July 1831, the four sees (Goa, Cranganore, Cochin and Mylapore) to which the Padroado had the privilege of appointing candidates were vacant. Gregory XVI (1831 - 1846) understood the difficulties with the appointment of candidates to these sees without recourse to Portugal, even if the situation warranted immediate action by the Holy See. Realising the delicateness of the matter, Cardinal Pedicini, the Prefect of the Propaganda Fide, sent a letter requesting Lisbon to fill the vacancies. Although Portugal was unable to fulfil its obligations as envisaged in the *Padroado* agreement, it insisted on its privileges granted by the Pope *ad perpetuum*. This was the beginning of a confrontation between Rome and Portugal. I. Padinjarekuttu tells us: "Instead of perceiving the problems and solving them, both Propaganda and the Portuguese authorities tried the method of confrontation, with damaging consequences to both sides and particularly to the Church."[50] Rome perceived that Portugal was not in a position to meet the needs in India. Therefore, Gregory XVI decided to take up some definite measures to improve the situation. Beginning in 1834, diplomatic relations between Portugal and the Holy See worsened, so that even the bishops who had been appointed to the sees of Goa and Mylapore could not get papal confirmation of their election.

After prolonged consultation and debate, Pope Gregory issued the Apostolic Letter *Multa Praeclare* on April 24, 1838.[51] Commenting on *Multa Praeclare*, E. Hull observed: "By these enactments the Holy See derogates from the past bulls by which the Sees of Cranganore, Cochin and Mylapore were erected; and also from the bull in which the See of Goa was erected in this sense, that in future the Archbishop of Goa cannot exercise any jurisdiction whatever over the countries of which we speak, viz., the diocesan areas of Cranganore, Cochin and Mylapore."[52] Commenting on the *raison d'être* of *Multa Praeclare*, the noted historian Stephen Neill wrote: "It was his [Gregory XVI] intention to put an end to the Portuguese claims, to make plain the full jurisdiction of the holy see over all the churches in India, and to assert that, when vicariates had been created, the vicars apostolic appointed by the Pope had full and perfect authority over all Christians of the Roman obedience in the territories assigned to them."[53] There was division in every corner of the Indian Church; between those who accepted the authority of the Vicars Apostolic and those who maintained the Portuguese authority. The apostolic letter of Gregory XVI led to long and bitter jurisdictional conflicts, which were mistakenly called a schism.[54] In the midst of such conflicts and confusion Propaganda went ahead with the erection of Vicariates Apostolic in India.[55] The Holy See encouraged and helped the missionary efforts and as a result many institutes, new and old, wanted to take up missionary activities.[56]

The End of Portuguese Padroado and its Effects

Instead of solving the problems affecting the missions, the efforts of Propaganda increased the tension. John Correia Alfonso identifies the struggles relating to the Padroado – Propaganda conflict: "Unfortunately, when Padroado clergy and Propaganda prelates came into contact, conflicts of jurisdictional matters often arose which in no way helped the Catholic cause. The un-edifying struggle covered the whole of the eighteenth and most of the nineteenth centuries, being especially fierce in the regions of Bombay, Madura (Madurai) and Madras".[57] In spite of various attempts – such as the *Concordats* of 1857 and 1886,[58] which were theoretically a victory for the Portuguese as the Holy See conceded in many aspects to the Padroado – the conflicts persisted, damaging the progress of the Church. Furthermore, the issue of 'double jurisdiction' continued to vex the Church.[59] Subsequent settlements between 1886 and 1890 ultimately led to a final agreement in 1928, which put an end to the double jurisdiction in India; new guidelines were issued in the final settlement that reduced the power of Portugal considerably. In 1950, Portugal renounced its Padroado rights in dioceses within the Indian Union and revised the boundaries of Goa accordingly. The final revision in 1953 put an end to this long struggle that had lasted for centuries.[60]

The effects of the *Padroado – Propaganda* conflict were disastrous. It weakened the Catholic ranks in India, and evangelisation work suffered. Internal conflicts and dissensions paved the way for various Protestant groups to flourish in their missionary efforts. The Catholic community was divided between the two factions, often resulting in violence when one of the parties went to take possession of a particular church. M. Dhall commented: "Under such circumstances the new religious force at work as W. Hunter observed in 1888, was not Catholicism, but Protestant and Anglican Christianity. Nevertheless, missionary activity from all sections of British Christianity increased and missions, Baptists, Congregational, Presbyterian, Wesleyan from England and USA were active in many parts of India. These organisations worked through voluntary societies with great earnestness and self-sacrifice, and often with abundant blessings."[61] Later during the second part of the nineteenth century, when the Catholic Church was able to set its own house in order by the laudable efforts of Propaganda, it felt the need to arrest the advance of Protestantism in India.

Malabar Rite Controversy

The Malabar Rite[62] controversy has been associated with the Jesuits who worked in the Madurai Mission. The Jesuit Mission in Tamil Nadu during the 16th and 17th centuries (as today) was faced with the inveterate problem of maintaining the caste distinctions in order to reach out to the people of higher castes. The word *parangi*[63] was a derogatory term used by non-Christians to refer to Christianity as *Parangi Margam*,[64] or the way of *parangi*. The term refers both to the vast number of its adherents who came from lower social origins and who were different to a ritually pure lifestyle, and the 'licentiousness' of the priests who ignored the rules of conduct expected by noble castes. Catholic priests ate beef, drank wine, and freely mixed with social outcastes, such as pariahs, and so the people of higher castes despised the religion the priests professed and preached.[65] The Jesuits, under the leadership of Fr. Robert de Nobili, decided to remove the stigma attached to Christianity by evangelising the Brahmins with the conviction that the "caste need not be regarded, just in and by itself alone, as a bar to the acceptance of the Catholic faith or vice versa".[66] De Nobili, in hopes of wiping out the stigma attached to Christianity, tried to adopt certain practices of the higher caste, maintaining that they had only a civil or social implication and never a religious significance. He was convinced that the conversion of Brahmins, who belonged to the priestly class or who were teachers of the *Vedas*, might serve as examples to their followers or members of the lower castes, since the people looked up to the Brahmins for religious instructions. After a prolonged reflection and study of the local customs and language, he adopted the lifestyle of Brahmins by living in a hut in their quarters.[67] He tried to win them over by becoming a Brahmin *sanyasi*, who was given utmost reverence, but such cultural adaptations or external transformations involved enormous sacrifices.

Concession accorded to certain practices of the Brahmins and commitment to minister to their members inevitably led to the formation of two distinct categories of priests among the missionaries: the *sanyasis* and the *pandarams*. The former were required to learn Sanskrit, engage in scholarly pursuits by studying the sacred scriptures of the Hindus, and serve the Brahmin Christians. The *pandarams*, in contrast, learned the vernacular and served Christians of low caste origins.[68] Such measures introduced to convert the Brahmins elicited outright suspicion. Opposition initially came from de Nobili's own confreres; his greatest adversary was Fr. Gonçalo Fernandes who criticised him till the end of his life and persuaded many priests and laymen alike to do so. Later others – such as the Archbishop of Goa, the Dominicans and the Franciscans -- joined the critics. But de Nobili also had supporters in the Church hierarchy. Besides his own relatives in Rome (including Robert Bellarmine who could not help him immediately), Archbishop Ros of Cranganore and Fr. Laerzio, the Provincial of Malabar, were his great patrons.[69]

The Bull, *Romanae Sedis Antistites* of Gregory XV, issued on January 31, 1623, gave provisional approval for appropriating the 'signs of nobility', such as *punul*, the sacred thread, the sandal paste and the ceremonial bath. S. Rajamanickam comments that "it marked the beginning of a new epoch, when the church came out to encounter and to win not only the Brahmins of Madurai but all the nations of the world".[70] Afterwards, the Jesuits in the Malabar province formally adapted to the Brahmin mode of life. Rajamanickam elucidates the *raison d'être* of this adaptation: "Nobili's method of evangelisation is precisely based on the principle of adaptation. To him the fundamental question is not whether this or that custom may be followed by his neophytes but whether the Indians as a nation would be given every legitimate facility to enter the Christian fold as pagan Rome and Greece were given by the primitive church."[71] The problem of adaptation surfaced again at the end of the 17th century, when the French Capuchins of Pondicherry disagreed with the Jesuits on this policy and reported them to Rome. Pope Clement IX sent Patriarch Charles Maillard De Tournon to settle this question permanently. The patriarch signed a decree on June 23, 1704, in which some of the practices of the 'Malabar Rites' were forbidden while others were retained.[72] The 'Malabar Rite Oath,' introduced by Pope Clement XII on May 13, 1739, obliged the missionaries to condemn 16 articles. Later Pope Benedict XIV in the Bull *Omnium Sollicitudinum*, issued on September 12, 1744 abolished the 'Malabar Rites'.[73] The oath remained in force till April 9, 1940, when it was finally abolished, a year after Pope Pius XII abolished the oath concerning the Chinese Rites.

Establishment of the Hierarchy in India

After much planning, Pope Leo XIII established the hierarchy of India by issuing apostolic letter *Humanae Salutis Auctor* on September 1, 1886.[74] The hierarchy consisted of eight archbishops with their suffragan dioceses (altogether nineteen units in India alone). In all there were about twenty-five ecclesiastical units both in India and in Ceylon, including those under the Padroado.[75] Following the promulgation of the apostolic letter, Pope Leo XIII appointed Msgr. Antonius Agliardi as his delegate to execute the decision. He organised meetings with bishops on a regional basis to settle matters. After the consultations he sent the acts and documents to the Holy See for approval. The Holy See published the brief *Post Initam* on June 7, 1887.[76] Referring to the Vicariate of Vizagapatam the apostolic brief mentions that "Adjoining the western vicariate of Bengal is the extensive mission deriving its name from Vizagapatam which takes in the whole territory between the boundaries of the Bombay vicariate and the Bay of Bengal up to the Godavery river on the south and was divided from Madras in the year 1850".[77] Together with the reorganisation of the Indian Church into several ecclesiastical provinces, efforts were intensified to train local clergy. This was one of the recommendations presented by Fr. Jean-Felix-Onésime Luquet[78] to Roman authorities in favour of the establishment of an ecclesiastical hierarchy for India, who would eventually take over from missionaries from the outside.

Indigenous Clergy

The idea of creating an indigenous clergy was very much present since the beginning of the Portuguese Mission in India, and the establishment of seminaries lends credence to this view.[79] The Synod of Pondicherry in 1844 marked a major milestone[80] not just for the mission of Pondicherry but also for the Catholic Mission in India as a whole. It provided the impetus for a new outlook or approach in the missionary endeavour, particularly in the formation of a native clergy, in the creation of more vicariates and in the establishment of a hierarchy for India. Following the Synod of Pondicherry, Luquet was sent to Rome to explain the 'Acts and Documents' of the Synod to the Sacred Congregation and get them approved. Formation of an indigenous clergy was very dear to him.[81]

Following the establishment of a hierarchy for India, the papal delegate looked for a suitable place to establish a seminary for India. This was finally founded in 1893 at Kandy (Ceylon), and it was intended for both India and Ceylon.[82] Pope Leo XIII's apostolic letter *Ad Extremas* (1893) clearly manifested the church's commitment to the promotion of native clergy, not as the ones who would be assisting the missionaries but as the ones who were well prepared to promote the interests of religion in their native land.[83] Writing on the formation of the Indian clergy, J. L. Miranda maintains that the indigenous priest is linked to "his compatriots by origin, character, feelings and aspirations, possesses extraordinary facilities for introducing the faith into their minds, and is endowed with powers of persuasion far superior to those of any other man".[84] The idea of creating an indigenous clergy was again affirmed by Pope Benedict XV when he issued the apostolic letter *Maximum Illud* on November 13, 1919, which was destined to have a profound influence on missionary attitudes and policies.[85]

The British Raj and Mission

The guiding principle of the religious policy of the British Raj in India was neutrality, since commercial success and political stability took precedence over any other concerns. Both depended largely on friendly relations with the people, regardless of their ethnic and religious background. Therefore, any action that might endanger those friendly relations was discouraged. M. Dhall illustrates in no ambiguous terms the neutrality observed by the British in matters relating to religion: "Between 1783 and 1813 the East India Company showed open hostility towards the introduction of Christianity and western ideas in India and followed a policy of neutrality."[86]

However, one could observe certain shifts in religious policy after 1813. The British East India Company, especially after the enactment of the Charter Act of 1813, was open to allow missionaries to pursue their mission in India. To quote M. Dhall again: "After 1813, mission societies did not follow colonisation. Countries which did not have any colonial stakes in India had also their missionary representatives in India."[87] However the British government meted out a step-motherly treatment towards Christians, which induced both Hindus and others to wonder whether the government had any religious policy at all. Already in 1853, the government introduced legislation regarding religious freedom. Even after the *Sepoy Mutiny* of 1857[88] the British government did not feel the need to modify this policy, but rather affirmed its commitment to neutrality in religious matters. Religious toleration became the hallmark of British rule, and this was the core of the proclamation of the Queen to her subjects in 1858.[89] Commenting on the religious policy of the British in India, J. Beckmann wrote:

> The external difficulties of the Indian mission included the relationship to the colonial power. The English East India Company had absolutely no interest whatever in missionary activity. It required a direct order from London before the work of Anglican missionaries in 1833 and of non-British protestant Mission societies in 1834 was permitted. The Catholic Church, which had been active in the country for centuries, did not seem to exist at all.[90]

However, the British later had to change the policy of neutrality in order to avail the services of the missionaries in providing education and other forms of social assistance to the people of the country. Missionaries ran charitable institutions and opposed several inhuman practices that had religious sanction, such as *sati* (burning of widows on the funeral pyre of their husbands), the Meriah sacrifices, the caste system, etc.[91]

The British official policy of religious neutrality initially helped the missionaries, since they did not face any serious challenges from other religious groups, thanks to the protection extended to all. A. Mayhew summed up the general attitude towards the Christian missions in India in the following words:

> the British government freed from nervous scruples about its association with the Christian faith, offered fair field and all necessary protection and opportunities for mission work. This was the general conclusion reached in the report of the international conference on Missions, which examined carefully at Edinbourgh in 1910 the attitude of government to the missions in all parts of the world.[92]

Commenting on the advantages that mission reaped during the British Raj, Stephen Neill said that "to the majority of missionaries and Indian Christians British rule no doubt presented itself as in every way a boon. The Government was doing many things that in less tranquil days they had longed to see done. It gave them the fullest possible liberty to do the things that Government could not itself rightly undertake".[93]

At the same time, the preference of the British for Anglicanism was obvious. This is attested to by the disparity in salaries of the military chaplains. Protestant chaplains received a monthly salary of Rs. 1,100/-, whereas the Catholic chaplains received only Rs. 50/-.[94] The Government's preference for Protestantism was obvious from the number of groups, such as the Anglicans and Baptists, who came from England. They were preferred on the pretext that they were subjects of the Empire, while the Catholic missionaries were mostly from outside, except the Irish missionaries who were working in the Madras Mission. Every Annual Report of the Presidency had a column on Ecclesiastical Matters, which invariably contained information pertaining to the Anglican Mission. Seldom one reads about the Catholic Church.[95]

However, one could argue that, although the British observed religious neutrality for all practical reasons, they did not prevent the missionaries from trekking into the mountains and crossing the valleys 'in search of souls'; the British recognised the missionaries as agents of social change and of the advancement of 'civilisation',[96] evident in the recognition of freedom accorded to the schools run by missionaries.[97]

The Theatines in Visakhapatnam

On their arrival at the Visakhapatnam Mission,[98] the Missionaries of St. Francis de Sales met Dom Joseph Xavier d'Attaide,[99] a Goan Theatine, who was the last of the missionaries of the Golconda Mission.[100] With him ended the history of the Theatines who, with a paucity of personnel and a vast territory to look after with two or three priests, maintained a few stations along the Coromandel Coast. The Theatines were sent to help out the missions in the kingdom of Idalcan. After having established themselves in Goa, they set out to find new stations nearby. Since they encountered some difficulties, they left Goa and sought a mission in the Kingdom of Golconda, whose capital was Masulipatnam.[101] The Indian Theatines were responsible for the Catholic communities of 'Bisanagar

(Vijaynagar) and Visapatan (Visakhapatnam)' in India under the Bishop of Mylapore, and for Sumatra and Borneo under the Bishop of Malaca. Since the missionaries were constantly exposed to the danger of ecclesiastical conflicts and prejudices, the superior at Goa wrote to Pope Clement XIV (1769 - 1774) asking for extraordinary faculties, so that the missionaries proceeding to the missions might not "be expelled on the occasion of every sinister event".[102]

The memorandum written by d'Attaide recalls some of the names of the Theatine missionaries who worked in Golconda mission.[103] In it he presents a list of missionaries who worked in the Visakhapatnam mission between 1806 and 1828.[104] From what is presented as the notes on "Vishak Mission", Joseph Baud (1890-1980),[105] the former Bishop of Visakhapatnam, writes that from 1806 until 1846 there were hardly one or two Theatine missionaries, most likely from Goa, visiting the scattered Christians living all along the Coromandel coast (from Masulipatnam to Puri and Cuttack). J. Baud recorded,

> From October 1816 to November 1818 Dom P. Celestino Paro Parais travels from Berhampur to Ichchapur, Chicacole, Vizianagram, Bimlipatam to Vizagapatam. In July 1826, Padre Gaitano Isao Godinho is in Ganjam and Berhampur. From June 1827 to December 1827 Dom Gaetano Gabriel de Sta Maria goes from Berhampur to Vizag via Chicacole and Vezianagaram (Vizianagram).[106]

Dom Joseph Xavier d'Attaide

Dom Joseph Xavier d'Attaide was the last Theatine missionary in Visakhapatnam. He was zealous and the only priest to serve the entire Catholic community all along the coast, from Madras to Calcutta.[107] He had been in Visakhapatnam since 1828 taking care of small Catholic communities in different military settlements.[108] The military garrisons in Cuttack, Ganjam, Aska and other places had the annual services of priests, who baptised children, heard confessions of the adults, rectified marriages, etc. In February 1848, d'Attaide made his first visit to Cuttack and on April 14, 1848, he sent a report of his voyage to Msgr. P. J. Carew, Vicar Apostolic of Calcutta, as Cuttack was under the ecclesiastical jurisdiction of the Vicar Apostolic of Calcutta. During his visit in Cuttack, d'Attaide had administered the sacraments of confession and communion to 36 persons. He received some adults and baptised 13 children.[109] Writing about d'Attaide's activities, Francis Moget notes: "He knew Portuguese and Tamil with some English, but with his extensive ministry, he could not do any mission work among the non-Christians. Besides, his poor knowledge of English limited his ministry among the British troops to the celebration of Mass and hearing Confessions."[110] However, it was he who provided the only link that existed between the cloudy and stagnant past and the bright future spearheaded by the MSFS.[111]

Fr. d'Attaide placed himself immediately under the jurisdiction of Fr. Henri Gailhot, the pro-vicar apostolic of Visakhapatnam, when the latter was appointed to lead the first team of missionaries from Savoy.[112] He never associated with other Goan priests who supported Padroado claims.[113] He was residing on the church premises of St. Anne, which was considered to be his private property.[114] But he bequeathed this property (including all the other chapels he had built or used for worship) to his successors, namely, the Missionaries of St. Francis de Sales. He signed a will to this effect and gave it to his clerk, M. Lobo, to execute it, lest some Goan priest claim the property. Subsequently, M. Lobo executed the will on the day of d'Attaide's death. Msgr. Neyret mentioned that after five years a priest arrived from Goa to claim the property of St. Anne. According to this priest, it belonged to the diocese of Mylapore (Meliapour) or to the see of Goa. He presented his case to the Collector, Mr. Robertson, a just man and a friend of the priests, who did not want to deal with the affair.[115]

Missionaries of St. Francis de Sales

The growth of the Catholic Church in India is influenced by the personal traits and labour of some religious congregations to which different territories were entrusted. Therefore, it is inevitable that in studying the history of the Visakhapatnam mission, or tracing the beginning of the Ganjam mission for that matter, one also encounters the history of the Congregation of the Missionaries of St. Francis de Sales, which was established on October 24, 1838 in Annecy, Savoy, when it was canonically erected by Msgr. Joseph Rey of Annecy.[116] The new religious fraternity began with six members under the direction of the founder Pierre-Marie Mermier (1790-1862), a diocesan priest.[117] Speaking of the founder, the Constitutions of MSFS mention that "in fulfilling the longing for the religious life which he had felt for several years, Father Mermier had in mind a community whose goal was perfect charity, learned in the school of Saint Francis de Sales, a master of the spiritual life who was filled with apostolic zeal".[118] Initially the missionaries envisioned a mission in Savoy where the Christian life was wanting in dedication and piety. Their mission originally consisted of preaching retreats and exhorting people to live according to Christian values.[119] Due to their initial success, the missionaries were viewed with hope. They were invited to preach missions in many parishes and to give retreats to priests.[120] With their simplicity and unwavering devotion the missionaries generated goodwill among the people.

In 1842 Cardinal Fransoni sent out letters to dioceses requesting missionaries for Africa. The letter which had been sent to the Bishop of Annecy was forwarded to Monsieur Mermier, who accepted it as a God-given opportunity to serve the mission. Warned of the usual delay by Rome, Monsieur Mermier was asked by the Bishop of Annecy to pursue the matter directly. Accordingly, he wrote a letter to the Cardinal Prefect expressing willingness to take up the mission in Libya with some conditions.[121] He personally went to Rome to discuss the matter with Cardinal Fransoni.[122] As a result, on June 2, 1843, Pope Gregory XVI, four years after founding, granted the congregation ecclesiastical approval. In the same year the "MSFS obtained the encouragements of the Holy See and many of the members consecrated themselves for (service in) the foreign missions. The founder, Mermier was very happy and approached Msgr. Rendu who welcomed it with great joy. This was also appreciated by the Roman Curia and Cardinal Fransoni, the Prefect of the Propaganda was very enthusiastic about it".[123] In his letter, Cardinal Fransoni informed Monsieur Mermier that there would soon be an establishment of vicariates in India and that the newly established congregation would get one or the other vicariate.[124] On March 15, 1845, the vast area of Central India was severed from the Vicariate of Madras and was made into the Visakhapatnam vicariate. The new congregation, just seven years old, was entrusted with a vast territory.[125] From then on Visakhapatnam became the focus of the newly-founded congregation's concern and the centre of their activities.[126]

The dispersed Catholic population of the time was composed of four principal groups: (1) Indians who had come from the Malabar coast to serve in the army along with their families; (2) Irish soldiers and their families; (3) Indians who had recently converted; and, (4) East Indians of Indian or Portuguese origin. There was also a small number of British and French Catholics in the area.[127] Even "before the arrival of the MSFS, there were only four priests to look after the 3,000 Christians of the vast territory: an Irish priest in Jalnah, two in Kamptee, an Irish and a Tamil. The fourth one is in Vizag".[128]

Upon their arrival in Visakhapatnam on February 19, 1846, the MSFS faced the arduous task of evangelising a vast territory of 435,000 square kilometres along the Coromandel Coast with a population of twenty million people, of whom mere 6,000 were Catholics.[129] Great distances, and a wide diversity of culture, language, and ethnicity posed major challenges to a congregation that was still in its infancy.[130]

Msgr. Clement Bonnand,[131] the vicar apostolic of Pondicherry, initially favoured the suggestion of sending two MEP Missionaries (Missions Étrangères de Paris) to help the MSFS in the Visakhapatnam Mission since the new arrivals were unfamiliar with the peculiar situations of the country. However, due to some constraints in personnel, he later informed them of his inability to send Frs. Metral and Ligeon to help them.[132]

Erection of Visakhapatnam Mission

Considerable progress in the mission occurred when Gregory XVI, through the proclamation of Apostolic letter *Multa Praeclare,* effected a reorganisation of the mission. In spite of the jurisdictional conflicts in India, it produced the desired results in Visakhapatnam mission, since the present Hyderabad and Visakhapatnam mission territories were attached to the Vicariate of Madras. This was a positive move as there were a good number of Christians serving in the army all along the coast.[133] This action by the Pope turned out to be of immense benefit to the faithful, particularly to the Catholic soldiers who had been working in the British army. In order to serve the dispersed Catholics, three priests were sent to some important centres in 1839. The second benefit was the erection of the Visakhapatnam Mission.[134] Since the priests from Goa were not generally liked – the Irish soldiers did not prefer the priests from Goa for confessions, since either the Goan priests did not know English well or their general conduct itself kept them aloof, while the Indian soldiers opted for European priests instead of ones with dark skins (a general prejudice of the time) - the change brought about by the proclamation of *Multa Praeclare* was hailed with great enthusiasm.[135]

At a time when the Propaganda was planning to reorganise the Catholic missions in India with the erection of new vicariates, Fr. J. F. Luquet, an MEP missionary from Pondicherry, was sent to Rome on a special mission to present the deliberations of the Synod of Pondicherry and to offer explanations if required. His mission earned him the purple hat, for he was appointed the coadjutor to Msgr. Bonnand, vicar apostolic of Pondicherry. Obviously, he succeeded in his initiatives to erect the Visakhapatnam vicariate with the intention of promoting his friend, Fr. Henri Gailhot, another influential priest in the Pondicherry mission and an active participant in the first synod of Pondicherry, to that see.[136] In the general congregation of the Propaganda (February 17, 1845) it was decided to erect the Visakhapatnam Vicariate and to give it to a non-English prelate. On May 2, 1845 Cardinal Fransoni conveyed the decision of the Sacred Congregation to the Missionaries of St. Francis de Sales, Annecy.[137]

The Holy See had also proposed to appoint a pro-vicar to look after the affairs of the mission territory. Since the missionaries were newcomers to the place, Rome appointed an experienced MEP missionary to help the community till they got used to the situation in India. Fr. Henri Gailhot, who at the time of his appointment was working in Bangalore, was to become the pro-vicar. With considerable experience in working at a military centre such as in Bangalore, he was a suitable choice for the new post. Thus, the foreign mission of MSFS began with six missionaries: four priests and two brothers.[138] The team embarked for India on June 5, 1845 and arrived in Pondicherry on September 7, 1845.

Misunderstanding and Delay at Pondicherry

Although Msgr. Bonnand welcomed the missionaries and did all he could to make their stay a memorable one,[139] they were eager to reach their destination. They were asked to learn Telugu. As the desire to reach their destination kept growing, Fr. Jacques Martin[140] wrote to Msgr. Fennelly, vicar apostolic of Madras, under whose jurisdiction Visakhapatnam was, requesting him to give the canonical faculties for their ministry in Visakhapatnam. But Msgr. Fennelly, without replying to Fr. Martin, wrote to Msgr. Bonnand explaining why he would not grant the requests of the Savoyards.[141]

The Sacred Congregation of the Propagation of Faith informed Msgr. Fennelly of the division of his vicariate that led to the formation of the Vicariate of Hyderabad and the Vicariate of Visakhapatnam.[142] Sensing that his plan could not be realised with the new arrangements of the Sacred Congregation, Msgr. Fennelly had posed some initial difficulties by not granting jurisdiction to the MSFS, which was later given at the intervention of the Holy See. Besides the monetary benefits they would have from the places where there were garrisons, the government also paid a meagre stipend to Catholic chaplains. Considering these factors, Fennelly may have thought that an individual coming from a subject nation would more likely be eligible for such grants from the government.[143] He may also have believed that the Irish Catholics would prefer their compatriots, since he had previously expressed his intention of bringing Irish clergy to India who might help to develop this region into a diocese. In his letter to the Propaganda, Msgr. Fennelly describes the nature of the Catholic communities: "Those Catholics were mostly Europeans, attached to the military troops stationed at important centres in the vicariate. There were also a few Tamil Catholics who were either *sepoys* (soldiers) or servants of the Europeans."[144] Because most of the Catholics of his Vicariate were Irish, he as an Irishman preferred that Irish priests should run the diocese.[145] Thus he decided to ignore the newcomers. He even wrote to the vicar apostolic of Pondicherry stating emphatically that until he received a letter from the Propaganda he would have nothing to do with the Savoyards.[146]

Right from the beginning the MSFS was faced with major financial constraints.[147] The missionaries had to depend on the *œuvre de Propagation de la Foi* for their expenses on the voyage. Even that allotted sum had been exhausted by the time they reached Pondicherry.[148] Fr. Henri Gailhot came to their help by providing some funds in the form of Mass stipends. As they waited in Pondicherry for further instructions, they utilised the time to learn both Tamil and Telugu. When finally, Msgr. Fennelly was asked by Rome to grant the faculties needed for the new missionaries,[149] they left for Madras immediately, reaching their destination in nine days on February 9, 1846. They were given a rousing welcome by the Irish Catholics who served in the military garrison. The Catholic community initially paid the rent of the missionaries, as they did not have any house to live in.

Growth of Visakhapatnam under the first three Leaders

a.　Fr. Henri Gailhot, the first pro-vicar 1845-1847

As mentioned earlier in the chapter, Msgr. Bonnand's plan of sending two MEP missionaries to introduce the Savoyards in the mission did not materialise because of certain unforeseen problems.[150] Meanwhile, Fr. J. F. Luquet[151] arranged with Propaganda Fide to appoint Fr. Henri Gailhot[152] as the pro-vicar of the new mission.[153] Though the Propaganda declared that Fr. H. Gailhot would be the 'Leader and Superior of the mission', Fr. J. F. Luquet, then in Rome on a special mission, promised him that he would later be appointed as the vicar apostolic of Visakhapatnam.[154] Fr. Luquet's promise was aimed at securing his friend's initial consent for the appointment. With that in mind he acted as if he were the vicar apostolic of Visakhapatnam. In contrast, the MSFS thought that Fr. H. Gailhot was only a temporary superior and that one of their confreres would be appointed the pro-vicar and eventually vicar apostolic. So friction between the two parties mounted.[155] However, the missionaries were full of praise for Gailhot's ability to organise and to provide material assistance to the mission. He was resourceful in making the acquaintance of the prominent people of the place. He was also very influential in Bangalore and probably for that reason he was promoted to this see, so that Msgr. Charbonnaux,[156] as the vicar apostolic of Bangalore, could administer the diocese without the interference of Fr. Gailhot.[157] When Theophilus Neyret was appointed the pro-vicar of Visakhapatnam, Gailhot left the place without waiting for the arrival of his successor.

b.　Msgr. Sebastian Theophilus Neyret 1847-1862

Sebastian Theophilus Neyret was born at Giez (near Annecy) in 1802. After his ordination in 1825, he was sent to Cluses where he became known for his piety. Beginning in May 1832 he worked as a chaplain for the Sisters of St. Joseph in Evian for 13 years. He entered the MSFS in 1845 and was appointed the chaplain of Les Allinges, but he expressed his desire to go to India. Realising the need to appoint a member of the congregation as the pro– vicar of Visakhapatnam, the Holy See asked for suitable names of individuals who could be appointed for the mission of Visakhapatnam. Fr. Sebastian Theophilus Neyret was the unanimous choice of all.[158] Before his departure for India he was in Rome in November and December 1846 to consult with the Holy See.[159] He arrived in Madras on

March 7, 1847 and waited there for the arrival of Fr. H. Gailhot, who had left Visakhapatnam without waiting for the new pro-vicar. Gathering whatever information, he could from Fr. Gailhot about the mission, he reached his pro-vicariate on April 24, 1847. When the pro-vicariate of Visakhapatnam was elevated to the status of a vicariate, Fr. Neyret was elevated to the episcopate with the title of Bishop of Olene *in partibus infidelium*. Msgr. Fennelly consecrated him in Madras on February 24, 1849.[160] He inherited a mission whose chapels were deteriorating because of declining resources. However, between 1849 and 1862, one could easily observe the growth of the mission by the number of its assets: seven churches, fifteen chapels and many presbyteries. He even extended an invitation to the Sisters of St. Joseph of Annecy to help the mission by establishing three convents.

Msgr. Neyret turned his attention towards the establishment of schools for children. He did all he could to establish schools wherever possible, and he was convinced of the need of establishing orphanages for poor children.[161] The Sisters of St. Joseph were equally busy with the education of girls for whom they maintained orphanages that proved to be beneficial. Many students who attended the mission school later continued their studies and eventually returned to their own villages in order to educate their people. Some of them entered the MSFS as well. Msgr. Neyret supported the promotion and formation of an indigenous clergy and recruited suitable candidates from Visakhapatnam.[162] In order to enforce the apostolic fervour and expedite evangelising efforts, Msgr. Neyret divided the vicariate into four districts: Visakhapatnam, Yanaon, Kamptee and Aurangabad. Despite the initial economic constraints of the mission, support arrived periodically from the *Propagation de la Foi* (which sent annual donations), from charity-minded people, from Irish soldiers who paid regular subscriptions and sometimes even from Protestants.

He had great appreciation for the missionaries and tried to help them in every way possible. He was convinced that there was nothing comparable to the values of a missionary in this country.[163] Describing Neyret's characteristics, Francis Moget writes: "his virtues equalled his talents. He was admired for his rectitude, his openness of mind, his courteous ways towards all. He had a great devotion to the Blessed Sacrament and was often seen with beads in his hands".[164] His simplicity and approachability won him the hearts of the people![165] He always practised both physical and evangelical poverty: whether it involved undertaking an arduous and tiring journey or meant lessening his Episcopal dignity in celebration, he did it happily for the mission and the poor.[166]

Msgr. Neyret undertook many hazardous journeys in order to administer the sacrament of confirmation, to exhort the faithful to be fervent in their calling, to encourage the missionaries, and to show care for the sick and the suffering. He never sought his own comfort. His last painful journey was when he accompanied the new superior to Kamptee, where he died on November 5, 1862.[167]

c. Msgr. Jean-Marie Tissot 1864-1890

Jean-Marie Tissot was born in Megeve, Savoy, on September 26, 1810. He lost his father two years later during the Russian campaign of Napoleon and received his Catholic education from his mother. He was ordained a priest on September 24, 1836 by Bishop Rey of Annecy.[168] After having worked in a parish as an assistant, he joined the MSFS in 1839. He was part of the first group of missionaries who came to Visakhapatnam in 1846. He undertook an expedition, at the request of Msgr. Neyret, with Fr. François Sermet[169] to the Kondh Hills to learn about the possibilities of evangelical work among the hill tribes. Besides his work as superior of the mission he was also the vicar general of the Vicariate of Visakhapatnam, a post he held until the death of Msgr. Neyret. So, it was no accident that he was chosen to succeed Msgr. Neyret. The choice was applauded by all, both in the mission and in the congregation, as Fr. Jean-Marie Tissot had been closely associated with the mission since its beginning. When Fr. Tissot was consecrated at Bombay on August 4, 1864, he immediately visited all the mission stations, starting from Kamptee, Nagpur, etc.[170]

Frequent visits and long journeys exhausted Msgr. Tissot, forcing him to return to Europe in 1866, where he could visit his native land and make his *ad limina* visit to the Pope. He met the directors of the Propagation of the Faith and requested them to continue their support to the mission in Visakhapatnam. He had the foresight to purchase a hillock near Visakhapatnam, what is now known as Ross Hill, that belonged to Mr. Ross, and built a shrine in honour of the Blessed Virgin. That shrine has grown into an important sanctuary in the state.[171] In 1870, he was back in Rome for the First Vatican Council. When Msgr. Tissot requested a coadjutor, he was given Fr. François Philippe,[172] who was known for his prudence and intelligence.[173] He visited the mission at the request of the superior general. Although his appointment brought joy to the missionaries initially, due to some problems Msgr. François Philippe never reached his destination. When the hierarchy in India was established, the vicar apostolic was raised to the dignity of a bishop and thus Msgr. Tissot became the first bishop of Visakhapatnam. In 1887, Visakhapatnam diocese was divided, and Nagpur was made a diocese with Msgr. Alexius Riccaz as its first bishop.[174]

During his last years, Msgr. Tissot spent much time visiting the missionaries. One of his great desires in India was to start a seminary for the training of future missionaries and this he did it at Gopalpur-on-Sea (near Berhampur) in Orissa in 1890. From Gopalpur he visited his beloved mission Surada, where he was attacked by mountain fever – just as he was when he made his first exploration with Fr. François Sermet. Previously he had been fortunate to survive but now he caught the fever that proved to be fatal. Bishop Tissot died completely alone in Thotavally near Surada on September 27, 1890. He was buried in the chapel of Surada.

To instil a spirit of self-help in his neophytes and orphans, Msgr. Tissot undertook many projects. One such project was meant to enable the local people to grow their own food. He thought that although the people were poor, they were used to agriculture and that they might not suffer from starvation if they could be provided with a small piece of land. In 1869 Msgr. Tissot acquired 1,000 acres of swampy land near Visakhapatnam, which became the site for the settlement of Catholics. Two Christian settlements, Gnanapuram and Kothavalsa (both of them are located in Andhra Pradesh), ultimately emerged on the site.

First Attempts

At the request of Msgr. P. J. Carew, the vicar apostolic of Calcutta, Msgr. Neyret went to Cuttack, accompanied by Fr. J. M. Tissot.[175] This visit was probably very important as it occurred after the death of Fr. Joseph Xavier d'Attaide, who was the sole missionary providing pastoral care of the Christians along the coast. Msgr. Neyret wanted to visit the mission stations in order to learn about their actual situation. So, after the rainy season, in September 1849, he proceeded to the Orissa coast: Cuttack, Ganjam and Berhampur. The journey seems to have taken them about a month as they travelled over 300 miles. The language barrier made it impossible to have any direct contact with the people. However, he came to the conclusion that very little evangelisation had been done and that the 1,500 Catholics found along the coast were all outsiders. There were Europeans, Goans and Tamils who had settled down in the towns because of government service or trade. They were found in Cuttack, Berhampur, Ganjam, Aska and Russelkonda.[176] He concluded that unless a priest resided with them the Christians would continue to live in ignorance.[177]

Msgr. Neyret also had a great desire to establish a mission station among the Kondhs. He appreciated their frankness and simplicity.[178] The evils of the caste system were unknown to them, unlike in other parts of Orissa. They differed in their culture and manners from the people of the coast. One of the positive aspects of a mission in the mountains was that the aboriginals seemed to have had no contact with Europeans nor with Protestants. The only contact that the Protestants had was when the Meriah children were rescued and sent to their orphanages in Berhampur. Thus Msgr. Neyret hoped that the mountains would bring the desired results which were not available on the plain.[179] Since their original attempts to evangelise the Hindus proved to be futile, the missionaries turned to the aboriginals who were not Hindus and who had no contact with Europeans. They thought that Kondhs would respond positively to the message of salvation, if it were offered to them.

Exploration in the Ganjam Mountains

Among the missionaries, Frs. Jean-Marie Tissot and François Sermet were chosen for the initial attempts. Fr. Jean-Marie Tissot, who was in Berhampur with Msgr. Neyret for the pastoral visit understood the desire of the vicar apostolic and was happy to explore the possibility of evangelisation among the Kondhs. If possible, he and Fr. François Sermet were also to choose a place where they could build the first station.[180] After performing spiritual duties for the small Catholic community situated at the foot of the mountains in Berhampur, they proceeded to the mountains. As they reached Russelkonda, they found a Kondh boy, who became their interpreter. He was poor and unable to work. They spoke to him in Tamil or in Telugu, and he in turn would interpret their words into *Kui*, the language of the Kondhs. He was very helpful, especially during the time of the missionaries' illness. He never left them. They appreciated the boy, since he was familiar with the forest, which was nearly impenetrable. One had to make one's way with the aid of a hatchet.

This was certainly an adventure on their part, since neither of them knew the terrain or the climate nor spoke the language of the tribals. Their initial enthusiasm waned through fatigue and insufficient water and food. Soon they were worn out completely. They had few provisions for the way, except some rice, fruit and wild roots. They had no shelter for the night. However, they used their trip in the mountains well by reaching out to as many people as possible. This exploration left an indelible mark on their lives as missionaries. They enjoyed the hospitality of the Kondhs and appreciated their humour and frankness.[181] They trekked through the mountain jungles, moving through thorny creepers, crossing deep rivers and visiting villages nestled on the crests of hills and ravines.

After a month-long journey and fatigue, these two enthusiastic missionaries reached a chapel and presbytery located about 120 miles from Visakhapatnam, at Ganjam. They were already exhausted when they reached that Christian community. But their health seemed unharmed. But on the 9th of September 1850, they had a violent attack of mountain fever. Msgr. Neyret in his letter to Mermier mentioned that "Fr. Sermet wrote me that both of them were ill. There is some hope of recovery for Sermet, but Tissot was very serious… that's the mountain fever, a doctor told here. Having heard that I sent two palanquins".[182]

Initially Fr. François Sermet was less affected; hence he went to aid his confrere. Fr. Tissot was so serious that he asked his companion to give him the last sacrament; after some time in his turn Fr. Sermet also asked for the same. Fr. Sermet was subject to violent attacks and the doctor had to be brought in. But there was no hope. He succumbed to the fatal fever on September 12, 1850, at the age of 26.[183] The following morning, the Catholic community of Ganjam came together to bid farewell to a young missionary. Dr. Adam, who treated the missionaries, also attended the funeral. With great difficulty and courage Fr. Tissot muttered a few words as he had become so feeble that he had to be carried on a chair to bury his companion.

As Fr. Tissot was still suffering, he was taken to Chatrapur where one of the Christians had prepared a mud hut covered with coconut leaves for him to rest. Sympathizing with the condition of the missionary, whose health worsened severely, the Collector took him to his bungalow where a doctor visited him regularly.[184] Fr. Tissot remained there till he was able to travel to Visakhapatnam.

The initial difficulties which they had encountered on the mountains, did not deter either Fr. Tissot or Msgr. Neyret. When Fr. Tissot recovered and was able to write, he furnished a detailed report about the expedition to Msgr. Neyret, who on the basis of favourable indications from the explorers, wrote to the Propaganda, informing them of the possibility of bringing the mountaineers (Kondhs) to the light of grace. Cardinal Franzoni, Prefect of the Congregation, replied favourably.[185] In the same manner Msgr. Neyret sent a letter to his superior at Annecy in France.[186] Monsieur Mermier responded by advocating prudence in undertaking such a major project without giving sufficient attention to the resources needed for the new endeavour. However, he promised to endorse Msgr. Neyret's decision in this regard as he understood the importance of the project.[187] They subsequently had to postpone the project until an opportune moment arrived.

Chotanagpur: Precursor to Gangpur

It was only after the Kol Insurrection of 1831-1832 that the British East India Company began to notice the problems of the tribals of Chotanagpur. During the next 30 years many commissions of enquiry would be appointed to make specific recommendations. However well intended the recommendations might have been, the administrative and judicial reforms were inadequate to solve exacerbating tribal problems such as land alienation -- in some cases the reforms even aggravated the problems. The ensuing struggle between the tribals and the *dikus* or foreigners led to the involvement of the police and the courts. However, the tribals were no match for their opponents. Legal proceedings, court language, as well as prejudiced and money-thirsty interpreters and lawyers made it impossible for the tribals to present their case properly before the judiciary.[188] When it became almost impossible to reach a settlement through the courts, the tribals tried to settle their differences with the zamindars by themselves. Unfortunately, such moves ended in favour of the latter. The landlords often demanded exorbitant rent, *bethbegari* or 'forced labour', and other services to which they had no legal right. The problem escalated when the landlords refused to give receipts for payments of rent so that they could exact even more the next time.

The Beginning of the Lutheran Mission

The Lutheran missionaries of the Berlin Gossner Mission[189] were the Protestant pioneers in the Chotanagpur region at the time of these disturbances.[190] They had already witnessed the suffering of the aboriginals from Chotanagpur who served as 'coolies' in the streets of Calcutta. The Lutherans were nevertheless impressed by their gaiety. Helped by friends, the Lutherans established themselves at Ranchi,[191] the capital of the Chotanagpur plateau. In 1850, after five years of dedicated service,[192] only four Oraons belonging to the *Kabir Panth Bhagat Movement*[193] had been baptised. On October 28, 1851 two Mundas were baptized.[194] But the missionary activities of the Lutherans attracted the tribal population and subsequently many joined them.

The rise in conversions to Christianity frightened the landlords who began to persecute Christians. The missionaries travelled to the villages that wanted to hear them, and many villagers also went to Ranchi to speak to the missionaries. By 1856 about 900 people had been baptised and another 2000 were in contact with the missionaries.[195] The *Sepoy Mutiny* of 1857 disrupted the administration of Chotanagpur, and no European felt safe. The missionaries were forced to abandon the neophytes and escape to Calcutta. The tribal Christians were once again at the mercy of the landlords. With the return of peace, the missionaries began to rebuild, and the government also offered relief funds to the aboriginals. This irked the landlords, who believed that the British government was now in favour of the aboriginals. By 1868 there were about 10,000 Christians under the care of the Lutheran mission.[196]

The Mission Work of the Lutherans

The Lutheran missionaries organized schools throughout the tribal areas. With the introduction of education, the tribals began to recognise their oppressed condition as well as their lawful rights and privileges. They refused to render more free labour than they were obliged to do.[197] As they grew in number, they felt confident enough to oppose the landlords. The missionaries advised the tribal Christians to endure the wrongs in humble submission, to speak the truth, to pay their rents, and to avoid taking recourse to the legal system. But they were not heeded.[198] Although the Tenures Act II of 1869[199] brought some improvement, it did not, however, specifically deal with the control of their ancestral lands. The official enactment was a failure because it did not directly treat the causes of the dispute between the Mundas and the *Dikus*. Moreover, there was no provision to protect the hereditary rights of the Mundas and the Oraons to cut wood from the village forests around which their life revolved.[200] The tribals became Christians in order to obtain help from the missionaries and they remained in the Church as long as the new religion served their purpose and protected them from the terror of the zamindari system.

In matters of church organization, the Lutherans tried to preserve as far as possible the social organization of the people. They used the services of the elders, catechists and teachers, almost all of whom were aboriginals, to propagate the faith. The success of the mission depended largely on the zeal and conscientiousness of these people. In November 1868, six of the older missionaries left the Lutheran Church and joined the Anglicans. About 3,000 converts followed them.[201] It should be noted that the landlords were not against the practice of Christianity as a religion but against the effect it produced on their adherents.

The Beginning of the Mission of Belgian Jesuits

In 1859 the Belgian Province of the Society of Jesus took charge of West Bengal, whose 15,000 Catholics were spread over the vast area of north-eastern Orissa, southern Bihar and West Bengal. Fr. Augustus Stockman[202] was very much impressed by his visit to Chaibasa and sent a favourable report to Msgr. Walter Steins[203] in November 1868. Two months later he was appointed parish priest of Chaibasa.[204] He arrived on the 10th of July 1869.[205] This is said to be the real beginning of the Chotanagpur mission. When Fr. Stockman settled at Chaibasa, people came to him to hear his preaching and teaching. However, it took almost four years for Mundas to adopt Christianity as their religion.[206] Gradually, the Jesuits established mission stations in four important places -- Sarwada-Doldo, Bandgaon-Burudi, Chaibasa and Buruma, which they called *Quadrilateral*.[207] De Sa stated that "the Fathers thought that the duty of the missionary was to preach the Gospel and to baptize those who wished to become Catholics. To help the people against oppression, they thought, was outside the scope of their apostolate".[208] North of the *Quadrilateral*, a mission station was started at Jamgain by Fr. De Cock[209] in 1882. Most of the Catholics belonging to this station were former Lutherans. Fr. De Cock, now the director of the mission, was against missionaries helping the people in their land disputes.

The younger missionaries, especially Frs. Müllender and John Fierens, [210] spent much time visiting the villages and getting to know the people.

The Internal Organization of the Bengal Mission of the Jesuits

The Chotanagpur mission was part of the Jesuit mission of West Bengal. The head of the mission was a `superior regular'. Fr. Sylvain Grosjean (1846-1915) was the superior regular between 1882 and 1892. The superior regular of the Bengal mission was under the provincial of the Belgian Province who resided in Belgium. A Jesuit was also at the head of the diocese; for example, Msgr. Paul Goethals (1832-1901)[211] held this position between 1878 and 1901. Until 1887, he was the vicar apostolic with the title of archbishop. In 1887 West Bengal was made an archdiocese with Msgr. P. Goethals as its first archbishop. The missionaries of the Chotanagpur mission came under the jurisdiction of both superiors, as religious under Fr. Sylvain Grosjean and as missionaries or helpers of the bishop under Msgr. P. Goethals.[212] The Catholic mission of Chotanagpur was not successful until the arrival of an intelligent and enthusiastic Jesuit, Father Constant Lievens, who reached Jamgain on the feast of St. Joseph in 1885.

First Missionary in Gangpur or Western Orissa

Fr. John Fierens was the first missionary to penetrate into the erstwhile kingdom of Gangpur in 1884. He was on his way to Sambalpur[213] to visit a Catholic community serving in the military garrison. This has some historical importance as it came not only before the apostolate of Lievens, but it helped to recognise the 'danger in the speedy spread of Lutheranism' and the possibility of starting a mission in that territory. Fr. J. Fierens took the longer way to reach Sambalpur, which put him in close contact with the people. Writing about the journey of Fr. John Fierens, M. Vermeire states,

> Father Fierens was then (the) missionary in charge of Bandgaon, 17 miles beyond Khunti on the road to the Bengal – Nagpur Railway. That side there were between 1000 and 1200 Catholics, the fruit of some 15 years of work in Chotanagpur, a poor gain obtained until then. The reason why Fr. Fierens went to, and crossed Gangpur, was that at Sambalpur in Orissa there was a military garrison, which apparently was maintained there till about 1902. At that time, i. e., in 1884 this garrison contained a certain number of Catholics, single or married. The Archbishop of Calcutta was responsible for sending them a priest from time to time. At first, the aged Father Sapart of Balasore Mission was charged with this duty. But he had

to cross the very broad Mahanadi river, besides others with plenty of rivers and canals. For a younger man like Fr. Fierens, riding the whole long way on a good horse, it was not so fatiguing (tiring) and probably was an interesting journey... Everywhere he found the Lutherans well established and nowhere did he meet any Catholics: so was it between Torpa and Basia and between Koel and Gangpur. A few miles from Kolebira, the Lutherans had a station at Takarma from where they were making converts throughout the neighbouring country and far even into Biru. They did not stop there for Fr. Fierens had hardly entered Gangpur than the road passed through Raiboga, a market place, where the Lutherans had a well-attended chapel; and so, until far beyond Gangpur, were there Lutherans in many villages.[214]

State of the Catholic Community in Sambalpur

In one of the letters to his sisters in Belgium, in October 1884, Fierens narrated his visit to Sambalpur. Some of its main features are as follows:

> I was in Sambalpur, which is about 200 miles from here, the western end of our mission. There is a regiment of indigenous soldiers, who come from South India. There are many Catholic soldiers among them. They live there with their wives and children. They are not recent converts, but Christians whose forefathers were converted by St. Francis Xavier. They are as active as Irish Christians. Once a year a missionary visit them (to administer the sacraments). They have a chapel where they come together for their morning and evening prayers. The catechist leads the prayers and teaches catechism to the children... They speak Tamil and Telugu. Men can speak some English and women, besides their mother tongue, a bit of Hindustani. It is in this language I manage to hear the confessions of women and children. Besides the catechist there is a headman who looks after the conduct of the people. Normally, he is competent to deal with some minor cases and give due punishment; however, the serious ones will be reported to the priest when he comes for the annual visit...Their good soldiers subscribe every month some fees for the maintenance of the chapel: they need to procure candles and they have the habit of burning incense in front of the statues. They are very much devoted to St. Antony of Padova. This devotion comes from the Portuguese as he is their compatriot. I had to baptise the children born during the year and most of them bear the name of St. Antony, Antony for boys and Antoniamma for girls. During his eight days of stay among them, the priest has to bless one day their houses, on other day the cemetery, see to the repair of the chapel, etc. I opened a list for subscription for the Europeans living at the station. It brought about 100 francs.[215]

In his letter to Msgr. P. Goethals and the superior regular of the mission, Fr. Sylvain Grosjean, Fr. J. Fierens sent a warning that, if rapid action was not taken soon, the territory would be lost forever, as the Lutherans were going about with relative facility. In his comments on the 'warning letter' sent by Fr. J. Fierens, M. Vermeire wrote: "About 20 years later when the Catholic missionaries began to penetrate Gangpur, they found Fierens' statements not only correct but they were astounded at the spread of Lutheranism in all directions."[216] Wherever the Jesuits went they were preceded either by the Lutherans or the Anglicans, except in Barway and Chotanagpur.

Three Great Missionaries of Chotanagpur

Of all the Jesuits who had lived and worked in Chotanagpur, the names of three individuals have become household names. Even today, the tribals remember these great men with respect and gratitude for their dedicated service. Here we have three great men of God, with their respective qualities, striving to attain the same end but with different means: Fr. Constant Lievens lit the fire that burst into flame; Fr. Sylvain Grosjean as superior regular organized and planned every campaign from his desk; Fr. John Baptist Hoffmann with his practical mind supplied the temporal needs by founding the Cooperative Credit Society and helped the government to enact laws protecting the tribal land holding system. In the final analysis their only aim was to spread the kingdom.[217]

a. Life and Achievements of Fr. Sylvain Grosjean

Fr. Sylvain Grosjean was born at Martilly in Luxembourg on March 4, 1846. Orphaned at the age of 9, he was educated by his maternal grandparents. He entered the Society of Jesus on September 24, 1864 in Belgium. In 1873 he arrived in Louvain for his philosophical and theological studies and was ordained a priest on September 7, 1879. During these years he kept up his interest in the Mission of West Bengal and finally arrived in India in December 1880. Two years later, he became the superior regular of the Bengal Mission of the Belgian Province of the Society of Jesus and remained in that office till 1892. Pope Leo XIII's call for the establishment of an indigenous clergy echoed in his heart. Later, when Msgr. Zaleski, the apostolic delegate in India, was given the task of founding a papal seminary for India, he chose Fr. Sylvain Grosjean as his assistant to complete the project.[218] During his tenure as the first rector of the papal seminary at Kandy (1893-1899), Fr. Sylvain Grosjean built the permanent structure of the seminary and also taught Latin, philosophy and later even theology.[219] When he was relieved as rector of the Seminary, he volunteered to help the Chotanagpur mission. When his term as rector of the Manresa House at Ranchi ended in 1909, he realised his longstanding desire by volunteering to work in the newly-established parish of Kesramal in Gangpur. At the age of 63, he became the parish priest and one of the co-founders of the parish, which is located at Kesramal, 6 miles north of Rajgangpur railway station.[220] After a long life of untiring service as a leader and a missionary, he died on September 6, 1915, and was laid to rest at Kesramal.[221]

After having taken over as the superior regular of the West Bengal mission in 1882, at the age of 36, Fr. Grosjean made his first tour of the Chotanagpur mission (1883-1884) with Msgr. P. Goethals in order to assess the missionary activities of the Jesuits and to understand the situation of the people. Fr. Grosjean wanted the missionaries in the field to probe into the vital social and human problems of the people and to offer effective help in order to eradicate their misery. This, he felt, would begin a broad movement, what the Belgian Jesuit Missionaries would call *Mouvement de la Grâce*. For this purpose, he had already earmarked two young and intelligent men: Frs. Constant Lievens and John Baptist Hoffmann.[222] His descriptive accounts of the mission, sent to the superior general and to the provincial, are examples of his intelligence and the keen interest he had in the development of the Chotanagpur mission.

As Jesuit superior of the growing mission, he had not only an enthusiastic vision but also agonizing concerns about the health of his over-burdened brethren. Often, he stressed the need for missionaries to have good housing, and he ordered that a 'Manresa House' should be built, which would serve as a house of formation and a place for missionaries to regain their physical and spiritual strength.[223] Fr. Grosjean cared deeply about the missionaries and felt one with them in troubled times. In one of his letters to his friends, he wrote: "I literally tremble when I receive letters from Ranchi."[224] In 1887 the Belgian province sent 10 new missionaries, whom Fr. Grosjean allocated according to the most pressing needs of the mission. In 1888 he visited Fr. Lievens' mission on horseback. He was deeply impressed by the way Fr. Lievens handled the mission. Later he wrote, "that within two years we shall have 100,000 baptized and catechumens. Three tribes, the Mundas, the Kharias and the Oraons are coming over. Now is the time or never".[225]

As a good leader, the superior spent the whole of March 1889 among his missionaries in Chotanagpur. He gave a Holy Week retreat to 200 catechists, many of whom were ex-Protestants; he animated the school and repeated his tour of the district. At the threat of the *Renny expedition*,[226] Fr. Grosjean engaged an eminent lawyer from Calcutta to appeal in favour of the missionaries and the jailed tribals. To ensure that the missionary work was carried on with sustained spirituality, Fr. Grosjean appointed a number of priests in charge of the major mission stations as *ministers*. They were to ensure that the missionaries faithfully adhered to a life characterised by poverty and obedience both to God and to the Church.[227] Fr. Grosjean's commitment to the work in the Chotanagpur mission was unmistakable. In his letter to the Belgian provincial in November 1891, he wrote: "I hope that after I have worked so long for Chota Nagpur, you will allow me to come to the help of the mission in danger (danger of the expansion of Lutheranism), a mission which in 1882 had 500 Catholics and is now threatened to lose 45,000. I shall do whatever obedience will require. I offer myself to go to Ranchi as Minister of Manresa House or to go to Barway."[228] He had a deep appreciation for Fr. Lievens, stating, "in my opinion, Fr. Lievens is the most qualified man to animate a great movement, for which he was exceptionally gifted; he is one of the very rare men, who, single-handed have made the missionary work significantly advance".[229]

Fr. Sylvain Grosjean also promoted the social services of the mission. In 1908 he forcefully pleaded with the British authorities, and even collaborated with them, to provide relief for the famine-stricken people of the plateau. He was one of the more dynamic superiors of his age, who provided the mission with extraordinary maps and statistics. In Belgium he was an accomplished public relations man and a successful fundraiser. The old worn-out parish priest of Kesramal saw himself as Christ on a mission from the Father, committed unconditionally to the salvation of the tribals of Gangpur. Through all his travels, preaching and teaching, he shared gradually with the people his own personal experience of the Crucified and Risen Lord. And it was here that he was laid to rest on September 6, 1915. The presence of his tomb in the soil of Gangpur will remind future generations of his untiring service and missionary zeal. He will live on in the hearts of the tribal population of Gangpur.

b. A Sketch of Fr. Constant Lievens' Life

Fr. Constant Lievens was born on April 11, 1856, in the Flemish town of Moorslede, Belgium. It was Fr. Callaert who pointed out to him the immense work that lay in the subcontinent, particularly in the Bengal Jesuit Mission, which had started a few decades earlier. Soon after taking his first vows he arrived in India (December 2, 1880) and was sent to continue his theological preparations at the Hill Seminary in Asansol. Along with his theological studies, Fr. Constant Lievens showed interest in learning the local languages, and he was able to converse fluently in both Bengali and Hindi within a short time. He was ordained to the priesthood on January 14, 1883 by Archbishop P. Goethals of Calcutta.

With the able guidance of Fr. Sylvain Grosjean, the superior regular of the Bengal Mission, Fr. Lievens reached his destination, Doranda, via Girdih and Hazaribagh on March 18, 1885. On the following day, the feast of St. Joseph, he was directed to move to Jamgain to begin the task of evangelisation. Later, he met his benefactor, Bisheshwar Dayal or Bisheshwar Singh, the *Jamadar* or the policeman in charge of the police station at Torpa, who not only gave him shelter but defined what his missionary endeavours should be in the future. The *Jamadar* told Lievens: "If you want to win over these people to your religion, you should take up their legal defence in court."[230]

Realising the tribal solidarity manifested in their communal living, Fr. Lievens insisted on receiving the Mundas into the church only in groups. He also observed that the people tended to be 'clannish', so that when the head of a family or a village became a Christian, the rest followed his example, thus preserving their social ties and diminishing any need for migration.[231] Therefore, at times, a whole family or a whole village came forward requesting baptism.[232] To mark their abandonment of their former religion, the converts would cut off their *chundis*, the tuft of hair on the head, which was a symbol of their traditional beliefs.[233] Sharp growth marked the fruit of Lievens' labour; records show that there were 56 Catholics at the arrival of Lievens in March 1885, and 50,351 in August 1888.[234] It is evident that as more people began to request baptism, Fr. Lievens was unable to handle the situation, especially when there was but a handful of priests to instruct them in the new faith. This apparent lack of foresight in his method of evangelisation brought him criticism from within the Jesuit community, including Msgr. P. Goethals and later Fr. J. B. Hoffmann.[235]

The mass conversions to Christianity soon assumed the form of a social revolution. The landlords were alarmed by the progressive changes in the attitudes of the usually docile and submissive tenants: in many cases the tenants refused to pay rents as well as to provide unpaid labour to the landlords. A great commotion erupted in those areas where the tribals faced persecution and atrocities from the landlords. Some were beaten up while others were forced to abandon the land.[236] Fr. Lievens was accused of leading a rebellion. Many false cases were filed against him in court. Archbishop P. Goethals ordered Fr. Lievens and his companions to discontinue their activities.[237] In March 1892, the superiors in Calcutta objected to the mass conversions. They asked Lievens and his companions to refrain from helping the people with their lawsuits. But by now Fr. Lievens was a sick man who was unable to continue in the mission. He left Calcutta for Belgium in September 1892. On November 7, 1893 he succumbed to his disease (tuberculosis), which snatched away a zealous missionary and left the mission bereft of a father and a leader.

Lievens' Work and Method

No doubt Lievens' own personality and charisma had much to do with people coming to him with the request for baptism. He made his objective quite clear: "I have come here among you for your eternal happiness. But in this life too I can make you happy. Confide your difficulties to me, I shall help you as much as the law allows. Believe me I know the law better than you do."[238] Having learned about the experience of the Protestant missionaries in dealing with the government, he was particularly careful not to alienate the authorities by supporting directly or otherwise any agitation; he even claimed that he had nothing to do with the *Sardar Movement*[239] which he considered a real socialistic agitation. He acknowledged the authority of the government in dealing with the situation, and he invoked the applicable laws.[240] Furthermore, two important factors led Father Lievens not to preach the gospel directly. First, the actual socio-economic condition of the people was so affected by the exploitation by the landlords that preaching about God and His liberative mission would have had no effect on them. Secondly, these people needed immediate help so that they could look for a better tomorrow. The usual methods practised by the older missionaries were insufficient and even irrelevant.[241]

The greatness of Lievens lies not so much in the many conversions he gained for the Catholic Church as in his selfless life of sacrifice, which emphasised charity, justice, human dignity, and equality. Fr. Lievens lit a spark at Torpa that would later spread throughout Chotanagpur and become a fire. In August 1888 he established himself at Ranchi, which was more centrally located than Torpa and more easily accessible to the ever-growing stream of village delegations that came to see and consult him, or even to request him to visit their villages. The defence of the aboriginals in matters of rent and forced labour was not at all a new phenomenon; in fact, the Lutherans and Anglicans had been advocating the same for many decades.

Fr. Lievens began to study the law more thoroughly in order to learn more about the traditional rights of the Mundas (Oraons). He learned of the illegal accumulation of land by the landlords, their practice of not giving receipts for rent paid, and their illegal demand for *Bethbegari*, forced labour. By listening to the villagers' troubles and helping them, he came to be regarded as their friend.[242] De Sa stated that "at the village meetings the catechists explained the advantage of the Christian Religion -- protection from the oppression of the landlords, protection from the evil spirits, blessings on their fields and on their cattle, medicines in time of illness and so on".[243] The impact of this apostolate of rendering help to settle land disputes was noticed by the superior regular of the West Bengal mission during a visit to Chotanagpur in February and March of 1888. Fr. Sylvain Grosjean accompanied Fr. Lievens during this visit in order to personally obtain information about the conflicts over peoples' lands.[244]

The effect of the *Mouvement de la Grâce*[245]-- this is how the Belgian Jesuits named the movement that added thousands of aboriginals to the Catholic Church -- was a steady growth in the number of adherents, and it was heart-warming. De Sa expressed the motives of the tribals in the following manner: "In the face of oppression and exploitation, the aboriginals were looking for justice. They were looking for the development of their human personalities, and for the way of life that would respect their human dignity. They could only achieve this goal as a community. And so when they were converted to Christianity, they came over either *to obtain justice, or because they had already obtained it*.[246] It is illustrative to note the steady growth in the number of tribals adhering to Christianity: in September 1886, there were 2,000 followers; in January 1888, the mission counted about 25,000 adherents; in March there were 40,000; and, in early October the total was 56,000.[247]

The British Government seemed to look favourably upon the Jesuit mission. The Mundas and the other tribes felt secure with the European missionaries, both the Jesuits and the Lutherans, who seemed to have the protection of the government. At such a favourable time it was natural for the missionaries to expand the mission. The plan which Fr. Lievens envisaged, according to Van der Schueren[248] was, "to convert all the Aboriginals of Chotanagpur, then penetrate into the independent states of Sirguja, Jashpur, Raigarh, Gangpur and Bonai and convert all the Aboriginals in these states, making one vast Christianity of them all".[249] Despite his heavy schedule with the villagers, Fr. Lievens found time to write prayer books and a catechism in Hindi; he even composed some Hindi hymns to Flemish tunes. Fr. Lievens also had a keen interest in the training of catechists. Since the aboriginals were illiterate, he thought that the work of conversion would be a failure, if education was not given priority. Hence, almost from the beginning, he took an active interest in establishing schools.

It is noteworthy that it was the people who came to the missionary. While they waited at the mission house to learn about the settlement of their court cases, they received instructions in the Christian faith and received baptism. Therefore, the real motives of the people are not clear, and some of the missionaries entertained serious doubts about them. One cannot categorically deny the socio-economic benefits that initially provided the motivation for their conversion to Christianity, but this does not rule out the possibility of a gradual assimilation of the tenets of Christianity. On the one hand, one cannot but applaud the *mouvement de la grace* inaugurated by Fr. Lievens that brought tens of thousands to the light of grace. On the other hand, a few questions remained to be answered regarding their entry into Christianity, such as preparation.

c. A Life Sketch of Fr. John Baptist Hoffmann

Born at Wallendorf, in the diocese of Trier, Germany on June 21, 1857, Fr. J. B. Hoffmann entered the Society of Jesus on April 20, 1877. After his ecclesiastical studies in India, he was ordained on January 18, 1891 in Calcutta. In 1892 he arrived in Ranchi to make his tertianship. He was asked to study both British law and the agrarian legislation pertaining to various practices in India, in the light of which he could understand fully the implication of the mutinous agitation that was simmering at that time throughout Chotanagpur. After his tertianship he was assigned to Bandgaon and later in 1895 to Sarwada, the heartland of the Mundas, who had been deeply affected by the agitation of tribal leaders against the landlords, the government and the missionaries.[250] Repatriated at the outbreak of World War I, Fr. Hoffmann dedicated the rest of his life to the publication of the sixteen-volume *Encyclopaedia Mundarica*, a lasting gift to the Munda world.[251] Fr. Hoffmann, with the help of Fr. Van Emelen (who was in Chotanagpur to collaborate with him), directed the work from Germany. The British government in India published these volumes at its expense. After the completion of his monumental work Fr. Hoffmann died in full satisfaction on November 19, 1928 in Trier.[252]

Hoffmann, a Missionary and Social Worker

Hoffmann was convinced that the complaints of the tribals, which he recognized as the real cause of the rebellion, were just. He proposed that legal recognition must be accorded to the customs and the rights under which a farmer had cultivated the fields. He also suggested that these fields be accurately measured and marked on the maps.[253] At Sarwada, Fr. Hoffmann conducted a thorough study of the *Khuntkatti* and *Bhuinari* lands (ancestral lands) of the aborigines. The Munda *Khuntkatti* tenancies are lands owned by the *Khuntkattidars*, the male descendants of the original founders of the village of Chotanagpur. The *Bhuinari* land means that the ancestral lands belong to the original settlers of the country. The word *Bhuinari* is a local variation of *Khuntkatti* with a slight difference in meaning. Based on his thorough understanding of the practices of the tribals, Fr. Hoffmann supported their struggle for the restoration of their ancient rights and privileges perpetuated by age-old custom and usage.[254] Together with Mr. Lister, he wrote a special memorandum on the Munda land system, and this document persuaded the government ultimately to enact the Chota Nagpur Tenancy Act of 1908, which recognized the age-old rights of the Mundas. Later the memorandum was included in the Act as an appendix.[255]

The Cooperative Societies

Economic self-reliance was one of the major objectives when Fr. Hoffmann founded various societies to help the tribals. As he analysed the concept of the *Mouvement de la Grâce*, he was convinced that inherent to the concept was the mundane object of liberation from economic slavery or servitude. The establishment of cooperative societies was his timely gift to the oppressed tribes of Chotanagpur. Before starting the cooperative Hoffmann wrote a small booklet entitled *Social Works in Chota Nagpore*, aimed at recommending his ideas to his fellow missionaries in hopes of getting their support.[256] To mention some of the main issues addressed by Fr. Hoffman in his work *œuvres sociales*:

> We all know that what they primarily and chiefly expected from us was assistance against the oppression and aggression of the alien invaders, and to obtain this they just barely accepted Christianity as part of the bargain... A good number of our neophytes consider the discipline of Christianity as an irksome restraint, which they submit to chiefly because they fear to lose our protection precisely in those matters where the settlement and the new law will in the future render that protection partly superficial and partly impossible...Christianity, so far from pauperising people, must necessarily tend to relieve poverty by the only means that are worthy of man, viz, by thrift and distinct rise in the intellectual and moral level of the masses... If we want this growth to continue we must offer the aborigines a new and powerful motive for joining Christianity, i. e., through sound economic organizations. But this economic organization is precisely the aim and object of the *œuvres sociales* and cannot be brought about without them. ... Let us teach them how to use their education for the development of a spirit of self-reliance, self-help and productive resourcefulness.[257]

He furnished convincing reasons for the founding of the cooperative.[258] He recognized the importance of the rural unit that is vulnerable and at the same time active in its participation of developmental activities. Therefore, the rural unit is the starting point for all Fr. Hoffmann's social activities. The aim of the village unit consists of education in thrift and good business habits of all the members of a village or of a small group of villages.[259]

The structure of the cooperative was based on the *Raiffeisen* system[260] in Germany but adapted to the local laws, customs and social background of the tribals in Chotanagpur.[261] Fr. Hoffmann also received recognition from the government when the Catholic Cooperative Society was registered on December 2, 1909, and the Cooperative Stores in 1913. The Catholic

Cooperative Credit Society met with great success. For the services rendered to the tribals, Fr. Hoffmann was honoured with a certificate, and in 1913 he was awarded the *Kaiser-i-Hind* silver medal on behalf of the King-Emperor for signal services rendered to the government.[262]

His monumental works and his dedicated services to the tribal community of Chotanagpur will live on for many centuries to come. Although he died in obscurity, away from the land he had come to love, his three outstanding achievements -- the Chota Nagpur Tenancy Act, the cooperative movement and his contribution to ethnological research -- will keep his name alive as long as there are Mundas and as long as the Chotanagpur mission continues operation among the tribals.

Christianity in the Neighbouring States

The work begun by Fr. Constant Lievens kept expanding. It soon spread to the neighbouring territories. The expansion of the *Mouvement de la Grâce* was not limited to a few northern districts of Chotanagpur but expanded towards the south, i.e., Biru. As a result, the Lutherans were compelled to expand their activities in Gangpur. They had a fairly large congregation at Raiboga, just across the Biru frontier.[263] The mass conversions in Chotanagpur infuriated the Lutheran Gossner Mission, since it lost about 7,000 adherents alone in the Gangpur mission because of the friendliness and unpretentious service of Fr. Louis Cardon (1857-1946).[264] The Lutherans considered the presence of the Jesuits a constant threat to their expansion. The activities of the Jesuit missionaries were, at the beginning, steered away from the district of Biru, as the local Raja was hostile to them. However, the enormous good that the mission brought to the tribals could not but attract attention; the tribals even travelled across the frontiers in search of missionaries, in order to experience the *Mouvement de la Grâce*. The three parishes of Biru district -- Rengarih, Samtoli and Kurdeg -- became centres of mission activities in Gangpur. Although a study of the expansion of the mission in itself would be worthwhile, this study will focus on the semi-independent state of Gangpur.

Deputations from Gangpur

After the initial success of Fr. Lievens in court, delegations came to him with requests that he should visit their villages. These delegations, often guided by the village *Panchayat* or council, consisted of the village headman and a few villagers. Obviously, the practice of a collective approach to the conversion of the people seems to have continued even after the death of Fr. Lievens. An assistant in the Noatoli-Basia Parish, Fr. Louis Cardon, recorded in his diary on July 10, 1898: "People are coming from the bottom of Gangpur to become Christians. In spite of our good will, we can not receive these people."[265] In his letter to Fr. Sylvain Grosjean on July 20, 1908 Fr. Cardon wrote:

> On my way back from Noatoli to Kompala (May 1901), deputations from Gangpur villages had met me at Sogra already, and continued coming in. I knew Msgr. Goethals was opposed to new openings. I could not receive them. As soon as Fr. Brice Meuleman (1862 - 1925)[266] was appointed as the Archbishop of Calcutta, I got leave to receive the *Gangpurias* (people of Gangpur), and in no time the rout was in the Lutheran camp, through the numerous accessions from their Christians.[267]

The number of delegations seemed to have increased as the people felt that it was convenient to approach Fr. Cardon whenever he came to Rengarih from Noatoli in 1901.[268] Although the total number of such deputations was not recorded, one can clearly notice the remarkable progress of the mission that drew tribals from the neighbouring states. The Rengarih statistics for 1903 indicates that, of the total number of about 9,600 Catholics under the care of the Parish, at least two thirds were from Gangpur.[269]

Biography of Fr. Louis Cardon

Fr. Louis Cardon was born at Néchin (Hainaut), Belgium, on December 25, 1857. He entered the Society of Jesus on October 25, 1876. His untiring missionary zeal brought him to India on November 25, 1884, where he pursued theological studies in the Jesuit Seminary of Asansol. He was fortunate to begin his missionary career with Fr. Constant Lievens, to whom he became an assistant in January 1889; Fr. Lievens in turn asked him to take charge of the mission of Tetara (Noatoli). Writing on the area of Fr. Cardon's activity, Peter Tete writes: "His area of apostolic activities included almost all that is now under the care of the whole of Noatoli Vicariate, Gumla, Soso and Majhatoli parishes; besides, the whole of Barway, Chechari and Biru."[270] He and his legendary horse, Raja, were kept busy travelling to distant places in search of people who invited him. When he was not away on mission tours,[271] he received the deputations coming to Tetara, the centre of his apostolic work.

Although he was well received among the poor people, he was hated by the Raja of Biru, the landlords and the police, who in 1889 had plotted a conspiracy against the missionaries. Even the British officials, such as Renny (the acting deputy commissioner of Lohardaga), accused Fr. Cardon and his confreres of revolt and warned them that they too would face the same fate as the German Jesuits under Chancellor Otto von Bismarck.[272] They were later vindicated with the help of a leading lawyer from Calcutta. Rather than relenting to such opposition, Fr. Cardon viewed it as a challenge to his apostolic endeavours. He continued to meet people even in the remotest places, including Barway, where he accompanied Fr. Lievens in December 1890. To quote again the words of P. Tete: "During three years he was not only one of the pioneers but also one of Father Lievens' most valued lieutenants, travelling throughout the length and breadth of Chotanagpur, preaching and baptising, gaining new villages, confirming the waverers (wayward), defending the oppressed, ever battling for the cause of Christ."[273]

Cardon's Work and Achievement

Fr. Louis Cardon was convinced that the development of the tribals was fundamentally linked to their education. During his mission tours he collected both boys and girls from the villages for schools. The boys were brought to the centre (where the missionaries resided) where there were schools, and the girls were sent to the Sisters in Ranchi.[274] During the famine of 1896-1897 the people witnessed the true nature of Christian charity, and as a result many tribals opted to become catechumens and many villages returned to Catholicism. Fr. Cardon was instrumental in establishing Rengarih station, with a church, a presbytery, a convent and a school. When Biru-Gangpur was made a separate unit in 1909, the superiors found in Fr. Cardon a suitable candidate to be the superior. He wholeheartedly supported the initiative taken by Fr. Hoffman for the development of tribals. He promoted the Catholic Cooperative Credit Society and the *Dhan Gola* or Grain Bank. Enumerating his works, P. Tete observed: "Father organised *Dharma Schools* where besides intensive religious instructions and prayers, they witnessed Christian life."[275] As he grew old, he withdrew from parish administration and spent much time in the garden. Since Fr. Cardon was also a botanist of some reputation, he discovered several orchids, one of which bears his name *–Microsotolis Cardoni*. He was totally at home with aboriginal laws and customs. He collected much Oraon and Kharia folklore. He was very affectionate to the aborigines. Vermeire writes that it is "a pity that he does not go out more often to visit them at their villages… The influence he exercised, even so from Rengarih, was such that it looked as if the whole of Gangpur would turn Catholic".[276]

In recognition of his meritorious work, the British government decorated him with a second class *Kaiser-i-Hind* medal on December 15, 1936. After long and eventful years as missionary in the jungles of Chotanagpur, Fr. Louis Cardon died at Samtoli on February 11, 1947.

The Visit of the Jesuits to Gangpur

There were already conversions in Gangpur during the time of Fr. Leo Scharlaeken[277] (July 1902). Rengarih was the centre from which the missionaries had contacted the tribals of Gangpur. A village delegation would visit the missionary with a request, and the missionary would then send the catechists to explore the feasibility of opening a station. In this way, by November 1902, the missionaries gained about 5,000 people.[278] As assistant priests in Rengarih, Fr. De Gryse and Fr. John De Smet[279] concentrated their activities in Gangpur where they met the Oraons and the Dhelki Kharias. Though they did not work long in Rengarih, they reached a 'good harvest' in Gangpur. Fr. Cardon wrote to Fr. Grosjean on June 10, 1904, informing him that a contact had been made in Gangpur and that 62 families were ready to become Christians.[280]

Fr. De Smet continued to visit Gangpur even when he was transferred to Samtoli in July 1903. In 1907 he received many deputations from Gangpur, and village leaders from Nagra came to Samtoli, expressing their desire to become Christians.[281] On May 13, 1907, he went on a tour to Gangpur. In spite of the scorching heat he continued to visit villages until June 4. Since no chapels existed in that part of the mission, Holy Masses were celebrated under the trees. During the visit Fr. De Smet baptised 11 adults and 558 children. Some of the landlords of Nagra began to harass the Christians because they were afraid that the latter would go to court to redress their grievances.

The Lutherans of Nagra joined the landlords (zamindars) in order to drive all the Roman Catholics out. Mentioning the difficulties of the Catholics in Gangpur, Peter Tete writes:

The Sub-Inspector of Police of Raghunathpali, reported Francis, the catechist, went with ten men taking guns, swords and sticks to Gaibira threatening to beat them. But the threat did not work. He (the catechist) was alleged to be a "disturber of peace". Then on September 29, 1907, the police wanted Francis and the men of Gaibira to sign a paper, the content of which was not known. The catechist and the people refused to sign it. Francis was then taken to Kuarmunda handcuffed. Meanwhile Father De Smet had written to Mr. Craven, the Dewan of Suadi (Capital of Gangpur, it is now Sundargarh) telling him that the matter would be referred to Archbishop Meuleman with whom the *Dewan* was on friendly terms. Later Francis was acquitted.[282]

The work of conversion continued from Kurdeg under the able direction of Fr. Edmund de Gryse,[283] who made it a point to visit the new adherents on different occasions and even to establish sub-stations at the border, for the Raja of Gangpur was hostile to the missionaries. He did this in order to strengthen the neophytes in their faith. On November 18, 1903, he visited Sakrabahar in Gangpur and visited four other villages. The Oraons were receptive. They invited him to visit their villages and were keen on sending their children to the schools run by the missionaries.[284] The diary entries of Fr. De Gryse provide much information on the various delegations that met him and on the many families and villages that requested him to receive them into the Church. He felt that a great change would occur both in Biru and Gangpur if a good school were established.[285] In September 1904 Fr. De Gryse was again in Gangpur, as he was on his way to Calcutta for a retreat. He made use of the occasion to visit Rengarbahar and Behrembasa in Biru and many villages in Gangpur.[286] Since Gangpur had a large territory, the visits of the missionaries were generally long as they grouped together a number of villages to be visited. The tour of Fr. De Gryse in Gangpur in 1904 lasted about two weeks (4-17 September). This gave him an opportunity to establish new contacts.[287] He was again in Gangpur in May 1905 to prepare for the visit of Msgr. Brice Meuleman. The visit of the two made such an impact on the people that more villages were added to the Catholic fold. The statistics of Kurdeg show that 2,345 Catholics out of 8,642 came from Gangpur State.[288]

On March 7, 1906, Msgr. Brice Meuleman paid a visit to Rengarbahar and Behrembasa (a place chosen as a sub-station for their activity in Gangpur); then with Fr. De Gryse he proceeded to Gangpur. Msgr. Brice Meuleman was back again exactly one year later to visit some of the villages in Gangpur; he did this on his way to Jharsuguda, the nearest railway station.[289]   As assistant parish priest of Kurdeg, Fr. Van Heck paid several visits to Gangpur.[290] He is said to have baptized 120 children when he visited to Craven, the manager of Gangpur, in September 1907, to obtain a grant of medicines.[291]

Yet the state of the mission was not all that encouraging. There were some recorded defections due mainly to the drunkenness and quarrelsome nature of the catechists.[292] There was also a general dissatisfaction among the Catholics of Gangpur, who felt that the Fathers did not provide them with the help they expected: protection from the *zamindars*.   In spite of the numerous difficulties and tensions, the missionaries continued their expansion work in Gangpur, especially under the able guidance of Msgr. Brice Meuleman, the Archbishop of Calcutta, whose periodic visits encouraged the missionaries. Their activities gained some enemies too; the political agent, Blakesley, recommended to the Viceroy in 1913 the expulsion of the Jesuits from Jashpur, but that did not happen.[293] Although the Jesuits continued to expand their work in Gangpur, the state of the Catholics was far from satisfactory. They were Christians in name only and would remain so until the Fathers decided to live among them.[294] The spiritual welfare of the tribals depended much on the visits of the Fathers to Gangpur and on the Raja allowing the missionaries to attend to the spiritual needs of the Christians.

Conclusion

This chapter has explored both the general background of the Church in India and some aspects of the Catholic Mission in Orissa, with all its shifting fortunes. The glorious past of Christianity in Orissa is first recalled in the Portuguese settlements along the coast, of which sadly nothing remains. Their premature end was like an eclipse, since Christianity reappeared or continued in some of the military settlements, such as Cuttack, Berhampur, Aska and Sambalpur. At the same time, small communities in Ganjam and Balasore emerged. Given the nature of the former, one would not expect continuity, as they were composed mostly of soldiers who served in the army of chieftains. Some of the salient important issues of 19th-century Christianity are then presented. These issues created unnecessary confusion and actually slowed the process of evangelisation, although they also contributed to the church's establishment in Orissa. One can only marvel at the rapid progress and expansion of the church in Orissa despite the long distances, the scarcity of personnel, the paucity of resources, and opposition from many agencies.

The tribal people were attached to their ancestral customs and conventions of landholding and cultivation. They were ignorant of the new laws, which were often contrary to their established practices. They slowly began to lose their property vis-à-vis their identity as tribal people or better *Adivasi*, the original settlers. In this atmosphere of cultural estrangement and economic oppression, the missionaries responded positively and did what they thought was best; it was in fact nothing more than humanitarian or social help motivated by the teachings of the Church. Missionaries began their work by protecting the tribals and dalits from the exploitation of landlords, moneylenders, contractors and other *Dikus* (foreigners). Although they did not go beyond the limits of the law of the land in offering assistance to the needy, their activities had a lasting impact on the people, who later sought admission into the Church. The community mentality of the tribals played a leading role in converting them *en masse*. In Ganjam, the MSFS was faced with the uphill task of penetrating the jungles infested with fatal mountain fever. The waning of their initial enthusiasm and the effects of the ill-fated explorations in the Ganjam Mountains called for reflection and better planning. This, of course, will be investigated in subsequent chapters.

Endnotes

[1] Till 1947 the city was known under the name Vizagapatam, a name that was widely used by the missionaries in their correspondence with their confreres and relatives in France. After the Independence of India, the city was renamed Visakhapatnam. For the sake of uniformity, the name Visakhapatnam is used, except when cited from the text. Cf. Histoire de la Mission, AMSFS, 5H4 Inde.

[2] Leo Kierkels, former Apostolic Delegate in India vents the tradition prevailing in India: "Legend and tradition speak of St. Thomas journeying overland, via Taxila in the north and arriving at Musiris (Cranganore) in the south by sea. The date for the latter event is traditionally placed at 52 A. D., a year or so after the Council of Jerusalem." L. KIERKELS, To Commemorate the Sixtieth Anniversary of the Catholic Hierarchy in India and Ceylon 1886 – 1946, Bangalore 1946, p. 12.

[3] Though the South Indian apostolate of St. Thomas is itself clouded in darkness, due to lack of, or rather in the absence of, documentary evidence, one cannot ignore the possibility of the apostolate of St. Thomas in India as there are persisting traditions that were handed down from posterity in the form of folksongs. If they are analysed critically and taken into consideration with the later evidence

like copper plate grants which are an authentic form of enquiry into the past of a people who had reasons in not conserving the documents, we could well arrive at some reliable conclusions with regard to the early beginnings of Christianity in India. A. MUNDADAN, History of Christianity in India: From the Beginning Up to Middle of the Sixteenth Century (up to 1542), Vol. I, Bangalore 1984, p. 29. Their consciousness of being the disciples of St. Thomas is attested by their adherence to the tradition that the Apostle established seven Churches: Palayur, Cranganore, Kokkamangalam, Parur, Niranam, Nilakkel and Quilon. Their belief in the South Indian apostolate of St. Thomas is brightened by the fact of their affinity to one or the other communities mentioned above. Cf. B. VADAKKEKARA, Origin of India's St. Thomas Christians, Delhi 1995, pp. 18, 137 ff.

[4] The archaeological evidence and the veneration of the tomb by not only Christians but also people of other religions are indications that the person buried there was a holy man. Concerning the historicity of the tomb, Benedict Vadakkekara observed: "The ancient tomb of Mylapore, the testimonies of the ecclesiastical writers, and the constant belief of the different churches serve as collateral evidences in vouching for this historical actuality". Ibid., pp. 469 – 470

[5] In order to recapture the spirit of the times the term 'conversion' is used.

[6] J. J. A. CAMPOS, History of the Portuguese in Bengal, Calcutta 1919, p. 12.

[7] M. DOMENGE, La Mission de Vizagapatam, p. 100.

[8] M. Mundadan writes: "Historians agree that the primary aim of the Portuguese expeditions to the East was not to establish a colonial empire but to gain control over profitable trade." M. MUNDADAN, History of Christianity in India: From the Beginning up to the Middle of the Sixteenth Century (Up to 1542), p. 432.

[9] H. Josson wrote that "le P. Nicolas Pimenta, Visiteur de la Compagnie de Jésus aux Indes, envoya au Bengale, en 1598, le P. Francois Fernandes, Supérieur de la Mission et le P. Dominique de Sousa. L'année suivante, vu les bonnes nouvelles qui lui parvenaient, le P. Visiteur désigna deux autres Pères pour la même Mission: les PP. André Boves et Melchior Fonseca". Thus, we could conclude that the Jesuits were the first ones to reach Bengal. H. JOSSON, La Mission du Bengale Occidental, vol. I, Bruges 1921, p. 51.

[10] The friars of St. Augustine, officially known as the order of the Hermits of St. Augustine, were among the most important mendicant orders formed during the 13th century. They belonged to a reformed branch of the order, known as the Discalced Augustinians, sometimes called the 'Barefooted Augustinians' or 'Augustinian Recollects'. The first batch of Augustinians arrived in Goa in 1572. There is a dispute among Augustinian historians themselves as to the time of their arrival in Bengal. Sicardo and other Augustinian historians place it in 1599. Manrique asserts that they came after the Portuguese settled in Hoogly in 1580. By living a more austere life, and by being faithful to something of their former hermitical status, they were more ready than others to go abroad and be preachers of Christianity. Cf. E. R. HAMBYE, "Christianity in Bengal of the 17th and 18th

Centuries: Some Notes and Remarks", in IES 9/1 (1970), p. 40. Campos is of the opinion that the Augustinians established themselves at Bandel which had a church, "on which depended all the churches and parishes in Dacca, Salicur, Chandpur, Banja, Pipli, Balasore, Tamluk, Jessore, Hijili, Tesgaon, Chittagonga, Dianga, Rangamati, Catroba, Sirpur and Arakan". J. J. A. CAMPOS, History of the Portuguese in Bengal, p. 107.

[11] G. C. RATH, "Impact of European Companies on the Foreign Trade of Orissa during the Mughal Era", in Indica 36/1 (1999), p. 5.

[12] Ibid., p. 6.

[13] Affirming the presence of the British in Orissa, J. J. A. Campos wrote: "Before the English had any footing in Bengal, they (Portuguese) settled in Pipli in 1625 and in Balasore in 1625." J. J. A. CAMPOS, History of the Portuguese in Bengal, p. 97.

[14] By the Portuguese period is meant the time when the Portuguese Padroado missionaries were active in various parts of India, i.e., the 16th and 17th centuries. The Christians of the Portuguese period could fall under three categories: 1) Europeans coming from different nations for commerce and other related matters who are found along the Hugli; 2) the descendants of Portuguese in the service of the Mughal government (they were strong in some centres: Hugli, Pipli, Chittagong, Dacca, etc.); and 3) the local converts, who were not many in number. Cf. H. JOSSON, La Mission du Bengale Occidental, vol. I, pp. 115 – 116.

[15] J. J. A. CAMPOS, History of the Portuguese in Bengal, p. 94.

[16] A. HARTMANN, "The Augustinian Mission of Bengal (1599 - 1834)", in Analecta Augustiniana 41 (1978), p. 175.

[17] The Augustinians built the two churches, and both of them were dedicated to Our Lady of the Rosary. The destruction of the churches was probably due to inundation and lack of maintenance in a climate affected by salt water. J. J. A. CAMPOS, History of the Portuguese in Bengal, pp. 94-96; E. R. HAMBYE, "Christianity in Bengal of the 17th and 18th Centuries. Some Notes and Remarks", p. 44; J. THEKKEDATH, History of Christianity in India: From the Middle of the Sixteenth to the End of the Seventeenth Century (1542-1700), Vol.II, Bangalore 1982, p. 466.

[18] J. J. A. CAMPOS, History of the Portuguese in Bengal, pp. 94 – 95. Since the term Feringhi could be same as Parangi, an explanation will follow later in the chapter when we deal with the Malabar rite controversy.

[19] Though Balasore corresponds to the present city in the eastern part of Orissa, it is now devoid of the sea which receded during the course of years. The long stretch along the Bay of Bengal was sometimes called the Orissa coast.

[20] Ibid., p. 99.

[21] Besides Balasore, there was another centre called Jampardo or Jampada, which was probably near Gabgaon, a village adjoining the old Balasore where there was

the Church of Our Lady of Salvation. There were never many Christians in the settlement. It was completely abandoned at the beginning of the 19th century. Cf. E. R. HAMBYE, "Christianity in Bengal of the 17th and 18th Centuries. Some Notes and Remarks", pp. 39 –53; J. THEKKEDATH, History of Christianity in India, vol. II, p. 465.

[22] Chrysanthus Sapart was born on October 25, 1816, at Châtelet (Hainaut). He entered the Society of Jesus on October 2, 1835 and arrived in India on January 31, 1861. He died at Ranchi on March 14, 1906. Cf. R. MENDIZÁBAL, Catalogus Defunctorum in renata Societate Iesu ab a. 1814 ad a. 1970, Romae 1972, p. 200.

[23] Fr. Sapart started the Balasore mission again in 1865. The principal activities of the missionaries were: instruction of catechumens and neophytes, visiting the dispersed Christians and doing some charitable work, like the care of poor children going to school. Though this mission deserves historical analysis, due to the extensive area under our purview, this study limits itself to the southern and north-western parts of Orissa.

[24] From August 1672 till March 8, 1673, Msgr. Pallau remained in Balasore. Cf. H. JOSSON, La Mission du Bengale Occidental, vol. I, pp. 85-86.

[25] It is not the present Pipli town found in Puri district of Orissa. It might have been located at the mouth of Subarnerekha River. Campos mentions: "In the beginning of the sixteenth century, that is, a short time after the discovery of the sea-route to India (1498) the Portuguese established themselves on the coast of Madras. Alarmed at the growth of a foreign power, the natives rose against the Portuguese, who escaped northward and in 1514 founded a town in Pipli about four miles from the mouth of Subarnarekha river, establishing their earliest settlement on the coast of the Bay of Bengal." J.J.A. CAMPOS, History of the Portuguese in Bengal, p. 97.

[26] Pipli was called the Little Port in comparison to the big one that was Hugli (sometimes, it is spelt as Hoogli). "Vers 1567, les ports fréquentés par leurs navires étaient: le Port d'Orissa, probablement Pipli; le Petit Port (Porto Pequeno), c'est-à-dire l'estuaire du bras le plus occidental du Gange". It is here that the Portuguese founded their first settlement. Cf. H. JOSSON, La Mission du Bengale Occidental, vol. I, p. 47.

[27] J. J. A. CAMPOS, History of the Portuguese in Bengal, p. 94.

[28] Campos wrote: "Early in the seventeenth century the Augustinians built a church and a residence in Pipli. The church was dedicated to Our Lady of the Rosary." Ibid., p. 98.

[29] A. HARTMANN, "The Augustinian Mission of Bengal (1599 - 1834)", p. 168.

[30] The decline of Pipli was due to the difficulty of navigation as sand began to gather. H. Josson explained the reason in the following words: "…que l'ensablement de la Subarnarekha rendait de plus en plus inaccessible aux naivres". H. JOSSON, La Mission du Bengale Occidental, p. 97. A. Hartmann thought that "Pipli had a

shallow harbour with not enough depth for ships to anchor in. So eventually it lost its trade to Hugli". A. HARTMANN, "The Augustinian Mission of Bengal (1599 - 1834)", p. 168.

[31] J. THEKKEDATH, History of Christianity in India, vol. II, p. 466.

[32] VINCENT URBANEJA, Notes on the History of Christianity in Orissa, A collection of Unpublished Documents, Gopalpur-on-Sea, p. 3; E. R. HAMBYE, "Christianity in Bengal of the 17th and 18th Centuries", p. 43.

[33] J. J. A. CAMPOS, History of the Portuguese in Bengal, p. 96.

[34] According to the Augustinian document of 1720, Tamboly was situated on the coast of Orissa. In the first half of the 17th century there was a parish church and a resident vicar there. It was Manrique, the official visitor of the Augustinian missions, who obtained the permission of the governor of Cuttack to erect a church at Tamboly.

[35] E. R. HAMBYE, "Christianity in Bengal of the 17th and 18th Centuries", p. 43; J. THEKKEDATH, History of Christianity in India, p. 466.

[36] E. R. HAMBYE, "Christianity in Bengal of the 17th and 18th Centuries", p. 43; J. J. A. CAMPOS, History of the Portuguese in Bengal, pp. 94-95.

[37] Summarising the condition of Christianity in Orissa, H. Josson wrote : "En orissa, la religion catholique était sur le point de disparaître ; comme Pipli depuis longtemps tombé dans l'oubli, Balasore était maintenant abandonné par les marchands européens : Danois, Hollandais, Portugais, Français et Anglais laissaient leurs factoreries tomber en ruines. Alors, raconte-t-on, 'le dernier Augustin assembla un jour les catholiques, restés de l'ancienne chrétienté, dans l'église peinte en noir pour la circonstance, et, après leur avoir reproché leur vices, il déclara qu'il allait les abandoner comme incorrigibles et qu'ils éprouveraient la malédiction de Dieu. En effet, divers événements dispersèrent tous ces chrétiens avec leurs familles. La plupart ont vu une fin malheureuse et il ne resta plus de trace de leur ancienne prospérité. Et comme pour confirmer cette tradition populaire, le cyclone de 1832 renversa l'église', ou plutot ce qui en restait. En 1825, les murailles seules existaient encore." H. JOSSON, La Mission du Bengale Occidental, vol. I, p. 141.

[38] A. HARTMANN, "The Augustinian Mission of Bengal (1599 - 1834)", p. 168.

[39] Propaganda Fide was officially erected on June 22, 1622 by the Bull Inscrutabili Divinae Providentiae of Pope Gregory XV. Propaganda was normally referred to as the 'Sacra Congregatio de Propaganda Fide'. The foundation of the Propaganda was certainly a welcome event in the history of the Catholic Missions. The Pope's intimate collaborator, Cardinal Ludovisi, writing on March 11, 1623 to the Bishop of Arras, mentioned the reasons for founding the Congregation. Regarding the motive of the Propaganda, J. Metzler wrote: "From the beginning of his pontificate, His Holiness had the special intention of doing all in his power to bring about the conversion of heretics and infidels and it is for that reason that he erected the Congregatio de Propaganda Fide." J. METZLER, "Foundation of the Congregation

"de Propaganda Fide" by Gregory XV", in Sacrae Congregationis de Propaganda Fide Memoria Rerum. 350 Years in the Service of the Missions 1622 – 1972, vol. I/1 1622 – 1700, Rom 1971, p. 81. A similar view is also expressed by S. Thanugundla. He wrote: this was 1) "to be an instrument in the hands of the Pope for furthering the interior reform of the Church in the European countries that had succumbed to Protestantism and for regaining areas; 2) she would be the link with the orthodox to foster closer relationship between Rome and the orthodox; 3) she would be responsible for the spread of the Catholic faith in America, Asia and Africa. In other words, she was meant to preserve, strengthen and to spread the Catholic faith throughout the world". S. THANUGUNDLA, Structures of the Church in Andhra Pradesh: An Historico – Juridical Study, PUU, Rome 1976, p. 124.

[40] I. PADINJAREKUTTU, The Missionary Movement of the 19th and 20th centuries and its Encounter with India, Frankfurt 1995, p. 13.

[41] Here are some of the important documents regarding Ius Padroado: (1) Romanus Pontifex (January 8, 1455) of Nicholas V gave the monopoly of conquering and subduing all the lands and kingdom of infidels and the faculty to found and construct churches in the conquered territories and provide the necessary clergy to King Alfonso and his successors; (2) Inter Caetera Quae (March 13, 1456) of Callistus III confirmed the right given by his predecessor and granted jurisdiction to the present and future possessions that will be acquired; (3) Ineffabilis (June 1, 1497) of Alexander VI clarified the duties relating to Padroado; (4) Dum Fidei Constantiam (June 7, 1514) of Leo X elaborated the rights attached to Padroado and these could not be revoked without the consent of the king; (5) Pro Excellenti Praeeminentia (June 12, 1514) of Leo X reaffirms the rights of the king; (6) Aequum Reputamus (November 3, 1534) of Paul III conveyed the erection of the Diocese of Goa and enumerated the duties of the Padroado personnel and their responsibility in promoting the cause of Catholicism; (7) Etsi Sancta et Immaculata (February 4, 1557) of Paul IV confirmed the rights of Padroado and the Diocese of Goa was raised to an Archdiocese. Cf. JORDÂO, LEVY MARIA, et al. (eds.), Bullarium Patronatus Portugalliae Regum in ecclesiis Africae, Asiae atque Oceaniae, Olisipone 1872-1879.

[42] J. COMBY, How to Understand the History of Christian Missions, trans. John Bowden, London 1996, p. 56.

[43] K. S. LATOURETTE, The Great Century in Northern Africa and Asia. A.D. 1800 – A. D. 1914, pp. 71 - 72.

[44] J. J. A. CAMPOS, History of the Portuguese in Bengal, p. 121.

[45] Ines G. Zupanov further reflects on the conflict between Rome and Portugal. The inability of the Portuguese crown to administer efficiently their overseas missionary enterprises and Rome's effort to reclaim for itself the jurisdiction over the distant missions was a sign of an even more 'important struggle between the

Papacy and the rising nation-states'. Cf. I. G. ZUPANOV, Disputed Missions. Jesuit Experiments and Brahmanical Knowledge in Seventeenth-century India, New Delhi 1999, pp. 91 & 114.

[46] S. NEILL, A History of Christianity in India. 1707 – 1858, vol. II, Cambridge 1985, p. 276.

[47] The suppression of the Society of Jesus (1773) had a catastrophic impact on the mission in India. They knew the people, their language and customs. They began with the education of youngsters and tried to propagate the faith through the press apostolate, by providing enough Christian literature in the vernacular. Therefore, the suppression of the Society of Jesus and the outbreak of the French Revolution had a negative impact on a degenerating mission. Cf. M. DOMENGE, La Mission de Vizagapatam, pp. 102 – 103. In view of the grim situation, very few of the clergy were willing to go to India, and such unwillingness clearly indicated a loss of missionary fervour compounded by the challenges involved in working under inclement weather. Under such circumstances it was not easy for the King of Portugal to find suitable candidates to fill vacant sees. T. ANCHUKANDAM, The First Synod of Pondicherry 1844, Bangalore 1994, p. 11.

[48] J. BECKMANN, "The Resumption of Missionary Work", in H. JEDIN (ed.), History of the Church. Vol. III, Abridged Edition, New York 1981, p. 108.

[49] Ibid., p. 109.

[50] I. PADINJAREKUTTU, The Missionary Movement, p. 50. Based on papal documents and existing tradition, the Portuguese government was convinced that the ancient privileges granted to Portugal by the papacy could not be revoked by succeeding popes without the consent of the other party. The Padroado was their national pride, for it recalled their golden epoch of their missionary endeavour and the enormous sacrifices that went with it. Therefore, any alteration in the granted privilege would invite wounded sentiments. Cf. G. MARTINA, Pio IX (1851 - 1866), Roma 1986, p. 379.

[51] It is interesting to refer to G. Martina's thoughtful statement here: "il 24 aprile 1838 col breve Multa Praeclare, frutto di lunghe consultazioni a Propaganda, aveva esplicitamente riconosciuto l'anarcronismo del patronato portoghese, ed aveva praticamente soppresso ogni giurisdizione delle diocesi di Cranganor, Cochin, Meliapur (probabilmente solo nei territori inglesi), sostituendola con quella dei Vicariati già costituiti". Ibid., p. 383. The apostolic letter Multa Praeclare did not abolish the Padroado dioceses, but it restricted its jurisdiction to the territory of Goa. Commenting on the letter, a renowned Anglican historian made a judicious statement: "Instead of effecting the rescue of Catholic Missions in India from almost complete collapse, its result was to inflict grave injury on the reputation of the Church in the eyes of the Protestants and non-Christians, to cause loss of the esteem in which bishops and priests had been held, to produce contest and conflict, and even blows, among Christians. And yet, all things taken into consideration, the Brief was far from being a failure. It aroused the Padroado

clergy from their lethargy, recalled to the Portuguese crown in the most urgent fashion its duties under the Padroado, laid on it the duty at once and vigorously to concern itself for the well-being of its missions in India, and prepared the way for a new agreement." S. NEILL, A History of Christianity in India (1707 – 1858), vol. II, p. 287.

[52] Here are some reasons that justify the action of the Holy See: 1) In granting patronage the Holy See never sacrificed its duty to 'provide for religion, or to deprive itself of the power of making new laws and arrangements'. 2) Portugal was no more in command of India, except in Goa. The changed scenario in India warranted such a step. 3) The Holy See did not innovate; but only repeated what it did in the past by carving out a vicariate apostolic from the dioceses. Cf. E. HULL, Bombay Mission History, vol. I, Bombay 1927, pp. 238 – 239.

[53] S. NEILL, A History of Christianity in India (1707 – 1858), vol. II, p. 286.

[54] The period between 1838 and 1857 is known as the 'Goan Schism', although according to some authors it is doubtful if it could be considered as such. E. Hull is of the opinion that there was no schism. To quote his words: "Hence it seems to me that whatever the convictions of the Vicars-Apostolic might have been, they were not technically justified at any time in publicly calling the Goa clergy 'schismatics' in the canonical sense of the word. (It is one thing to say there was schism, and quite another thing to call an individual person 'schismatic')." E. HULL, Bombay Mission History, vol. II, Bombay 1927, p. 123; Cf. I. PADINJAREKUTTU, The Missionary Movement, p. 55.

[55] In the early part of the nineteenth century a professedly Roman Catholic community in Bengal had neither public worship nor administration of the sacraments, nor gave any indication of its faith. It had a few images of the Virgin Mary and the saints. As late as the 1830s there was fear that Roman Catholic Christianity would disappear in Bengal because of the decline in the number of Christians and the failure to give religious instruction to the youth. Even the Augustinians, as a religious group, were unable to live up to their commitment in Bengal. Probably prompted by this state of affairs the Christians began to ask for missionaries who could speak English. "Alle, die er in dieser Angelegenheit befragt habe, stimmten überein, dass das Leben der Augustiner in Bengalen wenig lobenswert sei, dass man dort unbedingt gute Priester brauche, welche die englische Sprache beherrschen", wrote the Apostolic Vicar of London Msgr. Bramston. Cf. N. KOWALSKY, "Die Errichtung des Apostolischen Vikariates Kalkutta nach den Akten des Propagandaarchives", in ZMRW 36 (1952), p. 120. In 1800, there were four dioceses in Portuguese hands. In them the lives of the Goanese priests were often scandalous. It was at the request of some Irish Catholics in Calcutta, who wanted an English-speaking priest to cater to their spiritual needs, that the Holy See consented to sending some English-speaking priests.

[56] G. MARTINA, Pio IX (1851 - 1866), p. 415.

[57] J. CORREIA-AFONSO, "The Seventieth Anniversary of the Indian Hierarchy", in World Mission 7/4 (1956), p. 498.

[58] On June 23, 1886, a concordat was signed between the Holy See and Portugal that provided the elevation of the See of Goa to that of Patriarchate ad honorem. Cf. Ibid.

[59] By double jurisdiction it is meant that the two contending parties, the Padroado and the Propaganda, exercised their spiritual duty in the same territory under different religious superiors.

[60] The two clerical power centres offered nothing but division and confusion to the people. "The two sets of priests were trying to gain control over churches and parishes and, in the process, were favouring one or other caste group according to its perceived loyalty to themselves". M. AMALADOSS, "The Gospel, Community and Culture", in ZMRW 80 (1996), p. 246; Cf. K. S. LATOURETTE, The Great Century in Northern Africa and Asia. A.D. 1800 – A. D. 1914, pp. 72 – 73; I. PADINJAREKUTTU, The Missionary Movement, p. 76.

[61] M. DHALL, The British Rule. Missionary Activities in Orissa (1822 - 1947), p. 17.

[62] Malabar Rite has nothing to do with the Syrian rite practiced by the St. Thomas Christians of the Malabar coast. The controversy obtained its name from the fact that the mission area of Madurai, Mysore and Carnatik came under the mission or province of Malabar. It is basically connected with some concession in using certain cultural elements typical of the Zone. V. CRONIN, "Malabar Rite", in New Catholic Encyclopaedia, vol. IX, pp. 97-99; P. M. D'ELIA, "Contro i riti Malabarici in India", in Civ. Catt. 91/2 (1940), p. 331.

[63] Parangi is derived from the Persian word farang, which means "a Frank; an Italian; European; a Christian; all nations which wear short garments." It is probable that the word 'farang' comes from western Asia, which then was identified with the people of Western Europe. Later this word obtained a corrupt form in India, 'Parangi'. Though the word referred directly to the Portuguese as Parangis, it also stigmatised those associated with them. Cf. L. STANISLAUS, The Liberative Mission of the Church among the Dalit Christians in Tamil Nadu, p. 181.

[64] Margam is a Sanskrit word used in Tamil, meaning 'way of life'. It could also mean the way to attain salvation.

[65] The missionaries had to mix with the people of a lower origin as they, in the first place, responded to the call of the Lord en masse, and from whom the missionaries would take a cook to prepare non-vegetarian meals for them.

[66] The Portuguese who were called parangi "mixed freely with the low caste, ate beef, drank wine and took Indian wives, without bothering about the caste, untouchability or other social conventions. This did not matter in Goa and other Portuguese dominions, where they were ostracised. Those who associated with them also fared the same fate. Moreover, the Christian religion, which they followed, was

also despised. That explains why Fr. Gonçalo, in spite of more than ten years, was not able to convert a single Hindu". Cf. S. RAJAMANICKAM, "Founder of the Madurai Mission-Robert de Nobili", in S. L. GABRIEL et al. (eds.), Christianity in India. Its True Face, Thanjavur 1981, p. 112; J. E. WALSH, "De Nobili: Classic Example of Accommodation", in World Mission 9/2 (1958), p. 96.

[67] M. DOMENGE, La Mission de Vizagapatam, p. 100.

[68] The Sanyasis would be seen moving about on horseback or in a palanquin, eating rice, dressed like Brahmins and saluting no one as they went along, while the Pandarams covered with rags walked on foot surrounded by beggars and prostrated themselves when the Sanyasis passed, covering their mouths lest their breath should defile the teacher of the great.

[69] S. RAJAMANICKAM, The First Oriental Scholar, Tirunelveli 1972, p. 76.

[70] One of the great theologians of the time, Peter Lombard (1555 - 1624) was of the opinion that 'the thread (linea), the tuft of hair (curumby), sandal paste (sandalum), and the ablutions (lavatorias) were from their inception signs and marks of the political nobility and not superstition or of the cult of idols'. Cf. Ibid., p. 45. I.G. ZUPANOV, Disputed Missions, p. 242.

[71] S. RAJAMANICKAM, The First Oriental Scholar, p. 58.

[72] Patriarch Charles de Tournon was originally destined to go to China to settle the controversy over the Chinese rites. He was asked to look into the case of the Malabar Rites in India. From November 6, 1703 till July 1704 he remained in Pondicherry. Probably because he was sick, he never went to Madurai or to any other parts where the controversy was said to be raging. Writing about the mission of Tournon, P. M. D'Elia says, "Sembra dunque che l'informazione del Patriarcha, il quale non pareva in grado di fare personalmente le debite ricerche specialmente per il cattivo stato di salute, non fosse condotta con le dovute garanzie d'imparzialità e di oggettività, ma piuttosto sotto l'influsso degli avversari dei gesuiti". P. M. D'ELIA, "Contro i riti Malabarici", p. 340. Before leaving for the Philippines, the patriarch despatched copies to the provincial of the Malabar province, the superiors of Madurai, Mysore and Carnatic missions. The superiors were to see that the decree was kept under the pain of excommunication. The missionaries who refused obedience were to be suspended 'a divinis'. Cf. S. RAJAMANICKAM, The First Oriental Scholar, p. 59.

[73] In October 1744 Propaganda Fide, in the name of the pope, asked the superiors general of the Jesuits, Augustinians, Capuchins and Franciscans to execute the decree. Accordingly, the superiors in their name and in the name of the missionaries in the kingdoms promised to execute the prohibition of the Malabar rite. Out of 60 dioceses or missions under Propaganda, 26 were obliged to take the oath. Of the 26, eleven never bothered about it. Cf. P. M. D'ELIA, "Contro i riti Malabarici", pp. 428 – 429.

[74] For the text see ASS 19 (1886), pp. 176 – 184.

[75] The incumbents of these dioceses were designated by the apostolic brief *Apostolatus Officium* of November 25, 1886. Cf. J. CORREIA-AFONSO, "The Seventieth Anniversary of the Indian Hierarchy", p. 498.

[76] F. D'SA, History of the Catholic Church in India, vol. II, p. 297.

[77] "Finitima est Vicariatus occidentali Bengalico missio vastissima de Vizagapatam nuncupata quae universum territorium inter fines Vicariatus Bombayensis et mare Bengalicum usque ad flumen Godavery ad austrum comprehendit, et anno MDCCCL a Madraspatana divisa est". ASS 19 (1886), p. 181; Cf. L. KIERKELS, To Commemorate the Sixtieth Anniversary of the Catholic Hierarchy in India and Ceylon 1886 – 1946, p. 34. The English translation is taken from F. D'SA, History of the Catholic Church in India, vol. II, p. 309. Earlier, the apostolic letter Ex pastoralis ufficio muneris of April 3, 1850 announced Vizagapatam as a separate vicariate.

[78] Jean-Felix-Onésime Luquet was born at Langres on June 17, 1810. He left for Pondicherry Mission on December 21, 1842.While studying at the seminary he exhibited a great concern for the promotion of native clergy. His participation in the First Synod of Pondicherry in 1844 enabled him to represent the mission and explain the Acts and Documents of the Synod to the Holy See.

[79] In his booklet on The Native Priesthood, Willi Henkel cites one of the best authorities on India, Joseph Wicki, who arrived at the following conclusion: "It becomes clear from our observation how after initial difficulties the idea of the theological colleges and seminaries gained ground in India and generated greater success than one had dared to hope. Even during the first admissions to studies, it was noted that the boys came from respected castes and brought a patrimony with them, if they became secular priests. Their training was largely restricted to the essentials. The great importance attached to music and song is remarkable, evidently in order to adapt to national feelings. The talent for higher studies shown by the inhabitants of India is emphasised repeatedly. Whereas in Africa, China and Japan the question of a national priesthood was still in its infancy in 1600, India was already well supplied with priests from among its own peoples. However, the final consequence, the appointment of nationals to the bishop's throne and higher offices, could not be realised until a later epoch." W. HENKEL, The Native Priesthood, Aachen 1989, p. 3.

[80] "Le Synode du Pondicherry (18 Janvier – 13 Février 1844) procura une grande joie et une grande espérance à notre missionnaire, car on y traita en tout premier lieu de la formation du clergé indigène. On admit en consequence le prinicipe de l'education complète des indigenes, en vue du sacerdoce, on résolut la réorganisation du Séminaire d'après ce principe. Cette decision parut au P. Luquet l'oeuvre capitale du synode..." R. C. ROUSSEL, Un Précurseur. Monseigneur Luquet 1810-1858 des Missions Etrangères de Paris, Langers 1960, pp. 28 – 29.

[81] "Si je disais : le clergé indigène est nécessaire ; il est possible chez tous les peuples, je pouvais à cette autorité si puissante, ajouter le témoignage des faits

accomplis ; je pouvais montrer avec un saint orgueil des prêtres du sein d'une nation timide, versant néanmoins avec joie leur sang pour J. C. Or à ce témoignage du sang il n'y a rien à répondre, parce que N. S. l'a dit : majorem charitatem nemo habet ut animam suam ponat quis pro amicis suis". Cf. Synode de Pondicherry et instruction de la S. C. de la Propagande sur la formation du clergé indigène. Rapport sur les faits accomplis à Rome par suite du Synode du Pondicherry, p. 17.

[82] Leo XIII's benevolent action in favour of the formation of an indigenous clergy was lauded everywhere. Referring to this historic event Delacroix says: "Lui enfin qui voulut pourvoir aux frais de sa construction en adressant une encyclique aux évêques du monde entier, Ad extremas, du 23 juin 1893. Ce séminaire modèle fut confié aux jésuites belges du Bengale, en témoinage d'approbation pour leur réussite dans l'évangélisation des misérables aborigines du Chota Nagpur. Sur la médaille commemorative, Léon XIII fit graver une inscription qui exprima la règle d'or de l'apostolat: Filii tui, India, administri tibi salutis. Ce seront tes fils, ô Inde, qui t'apporteront le salut". Cf. S. DELACROIX (ed.), Histoire Universelle des Missions Catholiques, vol. III, Paris 1958, p. 98. The seminary itself was later transferred to Pune in 1955. For detailed information on the formation of indigenous clergy see C.M. DE MELO, The Recruitment and Formation of the Native Clergy in India (16th-19th century): An Historico Canonical Study, Lisboa 1955.

[83] For the text of the apostolic brief Ad Extremas see ASS XXV (1892 - 1893).

[84] J. L. MIRANDA, On the Formation of a National Indian Clergy, Trichinopoly 1920, p.15

[85] For a detailed explanation on the background and effects of Maximum Illud on the missions see A.MIOTK, Das Missionsverständnis im historischen Wandel am Beispiel der Enzyklika "Maximum Illud", Steyler Verlag, Nettetal 1999; Y. DE STEENHAULT, History of the Jesuits in West Bengal: 1921-1985, (Part I: 1921-1947), Ranchi (no year), p. 7.

[86] M. DHALL, The British Rule, pp. 22 – 23.

[87] M. Dhall wrote: "The American Quakers, Unitarians, Presbyterians, Freewill Baptists, Methodists, the German and American Lutherans, the Canadian Baptists and many others worked in the British Indian territories and beyond that." Ibid., p. 16.

[88] The rebellion of soldiers serving under the British, an event that occurred in almost all parts of India.

[89] In 1858, when the Queen took control of the government in India, she made a declaration: "We declare that it to be our Royal will and pleasure that none be in anywise favoured, none molested or disquieted by reason of their religious faith or observances, but that all alike shall enjoy the equal and impartial protection of the law; and we do strictly charge and enjoin all those who may be in authority under us that they abstain from all interference with the religious belief or worship of any of our subjects, on pain of our highest displeasure. And it is our further will that, so far as may be, our subjects of whatever race or creed, be freely and impartially admitted to offices in our service, the duties of which they may be

qualified by their education, ability, and integrity, duly to discharge". S. NEILL, Colonialism and Christian Missions, London 1966, p. 98.

[90] J. BECKMANN, "The Missions between 1840 and 1870", pp. 82 – 83.

[91] I. PADINJAREKUTTU, The Missionary Movement, pp. 58 – 62.

[92] A. MAYHEW, Christianity and the Government of India, London 1920, p. 198.

[93] S. NEILL, Colonialism and Christian Missions, p. 103.

[94] The amount is mentioned in the letter of J. F. Thomas, Chief Secretary to the Government of Madras, which was forwarded to the SCPF (Sacra Congregatio de Propaganda Fide) as proof of his claim that only the subjects of the British Empire should take up the mission of Visakhapatnam. Msgr. Fennelly to Cardinal Fransoni, Madras, July 10, 1845, APF, Indie Orientali: Scritture Riferite nei Congressi, vol. 10, ff. 473 – 482; S. GAL, Conversions et Christianisation en Inde au XIXe Siècle: la Fondation de la mission savoyarde de Vizagapatam. Vers 1845- Vers 1890, Unpublished Work, Université de Lyon 1991, p. 43.

[95] In talking about different churches, the British Government's Record shows the following category: Church of England (Anglican denomination), Church of Rome (Roman Catholics) and others (all the other denominations).

[96] J. Bruls observed: "Mission and colonisation buttressed one another: the missionary gave the coloniser a clear conscience and in return received support and protection. Christian missions supplied Europe's ambitions as a civiliser with the spiritual component they had hitherto fundamentally lacked." J. BRULS, "From Missions to 'Young Churches'", in R. AUBERT (ed.), The Christian Centuries, vol. V, London 1979, p. 391.

[97] Recognising the favour bestowed on the mission, Msgr. Tissot wrote : "Ici dans l'Inde, non seulement le Gouvernement anglais ne nous est pas hostile, mais il nous favorise. Il s'offre à subventionner nos écoles, nous laissant pleine liberté pour l'instruction religieuse. Il offre aux Soeurs de St. Joseph, à Nagpur, la direction d'une école normale. Les sujets manquent. Le moment serait des plus favorables, si nous pouvions faire face à la besogne qui se présente." Tissot to Messelod, Vizagapatam, November 26, 1884, AMSFS 5H5-2/2.

[98] Visakhapatnam, Vizagapatam, Visakh, Vizag and Waltair are all names for the same town. The town is situated in 17° 42' N. and 83° 18' E., about 484 miles by railway from Madras and 547 miles from Calcutta. The French missionaries and the British used the name of Vizagapatam frequently in their writings. For the sake of consistency and uniformity the current name in use is preferred, i.e., Visakhapatnam, except when referred to in documents. There is a legend attributed to the name of this maritime town. When Prince Kulothunga Chola of Vengi on his way to Kashi – Varanasi (Benares), halted in this town, he was attracted by its beauty and so decided to build a temple for his favourite deity, Visakha – the Lord of Valour. From then on, the town was called by the name Visakhapatnam. The Dutch, French and finally the British had their influence on the town. By the middle of 17th century, an English military garrison had settled

there. In 1803 Visakhapatnam was made the district headquarters. It was already a military centre of the British. Rajas of Vizianagaram, Bobbili, Jeypore, Chammudu and Gangpur had their summer resorts and residences at Visakhapatnam. These Rajas contributed to the development of the town. Cf. The Imperial Gazetteer of India, vol. XXIV, Oxford 1908, pp. 337 – 339.

[99] There are variations in writing his name. Some write Attaide, others d'Attaide and yet others de Attaide. The General Archives of the Theatines in Rome have no records on this part of the history, except that Fr. d'Attaide made his final profession on February 10, 1822. (AGT = The General Archives of the Theatines).

[100] Golconda was known for its diamonds and paintings in the 17th century. Founded in 1518 by Quli Qutb Sahih, the city, situated in the western part of Hyderabad, was destroyed in 1687 by Emperor Aurangazeb, who annexed the region. Golconda mission was a large territory stretching from Masulipatnam (Andhra Pradesh) to Cuttack (Orissa). Christians were scattered, and they were in the service of the rulers. The Congregation of Regular Clerics, founded at Rome in 1524 and popularly known as Theatines, sent its first priests to Goa in 1639. "It is known from different writers that from 1640 to 1750 there came 56 professed members of the order to Goa and 3 novices, all non-Portuguese, of whom 23 reached Goa, 13 died in the missions and 12 returned to Europe. As it was not possible for more religious persons to come from Europe, the prefect, as their superior was called, obtained permission from his General in Europe, confirmed by the king of Portugal, to admit Goans into the order. Limited to 4, it was extended to 12 and 4 lay brothers and finally to 20. Up to 1804 the number thus admitted was 39 and 1 lay brother. Of that number 20 died in the convent and 9 in the missions". Cf. F. D'SA, History of the Catholic Church in India, vol. II, pp. 369 – 370. At that time the jurisdictional battles between Bishop Mathew de Castro and the Archbishop of Goa were ravaging the territory. Realising the difficulties Bishop de Castro moved to Golconda. He went to the capital Masulipatnam to establish the church in the territory. J. THEKKEDATH, History of Christianity in India, p. 299. Manco, accompanied by a Goan priest, went to Bijapur, the capital of Adil Shah, to pick out the mission territory for the group. Manco was the third Italian Theatine who had come to India after Don Pedro Avitable and Joseph – Maria Anebiveri. He had a vast territory to look after, namely, from Masulipatnam to Balasore. Cf. Memorandum Left by Dom Xavier d'Attaide, La Mission de Vizagapatam. Extrait du Registre Officiel 1845. Dactylographhié et Photocopié par le Père Raymond Bosso, Jan 1990. MSFS Archives 8/2, Annecy. Propaganda Fide on 23 January 1663 found it necessary, however, to have the Superior General "seriously admonished" that it was "not the mind of the Sacred Congregation that his members reside at Goa simply as religious, but rather that they go out to the surrounding infidel regions and exercise their office as missionaries". But in 1682, they were again rebuked because they were still clustered around Goa. Cf. R.M. WILTGEN, "The Evangelisation Congregation at the Service of Java, Borneo, Sumatra (1622 - 1815)", in Regnum

Dei 28/98 (1972) p. 125. They did not succeed in their work in Golconda. After the death of Bergamora in 1693, the mission went over to the Augustinians who also experienced the same fate. J. THEKKEDATH, History of Christianity in India, p. 299. Before the arrival of MSFS there were 3 priests: a Goan stationed in Visakhapatnam and two Irish priests working as chaplains in the northern part of the vicariate. Cf. Anonymous, Notice sur la Mission de Visagapatam, Annecy 1866, p.10. The extension of the mission at that time was quite large, i.e., from Masulipatnam to Balasore. Neyret to Mermier, September 6, 1850. L'état de la Mission en 1850. Archives MSFS, 7Z/ 5 H 5.

[101] Annibale Spalla spells out the beginning of the Theatine mission in Golconda: "Quando la Sacra Congregazione de Propaganda Fide aveva inviato i Teatini alle Indie, aveva indicato il luogo dove essi avrebbero dovuto lavorare, cioè il cosidetto Regno di Idelcan [Idalcan]. Per questo, dopo di essersi stabiliti bene in Goa, nel dicembre del 1640, partiva il P. Manco, accompagnato da un sacerdote indiano, messo a sua disposizione dall'archivescovo di Goa, per la città di Vizapur (Bijapur) nel detto Regno. Ma pare che incontrasse difficoltà da parte di autorità religiose, che non desideravano altri religiosi sotto la propria giurisdizione. Ed il padre, senza per nulla insistere, mentre già gli era stata offerta una grande casa da un ricco signore fiammingo colà stabilito, pensò di non contraddire per nulla e si decise ad andare nel Regno di Golconda." A. SPALLA, "Le Missioni Teatine nelle Indie Orientali nel Secolo XVII e le cause della loro fine", in Regnum Dei 27/97 (1971), p. 17.

[102] R. M. WILTGEN, "The Evangelisation Congregation at the Service of Java, Borneo, Sumatra (1622 - 1815)", p. 138.

[103] Dom Xavier D'Attaide gives only the names of those who worked in Golconda mission. "As regards the mission of Golconda, the first missionary after Don Francisco Manco was Don Antonio Albuquerque; the second, Don Gajetan Astiao Farias who, after his ministry of 32 years in this mission died at Vizagapatam; the third, Don Joseph–Maria Miranda who died at Masulipatam. Don Pascal Lobo succeeded (Miranda) and died there also. The mission was for some time vacant, due to the fact that there were not a sufficient number of priests who could be spared. During this interval, the Masulipatam mission was occupied by a French priest and that of Vizagapatam by a Dominican friar, Joseph de Concicao. After some time, these missions were again supplied with priests of the Theatine Order namely Don Cajetan Saldanha and Don Pedro Viegas... In 1810, three Theatines and a secular priest were sent from Goa: Don Sebastian Xavier from (for) Massule, Don Riccardo from (for) Yanam (who died there); Don Emmanuel Mascarinhas for Vizagapatam and Fr. Celestino Joao Paes for Ganjam". Memorandum laissé par Dom Xavier D'Attaide, p. 32.

[104] Here is the list of the missionaries who served in Visakhapatnam: 1806 – 1810: Don João Cajetan Saldanha; 1811 – 1816: Don Emmanuel Mascarinhas; 1816 – 1822: Padre Celestino João Paes; 1822 – 1828: Don Roque Camillo Assumpção and Don Cajetan Gabriel de Santa Maria and 1828 – 1849: Don Joseph Xavier

d'Attaide, who died on July 6, 1849 after receiving the last sacrament from the hands of Bishop Neyret. He was about 66 years when he died. Cf. Ibid., p. 33.

[105] Msgr. Joseph Baud was born in 1890 at Bellevaux, Savoy. He came to India in 1911 and was ordained a priest in 1914. He was appointed the coadjutor bishop of Visakhapatnam in 1942. He succeeded to the see in 1947 and remained as the bishop of the same till 1967, when he retired. He died on March 13, 1980. Cf. F. MOGET, MSFS Obituary, Uchgaon 1999, p. 34.

[106] J. BAUD, Notes on the Stations of the Diocese of Visakhapatnam, Unpublished work found in Jnana Deepa Vidyapeeth, Pune 1959.

[107] "Le dernier de ces missionnaires mourut l'année dernière à Vizagapatam, après avoir desservi lui seul, pendant douze ans, toute la côte d'Orissa". Cf. Neyret to Mermier, L'état de la Mission en 1850, September 6, 1850, AMSFS, 7Z/5 H 5; Msgr. Neyret to Cardinal Barnabò, Vizagapatam, October 18, 1860, Relatio Vicariatus Apostolici Vizagapatami, APF Indie Orientali: Scritture Riferite nei Congressi, vol. 17, ff. 1408 – 1411.

[108] There were some military garrisons that had some Catholic soldiers: Cuttack, Berhampur, Aska, etc. Though the majority of the Christians were Catholics, and a considerable number of the soldiers in the king's regiments were Irish Roman Catholics, and therefore at that time British subjects, the government had a predilection for the national Church: Anglicans. Besides the Irish Catholic soldiers, there were Portuguese, French and Indians of Portuguese origins and Tamils. Cf. S. NEILL, A History of Christianity in India: 1707 – 1858, vol. II, p. 291.

[109] Cuttack was an important town where there was a military garrison, in which there were a good number of Catholics. Though Cuttack was under the vicariate apostolic of Calcutta, it was almost abandoned. That is why Msgr. Carew was willing to give this part of his vicariate to the Missionaries of St. Francis de Sales, as the city is closer to Visakhapatnam than Calcutta. "... il les pria donc d'y aller en son nom". Cf. H. JOSSON, "Histoire de la Mission: Les Dernières Années de Mgr. Carew", in MB (1920), pp. 197- 198.

[110] F. MOGET, The Missionaries of St. Francis de Sales of Annecy, S.F.S. Publications, Bangalore 1985, p. 60.

[111] Sources for the Golconda mission are limited except for a few references here and there. "There are two baptism registers, one for Yanam 1767 – 1837, another of the East Coast from Machilipatnam to Puri from 1806 to 1846. There are names of Capuchins, Theatines, Jesuits and Diocesan priests among the visiting missionaries. They used to visit Machilipatnam, Eluru, Kakinada, Yanam, Visakhapatnam, Vizianagaram, Bheemunipatnam, Puri, Cuttack, etc. The Catholics might have been European personnel, Tamils or Goans, employed or engaged in business". Cf. Anonymous, "Diocese of Visakhapatnam", in Visakhapatnam Diocesan Centenary (1886 - 1986), p. 3.

[112] A short biographical presentation of Fr. Henri Gailhot will be mentioned later in the chapter.

[113] Though he originated from Goa, he did not have any sympathy for the Portuguese Padroado. He never had any difficulty in accepting the jurisdiction of the Propaganda in the territory. "Don Xavier d'Attaide fut toujours un prêtre irreproachable dans ses moeurs et missionnaire zélé. Seul missionnaire de Goa qu'il y eut sur ces côtes depuis Madras à Calcutta, sa position le sauva au moins de la tentation ou du danger de tomber dans le malheureux schisme de ses compatriotes, soit de la presque totalité des missionnaires de Goa répandus dans les Vicariats Apostoliques. Comme par son testament il avait chargé son executeur testamentaire de remettre à son légitime successeur toutes les chapelles qu'il avait fait bâtire ou qu'il avait desservies, le dit exécuteur testamentaire, M. Lobo, son clerc et comme le P. d'Attaide natif de Goa, mit en possession de Ste. Anne les Missionnaires de S. Francois de Sales, soit le vicaire Apostolique, le jour même de la mort du P. d'Attaide". Notice de Msgr. Neyret sur Don Xavier d'Attaide, in La Mission de Vizagapatam, Extraite du Officiel 1845, Annecy, AMSFS 8/2, p. 33.

[114] M. DOMENGE, La Mission de Vizagapatam, p. 122.

[115] Notice de Mgr. Neyret sur Don Xavier d'Attaide, in La Mission de Vizagapatam, Extraite du Officiel 1845, Annecy, AMSFS 8/2, p. 33. The Collector is a government officer who is in charge of the revenue collection and law and order in the district.

[116] The new congregation had also to obtain the approval of the king. Accordingly, King Charle–Albert of Sardinia and Duke of Savoy granted the approval of the government on September 29, 1838. Cf. J. REY, Les Missionnaires de Saint-François de Sales d'Annecy, pp. 47-48; F. Moget, The Missionaries of St. Francis de Sales of Annecy, p. 29.

[117] Fr. Pierre–Marie Mermier, also referred to as Monsieur Mermier, a title common to the priests of his time, was born on August 28, 1790 at Vouray in the parish of Chaumont in Geneve. He came from a devout family. During the French Revolution some priests would go to his parish to celebrate Mass clandestinely. Since he came from a family of 'fortune and position', he experienced the brutal reality of terror during the French Revolution as General Montesquau proclaimed: Freedom, Equality and Fraternity. Brought up in great devotion to the Catholic faith, the young Mermier opted very early for religious life. He was ordained a priest on March 21, 1813 for the diocese of Chambery. As a young priest he worked untiringly in Magland and was later transferred to the College of Melan, where he taught. In 1819 he took charge of the parish of Le Chatelard where he met Monsieur Favre who 'changed the life and pointed him to the true vocation'. In 1823 he gave up the position of spiritual director of the major seminary at Annecy and decided to dedicate himself to mission. The constitution of the group began to develop in 1830. There are a number of aspects that influenced the first constitution: a major part is influenced by the Lazarists, some elements were added from the Jesuits, Oblates and Redemptorists. Cf. A. DUVAL, Monsieur Mermier : 1790 – 1862, Bangalore 1982, pp. 7 – 11 ; S.GAL, Conversions et Christianisation en Inde au XIXe Siècle : la foundation de la Mission savoyarde de Vizagapatam, Université de Lyon, 1991, pp. 10 – 11.

[118] Constitutions of the Missionaries of Saint Francis de Sales, The Mission of the Congregation, No. 3. Annecy 1984, p. 13.

[119] P. RIME, "Missionari di San Francesco di Sales", in DIP, vol. V, G. PELLICCINA AND G. ROCCA (eds.), Roma 1978, p. 1482, spells out the charism of the congregation in the following words: "L'Istituto ha i seguenti scopi: la predicazione delle missioni e dei ritiri nelle parrocchie, negli istituti e nelle communità religiose; la conversione dei non credenti nei paesi di missione; l'educazione cristiana della gioventù nei movimenti di azione apostolica."

[120] Since their foundation the Missionaries have been actively involved in the following apostolates: local parish missions, missions at far away places and the education of young people. They strive to live according to the ideals of St. Francis de Sales, their patron. Monsieur Mermier himself went around the parishes with enthusiasm, often spending three weeks continuously preaching retreats and teaching catechism. According to him, "this was the only way of bringing religious instruction to simple people and of breaking down their indifference and their mediocrity. It was with this in mind that Mermier gathered together his fellow-priests to form a religious congregation which would follow the example of Saint Francis de Sales, finding the enthusiasm they would need for their work". Cf. C. MOREL, "A Zealous Priest: Pierre–Marie Mermier (1790 - 1862)", in Missionaries of St. Francis de Sales. A letter to our Friends and Benefactors, October 1988. p.1.

[121] The conditions were proposed when the congregation was in its infancy stage and still needed approval from the Holy See. Jean Rey cited from the note of Fr. Granjux: "1. Your Eminence should request from His Holiness any kind of approbation in favour of our congregation, so that it may prove useful, please God, not only to the diocese of Annecy, but also to neighbouring dioceses and the foreign missions; 2. The Holy Father should grant to the Superior of the congregation, who offers to be one of the first volunteers, a delay of one year, so that he may complete and strengthen what he has begun for the congregation of the Missionaries and that of the Daughters of the Cross; and, 3. The third and the last condition is that the congregation does not undertake any financial burden". J. REY, Les Missionnaires de Saint-François de Sales d'Annecy, p. 84; F. MOGET, The Missionaries of St. Francis de Sales of Annecy, p. 37.

[122] On September 30, 1842 he reached Rome and on the 2nd of October he had a meeting with the cardinal. In order to get the approbation, Mermier was to produce the recommendation letters of the four Bishops in Savoy. J. REY, Les Missionnaires de Saint-François de Sales d'Annecy, p. 84; F. MOGET, The Missionaries of St. Francis de Sales of Annecy, pp. 38 - 39.

[123] The new congregation was ready to go wherever the Holy See would send them. M. Domenge recorded the outlook of the missionaries: "Lorsque, en 1843, peu d'années après sa naissance, la congrégation de Saint-Francois de Sales eut obtenu les encouragements et la<<laude >>[Decretum laudis] du Saint-Siège, plusieurs de ses members conçurent le pieux dessein de se consacrer aux missions

étrangères. Le P. Mermier, leur supérieur et fondateur, accueillit cette demande avec une grande joie, et se hâta de la transmettre à Msgr. Rendu, alors évêque d'Annecy, non mois heureux que lui d'un semblable projet". M. DOMENGE, La Mission de Vizagapatam, p. 109.

[124] "quod intra paucos dies de erigendis in Indiis orientalibus novis Missionibus agendum sit, quarum una vel altera electis tuis operaiis commendari queat". The letter was written on February 6, 1845. APF Lettre 1845, vol. 332, f. 85.

[125] "...Placuit autem S.C. selectis memoratis tuis presbyteris Vizagapatami Provincia a Vicaritu Madraspatano seorsim gubernanda curam committere...ad ducem, iis praeficiendum duxerunt alium aeque spectatum eximiumque operarium Puducheranae Missionis Henricum Gailhot qui Pro-Vicarii titulo Vizagapatami Missioni Praeerit". Cardinal Fransoni to Monsieur Mermier (May 2, 1845), APF, Lettere1845, vol. 332, ff. 269 – 270.

[126] "Cette Mission s'étend le long du golfe de Bengale, dans les Indes Orientales, de Cuttack aux bouches du Godavéry, sur une surface de cinq cents milles anglais (180 lieues de long sur 100 de large). Elle est borné au nord par le vicariat du Bengale, à l'ouest par celui de Bombay, au sud par celui d'Hydérabad, et à l'est par la mer, soit le golfe de Bengale". Cf. Anonymous, Notice sur la Mission de Visagapatam, Annecy 1866, p. 8.

[127] "La population catholique est composée de quatre elements principaux : d'Indiens originaires des côtes de Malabar, qui servent dans les armées ou qui les suivent avec leurs familles ; de soldats irlandais et de leurs familles, d'indigènes récemment convertis, et d'East-Indians, soit d'Indiens d'origine portugaise. On y compte aussi, mais en petit nombre, des Anglais et des Francais". Ibid.

[128] F. MOGET, The Missionaries of St. Francis de Sales of Annecy, p. 59.

[129] Anonymous, The Fransalians of Visakhapatnam. Yesterday, Today and Tomorrow, Visakhapatnam 1983, p. 2.

[130] From the original territory entrusted to the MSFS the Holy See eventually made many dioceses. At present there are about thirteen dioceses in the original territory that covered almost five States in the Indian Union: Andhra Pradesh, Madhya Pradesh, Maharashtra, Chhatisgarh, and Orissa.

[131] Clement Bonnand was born at Saint-Maurice-Dargoire on May 20, 1796. After his ordination on June 17, 1821, he joined the Seminary of the Paris Foreign Mission Society at Paris in 1823 and left for Malabar Mission on February 4, 1824. After the death of Msgr. Hébert, he took over the Mission and became the vicar apostolic of Coromandel. Following the delimitation of missions in 1836, he was named the apostolic visitor, a position which he retained till his death on March 21, 1861 at Benares. He was often called Msgr. de Drusipare as he was named the titular bishop of Drusipare in partibus infidelium. Concerning the papal visit, Beckmann writes: "In order to counter the lack of unity among the vicars apostolic and the missionaries of the propaganda, they suggested a papal visitation. In August

of the same year (1858) Pius IX appointed the vicar apostolic of Pondicherry from the Paris Mission Seminary, Clement Bonnand (1796 - 1861), as his visitor. He was charged with examining the deficiencies as well as determining the means of removing them in the areas subject to the Propaganda". J. BECKMANN, "The Missions between 1840 and 1870", pp. 180 – 181.

[132] M. DOMENGE, La Mission de Vizagapatam, p. 114.

[133] Msgr. Neyret wrote to Fr. Mermier concerning the effect of Multa Praeclare : "En effet Grégoire XVI, d'hereuse mémoire, venait de jeter un 3ème regard de miséricorde sur la Péninsule. Par la Bulle Multa Praeclare, il venait d'adjoindre au Vicariat Apostolique de Madras les vastes régions qui forment aujourd'hui les deux Missions d'Hyderabad et de Vizagapatam. Cette nouvelle disposition de la cour de Rome était un bienfait immense tant pour les anciens chrétiens de ces Missions que pour ceux, bien plus nombreux, dont la diffusion des troupes de la compagnie anglaise dans toute l'Inde avait doté le pays depuis un certain nombre d'années. Ces nouveaux Chrétiens étaient les Irlandais d'abord, puis les cipayes (soldat indigénes) venus des cotes de Malabar et du Coromandel". Neyret to Mermier, Vizagapatam, September 6, 1850. AMSFS, 7 5 H 5 – 2, p. 221.

[134] Neyret to Mermier, Vizagapatam, September 6, 1850, Lettres des Missionnaires 1845-1857. AMSFS 7Z/ 5 H 5.

[135] "Les 1ers, avec toute la foi qu'on leur connait, n'en avaient pas assez cependant pour se confesser aux prêtres de Goa. Ils n'accomplissaient pas même leur devoir pascal; c'est ce dont ils font tous généralement l'aveu. Pour les Cipayes et leurs familles, ils n'avaient sans doute pas le même éloignement ni les mêmes préjugés pour les Missres à peau noire que les Européens. Mais ils ne pouvaient les rencontrer, du moins que très rarement et plus brièvement encore". Neyret to Mermier, Vizagapatam, September 6, 1850. AMSFS, 7 5 H 5-2, p. 221.

[136] F. MOGET, The Missionaries of St. Francis de Sales of Annecy, p. 48.

[137] Cardinal Fransoni wrote that the Sacred Congregation had decided to entrust the mission to the MSFS priests. The superior was given the freedom to choose the ones who would be suitable for the mission. "Dein vero per Multa S.C. narrat de missionis Visagapatami exordio, ac statu quae plane suadent missionis ipsius bono congruere, ut ab illius regimen novus Pro-Vicarius, inter eosdem presbyteros/ Anncecienses eligendus, quamprimum statuatur, facta ex nunc R. D. Henrico Gailhot potestate, quod progressu temporis perficiendum erat, Puducherium reduend". APF Lettere 1845, part II, vol. 334, f.757.

[138] They are: Frs. Jacques Martin, who was the superior of the team, Joseph Lavorel, Jean Marie Tissot, Jean Thevenet and Bros. Pierre Carton and Sulpice Fontanel. F. MOGET, The Missionaries of St. Francis de Sales of Annecy, p. 51; Anonymous, Notice sur la Mission de Visagapatam, p. 9. There is no doubt that the first group of missionaries was very little informed of the country that they were entering, and they knew nothing of the people (their language, culture,

climatic and political conditions in which they lived) they were going to evangelise. All they probably knew about India was the exploits of General de Boigne, who made a fortune in the Maratha Army from 1781 to 1792. cf. S. GAL, S.GAL, Conversions et Christianisation en Inde au XIXe Siècle, p. 14f.

[139] It was Msgr. Rey of Annecy who lit the fire of apostolic zeal in the heart of Bonnand in one of his preaching missions. He persuaded the latter to enter Missions Étrangères de Paris. Anonymous, Notice sur la Mission de Visagapatam, p. 45. Probably owing to this initial contact he had with Annecy and the letters sent by Msgr. Rey and Monsieur Mermier, Msgr. Bonnand dealt very kindly with the newly-appointed missionaries. He did all he could to make them feel at home; "Msgr. Bonnand, leur vicaire apostolique, se montra d'une bienveillance toute paternelle. Conformément aux intentions du Saint-Siége, il donna à nos Pères, pour les initier aux travaux apostoliques dans l'Inde, un de ses prêtres, M. Gailhot, avec le titre de Provicaire apostolique, relevant de l'Evêque de Madras". Cf. Anonymous, Notice sur la Mission de Visagapatam, p. 9.

[140] Fr. Jacques Martin was born at La Cote d'Abroz, Savoy. He was the superior of the first group of the MSFS that took up the Mission of Visakhapatnam. He left for India on May 14, 1845. He was appointed as the parish priest of Yanam. Hardly three months after assuming his work he died of sunstroke on May 5, 1846. Cf. F. MOGET, MSFS Obituary, pp. 49 – 50.

[141] Msgr. Fennelly to Msgr. Bonand, Madras, February 13, 1846, APF Indie Orientali: Scritture Riferite nei Congressi, vol. 10, ff. 1079 – 1080. F. MOGET, The Missionaries of St. Francis de Sales of Annecy, p. 55. Martin had written to the vicar apostolic of Madras informing him of their arrival and their willingness to place themselves at the service of the pro-vicariate of Vizagapatam, but Msgr. Fennelly did not reply. Instead, he sent a letter to the vicar apostolic of Pondicherry informing the latter that he had sent a letter to the Sacred Congregation of the Propagation of Faith, registering his reservations about the work of the Missionaries of St. Francis de Sales in Visakhapatnam. Therefore, he did not want to have any communication with the missionaries until he received a reply from Rome. He suggested that the Savoyards remain in Pondicherry in order to avoid any potential friction with the Irish priests. Msgr. Fennelly had even made an appeal to the supreme government in Bengal against the assignment of Visakhapatnam to a French congregation. Cf. M. DOMENGE, La Mission de Vizagapatam, p. 114. The refusal of Msgr. Fennelly to grant jurisdiction either to the pro-vicar of Visakhapatnam or to the MSFS was probably based on the experience of his predecessor, Msgr. O'Connor, that the British government preferred a candidate from among their subjects. This may have been the reason for rejecting a French candidate, particularly at a time when the relationship between France and England was not friendly. Based on this presumption, the prelate may have recommended the Irish clergy. Cf. E. HULL, Bombay Mission History, vol. I, p. 271ff.

[142] For the division of Madras into three dioceses and the appointment of Henry Gailhot as the pro-vicar apostolic of Visakhapatnam: "Amplitudinem ejus

ita imminuere ut interim tres in partes, ac distinctos veluti missiones ille divideretur, nempe Visakapatam, Hyderabad, ac Madraspatani. Prioris limites constitui rite posse visi sunt ad orientem sinus Bangalensis, ad septentrionem Bombayna et Calcutta missiones; ad meridiem denique flumen Godavery... aut incomodo consuerunt Emi. Patres rogandum Drusiparensem Antistitem, ut provisoria item ratione operarium suum Henricum Gailhot regionum Vizagapatam curam gerere posse, haud graveretur. Supralaudato vero missionario, cui sub pro-vicarii a sui titulo, durante munere, regiones illas moderari tribuitur, facultatibus quoque sicuti de coadjutore innuimus, communicare poteris, iis exceptis, qua characterem Episcopalem quae ille caret, requirunt". APF Lettere 1845, vol. 332, ff. 293-295.

[143] M. DOMENGE, La Mission de Vizagapatam, p. 114.

[144] Anonymous, Notice sur la Mission de Visagapatam, p.2. Msgr. Fennelly writes, "In regionibus Vizagapatam intra limites a Sacra Congregatione definitos, octo sunt oppida, in quibus locantur undecim legiones (anglice Regiments) militum Angliae, una cum quatuor cohortibus Artilleriae (anglice artillery) et duabus cohortibus fossorum Castiensium (anglice sappers and miners) ex quibus licet quaedem constant praecipue ex aboriginibus, nihilominus plures sunt Indo-Brittani qui Anglice loquuntur, quaedam constant omnino ex Europaeis, et duces omnes sine exceptione sunt Angli aut Hiberni". Msgr. Fennelly to Cardinal Fransoni. Madras, July 10, 1845, APF Indie Orientali: Scritture Riferite nei Congressi, vol. 10 ff. 473 – 482.

[145] M. DOMENGE, La Mission de Vizagapatam, p. 116. In his letter to Cardinal Fransoni, Msgr. Fennelly informs him that they have enough personnel to take care of the mission: "In collegio Omnium Sanctorum apud Druncondra in Hibernia undecim sunt alumni hujus missionis qui ad sacros ordines promoti confectis studiis theologicis jamjam Madraspatanum navigare parati sunt. Praeterea in nostro seminario sunt decem juvenes optimae spei, qui Deo adjuvante, suo temporis ad vineam Domini excolendam apti reperiantur. Omnes isti juvenes sunt indigenae, sed non quales conatu parum efficaci apud Pudicherium instituuntur. Omnes sunt albis ex parentibus Hibernis, sed in India nati. In Collegio Sti. Patricii apud Maynooth quidam quoque sunt alumni, qui ad missionem Madraspatanum venire desiderant." Msgr. Fennelly to Cardinal Fransoni. Madras, July 10, 1845, APF Indie Orientali: Scritture Riferite nei Congressi, vol. 10 ff. 473 – 482.

[146]Msgr. Fennelly writes to Msgr. Bonnand: "I had a letter from one of the Savoy missionaries who were destined to Vizagapatam. But as I sent a strong remonstrance to the Sacred Congregation against this appointment, I consider it inexpedient pending the remonstrance to hold any correspondence with them. Indeed, it is not with them I should communicate in any case. It appears to me probable that your Lordship will have them all to yourself, and if it were so arranged, it would be perhaps the most convenient way of healing or preventing the bad feeling which will otherwise arise and has already been produced between the French and Irish missionaries". Msgr. Fennelly to Msgr. Bonnand, Madras, September 21, 1845, APF Indie Orientali: Scritture Riferite nei Congressi, vol. 10,

ff. 1079 –1080. Msgr. Fennelly was aware of the possible tension that might arise due to his interference in the assigning of mission territories to a congregation. Due to the humility of the Savoyards, more particularly due to the kindness of Msgr. Neyret, there was no tension. In fact, as a conciliatory measure Msgr. Neyret requested Msgr. Fennelly to leave two Irish missionaries, so that they could continue to serve as chaplains, an action very dear to Msgr. Fennelly. Later when Msgr. Neyret was made Bishop of Olene in partibus infidelium, he chose to be consecrated in Madras by Msgr. Fennelly.

[147] M. Domenge described the situation of their misery in contrasting colours, "Arriver seuls dans un pays absolument inconnu, affronter un climat meurtier pour ceux qui osent le braver, ignorer completement les langues dont la connaissance allait devenir indispensable, tout cela ne les inquiétait pas. Leur ideal du Missionnaire était de partir simplement avec leur Bréviaire et leur Bible à la main, comme saint Francois Xavier, et de s'en remettre, pour le reste, aux soins de la providence". M. DOMENGE, La Mission de Vizagapatam, p. 110.

[148] F. MOGET, The Missionaries of St. Francis de Sales of Annecy, p. 55.

[149] In his letter to the Propaganda Fr. Henry Gailhot informed them that Msgr. Fennelly refused to give him jurisdiction, in spite of the requests made to him: "Jurisdictionem a Reverendissimo Vicario Apostolico Madrapatanensi humillime petii, sed dare negavit". H. Gailhot to Cardinal Fransoni, Bangalore, October 10, 1845, APF Indie Orientali: Scritture Riferite nei Congressi, vol. 10, ff. 632 – 633.

[150] The two MEP missionaries were Frs. Metral and Ligeon, who were also from Savoy. They were asked to initiate the new arrivals in the Vizag. Mission, as the MSFS could not converse in Telugu. Cf. F. MOGET, The Missionaries of St. Francis de Sales of Annecy, p. 55.

[151] It was Luquet who surpassed the instructions given to him and used his influence in the erection of vicariates. "Msgr. Luquet avait outrepassé ses instructions et qu'en consequence nous lui ritirons nos pouvoirs. Je ne suis pour rien, Monseigneur, dans tous les arrangements qui ont été pris soit pour les limites de Vizagapatam soit pour les ouvriers evangeliques contre lesquelles reclame Votre Grandeur." Msgr. Fennelly to Msgr. Bonnand, Madras, September 21, 1845, APF Indie Orientali: Scritture Riferite nei Congressi, vol. 10, ff. 1079 –1080. Two letters addressed to the Propaganda (APF Indie Orientali: Scritture Referite nei Congressi 1947, Vol. 11, f. 28f) speak of the erection of Visakhapatnam as a vicariate and the following document suggests that Henri Gailhot be appointed as a pro-vicar of Visakhapatnam.

[152] Jacques Henri Gailhot was born on August 12, 1810, at Le Cheylard, Ardeche, France. After completing his ecclesiastical studies at Grenoble, he was ordained on December 20, 1834. He joined the MEP on September 16, 1835. He left for the vicariate–apostolic of Coromandel on September 3, 1838. He was sent to Bangalore as the military chaplain where he worked for 7 years. He was also an active participant in the First Synod of Pondicherry. On October 10, 1852 he quit

the MEP and returned to France. He died on October 15, 1890. F. MOGET, The Missionaries of St. Francis de Sales of Annecy, pp. 61-66; T. ANCHUKANDAM, The First Synod of Pondicherry 1844, p. 32.

[153] Pro-vicar is a title given to a person who serves as a leader of a 'missio sui juris'. The pro-vicar is neither a bishop nor a vicar apostolic. He depends on the vicar apostolic for the jurisdiction and faculties to exercise his mission in the said territory. For the details regarding the appointment see APF Lettere 1845, vol. 332, ff. 699-700.

[154] Due to the understanding that he would be appointed the vicar apostolic of Visakhapatnam, Gailhot acted as the supreme authority in the mission. He was of the opinion that the Missionaries of St. Francis de Sales were mere collaborators. He was autocratic in directing the mission. The missionaries found it difficult to listen to him. They were of the opinion that the Holy See had entrusted the mission to them and Fr. Gailhot was only a guide till they established themselves in the mission. Probably for this reason Gailhot kept Fr. Jacques Martin, superior of the group, in Yanam, which is located far from Visakhapatnam. This caused a tension between the two parties. F. MOGET, The Missionaries of St. Francis de Sales of Annecy, pp. 61- 66.

[155] F. Moget records some of the complaints of the MSFS regarding the way Pro-Vicar Gailhot acted in a mission which the missionaries thought was given to them. One of the interesting comments is that Gailhot "acts on his own authority, without consulting anyone else. He started a congregation of Nuns with teenagers and two of them were recent converts from Protestantism. He had taken the pariah servants and thus brings us all into contempt. He cares only for the British and Irish". Ibid., pp. 62 – 65.

[156] Etienne–Louis Charbonnaux was born at La Guerche, on March 20, 1806. He left for India on August 16, 1830. He was made Vicar Apostolic of Mysore in 1850. He continued the apostolic visitation after the death of Msgr. Bonnand in 1861. He died in Bangalore on June 23, 1873.

[157] Ibid., p. 65.

[158] Msgr. Neyret's devotion and simplicity attracted reverence and respect from all : "Sa modestie, son recueillement, sa piété, sa charité ne sont point encore oubliés dans cette ville. Le fond de son être était un mélange de gravité et de douceur qui commandait le respect et attirait à lui tous les cœurs". Anonymous, Notice Biographiques sur M. Pierre Mermier et Monseigneur Neyret, Annecy 1863, p. 37; cf. F. MOGET, The Missionaries of St. Francis de Sales of Annecy, p. 69. For the decree of nomination of Neyret: AMSFS, Mission de Vizagapatam, 73-74; For details regarding the Apostolic Brief that erected Visakhapatnam as an independent Vicariate: APF Lettere 1850, vol. 339, ff. 219-220 and Jus Pontificium de Propaganda Fide, vol. VI, Romae 1894, 90.

[159] "Pour correspondre à ses désirs, le supérieur de la congrégation le destina à la mission de Vizagapatam. Avant de faire voile pour l'Asie, il visita les tombeaux

des saints Apôtres a Rome". Cf. Anonymous, Notice Biographiques sur M. Pierre Mermier et Monseigneur Neyret, Annecy 1863. p. 39.

[160] Neyret considered his consecration as bishop as his second baptism. Every year he celebrated the anniversary of his consecration preceding it with a three-day retreat. Ibid., p. 40.

[161] The biographer of Monsieur Mermier praises the work of the missionaries: "Ces sont des espéces d'orphelinats qui donnent d'excellents résultats. Grâce à nos écoles, beaucoup de jeunes gens ont des positions honorables dans la société, car dans les Indes il est facile à celui qui a recu quelque education, de s'élever au-dessus de la foule, surtout si sa conduite est bonne, et s'il sait se garder de l'ivrognerie, vice si commun dans ce pays." Ibid., p. 42

[162] Concerning the initiatives taken by Msgr. Neyret to promote native clergy, see Anonymous, Notice sur la Mission, p. 15 : "Msgr. Neyret avait l'intention d'en élever aux orders sacrées, pour commencer un clergé indigène que tous désirent, mais jusqu'ici, les circonstances n'ont pas permis de réaliser ce voeu".

[163] Neyret used to say, "dans ce pays rien n'est comparable à la valeur d'un missionnaire". Cf. Ibid., p. 45

[164] F. MOGET, The Missionaries of St. Francis de Sales of Annecy, p. 69. The author of Notice Biographiques further writes: "entré dans la congregation sur la fin de 1845, le R. P. Neyret suivit les missions diocésaines pendant près d'une année. Dire l'édification qu'il donna pendant tout ce temps, et les vertus d'humilié, d'abnégation et d'obéissance qu'il fit paraître, n'est pas chose facile: il était vraiment comme une lime entre les mains des directeurs des saints exercices, plus jeunes et moins habiles que lui". Cf. Anonymous, Notice Biographiques, p. 39.

[165] To quote a sentence from the Notices Biographiques on Neyret, "Les Irlandais et les autres chrétiens disaient : 'cet évêque est un bel homme, son port est majestueux, il parle magnifiquement ; mais en voyant le nôtre, si humble et si pieux, nous ne pouvons nous empêcher de le préférer, et de dire que c'est un saint'". Ibid., p. 46.

[166] Ibid., p. 45.

[167] Anonymous, Notice sur la Mission, p. 15.

[168] Anonymous, "Bishop Jean Marie Tissot", in Visakhapatnam Diocesan Centenary (1886 – 1986), p. 15.

[169] Fr. François–Marie Sermet was born at Sallanches (St. Roch), Savoy. He belonged to the third group of missionaries who left France on June 18, 1848 and reached India in December 1848. He accompanied Fr. Tissot to explore the possibilities of establishing a mission among the Kondhs on the Ganjam mountains, where he contracted mountain fever. On reaching Ganjam he died on September 12, 1850. Cf. F. MOGET, MSFS Obituary, p. 81.

[170] Anonymous, "Bishop Jean Marie Tissot", in Visakhapatnam Diocesan Centenary (1886 – 1986), p. 15.

[171] Ibid. pp. 16 - 17.

[172] François Philippe was born at Cran, on July 12, 1835. He was ordained a priest on July 14, 1862. He worked as a chaplain of the Holy Cross Sisters of Chavanod for 8 years. He held important positions in the congregation. He was sent as a visitator to the MSFS mission in India in 1885. He was appointed coadjutor to Msgr. Tissot on August 14, 1886. He received his Episcopal consecration on November 30, 1886 but never succeeded Msgr. Tissot as his health did not permit him such an appointment. He died at Veyrier-du-Lac, on April 16, 1904. Cf. F. MOGET, MSFS Obituary, p. 44.

[173] Reference to the canonical visitation and to his elevation to the episcopate is dealt with in chapter four of this work.

[174] Alexis Riccaz was born at St. Jean d'Arves, Maurienne. He came to India in 1862. He worked in Visakhapatnam for many years. He worked in Gnanapuram, Ganivada, Kottadaba. He was appointed the vicar general in 1886. The following year he was appointed the first bishop of the newly erected Diocese of Nagpur. He died on September 7, 1890. Cf. F. MOGET, MSFS Obituary, p. 80.

[175] Cuttack was the place of Msgr. Neyret's first pastoral visit. Cuttack, a fortified town with a population of 100,000 people, is situated on the banks of the river Mahanadi. The distance from Visakhapatnam to Cuttack is about 300 miles. Tissot was there to baptise children and adults. He blessed marriages and rectified some of them. He heard confessions of the adults and instructed them. He continues his letter to Petitjean describing the caravan that would accompany them. He explained the need for a caravan where there was danger of theft and attack of wild animals. Besides these, men were required to transport the provisions for the missionaries and to cook their food. In all, the caravan was composed of about 23 or 24 persons. Neyret wrote: "huit pour porter l'Evêque en palanquin, vous dirai-je; 8 pour porter de même manière un autre personne nécessaire à notre visite; deux pour le service du cheval du P. Tissot; 5 ou 6 pour porter les différents articles ci-devant et autres, et faire notre cuisine". Neyret to Petitjean, December 29, 1849. Correspondance de Msgr. Neyret, AMSFS 7 5 H 5 – 2, p. 188.

[176] A military station was established at the foot of the Ganjam Mountains, at Russelkonda, with the view to extirpate the horrific crimes of human sacrifices that existed amongst the Kondhs. Every year, after the monsoon, troops under the leadership of a captain would enter the mountains to stop this superstitious practice. Cf. Neyret to Mermier, October 2, 1850. AMSFS 7Z/ 5 H 5.

[177] Msgr. Neyret's letter to the Propagation de la Foi, Lyons expresses his concern for the Christians living without the presence of a priest. "Je viens de faire une première visite pastorale. J'ai parcouru toute la côte maritime, depuis Vizagapatam jusqu'à Cuttack. Partout, les misères des chrétiens sont grandes, attendu que l'ignorance est profonde. Jusqu'ici, cette partie de la mission, ainsi que bien d'autres, n'avait participé que fort rarement aux bienfaits de la religion, par dèfaut de prêtres. Deux y seront envoyés dans le courant de l'année. Je l'espère; leur

presence y devient urgente. Deux autres seront encore nécessaries dans l'ouest de la mission." Cf. M. DOMENGE, La Mission de Vizagapatam, p. 179; F. MOGET, Early Days of the Visakhapatnam Mission 1846 – 1920, p. 142.

[178] In a glowing tribute to the Kondhs, Msgr. Neyret informs Monsieur Mermier : "Les habitants de ces vallées forment un peuple à part, n'ayant que fort peu de rapport avec les Indiens de la plaine, dont ils diffèrent par les moeurs aussi bien que par la langue. Chez eux, dit-on, le systeme des castes est inconnu, excepté sur les frontières de la côte d'Orissa, et encore y sont-elles moins tranchées et plus tolérantes que dans tout le reste de la péninsule... Ils ne sont pas d'un caractère féroce...la simplicité et la franchise... 'Aussi j'aime ces pauvres sauvages et je les crois bons'. C'est une terre toute neuve qui demande des ouvriers, mais de bons ouvriers. Les grands talents seraient utiles, mais bien moins nécessaires qu'une vertu à toute épreuve. ...A Dieu ne plaise que je vous dise, Mr. Le Superieur, que la mission de Vizag n'a pas besoin d'hommes savants et instruits; mais quand vous en envoyez, ils ne manquent pas ici de besogne. Il nous en faut pour attaquer l'hérésie, mais ils me semble, Mr. Le Superieur, qu'une vertu éprouvée nous est encore plus nécessaire. Nos pauvres khondes ne demandant pas des hommes capables de déraciner de vieux préjugés et de confondre des prétendus savants, car ils avouent franchement qu'ils ne savent rien. Si toutes les montagnes sont semblables à celles que nous avons visitées, nous n'avons nulle part rencontré une pagode. Ils font leur sacrifices sur une pierre. Je ne veux cependant pas dire qu'à la voix du missionnaire ces peuplades se convertirent en masse". Although Msgr. Neyret was unable to understand their language and to comprehend their culture, he was highly touched by their simplicity and frankness. Cf. Neyret to Mermier, Vizagapatam, September 6, 1850, AMSFS, 7Z/ 5 H 5. In another letter addressed to Monsieur Mermier, Neyret to Mermier, Visakhapatnam, October 2, 1850, AMSFS 7 5 H 5 – 2. Neyret wrote: "Je dois vous faire observer que ce peuple n'est pas, comme il apparaît d'abord par la nature de ses sacrifices, un people féroce et cruel...Ce people est bon, un peuple encore tout neuf si je peux m'exprimer ainsi, et par consequent simple et franc".

[179] "Ils n'ont pas encore été gâtés, disait-il, par le contact de Européens; la religion aura plus de prise sur eux. Les protestants n'y vont pas contredire la parole de Dieu, et créer, comme sur le littoral, cette multitude de sectes, qui toutes se disent chrétiennes, quoique toutes soient opposées les unes aux autres. Le succès, qui nous est refusé dans la plaine, nous attend peut-être sur ces montagnes". M. DOMENGE, La Mission de Vizagapatam, p. 186.

[180] Msgr. Neyret reported : "Le premiers missionnaires qui y seront envoyés, devrons prendre connaissance du pays, le parcourir et choisir pour commencer l'endroit le plus favorable, les peuples le mieuz disposés. Si cette enterprise réussit, il nous faudra plus tard des frères pour apprendre à ces pauvres gens à cultiver un sol qui paraît fertile, il nous faudra aussi des religieuses... Enfin il me semble que c'est une carrière intarissable à exploiter." Neyret to Mermier, Visakhapatnam, September 6, 1850, AMSFS 7Z/ 5 H 5.

[181] M. DOMENGE, La Mission de Vizagapatam, pp. 186 – 187.

[182] Neyret to Mermier, La Mort du Père François- Marie Sermet, 12 September 1850, Visakhapatnam, October 3, 1850, AMSFS 7Z/5 H 5.

[183] M. DOMENGE, La Mission de Vizagapatam, p. 187.

[184] Neyret to Mermier, La Mort du Père François-Marie Sermet, 12 September 1850, Visakhapatnam, October 3, 1850, AMSFS 7Z/5 H 5 ; Tissot to Mermier, Visakhapatnam, December 3, 1850, AMSFS 7 Z/ 5 H 5.

[185] Cf. M. DOMENGE, La Mission de Vizagapatam, p. 189.

[186] Msgr. Neyret reported : "Il me semble, bien respectable supérieur, que si vous aviez vu une seule de ces peuplades, votre bon coeur serait ému de compassion. Oh! qu'il est douloureux de les voir si bien disposés et de ne pas pouvoir les secourir; c'est bien le cas de dire: messis quidem multa, operarii autem pauci." Neyret to Mermier, Visakhapatnam, December 3, 1850, AMSFS 7 5 H 5 - 2.

[187] Mermeir wrote : "Cependant Rome se contente d'exhorter en applaudissant au projet que vous lui proposez de travailler à la conversion de ces montagnes sans vous promettre aucun secours, se fiant probablement aux resources que nous n'avons pas. Après l'essai qu'ont fait MM. Tissot, Sermet et les troupes Anglaises ne serait-ce pas prudent d'attendre que notre mission fut plus solidement établie tant ici qu'à Vizagapatam... D'où je conclus que si par cette nouvelle entreprise nous rendions notre position encore plus difficile, nous nous exposerions à ruiner les petits commencements...c'est vous Monseigneur, qui êtes sur les lieux, qui êtes en rapport immediate soit avec Rome, soit avec ces pauvres Condhas (Kondhs) et ceux qui les connaissant, qui pouvez mieux juger que nous, soyez-en toujours plus convaincu; nous approuvons dès ce moment et approuverons tout ce que Dieu vous inspirera de faire pour cette nouvelle Mission à laquelle Rome vous exhorte d'une manière si persuasive." Monsieur Mermeir to Neyret, Aux Allinges, August 6, 1851, AMSFS, 5 H 5 – 2/1.

[188] L. CLARYSSE, "Lievens and Zemindari System", in Sevartham 10 (1985), p. 11.

[189] Johannes Evangelista Gossner (1773-1858) was the founder of the group called 'Gossners Missionsverein = Gossner Mission Association', founded at Berlin in 1842. He remained the director of the Gossner Mission until 1858. He was a former Roman Catholic priest. In 1826 he became a Protestant and in 1829 the pastor of Bethlehem Church in Berlin. From there he sent out, on July 10, 1844, the first missionaries to India. Cf. ROEBER, Part of the History of Missions and History of the Church in India, pp. 4 – 8.

[190] Hoffmann to General, Memoir, ARSI, Beng. 2008, Fasc.III, p. 5.

[191] F. DE SA, Crisis in Chota Nagpur, p. 73.

[192] Peter Tete cites S. C. Roy for the names of the four Lutheran missionaries: Pastors E. Schatz, F. Batsch, A. Brandt and H. Janke. They arrived in Ranchi in November 1845. Cf. P. TETE, A Missionary Social Worker in India, p. 11.

[193] The Kabir Panthis were another Hindu sect enjoying the patronage of Oraons. Their beliefs and rites differ slightly from those of the other Bhakti Cults [Devotion]. The Kabir Panthi Gurus [masters] act not only as spiritual teachers but also as priests. Their ministrations are obligatory for the religious service that must be performed on important occasions such as birth, marriage and death. The Oraons who joined the movement did not completely abandon their tribal customs. Their regular ceremonies were always performed, either before or after the Kabir Panth rites. The vacillating Oraons could not comply with the tenets of the movement. A member was required to observe such practices as abstention from worship of idols and other visible symbols of divinity; abjuration of intoxicating drink and its use for libation; prohibition of blood sacrifices and of the eating of beef, pork and fowl meat; no worship of spirits and minor deities; belief in a single personal God; etc. Cf. S. FUCHS, Rebellious Prophets, pp. 44 - 46; A. KANJAMALA, Religion and Modernization of India, p. 61.

[194] P. TETE, A Missionary Social Worker in India, p. 12.

[195] F. DE SA, Crisis in Chota Nagpur, p. 77.

[196] Ibid., p. 79.

[197] P. TETE, A Missionary Social Worker in India, p. 14.

[198] F. DE SA, Crisis in Chota Nagpur, p. 93.

[199] In 1869, the Government introduced the Chota Nagpur Tenures Act setting into motion the Bhuinari Survey and Settlement operations, which went on till 1880. For various reasons the measure was a failure. Cf. F. DE SA, "The Crisis in the Mission of Chota Nagpur and the Reaction of the Landlords and the Police", in IES 8/3 (1969), p. 191.

[200] P. TETE, A Missionary Social Worker in India, p. 17.

[201] F. DE SA, Crisis in Chota Nagpur, pp. 95-96; Hoffmann to General, Memoir, ARSI, Beng. 2008, Fasc. III, p. 6.

[202] Augustus Stockman was born at Gand, in Belgium, on June 27, 1826. He entered the Society of Jesus on April 8, 1847. He arrived in India on April 2, 1860 and died at Khunti on April 23, 1897. Cf. R. MENDIZÁBAL, Catalogus Defunctorum in renata Societate Iesu ab a. 1814 ad a. 1970, p. 161.

[203] Walter Steins was born at Amsterdam on July 1, 1810. He entered the Society of Jesus on December 16, 1832. Joining the mission of Bombay, he eventually became the vicar apostolic there. He was transferred to Calcutta on April 14, 1867. He died on September 7, 1881, at Sydney. Cf. Ibid., p. 98.

[204] An interest in the mission was sparked by a letter that Fr. Stockman received from Fr. Sapart, the founder of Balasore, reporting the prospects of mass conversions among the tribals living between Chaibasa and Midnapur. This piece of information was given to him by the wife of the District Superintendent of Police. Msgr. Steins was also informed by a British official of the prospects of conversion in Ranchi. Cf. P. PONETTE, "Ranchi Mission: Before and After Lievens", in IMR 7/1 (1985), p. 34.

[205] F. DE SA, Crisis in Chota Nagpur, p. 116; Hoffmann to General, Memoir, ARSI, Beng. 2008, Fasc. III, p. 6.

[206] The first converts presented themselves to him in 1872. They were not Hos, one of the tribes belonging to the Munda family, who were the primary object of the missionary expedition, but Mundas. They came from six or seven families from Kontupai a few miles north of the town. They were baptized by Msgr. Steins himself. Since the Hos were hostile towards the neophytes, the missionary found a place for them to live in Tutui, just across the Singbhum border in Ranchi district. Then it was possible because the Ranchi ecclesiastical district went over to the Calcutta jurisdiction in 1871. Cf. P. Ponette, "Ranchi Mission: Before and After Lievens", p. 34.

[207] H. JOSSON, La Mission du Bengale Occidental, vol. I, pp. 409-411.

[208] F. DE SA, Crisis in Chota Nagpur, p. 119.

[209] Ferdinand de Cock was born at Alost on April 22, 1831. He entered the Society of Jesus on September 26, 1850. He arrived in India on December 23, 1868. In 1877 he became the chaplain of the Madras regiment stationed at Doranda (Ranchi). When he fell sick, he was replaced by Lachawietz. De Cock returned to Doranda in 1880. He died at Calcutta on August 6, 1890. Cf. R. MENDIZÁBAL, Catalogus Defunctorum in renata Societate Iesu ab a. 1814 ad a. 1970, p. 131.

[210] John Fierens was born at Anvers on October 8, 1844. He entered the Society of Jesus on September 27, 1863 and arrived in India on December 2, 1869. Msgr. Steins ordained him a priest on January 3, 1875. Due to illness he returned to Europe and died at Anvers on November 3, 1893. Cf. Ibid., p. 146.

[211] Paul Goethals was born at Courtrai on November 11, 1832. He entered the Society of Jesus on October 31, 1852. He was consecrated Bishop on December 3, 1877 and arrived in India on November 4, 1878. He died at Calcutta on July 4, 1901. Cf. Ibid., p. 180.

[212] F. DE SA, Crisis in Chota Nagpur, p. 150.

[213] Sambalpur, a town in western Orissa, lies between 20°43'N and 22°11'N latitude and 82°39'E and 85°13'E longitude. The fate of the inhabitants of Sambalpur depended on the Sai rulers. With the changing fortunes resulting from wars and destruction, "Maharaja Sai died in 1827, and his widow Rani Mohan Kumari was allowed to succeed. This was done against the local customs and laws of the land. Never in the history of Chauhan, ruler of Sambalpur, a woman had been raised to such a position. Disturbances immediately broke out, and for years there was constant internecine strife between the recognised ruler and other claimants to the chieftainship". N. SENAPATI et al. (eds.), Orissa District Gazetteers: Sambalpur, Cuttack 1992, p. 70. There was a rival claimant for the chieftainship supported by some zamindars. Matters became so serious that villages were plundered, and chaos prevailed everywhere. In this situation of anarchy, a military force from Hazaribagh was called to end the trouble. In order to end the dispute Captain Wilkinson deposed the Rani and appointed Narayan Singh, a

descendant of Bikram Singh, as the chief. In the eyes of the people he was not qualified for the throne, since his mother was from an inferior caste. As soon as the British withdrew the troops, rebellions broke out, including the more serious one in 1839, instigated by Surendra Sai who looked upon Narayan Singh as an usurper. As a descendant of the fourth Raja of Sambalpur, Surendra Sai claimed the throne. Narayan Singh died in 1849 and his wife Rani Mukhyapan Devi assumed the reins of Government as they did not have an heir to the throne. By virtue of Lord Dalhousie's 'doctrine of lapse', the kingdom was annexed by the British and the Rani was given a sum for her maintenance. When the Mutiny of 1857 broke out, the uprising continued in Sambalpur. On July 30, 1857, Ramgarh Battalion, stationed in Sambalpur, plundered the treasury, broke open the jail and released the prisoners among whom were Surendra Sai and his brother Udwant Sai. "Before the end of August, rumours of insurrectionary movements had begun to spread, though no actual outbreak occurred for some time, and early in September two companies of Madras troops were ordered from Cuttack to Sambalpur by G. F. Cockburn, the commissioner of Orissa". N. SENAPATI et al. (eds.), Orissa District Gazetteers: Sambalpur, p. 74. Later, the 40th Madras Native Infantry was despatched under Captain Knocker from Cuttack. Besides, Lieutenant Hadow of the Madras Artillery, who arrived at Cuttack with some light mountain guns, was also asked to reach Sambalpur. Even after the rebellion, the military troops continued to be stationed in Sambalpur. This explains why Catholics serving in the military were found in Sambalpur. Cf. Ibid., pp. 70 - 79.

[214] The journey from Balasore to Sambalpur might have been extremely tedious as they had to reach Cuttack by road where they needed to take a boat to cross the Mahanadi. It might take them several days before they reached Sambalpur. However, the road taken by Fierens from Bandgaon is less tedious, as he could cross a major part of the journey on horseback. M. VERMIERE, Gangpur Mission History, vol. I, Unpublished Collection of Documents, Bishop's House Rourkela, p. 1; M. VERMEIRE, Biru Mission History: Samtoli 1904 – 1940, vol. III, APBS India Lievens. General Sources, p. 23.

[215] This is a liberal translation, which retains faithfully the essential aspects of the text. Fr. Fierens wrote: "Je reviens à peine d'une excursion, j'ai été à 200 miles anglaises d'ici à un endroit nommé Sumbulpur (Sambalpur) vers l'extreme ouest de notre mission. Là il y a un regiment de soldats indigènes, qui viennent tout à fait du sud des Indes et dans ce régiment il y a un bon nombre de soldats catholiques avec leurs femmes et leurs enfants. Ce ne sont pas de chrétiens de date recente, mais leurs ancêtres ont ete convertis du temps de St. François – Xavier, ils ont une foi vive come les irlandais; ils sont visités une fois l'an par un missionnaire, mais ils ont une chapelle, dans laquelle ils se reunissent tous les jours, matin et soir, pour faire leurs prières en commun, il y a parmi eux un catechiste, qui préside aux prières à la chapelle, et qui doit apprendre les prières aux enfants quand ils sont en âge et aux néophytes qui se joignent a eux de temps en temps parmi les soldats paiens du régiment. Le catéchiste s'appelle dans leur langage, l'enfant

de l'église, ils parlent tamul et telugus, mais les hommes en assez bon nombre parlent un peu l'anglais, les femmes comprennent tant soit peu l'hindoustani, c'est par cette langue là que je me suis tiré d'affaire pour entendre la confession des femmes et de quelques hommes et des enfants en âge de comprendre. Il y a, outre le catéchiste, un headman ou chef des chrétiens du régiment, c'est lui avec son conseil qui arrange les differents qui surgissent pendant l'absence du prêtre; les cas un peu graves sont juges par le prêtre, président au conseil lors de la visite. J'ai (…) à présider un jour à un conseil ou un homme qui avait commis une faute pendant l'absence du prêtre devait être jugé et puni. Dans le cas actuel, la punition était une aumône à faire à la chapelle, quelques chandelles pour la chapelle et quelques coups de baguette sur les mains, que le cupable reçoit a genoux au milieu du conseil de guerre de la part d'un autre soldat qui est désigné pour cette besogne. Ces bons soldats souscrivent chaque mois quelque chose pour l'entretien de la chapelle et pour la lumière, car la chapelle est toujours illuminée au temps de la prière, ils ont aussi l'habitude de brûler de l'incens devant'autel pendant le temps des prières. Ils ont une grande devotion à St. Antoine de Padoue. Cette devotion leur vient des Portugais, dont St. Antoine était le compatriote. J'avais à baptiser les enfants nés pendant l'année et plus de la moitié devait porte le nome de Antony, ou Antoniama pour les filles. J'ai baptisé un païen et je l'ai marié à une fille des soldats. Le prêtre pendant un sejour de 8 jours parmi eux doit finir toute la besogne del'année, un jour on bénit toutes les maisons, un autre, le cimetière, on donne nom des directions pour les réparations de la chapelle, j'ai même ouvert une liste de souscriptions dans ce but parmi les habitants européens de la station, qu'a rapporté à peu près 100 francs." Fierens to Jeanne, Mathilde and Marie, Bandgaon, October 22, 1884, APBS, India / Lievens. Box 14/ 4.

[216] M. VERMIER, Gangpur Mission History, Vol. I, p. 1.

[217] C. TIMMERMANN, "Ranchi Mission", in Xavier's Footsteps. A Jubilee Souvenir of the 4th Centenary of the Society of Jesus, Anand 1939, p. 110.

[218] J. VAN TROY, "Fr. Sylvain Grosjean SJ (1846-1915). Jesuit Leadership", in P. TETE (ed,), To Chota Nagpur with Love and Service. Pioneers in the Ranchi Jesuit Province, Ignatian Commemoration Volume, Ranchi 1991, p. 15.

[219] Ibid., p. 16.

[220] Ibid., p. 23.

[221] H. JOSSON, Un Chef de Mission aux Indes, p. 396.

[222] J. VAN TROY, "Fr. Sylvain Grosjean SJ (1846-1915)", p. 4.

[223] Ibid., p. 6.

[224] Ibid., p. 8.

[225] Ibid.

[226] In the wake of numerous conversions of tribals, the landlords recognized the danger and were plotting against the Jesuit missionaries. They sought means to bring both the missionaries and their converts into conflict with the government,

and, they complained to the commissioner, Mr. Grimley. Noticing foul play in the motives of the zamindars, the Commissioner despatched an enquiry commission under the acting deputy commissioner of the Lohardugga district, Mr. Renny, in November 1889. The hostile attitude of Renny towards the Jesuits led to the suggestion of expelling the Jesuits from Chotanagpur. However, in their effort to mollify the so-called unrest, Renny and Lillingston condemned many tribals to imprisonment. Renny punished the people with severity. He saw proof that the disquiet was due to the actions of the priests. He felt obliged to punish the act of open resistance to authority with severity. By this means he hoped to show the people that the kingdom was not theirs (the missionaries) and that they would not be allowed in the future to take the law into their own hands. Cf. F. DE SA, Crisis in Chota Nagpur, pp. 203-215.

[227] J. VAN TROY, "Fr. Sylvain Grosjean SJ (1846-1915)", p. 11.

[228] Ibid.

[229] Ibid., p. 13.

[230] Hoffmann to General, Memoir, ARSI, Beng. 2008, Fasc. IV, p. 1; M. VANDEN BOGAERT, "Social Transformation of a Tribal Society. Fall-out of Evangelization in Chota Nagpur", in Sevartham 11 (1986), p. 25.

[231] F. DE SA, "The Crisis in the Mission of Chota Nagpur and the Reaction of the Landlords and the Police", p. 193.

[232] In his letter to Rev. Fr. General on January 7, 1889, Lievens wrote: "Actually the Lutheran missionaries are without funds, and their Christians in many places are ready to come and do come to us, provided we take care of them, give them instruction, build a chapel and hold a service. It is a most favourable time to convert a whole kingdom to Jesus Christ, time which probably will not last long, and which then passed away will be regretted forever." Lievens to the Superior General, January 7, 1889, ARSI, Beng. 1004, 3-XI, 4.

[233] The cutting of chundis took place at common meetings with the priest. After cutting off the tuft they would throw it far away with a hearty laugh. Cf. A. KANJAMALA, Religion and Modernization of India, p. 64.

[234] VAN DER SCHUEREN, The Belgian Mission of Bengal, vol. I, p. 9.

[235] According to Hoffmann, Lievens and his catechists whom he had sent to the villages, recommended three points that the tribal Christians/converts must take: (1) never to pay any rent without exacting proper receipts and if they are unable to read and write- most of them were illiterate- they are to pay only in the presence of an accredited mission servant; (2) to refuse absolutely any bethbegari, forced labour; and, (3) to refuse to pay any rent which Fr. Lievens considered exorbitant. The first point is perfectly legal. As regards forced labour Fr. Lievens was strictly right, for at times forced labour and its exaction had not acquired the force of law by prescription. But sometimes due to the cleverness of the landlords and the ignorance of the British officials, the forced labour itself had

an official sanction. Fr. Hoffmann accused Fr. Lievens of misusing the silence of the government to instruct the people to ignore its decisions. The rent fixed by Fr. Lievens as fair was in fact very low. Cf. Hoffmann to General, Memoir, ARSI, Beng. 2008, Fasc. IV, 1a - 1e; APBS India 1 – 14/3 Hoffmann letters: Hoffman to Provincial, Dortmund, March 11, 1925. Fr. Hoffmann is of the opinion that there is not much difference in the method of Lievens and that of the Lutherans. Fr. Lievens never promised independence, as did the Lutherans. He advised the aborigines not to pay the amount of bethbegari, which he considered exorbitant. The condition he put was that the people should accept Christianity.

[236] A. KANJAMALA, Religion and Modernization of India, p. 65.

[237] The motive for such a drastic action was the scarcity of personnel and the lack of finances. The view of Msgr. Goethals, archbishop of Calcutta, was very readily accepted by the then superior regular of the mission, T. Bodson. Cf. M. VERMEIRE, Biru Mission History: Common History to the Whole Mission, Vol.I, Part.II, ARSI, Beng. 2004, p. 5.

[238] L. CLARYSSE, "Lievens and Zemindari System", p. 15.

[239] Sardar means a leader , hence it was a movement of the leaders; and the Sardar Movement consisted of collecting money from the tribals to defray the expenses of sending petitions to the Government. The petitions sent in 1870 and in 1879 were rejected. The Government viewed this movement as political unrest and took many precautionary measures to curb the violence. Since the leaders were Christians, the British officials thought that the whole agitation was instigated by the Christian missionaries. As a result, most of the missionaries dissociated themselves from this movement. And since the expected support did not come from the missionaries, the Sardars did not hesitate to turn against the missionaries as well. Van Exem is of the opinion that the Sardars would have gladly become Catholics had the new missionaries supported their struggle. But seeing the havoc created in the Lutheran mission, the new missionaries did not show any sympathy towards the movement. Cf. IBID., pp. 14-17; A. VAN EXEM, "Early Evangelization in Chota Nagpur", in IMR 1/4 (1979), p. 352.

[240] L. CLARYSSE, "Lievens and Zemindari System", p. 15.

[241] Ibid., p. 13.

[242] F. DE SA, Crisis in Chota Nagpur, p.123.

[243] Ibid., p. 156.

[244] Ibid., p. 131.

[245] Hoffmann to General, Memoir, ARSI, Beng. 2008, Fasc.III, p. 1.

[246] F. DE SA, Crisis in Chota Nagpur,   p. 160.

[247] Ibid., p. 13.

[248] Van der Schueren was born at Erpe in Flanders on March 5, 1863. His effort to protect the mission from collapse during the First World War was lauded. He

died at Oak Park, USA on November 6, 1930. Y. DE STEENHAULT, History of the Jesuits in West Bengal: 1921 – 1985 (Part I: 1921 – 1947), p. 114.

[249] VAN DER SCHUEREN, The Belgian Mission of Bengal, vol. I, p. 22.

[250] P. TETE, "J. B. Hoffmann", in Idem (ed.), To Chota Nagpur with Love and Service: Pioneers in the Ranchi Jesuit Province, Ignatian Commemoration Volume, Ranchi 1991, p. 56.

[251] The reason for writing the Encyclopedia Mundarica was that the Mundari language, Fr. Hoffmann thought, was disappearing rapidly. This gradual extinction of their culture and civilization was the effect of the oppression of the Dikus or foreigners. Therefore, he thought it was his duty to expound the true picture of the race and their civilization and to preserve the true memory of that which is on the verge of destruction. It was Hoffmann who made the public aware of the wealth and beauty and significance of the Mundari folklore, thereby creating interest in the preservation of the cultural heritage of the Mundas. Cf. P. TETE, A Missionary Social Worker in India, pp. 145-154.

[252] Ibid., p. 157.

[253] P. TETE, "J. B. Hoffmann", p. 57.

[254] Ibid.

[255] Ibid., p. 58.

[256] Back from sick leave in Europe early in 1908 he set out to launch the Chota Nagpur Catholic Cooperative Credit Society. It was to be a common enterprise of the Jesuits and the people. He prepared a 17,000-word pamphlet to conscientise his brethren, sometimes using a language which we no longer commonly associate with his times: "If we should still maintain that for our Mundas and Oraons those organizations are out of question, quite impossible, or nearly sure to fail, well then, the best thing we can do is to pick up our little bundles and go back to Belgium." Cf. A. VAN EXEM, "Early Evangelisation in Chota Nagpur", in IMR 1/4 (1979), p. 90.

[257] J. B. HOFFMANN, Social Works in Chota Nagpore, 1904. ARSI, Beng. 1004, 4-IX, 13, pp. 4-10. Commenting on the work of Fr. Hoffmann, Fr. Grosjean informs the provincial in Belgium that the pages are remarkable and in order to make it realistic he proposes that a press be established in Ranchi, especially for periodic publications concerning the same matter. Cf. Grosjean to Provincial, Calcutta, March 4, 1909, APBS India 1 – 12/ Grosjean; Grosjean to Provincial, Calcutta, April 28, 1909, APBS India 1 – 12/ Grosjean; Grosjean to Provincial, Calcutta, June 26, 1909, APBS India 1 – 12/ Grosjean.

[258] Besides their eminently philanthropic and Christian aim, these organizations pursue a second and equally important aim — the economic education of the lower classes. They also teach the cultivators a simple and easy means of putting even the smallest savings into a perfectly secure and moderately profitable investment at any moment they choose and at their place of residence (or very close to it).

These organizations are managed by the very people for whose benefit they have been founded, and thus they train others in self-help and in a spirit of sound independence and activity which is so highly rational and Christian. Cf. J. B. HOFFMANN, Social Works in Chota Nagpore, p. 17.

[259] Ibid., p. 19.

[260] The Raiffeisen system is named after its founder Friedrich Wilhelm Raiffeisen (1818-1888), who drew inspiration from the Rochdale pioneers in England and adapted it to the economic needs and condition of Germany, especially after the famine of 1846-1847. Raiffeisen started these banks to rescue the peasants of Rhine Province from the clutches of the usurers who had brought them to the brink of destruction. The Raiffeisen system is made up of agricultural cooperative credit societies founded in 1848 to facilitate credit for small peasant proprietors. In 1849 loans were also granted to small farmers. The members of the cooperative were rich philanthropists who sold cattle to farmers on easy terms. In 1862 Raiffeisen founded at Anhausen the cooperative credit society of which the farmers themselves were members. These cooperative banks proved to be very successful and since then the system has been known as the Raiffeisen system. Cf. F. KARRENBERG (ed,), Evangelisches Soziallexicon, Stuttgart 1963, pp. 995-996; P. TETE, A Missionary Social Worker in India, pp. 84-85. As a result of the establishment of Raiffeisen banks in the Rhine Province, "those peasants are among the wealthiest and most Catholic of Europe, owing to the energy and enthusiasm with which the Catholic clergy, in the teeth of a narrow-minded government opposition, took up, spread and developed the work of Raiffeisen". J. B. HOFFMANN, Social Works in Chota Nagpore, p. 16.

[261] P. TETE, A Missionary Social Worker in India, p. 61.

[262] Ibid.

[263] Ibid., p. 29

[264] Fr. Louis Cardon's name is very much linked with the history of Chotanagpur as one of the founders of the mission together with Constant Lievens and Sylvain Grosjean. Though, due to his long years of service in the region of Biru, he merited the name the 'Apostle of Biru', his service to the nascent mission of Gangpur cannot be overlooked. Therefore, it is fitting that a brief biography be presented below.

[265] Missionaries were prohibited from carrying on their work without prior approval of residing among people outside the British territories in India — especially the princely states — since such activities could violate the treaty that the British had established with the local rulers. The government communicated this policy to the Archbishop of Calcutta, who in turn informed the missionaries. Cf. M. VERMEIRE, Gangpur Mission History, vol. I, p.3.

[266] Brice Meuleman was born at Gent on March 1, 1862. He joined the Society of Jesus on September 23, 1879 and came to India on November 4, 1886. On March 31, 1902, it was announced that he would succeed Msgr. Paul Goethals as

the Archbishop of Calcutta; at that time, he was superior regular of the Bengal mission of the Belgian Jesuits. After an eventful career for which he gave his best in organising the missions, he died in Marseilles, where he had gone to recuperate his health, on July 15, 1925. Cf. Y. DE STEENHAULT, History of the Jesuits in West Bengal: 1921 – 1985 (Part I: 1921 – 1947), pp. 106 – 107; R. MENDIZÁBAL, Catalogus Defunctorum in renata Societate Iesu ab a. 1814 ad a. 1970, p. 297.

[267] L. Cardon, July 20, 1908, APBS India 1- 13, Lievens/ Grosjean Memoir; Y. DE STEENHAULT, History of the Jesuits in West Bengal: 1921 – 1985 (Part I: 1921 – 1947), p. 29.

[268] Vermeire mentioned that there might have been many deputations, but they were left unrecorded, as Cardon was not consistent in maintaining a diary. "There is no doubt that deputations from Gangpur became more frequent as soon as they had no more to go to Noatoli to meet Cardon but found him at Rengarih so much nearer." M. VERMEIRE, Ganagpur Mission History, vol. I, p. 3.

[269] Ibid., p. 29.

[270] P. TETE, "Fr. Louis Cardon, S.J. ((1857-1946): The founder of the Biru Mission", in Idem (ed.), To Chotanagpur With Love, Ranchi, p. 67.

[271] The general pattern of the mission tour was as follows: the visit of the missionary is announced in advance, and the catechist prepares the people for the Holy Mass and other sacraments like penance, baptism and marriage; after the Mass the people sit for Panchayat, in which they discuss various issues concerning the mission station in question.

[272] Ibid., p. 69.

[273] Ibid., p. 71.

[274] Commenting on the work of Fr. Cardon, Fr. Alary wrote to Fr. General : "Notre Supérieur local, le Rév. P. Cardon, est un homme de beaucoup d'expérience, il a une grande influence sur les gens du pays. Il rend de grands services aux jeunes qui commencent la carrière, ces services pourraient être plus grands encore." Alary to General, ARSI Calcut. 1005 – XIII, 8, p.4.

[275] P. TETE, "Fr. Louis Cardon, S.J. ((1857 - 1946): The founder of the Biru Mission", p. 75.

[276] M. VERMEIRE, Gangpur Mission History, vol. I, p. 3; Fr. Perier wrote: "Le R. P. Cardon jouit d'une très grande autorité non seulement sur les indigènes du Biru, mai les notres l'ont en grande estime et recourent volontiers à ses lumières." Perier to Provincial, Calcutta, March 10, 1914, APBS India 2 Box 23/1.

[277] Before going to the Biru mission, Leo Scharlaeken was at Balasore (Orissa) since October 16, 1896. Scharlaeken was born on June 1, 1861 in Bruges (Belgium). He entered the Society of Jesus on September 27, 1879 and arrived in India on December 3, 1894. He died on November 20, 1902 at Calcutta. Scharlaeken was not an equestrian. Therefore, he went from village to village on foot. He had

brought along with him a bicycle, but in those days roads in Biru were bad even for bicycles.

[278] In his letter to his family in November 1902 Leo Scharlaeken writes, "These last months we have acquired a completely new country (Gangpur). Our parish now is as large as 3 Belgian provinces. We have not yet counted the number of those new Christians, but there will be about 5,000". VERMEIRE, Gangpur Mision History, vol. I, p. 4; P. TETE, The Kharias and the History of the Catholic Church in Biru, Ranchi 1990, p. 95.

[279] John De Smet was born at Swevezeele on May 17, 1852. He entered the Society of Jesus on September 24, 1874 and arrived in India on December 6, 1876. He died at Noatoli on May 5, 1921. Cf. R. MENDIZÁBAL, Catalogus Defunctorum in renata Societate Iesu ab a. 1814 ad a. 1970, p. 281.

[280] P. TETE, The Kharias and the History of the Catholic Church in Biru, p. 97.

[281] The names of the villages that came to Samtoli are: Bonai, Goghea, Ranakata, Konorkela, Demta and Katajor. Cf. Ibid., p. 174.

[282] Ibid., pp. 173 –174.

[283] Edmund de Gryse was born at Leeuw-St. Pierre (Brabant) on June 26, 1865. He entered the Society of Jesus on September 24, 1884 and arrived in India on November 24, 1885. He died at Rengarih on January 8, 1908. Cf. R. MENDIZÁBAL (ed.), Catalogus Defunctorum in renata Societate Iesu ab a. 1814 ad a. 1970, p. 208.

[284] M. VERMEIRE, Biru Mission History: Kurdeg, vol. IV, Sec.III, ARSI, Beng. 2006, p. 3.

[285] Ibid., p. 19.

[286] In addition to the regular visits of the missionaries and the village deputations, another important factor facilitated the spread of the faith in Gangpur: the presence of two important railway stations: Rajgangpur and Jharsuguda. The former is not far from Kesramal in eastern Gangpur and the latter is in western Gangpur. Sometimes they would take the train from Garpos station. The missionaries had to take the train to go to Calcutta for their annual retreat and other related matters. Most of them would spend a night in one or the other village hearing confessions, anointing the sick, baptizing and, above all, celebrating the Eucharist. This will be dealt with in the next chapter. Citing the diary of Fr. De Gryse, Fr. Vermeire writes: "In October (1904) he (Fr. De Gryse) went for his retreat to Calcutta, but visited on the way to the Railway (Station), Rengarbahar and Behrembasa in Biru, and many villages in Gangpur." Ibid. p. 21. In October 1908 Fr. Van Hoeck made a trip to Calcutta. He visited some places on the way: Timna, Katanjheria, Kusumdegi and Barokhata. When he returned from Calcutta on October 23, he also visited different places. M. VERMEIRE, Biru Mission History: Kurdeg, vol. IV, Sec.III, APBS India 1 – Box 4, p. 87.

[287] Some of the villages visited on the tour are: Sakrabahar, Saunamara, Rauldega, Gaibira, Simdega, Kirelega, Deogaon, Sahajbahal, Gorgabahal, Keetmunda, Latalaga, Kusumdegi, Katangjheria, Timan, Ambapani, Baiskar and Sakjor. He claims to have administered at least 104 baptisms in these places. Commenting on the people he writes: "The people are full of good will. The old people are the same everywhere. They drink a little too much. Most of the Christians are Oraons depending on Kurdeg and are emigrants from Palkot and Basia districts." Cf. Ibid., p. 22.

[288] Ibid., p. 28.

[289] Ibid., p. 47.

[290] He visited the following stations in Gangpur on April 1, 1906: Sakiabahar, Korai, Saunamara, Rauldega, Borobahal, Maiabahal, Gaibira, Deogaon, Kiralega, Simdega and Rengarbahar. On his way to Calcutta in March 1907, he visited the following villages: Timna, Borkata, Kusumdegi, Pachora, Katangjheria and Sakjor. Cf. Ibid., p. 55.

[291] Ibid. p. 57.

[292] Ibid., p. 34.

[293] Ibid., p. 48.

[294] Ibid., p. 62.

Chapter - 3

A New Beginning

Just as the growth of any social organism depends on the constant care of responsible people, so too did the nascent Catholic community in Orissa depend on the presence of the missionaries. Though the catechists did their best to strengthen the bonds that kept the community united and fervent in the faith, there was no progress in the quality of Christian life. In fact, there were even some defections from the community. Hence, the future of the Catholic community depended largely on the establishment of mission stations so that the missionaries, by means of schools, orphanages and other infrastructure, could nurture their faith in a systematic manner.

This chapter explores the circumstances relating to the establishment of the first stations in the Ganjam mission – i.e., Surada, Koussipanga and Gojolibady – which went through a difficult time of 'waxing and waning'. Though the established mission centres at Berhampur and Cuttack remained an attraction for the missionaries, these centres provided them with a *pied-à-terre* to spread into other areas, such as Puri and Khurda. This will be discussed in the following chapter. The sufferings that the Missionaries of St. Francis de Sales (MSFS) had to endure for commencing work in the ill-fated mountains and some of their missionary responses, especially in the face of natural calamities, are discussed here in order to analyse their efforts to win the people for Christ.

The centrifugal approach of the Belgian Jesuits was visible when they sought to expand their mission to the semi-independent states of

Gangpur (Orissa) and Jashpur (Chhatisgarh). The extension of the mission to Gangpur state was a long-cherished desire of the people, and the missionaries had the sympathy of those living across the border. But their desire could not be realised due to the intransigent attitude of the Raja of Gangpur. The Jesuits had even established a station at Behrembasa in 1905, on the western border of Gangpur with Chotanagpur, in order to extend the care of the missionaries to the neophytes living across the border. The missionaries used their influence with the government authorities in the hope of pressuring the Raja of Gangpur to grant a plot for a mission. But their efforts were futile until 1907, when the Raja finally gave his consent and turned over 7½ acres of land in Kesramal. The initial struggles and enthusiasm of the missionaries along with the approaches to win the tribes to Christ are considered in this chapter. Mention is also made of the beginning of two religious congregations of sisters in the mission: the St. Joseph Sisters of Annecy in Surada and the Daughters of the Cross in Kesramal.

Ganjam Mission

In spite of the paucity of personnel and the vast territory to be served, the Missionaries of St. Francis de Sales had registered considerable progress since their arrival at Visakhapatnam in 1845. By 1853 the progress was well marked by the construction of churches and convents, and almost all the centres had at least two resident priests. In fact, considering the existing circumstances, it was by no means a small achievement for a young congregation. When the congregation experienced steady progress, the missionaries felt the need to reach out to non-Christians, which was always very dear to the missionaries.[1] They looked for new avenues and opportunities to realise their desire.

The ill-fated exploration of 1850 forced the missionaries to retreat and to postpone their quest to spread the kingdom of God.[2] In spite of a positive report by Fr. J.M. Tissot,[3] which described the openness of the inhabitants of the Kondh Mountains[4] to God and the readiness of the tribals to ameliorate their life conditions, Msgr. Neyret was unwilling to sacrifice his confreres until they had acquired a better understanding of the mission and took every precaution against the fatal mountain fever. This required both time and personnel. However, the desire to establish a mission among the Kondhs and Panos did not diminish in the hearts of the missionaries. The 'almost savage life' of the tribals in the dense forests – content with whatever the forest offered them as food, often falling prey to wild and ferocious animals – cut them off from the *civilised world*[5] with no possibility of educating themselves and their children and deprived them of modern medical facilities. In short, the abject poverty of the Kondhs and the Panos attracted the attention of the missionaries.

However, the need to send missionaries to the northern part of the mission, particularly to look after the Christians in Berhampur and Cuttack, was realised after a pastoral visit by Msgr. Neyret, who, having seen the deplorable conditions of the Christians sent his priests to these stations.[6] Accordingly, Fr. Balmand was appointed to Berhampur to administer to the needs of Christians on the east coast, particularly in Ganjam, Berhampur, Russelkonda, Chatrapur and Cuttack.[7]

The First Expedition

In May 1853 Msgr. Neyret wrote to Fr. Jean Marie Dupont[8] in Berhampur, instructing him to proceed to the coastal area where the fishermen were said to have been open to the Word of God. Deterred by unpredictable climatic conditions on the coast, Fr. Dupont prolonged his stay. As he waited for a more suitable time to proceed to the proposed mission, he decided to explore the Kondh territory, especially the frontier.[9] He sought the assistance of Fr. Philippe Richard-Cugnet[10] in his search for a suitable place at the foot of the Kondh Mountains where they could begin their apostolic work. Initially, they set out without any precise plans or destination, depending totally on Providence to guide them to the right place.[11] After a few days, they reached a hut in Surada with the hope of staying there, but the people told them that it had been reserved for someone else. Expressing their indomitable courage and their resolve to win the people for Christ, Fr. Dupont wrote to Fr. Gaiddon:

> After we reached the place, the heat was very strong, and it was absolutely necessary to get a place where we could protect ourselves from the scorching heat. But there was no way of obtaining a hut where we could rest. However, we saw a miserable hangar and we were told that we could stay there. Thinking that this would be lesser grace, but even this favour was not accorded to us. Some people were found at the occasion of the anniversary of the death of one of their parents, in memory of whom a meal was held. For this reason, they told us that the place would be free in the evening. Therefore, we thought it would be better to go immediately to a forest nearby, situated on the banks of a river and at the foot of the mountain . . . Thus, instead of returning, I went ahead till the centre of the

village where I was surrounded by the majority of the inhabitants. As you may well think, I profited from a beautiful occasion to preach the truths of salvation. Till then, the poor people had never seen a person who preached the kingdom of God and who created them and the destination for which they were made. All that I announced was new for them.[12]

The servants of the missionaries warned them that the inhabitants of the village were 'thieves and assassins' and that there was no certainty that one would return safely upon entering the village.[13] By any standard it was a daring expedition as the missionaries were least prepared for any eventuality. The language of the people was unknown to them. It was very difficult for them to make themselves understood. Yet, they were courageous. These initial obstacles obviously did not deter them.

Montacallau (Surada)

The village they selected was called Montacallau,[14] situated on the outskirts of Surada. As Fr. Dupont approached the village most of the inhabitants surrounded him – their proverbial curiosity drew them to look at the 'white man' and to observe his manners and way of speaking. For a missionary who longs to make a breakthrough, everything is a god-sent opportunity to preach the message of love. So, Fr. Dupont used the chance to proclaim the Christian faith, despite the language barriers between the missionaries and their listeners. That was probably the first time that the villagers had ever met a missionary. Fr. Dupont sensed that their concept of God was very 'different and insufficient' as he came to know more about their superstitious practices, that he called 'offering sacrifices to demon'.[15] In the audience he found an old man, who served as a starting point for his future missionary endeavours. Narrating the incident to Fr. Gaiddon, Fr. Dupont wrote:

> One of the chiefs was moved by what I said regarding hell, of which he did not have any knowledge at all. I believe that the fear of hell forced him to convert himself immediately. But not knowing who I was, he asked: who would free me from my sins? Who would put me on the true path that leads to heaven? Where could I find someone who would instruct me in the true Religion in this country, is nobody capable of this? Then I said to him, if he truly desires to renounce the demons and serve only God, God himself would furnish all the necessary means. At that he told me: I am old and soon I will die, what is there, then, for me to do, if not to serve the Lord and to gain paradise for me? Seeing him well disposed, I said

to him, the person necessary for him to know the ways of salvation and all that was needed to reach heaven was there. That man has been sent to you by the Lord and toward that end he wished that I go after him, I was his minister and my work was to work for the salvation of souls.[16]

The man subsequently explained to the people the importance of the matter under discussion with the stranger. Since it was getting late, the villagers agreed to come on the following day to listen to him. Considering it to be a positive response, the missionaries hoped for a rich harvest. That motivated them to remain there and to look after the people who came into contact with them. The missionaries thus abandoned the idea of going to the seacoast for mission work, as Msgr. Neyret had wanted them. Without knowing the local language, it was not easy for Fr. Dupont to build a rapport with the people, much less discuss religion. He thought that his servant might be able to interpret what the missionary was saying in Telugu. But he later discovered that his translation was defective, and so he felt the need to learn the language. For the moment he memorised the translations of Christian truth, which he used to repeat in front of the gathered people. He insisted that his neophytes learn them by heart as well.

As the missionaries did not have a thorough knowledge of the people – their culture, their language, and their economic and political conditions – they had no specific method of evangelisation. Initially, they did not even bother with such concerns. All that they were interested in then was to find a breakthrough, which would bear fruit. Whatever they did, they did it to the best of their ability and according to the knowledge based on the only information available, which was an account of the military operations dealing with the insurgencies arising from *Meriah* and female infanticide.[17] Thus, one could conclude that the missionaries did not evangelize the people through the elegance of their discourses or by the lure of money, but by the simplicity of their lives and beliefs. This was confirmed by one of the village chiefs a few days after his baptism: "I don't know anything, but I believe in whatever you believe. I want to do all that you ask of me."[18]

Having experienced difficulties in finding a house, the missionaries had to be content with a simple place outside the village. Frs. Dupont and Richard sat under the big tree close to Montacallau, which became their favourite spot for teaching catechism and discussing topics on religion.[19] After six months, 184 persons were baptised.

As mentioned earlier, the missionaries' intention was to explore the possibility of establishing themselves at the foot of the Kondh Mountains, which, according to their calculations, would have kept them there for a short time. Therefore, they did not even take along enough provisions. However, they soon realised the openness of the people, and so they sought to establish a mission station at Surada. They chose a place by the riverside to build a provisional hut made of bamboo-and-foliage roof and mud walls. Since their hut was on the same level as that of the river, it was quite humid there. In his letter to Monsieur Mermier, Fr. Dupont wrote:

> During the first days, our place of refuge for the night was a hut. This place was open to all the winds, and it [the place where they chose to pitch their tent] was visible to passer-by and it was difficult for us to celebrate the sacred mystery. Every day we were obliged to go to the river. Soon we built a small hut closer to the river with the help of branches and leaves. We imitated the Kondhs who live around us.[20]

As the river rose during the monsoon, their hut was threatened, and they decided to leave the place till the end of rainy season, as suggested by Msgr. Neyret.[21] However, after four months they were back again in the same place to continue their apostolate among the Panos. Fr. Richard's transfer to Berhampur in March 1854 did not end the initial enthusiasm of Fr. Dupont. His enthusiasm was encouraged when he received a band of young and energetic missionaries to assist him in continuing the mission in Montacallau. They were: Fr. Antoine Guillermin,[22] Fr. Joseph Seigneur[23] and Br. Jean Pierre Piccot.[24] They were also instructed to extend their mission among the Kondhs.

Surada: The First Church in Ganjam

The participation of the Christians in Surada at Holy Mass and the evening prayers (e. g., the rosary) was encouraging, and one could witness the difference in their lives.[25] Placed at the foot of the Kondh Mountains, the nascent community of Surada had soon assumed a certain importance in the work of the Missionaries of St. Francis de Sales. It was the centre of their mission in the north, from where one could easily reach Berhampur, Cuttack and Ganjam. Therefore, they wanted to build a 'decent and beautiful' church in the 'desert'. Since they also had great hopes of winning more converts around Surada -- many villages invited the missionaries for instruction -- they decided to construct a presbytery there. They began the construction of the church in 1857, under the supervision of the superior of the mission, Fr. J. M. Tissot, who also had the difficult task of collecting money for the project. The missionaries even collected money from Protestants who contributed willingly.[26] They bought a suitable site in Surada, which was large enough even to have a dairy later on, and which included some paddy fields.[27] In one of the reports sent to the *Œuvre de la Propagation de la Foi*, Paris, Msgr. Neyret wrote that the number of Catholics in Surada in 1855 was 600, but all of them were dispersed in the forest.[28]

Obstacles

This initial work was not without obstacles that retarded the movement of grace, even if the missionaries had no power to avoid them. There were a number of issues that created an anti-Christian sentiment among the neophytes. To mention a few: there was a rumour among the people that the missionaries had a hidden agenda in the interest they had shown for the people and their families. The people believed that once the missionaries had learned the language and had become acclimatised to the ways of the villagers, they might kidnap some and send them to Europe, where they would become slaves or be forced into prostitution.[29] This obviously did not destroy the nascent mission, but it certainly slowed the movement that had begun with much promise. Even though there had been no reason to confirm their fears and doubts, the people were hesitant to cooperate with the missionaries when they asked the neophytes to come for prayers and worship.[30] The missionaries found it difficult to catechise the women, who were naturally shy and would not talk to strangers.

Their hut in Montacallau was inconvenient and unhealthy. In order to reach out to a growing community, they needed to move to a more central location. They decided to establish themselves in Surada, but obtaining land proved to be very difficult, since the British officials did not grant the necessary permission. Realising the difficulties in obtaining permission, the missionaries were initially resigned to living in solitary places in the forest. There they feared being attacked by wild beasts such as bears, lions, and other ferocious animals. There were also serpents, scorpions, etc., to deal with. Fr. Dupont described the situation:

> We are here more than a month, my confrere and I live at the beginning of
> the forest where the bears, lions and other ferocious animals roam around.
> Some have visited our house. When I went to sleep outside (the house)
> due to the heat, I was woken up to find a big serpent staying very close to
> my head. At that sight I pulled myself back for the moment. At another
> time we found a big black scorpion. We killed it and keep it as a souvenir.[31]

In addition, there were the initial difficulties of learning the language and
the culture of the people. Since the Panos were the ones who responded
to the missionaries, the missionaries had to learn Oriya, the common
language of the people, and to adapt to their culture.

Koussipanga

In March 1854, when more personnel arrived, the missionaries left their
first and provisional place (Montacallau) and went ahead to 'attack the
enemy' at the frontier. They ventured into the interior of the forest with
the hope of making more contacts. The number of villages in the Kondh
Mountains raised their hopes. One of the Kondhs who accompanied the
missionaries stated that on this trip they visited about 4,000 villagers.[32]
Urged by the desire to proclaim God's word to the Kondhs, Msgr.
Neyret, the vicar apostolic of Visakhapatnam, expressed his desire to
begin a centre among the Kondhs in the mountains. In the beginning
the missionaries were in favour of establishing themselves at Daringbadi,
where the climate was healthier. There were many surrounding villages
where the missionaries could preach the word of God.[33]

In their expedition to Daringbadi, the servants of the missionaries
were the ones who knew the language and the place. As they went along
they stopped at Koussipanga,[34] a commercial centre in the mountains,
where the servants had relatives. In the hope of obtaining the missionaries'
favour, the servants pre-arranged an impressive welcome for them. The
servants convinced the villagers that they were accompanying some
important, powerful and learned men, whose presence might bring them
good fortune. According to their custom, the village chief came forward
to meet the visiting dignitaries with fruit and other gifts. As a sign of
respect and welcome, the chief prostrated himself until Fr. Dupont asked
him to get up. The missionaries were highly moved by the unexpected
welcome accorded to them. At the request of the people, they pitched their
tents among them on March 25, 1854.[35] They were happy to announce
the Good News on the feast of the Annunciation, but soon realised that

their words fell on deaf ears. The situation did not improve either, for they met with indifference and hostility. They were quite different from the Panos of Montacallau.[36]

In view of the incomprehensible indifference of the Kondhs, the missionaries began to re-evaluate their strategy of reaching people. They thought that preaching in the streets and market places might bring similar reactions. The missionaries wanted to conform to the customs of the country and give the people enough time to realise that the missionaries were genuinely interested in them. So, they decided to learn *Kui*, the language of the people. As the vehicle of communication, *Kui* helped them to relate better to the people.[37] They were convinced that a personal rapport with the people was a precondition to any proclamation. The new situation demanded a different approach, and they decided to formulate a suitable strategy. They tried to introduce the great mysteries in 'little doses' – i.e., God, the soul and its immortality, sin and virtues, heaven and hell – so that these mysteries would be understood by the simple and illiterate people.[38]

Since they were ill-prepared for a long sojourn in the mountains, their physical endurance was drained when the temperature reached 36° or 37°C, leaving them prone to mountain fever. All fell ill at the same time. The people saw this as a curse from their god and kept themselves aloof, fearing that they too might be affected by the displeasure of their god. The situation worsened when their servants went to Berhampur to procure provisions and there was none to help them. But, in their dire need, a kind person came forward to collect water from the stream and to boil it.[39] Also, contrary to their expectations, the woodcutter smiled and showed them kindness. These were the first gracious signs that Fr. Dupont received from the people. Realising the goodness of the Kondhs, he asked them to help him in building their residence. So, they helped the missionaries to cut the wood necessary for their house.[40]

From that moment the missionaries were considered as friends, and the villagers did everything to help them. Nevertheless, their hearts were closed to accepting the Christian message. By the end of July 1854, after four months at Koussipanga, not a single person asked for baptism. Fr. Dupont did not want to give up, for he hoped to win the Kondhs one day. He wished that at least one person would be converted to justify prolonging his sojourn in Koussipanga -- even during the times of mountain fever. The hope of reaping a rich harvest was always present in the mind of Fr. Dupont, as can be seen from the letter that contains an account of conversions among the Kondhs.[41]

With the approach of the monsoon season the missionaries rightly thought of descending to Berhampur. Frs. Seigneur and Guillermin were sent first, while Fr. Dupont and Brother Piccot remained for a while longer. As he continued with his preaching, Fr. Dupont discovered to his great surprise that many were willing to receive baptism. Within two weeks he baptised about 250 persons. In spite of the invitations from other villages, he felt it prudent to retreat from the mountains but promised to come back once the rainy season was over.[42] However, the unexpected success brought a temporary cancellation of plans to establish a station at Daringbadi. Instead, they decided to build a chapel and a residence for the priest at the place indicated by the chief. Even though they later left Koussipanga for Surada, they continued to have contact with the people there, since they came down regularly to Surada to make purchases. It was quite natural for the Christians to pay a courtesy visit to the missionaries there.[43] The presence of the missionaries in Surada added colour to the festive mood when 18 persons received their First Holy Communion on September 15, 1854.

In order to foster a speedy evangelisation of the mission territory, Fr. J. M. Tissot persuaded Monsieur Mermier to appoint a superior to look after the northern part. He made clear that the suggestion was not meant to relieve him from the difficult task of organising the mission in the north but to organise it more efficiently. The great distance between Visakhapatnam and Ganjam was one of the reasons for the proposal.[44] At the annual retreat for the eight missionaries in Visakhapatnam, they had opportunities to reflect together on two important issues: (a) the observance of the rule of their congregation and (b) ways to advance the mission work entrusted to their care.[45] They wanted to put their reflections into a written form for their superiors.[46]

By 1860 the mission at Koussipanga had grown from its infancy to a developed station with a chapel and a small community of 360 Christians. The *pradhan*, the chief of the Kondhs, was very friendly to the missionaries, who recorded his kind treatment in a letter to the superiors and confreres in France. Undoubtedly the rapport the missionaries had with the *pradhan* helped the progress of the mission.[47]

Obstacles

In addition to the slow growth of Christianity, the missionaries were unhappy with the quality of life among the Kondhs. Fr. Dupont reported:

> Humanly speaking, looking at the happenings in Coussipanga [Koussipanga], especially at the beginning (of the mission), we could not expect great success. The drunkenness of the men, their indifference to salvation, their disinclination to receive us, the extreme savagery of the women who fled us because we looked dreadful, the state of health that each of us was in, none of these yielded a great hope for any success.[48]

The devotion and sacrifice of the missionaries did not produce the desired results. The attitude of the Kondhs gave the impression that they were not affected by the presence of the missionaries and that their efforts to bring about a qualitative change in the lives of the Kondhs were futile. The Kondhs were used to a free and easy-going life. It was very difficult for the missionaries to assemble them for instructions. Hence, they were Christians only in name, and they would resort to various superstitious practices. At the outbreak of any epidemic, for example, they would sacrifice a fowl to propitiate the angry god.[49]

The place where the missionaries lived was a good distance from the plain. The only provisions that they could procure such as salt, tobacco and other small items were sold locally by the merchants and were meant for the Kondhs. Time and again the missionaries had to send their servants to Berhampur. However, Mr. Snaize, a doctor who resided at Aska and was employed at its sugar factory, also helped them.[50]

A point of contention was the burial of the dead, a custom introduced by the missionaries.[51] The recently-converted Christians preferred to retain their tradition of cremating the deceased. But the missionaries, especially Fr. Dupont, insisted on burial. After much persuasion the people agreed. Unfortunately, an unpleasant incident marred the beginnings of this practice. At the insistence of Fr. Dupont, the family of a deceased young man agreed to bury him. But the villagers did not want the burial. As a result, they quickly dug a shallow grave and buried the young man there. The following night hyenas and jackals devoured the body. People were angry with the missionaries. However, they increased the depth of the graves and employed guards at night.[52] The missionaries felt the need to protect the cemetery from jackals, bears and other wild animals.[53]

Further Development in Koussipanga

In his letter to Monsieur Mermier, Msgr. Neyret wrote that before the missionaries came down to convalesce, they had prepared about 20 Christians for their First Communion and tried to train some of them as catechists. As the missionaries contracted mountain fever, they realised that it would require no small sacrifice on their part to continue the mission on the mountain.[54] Fr. Dupont received many invitations from the villages around Koussipanga but found it very difficult to travel with mountain fever.[55]

When he returned to his beloved mission, Fr. Dupont continued the work of evangelisation in the neighbourhood of Koussipanga. This time he was invited to one of the central places of the Kondh Mountains. He started his work in Arigadi, a village situated two *lieus* (four miles) from Koussipanga. While the disposition of the Kondhs was not encouraging, the enthusiasm of the Panos was more edifying. The missionaries often utilised the services of Panos as interlocutors when they approached a place where the Kondhs lived. In general, the Panos readily responded to the missionaries' invitation, whereas the Kondhs would wait and follow the Panos.[56] The Panos in Arigadi were so enthusiastic that they expressed their desire to have the presence of a priest among them. In fact, they went to Koussipanga twice in order to add weight to their request for a missionary who might stay in their village.[57]

Possession by evil spirits was common among the people, and they looked for a remedy to this problem. Often, they conducted rites and offered sacrifices with the hope that they would bring an end to the torment of the spirits' victims. In their desperation they turned to the missionaries for help. Fr. Dupont prayed over them and tried to drive the evil spirits away by sprinkling holy water. The people were discouraged when the prayers and blessings of the priest did not bring immediate healing.[58] However, there were some instances of successful exorcisms, which, besides creating an atmosphere of awe and fear among the people, provided a reason for them to trust the missionaries.

Since the Kondh mission did not bring the expected results – many Kondhs were still indifferent and converts often quickly fell away from the church-the missionaries decided to abandon the mission for a while. Added to this was the conviction that a longer stay was impossible without contracting the perilous mountain fever. Concerned for the well-being of his confreres, Msgr. Neyret decided to abandon the mission for a time.[59]

Mission at Gojolibady

When the missionaries returned to Berhampur during the monsoon, they were forced to halt at Gojolibady,[60] since the rivers were swollen. Unable to proceed further, their Indian helpers indicated a village where they took refuge. The *Bainihas* (Banias), a kolarian tribe, inhabited the village, and the servants had some relatives there. As Fr. Dupont preached, the people listened to him. They were even willing to be baptised. Thus, divine providence helped them to find a new community of Christians.[61] In his report to Msgr. Neyret, Fr. Dupont narrated their harvest in Gojolibady:

> On August 4, we reached Godervadi [Gojolibady] where we had the joy of meeting some Christians whom we had baptised last year in Surada. They seemed to be very happy to see us. Since we had the intention of reaching Berhampur at the earliest, we did not think of staying more than a night at Godervadi (Gojolibady). But someone told us that the rivers are full and that it is impossible to cross. We were obliged to stay a few days. But I did not want to spend the days doing nothing. I made an appeal to the inhabitants of a pagan village to adopt Christianity, and the majority of them appeared to be disposed. I hastened to baptise them, and 54 of them received it before our departure. With the other Christians who were there they formed a small congregation of 64. I hope that when we return the number may increase to about 20 more.[62]

In his indomitable courage and missionary spirit, Fr. Dupont proceeded to Ganjam (October 23, 1854) to build a hut among the fishermen, as there was some hope of instructing many of them. Fr. Richard accompanied him. He stayed there ten days for instructions, after which he went back to Koussipanga.[63]

Adaptation and the Emergence of Brahmin Christians

At a time when the missionaries were preoccupied with soul-winning, they were happy to employ any method deemed useful and relevant for their mission work among the people of Orissa. The missionaries were convinced that Christianity had to be preached in a way acceptable to all, irrespective of caste, and that restricting Christianity to the people of low-birth would only mean contempt. So far, the Missionaries of St. Francis de Sales (MSFS) found reception only among the Panos and Kondhs, both from humble origins. Therefore, they commenced evangelisation among those of higher castes, especially the Brahmins.[64] According to the missionaries, the Brahmins did not want to accept Christianity for the fear of losing caste, a social stigma that would bring ostracism.[65] The missionaries were convinced that the caste system could not be dispensed with, because it was embedded in the Indian psyche. To carry on the work among them, one had to be reconciled to this fact.[66] Although the missionaries sought Brahmin converts, they also realised that their hard labour among the Panos or others from a lower caste was justified-- despite the discouraging results--since true conversions marked deeper attitudinal changes on the part of such people who had been stigmatised as criminals.[67] Fr. Tissot stated that Fr. Seigneur had already found his first Brahmin followers in 1857. Fr. Seigneur had planned to instruct them in Christianity so that one day they could become catechists and would lead both Brahmins and others to Christ.

Opting for the Adaptation Method

The reasons for choosing the adaptation method became clearer when the missionaries read the work of Fr. Joseph Betrand, *La Mission du Maduré d'après les documents inédits*. The work illustrated the approach of the Jesuit missionaries in Madurai in converting both the Brahmins and other Hindus. The MSFS fathers in the Ganjam mission were fascinated by the content of the book; they admired particularly the method used by Fr. Robert de Nobili. They were searching for ways to penetrate into the interior areas, and so they were convinced that the best way of leading the entire populace to Christ would be through the conversion of the Brahmins, who had a respectable position in the caste hierarchy. The missionaries read the work several times and wanted to apply the methods used by Fr. De Nobili in the Ganjam mission.[68] Once their approach was even praised by a village chief, who stated that "If we come now, the others would not come; but if they start and if we follow, then they would not say anything".[69] Fr. Seigneur explained:

> Our progress in the ministry of the divine word met with great obstacles among the honourable portion of the Indian population. This difficulty comes, as you know, from the insurmountable horror that they have for foreigners or rather for those who do not belong by birth to both the faith and the strong fidelity to the customs of the caste, do not belong to the hierarchy of the pretended nobility. During the first years of our stay in Surada, knowing their touchiness on this point, we stayed in a village away from the capital. Our hut was hidden in the jungle. We could scarcely

have contact with anyone but pariahs. But afterwards, having placed our confidence in the infinite mercy of God and also foreseeing that we could not succeed even with the people of lower origin, when our holy religion became only the religion of latter, we chose a site for a chapel at the entrance of the big town of Surada.[70]

The missionaries recognised that the earliest converts from the lower castes did not have a favourable reputation among the rest of the population.[71] Therefore they wanted to begin their apostolic work among the Brahmins. In this way, they believed that they would remove the stigma attached to Christianity as *Parangi Margam* (the way of the Westerners or those who had been westernised). However, it is worth noting that the desire to obtain Brahmin Christians compelled them to refuse the request for baptism from none other than the village chief himself![72]

Some of the Customs Adapted by the Missionaries

In observing the practices of higher castes, one has to keep in view certain fundamental principles: (1) the Brahmins were forbidden to drink liquor and to eat meat; (2) they had to avoid any contact with the people of a lower origin, such as the Panos, the untouchables; (3) the higher castes did not like to leave a corpse in the house for fear of pollution; and (4) the use of saliva in the baptismal rite had to be dropped, as it is an unacceptable practice for an Indian. Fr. Seigneur tried to follow all the above-mentioned principles.[73]

Fr. J.M. Tissot, superior of the mission in the north, argued in favour of applying the adaptation method in order to convert more people to Catholicism. The principal accusations hurled at the missionaries were that they buried the dead instead of cremating them and that both the pariahs and noble people were allowed to worship in the same chapel. There were no purificatory ceremonies in Christianity, especially after the death of the family members. There were also other less significant accusations.[74] Fr. Seigneur insisted that the adaptation method was not the fantasy of a single person but a collective decision. He wrote: "Before we decided to live this way of life in Surada [as *gurus*, teachers or *sanyasis*, holy men], we went to Visakhapatnam for our annual retreat and examined the means or methods for the success of our project. The proposal to live a life of a *Sanyasi*, a scholar well-versed in religion [who commanded the respect of the people], was accepted as the method."[75] In order to avoid any misunderstanding, a certain distance was to be kept from other

Europeans, as they were considered to be *Sahibos* or lords (a title usually frowned upon as it recalled fear).[76]

Following the practice of Fr. Robert de Nobili, they learned and observed the manners and customs of the higher castes of the place. They wanted to imitate the lifestyle of the *Gurus* or *Sanyasis* by observing such practices as walking barefoot or using wooden sandals, eating only vegetarian food (rice, milk, vegetables and fruit) and avoiding the use of meat and any food prepared by someone other than a Brahmin. They also adopted certain purificatory rites: such as morning ablutions and cleansing oneself after contact with impure objects or persons.[77] They avoided interaction with the pariahs; whenever they had to deal with pariahs they followed the custom of maintaining a prescribed distance. They also preferred to give up their western habits of dress and used the saffron cloth for the cassock. Following the example of the *pundits*, the literati of Orissa, Fr. Seigneur used a pair of wooden sandals and a turban.[78]

Once a Brahmin from Benares who was on pilgrimage to Jagannath Puri with his two sons met Fr. Michel Périssin,[79] who was then in charge of the Cuttack Mission. As the missionary explained to him the true path to salvation, the Brahmin decided to embrace Christianity. He received baptism and was sent to Surada where he worked as a cook.[80] He thus made it possible for the missionaries, who had been eager to reach the higher castes like the Brahmins, to observe the typical mode of behaviour befitting a Brahmin. One of their subsequent successes in the village was the conversion of an influential Brahmin, who requested the missionaries to baptise him. He was known to be intelligent and commanded the respect of the people. The missionaries took pride in this conquest, as his presence in the village and his work would bring an immense benefit to the church.[81]

Fr. Joseph Seigneur, the 'Robert de Nobili' of Orissa

Since his appointment to Berhampur District, Fr. Joseph Seigneur was noted for his ability to learn the different languages of the place. He had been with Fr. Dupont on the Kondh Mountains for some time but was unable to remain there because of mountain fever. He was later sent to Surada to continue the work of evangelisation.

Following the illustrious example of Fr. Robert de Nobili, Fr. Seigneur adopted certain customs of the people, which, he thought, did not have any religious overtones. He used to meet the Brahmins regularly regularly to converse with them. Due to the constant flow of visitors, he was unable to keep a regular correspondence with Europe. Fr. Seigneur was also busy with the formation of catechists. However, he was concerned about the lack of good catechetical literature (prayers, hymns and songs in Oriya), which would serve the catechists when they went to the villages to evangelise. He wrote to Monsieur Mermier that he had a constant flow of Brahmin visitors who came to discuss religion with him.[82] Reporting on the manner of life of the confreres, Fr. Périssin wrote: "Our dear confreres of this station conform scrupulously to all the rules of caste, i.e. Brahmin. Their lives are like those of the Brahmins and even more perfect than theirs, because many things are allowed for the Brahmins but prohibited for our confreres. On this aspect I have no fear to propose this as an important model for all Indians to follow. Fr. Seigneur, this good father, would not even allow himself a slight transgression from the rules of caste."[83] Great were the sacrifices of the missionaries, and they did this willingly with the hope of winning souls for Christ.[84]

Unlike Fr. De Nobili, Fr. Seigneur did not build a hut in the Brahmin quarters, but he built one separate from the presbytery. He would retire there for study and prayer. He would receive visitors at certain hours only. The conversations with the Brahmins and other literati covered God, the soul, religion and some philosophical truths. Constant discussion about Hindu sacred texts obliged Fr. Seigneur to study Sanskrit.[85] Soon his fame spread, and people came from far and wide to discuss religion with him. He was also kind to those who would approach him for any blessing. He would bless the children brought by their mothers, who appreciated the fact that he held the children in his own hands, a symbolic gesture of special grace conferred by a religious person.[86]

He was so strict with the observance of vegetarianism that he reprimanded his cook one day when he found him roasting meat. He was aware that this could estrange people from the missionary, and it would be hard to remove any misunderstandings caused by this. In his heroic efforts of adaptation, he quickly ruined his health. Disappointed by the lack of interest shown by the Brahmins, Fr. Seigneur and the other missionaries freely decided to give up their efforts of evangelising them in Orissa. In 1860 Fr. Seigneur was transferred to Palkonda, where he died at the age of 36 of cholera contracted from the mangoes offered by one of his disciples.[87]

Fr. Seigneur and Aroto Misro, a Brahmin Convert

One of the Brahmins who had an influence on the people of Surada and who had the talent of composing lyrics in Oriya was converted by Fr. Seigneur. His name was Aroto Misro. Fr. Seigneur used the special talents of the Brahmin convert to compose lyrics in Oriya in order to explain the truths of the Christian faith, Christian morals and the sacraments.[88] With his knowledge of the sacred scriptures of the Hindus, he was a great help to Fr. Seigneur whenever the people came to him to discuss certain important aspects of the Christian faith. Together with Aroto Misro, Fr. Seigneur wrote the *Catholic Bhagavata,* considered to be on a par with the *Bhagavat Gita,* a pearl of the literature and philosophy of the Hindus. Some of the missionaries even thought that the *Catholic Bhagavata* replaced the *Bhagavat Gita* of the Hindus. Fr. Seigneur wrote: "Since we are the first missionaries in the Oriya land, we are obliged to write ourselves the prayers, songs, etc. I am in charge of this work and I have under me one of the important Brahmins of this place. He asked me to baptise him many times, but it needs to be seen. His little daughter is baptised, and she is called Mary. The name of the Brahmin is Aroto Misro."[89] Contrary to the claims of some of the missionaries, it is probable that Aroto Misro wrote the *Catholic Bhagavata* in its poetic form. Inspired by Dante's 'Divine Comedy', Fr. Seigneur might have encouraged the erudite Brahmin to put Catholic teaching into an epic form, modelling it after the current literary style. The work, the missionary claimed, was considered to be excellent by the educated and was generally appreciated.[90] Indeed, Aroto Misro was an invaluable addition to the mission. He had the intention of working as catechist. His first work was the 'Symbol of St. Athanasius', which included a short invocation to the Holy Trinity. He also busied himself with a treatise on paradise, which ran for thousands of verses.[91] The conversion of Aroto Misro raised the hope of the missionaries for a richer harvest.[92]

Failure

In spite of their earnest efforts to remove the stigma attached to Christianity, i.e., that it belonged to the lower caste people, the missionaries felt that their efforts were futile. In his letter to Monsieur Mermier, Fr. Dupont described the difficulty in getting the Brahmins into the Church: "In spite of our efforts to live and act like them, in the hope of winning more distinguished people, we need to wait. Whatever we do, there is always the indelible fact that we are Europeans and neither Brahmins nor penitent Indians. We cannot change our origin. Yet the Indians have a certain aversion to the Europeans, their manners and customs."[93]

The situation of Fr. Robert de Nobili was different. During the time of De Nobili Europeans were relatively unknown, and he could use his identity as a priest and his noble birth to influence the Brahmins. It proved to be effective, and the people readily accepted his claims. However, after several centuries of uninterrupted contact with Europeans, and more specially when people began to harbour a certain hatred for them, it was more difficult for Fr. Seigneur and his companions to touch the hearts of the Brahmins.[94]

Although Fr. Dupont emphasised in his letters that some individuals from higher castes had come to Christianity out of pure motives and showed interest in learning the prayers, their number was always negligible. He did not favour their service and was convinced that there was no hope for them. The only person who remained faithful was the cook, whose children were sent to the orphanage at Surada. In sum, the efforts at Surada to convert the Brahmins did not produce the desired results. There were only four Brahmin Christians, and these in fact were their domestic workers. Fr. Seigneur instructed them in view of training them as catechists.[95] However, one thing was clear: whether their converts were Brahmins or pariahs, they were all under the influence of the Hindus. If their chiefs were favourable to Christianity, they would have no problem in accepting it. Otherwise, even after having received baptism, they were inclined to return to their former religion.[96]

There was a rumour among the Panos that the missionaries received plenty of money from Europe for the people but spent it on themselves rather than distributing it among the newly-converted Christians. Without verifying such allegations, the Panos demanded their share of money. The missionaries protested against such calumnious attacks but to no avail. It was certainly for this reason that some of the village chiefs deserted Christianity. Fr. Dupont commented: "The Christian Panos, except the chiefs who received two *annas* on every Sunday, were no longer coming to the Church."[97] The Panos also resented the favouritism shown to the Brahmins and others of higher caste.

In their desire to convert the people of high caste, the missionaries adopted the local dietary practices, which ultimately affected their health. Hence, it proved impossible to live in such a difficult climate. Fr. Dupont complained that it was rare to find a conversion based on the purest of motives. The Panos and Kondhs looked for temporal rewards. Even Aroto Misro left the mission and took up the job of a priest in one of the temples because he thought that he had not been rewarded sufficiently for his conversion. It was said that some of the Brahmin Christians never received the sacraments of penance and Eucharist.

In view of such discouraging results and mixed motives on the part of the local Christians, the missionaries decided to send a memorandum to the vicar apostolic of Visakhapatnam asking to select a more favourable place for them to exercise their missionary activity. Instead in May 1859 Msgr. Neyret sent Fr. Tissot to study the situation of the mission and send him a report.[98] Having received the report, Msgr. Neyret went to Cuttack on a pastoral visit. On the way there he paid a visit to Surada (in 1860) to assess the situation personally. He finally decided to abandon the project of evangelising the people of higher castes in Surada.

Guiding Principles for the Orissa Mission

Once conversions began to increase, the missionaries felt the need to coordinate their efforts through certain common principles, which would secure the unity and continuity of the Ganjam mission. The missionaries gathered together for discussion in October 1858 under the leadership of Fr. Tissot, Superior of the Mission. This was the first time that they ever came together to decide on a course of action, which normally was left to the discretion of the individual. The Guiding Principles for the Orissa Mission were approved in October 1858 by Msgr. Neyret, vicar apostolic of Visakhapatnam. All missionaries working in Orissa were exhorted to read these rules during their retreat and to reflect on their implementation. The rules touched every aspect of their life and the mission.

A summary of these guiding principles (a rather long list divided into thirteen subsections) follows. [99]

Having recognised the role of the village chiefs (headman, catechist, clerk, *salvady*, etc.), the missionaries were asked to maintain a good rapport with them and to work in close collaboration with them, giving them due respect. The respect accorded to the chiefs should be equal to that shown to elder confreres. In general, the missionaries should not accept a candidate for the sacraments (i.e., baptism, marriage and confession) unless presented by the chief. Those guilty of an offence should be punished according to the local custom, but the chief should take the lead in rendering justice. Missionaries should intervene only when they felt that the punishment was unjust. The *salvady* and the poor of the chapel should be the priest's consultors. In case the missionary wished to talk to one of the Christians, it was best to call him or her through these consultors.

In general, the priest should not approve the chief's verdict of excommunication, since that affected the members of a family.

Baptism should be celebrated according to the custom of the universal Church. The children should be baptised within a period of ten days, in order to avoid mortal sin. The missionaries should ensure that the catechist knew how to administer baptism. However, he was not allowed to baptise, where a priest resided, except in *articulo mortis*. If he had to perform a baptism, he should do it in the presence of the chief.

Wherever the priest resided, First Communion should be celebrated with solemnity. The first communicants should be taught the catechism for a determined period. They should be asked to read a chapter of the catechism before Mass, instead of reciting prayers.

The first time a priest visits a community he should begin with a census, recording all the particulars possible. The visits of the missionaries should always be announced in advance. The missionary had to see to it that the faithful did not follow superstitious practices, visit temples, or visit the tombs of pagans. They also must not indulge in criminal activities. It would be good to bless their houses each year.

According to the local custom, the community on certain occasions forced some people to marry. On such occasions the priest should close an eye and allow them to do so. If the person refused to marry the girl he had seduced, he should be condemned and be made to pay for the damages according to the rules of the community. The gift offered to the priest during the time of marriage should be accepted in the presence of the village chief. The community should provide for the expenses of the priest.

Only priests, brothers and sisters on a journey could stay at the church. Without the permission of the parish priest no one should be allowed to bury their dead in the cemetery. The priest may or may not accompany the dead body to the cemetery. In all this local custom should prevail.

Missionaries should allow the people to celebrate the Christian feasts according to their custom, i.e., Christmas, Good Friday, etc. The beating of drums should be tolerated for the feast but should not be allowed in the church. Plays, if not scandalous to the manners of the locality, should be allowed.

The principal aim of the schools should be to impart religious instruction. Therefore, the missionary should ensure that the catechism is taught in the school. If time permits, he himself should teach catechism. The children from Malabar (Tamils) who study in English schools should be encouraged to learn the prayers in their own language. Non-Christians could be admitted to our schools. The offerings should be fixed for marriage, Mass and burial in the cemetery. The benefactors should be buried in the cemetery without any charge.

Every year there should be spiritual exercises conducted by one of the priests. Children before their first communion should also be asked to go through this spiritual exercise. It is desirable that the community recite the essential aspects of our faith before the Eucharist.

Reasons for Abandoning the Ganjam Mission

The missionaries decided to abandon the Ganjam mission temporarily for the following reasons:

First, experience proved that the missionaries could not penetrate the jungle and live in the area without contracting mountain fever, which forced them to leave the place. Those falling victim to the disease found it very difficult to regain their health and to continue their ministry there.[100]

Second, the missionaries found it difficult to employ suitable catechists to instruct the neophytes. A new mission like Ganjam could not prosper without the assistance of trained catechists. Being well-versed in the local customs and language, they could explain the Christian truth in a way acceptable to the simple people. The presence and work of one of their neighbours or relatives as a catechist motivated the people to enter the church in great numbers. Since the missionaries still did not have an adequate knowledge of the local languages, they often depended on their domestic servants, whose translations were defective and who themselves were in need of instruction in the Christian faith.

Finally, in spite of the presence of the priests and their prayers, superstitious beliefs and practices continued to reign among the Kondhs. Epidemics or natural calamities or accidents were thought to be the deeds of evil spirits. The people still offered sacrifices to placate them.[101] The missionaries did their best to stop all such superstitious practices, but their efforts were fruitless. In their frustration they decided to abandon the mission for a while. However, it was never a question of abandoning centres like Surada. They felt the need to leave a priest there to continue the work among the Panos, and if needed he could also help the Kondhs. Fr. Dupont made it clear: "Our ministry has met indifference, obstacles and contradictions everywhere. Those who are already converted do not correspond to their vocation. In addition to this, there is the usage and prejudices of the caste system, almost ready to ruin all our projects."[102]

These difficulties convinced the missionaries to abandon this part of the mission for the time being.[103] Reflecting on the information provided by the missionaries, Msgr. Neyret felt that the time for the conversion of the place had not yet arrived. Therefore, it was futile to sacrifice the health of the missionaries. He was convinced that their energies and goodwill could be used better elsewhere where they were most needed. Accordingly, he decided to leave Fr. Guillermin alone in Surada with the task of helping the existing Christians, while Fr. Seigneur accompanied Msgr. Neyret to Palkondah, where he concentrated on the conversion of the pariahs. [104]

Defection in Koussipanga

The initial enthusiasm of the Kondhs in Koussipanga soon died down. Christians were unwilling to take part in church activities, and their lukewarmness was accentuated by an incident that provided a cause for defection in 1862. In that year a severe famine was accompanied by an outbreak of smallpox, which ravaged the area. The Kondhs who had been afflicted by this calamity attributed it to the wrath of God because of the toleration and acceptance of the Christian faith and the missionaries in the Kondh Mountains. This view was held by their priest, who claimed that the God of the Christians was the cause for this misfortune in the country. This led to a widespread hatred of the missionaries. On the direction of the *Guru*, a general sacrifice was performed by the traditional priests of the Kondhs in order to propitiate the wrath of God. The people were advised to burn down the hut of the missionary, and if they were to do so in the dead of the night they might be able to burn the missionary as well. However, learning the villagers' evil intentions ahead of time, the missionary's servant removed the priest's belongings and advised him to escape. His belongings were hidden under a tree. Later, Fr. Guillermin found some coolies (porters) to transport them to Surada. Despite the prescribed animal sacrifices and the 'burning of the missionary' along with his hut, the smallpox remained unabated. The villagers were confused as to who could be the cause of this malady. They went again to the site where the hut of the missionary once stood to find out whether the missionary left anything that could continue to cause the calamity. At last they found a stone. Thinking it to be the God of the missionaries, they took it to Surada with due respect. The missionaries had a hearty laugh and explained to the Kondhs that the stone was used by Br. Piccot to sharpen his scythes and tools.[105] Ten years later the people came to Surada and requested Fr. Dupont to visit them. About 18 years after the missionaries left the place, Fr. Jean-Marie Descombes[106] visited Koussipanga.[107]

Defection in Surada (1864)

In spite of the painful decision in 1860 to refrain from seeking converts from higher castes and from the Kondhs at Koussipanga, the mission work among the Panos of Surada continued. Fr. Guillermin was left in Surada to keep the church alive in the two centres where there were some faithful. He also visited a few villages. However, his hard work in Surada met with indifference and coldness. This might have been due to the expectation of the village chiefs, who wanted monetary benefits for their role in bringing the people to the church. When they did not receive anything, they prohibited the Christians from going to the church. A warning was circulated that Christianity was incompatible with the traditional religion and that anyone continuing to practise the Catholic religion would be ostracised -- an undesirable state for the tribals.

The chiefs also convoked an assembly of elders and announced that Christianity was incompatible with the ancient practice of the caste system. They advised all Panos to follow their traditional religion.[108] This arrested the progress of the mission work. Fr. Guillermin consulted legal experts before he took action against the chiefs, who were acting against the law of the land. The case was brought to a superior court in Russelkonda, though the lower court at Surada was competent to investigate it. Realising that they were breaking the law of the land, the chiefs wanted to be reconciled with the priest and the Christians. They offered to revoke the excommunication and to pay a just compensation provided the case against them was withdrawn. However, Fr. Guillermin refused to withdraw it in the hope of teaching the chiefs a lesson so that they would neither trouble him nor the Christians in the future. In order to plead the cause, Fr. Dupont was called from Palcondah. But the verdict turned against the Christians, who did not explain themselves well in the court, whereas the pagan chiefs declared that they neither held an assembly nor prevented the Christians from practising their religion. In fact, the Pano chiefs denied all the accusations. The judge realised that there was little evidence to prove the claims of the Christians, and so he exonerated the chiefs.[109] This decision affected the Pano Catholics in Surada, since they were still a tiny minority within the community. It led to a general defection of the Panos in 1864.[110] Though they did not apostatise, their practise of religion was paralysed, and the number of conversions came to a standstill, resulting in the closing of the catechumenate.

In spite of the efforts of the missionaries, all but five families returned to paganism. What was most painful and difficult to understand was the attendant malice and hatred.[111] When Fr. Dupont came to the scene in 1865, the mission was practically in ruins. Writing to the *Propagation de la Foi*, Fr. Etienne Bonaventure[112] narrated:

> Because of the mischief and hatred, a schism was caused. In spite of the efforts and tears of the priests, with the exception of five families, all returned to their idols. The church was deserted, they abandoned the priest, the cohabitation was put on the agenda, the children were raised without baptism and the dead burnt in the forest according to their pagan rites.[113]

The church was empty, and no one bothered about the Christian faith. Fr. Dupont had the difficult task of rebuilding the community, which he did through his simplicity of life and knowledge of medicine. The Panos and Kondhs appreciated his service. People approached him to settle disputes. He gathered the children who had lost their parents and kept them in orphanages.

The Church during the Great Famine

The Orissa famine or the great famine of 1866 was one of the greatest natural calamities that befell the land. Due to the problem of communication with the rest of the country, Orissa remained isolated. It was especially vulnerable because there was no transportation to bring in the necessary commodities. It caused untold suffering for millions of people and left about 3,700,000 dead.[114]

Causes of the Famine

Since Orissa was located at the far corners of two presidencies (Bengal and Madras), the state remained a mere appendix. There was gross negligence of economic development, particularly in agriculture. Since the rivers had not been harnessed to provide irrigation, the people were left to the mercy of the rains.[115] Also, the Madras government did not implement any measure to provide help in times of drought and other natural calamities, and it had no reserve stocks of food. The rainfall in 1865 was scanty, which led to a scarcity of food.[116] The *Zamindars* and the other wealthy individuals had plenty of food and grain, but the government either took no control or relinquished its responsibility. Food was even exported to other parts of India. The price of grain rapidly doubled. Although the exorbitant price temporarily closed the markets, grain began to reach the district through the seaports and was available -- provided there was money to pay for it.[117] The poor were generally illiterate, shy and ignorant of the ways of reporting their misery to the authorities. In his description of the famine, Sahu observes:

> In January 1866 rice was not available at any price in Balasore and Puri. It became difficult for the Cantonment authorities to procure grains. In February numerous reports were received of incidents of grain-robbery and deaths on account of starvation. Conditions in the interior areas became so severe that some famine-stricken persons in Mahanga were reported to be eating human flesh by removing it from the dead bodies.[118]

The situation worsened in March 1866 with the outbreak of cholera and smallpox, which claimed a heavy toll in human lives. Drinking water became scarce, followed by widespread reports of deaths from starvation of both people and cattle in all corners of the district. Realising the gravity of the situation, the commissioner imported grain, but it could not be distributed on account of heavy rains and floods between July and September 1866. Although the government tried to maintain a number of famine centres where cooked food was provided to the poor, they were shut down due to the irregular supply of grain.

Effects of the Famine

The devastating famine depleted the resources of the people, who sold everything they had (jewels, animals, land, etc.) in order to procure rice, which was sold at exorbitant prices. Gradually the people began to lose their loved ones: many perished during the famine and some families even sold their children.[119] The poor in the district began to migrate to places where they could fill their stomachs, while others tried to survive on wild roots and leaves. Fr. Guillermin described the situation with a heavy heart to his bishop, Msgr. Tissot, who was on a visit to Europe: "Almost all the villages around here have suffered more or less. Some of the villages are almost half destroyed and others fully. The misery will not end for them with the harvest. Some people sowed a little part of their land and others nothing at all. What will these miserable people harvest?"[120] According to a report presented in the 'Annual Report' of the Madras Presidency, the effect of the famine was horrifying, since more than one third of the population of Ganjam district perished, and many were left as orphans.[121] The *Administrative Report of the Madras Presidency for the 1866-67* states:

> The superficial extent of the area affected by the famine in this district was 2,500 square miles, and the population 631,929 . . . After the distress was over, it was found that 550 orphans had been left without protectors. The Roman Catholic and Baptist missionaries took charge of 400, the government contributing 975 rupees monthly for their support. The maintenance of the remaining 150 was also undertaken by the State, till such time, as they may be able to earn their own subsistence.[122]

Sir Stafford Northcote (the secretary of state for India) gave a speech in the House of Commons which summarised the gravity of the tragedy and acknowledged the gross negligence of the British administration.[123]

As a follow-up, the government started many programmes for the social uplift of the people. Besides schools and irrigation canals, the government took the initiative to frame what is known as the Famine Code for India.

Response of the Missionaries of St. Francis de Sales

During the great famine a good number of Catholics (Panos) left their villages in search of food. Some of them moved into the mountains with the Kondhs with the hope of finding something to fill their stomachs.[124] In his letter to Msgr. Tissot, Fr. Richard described the misery of the Christians: "In Surada about 40 people (adults and children) slept in the Lord after having received holy baptism. Frs. Dupont and Guillermin have about 200 people without instruction, but till they are instructed and show a disposition to receive baptism, they cannot be accepted. They need someone in whom they can confide."[125] As the number of destitute children of both sexes increased, it required immediate attention on the part of the missionaries, who responded rather willingly but, as usual, struggled for funds to undertake such a gigantic enterprise.

Irrespective of their denominations the Christian missionaries were the first to respond to the calamity. Summing up the work of the missionaries in Orissa, Dasarathi Swaro commented: "They were the first men to sound a note of warning with a view to drawing the Government's attention to the impending problem and rousing the public conscience to the need of alleviating the distress of these people. They raised funds, efficiently organised relief operations, strongly criticised the Government's in-action and then heartily cooperated with it when it woke up to its responsibility."[126] The government established kitchens which distributed cooked food. The Brahmins refused this service fearing social ostracism from their caste for taking the food cooked by members of a lower caste.[127] The disastrous effects of the famine required immediate action from the MSFS for especially in favour of abandoned and orphaned children. The missionaries went around gathering children who could be brought to the orphanage, but some of them died on the way. Between June and September 1866, the priest in charge of Berhampur, Fr. Périssin, baptised about 544 children: a good number of them died and the rest were placed in the hands of their non-Christian parents. These were in addition to 125 children gathered at the beginning of September 1865.[128] Writing to Fr. Clavel in 1872, Fr. Périssin observed:

> When a few months later the great famine broke out and I had to shelter
> 5 caste children reduced to misery, I was happy to be in India. Soon, my
> family counted 15 children, then 20, then 100 – then several hundred
> which, with the help of Brother John Mary Punisset, I had to clothe,
> feed, shelter, instruct for baptism and burial. Within 6 months, helped by
> a few natives, I gave baptism to more than a thousand persons. 245 died
> in our arms out of 325 I baptised in the chapel, 88 of them during the
> month of October.[129]

Some of the tales were heart-rending, such as the child found on the dead body of his mother. Francis the catechist generally accompanied the missionary when they went looking for the children. The ones who were sick would be baptised immediately and the others would be taken home. Upon his return the missionary would offer a rupee or two to the family obtaining a promise that they would never reclaim the child after the famine. The children gathered this way would be sent to Berhampur.[130] The number of children under the care of the mission grew, as did the costs. The missionaries needed about 5,000 franks to build an orphanage to accommodate more children.[131] In any case, the missionaries were satisfied with the possibility of baptising them *in articulo mortis*. Mentioning the work of Francis, *Assainissement des marais* recorded: "Brother [catechist] Francis was sent by Father Richard to a place called Khurda, during the famine of 1865 [1866] to baptise the children *in articulo mortis*. When he had baptised nearly 700 of such children, he was accused by the people as a sorcerer and was put into prison, because they said that every child on whom he poured water died, as a rule."[132] The missionaries were thus constrained to maintain orphanages in Orissa. Every effort was taken to sustain the orphanages with funds collected from abroad and from the government,[133] which paid a monthly allowance of two rupees.[134]

Since the missionaries were busy gathering the children, their care was given to some of the women, who were also victims of the famine. They received food and protection from the missionaries. As the number of children grew, they felt the need to open yet another orphanage in Surada itself. Writing about the achievement of Msgr. Tissot, a newspaper cutting of July 25, 1891 says: "The foundation of the agricultural settlements of Surada and adjacent villages which he [Msg. Tissot] made to rise out of the jungles on the hilly tracts of the Ganjam district . . . provided comfort and provision for hundreds of orphans and a large number of paupers."[135] The missionaries thought of establishing it at

Surada, where they had vast enclosures that could serve the purpose. Frs. Dupont, and Guillermin were given charge of the orphanages. The children ranged between eight and ten years of age and sometimes even younger. The older ones were taught to take care of the younger ones. As the health of the little ones was so feeble, many of them soon fell ill. The orphanage looked as though it were a hospital. With their paltry resources the missionaries could not cope with the extra expenses, so they appealed to the charity of the public. The orphanage was enriched by the presence of Dr. Clarke and his wife who, after having served in the British army, came with a pension sufficient to look after themselves. He decided to help the mission in whatever way possible.[136] The order of the day in the orphanage consisted of 'attending class', which simply meant that they learnt to read and write Oriya and learnt the rudiments of arithmetic. Since the missionaries prepared the children to take up the cultivation of the fields, the basic knowledge provided, according to their view, would suffice. With the hope of bringing them up as solid Christians, an explanation of the faith was given them. In their free time the children learnt some hymns, which they sang joyfully whenever they went to work.[137]

In order to provide sufficient resources for the orphans and the poor Christians as well as to be self-sufficient, the missionaries purchased two villages: Dantholinghy and Caricotte. The government gave them these places at a minimal cost with the privilege of tax exemption, since they were for charitable purposes.[138] They bought the land at the rate of 10 franks per acre in the northern part of the mission. Though the property was well situated, it was covered with shrubs and needed a lot of work before it could be turned into arable fields. The boys were sent to this property, while the girls remained in Surada with the Sisters of St. Joseph of Annecy, who took care of the girls' orphanage. The boys went to the forest every day to fell trees and to demarcate fields for cultivation. Fr. Guillermin hired some Kondhs to help them, but due to fatigue compounded by the heat and the insalubrious air, he himself contracted a disease that led to his premature death on December 8, 1869, at the age of 47. On the death of Fr. Guillermin, Fr. François Louis Décarre[139] was called from Cuttack and was sent immediately to Thotavally. At this time the children wanted to visit their parents and relatives. Some of them left the orphanage without telling Fr. Dupont, but later they were brought back to the orphanage. Soon this became a precedent. The missionaries knew well that their return to their relatives was tantamount to returning to paganism. Therefore, they took all precautions to avoid that.[140]

When the boys grew up they married the young ladies brought up in the orphanage run by the Sisters of St. Joseph of Annecy in Surada. Such marriages were celebrated with solemnity and pomp. The newly-weds were settled in a small village set aside for this purpose; they were also given a plot of land for cultivation, bulls, and other items necessary for a family. This was the dream of the missionaries that the children raised in such manner would turn out to be faithful Christians.[141] In this way two Christian villages arose in Caricotte and Dantholinghy. As had been hoped, the Catholics brought up in the orphanages and settled on the land allotted to them by the mission proved to be faithful. In writing to the *Propagation de la Foi*, Fr. Bonaventure reported:

> We have now 47 families with a lot of little children. The number of the total orphans raised in the orphanage is 237 persons, fully under the charge of the mission. The missionary was their father, their judge, and their doctor. Without any doubt, modern civilisation has not yet reached them; but our children know how to read and write in Oriya; they are able to manage their accounts or counting; they know their morning and evening prayers by heart; and they are able to understand well the truth of their faith."[142]

There is no doubt that the orphanages brought a qualitative change in the life of the people.

Literary Activities

Language is the vehicle through which one can enter into the life or spirit of any cultural or linguistic group. The missionaries understood this very early, and they profited from the time allotted for learning the language. In the absence of a developed method for learning *Kui*, the language of the Kondhs, the missionaries spent a lot of time studying it. Initially, Fr. Dupont carried a pocket notebook and a pencil to note down the new words that he might learn from the people. In order to learn the right pronunciation, he repeated the sentence till they would approve his pronunciation.[143] In this way, he compiled a dictionary that would serve the French missionaries sent to the Kondh Mountains for mission work. Informing Monsieur Mermier about his activities, Fr. Guillermin wrote:

> As for me, when I had a few good moments, I used them to copy a Dictionary, written by the Rev. Fr. Dupont. Some time after I had finished this work that took me a lot of days, I lost it without finding any trace

of the same, which I consider a great loss. Such a loss that I did not have the courage to write it again, before the author revised and corrected the edition, because the first edition had many words that were not Cond [Kui]. In the meantime, I took down the words that I heard and understood. I had a good number of them when I came down. But unfortunately, I lost this new notebook. I recovered it however much later.[144]

As the MSFS were the pioneers in that part of Orissa, out of necessity they had to compose all the prayers and songs in Oriya.

Just as any beginning demands its price and sacrifice, so too did the planting of the church in the Kondh Mountains require dedication and toil. But the missionaries never wavered. In spite of the relatively short distance between Ganjam and Gangpur, the inhabitants of the semi-independent state of Gangpur had a different approach to the missionaries and to Christianity. The Gangpur mission was considered to be a place of punishment because of its isolation both from Calcutta and from Ranchi and because of the need to learn Oriya, Sadri and the tribal languages. But on the other hand, the Belgian Jesuits felt at home in Gangpur, because they did not encounter a new people and in fact, it was an extension of the Chotanagpur mission.

Gangpur Mission

An exceptional characteristic of the conversions in Chotanagpur was their spontaneity. Normally a village delegation conveyed to the missionaries its willingness to accept Christianity.[145] Having noticed the change in their kinsmen across the border, the Tribals of Gangpur sent deputations to Biru so that they too might receive the services of the missionaries.[146] The missionaries continued to receive such deputations from among the tribes of the remote jungles of Chotanagpur. The impulse on the part of the missionaries to extend the mission towards the semi-independent State of Gangpur came because of the ethnic affinity that the Tribals of Chotanagpur had with those of Gangpur.[147]

Like their kinsmen of Chotanagpur, the tribals of Gangpur experienced a similar hardship; an economic oppression that consigned them to the lowest state, a condition which the missionaries vowed to eradicate among the Tribals of Chotanagpur. Thus, the missionaries found it easy to apply the same methods which had produced good results in Chotanagpur.

The periodic visits of the priests to Gangpur prior to 1908 did not ameliorate the condition of the people. There were defections even among those who had been liberated from *Bethbegari*, the forced labour, while others had fallen prey to the mounting economic tensions. They did not receive the help they had expected from the missionaries; whose visits were infrequent. The presence of the missionaries among the neophytes was essential for their spiritual growth and economic progress.[148] The catechists appointed by the missionaries as contact persons and upon whom much of the expansion work depended were inefficient and often immoral. There were complaints of drunkenness and quarrels. However, the periodic visits of the missionaries kept the Christians together. The missionaries hoped that if the permission to commence a station in Gangpur were granted, the Jesuits would be ready to live among the people to guide them and protect them from the usurious moneylenders and landlords. Fortunately, some of the Catholics of Gangpur sent their children to schools across the border, i.e., to Kurdeg, Samtoli and Rengarih. This provided them with occasions to contact the missionaries and the catechists.[149]

Activities of the Jesuits: Frs. van Rabays and de Smet

After the historic visit of Fr. Fierens, which took him through Gangpur, Fr. de Smet was the pioneer of the Gangpur mission. While he was the assistant parish priest at Biru, he had the task of evangelising the people from the southern part of Biru. In his letter to the provincial, he wrote:

> It is necessary for me to build a second station at the limits of Biru and Gangpur, about 5 to 6 miles from here in a place called Salangabahar. I will dedicate the mission to Our Lady of the Immaculate Conception. This is the dream of my life. It was I who, in 1889, was the first missionary to set foot in Gangpur. I can remember it well; it was on a Saturday. I came back from the small kingdom of Anandpur, where a priest had never entered since Adam. I visited 11 Christian villages in a day, while passing by woods and mountains. I was told, 'this village far away is Naogaon, a Lutheran village. This is Gangpur'. They showed me the stone of separation (boundary stone). But in fact, there were at Gangpur only a few immigrant Catholics. All the others were pagan and a few Lutherans. I descended from my horse and, as it was Saturday, I consecrated myself, a poor missionary, and the Gangpur to the Immaculate. That happened in December 1889. My Reverend Father, may she who had destroyed all heresies . . . come to help us at Gangpur. The German Lutherans have two stations, but we only recently could acquire ground on which to build.[150]

Fr. van Rabays was interested in the work of the Gangpur mission in 1904. His diary is full of references to the mission in the eastern part of Gangpur (Nagra district or the present Rourkela and Jhunmur parish territories). He made his first tour of the mission in November 1904. Vermeire recorded the following entry from the diary of van Rabays:

> This month I went to Gangpur and visited all the villages except Goilo. I was everywhere very well received, and the Christians seem to be well disposed, but know very little. Jaedega and Babaimohan knew the most. I had to dismiss the *prachar* (catechist) of Ghaghari, Dharmdas, who it seems has left his wife in Barway and has taken a girl of Kadobahar."[151]

In his second tour, he visited most of the villages and recorded in his diary the conditions and the need of the Christians.[152] Explaining the condition of the Gangpur mission, Fr. van Rabays wrote:

> In Gangpur, 10 hours from here (Samtoli), there are 3000 Christians who ask for a chapel, schools and masters. The Lutherans have much money at their disposal. Over 5 years we have gained many of their villages and we have not lost any. Almighty God helps us visibly and I should not be surprised at all if in this year 1905, I might still win over 8 more villages to the Catholic Church.[153]

After the death of Fr. van Rabays, the work of evangelisation in Gangpur was placed in the hands of Fr. de Smet. In response to a village delegation that came to Samtoli to meet him, he sent both Johan *Munshi* (clerk) and Johan *Prachar* (catechist) to gather information about Gangpur, especially in the eastern part of the state, i.e., the Rourkela region. They spent about two weeks there and gave a positive report of their visit.[154] In the eastern part of the mission a considerable number of Catholics came from Lutheranism.[155]

During his first tour of Gangpur, Fr. de Smet was very impressed. He mentioned this in his diary:

> (On) 13 May 1907, I am off to Gangpur and the eastern part of Biru. Everywhere well received; people were well disposed; in many places Mass (was celebrated) underneath a large tree, because the chapels are not ready. I baptised people of at least 3 years adherence in the villages. I did not baptise any children of the *Berxa* [*Berga*] Uraons; that will be for the next time . . . In Gobira (Nagra) some people, all new catechumens, objected to going to Church, saying they would lose their caste! They wrote a *mchilka* [undertaking] stating that they would go regularly. In Nagra, the Zamindars

are against us because our people go to court for redress of grievances, not against Lutherans. Our fellows are threatened a great deal. [156]

Obstacles to the Progress of the Mission in Nagra

In the Nagra region the *Zamindars* were against the Catholics as the latter turned to the court to redress their grievances. Since the Lutherans did not do the same, they were preferred. Efforts were made to arrest the catechists and some of the leaders in order to intimidate the people. The threats were accompanied by visits of the police inspector and of armed policemen. Fr. de Smet described the situation in these words:

> The Ragunathpali Inspector with ten men with guns, swords and sticks went to Gobira on 20 September. He told the *prachar* [catechist] Francis: we do not want Romans in Nagra; go away, it is the order of the *Dewan Saheb* of Suadi [the capital of Gangpur]. Francis answered the Inspector: 'You and I are servants. If my *saheb* tells me to go away, I'll do so, but not before.' Then the Inspector went away to the *bhandar*. Thus, a vain threat![157]

The zamindars and the police harassed the Catholics and their catechist. Fearing that there might be resistance from the Catholics, they sought help from the armed police and obtained an order to shoot if there was any resistance when they arrested the catechist Francis. Realising that intimidation and threats did not produce results, the police wanted Francis and the Gobira people to sign a paper, but they refused, as the content was not disclosed to them. At this, Francis was arrested and taken to Ragunathpali, and none of his companions were allowed to meet him there. He was later acquitted on the intervention of the *Dewan* of Gangpur, M. Craven,[158] a Catholic and a friend of Archbishop Brice Meuleman of Calcutta.[159] However, these threats and difficulties did not arrest the progress of the mission.[160] Fr. de Smet had this entry in his diary:

> 5 April 1908. I went to Gangpur – Kinjir for 36 days. Everywhere well received by those poor children. A glass of beer [*Hanria* = rice beer], sometimes drinkable, sometimes wretched, yet I must take it, or when nauseous, give it to the small brats about me. In some villages the women and girls had never seen a European and they were shy like jackals, but later on they came to perform a dance, for their pleasure and in my honour. May the Lord have mercy on them. Goilo, Jorobahar, Chuanbahal, Kokrema, etc., were grand. In many villages Mass under a tree![161]

In spite of the pecuniary difficulties, Fr. de Smet sent catechists and *chaprasis*[162] wherever possible so that they might establish contact with the

people. During his second tour of 19 days in April 1908, he contacted
a large number of villages in the north of the Sankh river, particularly
in the Nagra and Kinjir region. Altogether one could count about 6,000
catechumens, and he felt that "to manage the north of Nagra – Kinjir and
the south of Nagra, we need a new Gangpur station, say in Rourkela . . .
otherwise the Anglicans of Chaibasa, who already have a few adherents
round about Ragunathpali, and the Lutherans of Chakradharpur will sweep
away Saranda, etc."[163] It was indeed the perseverance of the people that
brought the zealous missionary to them despite the scorching heat.[164]

A New Beginning

In 1907 the Gangpur mission had about 6,700 adherents (baptised and
catechumens). The first contacts seemed to have come from Noatoli
in 1901 when the missionaries established their residence in Biru, not
very far from the frontier of Gangpur at Kompala.[165] Until 1904 only
the Rengarih mission station was catering to the needs of the Gangpur
Catholics. Later Samtoli and Kurdeg were divided, and these continued
the expansion work. A geographical view of these stations would place
them along the length of Gangpur State. Rengarih, the central station,
was to take care of the expansion in and around the present Kusumdegi
station. Samtoli, in the eastern part of the mission, catered to the spiritual
needs of Kesramal, Hamirpur and Jhunmur. Kurdeg, in the western part,
served as a base for the expansion work in and around Gaibira and in
the next semi-independent State of Jashpur.[166]

Early Impediments to Missionary Extension

From the beginning the Catholic mission was ordered by the British
government not to start a mission in the native states without their
permission.[167] As noted earlier, the interest in the expansion of the
mission in Gangpur was sparked by the first deputations from Gangpur.
The missionaries could not take a decisive step until the appointment of
a new archbishop of Calcutta, Msgr. Brice Meuleman. In 1901 he gave
permission for an expansion into the independent states. However, the
raja of Gangpur was an absolute ruler, and he restricted the movement
of Europeans within his state. Therefore, no European missionary
could reside within Gangpur without his permission. Despite persistent
requests of the missionaries, the raja was reluctant to grant permission
for the acquisition of land.

Early Attempts to Establish a Mission Station in Gangpur

In 1903 Fr. Hoffmann, due to the good rapport he enjoyed with the British government officials, went to meet the raja at Suadi, the capital of Gangpur, carrying a letter of recommendation from Mr. Slacke, the commissioner of Chotanagpur. Although Fr. Hoffmann was initially reluctant to meet the Raja, he changed his mind after receiving the support of Craven, the *Dewan* or prime minister of Gangpur. Craven told the raja about Fr. Hoffmann, especially his work among the tribal population and for the British government in India. He suggested that an acquaintance with Fr. Hoffmann would benefit his state.[168] The raja consented to an audience, but he held to his position of not granting the permission to establish a mission station in Gangpur. Discouraged by the outcome of the meeting, Craven wrote to Msgr. Meuleman that the Raja had invited a man to travel the distance from Ranchi, at the height of the rainy season, simply to tell him that it was impossible to grant his request. Such an answer any civilized person could have conveyed through a letter. It seems clear that the Raja wanted to reject the mission in the most insulting manner he could find.[169]

Informing Fr. Grosjean about his excursion to Suadi, Fr. Hoffmann wrote that it was useless to try anything with the Raja, since he was angry with the missionaries because of the false charges made by Dr. Nottrott against him to the commissioner, viz., that he had made over his *rayats* in *Bethbegari* to a European timber merchant.[170]

Craven, the *Dewan*, was also present during an audience when the Raja became indignant and described the troubles that the missionaries (obviously the Lutherans) had caused. He underscored at least two of them: (1) the upset created in the local administration by Birsa and his followers[171] -- the Raja thought they were Catholics; and (2) the complaints that Dr. Nottrott had made to the British authorities in India against the Raja, who was said to have imposed the drudgery of *bethbegari* or forced labour.[172] The Raja was infuriated at the mention of these complaints and used certain derogatory remarks against the Lutheran missionaries. It is quite clear that the Raja was unable to differentiate between the various Christian denominations that were present in his kingdom.[173] Thus the Catholics had to expiate for the sins of the Lutherans.[174]

Before the submission of a formal application to the Raja of Gangpur through Fr. Hoffmann in 1903, Msgr. Meuleman had already sent a letter on May 20, 1903 to the Raja, explaining the advantages of allowing European missionaries in his state. He wrote: "The presence of a European missionary would highly contribute to the improvement of the Christians, already becoming numerous, and to the temporal welfare of his honour's subjects, by diffusing secular instruction and education, and by developing habits of thrift and industry."[175]

F. A. Slacke, the commissioner of Chotanagpur, was kind enough to send a letter of recommendation to the Raja of Gangpur, gratefully acknowledging the services that the missionaries rendered to the tribals of Chotanagpur. He recommended that the Raja grant his permission so that the tribals of Gangpur too could avail the services of the missionaries. However well intended might have been the recommendation, the Raja refused to be influenced by such and was very unrelenting in his decision.[176]

Reasons for the Entry in Gangpur

No sooner had the Raja of Gangpur turned down the request than the Fathers applied for general permission to visit the Catholics and administer the sacraments. Slacke, the commissioner, responded favourably without any appeal to the Raja.[177] As a result, the missionaries were able to enter Gangpur to administer the sacraments and to board the train to Calcutta, where they were expected to attend the annual retreat and meet their superiors. The train journeys to Calcutta and back enabled the missionaries to offer spiritual help to the Christians, who otherwise had only the services of the catechists. Each time a missionary boarded the train in one of the railway stations in Gangpur, he sent ahead a message to the villages to be visited. The catechists organised the people in these villages for receiving the sacraments, which was normally preceded by a *Panchayat* or village council.[178] The missionaries also hoped to check the growth of Lutheranism under the Gossner Evangelical Lutheran Church, whose work in the area had already been noted by Fr. Fierens in 1884. He noticed a large, well-organised congregation at Raiboga. Since the Lutheran mission prospered, Fr. Alary perceived that his mission was in danger, and he wrote to his superior general accordingly. Therefore, the missionaries of Gangpur made every effort to convert the Lutherans also.[179]

Kesramal: First Parish of Gangpur

Gangpur was a semi-independent state, and the Raja was its sole ruler, but it was under the suzerainty of the British Raj. Fr. Vermeire wrote that "the Raja depended for his semi-independence on the good graces of the Government [British] and dread[ed] nothing more than a commissioner's investigation into his behaviour".[180] The only control exercised by the British government was through the political agent[181] residing in Sambalpur and his control generally consisted of an annual visit to the state. An important feature of the state was the presence of a major railway line that promoted trade and commerce. The whole length of Gangpur, about 70 miles, was crossed by one of the chief railways of India, the Bengal - Nagpur Railway.

Kesramal lies in the plains which are surrounded on all sides by hills. During the summer the heat is intense, rising up to 112° F in the shade and about 160° F under the open sun.[182] The superior regular of the mission forbade his missionaries to leave the presbytery between 10 A.M. and 4 P.M. There were about 300,000 people, mostly Hindus, all of whom were subject to the Raja of Gangpur. As Kesramal was far from the mission stations of Chotanagpur, the missionaries felt isolated there. Sometimes they were unable to take part in meetings due to the distance and the rains, which made it difficult for them to cross many rivers.[183] However, a visionary like Fr. Grosjean would not fail to see the strategic importance of Kesramal as a central place in the central provinces. From Kesramal the missionaries could travel to Singhbhum territory in the east, to Orissa in the south and to the central provinces in the west.[184]

Despite the initial misgivings about allowing the Catholic missionaries in the territories and his adamant refusal to grant their petitions, the Raja seemed to have had a change of heart in 1907. This change was due to the presence of Mr. Craven, who was then appointed as the Raja's prime minister. Through his good offices and -- more effectively still -- through the good offices of Sir Andrew Fraser, the lieutenant governor of Bengal, the Raja was forced to concede. The hostility of the Raja did not deter the missionaries from pursuing their aim to establish a mission station in Gangpur. Regarding the purchase of land at Kesramal, Fr. Cardon wrote:

> Fr. Hoffmann had been sent to the Raja of Gangpur in August 1905, if I remember correctly, to ask for a plot of ground and leave to establish a station in his State. He was flatly refused. In May 1906, His Grace (Msgr. Meuleman) went to the Political Agent at Sambalpur. I was with him. The

> Political Agent then settled the business with the Raja, who then gave us a bit of land, 7 ½ acres, at Kesramal. This was gotten in the beginning of 1907.[185]

Earlier, Sir Andrew Fraser, the lieutenant governor of Bengal, had directed the Raja of Gangpur to concede a plot for use by the Catholic mission; should the Raja fail to comply he would then be forced to grant it. This move forced the Raja to permit the missionaries in Gangpur. They acquired 7 ½ acres of land at Kesramal, six miles to the north of the Rajgangpur railway station.[186] Fr. van Severen had the privilege of being the first priest of the newly-erected parish. In 1909, Br. Rotsaert, an architect-builder, was sent to construct a convent for the Sisters, Daughters of the Cross, from Liège, Belgium.[187]

The Contributions of the Three Pioneers

Two of the pioneers of the Kesramal station were Frs. Grosjean and Alary, whose years of hardships and hard work won thousands of Catholics to the Church.[188] A third pioneer was Fr. van Severen, who, as the first missionary, experienced considerable difficulty in undertaking this task alone.

Kesramal under Fr. Emile van Severen

Kesramal began on May 13, 1908 with the arrival of Fr. van Severen from Rengarih, the ecclesiastical district headquarters (at that time Fr. Cardon was the district superior).[189] When Fr. van Severen took charge of the mission he inherited 6,874 Christians.[190] Initially he lived in a *tugurium*, a peasant's hut. Describing the initial difficulties which Fr. van Severen had to endure, Fr. Camiel Lievens wrote: "Father van Severen crossed over in the heat of the warm season, since the rainy season would start soon. His only shelter was a small tent, which he arranged as a chapel, and an old hut of 7 x 10 feet. Soon he constructed a building, which, he thought, would later become a boys' school."[191] The charity of the mission during the famine of 1908, which affected the whole of India, brought about 2,000 new adherents to the Catholic Church, among whom about 700 were Lutherans.[192] The new Kesramal station had a distinct character from the rest of the mission in Chotanagpur. In addition to the local languages – Hindi, Sadri, Mundari, Kurukh and Kharia – the missionaries had to also learn Oriya, the official language of the state. In May 1908, when a school for the boys was built, it served also as a residence for the priest and as a chapel. During the monsoon, a severe outbreak of cholera killed about 20 people. This was immediately followed by smallpox.

In January 1909 Msgr. Meuleman and the superior regular of the Mission, Fr. Hippolite Waelkan, paid a visit to the new mission station of Gangpur to assess the situation.[193] Fr. Vermeire did not record the initial missionary endeavours of Fr. van Severen, but he explained the reason why he was transferred to Khunti: "As to Father van Severen remaining only one year, the chief reason was the shortage of missionaries. Since a new language had to be learned, Uriya [Oriya], for the schools of Gangpur, it was better to take a new and younger missionary like Father Alary than to keep the elderly Fr. van Severen there, accustomed to the Mundas and their difficult languages."[194]

Thus, Fr. van Severen gave way to a younger missionary, Fr. Alary, who took over the mission on February 9, 1909. It was during the time of Fr. Alary that systematic village visitation and socio-economic projects were implemented.

Kesramal under Fr. Alary

Fr. Alary was the head of the mission in Gangpur between February 1909 and November 1909 and again from September 1915 till his death in September 1918. During this time Fr. Alary spearheaded the evangelisation work. His diary is full of references to his many visits to Gangpur where his main responsibility was to gather the people and listen to their grievances. He used the visits to instruct them in the faith, to celebrate Holy Mass with them, and to hold the *panchayat*, the village council, with the *panches*, the village elders. He introduced the devotion to the Sacred Heart of Jesus on the first Friday of the month, which was always attended by many. The attendance was so great that the ordinary people, with the exception of children from the school, were unable to distinguish between Sundays and Fridays.

During his village visits Fr. Alary noticed the absence of women in the church.[195] This was because several of the women were Lutheran and their marriages were not rectified. He showed a special interest in settling marriage cases.[196] The marriage settlement, he thought, would restrict the spread of Lutheranism, which had always remained a constant threat to the Catholic missionaries. The Lutherans had enough funds at their disposal and were well organized. In contrast, the scattered villages and the difficult communication between the catechists and the missionaries caused great fatigue to the missionaries.[197] A breakthrough came with the blessing of several couples from the *Berga Oraons*, known as *Kisans*, a group that followed the tribal religion and was very orthodox in their beliefs.[198] In fact, Fr. Cardon declared, this was the first time that Berga Oroans accepted Christianity. Following the example of the first group, there were several couples from the Berga Oraons who were baptised in the Catholic Church. There were two or three 'rajas' among the baptised, a positive note for the mission, since they had a certain prestige in their tribe.[199] Kusumdegi, one of the Lutheran fortresses decided to join Catholicism. However, the distance created problems for the missionaries, since they were unable to make regular visits.[200] A distinguishing mark of the tribal Catholics was their numerous church-attendance on feasts and other solemn occasions, for example, Christmas and Easter.

Fr. Alary used his village visits to gather children for the new schools he had opened in the mission. The Jesuits considered this apostolate as an important one for the betterment of the tribals in Chotanagpur.[201] Even though the village visits were not very encouraging at times, he was still optimistic. His diary on August 28, 1909, reads: "I visited Kora. I see all the *tollas* (hamlets). It was not quite as bad as I thought. Parantolla is the only one that is going the wrong way. The Kharia *tolla* is not so bad. Perhaps the Gangapurias of *Khas Kokra* might have fewer rows. In the morning I had only a few people at church, it may have been due to the bad weather."[202]

In his attempt to eradicate illiteracy and teach *Dharam* (religion) to the adults, Fr. Alary established evening schools in Langiberna, in July 1910. This was followed by further requests from other villages as can be seen from his diary: "The Rengarbahar people also expressed their desire to have somebody to teach them at night. If possible, their wishes will be complied with. I believe it is the only means to check the Lutherans, whose emissaries are everywhere on the move."[203] Through his personal influence as a missionary, Fr. Alary also settled some land disputes without ever going to court.[204] Even the tropical heat did not deter him from reaching out to his neophytes, and his longing for new contacts prevented him from becoming sedentary.[205] Commenting on Fr. Alary's work, Fr. Vermeire observed that he was a true missionary, eager to bring over many to the Catholic Church, therefore carrying on a true apostolate, there is no doubt. A true apostle must be ready at all times, even very trying, to go and meet the lost sheep. Was he not this type? How often do we not see him abandon the little comforts he could find at the only station for a district several times the magnitude of Barway or Biru? Again, and again we see Fr. Alary plunge into this or that side, in the hope of conquering new groups hidden in Jungle.[206]

It was during his second appointment as parish priest in Kesramal that Fr. Alary died prematurely at the age of 44 on July 10, 1918. He succumbed to pneumonia.

Kesramal under Fr. Sylvain Grosjean

Fr. Grosjean arrived at Kesramal on November 26, 1909.[207] At the age of 63 he volunteered to work in the recently-established parish as a simple parish priest after having served in a number of leading posts of the Society.[208] He seemed to like the situation at Kesramal, which could not be described as a traditional parish: there was no presbytery, no church and no school. Everything had to be started from scratch, and Fr. Grosjean enjoyed such challenges.[209] His diary is full of references to Jhunmur (spelt Jhunmul, Jhurmul), where he took great care to establish a chapel for the growing community of Catholics.[210] Being very meticulous, he furnished the statistics on the number of people who had received the sacraments.[211]

Describing his apostolic endeavours, Fr. Camiel Lievens writes: "Father Grosjean, although in his mid-sixties, wanted to work like Fathers Lievens, Dehoy and Cardon, whom he had earlier seen at work on their wonderful journeys, and he wanted to forget his 35 years of missionary life. His zeal knew no limit. During his last years he was still studying *Sadri*.[212] He was travelling all the time from village to village through all kinds of weather."[213] He showed a great interest in the education of the Tribals. In order to improve their standards, he periodically inspected the schools, especially to control the absence of the teachers.[214] Fr. Grosjean's apostolic endeavour in Kesramal was not without hardships. He struggled to obtain funds to realise the plans for a new station. H. Josson quoted one of the letters of Fr. Grosjean to the latter's sister: "At the moment, my deposit with the procurator general in Calcutta has fallen to zero. 65 Catechists, 50 assistant catechists, 12 school teachers, domestic servants will be here next Tuesday (for their monthly payment). They will demand Rupees 500/-, very little for this army."[215] The financial constraints made Fr. Grosjean postpone his plans to build a church immediately, but he did build a hall, which served as a provisional church.

When Fr. de Smet arrived at Kesramal, he became the third missionary in residence there. The three divided the mission field into three parts: Frs. Alary and de Smet were assigned to the Bonai and Hamirpur areas respectively, whereas Fr. Grosjean looked after Kesramal and the district beyond the Sankh river, i.e., the present Jhunmur parish and its vicinity. Fr. Vermeire wrote: "Grosjean was entrusted [with] the part towards Jhunmur, which he developed with intrepid zeal, in spite of his great [advanced] age. After his death it was said that he had made (of) it the best portion of the vineyard."[216] When Br. Rotsaert was advised to return to Belgium for medical treatment, Fr. Grosjean had to carry on the construction work started by the brother, in addition to his own tasks of teaching, visiting the stations, and raising funds.[217]

The diaries of 1913 and 1914 are full of references to the village visits of the missionaries. In July 1913 Fr. Grosjean mentioned that the Catholic population of Gangpur, which included members 'inherited' from the three stations of the Biru district, was 22,252, of whom 7,958 were baptized and 15,194 were catechumens. There were 2,301 communicants.[218]

Kesramal after the Pioneers

When Fr. Alary died in 1918, Fr. Grignard succeeded him as the head of the Gangpur mission. After a short period, he was transferred to Ranchi, and Fr. Henry Floor succeeded him. Though there were changes in personnel, the mission progressed steadily, thanks to the common programme. A school had been built, and a convent with a large girls' school was entrusted to the Daughters of the Cross from Liège in Belgium. More than 50 chapels were built and served by the catechists, who instructed the new converts and prepared them for baptism and the other sacraments. Also, more than 50 schools were opened. Fr. van de Schueren recorded: "There are at present 5 missionaries in the Gangpur mission, viz., two Belgian Jesuits and 3 young native priests from the Seminary of Ranchi. A new church entirely of brick has been erected, and it was to be present at the solemn blessing of this church that I journeyed to Kesramal with His Grace."[219] Fr. van der Schueren furnished additional statistics of the

Gangpur mission in his extensive report of May 1921. The total number of converts was 22,000. There were 68 chapels presided over by catechists in which normally Mass could only be said only two or three times a year when the missionary was on tour. There were about 74 mission schools; but new schools were being added.[220]

Fr. Floor wrote: "There is a movement of conversion here, which we should try to keep up with God's grace . . . I have some centres with catechists at the head."[221]   The building of new chapels and 22 new schools had been started. Fr. Floor had over 1,000 communions and 230 baptisms; the total number of conversions for the year 1921 now exceeded 2,000.[222]

Assistance Given to get a Fortune outside Gangpur

a. Labour Corps

When World War I broke out in 1914, many Gangpur Catholics wanted to join the Labour Corps because they had heard about the possibilities for better treatment in France and the steady monthly income. Initially, the people were apprehensive of the initiatives taken by the missionaries. According to M. Vermeire, it was due to the rumours spread by the Lutherans.[223] However, when the tribals realised that it was only a rumour, some of them, mostly Oraons, decided to join the Labour Corps. But they insisted that they would join only if a missionary working in Chotanagpur accompanied them.[224] The first group of recruits from Ranchi left for France on June 13, 1917. A missionary from Chotanagpur was always present there to guide them. Although the agreement was for one year, some of them wanted to stay on, since their treatment in France was satisfactory. Besides, the work was not so heavy as dangerous -- they were exposed to constant dangers on the frontier. The first battalion returned to Ranchi on June 9, 1918, and it was accorded a joyful welcome. Their service in the Labour Corps improved the economic standard of some of the tribals. All those who had returned from France gave a subsequent contribution of Rs. 10/- towards the construction of the church at Kesramal, which had been delayed for want of money. Msgr. B. Meuleman, the Archbishop of Calcutta, solemnly consecrated the first church in Gangpur on February 2, 1921.[225]

b. Emigration to Tea Gardens in Assam

Even before the arrival of the Jesuit missionaries, the tribal people from the Chotanagpur plateau began to migrate to the Assam tea plantations to earn their livelihood. Their decision was motivated by a strong desire to escape from the oppression and land alienation in which they found themselves. They had lost their land to the usurious zamindars, and they feared that if they continued to live in the same village they might have to render *bethbegari* (forced labour) in perpetuity. Seeing no other possibilities locally and following their own natural instinct to survive, they left for the Assam tea gardens. The missionaries too followed their flock and visited them starting from 1908. Initially, the missionaries from Kurseong used to visit the Catholics living in Assam and helped those in need of assistance. They were also well received by the planters, in whose gardens the Catholics worked. Thus, they could build some chapels here and there.

With the arrival of German Salvatorians[226] the situation changed, since the people could finally have missionaries living among them. However, the dedicated efforts of the Salvatorians were brought to a halt with World War I, for the German missionaries were interned in different camps and some of them were even repatriated. But soon they were replaced by a handful of Belgian Jesuits who continued the mission until the arrival of the Salesians of Don Bosco in 1921.

While the mission was under the Jesuits, Fr. Stanislaus Carbery was asked to help the Catholics in the tea gardens. Fr. M. Vermeire quoted the diary of Kesramal which had the following entry under December 1913: "At a conference held at Rengarih, the fathers of Biru and Gangpur discussed the proposals of directing the coolies to the plantations of Assam and the Duars that are visited by the priests. But the plan failed due in particular to the bad will of those they intended to protect. Around the end of the war, it was studied again this time by the Catholic cooperative of Ranchi."[227] The tea garden coolies were settled in *bastis* or lanes, according to their nationality and caste, in different parts of the gardens; they worked in their vicinity. During the growing season the work was longer and steadier – but they earned more.[228] As a practical solution to improve the living and moral standards of the Catholics emigrating to the tea gardens in Assam, Fr. Stanislaus Carbery prepared a list of places where there was a catechist and sent the list to the *sar-panches* (the headman of the village) and missionaries for their reference. Although the list does not show the number of Catholics who had immigrated to Assam, it gives some information regarding their place of origin.[229]

Impediments to Growth

Not all the inhabitants of Gangpur viewed the work of the missionaries as constructive to tribal welfare. In the meantime, they also gained more opponents from among the zamindars. Some of the leaders of Nagra began to harass the Christians because they were afraid that the latter would go to court to redress their grievances. The Lutherans of Nagra were in league with the zamindars in order to drive all the Roman Catholics out. The harassment meted out to Francis the catechist and to the Catholics in Gobira is an example.[230]

Although there was considerable growth in the conversion of Oraons, the mission had a setback caused by an organisation called *mukti larai* that encouraged -- even forced the Christian Oraons to come back to the tribe they lost by becoming Christians.[231] In 1915 some of the influential tribal leaders, no doubt backed by zamindars, accused the women of pollution, as they took their meal with other tribes. In order to learn the catechism and to prepare for the reception of sacraments, the tribal women used to stay at times in the convent, where they were also fed. Though the women were cautious, the fear of losing their *Jait* (tribe) resulted in defections, and several families returned to their former religion.

About the same time, Christianity also had to face another powerful enemy, namely *Tana Bhagatism*,[232] which produced many defections from the Catholic faith -- including in Kesramal.[233] Following World War I, the movement spread among the Oraons and emphasised their independence, often with slogans against foreigners. While *Tana Bhagatism* was rampaging throughout the entire Chotanagpur plateau, Gangpur was more immune to it. The *Litterae Annuae* of Kesramal for 1916 mentioned: "[that two villages] that had not yet begun to learn the elements of the Christian religion, had gone over to the politico-religious sect, which goes here by the name of the *Bhagat* movement. There seems to be a real danger of several others following their example."[234] However, the situation began to change in 1919 when many villages that had adhered to the nefarious doctrine of Bhagat began to abandon the fold and started to return to Catholicism. Hence, there arose a great need for recruiting more catechists, whether or not they were trained or suitable.[235]

World War I had devastating effects on the mission. Deprived of their resources, the missionaries had to reduce the salaries of the catechists and teachers. With the reduction of their salaries, one could hardly get any cooperation from them. The schools and villages were practically neglected. The establishment of some industries in the area also had a share in the decline of faith. Since the supervisors and contractors of these factories were Hindus, they cared little for Sunday services. Rather they made the Christians work even on those days.[236]

Efforts of the Daughters of the Cross for the Upliftment of Tribal Women

In order to evangelise the tribal women, the Jesuit missionaries invited a group of religious Sisters who would have easier access to the timid tribal women. One of the first buildings to be built, after the provisional one which served as presbytery and chapel, was the convent. In 1909 a group of nuns belonging to the Daughters of the Cross agreed to establish their first convent in Gangpur. Regarding their arrival, H. Josson wrote: "On October 14, 1909, Fr. Alary bid them welcome when they alighted from the train at Rajgangpur; he also met Mother Provincial whose desire it was to preside at the installation of the community."[237] The Belgian province of the Society of Jesus was familiar with the congregation as most of the sisters were from Belgium. The Sisters had a convent in Chaibasa, which is geographically close to the Kesramal mission. Besides running a dispensary, they opened a school for children where they could also teach catechism to women and girls. Writing about the work of the Sisters in Kesramal, Fr. H. Josson recorded: "Only on one account was Kesramal a privileged station: immediately after its foundation it enjoyed the cooperation of religious women. They were of the greatest advantage for the instruction of children, marriage catechumenates, preparation of "old women" for baptism and the other sacraments."[238] They started a small workshop in August 1910 (later enlarged in 1912 with the hope of accommodating more women), for making lace.[239]

Besides their regular work in Kesramal, the Sisters took an interest in visiting villages where they visited the sick and distributed medicine. They gathered children for the school and hostel in Kesramal. To quote from the diary of Kesramal for October 21, 1912: "Sisters Xaveria and Julia go over to Sunkh. On Monday evening (October 21), (they go to) Jhurmul. Next day they see Kolabahar and all or nearly all the *tollas* (hamlets) of

Gulikhaman, reaching Ambadanr about 4 P.M."[240] They remained in the area till October 26, visiting most of the villages where the missionaries normally went. In the following month, Srs. Xavier and Mary Ann visited Kokrem and Goghea. They stayed in some of the neighbouring villages for a week.[241]

The Future of Gangpur Mission

In order to serve a vast territory and place it under efficient administration, Fr. Grosjean divided the parish into 62 circles, which he called *ilakhas*. Each *ilakha* was given to a catechist and a *chaprasi* (servant), who were given a small salary for the service rendered.[242]

Writing to the superior general of the Society of Jesus, Fr. Alary lamented the fact that the station of Kesramal had to provide for the spiritual needs of about 18,000 Catholics spread over an area of 2,500 square miles, with new converts living at a distance of 45 miles from the church and the missionary's residence. Under such circumstances, further development of the mission would be impossible. It had not been possible to obtain the permission of the native king to build another station in Gangpur.[243] It was absolutely necessary and urgent to divide the mission into three parts, each having at least 800 square miles. Kesramal would continue to remain the centre, but a new mission needed to be opened about 30 miles to the west and another new mission about 30 miles to the east. Sites for these new missions had been acquired at Behrembasa in the west and Hamirpur in the east.[244]

The efforts of the missionaries to evangelise the people in Gangpur did not stop with the Mundas, Oraons and Kharias. They approached one of the more populous but introverted tribal groups known as *Berga Oraons* or *Kisans*. These had not been ignored by the missionaries, but, the information on their entry into Catholicism is scanty, except for Fr. Cardon's comments on their marriages in the church. The tribal chiefs made it difficult for the *Kisans* to embrace Catholicism.[245]

Much of the missionaries' time was spent on visitation, which, due to the enormous distances between the villages, they were unable to undertake often. It was no mean task to live and move in a land of extremes: poverty, famine, sickness, oppression, illiteracy and religious fundamentalism. They were unable to start the proposed western station, since they ran short of funds and personnel. However, Fr. Lambot took up the work in the eastern part.

Changing Fortunes of Kesramal

The *Mouvement de la Grâce* initiated by the veteran missionaries of Gangpur, Frs. Grosjean and Alary, experienced a set-back after their departure (deaths). In January 1920, about 84 hamlets returned to paganism. A good number of the chapels were totally or partially ruined. In short, the flourishing mission of Gangpur seemed to be heading for an early demise. Reasons for this decline included World War I (which drained the available sources for evangelisation), *Tana Bhagatism*, (which blocked the people from practising their religion, since some of the Hindu employers did not allow Catholic workers to go to Mass on Sundays).[246]

Conclusion

Against all odds, the missionaries (both MSFS and Jesuits) managed to establish mission centres from which they could move to different places according to the needs of the people and the availability of personnel. In addition to the difficulties of acclimatisation, the MSFS suffered from their ignorance of local languages and of the customs of the people. There were some exceptions, like Fr. Joseph Seigneur and Fr. Dupont, who made great efforts at learning the languages, which in the long run helped them to have a lasting contact with the people. However, except for a few, all of them were unable to cope with the climate. The Jesuits did not feel that they were entering a new territory. Gangpur seemed to be an extension of Chotanagpur, particularly when comparing the people, the language and the culture. In fact, tribal affinities with Gangpur was one of the strong motives to pursue mission expansion. Except for the distances and extremes of weather, the missionaries did not feel that they were in a strange land. It is true that they felt isolated there, but they could continue the same methods they had used in Chotanagpur.

Since the initial responses were so encouraging, the missionaries realised that a renewed supply of personnel and resources could change the character of the mission. Therefore, they took the decision to send missionaries to different parts of the mission, often responding to the ever-growing number of requests, which ultimately resulted in establishing more centres, which in turn led to a good number of people adhering to Catholicism.

Endnotes

[1] Most of the reports sent by the vicar apostolic of Visakhapatnam contained some remarks about the work of missionaries. See Règles de conduite pour les Missions de la Côte d'Orissa, in Histoire de la Mission, AMSFS 5H4.

[2] For a brief report on the mission, especially the early attempts to evangelise the Kondhs in the Ganjam Mountains and the ill-fated expedition by Frs. Tissot and Sermet in 1850, cf. Msgr. Neyret to Cardinal Fransoni, Vizagapatam, September 2, 1851, APF Indie Orientali: Scritture Riferite nei Congressi, vol. XIII, f. 591.

[3] Writing to Monsieur Mermier, Fr. J. M. Tissot gave a positive report of the Kondh Mission : "Cependant il y a une chose, Mr. le Superieur, que j'ai besoin de vous répéter ici: c'est la réponse que nous avons partout et constamment recue lorsque nous parlions de Dieu, de la fin de l'homme. Ils ont une idée confuse de la Divinité, mais de la bonté de Dieu et des grandes destinées de l'homme, ils nous répondainent avec ingénuité: nous ne savons rien de tout cela; nous ne sommes que de pauvres condes (Kondhs). Nous n'avons pas de gros livres comme vous. Nous serions bien contents si quelqu'un venait nous enseigner la bonne voie. Nous l'écouterions volontiers et suivrions ses avis." Tissot to Mermier, Visakhapatnam, December 3, 1850, AMSFS 5H5-2/1.

[4] The word 'Kondh Mountains' denotes a chain of mountains, where the Kondhs and Panos live : "Le pays konde est affreux, couvert de nombreuses chaînes de montagnes, d'immenses forêts et d'horribles defis." Richard to Monsieur Billiet, Berhampur, March 15, 1856, AMSFS, 5H5-2/1; Cf. Msgr. Neyret to Cardinal Fransoni, Vizagapatam, November 5, 1850, APF Indie Orientali: Scritture Riferite nei Congressi, vol. 12, ff. 1107-1109.

[5] Often non-tribals tend to condemn the tribals as 'uncivilised' people as they do not conform to the manners of non-tribals. A similar attitude was found among the missionaries, especially when they narrated the horrendous practice of Meriah and the infamous practice of female infanticide among the tribal people of Ganjam. Therefore, the phrase 'civilised world' is used in italics. Cf. Ibid.; Msgr. Neyret to Cardinal Fransoni, Vizagapatam, February 22, 1852, APF Indie Orientali: Scritture Riferite nei Congressi, vol. 13, ff. 841-842.

[6] At the request of the vicar apostolic of Calcutta, Msgr. Neyret had agreed to send a missionary to Cuttack, Berhampur, Aska, Ganjam, etc. This decision was arrived at since Cuttack was geographically close to Visakhapatnam and was one of the important stations that existed prior to the arrival of MSFS; the Theatines had their ministry extended to Cuttack and other coastal towns. Moreover, the firsthand information regarding the state of Christianity obtained during the pastoral visit of Msgr. Neyret convinced him to send a missionary to the above-mentioned places. Cf. Msgr. Neyret to Cardinal Fransoni, Vizagapatam, July 30, 1850, APF Indie Orientali: Scritture Riferite nei Congressi, vol. 12, ff. 944-945.

[7] F. MOGET, Early Days of the Visakhapatnam Mission 1846 – 1920, Bangalore 1997, p. 57.

[8] Jean Marie Dupont was born on June 25, 1816, at Thônes, Savoy. He came to the Visakhapatnam mission in 1847. He spent his life in the missions: in Yanam 1847-1853, Surada 1853-1861, Palcondah 1861-1865, Surada 1865-1887. He attracted many to Christ with the simplicity of life and his knowledge of medicine. His decisions in the disputes were sought and accepted as just and impartial. He died on June 17, 1887, at Surada. Cf. M. DOMENGE, La Mission de Vizagapatnam, pp. 363 – 364; F. MOGET, MSFS Obituary, p. 62.

[9] In his letter to Fr. Gaiddon, Fr. Dupont described the beginning of the mission in the following sentences : "au lieu d'aller commencer ma visite des Païens du côté de la mer à l'Est, je me dirigeai, accompagné du Père Richard, du côté de Soorada pays des montagnes, au pied des Gondhes et à l'ouest de Berhampore". Dupont to Mermier, Berhampur, July 26, 1853, AMSFS 5H5-2 1. It is probable that after having realised that the climatic conditions were unsuitable for easy movement in the coastal area, Fr. Dupont might have thought of looking for a place at the foot of the Kondh Mountains. M. Domenge mentioned: "Mais, à cette époque, des vents extradordinaires soufflaient dans ces parages, balayant avec violence un sable desséché et subtil, qui aveuglait les voyageurs, rendait la circulation difficile et le pays malasin". It has to be borne in mind that due to the typical nature of the bay, coastal Orissa often becomes a victim of climatic aberrations, like inundations, cyclones, depressions, etc. Cf. M. DOMENGE, La Mission de Vizagapatnam, p. 212.

[10] Fr. Philippe Richard-Cugnet was born on October 22, 1824, at Serraval, Savoy. He was ordained a priest on April 5, 1851. In the same year he left for the mission of Visakhapatnam. He was a pioneer at Surada and Cuttack. He was the parish priest of Berhampur from 1852. He served as the vicar general of Visakhapatnam diocese from 1866. He was also the parish priest of Visakhapatnam, where he was at the same time a municipal councillor. He died on April 12, 1880, at Visakhapatnam. Cf. Tableau Genèral, in Histoire de la Mission, AMSFS 5H4, F. MOGET, MSFS Obituary, p. 44.

[11] F. Moget is of the opinion that: "Fr. Dupont knew only Telugu, Fr. Richard spoke English and Tamil. They were accompanied by a servant speaking Telugu and Oriya, who could be their interpreter". F. MOGET, Early days of Visakhapatnam Mission, p. 71. Moget is of the opinion that the first exploration that took the missionaries to Montacallau, a village near Surada, was in January 1853 and the people who listened to the preaching of Fr. Dupont were Panos or pariahs. The details of the expedition to Montacallau are mentioned in the letter of Fr. Richard to the central council members of the Society for the Propagation of Faith. For more details on the issue, Cf. RICHARD, "Lettre de M. Richard Cugnet, Vicaire general de la mission de Vizagapatam, à MM. les Membres des Conseils centraux de l'Oeuvre de la Propagation de la Foi", in Annales de la Propagation de la Foi 52 (1880), pp. 108 - 109.

[12] Fr. Dupont narrated his experience to Fr. Gaiddon : "Lorsque nous y arrivâmes, les chaleurs étaient très fortes et il nous fallait absolument un lieu pour

nous garantir contre les ardeurs du soleil, mais il n'y eut pas moyen d'obtenir la moindre maisonnette où il nous fut permis de nous retirer. On aperçut cependant un misérable hangar où on nous dit qu'on pourrait aller se placer. Nous pensions que ce serait au moins la moindre des grâces, mais encore cette faveur ne nous fut pas de suite accordé. Il s'y trouvait plusieurs personnes réunies à l'occasion de l'anniversaire d'un de leur parent défunt, en mémoire duquel on donnait un repas. Pour cette raison, on nous dit que la place ne pourrait être libre qu'au soir. Là-dessus, nous crûmes que le mieux était de nous aller promptement enfoncer dans une forêt voisine située sur les bords d'une rivière et au pied d'une belle montagne. . . Ainsi, au lieu de me retourner, je m'avançai jusqu'au sommet du village où je fus bientot entouré de la plupart des habitants. Comme vous le pensez bien, je profitai d'une si belle occasion pour leur prêcher les vérités du salut. Jusque là, ces pauvres gens n'avaient vu personne qui leur annonçait le Règne de Dieu, qui leur fit connaître celui qui les avait crées, et la fin pour laquelle il les avait fait. Tout ce que je leur annonçais était nouveau pour eux." Dupont to Gaiddon, Berhampur, July 29, 1853, AMSFS 5H5-2/1.

[13] M. DOMENGE, La Mission de Vizagapatam, p. 212.

[14] In a footnote M. Domenge mentioned that Montacallau was the place where Fr. Dupont fixed his tent. The village was close to Surada. Cf. Ibid., p. 219.

[15] The religious practices of Kondhs and Panos are dealt with in the first chapter (1.2.3.1.2 [Kondhs] and 1.2.3.2.1 [Panos]).

[16] Here is the text of Fr. Dupont's encounter with the elderly man in the village : "Un des principaux fut surtout ému de ce que je dis de l'enfer dont il n'avait pas connaissance et je crois que ce fut cette crainte qu'il en éprouva qui le détermina de suite à se convertir. Mais, ne sachant pas qui j'étais, il disait: qui pourra m'enlever mes péchés, qui pourra me mettre dans la voie qui conduit au ciel? Où pourrais-je trouver quelqu'un qui m'instruise de vraie Religion... dans ce Pays, il n'y a personne qui soit capable de cela. – Alors, je lui dis que, 's'il désirait vraiment renoncer au démon et ne servir que Dieu Seul, Dieu Lui-meme lui fournirait tous les moyens nécessaires'. A cela, il me répondait: 'je suis vieux et bientot je vais mourir, que me reste-t-il donc à faire, sinon servir Dieu et travailler pour m'assurer le paradis'. – le voyant ainsi disposé, je lui dis: 'Eh –bien! L'homme qui vous est nécessaire pour arriver au ciel, cet homme, le Seigneur vous l'a envoyé maintenant et c'est à cette fin qu'il a voulu que je me dirigeasse auprès de vous, moi qui suis son ministre et dont la fonction est de travailler au salut des âmes." Dupont to Gaiddon, Berhampur, July 29, 1853, AMSFS 5H5-2/1.

[17] See the first chapter for more information on Meriah and female infanticide. When Captain Macpherson visited Surada in 1842, there prevailed female infanticide. Since he was affected by the mountain fever, he was unable to continue with the expedition. Cf. J.C.B. CAMPBELL, Narrative by Major General John Cambell C. B. in hill tracts of Orissa for the suppression of human sacrifices and female infanticide, London 1861, p. 50.

[18] The following information is given by Fr. Dupont : "Peu de jours après son baptême, ce chef me disait : "je ne sais rien, mais je crois tout ce que vous croyez et je veux faire tout ce que vous me direz." Dupont to Mermier, Berhampur, July 26, 1853, AMSFS 5H5-2/1.

[19] Moget narrates the first encounter with these glowing words: "Fr. Dupont told them that God had sent him to teach them the means of purifying their souls and insuring their eternal salvation. These simple people were quite ready to believe in something. They were Panos, Pariahs, happy to learn that, despised by Hindu society, they were the children of God." F. Moget, Early days of Visakhapatnam, p. 72.

[20] Dupont to Mermier, Berhampur, July 26, 1853, in Lettres des Missionnaires 1845–1857, ASMFS 7Z/5H5.

[21] M. DOMENGE, La Mission de Vizagapatam, p. 214.

[22] Antoine Guillermin was born on April 5, 1822, at Poisy, Savoy. He came to Visakhapatnam mission in 1853. He spent most of his life on the Kondh Mountains with 'semi-savage' people. He was a pioneer missionary at Ganjam, Koussipanga and Surada. During the time of the temporary closure of the mission he was left alone in Surada from 1859-1865. He was instrumental in building the churches at Surada, Berhampur and many other places. He founded the orphanage at Thotavally. He died at Surada on December 8, 1869. Cf. M. DOMENGE, La Mission de Vizagapatnam, pp. 346-347 ; F. MOGET, MSFS Obituary, p. 104.

[23] Joseph -Eugène Seigneur was born at Megève, Savoy, in 1827. He was ordained in 1852 and in the following year he reached the Visakhapatnam mission. He was noted for his skills in learning Indian languages. He learned Sanskrit and studied Hindu scriptures. He was called "Singharayya Swami". He died on May 3, 1861. Cf. M. DOMENGE, La Mission de Vizagapatnam, p. 252; F. MOGET, MSFS Obituary, p. 49.

[24] Jean Pierre Piccot was born at Luillin, Savoy. He came to the Visakhapatnam mission in 1853. He worked in Koussipanga and other stations in Orissa. He was a carpenter and his help in the construction of churches in the mission was much sought after. He died on December 3, 1871, at Aska. Cf. F. MOGET, MSFS Obituary, p. 102.

[25] In his letter to Msgr. Neyret of April 27, 1855, Fr. Tissot says that there was a considerable change in the life of the people. People were pious and attentive during the Mass and prayers. Cf. Tissot to Neyret, Surada, April 27, 1855, AMSFS 5H5-2/1.

[26] Fr. Dupont mentioned Surada to Fr. Clavel : "Comme Sooradah est pour le présent le chef lieu de notre Mission Konde, un lieu d'où l'on peut se rendre de tous côtés dans les montagnes et que nous y avons en outre un assez grand nombre de chrétiens, nous nous sommes vus dans la nécessité de viser aux moyens de construire une Eglise et un presbytère un peu passable . . . J'ai même frappé à plusieurs portes protestantes pour trouver quelques secours à cette fin." Dupont

to Clavel, Surada, February 7, 1857, AMSFS, 5H5-2/1; Tissot to Gaiddon, Surada, April 29, 1857, AMSFS, 5H5-2/1.

[27] Dupont to Clavel, Surada, February 7, 1857, AMSFS, 5H5-2/1.

[28] Msgr. Neyret, La Mission de Vizagapatam, Extrait du Registre Officiel, 1845, ASMFS 8Z.

[29] At the time when there was a trade of coolies – very similar to the slave trade in the preceding centuries – a suspicion of 'white men' as secret agents was in circulation among the people of Surada. It might have been a weapon used by the Brahmins in order to arrest the spread of a new religion. Cf. Dupont to Gaiddon, Berhampur, July 29, 1853, ASMFS 5H5-2 1; Dupont to Mermier, Berhampur, July 26, 1853, in Lettres des Missionnaires 1845–1857, ASMFS 7Z/5H5; M. DOMENGE, La Mission de Vizagapatam, p. 216.

[30] Dupont to Gaiddon, Berhampur, July 29, 1853, ASMFS, 5H5-2/1; Dupont to Mermier, Berhampur, July 26, 1853, in Lettres des Missionnaires 1845 –1857, ASMFS 7Z/5H5.

[31] Dupont to Gaiddon, Berhampur, July 29, 1853, ASMFS 5H5-2/1.

[32] Dupont to Mermier, Berhampur, July 26,1853, in Lettres des Missionnaires 1845–1857, ASMFS 7Z/5H5.

[33] M. DOMENGE, La Mission de Vizagapatam, p. 224.

[34] Koussipanga was an ill-situated village in the mountains. One could not make a long sojourn there, as it was isolated and lost in a cluster of mountains. There was no possibility of contact with the outside world. Even communication with the neighbourhood was rare. Once a year a merchant came with some essential items. The villagers purchased these with wax, food grains and tiger skins. The climate was insalubrious. Therefore, the missionaries considered the village a provisory residence. Cf. M. DOMENGE, La Mission de Vizagapatam, p. 223. For a narration of personal experience in Koussipanga: see Ibid., p. 344.

[35] To quote the letter of Fr. Guillermin to Fr. Gaiddon : "La nuit venue ils nous envoyèrent des présents, ensuite une députation pour nous prier de les instruire avant d'aller plus loin, puis ils se rendirent auprès de nous dans la matinée et que l'on déciderait cette importante affaire. Les chefs qui sont au nombre de cinq, furent fidèles au rendez-vous, ils porteraient nos effects quand nous voudrions partir; ils nous donneraient des fruits, du riz, des poules, etc., etc. Voyant de si belles dispositions, le Père résolut d'évangéliser ce village, quoique ce ne fut pas celui auquel nous avions mission de nous rendre." Guillermin to Gaiddon, Koussipanga, May 1854, AMSFS, 5H5-2/1; M. DOMENGE, La Mission de Vizagapatam, p. 218.

[36] The impression of the missionaries was that it was their preoccupation with the after-life, which made the Panos readily accept the message of the missionaries. However, the Kondhs believed in the transmigration of souls, i.e. deceased people are born again as animals, persons, etc. It was probably for this reason that the missionaries were initially hesitant to kill animals. Cf. Ibid., pp. 219 – 220; NEYRET,

"Extrait d'une lettre de Msgr. Neyret, évêque d'Olène et Vicaire Apostolic de Visagapatam, à MM. les Directeurs de l'Œuvre de la Propagation de la Foi", in Annales de la Propagation de la Foi 27 (1855), p. 357.

[37] They even tried to take part in the hunting expeditions, but as it proved to be very dangerous, they sought an exemption with the sole condition that they be given a share in the hunt. "Lorsqu'on est bien avec le khonde, disait le P. Dupont, on trouve en lui un excellent ami; mais, si on a le malheur de se l'aliéner, il devient un ennemi implacable." M. DOMENGE, La Mission de Vizagapatam, p. 220.

[38] Ibid., p. 221.

[39] Ibid.

[40] Msgr. Neyret reported the event with following words : "Vous voyez, leur dit-il [Fr. Dupont], que nous périssons ici de chaleur, faute d'avoir un abri convenable contre les ardeurs du soleil; vous irez donc, dès demain, nous couper du bois dans la forèt, pour nous aider à bâtir une maison." NEYRET, "Extrait d'une lettre de Msgr. Neyret, évêque d'Olène et Vicaire Apostolic de Visagapatam, à MM. les Directeurs de l'Œuvre de la Propagation de la Foi", pp. 358 – 359; Dupont to Neyret, Koussipanga, April 10, 1854, AMSFS 5H5-2/1.

[41] Dupont to Mermier, (no place), October 10, 1854, AMSFS 5H5-2/1.

[42] Ibid.

[43] Cf. R. CUGNET, "Lettre de M. Richard Cugnet, Vicaire general de la mission de Vizagapatam, à MM. les Membres des Conseils centraux de l'Oeuvre de la Propagation de la Foi", in Annales de la Propagation de la Foi 52 (1880), p. 109.

[44] Tissot to Mermier, Surada, April 29, 1857, AMSFS, 5H5-2/1.

[45] Tissot to Mermier, Surada, January 20, 1857, AMSFS, 5H5-2/1.

[46] For details see Règles de conduite pour les Missions de la Côte d'Orissa, in Histoire de la Mission, AMSFS 5H4...

[47] Cf. E. BONAVENTURE, "Lettre du R.P. E. Bonaventure, de la Société de Saint François de Sales d'Annecy, Missionnaire au Vizagapatam, au T.R.P. Tissot, Supériéur", in Annales de la Propagation de la Foi 55 (1883), p. 52.

[48] Fr. Dupont wrote : "Humainement parlant en voyant comment les choses à Coussipanga surtout dans le commencement, nous ne pouvions pas beaucoup nous promettre grande réussite. L'ivrognerie des hommes, leur indifference pour les choses du salut, leur indisposition à notre égard, l'extrême sauvagerie des femmes qui nous fuyaient comme des êtres redoutables, ensuite l'état maladif où chacun de nous s'est trouvé, rien de tout cela n'était de nature à fournir grand espoir de succès." Dupont to Neyret, Berhampur, September 4, 1854, AMSFS, 5H5-2/1.

[49] Even a small viral fever could play appalling havoc among the Kondhs. The tiger, monarch of the forest, tormented the lives of the people, and could be controlled only by propitiating an angry god or by moving to a different place. Every calamity was taken as a sign of divine displeasure which had to be placated. Cf. M. DOMENGE, La Mission de Vizagapatam, p. 225.

[50] The missionaries had a benefactor in Mr. Snaize, who was probably the only expert in mountain fever in that part of the country. His house was open to the missionaries whenever they came down for health reasons. He not only treated them but also entertained them at his house till they were completely cured. If needed, he would send essential items to Surada and Koussipanga whenever the missionaries were in need of them. He would do their linen and send their letters. Even the superior would leave some money with Snaize, so that he would be able to procure whatever the missionaries needed. Fr. Guillermin referred to him in the following words: "C'est monsieur qui nous envoie toutes nos provisions à Souradah et à Coussi, qui fait blanchir notre ligne, qui nous envoie nos lettres etc.. . il se dit tout dévoué à la mission de Conde, et même il s'appelle le quatrième missionnaire Conde. De fait il est rare qu'il nous envoie des provisions sans qui il nous envoie quelque chose du sien. Sa maison est assez grande, pourtant il veut en bâtir une autre dans sa cour pour nous, afin que nous soyons plus libres. Il est marié et n'a encore qu'une héritière. C'est chez lui qu'on porta le cher P. Richard quand il fut malade en descendant des forêts condes". Guillermin to Mermier, Ganjam, October 22, 1854, AMSFS, 5H5-2/1. For more information regarding the services of Snaize, see Dupont to Neyret, April 18, 1854, AMSFS 5H5-2/1; Guillermin to Neyret, March 27, 1854, AMSFS 5H5-2/1; M. DOMENGE, La Mission de Vizagapatam, pp. 223 – 224.

[51] The local tradition was cremation, whereas the Catholic Church insisted on burial of the dead.

[52] M. DOMENGE, La Mission de Vizagapatam, pp. 216 – 217.

[53] Guillermin to Gaiddon, Surada, February 21, 1862, AMSFS, 5H5-2/1.

[54] Msgr. Neyret informed Monsieur Mermier : "Ils ont amené dernièrement des montagnes une vingtaine de Néophytes pour les préparer à la 1ère communion et essayer d'en former quelques-uns pour catechistes. Cette Mission nous coûtera beaucoup mais pas autant que nous désirerions à défaut être d'ouvriers necessaires pour récolter une moisson." Neyret to Mermier, Visakhapatnam, September 13, 1854, AMSFS, 5H5-2/1.

[55] Tissot to Mermier, Visakhapatnam, December 12, 1854, AMSFS, 5H5-2/1.

[56] Fr. Dupont reported the situation of Koussipanga to Monsieur Mermier : "Le père Dupont est dèja à Coussipanga au sein des montagnes Condes, où il a visité un village appelé Arigadi à deux lieus de Coussipanga. C'est un des principaux de tout le pays. Les dispositions des habitans ne paraissent pas encore bien favorables de la part des Condes proprement dits, mais elles sont très consolantes de la part des Panans dont vous avez peut-être entendu parler. C'est un peuple qui n'a pas de nationalité proprement dite. Il n'est ni conde, ni Oriya...Quand nous paraîssons dans un village Conde nos principaux interlocuteurs sont les Panans. Nos premières conquêtes, sont les Panans et nous nous servons des Panans pour gagner les autres. Les Condes se contentent de venir après, de répondre après et selon l'intelligence." Dupont to Mermier, December 4, 1854, AMSFS, 5H5-2/1.

[57] Dupont to Mermier, (no place) December 4, 1854, AMSFS, 5H5-2/1.

[58] Fr. M. Domenge wrote : "Cette fois-ci, le Père n'y rien pu, le diable est plus fort que lui". M. DOMENGE, La Mission de Vizagapatam, p. 218.

[59] To quote from Fr. Guillermin's letter to Fr. Gaiddon : "Le motif de la première décision est l'impossiblité de rentrer à Coussipanga, sans y ramasser une fièvre qui nous met à deux doigts du tombeau et l'impossibilité aussi de pouvoir faire un assez long séjour dans ces montagnes pour habituer les habitants à des pratiques religieuses." Guillermin to Gaiddon, Berhampur, September 14, 1859, AMSFS, 5H5-2/1.

[60] Gojolibady, often referred as Godolobadi, Godervadi, Gayelbadi, etc., a sub-station of the parish of Surada, was the village where Fr. Dupont seemed to have converted a few Banias, whom the missionaries called Bainihas. As the names of the villages in the mission were difficult, the missionaries pronounced them as close as possible. Very few took steps to spell them correctly. Sometimes the names of the villages are not spelt correctly; they may have found it difficult to record them. For the sake of uniformity, the name Gojolibady is used in this study.

[61] NEYRET, "Extrait d'une lettre de Msgr. Neyret, évêque d'Olène et Vicaire Apostolic de Visagapatam, à MM. les Directeurs de l'Œuvre de la Propagation de la Foi", p. 360.

[62] For a detailed report on the conversion at Gojolibady, Cf. Dupont to Neyret, Berhampur, September 4, 1854, AMSFS, 5H5-2/1.

[63] Guillermin to Mermier, Ganjam, October 22, 1854, AMSFS, 5H5-2/1.

[64] M. DOMENGE, La Mission de Vizagapatam, p. 227.

[65] Tissot to Gaiddon, Surada, April 29, 1857, AMSFS, 5H5-2/1.

[66] Dupont commented : "Pour l'indien, l'affaire de caste est tout et le reste l'intéresse bien peu. Généralement parlant, les choses de la vie future ne le touchent pas et le préoccupent encore moins." Dupont to Mermier, Surada, November 8, 1858, AMSFS, 5H5-2/1.

[67] Fr. J.M. Tissot informed Fr. Gaiddon : "Avant que l'Angleterre se rendait maître de ces contrées, ils (the panos) étaient la terreur de tout le pays, c'étaient de vrais brigands. Vous comprenez par là que l'oeuvre qui a été commencée n'est que l'oeuvre d'un jour, il faudra bien du temps pour les changer entièrement. Cependant, je dois vous dire, mon cher, que j'ai trouvé en eux un grand changement. Dimanche dernier, un bon nombre d'enfants ont reçu la sainte communion. Quand ils viennent confesser ils dissent: Père je viens vous trouver pour dire d'enlever mes péches. Si vous les voyiez à la chapelle prier, chanter, vous en seriez content, j'en suis sûr." Tissot to Gaiddon, Surada, April 29, 1857, AMSFS, 5H5-2/1.

[68] Fr. Seigneur wrote : "Pour avoir une idée de la réserve et du qui vive dans les quels nous vivons depuis ce changement d'habitudes vous n'avez qu'à lire, si vous la trouvez, l'histoire des missions du Maduré et du Carnatic sous les reverends pères Robert de Nobilibus (Nobilius), Conçalve Fernandez, Bouchet. Ceux là

étaient parvenus à déguiser leur origine." Seigneur to Gaiddon, Surada, February 12, 1859, AMSFS, 5H5-2/1; Fr. Dupont sent some favourable arguments for the method used by the missionaries to Clavel: "Comme ici les Brahms sont les plus considérés et qu'ils se regardent eux-mêmes comme de petits dieux, la conversion de quelques-uns d'entre eux fait plus de bien que celle de plusieurs autres personnes de basse condition." Dupont to Clavel, Surada, February 7, 1857, AMSFS, 5H5-2/1.

[69] Fr. J.M. Tissot narrated the incident in the following manner : "Nous voudrions bien vous trouver maintenant, nous autres pauvres gens, mais si nous venons les autres ne voudront pas venir : si eux commencent et que nous venions après, ils ne diront rien." Tissot to Gaiddon, Surada, April 29, 1857, AMSFS, 5H5-2/1.

[70] Fr. Seigneur described the importance of choosing the method : "Notre progress dans le ministère de la parole divine rencontre de grands obstacles parmi la portion honorable de la population indienne. Ces difficultés provient comme vous le savez de l'horreur insurmontable qu'ils ont pour les étrangers ou plutôt pour tous ceux qui par naissance et par une fidélité à toute epreuve aux usages de la caste, ne se trouvent pas ranagés parmi les degrés de leur prétendu noblesse. Durant les premières années de notre séjour à Sourada connaissant leur susceptibilité sur ce point, nous restâmes dans un village un peu eloigné de la capitale. Notre cabane était cachée dans un bois et nous n'avions guère de rapports qu'avec des parias. Mais ensuite nous confiant en l'infine misericorde de Dieu et prévoyant aussi que nous n'irons pas bien loin même avec les gens de basse naissance si notre sainte religion devenait seulement la religion de ces derniers. Nous choisîmes un emplacement pour une chapelle à la porte de la grande ville de Surada." Seigneur to Gaiddon, Surada, February 12, 1859, AMSFS, 5H5-2/1.

[71] Tissot to Gaiddon, Surada, April 29, 1857, AMSFS, 5H5-2/1.

[72] Ibid.

[73] The first principle does not require any elucidation as the Brahmins ate vegetarian food. Regarding the second principle: Though the majority of the Christians of the Ganjam mission were Panos, the missionaries who practised adaptation did not keep contact with them. Once one of the Fathers visited Fr. Seigneur at Surada to administer a certain medicine. Fr. Seigneur came out to meet the visitor, who was given a corner in which to sit, following the custom of the people. He was not invited by Fr. Seigneur to enter the house. So strong was the mentality that a Pano could not even touch their cooking utensils. The third principle: In order to avoid polluting the house, the higher castes took all precautions in not allowing a person to die in it. When the person was on his deathbed, they took his bed and other belongings to the rear side of the house. The fourth: Whatever touches the mouth cannot be used, as it is polluted. The higher castes do not touch the lips with the glass when they drink water. They have their own plates for a meal, i.e., a banana leaf, which can be disposed of after use. They use the right hand to take food. The Indians kiss a venerable object with the eyes, and not with the mouth. They never allow spitting in the house. Cf. Périssin to Faber, Surada, February 12, 1859, AMSFS, 5H5-2 1.

[74] Ibid.

[75] It is worth recording some aspects of the letter of Fr. Seigneur to Fr. Gaiddon here : "Car à proprement parler ce titre de Sanyacis ne vient de droit, qu'à nous seuls, puisque non seulement aux yeux des hommes, mais aussi sous les regards de la divine majesté nous nous vouons à une chasteté perpétuelle et que notre qualité de religieux et de chrétiens nous engage a ne nous attacher à aucune chose au monde. Ce qui est la soit - disant vie des Sanyacis. Car sachez le bien, le désir d'obtenir une place dans leur prétendu baïkonto (paradis) n'est pas ce qui les tourmente. La gloire de passer sur la terre pour une espèce de divinité est en general le dernier repos de leur ambition." Seigneur to Gaiddon, Surada, February 12, 1859, AMSFS, 5H5-2/1. Information regarding the retreat and the need to find a suitable method and some rules for guiding their missionary endeavours are mentioned in the letter of Fr. Tissot. Cf. Tissot to Mermier, Surada, January 20, 1857, AMSFS, 5H5-2/1.

[76] Perissin to Faber, Surada, February 12, 1859, AMSFS, 5H5-2/1.

[77] Here is a list of items that are forbidden for the caste: "1. Il faut quand on mange à la maison, que personne ne vienne regarder, soit à la fenêtre, soit à la porte. 2. Il ne faut pas toucher une personne de basse caste, pas même un morceau de bois, quand elle le toucherait en même temps. 3. Il faut bien se garder de mettre les pieds sur une natte où il y aurait une personne de base caste. 4.Il faut se moucher avec les doigts sans difficulté. 5. Il ne faut pas manger de la vache ni boire aucune liqueur. 6. Il ne faut pas manger d'oignons, ni d'oeufs. 7. Ni de la poule, ni du porc, ni de l'ours, ni du renard et d'un grand nombre d'animaux, surtout des oiseaux d'ici, et dont je ne sais pas les noms. 8. Il faut se baigner tous les jours et plusieurs fois par jour, il faut priser beaucoup de tabac. 9. Il faut bien se garder, quoi que vous mettiez, à le toucher; cet objet est souillé. Il faut bien se garder en cachetant une lettre de radoucir le cachet avec de la salive, s'ils le voyaient, ils ne voudraient pas la porter à la poste... 10. il faut chaque fois que l'on va manger, changer d'habit, etc". Piccot to Gaiddon, Surada, May 10, 1859, AMSFS, 5H5-2/1. Fr. Perissin recorded four important aspects held by brahmins: 1. prohibition of liquor and meat; 2. avoidance of any contact with pariahs and other polluting castes; 3. prohibition of a corpse at home; and 4. avoidance of saliva. Cf. Périssin to Faber, Surada, February 12, 1859, AMSFS, 5H5-2/1.

[78] Fr. Avrillon wrote : "Ainsi ils ont adopté une chaussure à la brahmine, un ornement ou un surtout a la bramine, une soutane de couleur des toiles de Brames. Il parait que le bon Dieu va bénir. N'est-ce pas le vieux principe de se faire tout à tous? Un célèbre missionnaire, le Rev. Père de Nobili disait: je me fais indien pour sauver les Indiens., et il n'en a pas peu converti. (Histoire du Maduré)." Avrillon to Clavel, Berhampur, February 14, 1857, AMSFS, 5H5-2/1; Dupont to Clavel, Surada, February 7, 1857, AMSFS, 5H5-2/1; P. ROSSILLON, La Croisade pour la Conversion du Monde. Les Missionaires de S. François de Sales dans l'Hindoustan, Chambéry 1926, p. 18; M. DOMENGE, La Mission de Vizagapatam, p. 227.

[79] Michel Périssin-Faber was born on June 14, 1827, at Grand-Bornand. He was one of the great grand nephews (on his mother's side) of Blessed Peter Faber, one of the first companions of St. Ignatius Loyola. Before his entrance into the Society he repaired the chapel built in the birthplace of Faber (Villaret). He was a missionary at Cuttack between 1857 and 1866. He also worked in Berhampur and Surada. He was very active during the great famine in collecting the children and providing help for them. He might have baptised about 1200 children during that epoch. He spent time with the orphan children and they had great respect for him. He died at Surada on November 10, 1874. Cf. M. DOMENGE, La Mission de Vizagapatam, op. cit. p. 350; F. Moget, MSFS Obituary, p. 95.

[80] Seigneur to Gaiddon, Surada, February 12, 1859, AMSFS, 5H5-2 1.

[81] Fr. Dupont wrote about a precious conquest of an influential and intelligent Brahmin : "Il s'impose déjà de traduire en vers les compositions... que fait le père Seigneur sur diverses matières. Sa première pièce a été le symbole de sainte Athanase avec une courte mais petite invocation à la Très Sainte Trinité qu'il a faite lui-même. Maintenant il s'occupe de la traduction d'un traité du paradis dont il a déja quelques milliers de vers. Un jour qu'il en lisait un chapitre il ne pouvait contenir ses larmes tant il paraissait ému du sujet." Dupont to Mermier, Surada, November 10, 1858, AMSFS, 5H5-2 1.

[82] Seigneur to Mermier, Surada, February 13, 1859, AMSFS, 5H5-2 1; Tissot to Gaiddon, Surada, April 29, 1857, AMSFS, 5H5-2 1.

[83] Périssin to Faber, Surada, February 12, 1859, AMSFS, 5H5-2 1. One could note the frustration in the letter of Fr. Guillermin, who felt that the adaptation method practised by the missionaries went to an extreme: "Nous avons eu beau nous assujetter à tous les usages de caste, aller même plus loin qu'eux sur ce point, faire des choses les plus révoltantes et les plus opposées à nos idées Européennes, nous ne passerons jamais pour des gens de caste." Guillermin to Gaiddon, Berhampur, September 14, 1859, AMSFS, 5H5-2 1.

[84] In his report to the Holy See, Msgr. Neyret wrote: "Per nonnullos annos quidam missionarii ex illa spe quod si semel infideles nobilioris castae conversaeiessent omnes ceateri facile illos sequerentur, toto animo et magnum cum privationibus et sacrificiis in illorum conversione incuberunt; sed frustra omnio ideo illos derelinquentes ad infideles infirmae castae". Msgr. Neyret to Cardinal Barnabò, Vizagapatam, October 25, 1860, APF Indie Orientali: Scritture Riferite nei Congressi, vol. 17, ff. 1408 – 1414.

[85] Fr. Decompoix illustrated the need to learn many languages in the mission to Gaiddon: "un ouvrier plein de zèle et de forces, pour qui l'étude des langues était un amusement, une jouissance; aussi savait-il le Malabar (Tamil), le Telingu, le konde (kui), l'oria (Oriya), l'Indoustani (Hindustani, which is now called Hindi), et l'anglais." Decompoix to Gaiddon, Vizagapatam, May 7, 1861, AMSFS 5H5-2 1; for Fr. Seigneur's linguistic abilities see, M. DOMENGE, La Mission de Vizagapatam, p. 230.

[86] Tissot to Gaiddon, Surada, April 29, 1857, AMSFS, 5H5-2/1.

[87] P. ROSSILLON, La Croisade pour la Conversion du Monde, p. 18.

[88] Ibid., p. 18. Speaking of the songs composed by the Brahmin convert of Fr. Seigneur, Fr. Domenge wrote that there were only two complete copies. The songs showed the verve and talent of the author. The latter claimed that those who knew Oriya appreciated the work. Unfortunately, no copy of the work is found in AMSFS. Cf. M. DOMENGE, La Mission de Vizagapatam, p. 229.

[89] Seigneur to Gaiddon, Surada, February 12, 1859, AMSFS, 5H5-2/1 ; P. ROSSILLON, La Croisade pour la Conversion du Monde, p. 18. For a detailed study on Catholic Bhagavata see I. SORENG, Odiyare o Odiya Sahithyore Khristodharmo (Christianity in Orissa and Oriya Literature) (in Oriya), Berhampur 1998, pp. 324 – 340.

[90] It is possible that Fr. Seigneur composed the Catholic Bhagavata based on Dante's Divine Comedy, for which Misro rendered the poetic form. This claim is substantiated by the similarity in structure. Fr. Dupont reported that in 1858, while translating the treatise on Paradise, Misro was in tears. Cf. Dupont to Monsieur Mermier, Surada, November 10, 1858, AMSFS, 5H5-2/1; I. SORENG, Odiyare o Odiya Sahithyore Khristodharmo, pp. 324 – 340.

[91] Dupont to Mermier, Surada, November 10, 1858, AMSFS 5H5-2/1.

[92] Fr. Dupont presented Aroto Misro to Monsieur Mermier : "Sans rien dire de plus de ce nouveau disciple, vous voyez combien la conquête en serait précieuse quand il viendrait : ex toto corde, son exemple et ses œuvres nous seraient un bien immense et on pourrait presque conclure à la réussite de notre œuvre." Dupont to Mermier, Surada, November 10, 1858, AMSFS 5H5-2/1.

[93] Dupont to Mermier, Surada, November 8, 1858, AMSFS, 5H5-2 1; Dupont expressed the concern that due to shortage of funds the missionaries could not have trained catechists to follow up the mission among the higher castes, especially where the Europeans were unwanted guests. They even resolved to sacrifice some their comforts in order to raise the resource needed for this end. Cf. Dupont to Clavel, Surada, February 7, 1857, AMSFS, 5H5-2 1.

[94] It is worth recalling the general hatred which exploded against Europeans during the Sepoy Mutiny of 1857, a violent rebellion of Indian soldiers in northern and central India. Dupont to Mermier, Surada, November 8, 1858, AMSFS 5H5-2/1; M. DOMENGE, La Mission de Vizagapatam, pp. 231- 232.

[95] In his letter to the superior Fr. Périssin wrote : "que tous les efforts de nos Pères furent inutiles. One ne voulut plus entendre parler de notre sainte religion". Périssin to Superior, (no place) September 12, 1858, AMSFS 5H5-2/1.

[96] M. DOMENGE, La Mission de Vizagapatam, p. 233.

[97] Domenge cites Fr. Dupont who wrote : "Les Chrétiens pâhnos à l'exception des chefs, à qui l'on donne deux annas par Dimanche, ne viennent plus à l'eglise."

Ibid., p. 234. An anna was the smallest denomination of money, which was equivalent to 6 paise.

[98] Apart from the reference found in M. Domenge's La Mission de Vizagapatam, no document relating to the report has survived in the General Archives of the MSFS. One is left only with the information that Fr. J. Tissot presented the report to Msgr. Neyret in view of the larger interests of the mission. Cf. Ibid., p. 235.

[99] The general archives of MSFS do not indicate whether these principles were actually in force in the Ganjam mission. The letters and reports consulted are silent about this.

[100] Guillermin to Gaiddon, Berhampur, September 14, 1859, AMSFS, 5H5-2/1.

[101] There was an outbreak of cholera in the environs of Surada in 1862. Many became victims of the disease. Some of them thought that the epidemic was the result of the anger of the devils; hence they started offering sacrifices to propitiate the angry spirits. Since the Christians lived among the pagans, they were also forced to participate in the sacrifices, which were offered at every full moon. Cf. Guillermin to Gaiddon, Surada, February 21, 1862, AMSFS, 5H5-2/1.

[102] Dupont to Mermier, Surada, November 8, 1858, AMSFS, 5H5-2/1.

[103] Perrissin to Faber, February 12, 1859, AMSFS, 5H5-2/1; M. DOMENGE, La Mission de Vizagapatam, p. 235.

[104] Ibid., p. 246.

[105] Ibid., pp. 341 − 343.

[106] Jean-Marie Descombes was born on January 11, 1856, at Savigny, Savoy. He was ordained a priest on April 24, 1881. He left for India in June 1881. He worked at the Surada mission establishing new mission stations. He was a pioneer at Torobady, where he was fondly called 'the eternal father' by his confreres. Due to illness he returned to France, where he died on arriving at the port of Marseilles on April 24, 1907. Cf. Tableau Genèral, in Histoire de la Mission, AMSFS 5H4, F. MOGET, MSFS Obituary, p.46.

[107] M. DOMENGE, La Mission de Vizagapatam, p. 343.

[108] Fr. M. Domenge recorded that : "On en vint à convoquer une assemblée générale de toute leur caste, où ils firent déclarer que le christianisme ayant été reconnu incompatible avec les antiques et invariables usages de la caste, défense était faite à tous les pahnos de se conformer à cette religion. Ceux qui l'avaient embrassée étaient invités à y renoncer pour toujours; que si quelqu'un persistait à s'en reconnaître l'adepte, il encourrait, par le fait même, le déplaisir de ses concitoyens et serait chassé de la caste." Ibid., p. 339.

[109] Refering to the verdict, Fr. M. Domenge mentioned : "Enfin dit-il [the Judge] aux chrétiens, ne pouvez-vous pas vous tirer d'embarras sans les païens? Quel besoin avez-vous d-eux? Nous n'en avons nullement besoin, répondirent-ils sans voir où tendait cette question. Alors répliqua le juge, réglez vos affaires entre vous, et laissez les païens traiter les leurs." Ibid., p. 341.

[110] Writing about the event, Fr. F. Moget commented on the effect of the court verdict: "The Pano chiefs were triumphant and the Christians crestfallen. It was the end of the Montacallau parish – these poor people did not declare themselves Christians and no conversion could take place any more." F. MOGET, Early days of the Vishakapatnam Mission 1846-1920, p. 153.

[111] E. BONAVENTURE, "Lettre du R. P. E. Bonaventure, de la Société de Saint François-de-Sales d'Annecy, Missionnaire à Vizagapatam, au T. R. P. Tissot, Superieur", in Annales de la Propagation de la Foi 55 (1883), p. 53.

[112] Etienne Bonaventure was born on April 26, 1851, at Dingy-St. Claire, Savoy. He entered the MSFS on January 29, 1872 and was ordained priest on May 26, 1877. In the same year he left for India. He served in the Surada mission up to 1885. In 1885 he was one of three who went to Koraput to explore the possibilities of starting a mission there. He was appointed to establish a station, but sickness did not permit him. He was the principal of St. Aloysius 1888-1891, SFS in Nagpur 1891-1894, St. Aloysius in Visakhapatnam 1894-1898. In 1901 he was made the vicar general of Nagpur, and he succeeded to the see in 1904. He died in France on March 12, 1907, while on holiday to recuperate his health. Cf. Tableau Genèral, in Histoire de la Mission, AMSFS 5H4, F. MOGET, MSFS Obituary, pp. 33-34.

[113] E. BONAVENTURE, "Lettre du R. P. E. Bonaventure, de la Société de Saint François-de-Sales d'Annecy, Missionnaire à Vizagapatam, au T. R. P. Tissot, Superieur", in Annales de la Propagation de la Foi 55 (1883), p. 53.

[114] For a governmental report of the famine see Report of the Commissioners Appointed to Enquire into the Famine in Bengal and Orissa in 1866, 2 vols., Office of Superintendent Government Printing, Calcutta 1867; N. K. SAHU et al., History of Orissa, Cuttack 1989, p. 415.

[115] For further information on the misery of the people and on the negligence of the administration, see: G.T. HALY, Appeal for the Sufferers by the Present Famine in Orissa, London 1866; N.K. SAHU et al., History of Orissa, p. 414; A.C. PRADHAN, A Study of History of Orissa, Bhubaneswar 1988, p. 285. For a general understanding of the cause of the famine, see Memorandum of the Scarcity and Drought of 1866-67, from the Report on the Administration of the Madras Presidency during the Year 1866-67, Madras 1867, Appendix iii, lxxvi.

[116] A general report on the mission of Visakhapatnam published in 1866 under the title Notice sur la Mission de Vizagapatam declares that there was no production in India and that there was a drought for three years. Cf. Anonymous, Notice sur la Mission de Vizagapatam, Annecy 1866, APF Indie Orientali: Scritture Riferite nei Congressi, vol. 19, f. 637.

[117] In his letter Fr. Guillermin lamented the exorbitant price they had to pay for essential commodities. People were leaving the villages for the towns with the hope of finding something to fill their stomachs. Cf. Guillermin to Tissot, Surada, September 30, 1866, AMSFS, 7Z 5H5.

[118] N. K. SAHU et al., History of Orissa, p. 418.

[119] The general report of the mission narrated : "Impossible de décrire quelles proportions a prises la misère en ces pays, dans ces dernieres temps : c'est par milliers qu'il faut chaque jour compter ses victimes. Dans les lieux où le gouvernement ne peut exercer sa surveillance - on trouve plusieurs cadavres sur les routes; personne, tant leur nombre est grand, ne prend soin de les enterrer. Nos missionnaires ont fait un supreme effort, ils ont rassemblé toutes leur ressources, frappé à toutes les portes, contracté de gros emprunts pour soulager une si epouvantable détresse. Leur résidences sont assaillis par les habitants affamés. D'apres une lettre recente, on en avait vu plus de cent demander à la fois un peu de riz à un de nos confreres." Anonymous, Notice sur la Mission de Vizagapatam, p. 637 ; M. DOMENGE, La Mission de Vizagapatam, p. 335.

[120] Fr. Guillermin observed : "presque tous les villages dans les environs ont plus ou moins souffert ; quelques uns sont à moitié détruits d'autres le sont entièrement. Pour eux la misère ne finira pas avec la récolte, car les uns n'ont semé qu'une petite partie de leurs terres, d'autres n'ont absoluement rien semé! Que récolteront-ils les pauvres malheureux!" Guillermin to Tissot, Surada, September 30, 1866, AMSFS, 7Z 5H5.

[121] A. C. PRADHAN, A Study of History of Orissa, p. 290.

[122] Initially the collector relied on the local contribution to overcome the tragedy: the zamindars organised free kitchens on their estates and with the local contribution, the government distributed cooked food in many centres. Besides the ordinary allotment of Rupees 110,215/-, Rupees 48,153/- was spent on relief works during the distress. The governor's [civil head of the Madras Presidency] visit to Ganjam expedited the relief measures. Cf. Memorandum of the Scarcity and Drought of 1866-67, from the Report on the Administration of the Madras Presidency during the Year 1866-67, Madras 1867. p. xxix.

[123] Sir Stafford Northcote, the then secretary of state for India, summed up the effect of the Orissa famine in the British House of Commons: "The catastrophe must always remain a monument of our failure, a humiliation to the people of this country, to the government of this country and to those of our Indian officials of whom we had perhaps been a little too proud. At the same time, we must hope that we might derive from it lessons which might be of real value to ourselves, and that out of this deplorable evil, good of no insignificant kind might ultimately arise." N.C. BEHURIA (ed), Orissa State Gazetteer, vol. I, p. 222; N.K. SAHU et al., History of Orissa, p. 425; A.C. PRADHAN, A Study of History of Orissa, p. 290.

[124] Cf. Richard to Clavel, Visakhapatnam, December 18, 1866, AMSFS, 7Z 5H5.

[125] Frs. Dupont and Guillermin were busy with the work of gathering the children and providing them help. They wanted to gather as many as possible, but they had neither personnel nor resources. Cf. Richard to Tissot, Visakhapatnam, October 18, 1866, AMSFS, 7Z 5H5

[126] D. SWARO, The Christian Missionaries in Orissa, p. 164.

[127] M. DOMENGE, La Mission de Vizagapatam, p. 335.

[128] Cf. Anonymous, Notice sur la Mission de Vizagapatam, p. 637. At the beginning of the great famine, Fr. Périssin was in charge of the two mission stations: Cuttack and Berhampur. He went around helping the people in their dire need. M. Domenge wrote: "Dès le commencement de la famine, il s'était mis à parcourir les villes et les villages de sa juridiction, cherchant surtout les enfants qu'il pourrait baptiser in articulo mortis, sans oublier les adultes, que ses aumônes ou leur extrême misère pourraient disposer à recevoir sa parole. Il n'eut que peu de succès auprès de ces derniers, mais il recueillit une riche moisson d'enfants. En temps ordinaire, il n'aurait trouvé personne; car, le Hindous ne lui auraient pas permis d'entrer chez eux. Mais, comme leurs maison seraient, selon les préjugés du pays, irrévocablement souillées, si quelqu'un venait à y mourir, ils en faisaient sortir tous les malades dès qu'ils étaient à l'agonie: aussi dans toutes les rues, rencontrait-on des morts et des mourants." M. DOMENGE, La Mission de Vizagapatam, p. 336; R. CUGNET, "Lettre de M. Richard Cugnet, Vicaire general de la mission de Vizagapatam, à MM. les Membres des Conseils centraux de l'Oeuvre de la Propagation de la Foi", in Annales de la Propagation de la Foi 52 (1880), pp. 109 - 110.

[129] Périssin to Clavel, Vizagapatam, May 20, 1872, AMSFS 5H5-2/1.

[130] M. DOMENGE, La Mission de Vizagapatam, p. 337.

[131] The resources of the missionaries were insufficient to meet the growing needs arising out of the great famine of Orissa. At some time, they had to stop taking children to the orphanage. Even the work of the Holy Childhood that was operative in the vicariate of Visakhapatnam was unable to provide for the ever-increasing needs of the people. Cf. Anonymous, Notice sur la Mission de Vizagapatam, p. 638 ; La Mission de Vizagapatam, Extraite du Registre Officiel, 1845, ASMFS 8Z.

[132] Brother Francis is none other than Francis, the catechist. He was arrested in Khurda for stealing children and giving some medicines that expedited the death of children. After three days, at the intervention of the collector Mr. Francis was released with the injunction that he should not set foot again in the district. Cf. Assainissement des marais, Coupres de Journeaux, October 17, 1891, AMSFS 5H5-2/3; Richard to Clavel, Visakhapatnam, December 18, 1866, AMSFS, 5H5-2/1.

[133] They were hoping that the number in the orphanage might increase, as the great famine in Orissa was rampant. Cf. La Mission de Vizagapatam, Extrait du Registre official 1845, AMSFS, 8Z.

[134] Writing on the condition of the orphanage in Orissa, D. Swaro commented: "The orphan boys were looked after by the money until seventeen years of age and for girls the age limit was sixteen. In orphanages boys were trained in various crafts such as weaving, carpentry and blacksmith work. Some were trained as tailors, cooks, servants, bearers, gardeners, etc.; in the mission schools several were engaged as monitors; girls were trained in house-wifery, knitting and needle work."

D. SWARO, The Christian Missionaries in Orissa, p. 171; A.C. PRADHAN, A Study of History of Orissa, p. 289.

[135] Coupures de Journeaux, July 25, 1891, AMSFS 5H5-2/3.

[136] M. DOMENGE, La Mission de Vizagapatam, p. 345.

[137] P. ROSSILLON, "Cent Kilomètres sur des Épaules Kondes", in Echos Saliénes 5/10 (1912), p. 153.

[138] Anonymous, Notice sur la Mission de Vizagapatam, p. 638 ; Msgr. Tissot to Cardinal Prefect, Vizagaptam, September 13, 1866, APF Indie Orientali : Scritture Riferite nei Congressi, vol. 19, ff. 652 -654 ; La Mission de Vizagapatam, Extraite du Registre Officiel, 1845, ASMFS 8Z.

[139] François Louis Décarre, native of Sales (Annecy, Savoy), was born on December 30, 1840. He was ordained on December 6, 1866. Arriving in India in 1867, he was sent to Vizianagram where he built a school. Upon his arrival in Cuttack 1867-1869 he continued with the school apostolate. As a priest in charge of Surada 1869-1870, he built the orphanage of Thotavally. He also worked as a missionary in Yanam 1870 – 1874. The last years of his life he spent in Cuttack 1874-1905. His end came on October 10, 1906, at Visakhapatnam. Cf. Tableau Genèral, in Histoire de la Mission, AMSFS 5H4, F. MOGET, MSFS Obituary, p.88.

[140] To instil fear in the children, the missionaries punished the children who left the orphanage without the permission of the missionary. Cf. M. DOMENGE, La Mission de Vizagapatam, pp. 348 – 349.

[141] Ibid.

[142] Fr. Bonaventure informed Propagation de la Foi about the progress of the mission : "Nous avons maintenant quarante-sept familles, avec de nombreux petits enfants. Le nombre total des orphelins s'élève à deux cent trente-sept personnes, entièrement à la charge de la mission. Le missionnaire est leur père, leur juge, leur médicin. Sans doute la civilisation moderne n'est pas encore parvenue jusqu'à eux; ils sont capables de tenir leur comptes; ils savent par coeur leur prière du matin et du soir; et peuvent comprendre les vérités de leur foi." E. Bonaventure, "Lettre du R.P. E. Bonaventure, de la Société de Saint François de Sales d'Annecy, Missionnaire au Vizagapatam, au T.R.P. Tissot, Supériéur", in Annales de la Propagation de la Foi 55 (1883), p. 55.

[143] 'History of Evangelisation: Method followed', in Histoire de la Mission, AMSFS 5H4 Inde.

[144] To quote the letter of Fr. Guillermin to Monsieur Mermier : "Pour moi, quand j'avais quelques bons moments, je les passais à copier un Dictionnaire, fait par le Rd. Père Dupont. Quelques temps après que j'eus fini ce travail qui me prit bien des jours, je les perdis sans jamais trouver aucune trace de cette perte, que je puis appeler grand. Tellement que je n'eu pas le courage d'en faire un second exemplaire avant qu'il eût une seconde édition revue et corrigée par l'Auteur parce qu'il s'y trouvait beaucoup de mots qui n'etaient pas Condes. En attendant je prenais les

mots que j'entendais et que je comprenais, et j'en avais un certain nombre quand je descendis: par comble de malheur je perdis ce nouveau cahier. Je le retrouvais cependant beaucoup plus tard." Guillermin to Mermier, Ganjam October 22, 1854, AMSFS, 7Z 5H5. M. Domenge makes a similar statement: "Dans les intervalles que leur laissait la fièvre, ils faisaient parler les khondes, cherchaient à deviner leur idiôme, enrichissaient leur trésor de chaque mot nouveau. Point de dictionnaire à consulter; point de grammaire où étudier les declinations, les conjugaisons et la syntaxe." M. DOMENGE, La Mission de Vizagapatam, p. 225.

[145] H. JOSSON, Un Chef de Mission aux Indes, p. 364.

[146] The origin of the Chotanagpur tribals is mentioned in the first chapter. It is apt here to recall that due to the population growth and in their natural inclination to seek new terrain the tribals migrated to the neighbouring states of Jashpur, Sirguja, Gangpur, Bonai and Bamra. M. Vermeire was of the opinion that "The aborigines of Chotanagpur, declining any other occupation, are accustomed to earn their livelihood through cultivating fields. When the latter are lacking they migrated southwards towards the interior Orissa, to the hilly and jungly tracts. There after having cut down the trees and levelled the ground they get the permission to prepare fields and fix a home." M. VERMEIRE, Biru Mission History: Biru Common, vol. I, Part II, APBS India Lievens. Ser. B. Box. 4, p. 49.

[147] In his letter to the Provincial, Fr. Grosjean mentioned: "Le Gangpur fait suite au Biru. Nous touchons par le nord aux territoires de Rengarih et de Samtoli. Les langues, le races et côutumes sont identiques". Grosjean to Provincial, Kesramal, September 12, 1912, APBS India 1- 12/ Grosjean letters. At the arrival of Fr. Grosjean at Kesramal in November 1908 the Catholic population of Kesramal consisted mainly of emigrants or the descendants of the emigrants of Chotanagpur. They were from the following tribes: Oraons (about 55%), Kharias (about 35%), and Mundas (about 10%). Cf. H. JOSSON, Un Chef de Mission aux Indes, p. 365.

[148] Waelkens to Provincial, Calcutta, 1906, APBS, India 2 – 22/5.

[149] Waelkens to Provincial, Calcutta, March 21, 1906, APBS, India 2 – 22/6.

[150] Fr. de Smet informed the provincial of the need to build a station for Gangpur and the possibility of the spread of Lutheranism. Cf. De Smet to Provincial, July 6, 1906, APBS, India Lievens: box 4, Samtoli.

[151] M. VERMEIRE, Biru Mission History: Samtoli 1904-1940, vol. III, APBS, India Lievens. General Sources, p. 21.

[152] Some of the villages he visited during the second trip were Babaimohan, Salangabhar, Jhamankera, Jhurmul (Jhunmur), Padrasilla, Kasbahar, Jharbera, Jaedega, Kadobahar, Dukatoli, Gaghari, Amko and Sakambahar. Ibid., pp. 22- 24.

[153] Ibid., p. 25.

[154] Ibid., p. 30.

[155] M. Vermeire wrote the following account from the diary of Fr. De Smet: "As regards Ragunathpali, the diary has the following: (p.53) Eliazar Kujur, Anglican

Uraon of Amba-Jharain, 4 kms from Ragunathpali (Bombay Railway), comes again to say that he and some 12 houses (some Anglicans and some Lutherans, who are or ought to be visited by the Chakradharpur Lutherans or the Chaibassa Anglicans but are not) complain of being abandoned and wish to come over to us". Ibid.

[156] Ibid., p. 31.

[157] Ibid., p. 32.

[158] Mr. Craven, the Dewan or the prime minister of Gangpur, was a former student of St. Xavier's College, Calcutta, where van der Schueren was also a professor. Fr. Vermeire stated that Mr. Craven was a Catholic and hence well disposed towards the spread of Catholicism. After the establishment of a parish at Kesramal in 1908, a priest would go to Suadi, now Sundargarh, to offer him the possibility to participate in the Christmas and Easter liturgy. There were also times when Mr. Craven and his family would drop in at Kesramal on a Sunday to participate in the Eucharist. On the eve of his departure to East Africa, he resigned in December 1919. He was succeeded by another alumnus of St. Xavier's college, M. Lucas. Cf. van der Schueren to Superior General, Calcutta, May 1921, ARSI, Calcut. 1005, XIV-13, p. 3; M. VERMEIRE, Gangpur Mission History, vol. I, pp. 7-8; H. JOSSON, La Mission du Bengal Occidental, vol. II, p. 410.

[159] M. VERMEIRE, Biru Mission History: Samtoli 1904-1940, vol. III, APBS, India Lievens. General Sources, pp. 32-33.

[160] Fr. De Smet's diary of January 22, 1908 reads: "Francis, the Gobira (Nagra) catechist comes with 16 men: they want a catechist, or better, two. Francis says that the following have become catechumens, all from paganism & that many more will join: 1. Banailata 43 houses, Uraons and Kharias; 2. Goghea 28 houses, Uraons, Kharias and Mundas; 3. Ranakata 15 houses, Kharias; 4. Bemta 4 houses, Kharias; 5. Olhaintola 10 houses, Uraons and Mundas; 6. Katajar (Katajhar) 11 houses, Kharias and Mundas; 7. Karanjua 8 houses, Kharias and Mundas; 8. Kusumtola 3 houses, Mundas." Ibid., p. 34.

[161] Ibid., p. 35.

[162] This was one of the institutions founded by Fr. C. Lievens in Chotanagpur. Their function is illustrated in the fifth chapter.

[163] Ibid., p. 39

[164] Fr. de Smet described his journey to Gangpur: "Very arduous, when it was terribly hot. Until now, for the sake of prudence, we had hardly baptised in Gangpur. But seeing the perseverance of those nice people and their good dispositions, I have baptised during this tour 11 adults and 558 children under 6 years." Ibid., p. 41.

[165] H. JOSSON, Un Chef de Mission aux Indes, p. 365.

[166] Frs. Cardon and his assistant de Smet did much of the expansion work from Rengarih, especially the latter with his periodic visits to Gangpur. Fr. van Rabays received the deputations from Gangpur with kindness and kept them in contact

with the mission, but his initiative was limited due to a lack of funds. Frs. de Gryse and van Hoeck spearheaded the expansion work in Kurdeg.

[167] M. VERMEIRE, Gangpur Mission History, vol. I, p. 2.

[168] Ibid., p. 7.

[169] Ibid., p. 8.

[170] Ibid., p. 9.

[171] The life of Birsa Munda and his activities are dealt with in the first chapter, footnote no. 218.

[172] H. JOSSON, La Mission du Bengale Occidental, vol. II, p. 399.

[173] M. VERMEIRE, Gangpur Mission History, vol. I, pp. 38-39.

[174] H. JOSSON, La Mission du Bengale Occidentale, vol. II, p. 399.

[175] M. VERMEIRE, Gangpur Mission History, vol. I, p. 7.

[176] The Raja wrote to the commissioner on July 16, 1903, informing him, "I have found that such missionaries as have hitherto been allowed to reside in the state have not refrained from interfering in matters of administration. I am thus unable to pass any order permitting the establishment of any new mission". Ibid., p. 7.

[177] There were three main reasons for the requests: (1) to baptise the children and those who were unable to come to the mission station; (2) to administer the Sacrament of Anointing the Sick; and (3) to visit the Catholics who were emigrants of Ranchi District or the relatives of those in Ranchi. Cf. Ibid., pp. 10-12. In order to visit the existing Christians and to administer the sacraments, it was sufficient to obtain the permission of the commissioner.

[178] Panchayat is a kind of 'home rule'. It is an assembly of five or more reputable elders selected from the community to settle issues relating to the community or tribe. They name themselves Panches; at their head is a man called, Sar Panch. The panchayat is responsible for law in the village. They are also responsible for the smooth running of schools and the bank. Fr. van der Schueren observed: "Truly the Panchayat is a great institution: by it the people are kept together, faults are combated, intelligence about a hundred things is conveyed to the people, quarrels are settled, and it is a very efficient school for the moral and social education and uplifting of our people". Van der Schueren to Superior General, Calcutta, May 1921, ARSI, Calcutta 1005-XIV, 13.

[179] In his letter to the superior general, Fr. Alary reported the situation of Gangpur : "Les luthériens avaient pratiquement conquis le pays avant notre arrivée. Ils étaient parfaitement établis au Gangpur (maisons, écoles etc.) alors que nous ne pouvions y faire que de rares visites. La plupart de nos chrétiens viennent de chez eux; mais impossible ou presque impossible d'attaquer ceux qui leur restent, ils sont absolument attachés à leur mission. Beaucoup de nos missionnaires ont fait cette remarque si les luthériens n'ont pas la masse, il est certain toutefois qu'ils sont réussi à s'attacher fortement un certain nombre de leurs adeptes. Actuellement, bien que les missionnaires luthériens aient dû quitter

le pays depuis tantôt 2 ans, les catéchistes continuent l'oeuvre, et du moins ici au Gangpur, nous ne faisons pas de nouvelles conquêtes. Que feraient nos chrétiens dans les mêmes conditions?" Alary to Superior General, Kesramal, July 14, 1916, ARSI, Calcutta 1005, XIII-23.

[180] M. VERMEIRE, Gangpur Mission History, vol. I, p. 9.

[181] The Political Agent was the representative of a group of semi-independent states in India. Generally, he did not interfere in matters unless the state itself asked for it, or when he found evidence of maladministration. Once a year the political agent toured the states that were under his control. The political agent for the state of Gangpur resided at Sambalpur. Cf. H. JOSSON, The Mission of West Bengal, trans. L. Clarysse, Ranchi 1993, p. 266.

[182] Van der Schueren to Superior General, Calcutta, May 1921, ARSI, Calcutta1005, XIV- 13.

[183] Cf. Grosjean to Provincial, Kesramal, July 30, 1913 APBS, India 1 – 12/ Grosjean letters.

[184] In his letter to Fr. Provincial, Fr. Grosjean wrote : "Le Gangpur est admirablement situé pour propager ce mouvement à l'Est, dans le Singhbhum ; au Sud, dans l'Orissa; à l'Ouest, dans les Central Provinces. Cela se fera si Dieu le veut. Ses dessins sont inscrutables; mais on peut croire qu'ils sont tels que la situation du Gangpur suggère." Grosjean to the Provincial, Manresa House, Ranchi, November 10, 1909, APBS, India 1 – 12/ Grosjean letters; H. JOSSON, Un Chef de Mission aux Indes, p. 363.

[185] M. VERMEIRE, Gangpur Mission History, vol. I, p. 38; M. Vermeire, Biru Mission History: Biru Common, vol. I, Part II, APBS, India Lievens. Ser. B, General Sources, Box 4, p. 30.

[186] M. Vermeire, Gangpur Mission History, vol. I, p. 42; The Indian mission found at Alken after the death of Camiel Lievens, APBS, India 2, Box15/5, p. 2; M. VERMEIRE, Biru Mission History: Biru Common, vol. I, Part II, APBS, India Lievens. Ser. B. Box. 4, p. 31.

[187] Alary to Superior General, Kesramal, July 11, 1916, ARSI, Calcutta 1005-XIII, 8; M. VERMEIRE, Gangpur Mission History, vol. I, p. 42.

[188] Van der Schueren to Superior General, Calcutta, May 1921, ARSI, Calcutta 1005, XIV-13.

[189] Alary to Superior General, Kesramal, July 11, 1916, ARSI, Calcut. 1005-XIII, 8; The Indian mission found at Alken after the death of Camiel Lievens, Archief Belges. India 2, Box15/5, p. 2.

[190] M. Vermeire cited the statistics compiled by Fr. Grosjean, a known statistician of the mission. Cf. M. VERMEIRE, Biru Mission History: Biru Common, vol. I, Part II, APBS, India Lievens. Ser. B. Box. 4, p. 22.

[191] The Indian mission found at Alken after the death of Camiel Lievens, APBS, India 2, Box15/5, p. 3.

[192] M. VERMEIRE, Gangpur Mission History, vol. I, p. 43; The Indian mission found at Alken after the death of Camiel Lievens, APBS, India 2, Box15/5, p. 4.

[193] M. VERMEIRE, Gangpur Mission History, vol. I, p. 43.

[194] Ibid., p. 39.

[195] During his visit to Tummura on March 17, 1909 and Dumloi on the following day, Fr. Alary noticed the absence of women in the church. He took on as a special task the winning over of the womenfolk to the Catholic fold. To quote the words of Fr. Alary as cited in the work of Fr. Vermeire: "The women do not come to the church, because they are afraid to lose caste. I saw they were keeping aloof from our cooking utensils. I am told they feared contamination." Ibid., pp. 45 - 46, 50.

[196] His diary of 16th of March 1909 under Katang reads: "[There was] a good assistance at Mass. I find in Litibera a couple whose marriage is surely illicit if not invalid. They were married years ago by a German catechist because the girl was a Lutheran." Here he felt the need to appoint a catechist for a Catholic village that could cater to the need of the neighbouring non-Catholic villages. Ibid., p. 45.

[197] Here is an entry from the diary of Fr. Alary on March 19, 1909, as recorded by Fr. Vermeire: "It seems my arrival was known too late, the catechist was in Raikani. I could visit only Mandaria and Kumarkela... The census is in awful state of confusion, catechist had to do it twice, there is still more gulmal (confusion or fight), than ever, and the fellow was not there. I was badly received in the houses. Lutheranism is everywhere. I shall go back to visit Panposh, Lachmimal, Noagaon and Jargara. Some new arrangements have to be made for working properly in that part of the district." Ibid., p. 46.

[198] In addition to the Mundas, Kharias and Oraons, the Berga Oraons or Kisans were a race that the missionaries had the fortune of evangelising in Gangpur. They were also sometimes referred to as 'Gangpuria Oraons', because they speak a similar language, i.e., Kurukh with slight variations. Kisans themselves say that they had a common origin with the Oraons, then they migrated to Gangpur in search of new terrain. Fr. H. Floor was of the opinion that it was probably the Kisans who migrated first to Gangpur and cleared the forest. Their habitat in the midst of the forest and the large property they own are cited as evidence of this claim. Due to their interest in cultivation the Kisans are called Koha Kisans, 'cultivators par excellence'. But unfortunately, much of the land was lost due to laziness, drunkenness and usury. This reduced the Kisans to a state of sukh-basi, without property, leaving them to find work in the mines and railways. Pointing out some of the habitual traits of Kisans, Fr. Floor wrote: "plus ivrogne, moins chaste, fanatiquement attaché à ses diableries, flatteur, menteur systématique, promettant tout, sans difficulté, mais bien determine à ne rien tenir". The first missionary who approached the Kisans in Gangpur was Fr. L. Cardon, and Fr. Alary followed him. Cf. V. GHEYSENS, "Hamirpur", in MB (1920), p. 142; H. FLOOR, "Les Kisans", in MB (1922), pp. 18-19.

[199] The 'rajas' of Berga Oraons, Kisans, have a special competence concerning the protection and observance of tribal laws and customs. If these were against the mission, then it would be difficult to get anyone from the group, since the 'rajas' can ostracise families and individuals from the tribe. Cf. Cardon to Provincial, Rengarih, July 23, 1909, APBS, India 2 – 29/1; Cardon to Provincial, Rengarih, January 13, 1910, APBS, India 2 – 29/1.

[200] M. VERMEIRE, Gangpur Mission History, vol. I, p. 48.

[201] Under the date of April 7, 1910, Fr. Alary mentioned: "(At Hatimunda I) scolded the people a good deal for not sending their children to school. They have no excuse, there are plenty of schools." Ibid., p. 49.

[202] Ibid., p. 46.

[203] Ibid., p. 51.

[204] In October 1912, Fr. Alary settled a land dispute at Bagpur. Regarding that he mentioned in his diary: "The Ganju (the landlord) was creating some annoyance for a widow, in fact, he has been cultivating her land for some time. This year again he ploughed a part. Before everybody the Ganju declared most emphatically that the land belonged to the old lady, and if he did not give it up, she was quite justified in prosecuting him before court... Of course, the Ganju felt somewhat ill at ease when I told him, that there and then he could be forcefully prosecuted for forcibly retaining the parcha (documents). The discussion was polite and courteous on both sides." Ibid., p. 56.

[205] Here are some villages that Fr. Alary visited during the summer month of April 1910: Simarmur, Hatimunda, Gyanpali, Bihaband, Tilaimal, Dahijira, Sahajbahal, Aludega, Pomra, Deogaon, Sakjor, Ambapani, Baiskar, Beratoli, Godratoli, Kumarkela and Kukurbuka. Cf. Ibid., pp. 48-50.

[206] Ibid., p. 56.

[207] Alary to Superior General, Kesramal, July 11, 1916, ARSI, Calcutta 1005-XIII, 8.

[208] Writing to the Provincial on November 10, 1909, Fr. Grosjean showed his enthusiasm for the new mission: "Je partirai tout aussi vite pour les jungles du Gangpur. Que je le veuille ou non, mes pensées s'envolent de ce côte. C'est bien la place qu'il me fallait. Il n'y a ni maison, ni église, ni école: c'est le rôle de pionnier, qui m'est devenu familier." Grosjean to Provincial, Ranchi, November 10, 1909, APBS, India 1 – 12/ Grosjean Letters.

[209] H. JOSSON, Un Chef de Mission aux Indes, p. 363.

[210] M. VERMEIRE, Gangpur Mission History, vol. I, p. 58.

[211] His diary on May 15, 1912 mentioned that there were four confessions and communions at Ambadanr. Cf. Ibid., p. 60.

[212] Sadri is a lingua franca of the tribal Catholics of Chotanagpur, Gangpur and Jashpur.

[213] The Indian mission found at Alken after the death of Camiel Lievens, APBS, India 2, Box15/5, p. 3.

[214] Fr. Grosjean wrote: "On my way back from Rengarih, at Danrpani, examination of the schools. Zacharias, our headmaster, who had accompanied me, helped to examine the boys. There are now three village schools at Jhurmul, Jomonkera and Danrpani, with about 20, 30 and 12 boys respectively. I examined the Jhurmul School on the 12th of May and found excellent results. Jomonkera was examined on Friday; it proved very raw, but there is much good, and the parents appear to take interest in the schools." M. VERMEIRE, Gangpur Mission History, vol. I, p. 61.

[215] Fr. Grosjean observed : "En ce moment, mon dépôt à la Procure générale de Calcutta est tombé à zéro! ... Nos 65 catéchistes, 50 aides-catéchistes, 12 maîtres d'école, nos domestiques, seront ici martedi prochain [pour la paie mensuelle]. Ils demanderont 500 Rupees; c'est peu pour cette armée." H. JOSSON, Un Chef de Mission aux Indes, p. 370.

[216]   M. VERMEIRE, Gangpur Mission History, vol. I, p. 39.

[217]   Ibid., p. 40.

[218]   Ibid., p. 97.

[219] Van der Schueren to Superior General, Calcutta, May 1921, ARSI, Calcutta 1005 - XIV, 13.

[220] Ibid., p. 7.

[221] Ibid.

[222] Ibid.

[223] M. Vermeire recorded one such rumour: "Among the rumours we find: The Padris (fathers) are sending their Christians to be slaughtered in Europe. They are selling your flesh and bones to the Sarkar (Government), and you will never come back from there. All the English are being killed, and they want you also to go and fight." Due to this calumnious attack by the Lutherans there was a rebellion among the Santals of Mayurbhunj. People burned and destroyed public property. Cf. M. VERMEIRE, Biru Mission History: Biru Common, vol. I, Part II, APBS, India Lievens. Ser. B. Box. 4, pp. 93 - 94.

[224] Responding positively to the request of the aborigines of Chotanagpur, the missionaries set two conditions for the recruitment of candidates for the labour corps: (a) each corps would be accompanied by a missionary from the Chotanagpur mission; and b) the money transactions would be carried out through the Cooperative Bank of Ranchi. Cf. M. VERMEIRE, Biru Mission History: Biru Common, vol. I, Part II, APBS, India Lievens. Ser. B. Box. 4, p. 100; VAN DER SCHUEREN, "Au Chota Nagpore", in MB (1921), p. 33.

[225] M. Vermeire, Gangpur Mission History I, p. 103; Fr. Camiel Lievens wrote that "Fr. A. Grignard suggested to 400 men of the 'Labour Corps' to dig in their pockets and bring out some savings to complete the Kesramal church. And that happened indeed! With this money Fr. H. Floor got the roof on the church. Msgr. Meuleman came to bless it on the 2nd of February 1921." The Indian mission found at Alken after the death of Camiel Lievens, APBS, India 2, Box15/5, p.

5; H. Josson, The Mission of West Bengal, p. 262; All those employed in the Labour Corps had agreed to pay Rupees 10 per head. Cf. H. FLOOR, "Lettre de Kesramal", in MB (1920), p. 193.

[226] The Society of the Divine Saviour (SDS) was founded in Rome, on December 8, 1881, by Fr. Franziskus Maria vom Kreuze Jordan (1848-1918). It was founded for the preservation and spread of the faith through the education of youth, retreats, and missionary work among non-Catholics. The society was recognised as a religious congregation in 1883 and received its present name in 1894. The society took up foreign missions when it counted only 6 priests and 17 lay brothers. With two priests (Frs. Otto Hopfenmüller and Angelus Münzloher) and two brothers (Brs. Josef Bächle and Marian Schumm) they began the mission work in the prefecture apostolic of Assam in 1890. Their apostolic zeal was evident in that they had to take care of a vast territory with a handful of people and by their interest in learning Khasi, Bengali and other local languages. For more details on the mission of the Salvatorians in Assam see, C. BECKER, History of the Catholic Missions in Northeast India (1890-1915), trans. G. Stadler and S. Karotemprel, Shillong, 1980; J. EDNARZ, "Missionstätigkeit der Salvatorianer in Assam", in KIEBELE et al (eds), Die Salvatorianer in Geschichte und Gegenwart 1881-1981, Rome 1981, pp. 283 – 291; R. MOLLEN, "Salvatorians", in New Catholic Encyclopedia, vol. XII, p. 1001.

[227] M. VERMEIRE, Biru Mission History: Biru Common, vol. I, Part II, APBS, India Lievens. Ser. B. Box. 4, p. 73. For detailed information regarding the work of the missionaries see pages 72-73, 100-101.

[228] 'Mission work among tea garden coolies and settlers in Assam', APBS, India 2, Box. 1, Ser. B. p. 3.

[229] Some of the places where the Gangpur Catholics migrated for work in the tea gardens in Assam: Dibrugarh district: Khobong, Hoogrijan, Nagarkatta and Hatigarh Bagans; Nowgang Distict: Misa Bagan and Tezpur District: Addabari Bagan. Cf. Assam ka Cha Bagan (Tea garden in Assam), Mission work among garden coolies and settlers in Assam, APBS, India 2, Box. 1, Ser. B. p. 5.

[230] P. TETE, The Kharias and the History of the Catholic Church in Biru, p. 174.

[231] They call their organization Mukti larai, fight for liberation, and it was prevalent in most of the Gangpur villages. They call their leader Raja and his assistant Dewan Sahib. They contended that the Oraon women who spent some time in the convent schools learning Dharam, religion, had taken food cooked in the utensils of other castes. While there, the pagan leaders claimed that the women had irrevocably lost their jait, caste, by eating rice cooked by others, a sure way of losing caste. Therefore, they would be readmitted to the caste by drinking the blood of goats, provided that they declare that they would in future sever all connections with Christianity. Fr. Grosjean claims that the Oraon women had their own utensils and they cooked separately to protect them from being contaminated. Cf. M. VERMEIRE, Gangpur Mission History, vol. I, p. 81; C. BECK "Three

Great Missionaries of Chotanagpur", in C. SRAMBICAL (ed.), Lead me to Light. Divine Word Missionaries 1875-1975 (1975), p. 92.

[232] Tana Bhagatism was a socio-political movement that began in 1915 with the idea 'Oraon land for Oraons'. This should logically conclude that all foreigners, i.e. Hindus, Muslims, Europeans without exception, should leave the land. But soon it took on a religious character, for they tried to reform the traditional religion by abandoning the spirits (bhuts) in order to reaffirm their belief in one God and by adopting an austere life – hence they received their name Bhagats, ascetics. Contrary to the former religious practice of appeasing the bhuts (spirits), the new method advocated that the bhuts be chased out. Fr. Walrave, a missionary in Chotanagpur, wrote, "In the incantations the refrain of Tana, Tana, Fire, Fire (i. e. chase them out) came back again and again, hence the name Tana Bhagats. To have the power to chase the bhuts, one had to purify oneself, externally through daily ablutions and internally by abstaining from drinks and forbidden food such as fish, pork-meat, chicken, a whole category of vegetables, intoxicating drinks, etc. Moreover, one had to be initiated in a whole ritual of incantations which was the noisy part of the programme to which they gave themselves whole night with unheard-of spirit. They practised their exorcisms on anyone they suspected of being possessed by evil spirits (the Dain Bisahis)." The bhagats declared that they would achieve their goal by peaceful means, but in some places, they were preparing ready with their traditional weapons for war. Cf. R.O. DHAN, "The Problems of the Tana Bhagats of Ranchi District", in Bulletin of the Bihar Tribal Research Institute 2/1 (1960), pp. 136 – 186; H. JOSSON, The Mission of West Bengal, pp. 249 – 250.

[233]Citing the diary of Kesramal for 28.9.1916, Fr. Vermeire wrote: "In Ambadanr nearly all the Oraons have become Bhagats. Some 20 families have promised to preserve (the faith) ... The movement has surely a political significance about it. In Nagra, the Rourkela side, Bhagatism seemed to be spreading too." M. Vermeire, Gangpur Mission History, vol. I, p. 105. The same author records the loss of a number of Christians in 1915-1917, which was due to the influence of Tana Bhagatism. Cf. M. VERMEIRE, Biru Mission History: Biru Common, vol. I, Part II, APBS, India Lievens. Ser. B. Box. 4, p. 26.

[234] Ibid., p. 99.

[235] The Indian mission found at Alken after the death of Camiel Lievens, Archief Belges. India 2, Box15/5, p. 4; Commenting on the quality of catechists, Fr. Alary wrote: "La plupart de nos catechists ne sont pas encore à la hauteur de la situation, aussi nos resultats, sont ils moins brillants. Nous avons toutefois obtenu des résultats passables." Alary to Superior General, Kesramal, July 11, 1916, ARSI, Calcutta 1005 XIII, 8, p. 4.

[236] In the beginning of the 20th century there were manganese mines as well as dolomite and lime quarries where Catholics were employed. Cf. H. Floor to Provincial, Kesramal, June 27, 1920, APBS, India 2 – 28/2.

[237] H. JOSSON, The Mission of West Bengal, p. 261.

[238] Ibid., p. 264.

[239] Van der Schueren to Superior General, Calcutta, May 1921, ARSI, Calcutta 1005, XIV-13.

[240] M. VERMEIRE, Gangpur Mission History, vol. I, pp. 67 – 68.

[241] Ibid., p. 70.

[242] The first section comprised the villages Alanda, Haathmunda, Koronga, Kahupani, Somloimunda, Raiberna, Gobarpiti, Simarmur, etc. The second consisted of Panrisila, Jhurmul, Ambadanr, Jambahar, Salangabahar, Babaimohon, Jomonkira, Amko, Jaidega, etc. Cf. Grosjean to Provinical, Kesramal, August 16, 1911, APBS, India 1–12/Grosjean letters.

[243] Alary to Suprior General, Kesramal, July 14, 1917, ARSI, Calcutta 1005 XIII, 23.

[244] Waelkens informed the provincial that the place bought in Behrembasa was well located. Fr. De Gryse, who purchased the property, had a plan of starting a school, which would be followed by a church and presbytery. Cf. Waelkens to Provincial, Calcutta, March 21, 1906, APBS, India 2 – 22/6; Van der Schueren to Suprior General, Calcutta, May 1921, ARSI, Calcut. 1005, XIV-13.

[245] Cardon to Provincial, Rengarih, July 23, 1909, APBS, India 2 – 29/1; Fr. Cardon mentioned the difficulties the missionaries faced with the Berga Oraons, Kissans: "Bon nombre de marriages chrétiens: même les Berga Oraons ont envoyé cinque couples. La providence s'est menagé deux ou trois hommes de cette tribu qui ont chez les leurs le titre de 'raja' et usent de leur autorité pour introduire les lois et coutûmes chrétiennes chez leurs gens. Si ces 'rois' étaient contre nous, humainement parlant, tous les efforts des missionnaires seraient vains pour christianiser ces bergas." Cardon to Provincial, Rengarih, January 13, 1910, APBS, India 2 – 29/1.

[246] H. Floor to Provincial, Kesramal, June 27, 1920, APBS, India 2 – 28/2.

Chapter - 4

The Spread of the Church

Encouraged by the initial success, the missionaries sought additional ways to spread the faith among the tribals and dalits. In their efforts to win the hearts of the people, the Missionaries of St. Francis de Sales (MSFS) received encouragement from their superiors, who appointed certain energetic missionaries well equipped for the difficult task that lay ahead of them. For example, Msgr. J.M. Tissot, vicar apostolic of Visakhapatnam, expressed his willingness to open new stations in the Kondh Mountains, though he lamented the scarcity of personnel and money and cautioned the missionaries to go slow. However, the missionaries were convinced of the need to spread the faith in the interior villages, and they felt that they were 'well prepared'— they were familiar with both the language and the culture of the people; they were confident that they had finally been able to develop an effective strategy for evangelisation; and they were eager to move into the interior and "attack the strongholds of paganism", as the missionaries would call it. It was natural, therefore, that the missionaries began to expand their activities from established centres such as Surada, Cuttack, and Berhampur. Whenever or wherever small Christian communities were established, the missionaries constructed a chapel and appointed a 'teacher-catechist', who not only taught the children but also instructed both adults and children in catechism.

Though the missionaries occasionally evangelised certain villages in Ganjam, they rarely had the opportunity to nurture these villages because of the distances involved. They were restricted to their annual visits and, as a result, the villages were almost abandoned or left to the goodwill of a few catechists. In this study, many of these villages are grouped together and linked to a number of leading centres in which a priest resided, or which he visited often.[1]

The Belgian Jesuits undertook arduous expeditions to the villages that sent deputations from various areas of Gangpur. Though the Hamirpur region in the eastern part was now a separate mission, with two resident priests, Kesramal felt the burden of evangelising a vast territory. The efforts to establish a station at Behrenbasa, in the western part of Gangpur, did not materialise. Somehow, the missionaries kept up the *Mouvement de la Grâce* by regular *tarikhs*,[2] usually conducted in Behrenbasa, and by regular visits. Fr. H. Floor took the initiative to contact both the raja and the dewan seeking permission to start a new station in Gaibira. These two parishes (Hamirpur and Gaibira) illustrate how the mission expanded in Gangpur.

Ganjam Mission

There were three established centres [Surada (1853), Cuttack (1850) and Berhampur (1851)],[3] from which the missionaries moved to the remote villages for evangelisation. Therefore, it is important to understand the development of these centres before describing the subsequent founding of new stations.

Surada: The Capital of Ganjam Mission

By 1870, Surada was a full-fledged parish with resident priests and Sisters, schools and orphanages. It continued to be one of the centres of expansion under the MSFS.[4] Even after almost seventeen years since the foundation of the Surada mission, the influence of Fr. J.M. Dupont continued. He maintained a good rapport with the local people, as he was fluent both in *Kui* and Oriya. In one of his letters to Fr. Clavel, Fr. Richard wrote that he would prefer that the mission was not so much the owner of the villages but that the priests were primarily concerned with the spiritual welfare of the people.[5] He added:

> I would like Fr. J. M. Dupont, who speaks Oriya fluently, if he recuperates his health well, to establish himself near the villages of Dantholinghy and Pipalpanga to work for their conversion. Before Pipalponga came to the mission, a good number of persons had started to receive instructions.

> However, for a long time they have continued to say: *hominem non habemus*.
> One more priest at Surada and a third at Thotavally (Joseph Konda) could
> have under them some confident persons. Besides our properties of Borady
> and Thotavally, we need to have six more villages there.[6]

Msgr. J. M. Tissot noted the progress when he went on a pastoral tour to
the northern part of his vicariate in 1881. Among the mission stations that
he visited, Surada was certainly better developed with all the infrastructure
that characterised it as an important centre. Local Catholics responded
positively to work there. However, he felt that more could still be done.[7]

When Fr. Descombes came to Surada in October 1881, it had two
resident priests (Frs. Bonaventure and Descombes) and two chapels.
However, this situation changed dramatically when Fr. Bonaventure left
for Koraput (Jeypur) on a fact-finding mission in 1885, and Fr. Descombes
was left alone with five chapels to care for. Besides, Dantholinghy was also
attached to Surada.[8] One can imagine the magnitude of the demands placed
on the shoulders of the young missionary. Even before the departure of
Fr. Bonaventure, Msgr. Tissot shared a similar concern. Writing in 1881,
Msgr. Tissot mentioned that Surada required more missionaries to attend
to the increasing number of Christians, including those orphans brought
up by the mission.[9] However, there was relief, in 1883, when Fr. Dupont
became the chaplain of the orphanage and the administrator of the paddy
field. These were tasks carried out previously by Fr. Bonaventure.

When Fr. Bonaventure left for Koraput (Jeypur), the catechumenate,
numbering between 60 and 100 persons, was entrusted to the care of Fr.
J.M. Descombes. Three catechists were also employed to teach them the
prayers. Their combined efforts brought many people into the church.
In response to the call of the missionaries, the Christians of Surada even
promised to lead an exemplary life. Although there was no serious direct
opposition from the Hindus at this time, the calumnious rumours that the
missionaries would take the Christians to their home countries persisted.
However, in some instances, the Christians themselves challenged the
rumours by stating that they continued to live in the same village for
many years without ever being transported to Europe.[10]

Surada, a Cursed Land?

The initial enthusiasm of the Catholics at Surada soon waned, and Christian
life became stagnant, which caused some concern to the missionaries.

Though perilous at times, the inhospitable Kondh mountains were not the real cause of concern for the missionaries, most of whom were brave and willingly went wherever their superiors sent them. In spite of the initial growth of the mission and the hard work of the missionaries, Surada did not record an increase in the number of adherents to the faith; the people continued with their superstitious practices. The villagers' critical attitude towards the mission led the missionaries to describe the Surada mission as a 'cursed land.' What was the reason? Fr. Bonaventure reported: "The mission, for long years, has given us no consolation. Among ourselves, we call it 'the cursed land.' We propose to make a last attempt. If it succeeds, all glory to the Sacred Heart! If it fails, it may influence the final decision to abandon this unfortunate country."[11]

Although the Catholics regularly attended Mass and prayers, they did not recognise the authority of the missionaries, who in their unsuccessful attempts to evangelise the villages, concentrated their efforts on the orphanages at Karicotte, Dantholinghy and Thotavally. These villages had large farms. They had hoped that the nucleus of Christian families would eventually produce a sizeable population that could bear witness to the faith in a non-Christian setting. Contrary to their expectations, however, the people were discontented and complained that the missionaries somehow failed to provide them with what they rightfully deserved.[12]

In 1883 Fr. Bonaventure lamented the decadence of Surada, once a flourishing and promising mission. This was partly due to the death of several pioneers, who could not be replaced and partly due to the fact that the priests were unable to visit many of the centres more than once a year. Some villages had not seen even the 'shadow of a priest'.[13] In spite of their toil, there prevailed the 'cult of the devil'[14] which no doubt saddened them immensely. Reporting on the manner of offering sacrifices to the local deities, Fr. Bonaventure wrote:

> Every Tuesday morning, crowds of pagans gather to the strains of a musical band, a few steps from our house, to offer sacrifices to *Tacorani* [*Thakurani*], the goddess of evil, represented by a red-painted wooden post; kids, young goats, are immolated to it and offerings of milk poured on it. A *pythoness* (a witch) who I believe to be really possessed, proclaims oracles and indicates with wild gestures the decisions of the goddess. The first time I saw this sight, I couldn't help weeping. And this is the people we have to convert.[15]

The missionaries seemed unable to inspire the people. The combination of a hardened disposition and the missionaries' nagging sense of failure forced them to take a final decision whether or not to continue the mission.

'Apostleship of Prayer' in Surada

The indifference and tepid outlook of the Christians at Surada challenged the missionaries to look for new ways to proclaim God's Word to the people. Committed as they were to the care of Christians, particularly the families in Dantholinghy and other villages, the missionaries made several attempts at instilling a spirit of fervour in the people. Fr. Bonaventure introduced the 'Apostleship of Prayer'[16] among them, and soon he realised that the people themselves responded positively, because of the elaborate nature of the initiation rites that called forth their enthusiastic participation. Many enrolled in it. On feast days the priest gave a short explanation highlighting the importance of the organisation.[17] A good number of orphans were also happy to register their names.

One of the devices that Fr. Bonaventure followed was to give more solemnity to simple religious occasions such as receiving the scapular. The people were fond of solemnities and feasts. He described the manner of the celebration: "I keep a small table in the centre of the church, with a picture of the Sacred Heart, a register and some Sacred Heart scapulars sent by my sister. After a short talk and a hymn to our Lord, I write down the names. Then I call the boys one by one and place around their neck the scapular. I bless each with the sign of the cross and send him back to his place."[18] In order to make it an association, he planned to introduce the enrolment card. Since he found a positive response in Surada, Fr. Bonaventure asked that a director for the Apostleship of Prayer be appointed for the vicariate.

Activities of Fr. Descombes

Fr. J.M. Descombes' work was very much connected with the growth of the Surada mission. On his arrival in 1881 he decided to lead an austere life. He practised one of the methods of Fr. Robert de Nobili, namely, preaching the gospel as an itinerant monk. His principal desire was to go to the villages and preach our Lord.[19] He was encouraged in his efforts by missionaries like Fr. Thevenet, who used to tell him: "Take with you a small tent and settle in a village to preach Christianity. If they listen to you, convert them. If they don't, shake the dust off your shoes and go elsewhere."[20] Fr. Dupont also encouraged him in his efforts. Fr. Descombes was convinced that his duty was to proclaim the gospel and that conversions depended on God. He was not alone in this way of life; other itinerant monks included Frs. Payraud and Buttay.[21]

Fascinated by the methods of evangelisation adopted by Fr. Robert de Nobili, Fr. Descombes desired to become a Brahmin in order to convert that race. However, both Msgr. Tissot and the confreres were against such an initiative for two reasons: (1) it might become a stumbling block to the conversion of Panos and others of lower origin; and (2) the method proved to be ineffective in the Ganjam mission.[22] Even a great linguist such as Fr. Joseph Seigneur could not convert the Brahmins. Hence Fr. Descombes was persuaded by his confreres to abandon these initiatives despite his own convictions that if he lived alone, avoiding any contact with people of lower castes and the missionaries who served them, he might be able to win a few Brahmins.[23]

In his wanderings Fr. J.M. Descombes soon realised the importance of caring for those who were already Christians. Fr. Descombes described his way to his superior general: "When I began to convert the villagers of Badossai and Alossai, I first gained the important men of these villages, who declared themselves favourable. Winning other villages up to a distance of 50 km took place at the meetings with the villagers. How great were the fears of our catechists at the time of these meetings. Two days later, one of the catechists told me, 'Ah, father, all went well, but I lost my appetite for several days'."[24] Due to his charismatic leadership, many Panos began to attend the prayers. Some Protestants (Baptists) wanted to join them as well.[25] Fr. Descombes distributed medicines, which the people took regularly. They had a preference for the holy water, blessed by the priest, which they took home after the Sunday services.[26]

The Court Case of Surada

A particular court case severely tested the mission. The missionaries thought that if they lost the case, it would send a negative signal to the people and might even be ruinous to the objectives of the mission. They took all the precautions because they did not want it to appear to the Protestants that their efforts to convert the Kondhs and Panos had been futile. They wanted to be victorious in this particular case, since the missionaries claimed that the Wesleyan Protestants were helping Andrew, who denounced the missionaries in court. The missionaries were of the opinion that a person who had worked with them for many years could only turn against them if he was influenced by the Protestants. In order to help Fr. Bonaventure with the case, Fr. Dupont, who knew the laws well and had solved many disputes in the mountains, volunteered to go to Surada.[27] Fr. Bonaventure wrote: "Since my arrival at Surada [1878], I have been busy with court cases. It is an inheritance from Fr. Dupont who was so fond of chicanery. Up to now, I have always won the cases. I have still one to be decided by the Madras High Court, the last one."[28]

Fr. Dupont's liberal policy, particularly in the administration of the farms, suffered a setback. In order to redeem the situation and revitalise the mission, Fr. Riccaz[29] was sent to Surada with a clear mandate to keep the mission in order, especially the farms. Having seen no reliable person to supervise the farm, he decided to lease it out for five years in 1878 to Andrew, one of the orphans educated in the mission, in 1877. Since Andrew produced a written document, the mission advanced him 400 hectolitres of rice and 73 pairs of bullocks. However, Andrew did not get along well with Fr. Dupont, when the latter was the parish priest. In the meantime, when Fr. Bonaventure took charge of the mission, Andrew assured him that he would abide by the previous agreement. However, in view of his worsening drunkenness, Fr. Bonaventure dismissed Andrew and asked other farmers in the village to seize all the bullocks given to him. He even took on himself the management of the fields. Infuriated by these developments, Andrew denounced the missionary for theft and usurpation of property and took him to court. When the outcome was unsatisfactory, Andrew appealed to the court in Berhampur. However, the judge was not favourable to the mission and ruled in favour of Andrew, releasing those who had given false witness. In his attempt to defame the missionary further, Andrew lodged another complaint in the court of Aska where the judge decided against him. But when he appealed to the judge in Berhampur, the latter sent the papers to Madras, which in its turn remanded the case to Aska. Fr. Bonaventure thought that the Protestants were behind this prolonged legal battle.[30] The judge at Berhampur was unfavourable toward the missionaries, since Msgr. J.M. Tissot complained against him in the Madras High Court.[31]

In the meantime, Andrew also lodged a complaint at the court of Berhampur in the hope of obtaining a compensation of Rs. 7000/-. This time he pleaded his case as a pauper. Since the mission had neglected to follow the procedures in dismissing Andrew, the judge awarded him Rs. 700/- as remuneration for his services. But since he had admitted in court that he owed Rs. 1000/- to the missionaries, they actually received Rs. 300/- from him instead.[32]

Thotavally

Thotavally was a small village eight km away from Surada. In 1867 Fr. Guillermin purchased a forest here, with the intention of settling the families of orphans gathered during the great famine. Since trees and bushes covered the land, a number of Kondh families were engaged to clear the forest.[33] Though the Kondhs were exposed to Christian influence, they were not touched by the missionaries' preaching. Only in 1881 did they begin to respond. Initially Fr. Guillermin spent much time and money in establishing the station, which was called *Josepattah* or *St. Joseph Kondah* (village of St. Joseph). The missionaries intended to transfer the boys' orphanage to Thotavally, thus separating it from the girls' orphanage, which had been entrusted to the Sisters of St. Joseph of Annecy.[34] In 1871 Fr. H. Moenne-Loccoz came to Thotavally to take charge of the orphanage and its 67 children. The girls' orphanage in Surada had about 130 to 150 children and 20 widows. These were looked after by three St. Joseph Sisters, two native Sisters and a helper.[35]

Some of the grown-up boys from the orphanage were asked to clear the forest and help with farming. They learned to plough as well as to read and write. The missionaries thought that if the orphan children married and settled on the land cleared for cultivation, eventually a number of Christian villages would emerge. Such settlements, they hoped, could carry on the work of evangelisation. Writing in March 1872, Fr. Moenne-Loccoz described the beginning of this settlement: "There were already eight families, of which three families had a child each."[36] Two more villages also belonged to the mission-Dantholinghy and Pipalpanga. For these the missionaries paid a nominal tax to the government. Fr. Dupont seemed to have converted a good number of people in Pipalpanga when he was appointed to look after the orphans.[37] However, their preparations for baptism were minimal.

The first to enter the Catholic Church in Thotavally was a Protestant woman, Jesse, who as a girl was probably rescued from being sacrificed as *Meriah*. The Protestants brought her up in an orphanage. She was married to one of the Kondhs working as a woodcutter in Thotavally. Jesse knew how to read and write. When she came to Thotavally with her husband she listened to the instructions of Fr. Dupont and requested to be received into the church. Soon a catechumenate began in order to instruct other Kondhs. Despite the missionaries' efforts, the catechumenate did not progress well due to the disturbance caused by a sorcerer who frightened the Kondhs. When the cause for the disturbance was discovered, the sorcerer was chased out of the village. Soon a dozen families received baptism.

The nascent Christian community of Thotavally grew under the guidance of Fr. Décarre, who was appointed the priest in charge of the mission in 1889. He spent much time with the people. He built a new village with a spacious church in Thotavally. He saw to it that the instructions continued. Under his influence some 20 families accepted the Christian faith. He offered work in the fields to the pagans, provided that they agreed to take part in prayers and instructions. In this way he managed to convert about 200 of them. Under Fr. Décarre, Thotavally became an important centre with a flourishing parish with a church, a cemetery and a catechumenate.[38]

Torobady

Torobady, a village inhabited both by Kondhs and by Panos, lies about 50 km from Surada and about 12 km from Koussipanga, where the missionaries established their first church among the Kondhs. The Kondhs, who lived with a tiny minority of Panos, were free here, as there was no dominance by the *Oriyas*.[39] The story of the conversion of Torobady began in May 1886, when a strange disease that claimed quite a number of lives was rampant in the village. Since the Panos became the first victims, the Kondhs ordered them to leave the place. Not knowing a way out, the Panos returned to their relatives who were living in Surada, who advised them that only the Catholic priests could relieve them of their affliction. The afflicted Panos approached Fr. J.M. Descombes, who agreed to visit Torobady on the assurance that if they were delivered from the evil spirits, they would become Christians. In June 1886 he moved into a hut and celebrated Mass on the feast of the Ascension, which was attended by many villagers. During the Mass he was informed of two possessed women who could not be controlled. He went there with the assistance of boys carrying the cross. No sooner did the possessed women see him than they became violent, causing panic among the bystanders who had gathered to observe the responses of the missionary. After reading the prologue of St. John, the priest sprinkled holy water on the possessed women. They became calm and normal. The people considered this a miracle and asked the priest to bless every house with his '*mantram*',[40] which contained supernatural power. The priest obliged the village chief to accompany the procession with a bucket of holy water on his head. From that day everyone in the village wanted to be instructed in the new faith.[41] By 1889 all of them had abandoned their superstitious ways and were baptised, leading a Christian life.

Cuttack

Cuttack[42] attracted the attention of Catholic missionaries not because of its political importance but for its growing Christian community, which existed even before the arrival of the Missionaries of St. Francis de Sales. The Imperial Gazetteer refers to the Catholics in Cuttack as follows: "A Roman Catholic mission, founded in 1845, maintains in Cuttack city a chapel, a church, a convent, and a boys' school."[43] Before the arrival of MSFS, the Catholic community was composed of those who came from outside Orissa, and it was under the jurisdiction of Calcutta. Later, for practical reasons, such as geographical proximity and the scarcity of priests, Cuttack was attached to the mission of Visakhapatnam, from which a missionary visited it annually. Fr. Domenge provided some information regarding the early history of the mission dating as far back as to 17th century, when the Jesuits from Balasore visited Cuttack to administer the sacraments.[44] A year after the death of Fr. Francis Sermet (1850), Fr. Balmand was appointed to look after the vast territory that included Ganjam, Berhampur and Cuttack. Because he could not remain in Cuttack, he chose Berhampur, a central location, for his residence. Only in 1855 did Cuttack have its own resident priest in Fr. Richard, who purchased land for the mission and built a modest chapel in 1859 dedicated to Our Lady.[45]

In 1868, when Fr. Décarre was transferred from Vizianagram to Cuttack, the town had a population of 35,000 to 45,000, of which the Catholics numbered about 600, composed of Europeans, East Indians and Malabars or Tamils who worked in the army (32nd Madras Regiment). A few high-ranking officers--such as the commissioner of Orissa and his wife, Lady Thompson-- were the patrons and protectors of the work of the missionaries.[46]

Activities of the Sisters in Cuttack

In 1872 a group of Sisters of St. Joseph of Annecy came to Cuttack at the invitation of the missionaries to work among the women and the girls. Their arrival in Cuttack brought an added joy to the missionaries.[47] Initially the Sisters were living in a house formerly used by the Fathers, who vacated it for them. The Sisters used the church building for a school. Due to some difficulties, the Sisters left Cuttack in January 1877 and returned in November 1879.[48] Realising the need for a more spacious place for their activities, Fr. Décarre requested a site on the northern side of the church. Fr. Foulex[49] considered it a beautiful location near the sea. Thanks to the kindness of the colonel of the 32nd Madras Regiment and also of the commissioner of Orissa, that land was given to the mission for constructing a new school for girls and a convent for the Sisters.[50]

In July 1881 the foundation was laid, which was attended by the commissioner of Orissa and his wife, Lady Thompson, as the chief guests, plus other important personalities of the city. In a letter to Sr. Cèsarie, Sr. Claire reported:

> Last Thursday (July 6, 1881), we had a beautiful ceremony; the blessing of the first stone of our new convent. You need to know that the government has given to the mission a very big plot of terrain. Our good Fr. Décarre has done a good job in taking the work ahead: the foundations are already completed; the compound wall is almost finished. Returning to the blessing of the first stone, the Chief-Commissioner [commissioner], who takes the place of the Viceroy, had agreed to preside over the musical band, instead of the colonel of the regiment, who consented to assist. The music was pleasant. All the top officers of Cuttack wanted to be present for the ceremony.[51]

Many of those who attended the inauguration greeted the Sisters in appreciation of their dedication. For the construction of the convent and for the running of the orphanage, the Sisters had organised a fair, which turned out to be a great success.[52] It covered a part of the expenses, which reached a sum of 50,000 francs. However, the vicar apostolic was displeased, since the other convents in the vicariate apostolic had cost far less.[53] When in 1882 the number of orphans reached 30, the Sisters accommodated the little ones in the convent because of the limited space available in the orphanage.[54] By 1884 the construction was finished, and the Sisters started to use the convent.

In November 1885, Fr. Décarre started a dispensary in Cuttack under the patronage of Lady Thompson, the wife of the commissioner of Orissa, whose subsequent visits to the dispensary encouraged the missionaries. Since Cuttack was an important centre for the province, the missionaries felt the need to establish such a dispensary, where the missionaries could also recuperate and rest. The Sisters baptised several children *in articulo mortis* and treated about 110 patients during October 1887. In spite of their devotion to their work and the recognition from the people, the British government required them to have a professional qualification--which they did not have. So, there was the danger of having to turn the dispensary over to some certified nurses.[55] Fr. Décarre wrote to the Mother General about the Sisters:

> I am sure Mother St. Charles might have written to you about our good work in Cuttack and the need to begin a dispensary that would bring an abundant harvest of people to heaven. I have written to our bishop requesting him to give you the details of the project and I ask your help in providing personnel for the work. I have no doubt that you are ready for any type of sacrifice so that we may obtain success and prove to the government that the Sisters are capable of taking control of the work.[56]

The Cuttack municipality wanted to open a dispensary exclusively for women which would be run by women doctors and attendants to avoid receiving treatment from men. Many women would rather die than submit themselves to the gaze of a male physician. When the municipality requested help from the mission, one of the Sisters was made available for this apostolate.[57] It required learning both Oriya and *Hindustani*, both spoken by most people.[58] Later, in 1908, when the Government built a hospital, two Sisters took up residence there and served as nurses. Initially they looked after the laundry and the kitchen, but later the Sisters were asked to supervise everything. Their good work and their devotion brought general satisfaction among the people, including the Hindu doctors.[59]

Mission Schools in Cuttack

Initially, the work of the MSFS in Cuttack consisted mainly of administering sacraments to the Tamils of the 32nd Madras Regiment and in running the school for boys. As soon as he arrived in Cuttack in 1868, Fr. Décarre was busy starting a school for Catholic boys. His experience in Vizianagram, where he had set up a school with 160 students and 6 teachers, prompted him to begin one in the new station. Initially, he had 30 students and a teacher who had studied at St. Xavier's College in Calcutta.[60] Time permitting, the missionaries also involved themselves in the schoolwork. For example, Fr. Girard used to spend five hours each day teaching algebra, geometry and English literature.[61] Fr. Foulex described the nature of his work as follows: "I am the headmaster. I am happy to supervise and to take some classes to earn Rs. 20 per month. Our school is a small *Babil* (tower of Babel)."[62]

The quality of education was high, and by 1872 there were 90 boys in the school -- mostly Catholic students. Even though non-Christian students expressed their willingness to pay, the missionaries turned down their requests for admission. They did not take more students because they wanted to apply to the government for the grant-in-aid intended for religious minority schools.[63] Fr. Souchon had cultivated a personal rapport with the officials, especially with the commissioner and the inspector of schools, and he applied for the grant-in-aid. Not only did the missionaries excel in imparting the prescribed courses to the pupils but also in instilling certain moral values. The Catholic students, as a rule, had to attend catechism classes and pass the examinations conducted by the Fathers from Visakhapatnam. For example, in 1911 Fr. Rossillon[64] went to Cuttack for a dual purpose: (1) to conduct exams in catechism at the school; and (2) to preach a retreat for those receiving their first communion.[65] In December 1898, Sir Jean Woodburn, lieutenant governor of Bengal, visited the Cuttack school. Although the annals refer to the favour received from his official visit, it is not clear what this favour actually was. However, the visit itself must have been an honour bestowed on the Fathers and Sisters in recognition of their dedication.[66]

Growth of the Cuttack mission

Though Cuttack never recorded any mass conversions, there were occasional adult baptisms that marked the growth of the mission. In 1882 Fr. Foulex began a 'Reading Club', which was strongly criticised by his colleagues, since the journals read were Protestant, although they were subscribed by those who had been educated in the mission's orphanage.[67] Since there was a general feeling that exposing Catholics to Protestant literature would create unnecessary tensions, Fr. Foulex was encouraged to spend his time more usefully with the conversion.[68]

After a three-year absence, on June 28, 1884, Msgr. Tissot, vicar apostolic of Visakhapatnam, made a pastoral visit to Cuttack. He received a warm reception with the 32nd Regiment playing the band. When the vicar apostolic celebrated Mass, the church overflowed with a large number of participants, both Catholics and non-Catholics, who came to witness that great event. The occasion was also used to confirm 60 adults, and 40 children received Holy Communion for the first time.[69] By the time his successor Msgr. Clerc[70] took over, Cuttack had grown into an established station. In his report to the Holy See, Msgr. Clerc conveyed that Cuttack with its two small stations, Khurda Road and Puri, was the principal centre of the northern part of his vicariate. He wrote:

> Cuttack is the principal and more ancient of the cities. It possesses a resident priest, a beautiful church with three naves and a convent of the Sisters of St. Joseph of Annecy, who are in charge of the hospital of the city, an English school and an orphanage for the European and Eurasian children, for the expansion of which the new provincial government of Bihar and Orissa allotted a sum of Rs. 20,000.00.[71]

Hostilities with the Baptists

The relationship between the Catholics and the Baptists was never very good, since each perceived the other as intruders. From its inception the girls' school run by the Sisters annoyed the Baptists who started their own school on July 1, 1881. The Baptists forbade their own children from studying at the Catholic School.[72] They were hostile toward the school in Cuttack and toward the Catholic missionaries.[73] In November 1898 the Annals of the Sisters of St. Joseph of Annecy reported that their work in the school had suffered from Baptist competition, since some of their students transferred to the Baptist school. However, the Sisters were pleased with the growth of the orphanages and of the home for the widows. They were also pleased with the dispensary, where they had baptised about 200 people.[74] However, Fr. Descombes acknowledged the contribution of Protestants when he was in need of money to print a book in Oriya.[75]

Puri

Puri,[76] situated about 80 km from Cuttack on the Bay of Bengal, has been and still is one of the most important Hindu pilgrim centres. It attracted (and still attracts) not only tens of thousands of pilgrims for its annual *Ratha Yatra* (car festival) but also Protestant preachers who used this opportunity to preach the gospel. There were also other festivals that attracted pilgrims, and which provided the Protestant missionaries opportunities for conversions.[77]

The Catholic missionaries similarly wanted to make use of the opportunity. In one of his letters to Cardinal Simeoni, Prefect of the Propaganda Fide, Msgr. Tissot stated that it was impossible to get a piece of land in Puri. However, thanks to the generosity of a Protestant who became Catholic, the mission was able to buy a plot with a small house.[78] At that time (1881), there were two local families whose Christian background could be traced to the conversion of their grandfather, an orphan baptised and instructed by Mr. Madeira, a Catholic who was a local health care officer.[79] The Catholic missionaries planned to start a school which would provide a platform to launch their mission work. However, Fr. Riccaz (missionary in Visakhapatnam) suggested that several factors must be kept in view before opening a school as proposed. First, the school should not be established in order to seek converts but to educate them, whenever a sufficient number of Christian boys is found. Thus, the school would become a medium for instructing Catholic students in the faith. Second, once established, the school could provide a favourable setting for the conversions of non-Catholic students who might attend the school. The missionaries were to emphasise that those who wished to enrol in the school had to participate in the prayers and attend catechism classes.[80] As the assistant priest of Cuttack in 1882, Fr. Foulex went to celebrate Easter at Puri, where there were about 25 communicants. The small Catholic community consisted of a few government officers and their servants from Madras. Having seen the growth of the community, Fr. Décarre (the Parish Priest of Cuttack) and his companion, Fr. Foulex, decided to build a chapel, which they hoped would compete with the temple of Puri.[81]

In June 1884 Msgr. Tissot visited Puri, where he found a good number of Christians. This pleased him, as there had been none during his previous visit.[82] Fr. Rey disclosed the plan for Puri in the following sentences: "We are making plans for Puri. We are planning to install a beautiful statue of Our Lady in a small chapel, close to which we will have a hospital for cholera victims and dying persons, all these in view of ...

starting a pilgrimage for Our Lady in place of Jagannath."[83] Although the plan appeared plausible, it had to wait many years before it was realised.

In 1887 Fr. Décarre requested Fr. Superior to send him a statue of St. Benedict to be installed in Puri, where, he said, Hinduism was very strong.[84] Fr. Décarre was convinced that the acts of kindness of the missionaries would naturally attract the people. Realising the religious fervour of the Hindu pilgrims who visited Puri, the missionary rightly thought that proselytism not only would produce a negative result but also might bring more difficulties for the missionaries. So, he proposed to start a hospital to care for the abandoned sick in the city, especially during the time of the annual *Rath Yatra* (car festival). Fr. Décarre observed:

> For one who has seen with his eyes the manner in which the poor miserable pilgrims were abandoned to their sad lot, especially when death is imminent, there is no doubt that the Sisters with a hospital could do an immense good. Under such a treatment filled with charity, who could resist the grace?[85]

With this in mind, Fr. Décarre obtained the permission of Msgr. J.M. Tissot to correspond with the collector of Puri in order to purchase a dilapidated house, which could initially serve as the accommodation of the Sisters. From there they could go to the hospital, which was about to be built in the neighbourhood.

Most of the early Christians came from among the pilgrims who were on the threshold of death and who needed gentle care. They were baptised immediately without giving much thought to instruction or to their understanding of the faith.[86] Fr. Décarre also planned to establish a leprosarium, which would be of immense help to those with leprosy who came to Puri. His vision received further encouragement from the Puri municipality, which offered him both a site and the money for the construction. It also expressed willingness to allocate Rs. 60 per month for the support of the Sisters. Fr. Décarre offered the services of a catechist known for his goodness and helpfulness to the Sisters.[87] Although the documents are silent whether or not the proposed plan was executed, one can conclude that it was not, since there were only a handful of Christians whom the missionaries visited regularly.

In 1890 the MSFS acquired a plot of land and constructed a chapel in Puri. For unknown reasons the chapel deteriorated and was abandoned by 1900. It was auctioned subsequently without the knowledge of the missionaries, who continued to pay taxes on the property. When the missionaries learned that the chapel was being demolished, they presented a petition to the judge seeking a restraining order. The judge found the new buyer, a government employee, negligent for failing to realise that the missionaries owned the property. In 1905 the missionaries applied to the collector for a plot of free land on which they could construct a church, an orphanage and a school for poor children. The collector granted the request, and a chapel was built there in 1910.[88]

Berhampur

Berhampur[89] was another mission, founded before the arrival of MSFS, where many Catholic merchants and soldiers lived. They were under the pastoral care of a priest from Balasore. In the 17th century, Fr. Martin, a Jesuit, visited the Christians a few times. Later the Goan priests belonging to the Golconda mission built a chapel. But the station remained underdeveloped due to the unavailability of priests. The first priest to reside at Berhampur was Fr. Balmand in 1851, when he was appointed to the northern part of the vicariate. Later, in 1854, when Fr. Richard was appointed to Berhampur, he took care of Cuttack as well. Within the precinct occupied by the troops there was a small-dilapidated chapel built of mud and a few logs. Since this was in poor condition and its space inadequate for a growing community, Fr. Richard asked the commandant if he could undertake the construction of a new chapel. He initiated a monthly subscription to which the soldiers could contribute towards the project. It was said that even Protestants and Brahmins contributed generously, and the church was dedicated on July 16, 1865. The chapel survived until 1909.

Fr. Michael Perissin, who replaced Fr. Richard in 1866, rendered valuable service in Berhampur during the great famine of 1866. Besides baptising many children *in articulo mortis*, he brought them to the orphanage, which was later transferred to Surada. The Catholics in Berhampur were mainly Tamil soldiers and their families and a handful of Eurasians. During the time of Fr. Riccaz (1883) the existing chapel was converted into a presbytery, and a new church was built in 1884. The chapel remained unaltered till the arrival of Fr. Gangloff, who rebuilt the church in 1909 after a violent cyclone caused enormous damage to the property.[90] Once the troops left the city, the Christian community of Berhampur was reduced to a small community.[91]

Gopalpur

Gopalpur[92] was and still is a maritime town situated about 14 km. from Berhampur. Unlike other stations founded by the MSFS, it had neither the presence of a para-military force nor of a strong community of Kondhs and Panos. The motives for starting a mission station at Gopalpur were to have a place for convalescence from the fatiguing expeditions in the mountains and to recuperate from the effects of malaria. The first reference to Gopalpur is found in the letter of Fr. Chéminal to *La Feuillette* (Mother house of the MSFS in Annecy, France) in 1855, after he had met with the colonel appointed to civilise the Kondhs. On arrival of Frs. Chéminal and Balmand in Gopalpur they met a small Catholic group.[93] But, there was no mention of the missionaries until 1881 when the missionaries went there to request the governor to grant them some land to construct a home. The governor granted their request but stipulated that they had to construct the house within six months and that the property should revert to the government when the missionaries left the place.[94]

With its artificial bay, a small dock and a huge storehouse, Gopalpur functioned as a seaport from 1880 to 1895. There were many merchants and immigration agencies involved in the transportation of labourers to Burma, among whom there were a few Christians. Probably this was one of the reasons for constructing a house in Gopalpur.[95] Fr. J.M. Dupont founded a Christian community among the fishermen, and the nascent community had a church in 1883.[96] The missionaries also built a sanatorium for the Kondh mission.

In the absence of a resident priest in Gopalpur, the church did not register any significant growth until 1889, when cholera broke out, claiming a heavy toll.[97] The missionaries, both priests and Sisters, provided relief to the affected people. Fr. Alphonse Voisin,[98] the priest in charge at the time, informed the Mother General of the Sisters of St. Joseph of Annecy that Sr. Hippolyte had already baptised a few children *in articulo mortis* but that most of them died immediately. While Sr. Hippolyte was busy baptising children, Fr. Voisin was busy burying the dead. In their misery the parents were eager to sell their little children. Fr. Voisin reported that Sr. Hippolyte even bought a little girl for a rupee.[99] Once the famine and cholera were over, the mission was faced with an inundation which carried away people and property. Most of the livestock also perished.

The brave and timely demonstration of Christian charity performed by both Fr. Voisin and the Sisters of St. Joseph of Annecy brought about 400 people into the church.[100]

The missionaries succeeded in purchasing a substantial piece of property on which they could develop a number of institutions, including a school and a seminary that offered instruction in philosophy and theology under Fr. Marie Eugène Gojon.[101] The Sisters of St. Joseph of Annecy, who started a convent in Gopalpur in 1890, ran the school.[102] Informing their Mother General about their work in Gopalpur, Sr. Hippolyte wrote: "We arrived on March 14 (1890). They asked us to open a school. We could not do it immediately since we did not have anything. But we are going to begin a school on the 12th of this month (May 1890) under the protection of the Holy Virgin. Sr. Stanislas is with me, who took final vows."[103]

Apart from the conversions during the natural calamity, there were a few additions to the church. Reporting on such events, Fr. Voisin wrote: "Conversions do take place; yesterday I was happy of being able to baptise 42 adults, of whom 3 have already reached 70 years of age, and 17 children in young age. Entire villages come for learning prayers. All are submissive and very docile . . . They learn prayers and catechism with an extraordinary facility."[104] The number of Christians diminished once many left for Assam to work in the tea gardens, which was considered to be lucrative.[105] Although the people who grew up in the orphanages were settled in the territory with some rice fields, a hut, a pair of bullocks and a plough, they felt it was too much work. Therefore, they sold the property and moved to Assam.[106] Writing to his uncle, Fr. Allard mentioned: "The fisher folk of Gopalpur have just started to listen to our religion. Their chief is also well disposed. Two months back, when many of them were affected by fever, they came to the chapel to receive a blessing. One week ago, Fr. Descombes told that he converted 50 people this year [1892]."[107]

Between 1895 and 1924 Gopalpur deteriorated as the seaport was closed by 1895 and the huge storehouse was also abandoned. Except for the Immigration Agency, there was no activity. The seminary itself was moved to Visakhapatnam after complaints from both Fathers and students.[108]

The Seminary at Gopalpur

Two major considerations -- both political and pragmatic -- underlay the missionaries' motivation for establishing the seminary at Gopalpur. First, at the end of the 19th century, the French chamber voted a law that obliged the clerics to perform a year of military service. This law, known as *'les curés sac au dos'*, came into effect in the autumn of 1889. One of the articles stipulated that an 'ecclesiastical student' would have to complete three years of military service (normally it was two) if he did not persevere in his vocation. Another article stated that all priests who had attained the age of twenty-six and had not occupied a post recognised by the state would be called to the barracks if they had not received the benefit of exemption. This law created consternation among ecclesiastics, resulting in a number of defections. In order to limit such dangers and to safeguard the vocations of youngsters, the superiors of MSFS decided to start a seminary in India. Second, the missionaries who had been trained in the West had to learn the language and customs of the people before they could commence their missionary activities. A seminary established in the area of their labour could therefore formally introduce them to the local culture and enable them to become acclimatised. Thus, the superiors thought, future missionaries would be better prepared and could avoid military service altogether.[109]

Thus in 1889 Fr. J. Tissot, superior general of MSFS, decided, along with the bishop of Visakhapatnam, to find a seminary for those who had completed high school.[110] The seminary began in 1890 with 3 students and Fr. Gojon, as the first Rector. The curriculum and rules were similar to the ones that existed in Europe, namely, long hours of study and short period of recreation. But because of the ill health of some of the students, the rules had to be modified, allowing more time for recreation, games and walks. Besides English, the students had to learn Oriya and Telugu under Brahmin teachers. Fr. Gojon continued to be the rector until his election as the superior general of the congregation in 1895, when Fr. Anselme Rey replaced him. Later, in December 1898, the seminary was transferred to Visakhapatnam Cathedral.[111] The seminary was closed between 1912 and 1915, and later the seminarians were sent for a short period to Ranchi.[112] Besides theology and philosophy, the seminarians were given homework on Sundays to improve their knowledge of French.[113]

Other New Centres

The urge to proclaim Christianity to as many as possible took the missionaries to some interior places. Some of them were set apart for what is known as *missio extra muros*, where they concentrated on some simple ways to draw the attention of the people.

Katingia

Katingia, the domain of the Kondh raja, was an interior village surrounded by mountains and valleys. Situated at a distance of about 28 km. from Surada, it counted a population of about 600 people. It became a centre for many villages of Kondhs and Panos. Since it was located in the interior, there was very little possibility of finding essential commodities. However, the British government established a police station there in order to maintain law and order among the Kondhs.[114] The territory was under the rule of a tribal chief, and the people had to pay a nominal tax regularly plus an extraordinary tax whenever someone died, or some important function took place in the family of the chief. In their status as outsiders, the Panos refused to pay the tax, although the chief demanded that they pay like everyone else. He prohibited them from cultivating the land and denounced them in the court of Berhampur. Because of their unfamiliarity with the language and court procedures and being unable to employ a competent lawyer, they decided to approach Fr. Dupont, who was known to be both knowledgeable and just in all his dealings. A delegation was sent to the missionary in 1883.

So just when the Fathers of Surada were contemplating a *missio extra muros* the deputation of Panos arrived from Katingia. Fr. Dupont agreed to help them. As anticipated, the judge passed a verdict in favour of the Panos, and the chief was found guilty. Touched by the kindness of the missionary, the Panos requested him to establish a mission station in their place so that they could benefit from the religion of the missionary. Fr. Dupont, encouraged by this overwhelming response, decided to live in the village. He started his apostolate on the Feast of the Immaculate Conception of Mary (December 8, 1883), the protector of the mission. Initially the priest lived under a tree, a fairly normal practice in starting a new mission.[115] Afterwards Fr. Dupont had to be content with a hut. He thought that if he succeeded in converting some people, he might build a better house. He began instructing a small group, and others later followed. As Christmas approached, he decided to celebrate the feast with solemnity. Soon a good number of people asked for baptism.[116]

The Influence of Fr. Dupont

One of the institutions that Fr. Dupont established after his arrival in Katingia was a school for children. Right from the beginning, the Roman Catholic School at Katingia exerted its influence on the people. It attracted converts from among the Panos in Katingia and in Goddapur. By becoming Christians, the people of Katingia thought that they were no longer under the control of *Potros*; they even refused to collaborate with the government. These difficulties were later settled through the intervention of the missionaries. In order to encourage his neophytes, Fr. Dupont used to organise activities for certain church feasts, depending on the availability of funds. He used such occasions to impart knowledge about the faith.[117]

In his long career as a missionary Fr. Dupont was also known as a doctor. He had a practical knowledge of Indian diseases, and he distributed medicines accordingly. Often the diseases were minor and were caused by malnutrition. His services brought certain relief to those Kondhs and Panos who generally went to the sorcerers (often village medicine men). In their ignorance, the latter attributed the diseases to the wrath of offended spirits that needed to be appeased through sacrifices. Adjacent to his hut Fr. Dupont erected a shed, which served as a hospital where he often shared his food with the patients. His reputation as a caring doctor spread, and he did not fail to speak about God and salvation to anyone who sought medicinal help. Through this simple technique he won over a good number of Catholics in the vicinity, especially in the villages of Solima, Saragoudi and Possopodoro.[118]

Hardships and Obstacles

However, Fr. Dupont was faced with numerous obstacles when he decided to construct a church. The chief of Katingia prohibited him from collecting the wood needed for the chapel from the ruler's territory. Moreover, the raja vented his displeasure by driving away the person who had given the land to the missionary and by ordering the Kondhs to have no contact with him. Undeterred by such restrictions, he approached the raja of Bodogoro, who gave all the timber necessary for the construction. Furthermore, the raja dragged the missionary to court for encroachment upon a plot of land that did not legally belong to the latter. However, convinced by the missionary's respect for the law, the judge decided in his favour. The chief was not the only opponent that Fr. Dupont had to deal with; there were also the *Potros* and *Karnams* who incited the hatred of the chief towards the missionary. Since the *Karnams* were the ones who knew how to read and write, the Kondhs depended on them for their links with the government. Realising their vulnerability, the *Karnams* tried to turn the Kondhs against the missionaries by preventing their children from attending the missionary school. They forbade the villagers to sell the missionary essential items, and they even barred him from entering their village. Fr. Dupont was also accused of illegally involving himself in the sale of properties that did not belong to him. Yet all this did not deter the people from placing their trust in him and rendering the support that he needed for establishing the mission.[119]

Katingia after Fr. Dupont

Katingia became one of the flourishing communities in the mountains established by the hard-working and kind-hearted missionary, Fr. Dupont. He chose a catechist who could also work as a teacher in the school and who wielded much influence among the Kondhs. After the death of Fr. Dupont (June 17, 1887), Fr. Descombes took over the care of the community. The provisional church was almost collapsing, so the people requested him to build another one. Fr. Descombes was interested in building a chapel with stones and mortar, which would cost him Rs. 800. He asked Msgr. Tissot to approve a plan of constructing a small residence for priests, where the missionaries could live during their annual visits. Msgr. Tissot approved it.[120] Thanks to the school the number of Christians who knew how to read and write increased. This fact increased interest in printed prayer books, just like the Protestants had. Looking at the prospects of conversion in the mountains, Fr. Descombes commented:

> The ground is quite suitable for conversion. Except in the mountain district of Goomsur, the Protestants have not touched the populations, the Brahmins do not keep them under their yoke, and Europeans are almost unknown. The great obstacle is that we are not able to travel by bullock cart, and that communications are more difficult than anywhere else. Besides, it is difficult to find in these parts fruit, sugar, eggs, and milk. We have to carry along all provisions for the journey.[121]

By the time Fr. Descombes took over the mission, there were changes in the village. Fr. Descombes visited the station only four times a year, but in his absence the people gathered for evening prayers and recitation of the rosary. The missionary was elated when people greeted him by genuflecting, while the children called out 'praised be Jesus Christ'. When they met the priest, they knelt down to receive his blessings. Fr. Descombes went to the villages around Katingia to gather the people for Christ.[122] In 1897 he administered baptism to 36 catechumens, both children and adults, at Didrobady. Most of them were victims of famine. He recorded that one of the neophytes had practically nothing, except some herbs and roots for food.[123] During his sojourn at Gojolibady he sent messengers to invite the Christians of Gosta and Pondacalo for worship, but they discovered that the men were away seeking work in the mountains and that the women were so debilitated that they could not undertake the two-hour journey. The missionary therefore arranged for the distribution of rice, which brought them momentary relief.[124]

Even in difficult times when very little progress was visible, the plan of abandoning the mission at Katingia was abandoned, due to the toil of the veteran missionaries. They felt it would be a great loss to give up a place where the missionaries had spent so much energy in spreading the gospel.[125] In 1911 Fr. Descombes received 2500 francs for the construction of the mission in Katingia. It was proposed that a more comfortable house be built for the missionaries there.

Conversion of the Villages around Katingia

In the last decade of the nineteenth century Fr. Descombes spearheaded the process of conversion in the Ganjam mission. It was at Katingia that he came in contact with the people who needed his help against either the police or the usurious zamindars. Advised by the Christians of Katingia, the people came to the missionary and expressed their willingness to place themselves under his protection. Sometimes as a sign of gratitude the chief would offer the missionary a plot of land to construct a church, as happened in Cutruca.[126] Once the missionary pitched his tent among the Kondhs, interest in Christianity grew--even from the neighbouring villages.[127] Gutuli,[128] Eperma, Solima,[129] Goomsur, Saragood and Killama were all attracted to the faith.

Kondhs in general are a shy people. If they do not know someone, they will hide behind the door and peep through the little opening to observe the person. Such was the behaviour of the Kondhs in Cutruca, Eperma and other villages, which Fr. Descombes had visited. But their behaviour changed when the missionary started to live with them. They were now used to the missionaries. However, some of their traditional religious beliefs still impeded the growth of the mission. For example, if a person died of smallpox, the Kondhs would not even the touch the body much less take part in the funeral.[130] They were also obsessed with their prescribed sacrifices.[131]

It was also not easy for the people (Kondhs and Panos) to accept the new religion of the missionary because their oppressors continued their threats and intimidations. Although the manager of the raja of Boroguda threatened the new Christians with sanctions, they remained faithful. Convinced of their positive response and their interest in the new religion, the missionary built a chapel wherever he had baptised the people. By 1900, most of the villages had chapels.[132]

Additional Centres visited by Fr. J.M. Descombes

The Kondhs invited the missionaries to open a station in Baliguda, where there was hope of a good harvest.[133] The itinerary of Fr. Descombes in March 1905 indicates the immense work that he undertook. Here is his account:

> In this valley (Didrobady) all the villages except one are learning prayers. At Koussipanga, 60 families are under instruction. On Tuesday, 2 hours walk took us to Dighy where I met dear Fr. Suiffet . . . Eight villages are favourable to us. Only in one village is the chief our adversary. Next day, we left for the valley of Raikia, where 6 villages are under instruction. We visited 3, two of them are to be baptised soon. It's from here that 18 families had sent delegates to Fr. Suiffet, requesting the missionary to make them Christians. On the road for 3½ hours, we went through 3 big villages Kritigia, Tsantsiri, Krootigiah, which look like towns, with well laid-out houses. A crown of big mango trees surrounds each village.[134]

Continuing his tour in the mountains, he wrote:

> We arrived finally where there was a cluster of villages, Cuttoghia, with Gumagarra as the head of the villages. A chief who was guiding us, said: 'here is your house'. There are three rooms, the chapel, in the middle, with the kitchen on one side and the stable on the other. Entering the chapel,

we knelt down to thank God for our safe journey. We got out: the village is there to see us. This village counts 200 families of diverse castes, the Kondhs in the majority. I begin the conversation in *Kui*. At once, people smile. We are considered old friends . . . On Sunday the crowd of onlookers in front of the chapel was numerous. Twice a day, morning and evening, catechism and prayers are held for men in the chapel, and for women in the village. One of my two catechists have opened a small dispensary and distributes medicines . . . I am resolved to remain here as long as possible. We can hope for good results. 9 other families have joined the initial 18 families. Some local chiefs' tyranny was the occasion for people to seek the protection from the missionaries. One of the chiefs said: 'We are going to unearth the treasure of our ancestors to fight against the sahibs (Europeans) and drive them out'. While this house was under construction, these chiefs sent people to take out the pillars, threatening the catechumens.[135]

Russellkonda

A small chapel along with a cemetery existed since the establishment of a military outpost in Russelkonda.[136] Soldiers had been sent there in order to capture the fugitive raja of Goomsur and to eradicate the horrendous human sacrifices. The Vincentians, who later took over from the MSFS, found a document that referred to the presence of Christians in Russelkonda. It deals with the resolutions that the soldiers of the 18th Regiment had sent to the vicar apostolic of Visakhapatnam. The resolutions stated:

> (1) That no Christian would participate in the pagan religious ceremonies; (2) that all should fulfil the Easter obligations, under the threat of being marginalized from the community and being denied a Christian burial; and (3) that everybody should attend on Sundays the divine cult in the big chapel, and to solve disputes Christians should appeal to the community council without any kind of interference on the pagan side. Should anybody dare to infringe these laws, the document ends, he would be punished with 40 strokes or 30 rupees and 20 candles.[137]

This document reveals that the Christian community had existed even before the arrival of MSFS, although one cannot be certain when it actually began. The chapel was maintained at the expense of the state due to the presence of some important monuments.[138]

Dighy

Dighy[139] is situated about 30 miles from Surada. This was a centre where the Kondhs were living in large numbers. Until 1900 they were victims of injustice and oppression by the chiefs and merchants, who even took away their lands. On hearing that they could get help from a missionary, they sent a delegation to meet Fr. Descombes and possibly to bring him to their village. In 1900 he visited the place for the first time and decided to begin a station there.[140] By the end of 1901 almost all the people of Mondosoro were Christians. In 1902 the missionary visited about 118 villages, resulting in an increase of 173 families. At this time Fr. Suiffet began to reside in Mondosoro with a view to move on to other villages. Between 1903 and 1905, forty-three families became Christian when the missionary visited Boregada and Padangui. Since many nearby villages requested the services of a priest, Msgr. J.M. Clerc advised Fr. Suiffet to build a presbytery in Dighy.

In July 1909 Fr. Suiffet claimed that he had baptised 850 individuals living in 3 large villages. The new Christians built a hut for the priest as evidence of their changed faith, and they requested him to visit them regularly. It was not easy for the missionary to convince the people of Christianity. Sometimes they ignored the priests' presence among them and continued their pagan practices. Fr. Petitjean wrote: "Five days ago in one of the turns to visit villages I stayed in a village where they speak Oriya. In my six days of stay there I never received any consolation from the Christians. There is a school. However, when I was about to depart I was given a fowl as a gift by them."[141] When he made his pastoral visit to the northern mission, Msgr. Clerc deputed Fr. Rossillon to visit Dighy. He did so with much enthusiasm, braving difficulties, crossing rivers and trekking the mountains. In his short stay in Dighy (1909) Fr. Rossillon witnessed the positive response of the Kondh chiefs. He narrated for the readers of Echos Salésiens:

> Forty-one chiefs came to meet us at Dighy on Sunday, where we had given them the appointment. As each had brought two or three men from their respective villages, we had there a feast the likes of which I have not seen in my life. Though pagans they (villagers) followed the Mass with respect and approved the sermon with head movements and small cries. Once the Mass was over, in order to manifest their joy, they executed mock hunts of buffaloes and dances with raised axes. All danced to the rhythm of their drums![142]

The representatives came with the request that the Fathers and the catechists be sent so that they might have the opportunity to love God. The representatives claimed that they were the spokespersons for seventy villages that wished to become Christians, if the missionaries were interested.[143] Looking at the Dighy mission in 1924, Fr. J.M. Fernandez (a Spanish Vincentian and the superior of the first group of missionaries who had inherited the Ganjam mission from MSFS) acknowledged the hard labour of the missionaries full of hope and apostolic zeal, but who had had to abandon the mission in the face of their dwindling numbers caused by the First World War.[144]

At times the Sisters from Surada went to Dighy to provide medicines for the remote villages. Their presence added a certain glimmer of hope to the mission. Fr. Petitjean recorded one such event: "Recently one of the Sisters from Surada came here to explore the terrain. She was carried in an armchair. Her coming here raised the curiosity of many Kondh women. During her stay of three weeks in Dighy she had an attack of fever that prevented her from visiting the sick in the villages."[145] In 1913 Frs. Fleury and Bouchet were appointed to Dighy. While the former remained in Dighy to help Fr. Suiffet, the latter was asked to look after Padangui. But when both were asked to serve in the war, their work was interrupted considerably. Fr. Suiffet was again left with the burden of taking care of a large area, including Dighy, Daringbadi and Padangui, until Fr. Rey joined him in 1914.

Though Frs. Fleury and Bouchet returned to Dighy after the war in 1918, they could not accomplish much, as Fr. Suiffet died that year and Fr. Fleury in 1921. Fr. Rey remained alone in Dighy, since Fr. Bouchet was transferred to other places with greater needs. Since it was difficult to struggle alone, Fr. Rey was forced to close the orphanages in 1919. Realising the challenges that he was faced with, the superior appointed him to Surada with the possibility of visiting Dighy occasionally to take care of the Christians. At the request of the bishop of Visakhapatnam to furnish the statistics of the mission, Fr. Rey wrote: "In my districts of Dighy, I have 500 baptised (Christians). They are from Kondhs and Ghazis. The majority of them live in the valleys of Daringbady, Kerubady, and Didrovadi, and there are 22 'criados de la Mission' (employees of the mission), both teachers and workers."[146]

Padangui

The impact of Christianity might have been felt in Padangui in 1901, when the Kondhs of Mondosoro (Dighy) invited the missionary to mediate in their disputes. Recognising the influence of the missionary, the timid tribals of the area accepted Christianity slowly. Padangui's turn came in 1905, after many other villages between Raikia and Boregada had already taken a positive step. Fr. Suiffet was sent to visit the new communities in Raisinguia, Sukamanda and Boroga, near Baliguda. Fr. Tohu and Fr. Julien Vulliez later assisted him. Fr. Bouchet took up residence in Padangui in 1913, where he led 200 families to Christianity.

Writing in *Les Missions Catholiques*, Fr. Bouchet commented that on January 29, 1914, the missionaries acquired a patch of land on which they had intended to build a church and a priests' residence. This was believed to be a central place for the valley.[147] The people donated some trees that were consecrated to their gods (Lona Penu). The missionaries later re-consecrated them through the sprinkling of holy water. Writing on March 4, 1914, Msgr. J.M. Clerc informed Cardinal Gotti that they were planning to open a new station in the eastern part of the Kondh mission at Padangui, a central place for the surrounding villages where there were many catechumens.[148] However, Fr. Bouchet had to leave for France and serve as a soldier during the First World War, which unleashed disastrous consequences for the mission. Writing about the conditions of the mission when Fr. Bouchet returned to Padangui, Fr. Jesús Taboada commented:

> On his return from France in 1918, he didn't find the result of his labour but rather ruins and smoking ashes. Sheltered under a miserable hovel of three metres large and three metres wide, he resolved to reconstruct the ruins. Only a few came after the 'whistle of the pastor,' and before being able to organise an effective plan of re-evangelisation, he was called to Visakhapatnam in 1919. Two years later the mission was handed over to the Spanish Vincentians of the Province of Madrid.[149]

Expedition to Jeypore

On hearing that there were great opportunities for evangelisation in the kingdom of Jeypore,[150] Msgr. Tissot despatched three MSFS (Frs. Bonaventure, Payraud and Domenge) to ascertain the prospects for starting a mission in the kingdom, where a good number of Kondhs lived. Msgr. Tissot appointed Fr. Bonaventure as leader of the expedition, since he was able to speak Oriya. At the time of the expedition (1883), Jeypore was a town of about 4000 to 5000 people. The streets were narrow, and the houses were built with mud, including the palace.[151] The people worshipped *Tacorani* [Thakurani], a goddess and the presiding Hindu deity who was also part of the Kondh pantheon. Narrating his journey to Jeypore to his uncle, Fr. Philippe, Fr. Bonaventure wrote:

> I am today at Sonky, in the centre of the forests of the southern Range of the Kondh country. I walked 85 miles in three days. I am the guest of a good (brave) Catholic Irish engineer, (his name was Harris), in charge of the building up of a road through the forests. I shall leave tomorrow for Koraput where I will arrive after a three-days' walk. The carriers are there to take my bag. As for me, I walk. Monsignor has sent me to try a mission among the Kondhs. I recommend this mission to your prayers. I am full of courage and everybody gives me hope.[152]

When they arrived in Jeypore, the missionaries were welcomed with all the formalities that the small kingdom could afford. The dewan and a few senior ministers were at their service and as a token of recognition for the missionaries, the raja himself sent some fruit for the priests and expressed his willingness to pay a visit. The missionaries declined the offer, since the protocol was that they should first call on the king. However, the intended meeting did not take place, as the king himself was busy with state affairs. The dewan took the missionaries to a school, where the king desired them to work. This visit was an eye-opener when the missionaries discovered the people's expectations and fears: namely, (1) that the missionaries had come to preach a new religion or new English gods; (2) that by introducing a new religion the priest might make the people lose caste (the Brahmins of the place were especially concerned about this); and (3) that they had come to teach European science and civilisation. The missionaries stated in no uncertain terms that their motive was to preach Christianity.[153]

In his report to Msgr. Tissot, later published in the journal *Propagation de la Foi*, Fr. Bonaventure explained the advantages of opening a station either in Koraput or Pottinghy. The following were the reasons for starting a station at Koraput: First, though situated beyond the chain of mountains, Koraput could be well connected with the rest of the mission, as the missionaries could easily reach Nagpur, Kamptee and Visakhapatnam for retreats and meetings.[154] Second, the climate was pleasant, almost like the climate in Europe, and certainly not feverish (as in the Kondh mountains). Third, the missionaries liked the picturesque mountains of Koraput, and they were also encouraged by the welcome they had received from the local authorities and the people. Fourth, the missionaries felt that their mission in Jeypore might bring them some success,[155] for despite the dominance of the Brahmins, they wielded little or no influence on the Kondhs.[156] Even the Protestants were not there to compete with the Catholics.[157] In sum, satisfied with the visit, the Fathers presented a recommendation to Msgr. Tissot to start a mission immediately. However, only after an informal consultation between the bishop and the missionaries and the superior in Annecy, did Msgr. Tissot decide to start in Koraput. He appointed Fr. Bonaventure, young and energetic, to commence the mssion.[158]

The Attempts to Establish a Mission in Koraput

Though in one of his letters to his uncle, Fr. Philippe, Fr. Bonaventure mentioned that the project to open a station in Koraput was beyond his strength, he accepted the request of Msgr. J.M. Tissot.[159] Following his experience in Surada, Fr. Bonaventure wanted to purchase a large farm in Koraput, with the hope of working like a benevolent landowner, where he could employ people as he did in Thotavally.[160] It was widely known that such a method had worked well in Thotavally, especially among the Kondhs or Panos, whereas the people he encountered in Koraput were a mixed population of both Kondhs and Oriyas.[161] However, Fr. Bonaventure was unable to assume responsibility because he fell ill. Later, when he had recovered, he was transferred to Nagpur (1898) and eventually he became the fourth bishop of Nagpur (1904).

The Missionaries' Outlook and Strategies

Orissa experienced yet another famine in 1889, caused by poor rains in 1888 that resulted in scarcity and misery. Though the market price for a measure of rice was Rs. 4, it was very difficult to obtain any even at the rate of Rs. 10. Fr. Décarre reported that he had sent servants more than 150 km away to buy rice for the boarding school in Surada. The people were scavenging for food. When they found nothing, they ate grass, roots, leaves and even tree bark. Some of them ate mud.[162] The tragedy struck the families immeasurably: some parents killed their children, sold them for a few rupees, or abandoned them along the roadside in hopes that someone would show pity and give them a chance to live. Many such children were brought to the mission orphanages, where some died before they could be nurtured back to life.

The governor of the Madras Presidency, Lord Connemara, visited Ganjam district to avert criticism of administrative negligence. Msgr. Tissot went to Gopalpur to offer his respects to the illustrious visitor. Fr. Décarre went to meet the governor at Aska, where he was taking care of about 400 to 600 people. Having noticed such acts of mercy and kindness, the governor acknowledged the services of the missionaries and gave orders to open a distribution centre in Surada, under the supervision of Fr. Décarre.[163]

In the face of this natural calamity many sought relief from the church. The selflessness and charity of the missionaries had positive influence on the people; some of them became Christians. Writing on November 8, 1889, Fr. Descombes recorded: "Thanks to the famine, a good number of souls have found the way to heaven, that is opened for them through baptism."[164] The famine had dramatically increased the number of orphans, for whom the missionaries sought help from the outside. When the much-needed help failed to arrive, they reluctantly had to limit the number of children granted admission to the orphanages.

The Motives for Conversion

The missionaries utilised every possible opportunity to gain people for the kingdom of God, but at the same time they were fully aware of the mixed motives of people who accepted Christianity. But what mattered ultimately was their adherence to the faith. One of the recurring motives for the conversion of Panos and Kondhs was the belief that the 'white' missionaries, with their easy access to the British government, would protect them from the tyranny of landlords, *Karnams*, *Patros* and others who oppressed them. The missionaries would also prevent the destruction of their harvest by the *Karnams* and *Patros* and Oriyas when they wanted to instil fear among the people. The missionaries had certain medicines that could cure their sickness. The charitable-minded missionaries were the first ones to provide food during the famine.[165] Unwilling to divulge their real motives initially because the missionary might refuse to visit their village, the villagers as a rule would send a delegation stating that many of them were willing to receive baptism. Once the missionary arrived in their midst, they would reveal to him the extent of their troubles, such as exploitation by the moneylenders, who took away their lands.[166] Then the missionary would have a meeting with the villagers that might last for a few days, and he would attempt to persuade the usurers to return the lands.[167] In sum, the presence of missionaries in their midst brought assurance, protection and opportunity. The people became ever more confident when the missionaries continued to visit their villages.

Problems in Sending the Children to School

In spite of the missionaries' efforts at establishing schools even in the remotest villages, the Kondhs and Panos showed little enthusiasm for education. Although there were a few schools on the mountain, they were established by the government, and they were far from Kondh territory. Moreover, the teachers taught in Oriya and did not speak *Kui*, while the Kondh children did not know Oriya. Also, the Kondhs felt that in order to eat one must work, and that included children. Fr. J.M. Descombes observed: "The Kondhs will eat only if they work. They say: It's fieldwork and not reading books that feeds us.' Parents hesitated to send their children to school saying that if they were educated, the missionaries would appoint them as catechists and teachers in the school. Hence they would not be with the family."[168] These were some of the obstacles in sending the children to the school. It took many years to remove this unfounded fear from the minds of the ordinary people.

The Plan for the Ganjam Mission

In 1906 Bishop Jean Marie Clerc and the regional superior, Fr. A. Rey travelled, to the missions in the north and visited (among other places) Dighy, Katingia and Dantholinghy. Fr. Rey was on horseback while the Kondhs, sent by Fr. Suiffet from Dighy, carried the bishop on a chair.[169] Ever since his return from Europe, Bishop Clerc gave importance both to the spiritual as well as the material growth of the diocese. In his letter to Fr. Bouvard, the bishop wrote that the missionaries working in the northern part of the Visakhapatnam mission had agreed to divide Surada mission into four units: Surada, Dantholinghy, Katingia and Dighy.[170]

In 1906 Fr. Petrus Descombes, nephew of Fr. J.M. Descombes, became the priest in charge of Surada. He was also in charge of the farms. The Catholic population at that time was about 500. There were two separate schools, one for boys and another for girls. An orphan girl, supervised by the Sisters of St. Joseph of Annecy, taught 30 girls catechism, sewing, reading and writing. An intelligent Pano Christian, who prepared the students for a certificate course at the primary level, ran the school for boys.[171] Fr. Petrus Descombes wrote that he was happy to bless the marriage of the orphans brought up in the orphanage.[172]

Planning for the future of Surada, Fr. P. Descombes said: "We are trying to provide local resources for our maintenance. The Surada mission has much land, about a thousand acres of land, a part of which is made of forests, which could be cleared and turned into rice fields, but that needs much work, time and money. The Fathers from the mountains come to Surada to rest and get cured of their fever."[173]

Though the death of several missionaries (including Fr. J.M. Descombes who established about 30 stations in his 27 years as a missionary in this inhospitable region) was a blow to the mission, it continued to flourish. Fr. P. Descombes witnessed a great conversion movement among the Kondhs in Dighy and Didrobady in 1907. He felt that the times had changed. Formerly the missionaries went to the people with the intention of converting them, and now it was their turn to come to the missionaries. Accompanied by the village chiefs, they came to the missionary with the request to establish a station in their village.[174]

Difficulties in Explaining Christian Beliefs and Literary Work

Explaining the major tenets of Christianity – such as the concept of God, the Holy Spirit, original sin, etc. – to a simple and illiterate group of Kondhs was never easy for the missionaries. Since the Kondhs understanding of God and the 'other world' was different, the missionary found it difficult to explain a concept such as 'God is formless'. Fr. Descombes tried to compare God with wind, heat and life, but he did not receive the peoples' usual nod of approval, which meant that they understood the preaching of the missionary. He wrote:

> One day, a catechumen provided the proper word, *'Ishwaro eloo maneru'*, God is spirit. *Eloo* could also mean either memory or intelligence. They also found a suitable word for original sin or *vele papo*, which meant the first sin. Moreover, very few Kondhs understood Oriya and particularly the women did not understand it at all. Therefore, the missionaries were forced to translate Bible history into *Kui*.[175]

Fr. Descombes took up the challenge and by 1905 his manuscript was available. With the help of a teacher he wrote the prayers, catechism, songs in *Kui*.[176]

Besides Fr. Descombes, others were also involved in literary activities. Fr. Jules Rey was busy composing songs in Oriya and translating the life of the saints.[177] In their efforts at disseminating the Word among the literate population, the missionaries felt the need to start a press in order to publish the books they needed in Oriya.[178] There was a sense of urgency because of the infiltration of Protestant literature, which was published at their press in Cuttack and to which the Catholics were exposed.

The Importance of Catechists

Among the many things thought to be fundamental to the growth of the mission were trained catechists and money, but the Ganjam mission lacked both.[179] Catechists were considered to be vital to the progress of the mission which to a large extent rested on their formation and dedication. The missionaries used to organise three-day annual retreats for catechists so that they would receive some spiritual formation besides the usual discussion on mission matters.[180] The appeal for good and dedicated catechists was constant in the letters of the missionaries.[181] The Synod of Visakhapatnam recognised that the formation and the role of catechists was indispensable for the progress of the mission.[182] Catechists, despite their modest salaries, were responsible for children, who attended classes on religion, and for the catechumens, who learned the prayers and the principles of Christianity. The Synod rightly recognised the dedicated life of catechists when it stated: "The life of a good catechist is in fact a life of devotion, of plenty of work and of tiredness. One can never easily find a catechist for the modest salary we offer them. They are disposed to all kinds of sacrifices."[183]

The catechists conducted monthly meetings at the centre in the presence of the missionaries. The annual retreats, as a rule, were followed by a general assembly, where certain issues vital to the progress of the mission were discussed. In 1906 there were two separate retreats for catechists – one for Telugu-speaking catechists and the other for Oriya speakers – preached by Fr. P. Descombes in clear and practical language. Both Fr. Muffat and Fr. Suiffet were also present at that time.[184] At the end of the retreat, on November 1, 1906 a *Panchayat* (general assembly) for the Catholics of the mission was held. After listening to one of the catechists, who made a long but inspiring presentation, the assembly took three important decisions:

- that everyone should pledge to give up pagan sacrifices;

- that if someone was found guilty, he would pay Rs. 50 as a fine; and

- that if the entire village was found guilty, it would be punished.[185]

Establishment of a Catechetical School

The Baptists in Orissa had a centre in Udaygiri for training catechists. Probably due to the quality of catechists who came out of the centre, the Baptists were able to reap a 'good harvest' in Orissa. The catechists employed in the Catholic mission were recent converts who lacked proper training. Therefore, their understanding of Christianity was limited and there was little difference between them and the menial labourers.[186] These reasons, among others, prompted the missionaries to start a catechetical school. Fr. J. Vuillez wrote:

> This work is going on at Surada. This is an important work. Without the catechist the missionary can do nothing. The native population has always some reservation about the Europeans. They will never share a secret with a European, even if he is a respected and known priest, whom they know and esteem. Left to himself the missionary would never know the detailed history, the background of things.[187]

Generally, the priest never went to minor stations except during the annual visit. Therefore, the following questions might be asked: How did the priest instruct the people? Who kept them united? He had no one to go to except the catechist, who was a resident of the village. In fact, it was the catechist who often represented and sometimes even replaced the missionary in that village. In order to be effective in persuading the people to accept Christianity, he needed special training. The training lasted generally for five or six years. When a catechist got married, the couple was sent to a village with a double charge: to be the catechist as well as the teacher of the local school.[188] Fr. Cyrille Ailloud was busy digging the foundation for the proposed school for the catechists in Surada in 1911.[189] Fr. Alphonse Favrat, delegate of the superior general, inaugurated it in March 1912. Writing on the importance of such a school, Fr. P. Descombes wrote:

> The formation of catechists is essential. That's why I started a catechists' school in Surada. I have accepted two candidates: a Pano and a Kondh. Candidates are not lacking, but we need a building, money, and a Father to

be in charge. These young men should be kept here several years, to pass
the exams required to be school masters whilst getting a good training in
religion and catechism.[190] In 1915 another school was established at Dighy
for Kondh catechists.

Rayappa Sanyasi Das: A Devoted Catechist

While everyone acknowledged that the service of the catechists was
pivotal to the progress of the mission, hardly any one remembered
their self-effacing sacrifices at a time when the church revolved around
clerics and religious. Their work was either deemed secondary to that of
priests and religious. However, the life and service of catechist Rayappa
Sanyasi Das was so outstanding in that he found a place in the annals of
Ganjam mission. A polyglot, he was able to converse fluently in Telugu,
Kui and Oriya. In fact, he was the only interpreter for many missionaries
who worked in Surada. Fr. A. Rey acknowledged that he had personally
received much help from Rayappa, who had a great influence on the
new converts.[191]

During the 1867 famine, the parents of Rayappa brought him to
Surada while he was still an infant. At the age of 12 his mother came
to take him back so that he would be received into the caste. But to her
dismay Rayappa refused to accompany her, as it would mean that he had
abandoned Christianity. He chose to remain with the Fathers, who educated
him and later employed him as a catechist. People had much respect for
him, as he was strict with his caste practices and prudent in his dealings
with women. Fr. Décarre sent Rayappa to Puri as a catechist, where he
converted two or three families. Fr. A. Rey wrote: "For the service rendered
to me I gave him Rs. 12/- per month. He offered something from that
to the poor. He never took drinks with the Kondhs, nor meals, except
one in the evening after work. The people used to call him "Sanyasi" [a
monk or religious] and in reality, he was."[192]

Rayappa Sanyasi Das' influence within the mission was so great that
in the absence of the missionary he could sanction certain punishments
against the guilty and impose fines. He organised meetings to settle
disputes among the parishioners, and in so doing he had made certain
crucial decisions on matters pertaining to the operation of the mission.[193]
Rayappa Sanyasi Das' good service was widely acknowledged in the final
settlement of the lands at Dantholinghy. He died in 1919 as peacefully

as he had lived. Though unwell at times, he never missed his daily Mass and Holy Communion. Reporting on the way he died, Fr. Cyrille wrote:

> In the evening he said his prayers as usual and went to bed in the dormitory of the children of Dighy and Katingia. At about 1 a.m. the children came to call us, and we found him in his last agony. After giving him the last sacraments and a plenary indulgence, the children kept watch over him, while (he) went to say Mass. He died about at 6 a.m. as the children were praying for him, their arms extended in the form of cross. The first thing that the children told us was: 'See, how happy he is, he's laughing.' He was about 65.[194]

A Time of Trial for the Orphanages

Again, there was both famine and cholera in 1918, when children in the orphanage (Surada) suffered. The orphanage had about 60 children. The people did not expect the plague, but it broke out in Ganjam. In June 1918, it arrived in Surada and its surroundings in the shape of cholera, which claimed the lives of a number of children despite all precautions. Some of them, especially those who were in good health, were sent to Berhampur, where the missionaries attended to the sick and dying. The entire presbytery, it seemed, was turned into a hospital for two months. Mother Fabienne and the Sisters devoted themselves day and night to the care of the little ones.[195]

Exhorting the work of the Sisters of St. Joseph of Annecy, Msgr. Tissot shared his concerns for the orphanage for girls:

> I am happy with our poor orphans. They have lost their uncouth manners and in general they are good and very attached to their teachers and the establishment. I had to announce to them the bad news of the stopping of the subsidy from the government. I have them to producing castor oil that I have promised to sell for their profit. Others go to collect cotton and spin it. We have two looms to make canvas. Unfortunately, it all goes at the pace of the country, slowly, in a way a little bit uncouth. They receive the sacraments and pray a lot, even when they go to the forest to cut trees. I will do all I can to feed and clothe this brood.[196]

Whenever there was a financial crisis, the farms helped the mission considerably, particularly the orphanages. Writing in 1919, Fr. Cyrille recorded how useful were the farms maintained by the mission:

> It is due to the fields that the orphanage and the school have been maintained. This year alone, I was able to get back the Rs. 3,000 I had spent on the

pond of Dantholinghy. I have still some bags of rice for sale . . . if we
had a brother who could look after the fields and someone who loved
God and was ready to work for him, what a difference it would make! ...
This year the harvest is excellent. But here is another cross. Hilary, our
supervisor, has been ill for a month, just at the most critical moment of
harvest. I leave to God   for the feeding of his children.[197]

Some of the Major Events of the Mission

a. Canonical Visit (1885)

The need for a canonical visit to assess the mission was felt by the
Missionaries of St. Francis de Sales, both in India, where the first mission
of the congregation was operative, and in Annecy, France.[198] Though
the superiors general had desired to visit the mission at Visakhapatnam,
neither Monsieur Mermier nor his successor Fr. Clavel could manage the
long and tiring voyage, the prolonged absence from the office, and the
huge expenditure. Though epistolary communication with the mission
was useful, personal contacts with the missionaries in the field would
expose the circumstances under which they lived and worked, as well
as the culture and linguistic barriers that impeded evangelisation. This
probably persuaded Rev. Fr. Joseph Tissot, the superior general of the
congregation, to visit the mission in India. Yet his confreres and doctors
advised him to be prudent, as he was suffering from an illness that could
prove to be fatal if care was neglected. So, he delegated Fr. François
Philippe to visit the mission.[199]

Overwhelmed by the announcement of the visitator, Msgr. J.M. Tissot
wrote to Fr. Philippe: "You have accepted the proposal of our dear
Superior to do the visitation of the mission in his name. I will do all I
can in my power, so that this may not be a penance. I repeat that I will
accompany you everywhere and I will furnish all information either by me
or by our Fathers, so that you may get a clear picture of the mission."[200]
In preparation for the general visit, Fr. J.M. Dupont was asked to write
a history of the mission of Surada.[201] Despite his carefully made plans,
Fr. Philippe did not visit either Surada or Cuttack.[202] Informing Cardinal
Simeoni about Fr. Philippe's travels in India, Msgr. Tissot observed: "Fr.
Philippe, who came to visit the mission, had to return to Savoy towards
the end of February without having visited all the stations of the southern
and the northern part of the mission. He has seen the principal localities
and all the principal establishments."[203]

Having recognised the talents of Fr. Philippe, Msgr. Tissot petitioned the Holy See to appoint him as his coadjutor. He also sent letters to Father Superior General Tissot requesting him to recommend his proposal to the Holy See. With strong recommendations both from Bishop Tissot and the superior general, Fr. Philippe was appointed against his own wishes. Even after the consecration, Msgr. François Philippe kept postponing his departure for India, citing ill health. Frustrated by this, Msgr. J.M. Tissot wrote to Fr. Berod:

> I asked him (Card Simeoni) once again to give me Msgr. Philippe as coadjutor, at least provisionally. I must tell you, my dear confrere, that Msgr. Philippe completely ignores the request I made. He writes me time to time, but never a word regarding this affair nor a word of blame against the superior and the council. My aim in not interrupting the correspondence with him was not to give him an occasion to say that I don't want him any more. He has written• to me that he never asked for the office of coadjutor, but it was given to him, based on the explication of the state of his health, as someone explained to him. I must necessarily be taken for somebody who holds on to his see and who seeks by all means to remain at the head of the mission.[204]

Msgr. Philippe never exhibited any keen desire to work in the missions. His presence in *La Feuillet*, the mother house of MSFS, was not received well by the confreres. Finally, the Holy See released him of his obligations. He spent his days at Les Allinges and Evian until his death on April 16, 1904.[205]

In 1912 Fr. Alphonse Favrat was delegated by the superior general to visit the mission. He appreciated whole heartedly the work of the missionaries and marvelled at the way that they lived in such difficult places. He spent much time in the Orissa mission. On his return to Annecy, he gave a positive report to Rev. Fr. Bouvard, the superior general.[206]

b. The Synod of Visakhapatnam and its Impact on the Orissa Mission (1888)

Msgr. J.M. Tissot convoked a synod when the missionaries were in Visakhapatnam for their annual retreat. The reasons for the synod were clearly spelt out in the very first paragraph of *Actes et Ordonnances du Synode de Vizagapatam tenu en Septembre 1888*: (1) to discuss the principal difficulties of ministry in the country; (2) to formulate certain rules for guiding the apostolic endeavours of the missionaries; and (3) to have a uniform approach both to the Christians already living in the mission and to the non-Christians who would be converted.[207] Sixteen priests as well as the bishop attended the synod, which took place September 10-17, 1888. In general, the deliberations were similar to those of the Directory of Pondicherry Mission.

First, the synod declared that every missionary should work towards the formation of an indigenous clergy. It was recommended that the missionaries choose suitable pious and intelligent candidates from their congregations and teach them the rudiments of Latin and other required subjects in preparation for the seminary. In theory, the children of all castes could be candidates, but prudence dictated that those who belonged to a higher caste should be generally selected. The missionaries of St. Francis de Sales had always considered caste a purely civil institution outside the purview of religion.[208] Just like the missionaries of Pondicherry, so too did the Missionaries of St. Francis de Sales bring into the church those customs which did not militate against either sound faith or good manners.[209]

Second, the synod listed the missionaries' duties in the care of souls (*cura animarum*):

(1) residing at his assigned station; (2) visiting and instructing the faithful regularly; (3) administering the sacraments and leading a life of piety; (4) caring for the sick and the poor; and, finally (5) safeguarding church property and revenue.

Third, the synod encouraged the missionaries to correspond regularly with their superiors and with confreres, sharing with them both successes and failures.[210] Every missionary was recommended to organise an annual retreat of three days for the parishioners, to which one of the confreres could be invited to guide the spiritual exercises. Finally, the missionaries were exhorted to start primary schools, so that the children might avoid negative influences and have regular religious instruction.[211]

c. *The Visit of the Apostolic Delegate*

The visit of Apostolic Delegate Msgr. Zaleski (January 3-10, 1913) was very beneficial to the mission of Visakhapatnam.[212] He visited some of the most important stations and manifested an appreciation for the work of the missionaries of St. Francis de Sales. He wished that the Visakhapatnam mission would flourish like the Chotanagpur mission begun by the Belgian Jesuits.[213] A meeting was organised in which not only the ecclesiastical dignitaries but also the council of the bishop of Visakhapatnam took part. During the meeting some important decisions were made: 1) the areas in both Orissa and the Central Provinces which were dependent on Visakhapatnam Mission should be turned over to a congregation which had both the personnel and the resources for further expansion; 2) a minor seminary should be established for Europeans, Eurasians and Indians at the cathedral of Visakhapatnam; 3) priests should be freed mainly for sacramental work, whereas the responsibilities for the schools should be given to a community of Brothers who were specialists in the educational apostolate; and 4) two new schools should be opened for catechists -- one in Surada for those who spoke Oriya and Kui and the other in Kottavasala for Telugu speakers.[214]

Though the MSFS welcomed the decision, they realised that it entailed a great sacrifice to give up the two districts of Cuttack and Ganjam. The thought about leaving Surada, where many of their confreres had worked and died and where the mission had spent a lot of their resources, was disturbing. Though it was painful to cede a part of the mission, there were also some advantages: they could avoid a place of endemic fever and they could concentrate their work in Visakhapatnam, where only Telugu is spoken.

d. *The Reasons for Separation*

Realising the immense task entrusted to the small congregation, the apostolic delegate in India searched for a way in which to relieve the MSFS of that part of the mission which called for greater sacrifices.[215] In one of his letters to the superior general, Msgr. Pierre Rossillon (coadjutor bishop of Visakhapatnam) explained the state of the mission and the position of the congregation in the following words: "In giving up Ganjam and Orissa, we cede a part that is feverish. We free ourselves from Oriya, in order to learn Telugu as our principal language. The advantages of the language are enormous. While making their tours till now, the Fathers of Surada spend about two thirds of their lives in travel and in being ill."[216] In another letter Msgr. Rossillon stated:

> It is sufficient to note that at this moment among the missions in India, only our mission is static for twenty years. Recently I wrote to the apostolic delegate in India explaining the status of our mission and I did not hide

anything. He has given me an appointment to meet him at Madras to discuss more about it at the Marian Congress that takes place in Madras on the 12th, 13th and 14th of January 1921.[217]

It was no secret that some of the Fathers – namely Vulliez, Baviel and Descombes --working in the Ganjam mission were unable to withstand the inclement mountain weather.[218]

The bishop of Visakhapatnam and his council agreed subsequently to separate both Cuttack and Ganjam districts in Orissa and entrust them to a new congregation. The missionaries who had worked in Orissa felt that handing over Surada and the northern mission entailed an enormous sacrifice. Fr. J.J. Vulliez expressed a similar feeling to Fr. A. Favrat, the superior general: "Materially, and also spiritually, we abandon the best part of our diocese, the part which holds the most promise for the future."[219] Msgr. Rossillon, however, was determined to divide the mission:

> We would leave a country of endemic fevers, where the Fathers have not been able to live, and would be freed from the Oriya language and a territory which we could never evangelise fully. Two things were to be sought: the consent of the Fathers of Surada, who would certainly find it difficult to accept, and the acceptance of the Fathers of La Salette to whom I wrote.[220]

It was not easy for the missionaries to abandon a part of the mission that represented their identity as a congregation and whose work had been significant. Besides, there were the tombs of those who had sacrificed their lives amidst the inclement weather. However, they needed to decide.[221] The blessing of the new church in Surada took place on March 7, 1920, after which the coadjutor announced that the Ganjam mission comprising Cuttack and Ganjam would be given to a new congregation. Initially the La Salette Fathers were contacted, but they declined the offer. Meanwhile, Propaganda Fide contacted the Congregation of the Mission, popularly known as the Vincentians.[222]

e. *Arrival of the Spanish Vincentians*

Even before the MSFS felt the need for a change, Propaganda Fide was urging the Congregation of the Mission to concentrate on one or the other territory in India and to develop it.[223] When the urgent need arose to substitute the MSFS working in the Ganjam Mission, Cardinal Van Rossum requested Rev. Fr. F. Verdier, the superior general of the Congregation of the Mission, to accept the separated part of the

Visakhapatnam mission with the hope that the Vincentians would be able to provide the reinforcement that the MSFS could not.[224] The request of Propaganda Fide was forwarded to the Province of Madrid, which accepted after some hesitation.

Once the acceptance of the Province of Madrid was communicated to Propaganda Fide, Cardinal Van Rossum sent an immediate reply thanking them for their positive response.[225] Fr. Joaquin Atienza, visitor of Madrid Province, initiated a dialogue with the Vincentian superior general and Cardinal van Rossum, the prefect of the Sacred Congregation of the Propaganda Fide, and made arrangements for the first group of missionaries to travel to India. Arriving in Berhampur on January 10, 1922, the four Spanish Vincentians were sent to different parishes to get acquainted with the place, language and culture of the people. On February 3, 1922, on the occasion of confirmation at Surada, Bishop Rossillon formally announced the separation of the mission and handed over the mission to the Spanish Vincentians.[226] However, a few MSFS Fathers were asked to remain till the newcomers got used to the mission. The Vincentians exhibited a genuine interest in learning from their predecessors, who had begun earlier their apostolic work in a *terra ignota*.[227] On the eve of the Feast of Immaculate Conception in 1922, the Vincentian Fathers took over the Cuttack parish.[228] The departure of Frs. Jules Rey and Cyril Ailloud, the last MSFS to leave Surada on December 8, 1923, marks the end of the mission work of MSFS in Orissa.[229]

f. The Cuttack Mission

The division of the diocese of Vizagapatam was approved by Rome and the districts of Ganjam and Orissa were formally offered to the Spanish Vincentians. Reporting about the beginning of a new mission, one of the leading Catholic weeklies in India, 'The Examiner' commented:

> Five missionaries are expected at the end of the year, but the actual transfer of the mission will not take place before a year or two. Their chief work in the beginning will be to study the vernacular, namely Oriya and get acquainted with the country and customs and manners of the people. It is only after acquainting themselves with the special circumstances and conditions of ministry in this country, that they will take charge. The present territory of Visakhapatnam extends over an area of 62,567 square miles with a Catholic population of nearly 14,000.[230]

The Vincentians were not fully aware of the extension and the nature of the territory of the new mission entrusted to them. Meanwhile, a rumour began to circulate that certain parts of the Orissa mission – namely, Balasore, Krishnachandrapur and Gangpur, would be integrated into the Cuttack mission. The Jesuit missionaries working in Balasore and Krishnachandrapur did not feel the loss, since there was never a *mouvement de la grace* in those areas. However, when the rumour was purported about the severance of the Gangpur mission as well, many Jesuits working in the Ranchi mission thought that such action needed to be re-evaluated.[231] On February 3, 1922, the Spanish Vincentians clarified all doubts when they took over the mission territory where the MSFS worked. A letter from Rome, which arrived on July 28, 1928, formally constituted the Orissa and Ganjam districts[232] into an independent mission, *missio sui juris*, with its centre at Cuttack. The newly created Cuttack mission was placed under the administration of Fr. Valeriano Gümes C. M., who was called the 'Ecclesiastical Superior' of the Mission.[233]

It is worth noting here once more that the scarcity of missionaries was one of the major problems that impeded the spread of Christianity, forcing the MSFS to cede certain parts of their mission to a new congregation.

Gangpur Mission: Establishment of Hamirpur and Gaibira

Even after the foundation of Kesramal in 1908, the new parish did not include all the Catholic villages that were found in Gangpur. Considering the distance, some villages were allowed to remain with the parishes in Samtoli, Kurdega and Biru. But they were gradually given to Kesramal. "At the beginning of 1912", wrote Fr. Alary, "some Gangpur villages belonging to Samtoli and Kurdeg were added to Kesramal. The distances were increased, so also the number of catechumens. As a result, a third missionary was sent to Kesramal. Finally, towards the end of 1912, the last part of Gangpur was detached from Biru and given to Kesramal."[234]

Being a new parish, Kesramal had the difficult task of caring for the pastoral needs of Christians spread over a vast area of 2,492 square miles. There were four priests assigned to the parish, which by 1914 had a population of 22,252 Christians.[235] Of the four priests assigned to Kesramal, two were sent to the eastern part of Gangpur (Nagra-Khinjir area) to establish a new mission station. The distances involved made it impossible for the missionaries to pay an annual visit to many Christian villages, although the catechists had done much of the groundwork. It was the promise of regular help and the presence of the missionaries that motivated the tribals to agree to cut off their *chundis*, the tuft of hair, and to profess the Christian faith.[236] The initial difficulties with the raja of Gangpur seem to have dissipated. No reference could be found whether the young raja had given permission to begin a new station or had forbidden it.

The Status of Gangpur Catholics

Even though the eastern part of Kesramal was taken care of by the missionaries, they seemed to have neglected the western and northern regions of the mission in Gangpur. Kesramal had its difficulties in the expansion of the mission. One such difficulty was reported in the *Missions Belges* of 1920. No sooner had Fr. Henry Floor[237] taken charge of Kesramal than he undertook two important visits. In February and March 1920, he visited the northern area (towards Biru), and in April 1920 he travelled to the southern region around Bamra and Jashpur. He passed through about twenty villages during each visit and was able to observe the conditions of the mission in that part of Gangpur. He felt obliged to send a report of his observations to the archbishop of Calcutta.

Most of the village chapels had deteriorated due to neglect by the catechists and others in maintaining them. Fr. Floor's report also contained a number of very significant observations on the state of the Christians. First, a large number of kisans (Berga Oraons or Gangpuria Oraons) were leaving the church because they could not find suitable marriage partners within their own Catholic tribal groups. As a result, many sought partners among the non-Christians. Second, these defections were also due in part to the scarcity of visits by the missionaries, who ministered to a vast territory with numerous villages scattered far from one another. Moreover, some of the catechists were notorious for their moral depravity.[238] Third, *Tana Bhagatism* continued to play havoc in the lives of the tribals, as it lured away many from Christianity.[239]

Fr. Floor proposed the following measures to remedy the situation: (1) by 1921, Behrenbasa, in the western region of Gangpur, should have a resident priest, since the priest's presence had been limited to the *tarikhs* (monthly meetings); (2) the ruined chapels should be repaired as soon as possible, assuring continuity of worship and regular schooling for the children; (3) the catechumenate that had been closed because of financial difficulties and World War I should be resumed;[240] and (4) teachers and catechists should be brought from Biru, since the local catechists were unable to make an impact on the people and their behaviour was often odious.[241]

However, as Kesramal grew steadily it required an additional reinforcement of personnel and money for consolidating the existing Christian community. By1921 the parish had 22,000 Catholics, 68 chapels with catechists (where the Holy Eucharist was celebrated two or three times each year) and 74 mission schools.[242]

Eastern Gangpur

The steady growth of the Gangpur mission demanded a new centre to meet the numerous deputations that came from villages far and near to meet the missionaries in Kesramal. The missionaries initially concentrated on the east as it was geographically close to Kesramal, the centre of their activities since 1908.

An Account of the Early Evangelisation of Nagra-Khinjir

The first reference to the presence of Christians in the Nagra-Khinjir area (Hamirpur station) is found in the diary of Fr. Robays. The entry in February 1904 stated: "In Gangpur I am supposed to look only after the people of Nagra district. It would be preferable to give me Nagra and all the Christians that are living to the East and North of the Sunkh, except the small corner of the west of Borkhonda wali [river]."[243] He also mentioned a visit to Gangpur in November 1904, when the Christians received him warmly. In November 1905 Fr. Robays visited a number of sub stations, including Babaimohan, Salangabahar, Jhamankia, Jhurmul, Kasbahara and Goilo.

According to the 1905 statistics, Samtoli had about 8680 Christians, of whom 2590 were supposedly from Gangpur.[244] A look at the map reveals that the eastern part of Gangpur is closer to Samtoli. In 1904, when Fr. de Smet joined Fr. Robays in Samtoli, the latter asked the former to concentrate on his efforts on Gangpur. Subsequently many delegations from Gangpur villages met Fr. de Smet, requesting him to accept them into the church. The village of Gobira (Nagra region), for example, sent a delegation on November 9, 1906, to convey to the missionaries their willingness to profess the Christian faith. Fr. De Smet sent Johan the *Munshi* (clerk) and Johan the catechist to gather information about the possibilities of starting a station in the Nagra region. They were optimistic about the area but felt that several catechists would be needed. On January 12, 1907, the catechists from Nagra brought the news that some tribal groups, including some Lutherans of Joketa, were willing to become Catholics.[245] The willingness of these tribals was also conveyed to the missionaries at Samtoli on November 29, 1907 by two *Zamindars* from Nagra, who were ready to donate land for a mission station.[246] They later provided detailed information on the families willing to become Christians.[247] Yet some *Zamindars* in Nagra were opposed to the progress of the mission, since they thought that the Catholics would seek redress in court against them.

The deputations continued to arrive from other villages in Gangpur, such as Tangarani and Ragunathpali. On January 22, 1908, Francis, the catechist of Gobira, came to Samtoli with 16 men, to announce that a good number of people from the Nagra area had been added to the catechumanate.[248]

Proposals for a Mission Station in Eastern Gangpur

Fr. De Smet thought that "to manage the north of Nagra-Khinjir and the south of Nagra, we want a new station, in Rourkela . . . Otherwise the Anglicans of Chaibasa, who have already adherents around Ragunathpali, and the Lutherans of Chakradharpur will sweep away Saranda".[249] He added that "from Ambadanr (Raiboga), where Samtoli has built, with Government consent, a school-chapel and rooms for the priest, we can easily visit Nagra-Khinjir north of the Sunkh and keep our people in trim".[250] The distance between Kesramal and Nagra-Khinjir, the difficulties of transport, and the enervating climate were factors that influenced the missionaries' decision to search for a suitable place in the eastern part of the mission where they could settle.

Setting of Hamirpur

Hamirpur is adorned with hills and valleys, among which runs a dangerous and wide river, the Koel. It often ran dry during the summer and produced catastrophic floods when it rained.[251] This annual phenomenon often isolated the poor tribals from the rest of the country, and there was very little possibility of reaching them except by boat--something they could not afford.[252]

During the monsoon season Gerdhai[253] was an inaccessible island. The acts of charity of the Catholic mission during the flood of July 1920 gained considerable numbers to its fold. In times of inundation the victims sought shelter at the mission, thus providing an occasion for the missionaries to instruct those who were willing. Therefore, the presence of the missionaries in Hamirpur helped the people to prepare themselves for the reception of the sacraments.[254] An examination of mission documents reveals a backward and needy people.

The climate was difficult if not dangerous for the missionaries.

Gangpur was a country where people could almost suddenly be exposed to a terrible danger . . . Fr. Lambot, then in charge of Hamirpur, went to the district for 8 days touring. It was during the hottest time of the year, this was rather dangerous. The first day he visited a Catholic centre called Bispur. "The chapel had lost a good deal of its roof, carried off by a storm. To save me from lodging there, the Christians had quickly prepared a thatched shed for me. The roof was so badly made that during the Mass, I had hardly any protection against the burning rays of the sun. The people were on their knees in the blazing sun and yet seemed not to mind it at all. From my part I had to bear that heat till mid-afternoon when it was time to move to the second Catholic centre."[255]

In the second place a torrential rain interrupted the Mass, and he was forced to give the final blessing after reading the Gospel.[256] The Easter ceremonies of 1917 were celebrated in a rickety barn. The people were so poor that they could not afford a place that could protect either the missionaries or themselves from the extremities of the weather.

A New Start

Fr. H. Grignard,[257] who used a tent as a chapel in some places, began constructing chapels in several villages. But he was told that there was no hope of building a presbytery in the Nagra area, where it was difficult to obtain land. But Fr. Grignard happened to meet Mr. Craven, the dewan of Gangpur, when they travelled together on a train. Utilising the opportunity, Fr. Grignard quietly broached the topic of granting some land for the mission, as the officers of the king obtained land freely. In his willing response, the dewan asked the missionary to submit a formal request, which he promptly did. Archbishop Meuleman of Calcutta also sent a request to the dewan, once he had chosen the place where he wanted to build the mission. Meanwhile, the old raja, who had been opposed to the missionaries building a residence in Gangpur, died on June 16, 1917.[258] Since the crown prince was a minor, Mr. Craven became the superintendent of the state.

The new ruler, Raja Bhawani Sanker Deo, gave permission to purchase land and to open a station in Gerdhai (July 8, 1917).[259] This allowed the missionaries to purchase seven acres of land at Hamirpur along the Koel, three miles north of the Bengal-Nagpur Railway.[260]

Hamirpur under Fr. Grignard

In March 1918 Fr. Grignard went to Gerdhai-Hamirpur for a pastoral visit, spending several days with the Christians and helping them in their struggles. His rather frequent visits were facilitated by the railway connections between Rajgangpur and Rourkela.[261] He was also keen to take part in the *tarikh* days (monthly meetings) of the Nagra region. Chapels had already been built in several places--Olhain, Potob, Kansikon, Godha, Bailmunda, Bispur, Joketa, Harumunda, Tangrain, Gerdhai, Dudenta (Bisra), Dunetra, Jorobahar and Goilo[262]--and he began to build more in different villages. The diaries of 1918 and 1919 mention regular visits of Fr. Grignard to the Nagra region, where he settled disputes and prepared the ground for the future Hamirpur station.[263] He wanted to build a presbytery in a central place, and he invited the Archbishop to choose a convenient spot. After having visited Tumkera and Ramkela, "(Tumkera is first visited, and he [Archbishop] is not much pleased. Archbishop and Fr. Grignard pass the night in Gerdhai chapel) in the morning they take to Ramkela. Waiting for the train, the Archbishop manifests a liking for Gerdhai: near the railway station. Fr. Grignard jumped at it. Gerdhai is chosen. Fr. Grignard settles in Gerdhai chapel, on the bank of the river ".[264]

The Nature of Hamirpur Station

In an article in *Missions Belges* (1920), Fr. Victor Gheysens,[265] one of the pioneers and companions of Fr. Theophile Lambot,[266] described the nature and prospects of evangelisation at the station that had just been started. He obviously felt encouraged by the numerous delegations that sought admission into the Church. He wrote:

> I feel sure that our Hamirpur station is developing so fast that in the near future it will officially take rank among the oldest stations of our great mission... At present two schools, one for the boys, the other for the girls are being built. We hope to have them ready in months. In the meantime, we are lodged, all of us Fathers, masters and pupils in the small buildings constructed last year. We have at present some 30 boarders and some 20 externs, a crowd is expected as soon as there are more rooms. Most of our Christians are people that have left Chotanagpur, to acquire fields

by clearing jungles in Gangpur. Among them there are Oraons, Mundas, Kharias, Gangpuria Oraons [Kisans]. The different languages spoken by each clan are a great difficulty in our ministry.[267]

In 1920, when Fr. Floor took charge of Kesramal, he assigned two priests to Kesramal and two to Hamirpur.[268] Though the exact date when missionaries took residence in Hamirpur is not clear, one could conclude from the letters of Fr. Floor and Fr. Fédéric Ernest that by the first week of January 1920 the two priests (Frs. Grignard and Lambot) took up their residence there.[269] Although Fr. Grignard spent much time in Hamirpur, the beginning of the mission was attributed to a later date due to its dependence on Kesramal.[270]

With the establishment of the mission stations at Kesramal and Hamirpur, the missionaries now had easy access to the villages that were sending delegations. A friendly government at Suadi helped with the evangelisation of a vast territory, where a number of mission stations were established quickly. Fr. Grignard and Fr. Lambot, who were later joined by Fr. Gheysens, undertook the construction of the buildings in Hamirpur.[271] The Hamirpur diary for October 1920 recorded: "Ten houses of Loakera (the Oraon hamlets) came over in a body. Incidentally they were asking protection against their *Ganju*. As the settlement is soon to take place, the *pauchas* of the rayats should be put in order . . ."[272]

The Missionaries' Response to the Flood of 1920

The monsoon of 1920 was devastating, since the Koel River destroyed crops, fields, and even some houses. There were times when people were stranded by the swollen waters. The missionaries provided them with shelter and fed them in the mission station till they could return to their villages. During their stay at the mission house in Hamirpur, the people were instructed, and a few were even admitted to the catechumenate. Fr. Vermeire recorded: "The mission gained by the catechumenate for the whole of Gerdhai, as they could easily be prepared for the Sacraments during their stay at Hamirpur. What had caused the greatest loss to these poor people was a good part of their fields now covered with sand, in some places so thick that there may be no hope of redeeming them."[273]

Growth of Hamirpur under Fr. Lambot

Fr. Lambot and his companion, Fr. Gheysens, had to endure the initial difficulties of establishing a mission station. They lived in extreme poverty and persevered through all sorts of privations. Fr. H. Floor lauded the natural talents of Fr. Lambot in the following words: "Fr. Lambot is zealous, active and prudent. He follows the directions given with a laudable punctuality. Left to himself, I don't think he would be able to manage."[274] Despite financial constraints, he built many chapels in the mission. In order to sustain progress, the Hamirpur mission needed money and catechists. In the 1920 issue of *Missions Belges*, Fr. Lambot wrote that Hamirpur, formerly called Gerdhai, had become an independent station separate from Kesramal.

> We are two Fathers. Gheysens (is) in charge of the school and I (am) of visiting the district; more than 8000 Christians had to be visited and instructed; there were 39 catechists; plus 7 school masters. We must increase the number of Christians and acquire still more lands. From several places, villagers want to become Christians, wish to have a chapel, catechists and schoolmasters. I have to find 10 more catechists, build many chapels, revive groups of Christians that were dying from want of instruction. These last years, the Nagra region has suffered very much from the loss of the missionaries and catechists who disappeared and were not replaced. Many Christians here, on that account, suffer from want of instruction, because they think that we had neglected them. I have visited them and now they renew their appeal to us.[275]

Fr. Lambot noted both the willingness of the youth and the stubbornness of the old. He saw a change in the people, as they were willing to be instructed. The people of Dalki, including three Lutheran families, showed a keen interest in learning the *Dharam*, the religion of the Catholic missionaries. Some of the Anglicans of Bajnathpur were also willing to come over to the Catholic Church.[276] Since January 1920 there was a great movement of conversions in Bonai, one of the native states situated in the southern part of Hamirpur.[277] Villages sent deputations to the Fathers at Hamirpur. For example, a deputation from Banrutola (Tumkera) arrived on November 21, 1920. It was led by the village head himself, and it sought assistance in curbing a cattle disease that devastated their village. Normally such villagers would have consulted a sorcerer for the cure.[278] The catechists played a leading role in bringing people to the Catholic Church. However, since the abrupt stopping of *Bethbegari* (forced labour) on Sundays which often escalated the tensions,[279] the catechists were requested to report, if any problem, to Hamirpur so that the missionaries themselves could handle them.

Missionary Activities in Hamirpur

Initially the activities of the missionaries were mainly to invite the people to attend the Holy Mass and the *Panchayat*, at which there were discussions on cooperative banks, schools, the *Dhan Gola*, the *Dharam* School and drunkenness.[280] During his visit to Goelo on December 13, 1922, Fr. Lambot preached on the villagers' negligence in maintaining their cooperative bank and on other matters. He condemned their celebration of the *Ind*, their night dances and their practice of *Puja*.[281] As he went through the villages, Fr. Lambot noticed the poor conditions of the village chapels and did all he could to repair them.[282]

School Apostolate

Since the missionaries gave priority to education, each village that accepted the faith, as a rule, had a school. According to the missionaries, the school was an important way of conserving the faith. Fr. Lambot encouraged his catechists through a one-rupee increase in their monthly salaries for their efficiency in teaching religion and in attracting others to the faith. The results were brought to the presbytery every two months, where they were examined and rewarded if found worthy.[283] A school for boys was constructed in Hamirpur by April 1920, and one for girls by June 1920, in addition to the lower primary school that had already been in operation.[284] School attendance in the district improved, and it was given further impetus when Mr. Lucas, the *dewan* of Gangpur, showed interest in education. The schoolmasters were required to submit reports, which were later sent to the District Inspector of Schools at Kuarmunda. In this way the laxity of the schoolmasters was controlled.[285]

Fr. G. Pierret[286] described the need for the schools in an article in *Missions Belges* of July 1922: "We must develop our schools in order that our Christians may find among the youth that leave the school future chiefs who can defend them against pagan strangers who arrive from all sides and want to crush the Christians and to occupy all the most remunerative posts."[287] He added: "If our people advance morally from their religion, intellectually from our schools, materially from their work, after some years they will be able to maintain their religion, as they already do partly by keeping up their schools."[288]

Despite the lofty idealism of the missionaries, a number of the schools operated poorly, and the students were unable to acquire proper skills in reading and writing. In his effort to teach them, Fr. Lambot ordered the children to bring sand. Then he made them write in it with their fingers. The people became curious and began to show some interest in the education of their children.[289] Low attendance in the schools was regular during the harvest season, because the children were expected to perform household activities, such as tending the cattle, babysitting, etc., while their parents were away in the fields.

Programme of Self-help

The missionaries instilled in the people's minds the importance of contributing to the maintenance of the church even if their donations were meagre. Their contribution was called *Mission Madait* or Mission Help, and it was collected at the end of the month by the catechist and submitted to the missionary at the *tarikhs*. Every Catholic family, as a result, paid *1 anna*[290] to help the mission. Often people contributed in kind, especially with rice. On September 16, 1922, for example, the Christians of Hamirpur asked the missionaries to bless the harvested new rice and each family offered a cupful for the maintenance of the missionaries.

A Crusade against Oppressive Traditions

The missionaries condemned the practices of *Ind*[291] (a communal feast accompanied by night dancing) and *Puja*,[292] (sacrifice). In Goghea the zealous missionary refused to administer sacraments to those who took part in *Ind* and *Puja* and delivered a strong homily against the non-Christian practices.[293] They were convinced that strong measures alone would dissuade the tribals from such non-Christian practices and would help them to realise the differences between good and evil. When the *Panchayat* or the village council on December 22, 1922, imposed a fine for participation in the *Ind* and its resultant drunkenness, it could not be collected, since most of those were very poor. However, in some villages, like Konsikona, the strong measures taken by the missionaries produced positive results.[294]

During the *Panchayat* at Tunmura on November 27, 1922, all those present took a pledge that they would give up drinking *Daru* or country liquor. They also decided that any one violating the decree would pay a fine of Rs. 1, while any catechist found guilty would pay Rs. 10.[295]

Rapport with Officials

The missionaries realised that good relations with local officials would not only keep them out of trouble but would also help to obtain certain benefits for the church in the long run. For example, during his visit to Panposh on November 29, 1922, Fr. Lambot obtained various gifts from the manager of the quarries: lime for the chapel, boxes, wires and a rope for the well.[296] When the *dewan* of Gangpur offered to help the people buy bullocks, the Khinjir people responded in large numbers, while those at Nagra were very diffident. Only one Christian and a few pagans applied. Fr. Lambot, saw this as a sign of the oppression suffered by the *rayats* in Nagra.[297] In October 1922, he visited Lal Sahib, the *Thakur* or Zamindar of Khinjir, who had been satisfied that the Catholics had not joined either the Germans (Protestants) or the pagans in creating trouble by sending petitions to Sundargarh. Fr. Lambot said: "I showed them that we give much to the State; the result obtained in the Kesramal area is proof of it, for we help the police and State officials. We are a conservative power in the state. The *Daroga* of Hathibari told me that he had least troubles where there are Catholics."[298]

Troubles and Opposition

The steady progress of Christianity did not fail to draw the attention of the zamindars, the lords of the land, who often punished the catechists for their free-lance preaching. However, troubles in the villages could be controlled by an able catechist, either by timely intervention or by reporting it to the authorities. Therefore, the progress of the mission largely depended on the initiative and character of the catechist, who also had a moral duty to educate and gradually prepare the people for Christian living.[299]

During the first week of October 1922, Marcus, the catechist of Hamirpur, responded to an urgent call from Olhain, where trouble had been brewing. It was caused by a former Hindu *chowkidar*, a lower-grade government employee. He not only ignored the decisions of the *Panchayat* but also seemed to have instigated some people to return to their former religion. Fr. Lambot said: "He uses his *sarkari*, the governmental kit (uniform), to bring others back to paganism. Peace is to be re-established by getting rid of that undesirable person, as he refuses to pay all fines as well as to amend his ways and he is cut off from the Bank and from the *Dhan Gola*, I am taking steps to have his *chowkidari* also cancelled."[300] There was also trouble in Konsikona, where nine girls were alleged to have taken part in the *Ind* and where a villager had been performing *puja*. They were fined. In Goghea, all who had contributed to start the *Ind* refused to pay any fine. The missionary had to intervene and settle the matter, as the villagers were unwilling to listen to the catechists. It was reported from Potob that on *Karam*[301] night, the apostates of Jamdara deliberately desecrated the chapel.

Since the people were insolent and unwilling to make reparation, a complaint was lodged with the police to take necessary action.

A *Panchayat* was held in Kerketa on October 8, 1922, to discuss various local issues: the formation of a cooperative bank, the Dhan *Gola,* schools, complaints against the *Dharam,* and other difficulties. The missionary took immediate steps to implement the decision of the *Panchayat.* He wrote: "I have asked for a new license for a chapel. There is hope. Kerketa is turning around for good. The young people are very good."[302] In his visit to Bispur on October 9, 1922, Fr. Lambot noticed that the ignorance of the catechists was causing a great deal of troubles to the villagers. He was unable to bring the people together and was drinking. Fr. Lambot commented: "Bispur has no chance. The actual catechist is worth nothing. The school is ill [in poor condition]. That shows the catechist's worth. So, he must be changed or discarded."[303] Seeing the miserable condition of the school in Arundah, the missionary had a *Panchayat* on October 15, 1922, with the parents of both the Christian and non-Christian children. He was satisfied to establish contacts with the Christians who did not practice Catholicism. In some villages, the people wanted the mission schools but declined to accept Christianity.[304]

Even though he was well received at Balenda in November 1922, Fr. Lambot was unable to baptise any one there. The catechist did not prepare them for the sacrament, and the people were also not interested. The missionary was disturbed to discover that the girls were not attending church and seemed to have been working on Sundays. The people felt that they should go to the church only if their case against the *Ganju* was settled.[305] Fr. Lambot observed that similar situations persisted in both Jorodabiri and Garjan. Certain industries in the region were also a cause for concern, as Catholics were obliged to work on Sunday. However, the missionaries thought that the problem could be addressed with the management and that the Christians, even if they did not get a holiday for the entire day, could attend Sunday services at chapels established by the owners. There were 28 such chapels in Kesramal parish, they helped to bring about an increase in Mass attendance from the *Girja Ilaka* (church zone).[306]

In spite of the challenges and difficulties, the socio-religious movement spearheaded by the dedicated and talented missionaries did not diminish. Fr. Vermeire wrote: "The Hamirpur diary in Fr. Lambot's time was very well kept up. It gives an insight in many aspects, most of all, the mission progress, as was to be expected. Much is said about the villages where Christianity is penetrating. Regular tours were made among them by the missionaries in charge."[307]

Western Gangpur

In the second chapter reference was made to the beginning of the conversion movement, originating from Kurdeg station in Rengarih district under the able leadership of Fr. Edmund De Gryse. He made extensive journeys in western Gangpur, visiting villages and bringing them into the Catholic fold. The visits of Msgr. Brice Meuleman, Archbishop of Calcutta, in 1905 encouraged the people and increased the prospects of conversion in Gangpur.[308] The annual retreats and missionary meetings in Calcutta provided opportunities for the missionaries to pass through Gangpur and thus spend some time with the neophytes. They celebrated the Holy Eucharist together and discussed their concerns.[309] The missionaries had to pass through western Gangpur in order to catch a train either at Bamra or at Jharsuguda.

The Reasons for an Extension

In a report to the archbishop Fr. Floor mentioned some of the difficulties in the region:

> Evidently the district is too big, and the good Fathers 'kill' themselves, unable to give sufficient care to the people. This situation still goes on, and it is impossible for me to take the responsibility of Kesramal and Behrenbasa. Most of the villages of the Kharias and Oraons left no account of the visits of the catechists and the *Bhagat* movement was to be taken into account . . . The *Labour Corps* had also contributed its share in disrupting the progress, for many catechists and teachers left their work at home to join the *Corps*; the mission was left without any replacement. There were also insufficient schools for a large territory.[310]

As it is clear from the report, the arduous journeys from station to station, which was often about 50 miles apart, which exhausted the already over-burdened missionaries. The constant presence of the missionaries was also required to assist the 32 catechists employed in the Behrenbasa substation, as some of them seemed to be of dubious character. Eager though they were, no progress was being made in the instruction of about 4700 Christians.[311] There were about 20 chapels and another 20 under construction in Behrenbasa.[312] Yet the lack of personnel did not allow for a resident priest in Behrenbasa. Fr. Floor felt strongly that the Christian population in Behrenbasa would grow steadily under the leadership and guidance of an able missionary.[313]

Establishment of a Substation at Behrenbasa

A mission station was established at Behrenbasa, situated close to the border of Gangpur in 1905.[314] It remained one of the important stations of western Gangpur, as it often provided temporary shelter for the travelling missionaries and a contact place for the people of the area.[315] In 1915 it became a secondary station of Kesramal without a resident priest. Visits by priests were restricted to a few days, especially for *tarikh* or monthly meetings, when both the catechists and schoolteachers rendered account of their activities. Such visits were often concluded with spiritual exercises and instructions for the coming month.[316] However, the visits grew more frequent in 1920. Although the missionaries' regular visits had stopped the tribals' defections *en masse* to their former state, they did not improve their way of life.[317] The missionaries themselves realized that a practical solution was to establish a mission in western Gangpur. As a result, they chose a place, more or less at the centre of western Gangpur, to nurture the more than 6500 Christians (3000 baptized and 3550 catechumens) there. Writing in 1920, Fr. Floor remarked that a house had been constructed but no priest had yet been appointed. A resident priest in Behrenbasa was necessary to stop the defections in the area.[318] Fr. H. Floor wrote to the provincial in Belgium: "This year we have organised this part (well). Out of 25 chapels to be built, we have completed 19 of them. There are catechists everywhere and a good number of teachers. Due to the distance, this part [Behrenbasa] should be separated from Kesramal."[319]

A Mission at Kusumdegi?

In 1921 a consultation took place with regard to the beginning of another station in Gangpur. The superior and consultors decided that it could be started at Kusumdegi, one of the important villages in western Gangpur. But this decision did not materialise. Fr. Djardin accused Fr. Floor of manipulation when he asked for and received the approval of the archbishop of Calcutta for a station in Gaibira. He wrote: "Last year we were consulted on the location of the new station in Gangpur. The consultors and I decided on Kusumdegi. This year Fr. Floor went for his retreat (to Calcutta), where he spoke with the Archbishop. What happened there, I don't know. The fact is that I received a letter after a month informing me that the new station would be Gaibira."[320]

Evangelisation in Gaibira

Fr. De Gryse undertook an extensive tour in the western part of Gangpur mission in July 1905. he reported that he had lost about 35 families, of whom 8 fled and 27 returned to paganism. Those who left the church did so because they had gotten married to non-Christian tribals; they were repulsed by the drunkenness and contentious behaviour of the catechists (who had imposed exorbitant fines on the neophytes), or they were disillusioned that they had not received anticipated material benefits.[321] In April 1906 Fr. Van Hecke visited 11 villages in western Gangpur. Similar visits took place in June, September, October and November.[322] One of the remedies suggested to stop defections was to increase the number of catechists and schoolteachers.[323] With more frequent visits by the missionaries and constant guidance and instruction given to the catechists, the defections were arrested to a large extent.

Fifteen years later Fr. Floor could report: "There is a movement of conversion in Gangpur. In 1921 there were 2000 conversions before the month of July and conversions in December there were about 1500."[324] The Oraons in the west as far as the native State of Jashpur were ready to become Christians. There was a possibility of a true *mouvement de la grace,* where tens of thousands of Christians could be ascribed to the Church.

The Founding of a Mission in Gaibira

Gaibira is situated 34 miles west of Kesramal and 15 miles northeast of Suadi, the capital of Gangpur. It is located not far from the Ib river. Its territory covered an area of 800 square miles.[325] The people of Gaibira had been waiting a long time for the arrival of the missionaries. Their village deputations started arriving in 1906, inviting the missionaries to baptise them and to receive them into the church. In 1922 alone 21 villages sent deputations to Fr. Floor at Kesramal, requesting him to baptise them.[326]

It made good sense to start a mission at Gaibira: (1) Gaibira was the centre of the conversion movement in western Gangpur; (2) Gaibira was in the semi-independent state of Gangpur, whereas Behrenbasa was in British territory;[327] and (3) there was no difficulty in obtaining land. In fact, the people had already built a hut for a missionary there.

On July 1, 1922, Fr. H. Floor visited the raja at Suadi to seek permission to purchase a few acres of land at Gaibira. The raja rejected the request because he had been displeased with the Christians and the catechists of Talsera, near Gaibira. When Fr. Floor tried to explain the cause of the agitation, the raja refused even to listen to him. When the Raja had finally finished with his litany of accusation against the Christians, the missionary took responsibility for their behaviour and suggested that the situation would have been different had a missionary been residing among them. This seemed to persuade the ruler. Fr. Floor received a positive reply from the *dewan*, Mr. H. D. Christian, authorising him to buy 20 acres of land for the Gaibira mission.[328]

In his letter to the archbishop, on July 10, 1922, Fr. Floor wrote: "I secured 15 acres of land at Gaibira, the lease of which will be written in Your Grace's name."[329] He wrote again, on August 12, 1922: "With your approval I can start residing there from the beginning of September. My dwelling will be the boys' school, which is ready. It has four rooms. I intend pushing actively the erection of the convent and girls' school, as I would like to get native Sisters already in January for the marriage catechumenate. Many pagan marriages have to be settled."[330] Initially Fr. Floor had to endure numerous inconveniences, which Fr. Camil Lievens later described: "His Church, a small hut! His rectory, another hut! His furniture, a bed, a table, a chair, and… that was it! His parish carried the burden of 6000 Christians and all who had to be converted in an area of 2200 square kilometre."[331]

Fr. Pierret in his rather short diary of nine pages has an entry for August 19, 1922, which reads: "Father Floor receives news. He is to settle in Gaibira on September 1,1922. There will be 3 stations in Gangpur from that date; Gaibira with Fr. Floor, Hamirpur with Fr. Lambot and Kesramal with Fr. Pierret."[332] Though the founding of Gaibira as a separate parish came into effect on September 1, 1922, Fr. Floor actually took possession on September 8, 1922.[333] The missionaries adopted the native system in the construction of the house. The roof was to be covered with native Mangalore tiles. Local carpenters would make the needed furniture. The missionary adhered to this style of construction for two reasons: (1) the financial difficulties faced by the mission during and after the war; and (2) the uncertainty regarding the status of the Gangpur mission, namely, whether it would remain with the Jesuits or it would be passed on to the new Orissa mission of the

Vincentians.[334] The dewan, a Protestant European, was sympathetic to the Catholic mission and helped it in every way possible, such as granting permission to fell the trees for the construction of the house or fixing a nominal tax on the land (about 15 acres). With such generosity on the part of the dewan, plans were finalised to build a chapel, a presbytery, schools for boys and girls, and a convent for the Indian Sisters.[335]

The news of a parish established at Gaibira spread throughout the immediate area: four villages around Dirga and three villages near Sundargarh approached the missionary. In a letter to the archbishop, Fr. Floor underscored the prospects of the new station: "I have studied the map with the catechists: there is hope of conversion for the 16 Uraon (Oraon) villages, and 15 Kharia villages and 7 Gangpuria villages. These 38 villages should give between 3 and 4 thousand souls. This refers to the vicinity of Gaibira, and the country along the west of the Ib river up to Sundargarh [Suadi]."[336] There were also other villages that sent delegations, such as Dipatoli, Kitgaon, Tangarbhauri, Suadi, Tumulia, Sadagar, Pataimunda, Chatasarga, Koensera and Kirelaga.[337] The *dewan* offered a sum of Rs. 2000 to purchase cattle for the people after the tribals had sustained a heavy loss of livestock with the outbreak of rinderpest (cattle plague). This indirectly influenced the conversion of the tribals.[338]

Archbishop Meuleman declared on August 20, 1922 that the three stations of Gangpur -- Kesramal, Hamirpur and Gaibira -- would become independent. They would be detached from the district of Rengarih and form a separate district of their own.[339] There were 6,051 Christians in the new station of Gaibira, while Kesramal had 12,019 and Hamirpur 8,500. This made a total of 26,570 Catholics in Gangpur.[340]

Obstacles

One of the difficulties that Fr. Floor had to face in the new Gaibira mission was an insufficient number of catechists (who were often ill-formed and unmotivated) to meet the growing requests of the villages in and around Gaibira. In order to respond to the village delegations, he needed a minimum of 28 catechists. Yet Fr. Floor could not even afford to provide the meagre salary he was paying to his present catechists.[341] The missionaries had also to address the drunkenness of both the catechists and the people.

Conclusion

The establishment of new centres signalled the vitality and the dedication of the missionaries, who, despite their foreign appearance and attire, could feel at home among the Tribals and the Dalits. Their sufferings and trials were not in vain. Their exhausting expeditions across the mountains and their frequent exposure to various dangers brought the desired results, for the simple people recognised the missionaries' sacrifices on their behalf. As ignorance and superstition reigned supreme, the missionaries established schools, although they were fully aware that education would not automatically guarantee the social and moral regeneration of the people. Therefore, they appointed an Inspector of Schools, whose duty, besides efficiency and good results, was to provide direction for a value-based education.

Though the First World War paralysed mission activities, the church did not register a great loss, thanks to the handful of missionaries who remained in India and took care of the flock. Once the War was over, the MSFS looked for another congregation that could provide more personnel and resources for the Ganjam Mission. As a result, in 1922 the Spanish Vincentians arrived to take over the Ganjam Mission, later known as the Cuttack Mission. In the north-western frontier of Orissa, the Belgian Jesuits enjoyed a springtime of missionary activity, though they had to manage with a handful of missionaries. Certain of their methods, the Jesuits continued the expansion of the mission by establishing some new parishes during the subsequent years.[342]

Endnotes

[1] The following areas are examined in the first part of this chapter: 1) Surada, Thotavally and Torobady; 2) Cuttack and Puri; 3) Berhampur and Gopalpur; 4) Katingia; 5) Dantholinghy and Russellkonda 6) Dighy, Jeypore, Koraput and Padangui.

[2] *Tarikhs* were monthly meetings of catechists and teachers which were usually conducted on the first Friday, when they rendered the monthly account of their activities to the priest. The missionary usually gave some instruction either on Christianity or the course of action for the coming month. Before leaving for their villages they received their salary.

[3] The years within bracket refer to the time when the MSFS began to reside in those centres. Cf. F. MOGET, *Early Days of the Visakhapatnam Mission 1846-1920*, pp. 146-149.

[4] Since Surada was located at the foot of the mountains, it served as a resting place for those coming from Visakhapatnam before they continued

their upward journey. The Sisters at Surada sent provisions for the missionaries while they were on expedition, and if they fell ill, they came back to Surada for treatment.

[5] Fr. Richard wished that : "Dans le district de Souradah (Surada), je ne voudrais pas que la mission se contentât pour-ainsi-dire, d'être un gros propriétaire, ayant de villages ; j'aimerais que les prêtres eussent à s'y occuper principalement du spirituel". Then he desired that Fr. Dupont's service might be made available for Surada. Cf. Richard to Clavel, Visakhapatnam, August 8, 1870, AMSFS 5H5-2/2.

[6] Ibid.

[7] Attendance during Mass on Sundays and feast days, the work of the Sisters in the orphanage and the school, and other activities were advanced compared to other stations in the Ganjam Mission. Cf. Bonaventure to Philippe, Surada, November 19, 1881, AMSFS 5H5-2/2.

[8] Torobady, Karikotte, Thotavally and Dantholinghy were centres that were under Surada where Fr. J.M. Descombes used to offer Sunday Masses. Cf. J.M. Descombes to Allard, Dantholinghy, May 19, 1885, AMSFS 5H5-2/2.

[9] J.M. Tissot to his friend in France, Surada, March 14, 1881, AMSFS 5H5-2/2.

[10] Descombes to J. Tissot, Surada, May 8, 1883, AMSFS 5H5-2/2.

[11] Fr. Bonaventure described : "Surada est une station qui, depuis de longues années, ne nous donne aucune consolation. On dit parmi nous que c'est la 'terre maudite' [cursed land]. Nous nous proposons d'y faire un dernier essai: s'il réussit, toute gloire en sera rendue au Sacré Coeur, s'il ne réussit pas, celà pourrrait influer sur la decision definitive d'abandonner ce malhereux pays." Bonaventure to Clavel, Surada, December 12, 1879, AMSFS 5H5-2/2.

[12] For the decline of the Surada mission see F. MOGET, *Early Days of Visakhapatnam*, pp. 161 – 162.

[13] Bonaventure to J. Tissot, Berhampur, March 19, 1883, AMSFS 5H5-2/2.

[14] This is how the missionaries viewed the worship of Hindus.

[15] Bonaventure to Clavel, Surada, December 12, 1879, AMSFS 5H5-2/2. Fr. Bonaventure is referring to the *Thakurani Jatra*, which is one of the most important festivals in Berhampur. It is celebrated with pomp and splendour for a period of about one month. Each day seven women carried in procession the consecrated *Kalasas* (small earthen pots containing some holy objects) to different sectors of the town. Cf. N.C. BEHURIA (ed.), *Orissa State Gazetteer*, vol. II, Cuttack 1991, p. 268.

[16] The Apostleship of Prayer, a pious association, which is neither a sodality nor a confraternity, and which is otherwise known as a league of prayer in union with the Heart of Jesus, was well diffused in the second part of the nineteenth-century Catholic world. It was founded at Vals, France, on December 3, 1844 by Fr. Francis X. Gautrelet S.J. The growth and diffusion of

the association was due to the work of Fr. Henry Ramière, S.J., who in 1861, adapted its organization for parishes and various Catholic institutions, and made it known by his book *The Apostleship of Prayer, the Holy League of Hearers United to the Heart of Jesus* and by the *Messenger of the Heart of Jesus* which were translated into many languages. In 1879, Pope Pius IX approved the statutes of the association. The motives, as mentioned in the statutes, clearly indicate the promotion of prayer for the mutual intentions of the members in union with the intercession of Christ. The members are also urged to observe the practice of the Holy Hour, spent in meditation on the Passion. Cf. F. SCHOBERG, "Apostleship of Prayer", in *The New Catholic Encyclopaedia*, vol. I, p. 687; LUDWIG KOCH, *Jesuiten – Lexikon. Die Gesellschaft Jesu einst und jetzt*, Paderborn 1934, p. 21.

[17] Bonaventure to Philippe, Surada, February 21, 1882, AMSFS 5H5-2/2.

[18] Bonaventure to Philippe, Surada, February 21, 1882, AMSFS 5H5-2/2.

[19] Ibid.

[20] Descombes to J. Tissot, Surada, January 8, 1883, AMSFS 5H5-2/2; It is obviously an allusion to the mission discourse of Jesus (Mt.10: 14). Fr. Bonaventure observed: "Son principal désir est de voyager dans les villages pour prêcher notre Seigneur. P. Thevenet l'incourage. 'ayez une petite tente, lui dit-il, et établissez vous dans un village pour y prêcher la religion, se l'on vous écoute, convertissez, se non, secouez la poussière de vos soulliers et allez ailleurs'". Bonaventure to Philippe, Surada, February 21, 1882, AMSFS 5H5-2/2.

[21] Bonaventure to J. Tissot, Surada, October 30, 1881. AMSFS 5H5-2/2.

[22] In the previous chapter (3.1.9) the adaptation method followed by the MSFS in Ganjam and its failure are presented.

[23] J.M. Tissot to J. Tissot, Visakhapatnam, August 10, 1883, AMSFS 5H5-2/2.

[24] Descombes to J. Tissot, Surada, May 8, 1883, AMSFS 5H5-2/2.

[25] Riccaz to Bonaventure, Surada, May 10, 1883, AMSFS 5H5-2/2.

[26] Descombes to Allard, Dantholinghy, May 19, 1885, AMSFS 5H5-2/2.

[27] Dupont to his friend, Visakhapatnam, September 14, 1882, AMSFS 5H5-2/2.

[28] Bonaventure to Philippe, Surada, October 30, 1881. AMSFS 5H5-2/2.

[29] Alexis Riccaz was born on January 26, 1834, at St. Jean d'Arves, Maurienne. After his ordination on June 23, 1861, he arrived in the Visakhapatnam mission on January 22, 1862. He worked as a teacher in St. Aloysius School (Visakhapatnam) and as a pioneer in Gnanapuran (1872-1881). In 1877 he was sent to Surada for a short period to help the mission. He served as the vicar general till 1887, when the diocese was divided, and he became the first bishop of Nagpur. He was consecrated in Nagpur on November 20, 1887. He worked tirelessly for the new diocese until his death on September 8, 1892, at Jabalpur. Cf. *Tableau Genèral*, in *Histoire de la Mission*, AMSFS 5H4; F. MOGET, *MSFS Obituary*, p. 80.

[30] Describing the situation of the mission, Fr. Bonaventure wrote to Fr. Philippe: "This year (1882) I had conversions everywhere. The process takes a lot of my time. In spite of my desire I can't do anything. I came to know that this was a conspiracy. The Wesleyans of Berhampur helped our adversaries. The judge is against us, specially his secretary. Given these difficulties, we cannot think of any success. We have nothing but God and the constitution on our side." Bonaventure to Philippe, Surada, September 30, 1882. AMSFS 5H5-2/2; Foulex to Philippe, Cuttack, January 27, 1882, AMSFS 5H5-2/2.

[31] Bonaventure to Philippe, Surada, October 30, 1881. AMSFS 5H5-2/2; Foulex to J. Tissot, Cuttack, August 9, 1881, AMSFS 5H5-2/2.

[32] Bonaventure to J. Tissot, Visakhapatnam, April 12, 1883, AMSFS 5H5-2/2.

[33] Bonaventure to Philippe, Surada, December 5, 1881, AMSFS 5H5-2/2. Fr. Décarre wrote that Fr. Guillermin was instrumental in the purchase of 200 acres of land from the Government at a cost of Rs. 1000/-. Cf. Décarre to J. Tissot, Thotavally, March 1889, AMSFS 5H5-2/2.

[34] Souchon to Clavel, Berhampur, May 16, 1867, AMSFS 5H5-2/2.

[35] H. Moenne–Loccoz to Clavel, Surada, September 1, 1871, AMSFS 5H5-2/2.

[36] H. Moenne–Loccoz to Clavel, Thotavally, March 1872, AMSFS 5H5-2/2.

[37] Ibid.; H. Moenne–Loccoz to Payraud, Surada, March 17, 1872, AMSFS 5H5-2/2.

[38] Cf. Bonaventure to Fr. Philippe, Surada, December 5, 1881, AMSFS 5H5-2/2.

[39] *Oriyas* were synonymous with the oppressors or moneylenders. They spoke *Oriya* as their mother tongue. They were Hindus and belonged to a higher caste. They were literate and occupied the influential jobs, like *Patros* and *Karnams*.

[40] A short formula, generally recited by a *guru*, is said to be efficacious when repeated by the individuals who received it in piety.

[41] Descombes to Allard, Dantholinghy, May 19, 1885, AMSFS 5H5-2/2.

[42] Cuttack, the capital city of Orissa division, is situated in 20° 29' N. and 85° 52' E. Writing on the meaning of the word Cuttack, the Orissa Gazetteer remarks: "The word 'Cuttack' is anglicised from the Sanskrit word '*kataka*' which signifies seven different meanings out of which the two noted below are applicable here. The first meaning is the military camp and the second is the fort of the capital or the seat of the Government." The city stands at the apex of the delta of the Mahanadi, the great river. The place gained its importance in the tenth century, 'when protecting dykes were built and a fort was constructed by the Hindu king Makar Kesari.' Barabati Kila, an ancient fort built by one of the Hindu kings, is still one of the conspicuous monuments in the city. Cuttack was declared a municipality in 1876 and became the headquarters of Orissa division. The city is noted for filigree work. Towards the last quarter of the nineteenth century Cuttack had some important educational institutions, obviously founded by Christian missionaries, i.e. Baptists and Roman Catholics.

Cf. *The Imperial Gazetteer of India*, vol. XI, Oxford 1908, pp. 85-99; N. C. BEHURIA (ed.), *Orissa State Gazetteer*, vol. II, pp. 283-291.

[43] *The Imperial Gazetteer of India*, vol. XI, Oxford 1908, p. 90.

[44] For details of the early history of the church in Cuttack, cf. M. DOMENGE, *La Mission de Vizagapatam*, pp. 452, 453 and 456.

[45] J. TABOADO, *En las Selvas del Ganjam*, pp. 141 – 147.

[46] Décarre to Philippe, Cuttack, May 1868, AMSFS 5H5-2/2; Décarre to the Mother General of the Sisters of St. Joseph of Annecy, Gopalpur, December 18, 1885, Archives of the Sisters of St. Joseph of Annecy, 2H, J4. A.

[47] Girard to his friend, Cuttack, February 9, 1872, AMSFS 5H5-2/2.

[48] The 'Annals of the Sisters of St. Joseph' mentioned that the Sisters had to leave Cuttack because of the false propaganda of the Baptists. Though the reason in itself might have been trivial, the competition between the Catholics and Baptists was a cause of concern. They came back in November 1879 when the situation was favourable. Cf. *Annales des Soeurs de Saint Joseph. Diocese de Vizagapatam. 1897 – 1906*, vol. II, Archives of the Sisters of St. Joseph of Annecy, Annecy, 161-162, 219.

[49] Jean François Foulex was born on September 19, 1851, at Charvonneux, Savoy. He reached Visakhapatnam mission in October 1874. He was ordained a priest on May 26, 1877. He worked in Cuttack as assistant priest in 1881. In 1894, he was transferred to Nagpur. He worked in Kamptee, Khandwa, and in the last years of his life served as vicar general of Nagpur. He died on June 6, 1923. Cf. *Tableau Genèral*, in *Histoire de la Mission*, AMSFS 5H4, F. MOGET, *MSFS Obituary*, p. 59.

[50] Foulex to J. Tissot, Cuttack, July 7, 1881, AMSFS 5H5-2/2.

[51] Sr. Claire wrote : "Nous avons eu une belle cérémonie Jeudi passé ; la bénédiction de la première pierre, de notre nouveau couvent. Vous devez savoir que le gouvernement a donné à la mission un très grand morceau de terrain. Notre bon père Décarre a déjà bien fait avancé son ouvrage; les foundations sont déjà tout creusées; le mur de clôture est presque tout fini. Revenons à la bénédiction de notre première pierre le Chief Commissioner celui qui tient la place du Vice-Roi à bien voulu présider la bande de musique, ainsi que le Colonel du régiment ont bien voulu y assister. La musique a été très agreeable. Toutes les personnes de première rang de Cuttack ont bien voulu aussi y assister." Sr. Claire to Sr. Césarie, Cuttack, July 10, 1881, Archives of the Sisters of St. Joseph of Annecy, 2H, J3. B.

[52] Décarre to companion, Cuttack, November 2, 1881, AMSFS 5H5-2/2.

[53] J.M. Tissot to Philippe, Surada, Vizagapatam, August 9, 1884, AMSFS 5H5-2/2.

[54] Foulex to Philippe, Cuttack, January 27, 1882, AMSFS 5H5-2/2.

[55] Décarre to J. Tissot, Cuttack, September 15, 1887, AMSFS 5H5-2/2.

[56] Décarre to Mother General of the Sisters of St. Joseph of Annecy, Gopalpur, December 18, 1885, Archives of the Sisters of St. Joseph of Annecy, 2H, J4. A.

[57] M. DOMENGE, *La Mission de Vizagapatam*, p. 454.

[58] Foulex to J. Tissot, Cuttack, August 9, 1881, AMSFS 5H5-2/2.

[59] The work of the Sisters consisted of supervising the kitchen, the laundry and the general cleanliness of the hospital premises. They helped the doctors in the operations and with nursing. P. Rossillon to Superior, Kottavasala, July 23, 1911, AMSFS 5H5-2/2. 5H4; A. Rey to Constant Bouvard, Visakhapatnam, May 20, 1908, AMSFS 5H5-2/2; F. MOGET, *Early Days of Visakhapatnam*, pp. 144 – 145.

[60] Writing to Fr. Philippe, Fr. Décarre narrated : "Votre serviteur est dans la station de l'état, station isolée où je suis de nouveau en train avec une école; j'ai déjà 30 élèves avec un bon professeur qui a fait son éducation au Collége des jésuites à Calcutta. J'espère que cette école ira bien aussi, Dieu aidant, et que les écoles du diable tomberont aussi en présence de la nôtre comme cela est arrivée à Vizianagram par la grâce du tout bon Jésus." Décarre to Philippe, Cuttack, May 1868, AMSFS 5H5-2/2.

[61] Girard to his friend, Cuttack, February 9, 1872, AMSFS 5H5-2/2.

[62] Besides English, Oriya, Tamil, Telugu and Hindustani were also taught. The missionaries had to learn all these languages. Tamil was used with the Catholics who worked in the 32nd Madras Regiment, since most of them were from the south. Telugu was also widely spoken among the Catholics. In addition to these languages, the missionaries had to acquire a working knowledge of Oriya. Cf. Foulex to J. Tissot, Cuttack, August 9, 1881, AMSFS 5H5-2/2.

[63] It is a form of subsidy from the government to pay the salary of teachers in non-governmental institutions. Cf. Girard to his friend, Cuttack, February 9, 1872, AMSFS 5H5-2/2.

[64] Pierre Rossillon was born on September 22, 1874, at La Biolle, Savoy. He entered the MSFS in August 1893. He came to Gopalpur in India to continue his philosophical and theological studies under Fr. Anselme Rey. He was ordained a priest on June 5, 1898, at Visakhapatnam. He served the mission in various capacities: as teacher in St. Aloysius School, as parish priest of Gnanapuram (1899-1908), as a missionary in Kottadabah. He served as the regional superior in 1911. During the war years, 1914-1918, he worked as a teacher at Florimont, Geneva. He was consecrated the coadjutor bishop of Visakhapatnam on May 7, 1919, at Annecy. He guided the diocese of Visakhapatnam for 21 years and gave new life to the mission through his organisational skills. He was one of those prolific writers who explained the missionary situation to the West. He died at the age 72 on March 22, 1947. Cf. F. MOGET, *MSFS Obituary*, p. 37; J. REY, *Son Excellence Msgr. Pierre Rossillon*, in *Histoire de la Mission*, AMSFS 5H4.

[65] In preparation for their first communion, a retreat was organised for the communicants. Fr. P. Rossillon preached the retreat in 1911. Cf. P. Rossillon to Bouvard, Kottavasala, July 23, 1911, AMSFS 5H5-2/4.

⁶⁶ *Annales des Soeurs de Saint Joseph. Diocese de Vizagapatam. 1897-1906*, II, Archives of the Sisters of St. Joseph of Annecy, Annecy, p. 28.

⁶⁷ Bonaventure to Philippe, Berhampur, November 1882, AMSFS 5H5-2/2.

⁶⁸ Fr. Décarre distinguished Baptists from other denominations by using the expression 'Baptists and Protestants'. Expressing his impressions of the Baptists, Fr. Décarre wrote: "Cuttack est une assez belle et grande ville pour l'Inde, mais les gens n'y sont pas meilleurs que dans les autres stations; nous avons surtout ici les fameux Baptistes qui sont vraiment le cauchemar du missionnaire catholique, et Cuttack est leur rampart dans l'Inde. Les protestants proprement dit, sont, en general, assez tolerants, nous aidant même assez volontiers; tandis que catholiques et Baptistes ne pourront jamais tirer à la corde ensemble. On dirait que le principe fondemental cette secte est une haine implacable pour le catholicisme, inde irae." Décarre to Philippe, Cuttack, January 15, 1884, AMSFS 5H5-2/2.

⁶⁹ The presence of non-Catholics might have been due to the innate curiosity of Indians for a stranger and for the colourful pageantry. Cf. Décarre to Tissot, "Informations Diverses: Vizagapatam (Hindoustan)", in *LMC* 16 (1884) p. 423.

⁷⁰ Jean-Marie Clerc was born on March 21, 1841, at Ballaison, Savoy. He was ordained a priest on May 25, 1872. Between 1872 and 1880, he was known to be an accomplished preacher in Savoy. In May 1881, he went to India with the special mandate of helping the administration. He served the mission in various capacities, i.e., regional superior and vicar general of Visakhapatnam. He succeeded Bishop J.M. Tissot on July 26, 1891, when he was consecrated as the Bishop of Visakhapatnam. He died on June 18, 1926. Cf. *Tableau Genèral*, in *Histoire de la Mission*, AMSFS 5H4; F. MOGET, *MSFS Obituary*, p. 62.

⁷¹ Msgr. Clerc reported : "Cuttack est la principale et la plus ancienne (ville). Elle possede un prêtre résident une belle église à trois nefs (naves) et un couvent de Soeurs de St. Joseph en charge de l'hôpital de la ville, d'une école anglaise et d'un grand orphelinat de filles européns ou eurasiennes pour l'agrandissement duquel le gouvernement de la nouvelle province du Bihar et Orissa vient d'accorder un subside de 20000 roupias." Msgr. Clerc to Cardinal Gotti, March 4, 1914, APF Rubrica 128/1914, vol. 534, ff. 44–45.

⁷² Sr. Claire to Sr. Césarie, Cuttack, July 10, 1881, Archives of the Sisters of St. Joseph of Annecy, 2H, J3. B; Foulex to J. Tissot, Cuttack, July 7, 1881, AMSFS 5H5-2/2; *Annales des Soeurs de Saint Joseph. Diocèse de Vizagapatam. 1897 – 1906*, vol. II, Archives of the Sisters of St. Joseph of Annecy, Annecy, p. 226.

⁷³ Décarre to Bonaventure, Cuttack, May 8, 1883, AMSFS 5H5-2/2.

⁷⁴ This was the number of children whom they baptised *in articulo mortis* in 1906. Cf. *Annales des Soeurs de Saint Joseph. Diocèse de Vizagapatam. 1897 – 1906*, vol. II, Archives of the Sisters of St. Joseph of Annecy, Annecy, p. 17.

⁷⁵ Descombes to Superior General, Torobady, November 14, 1900, AMSFS 5H5-2/3.

[76] Puri is generally believed by Hindus to be the city of Lord Jagannath, the Lord of the Universe. Hence it is considered to be one of the most important holy cities in India. It is situated on lat. 19°47'55"N., long. 85°49'5" E. It possesses a natural beauty, as it lies on the shores of the Bay of Bengal. A map of the city would appear like a conch shell, the symbol of Lord Jagannath. At the centre of the town is the temple of Jagannath. The main road of the town is called *Badadanda*. It is a spacious street, at the end of which the Gundicha temple is found, where the three deities are housed for ten days during the *Ratha Yatra*. Among other edifices, one finds the palace of the raja of Puri on this street. It is said that more than 6,000 adult male priests are employed in the temple. Cf. N.C. BEHURIA (ed.), *Orissa State Gazetteer*, vol. II, pp. 366 – 380.

[77] The *Ratha Yatra*, Car Festival, is celebrated in the month of Asadha (June or July). The Protestant missionaries of almost all denominations that worked in Bengal and Orissa made it a point to attend it. At the festival the European missionaries and native preachers explain the gospel to small groups. In order to attract the attention of the crowds the missionaries and native preachers would sing a hymn in Oriya. As soon as a considerable number had gathered, they would present the Christian doctrines with occasional attacks on idolatory. They used the occasion to project themselves as friends of the poor and destitutes. Except for 1857, when the Sepoy Mutiny occurred, the Protestant missionaries gathered at Puri uninterruptedly between 1822 and 1900. Cf. M. DHALL, *The British Rule. Missionary Activities in Orissa 1822-1947*, New Delhi 1997, pp. 110-112.

[78] Msgr. Tissot to Cardinal Simeoni, Vizagapatam, April 20, 1881, APF Indie Orientali: Scritture riferite nei Congressi, vol. 22, ff. 1252-1253.

[79] J. TABOADA, *En las Selvas del Ganjam*, pp. 189-190.

[80] Riccaz to Foulex, Visakhapatnam, October 20, 1881, AMSFS, 5H5-2/2. However, there is no mention of a school begun by the MSFS in Puri.

[81] Fr. Décarre wrote : "Père John revient de Puri où il est allé passer quelques jours pour les Pâques; il a eu 25 communions. Aussitôt que faire se pourra, nous pensons bâtir une petite chapelle dans cette dernière station pour essayer de faire concurrence au fameux Jaggernath." Décarre to Bonaventure, Cuttack, May 8, 1882, AMSFS 5H5-2/2.

[82] Décarre, "Informations Diverses : Vizagapatam (Hindoustan)", in *LMC* 16 (1884), p. 423.

[83] Rey expressed the plans for Puri : "Nous faisons des plans pour Pouree (Puri); nous nous proposons d'obtenir une jolie chapelle puis à côté une espèce d'hopital pour les cholerias et les mourants, tout cela pour attaquer le diable dans sa place forte et pour ériger une pelérinage à la bonne Mère au lieu de Jaganath." Rey to the Director, Cuttack, August 6, 1884, AMSFS 5H5-2/2.

[84] There used to be a common practice of immolating oneself by placing under the wheels of the car of Jagannath. This is obviously motivated by the

belief that once killed under the wheels of the car of Jagannath one attains salvation. The missionaries found it difficult to accept such practices. Décarre to the Superior, Cuttack, September 15, 1887, AMSFS 5H5-2/2.

[85] Décarre observed : "Pour un qui a vu de ses propres yeux la manière dont ces pauvres misèrables pélerins sont abandonnés à leur triste sort, surtout lorsqu'ils sont aux étreintes avec la mort, il n'y a pas de doute que des sœurs chargées d'un hopital pourraient faire un bien immense. Sous leur traitement tout de charité, il y en aurait bien peu qui resisteraient à la grâce. Tout autre moyen de conversion que l'on pourrait tenter à Pooree (surtout au debut) serait loin de présenter les mêmes chances de succès, et je dirai même, pourrait nous susciter bien des difficultés." Décarre to the Superior, Cuttack, September 15, 1887, AMSFS 5H5-2/2.

[86] M. DOMENGE, *La Mission de Vizagapatam*, p. 410.

[87] The catechist was Rayappa Sanyasi Das. There is no information on how the Sisters responded to the plan. Cf. Décarre to Mother General of the Sisters of St. Joseph of Annecy, Cuttack, July 7, 1900, Archives of the Sisters of St. Joseph of Annecy 2 H. J4. B.

[88] J. TABOADA, *En las Selvas del Ganjam*, p. 190.

[89] Berhampur, situated on lat. 19°20' N. and long. 84°50' E. is the headquarters of Ganjam district. The name is derived from Lord Brahmeswar, whose temple is situated at Lathi about 4 Km from the town. Due to the Ganjam fever in 1815, the collector's office was shifted to Berhampur in 1816. The *Thakurani Jatra* is one of the most important festivals in Berhampur, which is celebrated with pomp and splendour. For 15 days the town takes on a festive look with colourful decorations, dances, jatra parties, sweetmeat stalls, etc. Cf. N.C. BEHURIA (ed), *Orissa State Gazetteer*, vol. II, pp. 267- 269; *The Imperial Gazetteer of India*, vol. VIII, Oxford 1908, pp. 2-3.

[90] Cf. F. MOGET, *Early Days of Visakhapatnam*, pp. 146 – 148. Besides constructing the church in 1909, Fr. A. Gangloff, who came to Berhampur in 1909, contacted Mme. Ross, the owner of a house, who expressed her desire to sell it since she was leaving Berhampur definitively. The price proposed was Rs. 7000. The club (soldiers) wanted to purchase it, but it gave the mission precedence, which was ready to rent it for Rs. 70 a month. Mme. Ross was willing to accept Rs. 5000 immediately; the rest could be paid in instalments. Fr. Gangloff felt that the old house of the mission could be sold to the government for a reasonable price, since the engineer who appraised the house was known to him personally. Fearing that the renovation of the old house might consume more money, it was sold and the money from the sale of the seminary in Gopalpur was advanced for the purchase of the clubhouse in Berhampur. Cf. Gangloff to J.M. Clerc, Berhampur, January 22, 1916, AMSFS 5H5-2/4. For some details of the cyclone that affected the Berhampur mission on October 29, 1909, see J. REY, *Les Missionnaires de Saint François de Sales d'Annecy*, p. 418.

[91] The year when the soldiers departed is not known. Cf. J. TABOADA, *En las Selvas del Ganjam*, pp. 183-184.

[92]   Gopalpur or Gopalpur-on-Sea (then known as Mansurkota) was a flourishing port town that served as a harbour for the maritime trade activities of Kalinga with the Southeast Asian countries. It lies in latitude 19° 31'N. and 85° 0' E. One of the chief ports during British rule, it was frequented by steamers of the British India Steam Navigation Company. Regarding the origin of its name, nothing is known for certain. The *Orissa Gazetteer* says: "It is said that towards the end of the 19th century A. D. [18th century], one Gopal Rao, a leader of the Telugu fishermen community (Nolias) established a large settlement near the sea-beach after whose name the place was named Gopal Rao Petta which was abbreviated into Gopalpur in the course of time." N.C. BEHURIA (ed), *Orissa State Gazetteer,* vol. II, p. 301.Another version, which seems plausible, is that the village is named after Lord Gopal Krishna, who is the presiding deity of the place. Even today, he is highly revered by the people of this area.

[93] Frs. Chéminal and Balmand had met the general of the Agency Tract to obtain his permission to start a mission among the Kondhs. The general received them well, but he declined to give them the permission, as the Protestants had also been refused. However, they were still hopeful of receiving permission. Cf. Chéminal to La Feuillette, Yanaon, August 3, 1855, AMSFS 5H5-2/1.

[94] J. TABOADA, *En las Selvas del Ganjam*, p. 227.

[95] Ibid., p. 228.

[96] Riccaz to Bonaventure, Surada, May 10, 1883, AMSFS 5H5-2/2; Msgr. Tissot to Cardinal Simeoni, Vizagapatam, March 23, 1885, APF Indie Orientali: Scritture riferite nei Congressi, vol. 25, f. 890.

[97] Fr. Alphonse Voisin narrated the situation in these words : "Le plupart n'osant sortir de leur maison à cause du choléra, meurt de misère chez eux. D'ordinaire les païens brlent les cadavres, mais maintenant, pour ne pas épouvanter les gens, ils se contentent de les jeter derrière les buissons, ai ils deviennent la proie de bêtes fauves. Aussi de longtemps dit-on, on n'avait vu les chacals, les tigres, les ours et les sangliers sauvages si bien portant." Alphonse Voisin to Mother General, Jeanne Marie Louise, Gopalpur, May 24, 1889, Archives of the Sisters of St. Joseph of Annecy, Annecy, 2H, J4. A.

[98] Alphonse Voisin was born on December 25, 1864, at Duingt, Savoy. He came to the Visakhapatnam mission in October 1887. He was ordained on May 10, 1888. Between 1888 and 1893 he worked in the Surada mission. Between 1893 and his death (June 14, 1931) he worked in Vizianagram. Cf. Tableau Genèral, *Histoire de la Mission,* AMSFS 5H4; F. MOGET, *MSFS Obituary,* p.61.

[99] Alphonse Voisin to Mother General, Archives of the Sisters of St. Joseph of Annecy, Jeanne Marie Louise, Gopalpur, May 24, 1889, Archives of the Sisters of St. Joseph of Annecy, Annecy, 2H, J4. A.

[100] *Annales des Soeurs de Saint Joseph. Diocese de Vizagapatam. 1897-1906*, vol. II, Archives of the Sisters of St. Joseph of Annecy, Annecy, 312 -318.

[101] Marie Eugène Gojon was born in Savigny, Savoy, on April 2, 1849. He entered the MSFS in 1873 and was ordained a priest on May 25, 1875. Between 1875 and 1886 he served in Savoy and was professor at Evian College. He reached India in August 1886 and taught at the SFS School for two years (1887-1889). He became novice master and rector of Gopalpur seminary from 1889 until his election as superior general of the congregation on September 26, 1894. After having guided the Society through a difficult time of persecution, he resigned in August 1904 for health reasons. He died on October 25, 1905. Cf. *Tableau Genèral*, in *Histoire de la Mission*, AMSFS 5H4; F. MOGET, *MSFS Obituary*, p. 91; F. MOGET, *The Missionaries of St. Francis de Sales of Annecy*, pp. 171 - 173.

[102] Once the missionaries were in Gopalpur, they became familiar with the surroundings. There was a huge ranch of 13 acres which belonged to Madame Camil, widow of the Count of Salaberri. She lived at that time in France. Probably the property was acquired a quarter of a century earlier when Ganjam was under the French. Now under the British government, the proprietor wanted to get rid of the possession and sold it for 3,500 pesetas, which was definitely an act of charity. Cf. J. TABOADA, *En las Selvas del Ganjam*, p. 228.

[103] Sr. Hippolyte to Mother General Jeanne Marie Louise, Gopalpur, May 10, 1890, Archives of the Sisters of St. Joseph of Annecy, 2H, J4. A; Alphonse Voisin to Mother General Jeanne Marie Louise, Gopalpur, May 22, 1890, Archives of the Sisters of St. Joseph of Annecy, 2H, J4. A.

[104] Alphonse Voisin to Mother General Jeanne Marie Louise, Gopalpur, May 22, 1890, Archives of the Sisters of St. Joseph of Annecy, 2H, J4. A.

[105] A. Voisin recorded : "Notre congrégation de Surada a perdu plus de 500 chrétiens ; des enrôleurs d'hommes et de femmes ont parcouru le pays et en ont ammené un très grand nombre dans le pays d'Assam. Tout ce monde a été enrôlé sous de fausses promesses, et nos 500 chrétiens de Surada ont été des dupès comme les autres." Alphonse Voisin to Mother General Jeanne Marie Louise, Gopalpur, May 22, 1890, Archives of the Sisters of St. Joseph of Annecy, 2H, J4. A.

[106] J. REY, *Les Missionnaires de Saint-François de Sales d'Annecy*, p. 444.

[107] F. M. Allard to his uncle, Gopalpur, October 19, 1891, AMSFS 5H5-2/3.

[108] J. TABOADA, *En las Selvas del Ganjam*, p. 228.

[109] J. Rey cited from the Missionnaire Indien : "Ces jeunes gens, lisons-nous dans le Missionnaire Indien, sortiraient de cet établissement tout équipés pour le travail des missions, acclimatés au pays, avec une connaissance des ses

coutumes, des ses mœurs et de ses langues que seules peuvent donner la vie sur place et des études commencées alors que la mémoire conserve encore toute son activité." J. REY, *Les Missionnaires de Saint-François de Sales d'Annecy*, p. 329.

[110] F. MOGET, *The Missionaries of St. Francis de Sales and the formation of an Indian Clergy*, (MSS) in *Histoire de la Mission*, AMSFS 5H4.

[111] When the seminary was established in 1890, the Sisters were invited to take care of the laundry of the Fathers and the seminarians. Later, they were requested to run a school and a dispensary. The Sisters accepted this invitation because the climate was better in Gopalpur, compared to the climate in the mountains. Cf. *Annales des Soeurs de Saint Joseph. Diocèse de Vizagapatam. 1897-1906*, vol. II, Archives of the Sisters of St. Joseph of Annecy, Annecy, p. 322; F. Moget, *The Missionaries of St. Francis de Sales of Annecy*, p. 165.

[112] F. MOGET, *The Missionaries of St. Francis de Sales and the formation of an Indian Clergy*, (MSS) in *Histoire de la Mission*, AMSFS 5H4.

[113] F. M. Allard to his uncle, Gopalpur, August 4, 1895, AMSFS 5H5-2/3.

[114] Bonaventure to Philippe, Surada, February 21, 1882, AMSFS 5H5-2/2.

[115] Descombes to Superior, Torobady (Surada mission), November 14, 1900, AMSFS 5H5-2/3.

[116] Writing on the arrival of Fr. J.M. Dupont in Katingia and the welcome given to him, Jean Rey narrated: "Cédant à leurs instances, le P. J.M. Dupont arriva le 8 décembre dans leur village. Son renom de défenseur des faibles et des pauvres, de père des orphelins l'y avait précédé et ses amis le reçurent avec force demonstrations de joie et de reconnaissance. Douze familles de Pahnos vinrent tout de suite apprendre les prières et le catéchisme. Sous un toit de feuillage, devant un autel garni de belles images et de lampions, la fête de Noël revêtit un grand éclat." J. REY, *Les Missionnaires de Saint-François de Sales d'Annecy*, p. 255; M. DOMEGE, *La Mission de Vizagapatam*, p. 354.

[117] Ibid., p. 355.

[118] Ibid., p. 358.

[119] Ibid., pp. 355-357.

[120] The letter is written in the form of an appeal for funds to construct a church in Katingia. Cf. Descombes to Superior, Torobady (Surada mission), November 14, 1900, AMSFS 5H5-2/3.

[121] Descombes to J. Tissot, Surada, December (no date) 1892, AMSFS 5H5-2/3.

[122] Ibid.

[123] Descombes to Clerc, Merycot, (no month and date) 1897, AMSFS 5H5-2/3.

[124] Ibid.

[125] Descombes to Bouvard, Surada, March 29, 1911, AMSFS 5H5-2/4.

[126] Descombes to J. Tissot, Surada, December (no date) 1892, AMSFS 5H5-2/3.

[127] P. DESCOMBES, "Diocèse de Vizagapatam: Lettre du R.P. Petrus Descombes", in *Annales de la Propagation de la Foi* 72 (1900), pp. 111-112; Descombes to Clerc, Merycot, (no month and date) 1897, AMSFS 5H5-2/3.

[128] Gutuli was one of the centres where freed *Meriahs* lived. The British government took several measures to rehabilitate them. One of them was the distribution of land for cultivation. It was then that Fr. Descombes helped them to obtain the privilege from the government. He even helped them to purchase bullocks and seeds for cultivation. He redeemed the land that was sold during the famine. Realising the goodness of the missionary, the people of Gutuli expressed their willingness to become Christians and invited the priest to build a chapel in their village. Cf. Descombes to Clerc, Gutuli, (no month and date) 1900, AMSFS 5H5-2/4.

[129] The conversion of Solima was the work of Alex, the trusted mason of Fr. Descombes. In spite of the intimidation of the raja of Bodogodo, he kept the people together and helped the priest in the construction of chapels in the mountains. Descombes to J. Tissot, Surada, December (no date) 1892, AMSFS 5H5-2/3.

[130] P. DESCOMBES, "Diocèse de Vizagapatam : Lettre du R.P. Petrus Descombes", in *Annales de la Propagation de la Foi* 72 (1900), p. 97.

[131] Fr. Descombes clearly indicated: "One of the main obstacles in the conversion is their attachment to sacrifices. They hold this belief above all others; 'no sacrifice, no harvest!' is their principle. According to them, it's the sacrifice that brings the rain. It's the sacrifice that stops it when it's abundant. 'There is no means more efficacious to cure fever, to drive away the tiger, to preserve from epidemics'. Every harvest requires 3 sacrifices; the victim being a he-goat or a pig: (1) at the time of sowing; (2) when the ears come out; and (3) on the eve of the harvest." Descombes to J. Tissot, Surada, December (no date) 1892, AMSFS 5H5-2/3.

[132] Descombes to Clerc, Gutuli, (no month and date) 1900, AMSFS 5H5-2/3.

[133] Ibid.

[134] Descombes to Clerc, Gumagarra, June 25, 1905, AMSFS 5H5-2/3.

[135] Ibid.

[136] Russellkonda or Russell's Hill is known today as Bhanjanagar, which after independence was named after the Bhanja dynasty that ruled the area for a long time. Russellkonda, situated in lat. 20°56'N. and long. 84°37'E. was a sub-divisional town in Ganjam district. The climate is generally salubrious during the year, except March, April and May when the heat is oppressive. Maltby wrote: "This small town, situated in the midst of a charming scenery, was named in 1837 at the termination of the second Goomsur campaign after Mr. Russell, the able special Commissioner in Ganjam." T.J. MALTBY, *The Ganjam District Manual*, Madras 1882, p. 53; N.C. BEHURIA, *Orissa State Gazetteer*, vol. II, pp. 255 – 256.

[137] J. Taboada, in his book, *En las Selvas del Ganjam,* refers to the document of 1850, which is said to have been preserved in the Cuttack diocesan archives, but he did not cite the content of the document. If the document dates to 1850, then the bishop's name should read Msgr. Neyret, who was the vicar apostolic of Visakhapatnam from 1849 until his death in1862, instead of Msgr. Tissot, who was appointed his successor. Cf. J. TABOADA, *En las Selvas del Ganjam,* p. 207.

[138] Cf. P. Descombes, "Chez les Khondes 1891", in *Extrait du Petit Salesien* (1891), AMSFS.

[139] The village of Mondosoro and the surrounding area were called Dighy. The same name was also used in government records.

[140] P. ROSSILLON, "Cent Kilomètres sur des Épaules Kondes", in *LMC* 44 (1912), p. 63.

[141] Petitjean to a confrere, Dighy, April 6, 1908, AMSFS 5H5-2/3.

[142] Rossillon narrated : "Quarante et un chefs vinrent un dimanche nous trouver à Dighy, où nous leur avions donné rendez-vous. Comme ils avaient amené chacun deux or trois hommes de leur village respectif, nous eûmes là une fête comme de ma vie je n'en avais encore vue. Quoique païens, ils entendirent la messe avec respect, approuvant le sermon par des signes de tête et de petits cris significatifs; et la messe finie, pour nous manifester leur joie, ils exécutèrent divers simulacres de chasses aux bisons et des danses à la hache de mieux enlevées, le tout au son rythmé de leurs tambourines." P. ROSSILLON, "Au lendemain des Cyclones. Une visite èpiscopale dans le district de Ganjam", in *Echos Salésiens* 4 (1910), p. 159.

[143] Jean Rey cited from the letter of Fr. Rossillon: "Nous voulons des prêtres et catéchistes pour nous apprendre à aimer Dieu. Nous sommes ici les porte-voix de soixante-dix villages qui se feront chrétiens si vous venez." J. REY, *Les Missionnaires de Saint-François de Sales d'Annecy,* p. 415.

[144] Fernandez to Verdier, Surada, May 30, 1924, Archives of the Congregation of the Mission, Superieur de la Mission Cuttack Indes 1922-1927 ; J. REY, *Les Missionnaires de Saint-François de Sales d'Annecy,* p. 447.

[145] Petit Jean to a confrere, Dighy, April 6, 1908, AMSFS 5H5-2/3.

[146] J. Taboada cites Fr. Rey in the following words: "En mi Distrito de Dighy, dice, tengo 500 bautizados entre kondos y ghazis, la mayoria de los cuales viven en los valles de Daringobadi, Keruvadi y Didrovadi, y 22 criados de la Missión entre maestros et jornaleros." J. TABOADA, *En las Selvas de Ganjam,* p. 168.

[147] BOUCHET, "Informations Diverses: Vizagapatam (Hindoustan)", in *LMC* 46 (1914), p. 522.

[148] Msgr. Clerc to Cardinal Gotti, Vizagapatam, March 4, 1914, APF Rubrica, vol. 546, ff. 41 – 42.

[149] Jesús Taboada wrote: "Al volver de Francia, en 1918, no encontró de su labor más que escombros y cenizas humeantes. Albergado en un tugurio miserable de tres metros de largo por tres de ancho, se resolvió, animoso, a levantar tanta ruina. Pocos acudieron al silbido de su antiguo Pastor, y antes de poder organizar de nuevo un plan efectivo de reconquista, fué llamado a Vizagapatám en 1919. Dos años más tarde, la Misión fué transferida a los Padres Paúles españoles de la Provincia de Madrid." J. TABOADA, *En las Selvas del Ganjam*, p. 172.

[150] Jeypore, or the 'city of victory,' is the most important town in the district of Koraput where the ex-maharaja lives. The town gained its prominence when Vira Vikram Deo (1648 -1660) shifted his capital from Nandapur in the middle of the 17th century A. D., which was considered to be auspicious. Sometimes the name of the town is spelt as Jeypur. Cf. N.C. BEHURIA (ed), *Orissa State Gazetteer*, vol. II, pp. 320-323.

[151] Even though establishing a station in Jeypore did not materialise, the expedition was considered for the sole reason of founding some stations that would be conducive to the missionary enterprises. The information thus gathered helped the missionaries in founding a station at a later period. Cf. M. DOMENGE, "Au pays du Khondes : Voyage Raconté par le P. Domenge", in *LMC* 15 (1883), p. 484.

[152] Bonaventure wrote : "Je suis aujourd'hui à Sonky, au centre des forêts du sud. J'ai fait 85 miles en trois jours. Je suis l'hôte d'un brave ingénieur irlandais et catholique, en charge de la construction d'une route à travers les forêts. Je partirai d'ici demain pour Koraput où j'arriverai après trois jours de marche. J'ai des porteurs pour mon baggage, moi je marche à pied. Msgr. m'envoie pour essayer une mission parmi les Khondes. Je recommende cette mission à vos bonnes prières. Je suis plein de courage et tout le monde me donne des espérances." Bonaventure to Philippe, Visakhapatnam, April 11, 1883, AMSFS 5H5-2/2. For another account of the expedition see M. PAYRAUD, "Lettre du M. Payraud, missionnaire apostolique, à M. Tissot, supérieur de la Société de Saint-François de Sales d'Annecy", in *Annales de la Propagation de la Foi* 55 (1883), pp. 238-242.

[153] M. DOMENGE, "Au pays du Khondes : Voyage Raconté par le P. Domenge", pp. 484-486.

[154] Bonaventure wrote : "En outre, je dis qu'il est nécessaire que nous ouvrions cette station sans délai. La gloire de Dieu l'exige; c'est la ligne qui va enfin relier la mission du Sud avec celle du Nord, le missionnaire de Koraput pourra faire sa retraite aussi facilement à Nagpore qu'à Kamptee et à Vizagapatam. Les protestants d'ailleurs veulent s'y implanter: or, les premiers venus seront les premiers servis; et les bonnes places sont rares soit à Pottinghy, soit à Koraput." E. BONAVENTURE, "Lettre du R. P. Bonaventure, de la Société saint François

de Sales d'Annecy, à Msgr. J.M. Tissot, Vicaire apostolique de Vizagapatam", in *Annales de la Propagation de la Foi* 55 (1883), p. 237.

[155] Here Msgr. J.M. Tissot expressed his eagerness to begin a mission, since the place is well situated and the climate salubrious. The climate is similar to the one in Europe. For more details: J.M. Tissot to Philippe, Vizagapatam, January 20, 1883, AMSFS 5H5-2/2; Bonaventure to J. Tissot, Visakhapatnam, January 6, 1883, AMSFS 5H5-2/2.

[156] Domenge observed : "Mais le pays est tout entier sous l'empire des brahmes les plus fanatiques et les plus arriérés de toute l'Inde, et l'on y aurait en général plus de difficultés et moins de chances de succès qu'en beaucoup d'autres endroits". M. DOMENGE, "Au pays du Khondes: Voyage Raconté par le P. Domenge", p. 485.

[157] Domenge commented : "Chez le Khondes, c'est un pays nouveau, où les brahmes n'exercent aucune influence, le climat nous y offre des avantages que nous ne trouverons nulle part ailleurs dans notre mission, et pour longtemps encore les protestants ne viendront pas empêcher les conversions par les contradictions de leurs doctrines. Le missionnaire de Khorapett pourrait faire une visite à Jeypoor une ou deux fois l'an, pour sonder les dispositions et préparer les voies. Si une mission s'y établissait, elle dépendrait plus naturellement de Kamptee que de Vizagapatam." Ibid., pp. 485 - 486.

[158] The choice of Fr. Bonaventure was based on the consultation that Msgr. J.M. Tissot had with the missionaries, who were unanimous in favour of starting a mission immediately. Cf. J.M. Tissot to Philippe, Vizagapatam, March 15, 1883, AMSFS 5H5-2/2; M. DOMENGE, "Au pays du Khondes: Voyage Raconté par le P. Domenge", p. 485.

[159] Bonaventure to Philippe, Koraput, May 16, 1883, AMSFS 5H5-2/2.

[160] Domenge declared: "Nous y avons donc choisi un terrain assez vaste et bien situé, que le gouvernment paraît disposé à nous céder, pour y former notre future établissement." M. Domenge, "Au pays du Khondes: Voyage Raconté par le P. Domenge", p. 478.

[161] Domenge to Montagnoux, Vizianagram, August 9, 1883, AMSFS 5H5-2/2.

[162] To understand the intensity of the famine and the sufferings of the people, see P. DESCOMBES, "La Famine & le Cholèra à Vizagapatam", in *LMC* 21 (1889), pp. 591 – 594.

[163] Here is a moving account of the effect of the famine: "Un jour, Mgr. Tissot traversait notre village de Dantholinghy. Il vit ce bois que l'on faisait sécher devant chaque maison, et en demanda la raison. C'est pour faire de la soupe: fut-il répondu. Notre bon évêque goûta de cette farine et, la voyant extrêmement insipide, il prit des measures pour faire donner du travail immediatement à ces neophytes." P. DESCOMBES, "La Famine & le Cholèra à Vizagapatam", p. 592. On May 1, 1889, Lord Connemara, the governor of

Madras Presidency, was in Gopalpur. He spent about a week in Ganjam to assess the severity of the crisis and to provide relief.

[164] P. Descombes wrote : "Grâce à la famine, un bon nombre d'âmes ont trouvé le chemin du Ciel ouvert devant elles par le baptême." Ibid., p. 594.

[165] Descombes wrote : "Le Swami, se disent ces païens, est un homme influent. Le Swami me protégera. Le Swami empêchera qu'on détruise mes moissons. Le Swami, qui est quelque peu médecin (puisque, pour ces gens-là, la science de la médicine est un don inné dont le bon Dieu fait cadeau à tous les blancs), le Swami me donnera des remèdes, si je tombe malade. Le Swami est un homme charitable; en temps de famine, il me fera l'aumône. Allons donce à lui, car un être aussi parfait ne peut qu'enseigner la vérité. Et ils viennent par certaines." P. DESCOMBES, "Lettre du R.P. Descombes", in *Annales de la Propagation de la Foi* 72 (1900), p. 112.

[166] Fr. J.J. Vuillez commented : "Le motif qui les amène n'est pas très surnaturel. C'est la plupart du temps la protection du missionaire à obtenir contre certains chefs trop exigeants, c'est une dette à payer, un different à juger, des semences à avancer etc. Comme vous le voyez, le motif n'est pas très surnaturel, mais du moins la volonté est sincère. Si en ces moments critiques nous pourrions prendre leurs cas en mains, et commencer de suite leur instruction religieuse, nous obtiendrions de bons résultats. Une petite banque agricole qui consisterait à avancer une certaine quantité de graines au début des semailles quite à nous les faire rendre à la récolte avec un petit intérêt, constituerait à Dighy un moyen de persévérance après le baptême. Nous avons actuellement à Dighy près de 800 baptisés et entre cinq à six mille catechumènes." J.J. Vuillez to Superior, Ranchi September 18, 1910, AMSFS 5H5-2/2.

[167] After the arrival of Fr. J.M. Descombes in Gumgarra, the catechumens gave him the names of usurers who took away their lands. As a result of the persuasion of the missionary, 12 paddy fields, the property of 6 families, were returned to their owners, and the legal deeds were made in the presence of witnesses. According to Fr. J.M. Descombes, this was only one quarter of the work. They might have to approach the court in order to deal with other usurers. Since some of them had their accountants in the town, it was difficult to persuade them. Cf. Descombes to Clerc, Gumagarra, June 25, 1905, AMSFS 5H5-2/3.

[168] Ibid.

[169] Clerc to Bouvard, Surada, February 17, 1906, AMSFS 5H5-2/4; P. Descombes to Bouvard, Surada, February 20, 1906, AMSFS 5H5-2/3.

[170] Clerc to Bouvard, Surada, March 6, 1906, AMSFS 5H5-2/3.

[171] Descombes to Bouvard, Surada, April 23, 1906, AMSFS 5H5-2/3.

[172] Descombes commented that marriages always took place in the morning at the Mass, where the couple received Holy Communion. The whole village accompanied the couple to the church, followed by a festive meal offered

by the newly-weds. Cf. P. Descombes to Bouvard, Surada, February 20, 1906, AMSFS 5H5-2/4.

[173] Descombes to Bouvard, Surada, February 20, 1906, AMSFS 5H5-2/3.

[174] Descombes to Bouvard, Surada, June 21, 1907, AMSFS 5H5-2/3.

[175] Descombes to Clerc, Gumagarra, June 25, 1905, AMSFS 5H5-2/3.

[176] Unfortunately, the General Archives of MSFS do not have any of the works mentioned above. Cf. A. Rey, *Souvenirs*, Rédigés à la demande du P. Comerson en 1933 (MSS), AMSFS.

[177] Descombes to Constant Bouvard, Surada, March 29, 1911, AMSFS 5H5-2/4.

[178] Fr. Descombes wrote from Surada : "Nous avons de multiples besoins dans notre pauvre mission, et l'un des plus urgents est de nous procurer une petite presse à bras, pour imprimer nous-même les divers livres qui nous sont très nécessaires. Nous venons de faire imprimer, en Oryah, une histoire Sainte; cela nous a coûté 230 francs. C'est maintenant le tour d'un grand catéchisme (coût 300 francs), qui sera suivi d'un petit catéchisme à l'usage des premières communiantes. Pour l'année prochaine, nous préparons une Histoire de l'Eglise; après quoi viendra un proissen." P. DESCOMBES, "Informations Diverses: Vizagapatam (Hindoustan)", in *LMC* 44 (1912), pp. 100 -101

[179] SUIFFET, "Informations Diverses : Vizagapatam (Hindoustan)", in *LMC* 41 (1909), p. 39.

[180] P. ROSSILLON, "Cent Kilomètres sur des Épaules Kondes", in *LMC* 44 (1912) p. 342.

[181] Fr. P. Descombes observed: "On the plateau of Didrobady, there are 8 villages with a population of 1100 Kondhs, some of whom are baptised and others under instruction. Another dozen villages, with 1,500 Kondhs have approached us. We need an army of good catechists to teach catechism and prayers. And we have only 2 real catechists." Cf. Peter Descombes to Constant Bouvard, Surada, June 21, 1907, AMSFS 5H5-2/3.

[182] The Synod of Visakhapatnam stated in the 4th article of the fourth day : "La formation de bons catechists est de la plus grande importance ; ils sont indispensables aux missionnaires et les aident beaucoup, lorsqu'ils sont dignes de leurs fonctions, soit pour l'instruction des enfants et des catechumènes, soit pour le mantien des bonnes mœurs dans les congrégations. Ils gagnent aussi plus facilement que le prêtre, l'amitié et la confiance des païens, lui préparent les voies dans les endroits où il n'est pas encore connu. S'ils sont de bonne caste leur exemple même est une preuve que l'on peut être chrétien, à quelque race qu'on appartienne." *Actes et Ordonances du Synode de Vizagapatam tenu en Septembre 1888*, in *Histoire de la Mission*, AMSFS 5H4 Inde.

[183] Continuing on the life of catechists, the Synod stated : "La vie d'un bon catéchiste est, en effet, une vie de dévouement, de beaucoup de travail et de

fatigue, et l'on n'en trouvera jamais facilement qui, pour le modeste salaire que nous leur offrons, soient disposés à tous ces sacrifices." Ibid.

[184] Henri Petitjean to Constant Bouvard, Surada November 12, 1906, AMSFS 5H5-2/3.

[185] Ibid.

[186] Fr. J.M. Descombes wrote : "Nos catechistes sont généralement des convertis de date assez récente; sans aptitudes littéraires, laissés à eux seuls, ils ne différeraient en rien des gens de peine." P. Descombes, "Lettre du R.P. Descombes au R.P. Messelod, Solima, de la même Congregation (September 10, 1890)", in *Annales de la Propagation de la Foi* 63 (1891), p. 120.

[187] Fr. J. J. Vulliez confided that : "Cette oeuvre est actuellement à Surada, l'oeuvre la plus importante, sans catéchiste, le missionnaire ne peut rien faire. Le natif a toujours une certaine réserve avec l'européen. Il ne lui fera jamais ses confidences, même a un prêtre qu'il connaît et estime. Le misssionnaire ne pourra jamais par lui seul connaître les petites histoires, les dessous des choses etc." J. J. Vuillez to Superior, Ranchi September 18, 1910, AMSFS 5H5-2/4.

[188] J. J. Vuillez to Superior, Ranchi, September 18, 1910, AMSFS 5H5-2/4.

[189] Descombes to Constant Bouvard, Surada, March 29, 1911, AMSFS 5H5-2/4.

[190] Descombes to Constant Bouvard, Surada, June 21, 1907, AMSFS 5H5-2/3.

[191] A. Rey, *Souvenirs*, Rédigés à la demande du P. Comerson en 1933, AMSFS.

[192] Fr. A. Rey recalled : "A mon service, je lui donnai 12 Roupees par mois. Il en donnait quelques unes aux pauvres. Il ne prenait jamais de boisson avec les khonds, ne prenait qu'un repas le soir après son travail. Les gens l'appelaient "Sanyassi" (religieux) et il l'était en réalité." A. REY, *Souvenirs*, Rédigés à la demande du P. Comerson en 1933, (MSS), AMSFS.

[193] Here are some examples that clearly indicate the respect that Rayappa Sanyasi Das had in the mission. In June 1909, Anthony Nidhi, catechist and teacher of Didrobady, went to Mondsoro for the salary. Catechist Rayappa Sanyasi Das was there in the absence of Fr. A. Suiffet who was in France for holidays. He found out that Kobi was offering sacrifice and he was fined Rs. 3/-. He was fined in the presence of Rayappa Sanyasi Das. Yet another sacrifice was found in Koruma, where Tatty was preparing a sacrifice with a he– goat. The catechist snatched the he-goat and took it to Rayappa. The goat had a value of Rs. 4. After a few days Rayappa came to Didrobady and convoked a meeting of the Christians of Koruma, Kudevaḍy, Padassy and Laurano. Catechists Anthony Mondalo and Anthony Nidhi were also invited for the meeting. In the meeting Rayappa Sanyasi Das condemned Tatty to a fine of Rs.10 and five strokes with a cane. Cf. Anthony Nidhi to Suiffet, Didrobady, July 1909, AMSFS 5H5-2/3.

[194] Cyrille wrote : "Le soir il a fait sa prière comme de coutume et s'est couché avec les enfants de Dighy et Katingia. Vers 1h du matin on est venu

nous appeler, nous l'avons trouvé à l'agonie. Après l'avoir administré et lui avoir donné l'Indulgence plenaire, les enfants l'ont veillé et nous sommes allés dire nos messes. Il est mort vers les 6h du matin alors que les orphelins priaient les bras en croix par lui. La première chose que les enfants ont dite, c'est : voyez comme il est content, il rit. Il était agé environ 65 ans." Cyrille to Rossillon, Surada, December 5, 1919, AMSFS 5H5-2/4; Jacob Malico to J. Bouchet, Surada, November 30, 1919, AMSFS 5H5-2/4.

[195] J.J. Vuillez to Constant Bouvard, Visakhapatnam, October 21, 1919, AMSFS 5H5-2/4.

[196] Msgr. J.M. Tissot writes : "Je suis content de nos pauvres orphelines. Elles ont perdu leur air et leurs manières sauvages, en général elles sont bonnes et très attachées à leurs maitresses et à l'établissement. J'ai eu à leur annoncer une assez mauvaise nouvelle, la cessation du subside que nous passait le governement pour elles... Je leur fais faire de l'huile de ricin que je leur ai promis de faire vendre à leur profit. D'autres vont ramasser le coton, le filent et nous avons deux metiers pour faire la toile. Malheureusement tout cela se fait à la mode du pays, d'une manière un peu sauvage, l'ouvrage va lentement... Si vous les voyiez à la chapelle. Elles fréquentent souvent les sacrements, elles prient beaucoup, même en allant couper leur bois à la forêt. Je fais prendre tous moyens possibles pour trouver de quoi nourir et habiller tout ce petit monde." J.M. Tissot to Mother General of the Sisters of St. Joseph of Annecy, Surada, March 16, 1874, Archives of the Sisters of St. Joseph of Annecy, Annecy, 2H, J3. B.

[197] Cyrille to Rossillon, Surada, December 5, 1919, AMSFS 5H5-2/4.

[198] In one of his letters to the director, Msgr. J.M. Tissot wrote : "Je crois qu'il est de la plus haute importance, pour ne pas dire indispensable, que Mr. le Supérieur ou vous veniez visiter la Mission *in persona*, si notre chère congrégation veut la garder." J.M. Tissot to Philippe, Vishakapatnam, July 7, 1883, AMSFS 5H5-2/2.

[199] In his letter to Cardinal Simeoni, Rev. Fr. Joseph Tissot, the superior general, reiterated the importance of the visit and justified the choice of the person who was appointed for such task. Cf. Fr. Joseph Tissot to Cardinal Simeoni, Annecy, November 15, 1884, APF Indie Orientali: Scritture riferite nei Congressi, vol. 25, f. 456; J. REY, *Les Missionnaires de Saint-François de Sales d'Annecy*, pp. 287-295.

[200] Tissot to Philippe, Surada, July 23, 1884, AMSFS 5H5-2/2.

[201] Tissot to Philippe, Surada, August 25, 1885, AMSFS 5H5-2/2.

[202] In a letter to the Sisters, the visitor excused himself for his inability to visit them in Cuttack and Surada. Cf. *Annales des Soeurs de Saint Joseph. Diocese de Vizagapatam. 1897-1906, II*, Archives of the Sisters of St. Joseph of Annecy, Annecy, p. 265.

[203] Msgr. Tissot wrote : "Le père Philippe, qui était venu visiter la mission, a dû rentrer en Savoie vers la fin de Février sans avoir pu visiter toutes les stations de Sud et du Nord de la mission. Il a vu les principales localitès et toutes les principaux etablissements." Fr. Joseph Tissot to Cardinal Simeoni, Annecy, April 6, 1886, APF Indie Orientali: Scritture riferite nei Congressi, vol. 26, ff. 487-488.

[204] "Je lui demandais de nouveau de me donner Mgr. Philippe pour le Coadjuteur au moins provisoirement. Je dois vous dire mon cher confrère, que Mgr. Philippe ignore complétement la demande que j'ai faite. Il m'écrit de temps en temps, mais jamais de ce qui le regarde, ni un mot de blâme contre Mr le Supérieur ou contre le Conseil. Mon but de ne pas rompre toute correspondance a été de ne pas lui fournir l'occasion de dire que je ne voulais plus de lui. Il m'a écrit qu'il n'avait jamais demandé sa décharge de Coadjuteur mais, qu'on la lui avait donnée, sur l'exposé qu'il avait fait de son état. Je dois nécessairement passer pour un homme qui se cramponne a son siège et qui veut a tout prix rester à la tête de la mission." J.M. Tissot to Berod, Surada, August 20, 1890, AMSFS 5H5-2/3.

[205] F. Moget, *MSFS Obituary*, p. 44.

[206] J. REY, *Les Missionnaires de Saint-François de Sales d'Annecy*, p. 445.

[207] The Synodal document clarified its aims : "...discuter avec eux (les missionnaires) les prinicpales difficultés du ministère dans ce pays ; pour formuler quelques régles pour la direction des missionnaires et établir par là une certaine uniformité dans leur manière d'agir soit avec les chrétiens déja existants, soit auprès des infideles qu'ils ont à convertir". *Actes et Ordonances du Synode de Vizagapatam tenu en Septembre 1888*, in *Histoire de la Mission*, AMSFS 5H4 Inde, p. 1.

[208] The synodal document stated : "Fondés sur cette recommandation, les missionnaires de St. François de Sales se sont toujours fait un devoir de considérer la caste comme une institution purement civile, séculier et étranger à la religion ; et de n'en danner que les abus qui seraient très évidemment (certissime) contraires à la religion et aux bonnes mœurs". *Actes et Ordonances du Synode de Vizagapatam tenu en Septembre 1888*, in *Histoire de la Mission*, AMSFS 5H4 Inde, p. 12.

[209] They have taken the instruction given by the Sacred Congregation to the first bishops of Missions Étrangères de Paris. Cf. Ibid., p. 11.

[210] Ibid., p. 9.

[211] The Synodal document exhorts : "Les missionnaires sont invités à établir une école primaire dans toutes les principales stations, où il n'en a pas encore. C'est un des meilleurs moyens pour éloigner les enfants de la rue et des mauvais exemples qu'ils y rencontrent, de les prévenir contre l'oisiveté, les habituer au travail, enfin leur assurer une instruction religieuse plus pratique et plus complète." Ibid., pp. 25 – 26.

[212] J.M. Clerc to Constant Bouvard, Visakhapatnam, March 14, 1914, AMSFS 5H5-2/4.

[213] Msgr. Clerc to Cardinal Gotti, Vizagapatam, January 28, 1913, APF Rubrica 128/1913, vol. 533, f. 18; Msgr. Clerc to Constant Bouvard, Visakhapatnam, April 9, 1914, AMSFS 5H5-2/4.

[214] Msgr. J.M. Clerc reported: "Les vastes territories du diocèse de Vizag (Visakhaptnam) qui dépendent de l'Orissa et des provinces centrales, seront confiés à d'autres congrégations, et notre diocèse se trouvera ainsi restreint aux districts du Godavery, de Vizag et de Ganjam... Comme moyen efficace d'augmenter et de fortifier notre personnel, Son Excellence le Délégat a insisté sur la necessité d'un petit séminaire, le remplacement des pères au college par une congregation de frères enseignants et la fondation d'écoles de catéchistes... deux écoles de catéchistes seront fondées, l'une à Surada pour les aspirants catéchistes Oriyas et Khonds, e l'autre à Kottavasala pour les aspirants Telugus". Msgr. Clerc to Cardinal Gotti, Visakhapatnam, January 28, 1913, APF Rubrica 128/1913, 533/18ff.

[215] Fr. Jules Rey recalled that "Depuis 1912, sur les conseils de Msgr. Zaleski, alors Délégué Apostolique pour l'Inde, Msgr. Clerc était en tractation avec Rome en vue d'une division du diocèse de Vizagapatam. L'affaire traîna. Il était dur à l'évêque de céder ce Ganjam et cet Orissa, pays de langue oryia, où ses prêtres avaient le plus travaillé et possédaient autour de Surada leur centre de mission le mieux équipé comme le plus florissant. En 1920, Msgr. Rossillon hâta cette cession et, dès que les Lazarists espagnols arrivèrent, en 1921, il commença à retirer ses missionnaires pour les utiliser à l'intérieur de son diocese. Afin d'augmenter leur nombre et de suppléer aux recrues d'Europe alors presque inexistantes, il amorça tout de suite le mouvement des vocations indigènes." JULES REY, *Son Excellence Msgr. Pierre Rossillon*, AMSFS.

[216] Msgr. Rossillon wrote : "En donnant le Ganjam et l'Orissa, nous cèdons la partie la plus fièvreuse. Nous nous débarrasons à peu près de l'Orya, pour ne garder que le Telugu comme langue principale à apprendre. Ces avantages, à la langue, sont énormes. En faisant le total, on trouve jusqu'ici, que les pères de Surada passent les deux tiers de leur vie à voyager et à être malades." P. Rossillon to Favrat, Vizagapatam, July 7, 1920, AMSFS 5H5-2/5.

[217] Msgr. Rossillon explained the state of the mission in Ganjam : "Il suffit de constater qu'en ce moment toutes les missions de l'Inde sont en progrès excepté la nôtre qui est en recul depuis 20 ans... Dernièrement, j'ai dû écrire au Délégué Apostolique pour lui expliquer cet état singulièr et, ma foi, je n'ai rien caché. Il m'a donné rendez-vous à Madras pour plus amples explications. Au congrès Marial, qui doit avoir lieu à Madras le 12, 13 et 14 Janvier 1921." P. Rossillon to the Superior General, Vizagapatam, October 11, 1920, AMSFS 5H5-2/5.

[218] Health problems plagued the missionaries. Fr. Julien Vulliez died at Surada on July 21, 1921 at the age of 45 and Fr. François Fleury died at Surada on November 29, 1921 at the age of 39. Cf. F. MOGET, *MSFS Obituary*, pp. 69, 100.

[219] J.J. Vulliez to A. Favrat, Surada, April 4, 1921, AMSFS 5H5-2/5.

[220] Msgr. Rossillon thought that : "Nous quitterions un pays très fièvreux où les pères n'ont, jusqu'ici, pas trouvé le moyen de vivre, et nous serions dèbarrassés de la langue Oriya et d'un territoire que nous n'avons jamais pu embrasser. Il ne reste plus qu' à obtenir deux choses: le consententement des pères de Surada – ils auront de la peine à accepter – puis l'acceptation des pères à La Salette auxquels je me suis adressé." P. Rossillon to Constant Bouvard, Visakhapatnam, February 26, 1920, AMSFS 5H5-2/5.

[221] Fr. Vuillez wrote about the cessation of the mission : "La cession du Ganjam et de l'Orissa à une autre congrégation étant chose reglée! Cette question, comme vous pouvez le supposer, ne nous laisse pas indifferents. Nous abandonons la meilleure partie de notre diocèse, celle où nous avons le plus travaillé et aussi celle qui nous donne le plus d'éspérances. Tout cela évidemment ne nous regarde pas, c'est l'affaire des supérieurs et ils connaissent assez le pour et le contre de la question. Pour nous, nous n'aurons qu'à obéir quand le moment sera venu. Malheureusement en attendant ce moment, qui est long à venir, notre situation n'est pas des plus brillantes. A la retraite on nous avait annoncé que la cession se ferait dans quelques mois - mainternat nous apprenons que les pères de la Salette ont refusé. Entre-temps nous avons l'ordre de ne rien entreprendre d'important, de ne commencer aucune œuvre nouvelle." Vuillez to Constant Bouvard, Surada, April 4, 1921, AMSFS 5H5-2/5.

[222] A sermon, an exhortation and an invitation to make a general confession, given by St. Vincent de Paul on January 25, 1617, in the church of Folleville laid the foundation for a future congregation officially begun in 1625, that was known as the Congregation of the Mission. Its members are generally called Vincentians in English, Lazarists in French and Paules in Spanish. Vincent and his first companions declared that they had joined together "to live in a community or confraternity and to devote themselves to the salvation of the poor country people". Edified by their labour, Jean-François de Gondi, Archbishop of Paris, approved the first community on April 24, 1626. This is one of the rare cases in history where a community was approved before it even existed physically. The pontifical authorisation of the community took place with the Bull 'Salvatoris Nostri', on January 12, 1632. On January 8, 1632, Vincent took possession of the house of St. Lazare, which became the headquarters for the Congregation of the Mission. For a detailed history on the Congregation of the Mission in English, see, S. POOLE, *A History of the Congregation of the Mission, 1625-1843*, California 1972.

[223] A few territories had been suggested for their consideration: a part of Hyderabad diocese or the Arakan which actually depends on Dacca, situated on the Bay of Bengal closer to Burma. Cf. S. Congregazione 'de Propaganda

Fide' to Francesco Verdier, August 9, 1920, Protocollo N. 1229/920, Archives of the Congregation of the Mission, f. 79.

[224] S. Congregazione 'de Propaganda Fide' to Francesco Verdier, November 20, 1920, Protocollo N. 3346/20, Archives of the Congregation of the Mission, f. 86; S. Congregazione 'de Propaganda Fide' to Francesco Verdier, December 30, 1920, Protocollo N. 3957/20, Archives of the Congregation of the Mission, f. 90.

[225] S. Congregazione 'de Propaganda Fide' to Francesco Verdier, April 30, 1921, Protocollo N. 1213/21, Archives of the Congregation of the Mission, f. 112.

[226] Vuillez to Constant Bouvard, Surada, April 4, 1920, AMSFS 5H5-2/2.; Rossillon to Bouvard, March 20, 1920; J. J. Vuillez to Favrat, Surada, April 4, 1921; Msgr. Joseph Baud expressed that, "Enfin la mission de Surada qui fut cédée, âmes et biens aux Lazaristes espagnols dès 1922, pour le plus grand bien de Surada et de Vizag." J. BAUD, *L'œuvre de Msgr. Rossillon*, Vishakapatnam, May 5, 1947, AMSFS 5H5-2/5.

[227] The names of the first group of missionaries are: Frs. Jose Maria Fernandez (who was the first superior), Ramon Ferrer, Valerian Guemes and Rey Coello. Cf. C. WILSON, "Vincentians in India", in Idem (ed.), *Silver Jubilee Souvenir of the Indian Province of the Congregation of the Mission*, Vijoy Bhavan, Berhampur 1995, p. 5.

[228] Fernandez to Verdier, Cuttack, December 12, 1922, Superior of the Mission 1922 – 1927, Archives of the Congregation of the Mission.

[229] V. URBANEJA, *El Padre Guemes al Descubìerto. Cincuenta Añños de su vida. Dia a Dia su diario el Diario de una mision, 1921-1978*, St. Vincent's, Gopalpur-on-Sea, Unpublished Manuscript, pp. 3-4.

[230] The Examiner, 72/39 (1921), 389 – 390.

[231] Mauritius Veys to Provincial, Calcutta, January 11, 1922, APBS India 2 – 23/4.

[232] It is to be borne in mind that Ganjam district was in Madras Presidency and the Cuttack and Puri districts were in Orissa division of the Bengal Presidency.

[233] C. WILSON, "Vincentians in India", in *Silver Jubilee Souvenir of the Indian Province of the Congregation of the Mission 1970 – 1995*, Vijoy Bhavan, Berhampur 1995, pp. 10-11; F. MOGET, *Early days of Visakhapatnam*, p. 277.

[234] Alary to Superior General, Kesramal, July 11, 1916, ARSI, Calcut. 1005-XIII, 8.

[235] It was S. Grosjean who made detailed statistics of Gangpur for the year 1914. Cf. M. VERMEIRE, *Gangpur Mission History*, vol. I, p. 99.

[236] The decision to receive baptism was generally decided with the missionary in a Panchayat. Generally, the missionary promised to extend help to the village and villagers who expressed their readiness to receive baptism. As a sign of their agreement, the tribals cut off their *chundis* (tuft of hair). With this act they often resorted to hearty laughter, saying that the evil spirit had been gotten rid of.

[237] Henry Floor was born on June 1, 1874, at Brugge, Belgium. He entered the Society of Jesus on September 23, 1893. He took his fourth vow on February 2, 1910. He was instrumental in establishing a parish in Gaibira in 1922, and he served as its first parish priest. He died on December 12, 1947, at Ranchi. Cf. R. MENDIZÁBAL, *Catalogus Defunctorum in renata Societate Iesu ab a. 1814 ad a. 1970*, p. 439.

[238] In a letter dated May 3, 1920, Fr. Floor reported on the status of the mission he had inherited and proposed certain remedies for the improvement in the quality of life. Cf. M. VERMEIRE, *Gangpur Mission History*, vol. I, p. 180.

[239] Cardon to Superior General, Rengarih, July 10, 1917, ARSI Calcut. 1005-X, 7. A short description of Tana Bhagatism is mentioned in the third chapter of this study (foot note no. 232).

[240] H. FLOOR, "Simples Réflexions d'un Missionnaire VII", in *MB* (1920) pp. 226 – 227.

[241] In 1917 when the missionary visited the villages near Kutra, he chose a common place for celebrating the Mass. The catechist of Kutra and his wife came to the place after entrusting the key to their house with a neighbour. When they returned, the catechist discovered that he had lost Rs. 60 that he had in the house. He lodged a complaint. The police, instead of nabbing the culprit, threatened the whole village and imposed a fine of Rs. 30 for them and Rs. 60 for the catechist. In order to pay the fine some villagers had to sell their cattle and mortgage their fields. They felt that the fine had been imposed on them unjustly, because, they said, 'it is the fault of the catechist, we don't go any more to the church'. Later, with the help of two youths from Tunmura, Fr. Floor turned the situation into a favourable one for the church when he appointed two dynamic persons as a catechist and a master of the school, replacing the old catechist who had lost his credibility when he complained to the police. Fr. Floor wrote: "Ils vendent leurs bœufs, hypothèquent leurs champs, ils sont appauvris, endettés. 'C'est la faute du catéchiste! Nous n'allons plus à l'église'." H. FLOOR, "Simples Réflexions d'un Missionnaire", in *MB* (1920), p. 40; M. VERMEIRE, *Gangpur Mission History*, vol. I, pp. 186-187.

[242] VAN DER SCHUEREN, "Au Chota Nagpore", in *MB* (1921), p. 32.

[243] M. Vermeire, *Biru Mission History: Samtoli*, vol. IV, Section II, ARSI. Beng. 2004, p. 21.

[244] Ibid., p. 29.

[245] Ibid., p. 30.

[246] It is possible that these *Zamindars*, having seen the work in Chotanagpur and the influence of the missionaries with the government, wanted to avail of their friendship. Ibid., pp. 30-31.

[247] The following families of Nagra were ready to become Catholics: 40 families from Banailata, 20 from Goghea, 60 from Ranakato, 15 from Konokela, 5 from Demta and 60 from Katajir. Cf. Ibid., p. 31.

[248] The new catechumenate villagers of Nagra were: 43 from Banailata, 28 from Goghea, 15 from Ranakata, 4 from Bemta, 10 from Olhaintola, 11 from Katajhar, 8 from Karaqua and 3 from Kusum *Tola* (hamlet). Cf. Ibid., p. 34.

[249] M. VERMEIRE, *Biru Mission History: Samtoli*, vol. IV, Section II, ARSI. Beng. 2004, p. 39.

[250] Ibid.

[251] In a moving narration of the catastrophic effects of the floods that took place in July and August 1921, Fr. T. Lambot portrayed the precarious life conditions of the tribals living in the Nagra region because of the 'capricious and cruel river' called Koel. Cf. T. Lambot, "Scènes Tragiques", in *MB* (1921) pp. 129-131. In another article, Fr. H. Floor narrated how it was difficult for the missionaries to respond to invitations during the monsoon. He was unable to move in the torrential rain, when the rivers were usually full, which prompted him to build a boat, called *Patras*, Peter, for the parish of Kesramal. Cf. H. Floor, "La Barque de Kesramal", in *MB* (1921), pp. 369 - 370.

[252] M. VERMEIRE, *Gangpur Mission History*, vol. I, p. 149.

[253] Gerdhai was a village situated in the Nagra region, which was close to Hamirpur. Now it is part of Rourkela city. Cf. Ibid., p. 131.

[254] Ibid., p. 150.

[255] Ibid., p. 146.

[256] Ibid.

[257] Hadelin Grignard was born on September 1, 1875, at Verviers in Belgium. He entered the Society of Jesus on November 21, 1893. He was ordained a priest on February 2, 1912. After having worked hard for the progress of the mission, he breathed his last on May 31, 1942, at Ranchi. Cf. R. MENDIZÁBAL, *Catalogus Defunctorum in renata Societate Iesu ab a. 1814 ad a. 1970*, p. 402.

[258] The Indian mission found at Alken after the death of Camiel Lievens, Archief Belges. India 2, Box15/5; M. VERMEIRE, *Gangpur Mission History*, vol. I, p. 107; H. JOSSON, *La Mission du Bengale Occidental*, vol. II, p. 409.

[259] M. VERMEIRE, *Gangpur Mission History*, vol. I, p. 134.

[260] H. JOSSON, *La Mission du Bengale Occidental*, vol. II, p. 409.

[261] M. VERMEIRE, *Gangpur Mission History*, vol. I, p. 108.

[262] Ibid., p. 134.

[263] Ibid., pp. 109-110.

[264] Ibid., p. 134.

[265] Victor Gheysens was born on July 12, 1886, at Gentbrugge, Belgium. He entered the Soceity of Jesus on September 23, 1908. After an exemplary career in the mission he died on July 29, 1948. Cf. R. MENDIZÁBAL, *Catalogus Defunctorum in renata Societate Iesu ab a. 1814 ad a. 1970*, p. 443.

[266] Theophile Lambot was born on December 28, 1882, at Petit-Fayt (Namur), Belgium. He entered the Society of Jesus on September 13, 1909. He took his fourth vow on February 2, 1918. After having worked in India, he died on May 5, 1927, at Calcutta. Cf. Ibid., p. 314.

[267] M. VERMEIRE, *Gangpur Mission History*, vol. I, p. 132.

[268] Ibid., p. 130.

[269] Floor remarked : "Depuis 1920 en janvier, deux pères y eurent leur résidence fixé." Floor to Provincial, Kesramal, December 29, 1920, APBS India 2 – 29/2. In his letter to the Provincial Fr. Fédéric Ernest mentions that due to the division of the district two priests could take up residence in Hamirpur. F. Ernest to Provincial, Rengarih, July 15, 1920, APBS India 2 – 29/2.

[270] From a letter of Fr. H. Grignard, dated Rajgangpur, near Kesramal, October 27, 1919, one can understand that he had been put in charge of the whole Gangpur area by Fr. Alary. At that time Fr. Grignard was busy building the new residence of Hamirpur. Due to his rigorous work schedule combined with bouts of malaria attacks, he fell very ill and endured all sorts of privations until January 1920, when someone else joined him. In the beginning Fr. Grignard used to live under a tent next to a stable. Later he lived in a godown (hut), as the missionaries called it, and finally in a corner of the kitchen. Cf. M. VERMEIRE, *Gangpur Mission History*, vol. I, p. 130.

[271] Ibid.

[272] Ibid., p. 137.

[273] Fr. Lambot reported this tragic incident, which took place in July 1920. Cf. M. VERMEIRE, *Gangpur Mission History*, vol. I, p. 150.

[274] Floor to Provincial, Kesramal, December 29, 1920, APBS, India 2 – 29/2.

[275] M. VERMEIRE, *Gangpur Mission History*, vol. I, p. 131.

[276] Ibid., p. 147.

[277] Bonai, named after its capital Bonaigarh, was a semi-independent state ruled by a native chief. The state had an area of 1,296 square miles and a population of about 68,186 at the beginning of the nineteenth century. It experienced a similar fortune as Gangpur, its neighbour. It was ceded to the British government in 1803 by the treaty of Deogaon by Rahuji Bhonsla, to whom it was restored by a special arrangement in 1806. It reverted to the British in 1818 and was finally ceded by a treaty in 1826. In order to maintain its semi-independence, the raja was required to pay a tribute of Rs. 500 per annum, which was liable to revision. The relationship between the chief and the British government was regulated by the *sanad* granted in 1899 and reissued in

1905, when the state was transferred to the Orissa division from Chotanagpur. Raja Dharanidhar Indra Deo Deb, a *Kshatriya* by caste, succeeded to the *Gadi,* crown on February 13, 1902. Babu Bharat Chandra Naik was appointed dewan of the state. Cf. *Feudatory States of Bihar and Orissa. List of the Ruling Chiefs and Leading Personages*, Government of India Central Publication Branch, Calcutta 1924, pp. 7- 8; M. VERMEIRE, *Gangpur Mission History*, vol. I, p. 139.

[278] Ibid., p. 138.

[279] Joseph, the catechist of Vigera, was punished severely at the police station of Banki, where, in his effort to stop all *begari* (labour) on Sundays, he stopped a group of Catholics from the important work of carrying ice to the raja who was ill. With the intervention of the dewan, the raja himself agreed to drop the procedure against the catechist. Cf. Ibid., p. 138.

[280] Ibid.

[281] Ibid., p. 160.

[282] For more details see the article of T. LAMBOT, "En Tournée Apostolique", in *MB* (1921), pp. 85-87.

[283] M. VERMEIRE, *Gangpur Mission History*, vol. I, p. 141.

[284] H. JOSSON, *La Mission du Bengale Occidental*, vol. II, p. 409.

[285] M. VERMEIRE, *Gangpur Mission History*, vol. I, p. 138.

[286] Gustav Pierret was born on May 17, 1855, at Etalle (Luxembourg). He entered the Society of Jesus on September 26, 1918. He died on June 14, 1926, at Kesramal. Cf. R. MENDIZÁBAL, *Catalogus Defunctorum in renata Societate Iesu ab a. 1814 ad a. 1970*, p. 309.

[287] M. VERMEIRE, *Gangpur Mission Hisotry*, vol. I, p. 189.

[288] Ibid., p. 189.

[289] There was an inspection of the district schools at Hamirpur. Only a few of the catechists, who also served as schoolteachers, turned up. The Inspector of Schools was unhappy with the inspection he conducted in Dumandiri on October 25, 1922. Cf. Ibid., p. 147.

[290] An *anna* was the last category in pre-independent Indian currency. Sixteen *annas* constituted a rupee. A missionary residing at Kurdeg at that time (1905) claimed that he bought 23 *sers* of uncooked rice for a rupee. A *ser* of uncooked rice would weigh more or less about 900 grams. Cf. M. Vermeire, *Biru Mission History. Section. III. Kurdeg*, ARSI. Beng. 2005, p. 16.

[291] *Ind* was a Hindu festival imitated in some villages by the Mundas (tribes) and consisting essentially of a sacrifice followed by dancing. In a few villages where the *Ind* was regularly celebrated, a high ground was set apart for it, where a heavy wooden frame remained firmly and permanently fixed. People gathered in the afternoon at the pole. "The crowd", wrote Fr. Hoffmann, "is made up of dancers and few spectators. Only youths and maidens visit the *Ind*

ground, with, may be, a slight sprinkling of married people, not to be taken into account". The spinsters and bachelors of the same village visit the fair in separate groups. And on their way back from the *Ind*, the group of youths of one village often exchanges lewd jests with the girls of another village. Cf. J.B. HOFFMANN, *Encyclopedia Mundarica*, vol. VII, Patna 1932, pp. 1911-1913.

[292] *Puja*, as performed by Hindus, is ritual in which certain articles — such as flowers, fruit or milk — were offered to the deity. Sometimes fowls and animals were slaughtered for the deity. Here it was mainly applied to the offerings of inanimate objects to a deity by magicians, witch-finders, snake venom "sweepers" and the like. Cf. J.B. HOFFMANN, *Encyclopedia Mundarica*, vol. XI, Patna 1938, p. 3419.

[293] M. VERMEIRE, *Gangpur Mission History*, vol. I, p. 146.

[294] Ibid., p. 146.

[295] Ibid., p. 151.

[296] Ibid., p. 151.

[297] Ibid., p. 152.

[298] Ibid., p. 140.

[299] Ibid., p. 143.

[300] Ibid., p. 142.

[301] This feast is observed in honour of the Hindu Divinity Karma. Fr. J. B. Hoffmann writes: "His cult starts when the consultation of the witch finders or sorcerers has revealed him to be responsible for the harm which has befallen a certain person or his family. From this moment the latter become Karma's devotee, promising him a yearly sacrifice at the *Karam* feast, blessed by him with material prosperity if faithful to his cult; punished if remiss. As a token of the promise a *dali* basket is hung up under the roof of the house or on the wall". The Hindu *Karam* feast is kept on the *chautha* (4th day) of *Bhado* (August-September) but the Oraons only plant their *Jawa* (maize grains that have just germinated) some days later, in preparation for their *Karam* which is celebrated on the *'ekha dashi'* day of *Karam* (on the eleventh day). On this day many boys and girls keep a strict fast from 0600 hrs till 1900 hrs. The youth put on their nice dresses and feathers and yak's tails and *Jawa* only for the narration of the legend and for the night dance. They dance at the foot of the *Karam* tree (Nauclea parvifolia). Cf. E. CAMPION, "Uraon Customs", in *The Chota Nagpur Mission Letter* 9 (1935), pp. 118-121, 151-155; J.B. HOFFMANN, *Encyclopedia Mundarica*, vol. VIII, Patna 1933, pp. 2227-2231.

[302] M. VERMEIRE, *Gangpur Mission History*, vol. I, p. 143.

[303] Ibid., p. 144.

[304] Tahinda, a new village that had appealed only for a schoolteacher i.e., they did not want to learn *Dharam* but only to have a school. Cf. Ibid.

[305] Ibid., p. 151.

[306] Ibid., p. 138.

[307] Ibid., p. 150.

[308] M. Vermeire, *Biru Mission History: Kurdeg,* vol. IV Section III, ARSI, Beng. 2006, pp. 46-47.

[309] H. Floor to Provincial, Kesramal, June 27, 1920, APBS India 2 – 28/2.

[310] M. VERMEIRE, *Gangpur Mission History,* vol. I, p. 182.

[311] H. Floor to General, Kesramal, July 1, 1920, ARSI, Beng. 1006, II-16.

[312] H. Floor to General, Kesramal, June 29, 1921, ARSI, Beng. 1006, III-49.

[313] M. VERMEIRE, *Gangpur Mission History,* vol. I, p. 183.

[314] It was Fr. De Gryse who purchased the land for a church and presbytery at the border between Biru and Gangpur. The place was considered to be suitable for evangelisation in the western part of Gangpur, which depended on Kurdeg mission. cf. Waelkans to Provincial, Calcutta, March 21, 1906, APBS India 2 – 22/5.

[315] M. VERMEIRE, *Biru Mission History: Kurdeg,* vol. IV Section III, ARSI. Beng. 2006, pp. 46-47.

[316] Fr. H. Floor wrote : "Il n'y a pas encore de prêtre résident, mais un prêtre vient ici pour la réunion des catéchistes, le premier vendredi de chaque mois, il reste pour le dimanche suivant et ainsi les gens ont souvent l'occasion de communier. Le père est également ici les jours de grandes fêtes." H. FLOOR, "Simple Réflexions d'un Missionnaire VI", in *MB* (1920), p. 206.

[317] Fr. Floor reported: "Cette partie s'étend jusqu'à 50 miles (75 kms) à l'ouest, c'est assez dire qu'il n'y a pas moyen d'administer et de développer cette partie d'ici. Il faut absolument un prêtre résident à Behrenbasa. Ni les catéchistes ni les chrétiens ne viennent ici. La réunion mensuelle et le payment des salaires se fait là, causant un long et pénible voyage aux pères." Floor to Provincial, Kesramal, December 29, 1920, APBS India 2 – 29/2.

[318] Ibid.

[319] Fr. H. Floor reported : "Nous avons organisé cette partie cette année, sur 25 chapelles à bâtir, 19 sont terminées, partout il y a des catéchistes et déjà un bon nombre de maîtres. Il faut séparer cette partie de Kesramal a cause des distances." Floor to Provincial, Kesramal, June 22, 1921, APBS India 2 – 29/3.

[320] Djardin complained : "L'année dernière nous avons consulté sur l'emplacement d'une nouvelle station au Ganpur. Les consulteurs et moi même, nous tombons d'accord sur Kusumdegi. Cette année le P. Floor va pour sa retraite, où il a parlé avec l'Archêveque, que s'est-il passé, je n'en sais rien. Le fait est-il qu'il y a un mois je reçois une de ses letters me disant que la nouvelle station sera Gaibira." Djardin to Provincial, Rengarih, August 10,

1922, APBS India 2 – 29/2, Djardin to Provincial, Kesramal, August 26, 1922, APBS India 2 – 29/2.

[321] M. VERMEIRE, *Biru Mission History: Kurdeg*, vol. IV, APBS India 1 – 3 / Ser. B, India Lievens, Gen. Sources, p. 55.

[322] Some of the main villages visited in western Gangpur were: Sakiabahar, Korai, Saunamara, Rauldega, Borobahal, Maiabahal, Gaibira, Deogaon, Kirelega, Kusumdegi. Cf. Ibid.

[323] Floor to Provincial, Kesramal, October 20, 1920, APBS India 2 – 29/2.

[324] Fr. Floor wrote : "Au Gangpur, il y a un mouvement de conversions. En 1921 avant juillet il y a eu 2000 conversions et en decembre environ 1500." Floor to Provincial, Kesramal, January 14, 1922, APBS India 2 – 29/2.

[325] T. VAN DER SCHUEREN, *The Belgian Mission of Bengal. Among the Aboriginal Tribes of Chota Nagpur*, vol. II, Calcutta 1922, p. 81.

[326] Ibid., p. 80.

[327] Fr. Floor wrote : "Gaibira est à 50 kms à l'ouest de Kesramal, au centre même du mouvement des conversions. C'est pour ce motif que Monseigneur a préferé Gaibira à Behrenbasa. Un second motif: il desire traiter le Gangpur comme une unite séparée. Behrenbasa est situé sur la frontière du Gangpur. Biru est sur territoire anglais." Floor to Provincial, Kesramal, August 26, 1922, APBS India 2 – 29/2

[328] M. VERMEIRE, *Gangpur Mission History*, vol. I, pp. 131, 253.

[329] Ibid., pp. 204 – 205. Fr. Floor wrote: "Nous venons d'obtenir un terrain de 15 acres." Floor to Provincial, Kesramal, July 13, 1922, APBS India 2 – 29/4.

[330] Floor to Provincial, Kesramal, July 13, 1922, APBS India 2 – 29/2; M. Vermeire, *Gangpur Mission History*, vol. I, p. 205; VAN DER SCHUEREN, *The Belgian Mission of Bengal*, vol. II, p. 81.

[331] The Indian mission found at Alken after the death of Camiel Lievens, Archief Belges. India 2, Box15/5.

[332] Mauritius Veys to Provincial, Calcutta, August 17, 1922, APBS India 2 - 23/4; Van der Schueren to Josson, June 7, 1923, APBS India 2 - 15/4; M. VERMEIRE, *Gangpur Mission History*, vol. I, p. 199.

[333] Fr. Floor wrote : "J'ai pris possession de Gaibira le jour de la nativité de la Ste. Vierge. Puisse notre mère du ciel la prendre sous sa protection." Floor to Provincial, Gaibira, October 18, 1922, APBS India 2 – 29/2.

[334] Ibid.

[335] Floor to Provincial, Gaibira, October 18, 1922, APBS India 2 – 29/2.

[336] M. VERMEIRE, *Gangpur Mission History*, vol. II, Diocesan Archives, Bishop's House, Rourkela, (Unpublished Manuscripts), p. 213.

[337] M. VERMEIRE, *Gangpur Mission History*, vol. I, p. 205. Fr. Floor wrote to the Archbishop on December 12, 1922, "Since my last letter 3 Kharia *tollas* (hamlets)

on the side of Behrenbasa came over . . . So far the Uraons are afraid of the Raja and do not join us." M. VERMEIRE, *Gangpur Mission History*, vol. II, p. 215.

[338] Fr. Floor remarked : "Le Dewan m'a offert 2000 roupies pour aider les natifs ruinés par les peste bovine. Les largesses que cette décision me permettre de faire, contribuent sans doute à étendre la mission." Floor to Provincial, Gaibira, October 18, 1922, APBS India 2 – 29/2; M. VERMEIRE, *Gangpur Mission History*, vol. II, p. 214.

[339] The members of the Society of Jesus were grouped in districts under a district superior. They used to gather in a common place at least four times a year, mainly to conduct the examination of conscience and to discuss matters relating to the mission. This division was necessitated by the long distances and the difficulties of travel during the monsoon season. Cf. Cardon to Provincial, July 12, 1920, Samtoli, APBS India 2 – 29/2.

[340] M. VERMEIRE, *Gangpur Mission History*, vol. I, p. 206.

[341] Van der Schueren to Josson, June 7, 1923, APBS India/Lievens Box. 15/4.

[342] The Belgian Jesuits' work of expansion came to a halt with the establishment of Kusumdegi, the 5th parish of the Gangpur mission, in 1933. Jhunmur, the fourth station, was established in 1925. Unable to provide personnel for the growing needs of the Gangpur mission, they also looked for a congregation that could provide for the needs of the mission. When Gangpur state merged with Orissa, they were obliged to learn Oriya, the state language. The Divine Word Missionaries took up the task of guiding a mission that required rejuvenation and expansion. Their arrival in 1948 marked a new phase in the history of the Gangpur mission.

Chapter - 5

Missionary Methods

India has always been a magnet for missionary efforts, and those who had the 'quest for souls' never lost their passionate attachment to it.[1] Though challenging, India with its multi-racial and multi-religious background offered an ideal field for missionaries, provided they went into the interior villages. There is no doubt that the ultimate goal of the Catholic missionaries in preaching to the aboriginals and dalits of Orissa was their conversion. The missionaries considered it their sacred duty to save souls and to bring the people to the knowledge of the truth. The number of converts a missionary gained measured his success and failure.

To obtain their goal, the missionaries of the nineteenth century used methods and approaches that were both traditional and new. They were convinced that they were called to 'civilise' a people that was still primitive and 'groping in darkness'.[2] The opening of schools, dispensaries and hospitals, orphanages, maternity centres, vocational institutions, cooperative societies and other social works were the methods usually adopted. Though it is said that these institutions were primarily meant for Christians, non-Christians could also benefit from their services. Therefore, the establishment of schools, hospitals, orphanages and other charitable institutions were primarily oriented to this singular purpose.

The passing of time and an appropriate distance from the field of their work might permit us to evaluate the mission in Orissa. The method used there was the best that the missionaries knew. They saw themselves as coming from a superior civilisation, and they had an absolutist understanding of Christianity. Hence, they felt the obligation and urgency to give the treasure they had to the underprivileged 'primitive people'. It was typical of the epoch to follow the methods that were suitable for the particular territory and the particular religious congregation. Since religious orders spearheaded the missionary movements, they not only unified their efforts but also made sure of its continuity. Stephen Neill commented: "On the Roman Catholic side, there were considerable varieties in missionary practice as between the various religious orders, and as between the orders and the secular clergy."[3]

In the absence of a common method for the Ganjam mission, the MSFS sought those approaches that were suited to their particular situation. Apart from some limited instructions from their superiors, the missionaries in Ganjam had little guidance in their efforts to 'save souls'. The Jesuit mission in Gangpur was better placed, as the missionaries could follow the pattern of the Chotanagpur mission. This chapter will attempt to highlight and evaluate the methods of both missionary congregations in attracting the tribals and dalits of Orissa to the faith. In their zeal the missionaries sometimes exhibited negative features that even though did not cause the demise of the mission, certainly did not foster friendly relations with the people. However, it is to be borne in mind that there was no single method that was applicable to all the mission stations and accepted by all the missionaries.

Ganjam Mission

Though the missionaries working in the Ganjam mission did not have a highly organised method like the Jesuits in Chotanagpur, they used the strategies they believed would bring them conversions. The missionaries were at liberty to choose the method suitable to the place where they were posted.[4] Keeping in mind the socio-economic condition of the people, the missionaries framed a method that they thought would bring them the desired results.

Spiritual Activities

Spiritual activities such as popular devotions did not directly produce conversions. Nevertheless, besides providing a way of conserving the faith of the neophytes, they bore testimony to the non-Christians, particularly those who came into frequent contact with the missionaries and Christians.

Establishment of Catechumenates

The establishment and running of catechumenates were some of the important duties of the MSFS in the Ganjam mission. It was the sure means of teaching religion to the Kondhs and Panos. Possibly the catechumenate programmes gave the missionaries an occasion to maintain close contact with the people, at least in the initial stage of their apostolate. It was also an occasion for the missionaries to teach the people 'civilisation', as they would claim.[5] Catechumens were divided into small groups based on the number in a village and on the level of the people's understanding. One of the main activities of the catechumenate was teaching the prayers and some fundamental truths of Christianity. In teaching the prayers the missionaries claimed to follow the instruction of St. Francis Xavier, who recommended that the missionary himself teach the prayers to his neophytes.

The instructions preparing the people for baptism generally lasted a month.[6] Fr. Bonaventure found the catechumenate method effective, since it provided an occasion for him to give thorough spiritual formation to small groups of catechumens. Citing one of the letters of Fr. J.M. Descombes, F. Moget wrote: "Catechumens in villages are divided into groups and are given a course of instruction lasting a month. We teach them the knowledge of God, creation, providence, sin and forgiveness, the incarnation of Christ, the redemption, the sacraments, the study of prayers."[7] Commenting on the suitability of the method for the Ganjam mission, Fr. Bonaventure wrote:

> My way of evangelisation is a little different, peculiar to Surada mission. The priest gathers two or three pagan families and gives them hospitality on our lands, a little material help. And I throw off the seed of the word of God. I had good success at times. Just now, I have 18 families of catechumens whom I am instructing, and with God's grace, hope to baptise before the end of the year. How difficult it is to bring pagans to the service of God. The more educated are the most obstinate. We get only the poor.[8]

This method was directly opposed to that of Fr. Dupont, who concentrated on baptising as many people as possible without any preparation or an infrastructure to follow them. Though the method was inspired by the theological thinking of the time -- saving as many souls as possible for the glory of God -- it suffered a great setback when many of them defected for various reasons.

Retreats and other Spiritual Activities

Once a year the missionaries gathered Catholic men and women for the annual retreat, which as a rule was organised at the centre where the priest resided. During their stay, which lasted about three days, the participants were given further explanation of Christian doctrine or catechesis. The preachers helped the people to make a good confession and to receive communion. At the end of the retreat, the participants would promise to amend some of their old habits, such as drinking, smoking, etc. As far as possible the missionaries tried to invite the same priest for three consecutive years for the following reasons: (1) to evaluate whether the people understood what was said in the last retreat; (2) to continue the catechesis begun in the previous retreat; and (3) to evaluate whether the people were faithful to the promises made during the previous retreat. They believed that only in this way would they help the people in their faith-formation. Attendance in such gatherings was generally satisfactory.[9] In tune with the universal church and in the hope of improving the spiritual life of the people, the missionaries introduced the Apostleship of Prayer, which they claimed improved the faith-lives of the people.

Humanitarian Projects

The missionaries' immediate and unreserved response to natural calamities produced positive results, that is, people asked to join the church. Though the missionaries were seldom prepared for such disasters, the mission's growth often resulted from them. The MSFS were contemplating the abandonment of the mission when the Great Famine of 1866 occurred. This was followed by another famine in 1889. There were inundations, cholera and epidemics like smallpox that required medical and humanitarian assistance. In the absence of government services, the people had no other option but to accept help from them. The missionaries used these opportunities to show their kindness and generosity. When Kondh Christians were asked to state the reasons for their conversion, a sizable number stated that, "It is well to become part, that is, to find security with the Christian community."[10]

Charity during Epidemics

Right from the beginning, the MSFS responded promptly and positively to natural calamities like famine, flood, cholera, etc. Very often these calamities left numerous orphans and widows, who wandered on the streets or came to the mission with the hope of finding something to fill their stomachs. There were occasions when parents sold their children or abandoned them on the roads. They did this for two reasons. First, they hoped some kind people, like the missionaries whose charity extended to all, might take them into the orphanages. Second, the purification rules of the Hindus do not permit the presence of a dying person in the house. The missionaries took up the challenge by providing help to the starving and to the dying -- particularly the children. After all, they believed that they were called to help people in need. Hence, this was a unique opportunity to exhibit their charity. Though initially they lacked a definite plan, apart from nourishing the sick and baptising them *in articulo mortis*, the missionaries eventually arranged for the children to be brought up in the Christian faith and to be educated in schools.

Orphanages

As the gathered children increased in number during and after the Great Famine of 1866, the missionaries were obliged to open an orphanage in Surada. Initially they had no specific plan for the orphanage, apart from caring for the children's health. Once they were settled, they began to educate the children. Their education consisted of 'reading and writing', since, the missionaries thought that would suffice for those who would be involved in agriculture.

Since funds for the maintenance of the orphanages were limited, the missionaries purchased some fields that could be cultivated in order to make the orphanage self-sufficient. The governmental scheme of leasing forestland inspired the MSFS to lease large tracts of forest for a nominal price so that they could be converted into arable fields. Grown-up boys from the orphanage were engaged in the cultivation of the land, while a priest supervised the work. Later, the cleared property was given to married couples for settlement. Such settlements paved the way for the birth of Christian villages like Dantholinghy, Karicotte and Thotavally. These settlements were under the rigorous supervision of a priest, who even meted out physical punishment to wrongdoers. The missionaries took the liberty to correct the mistakes of the orphans and the Christians with the use of the cane.[11]

There were often tensions between the missionaries and the orphans who settled on the property and who were expected to repay something for the maintenance of the mission. It was very difficult for the people who had received so much from the mission to return something to it. Not only did they think that the mission did not require their help, but they were also of the opinion that the missionaries did not distribute what lawfully belonged to them. Dissatisfied with their situation in the orphanage, some of those who grew up there left Surada and went elsewhere to seek jobs. A small group left for the tea gardens in Assam. Since the residents of the orphanages were leaving the settlement, the missionaries decided to reduce the property. They sold some of the fields in both Thotavally and Surada.[12]

Considering the work of MSFS in Ganjam, one is rather certain that the missionaries' help was timely and liberative, as it provided immediate relief from the miserable condition of the orphans and widows. They also tried to provide a future for them. However, the settlements were not well-organised and provided limited educational advancement.

Distribution of Medicine

The medical mission was considered to be an effective *preparatio evangelica* in India. However, there was but a handful of medical personnel, and only a few were willing to move to the interior. The missionaries, who were convinced that the work of helping the poor and oppressed was an effective method of revealing the goodness and love of God, were happy to distribute medicine, since it brought them in close contact with the suffering and vulnerable people. In his simplicity, Fr. Descombes did all he could to alleviate the suffering of the sick. His knowledge of tropical diseases and the medicines to cure them came in handy, as the people could not afford to go to a hospital – which in any case was far from where they lived. The long distances and the poor means of transportation discouraged the sick and made them resign themselves to the skills of the village medicine man.

Under such circumstances, finding someone who knew the cure for a sickness and provide free medicine was a blessing for the Kondhs and Panos.[13] We should recall that one of the first huts established in Katingia beside the chapel-cum-residence of the priest was a dispensary. The missionary's fame as a caring doctor spread throughout the vicinity, and people came to receive medicine from him. Dispensaries were also established in Surada, Gopalpur and Cuttack where the Sisters treated the people for all kinds of diseases.

The dispensaries established in the mission treated both Christians and non-Christians. Sometimes the non-Christians, when they came to the priest for medicine, would go to the chapel out of curiosity and then seek an explanation of the statues. This allowed the priest to give a short introduction to Christianity and its beliefs. The missionaries not only blessed the sick but also encouraged them to pray to the Virgin Mary for a cure.[14]

Schools

The spread of education in India today is to a large extent the merit of the Christian missionaries. Missionaries of all denominations took upon themselves the task of establishing schools, even in small villages in the remotest corners of India. Missionaries, irrespective of their denomination, considered educational institutions essential to the progress of the mission. The establishment of schools in the Ganjam Mission was very dear to the MSFS.[15]

The school in Surada provided education to a large number of children. However, the Kondhs had a tendency to avoid the school, for the simple reason that going to school would not feed them. So, the missionaries looked for various ways to attract the Kondhs. They finally decided to provide midday meals for the children attending the school. This did attract students, but it added another problem to the poor mission: finding the money to pay for the meals. The missionaries felt the need to sacrifice some of their personal expenses to help the poor people.[16]

Friendly Relations

Simplicity of life and personal rapport with the people were hallmarks of the missionaries' efforts to evangelise them. There were times when the missionaries felt that their preaching fell on deaf ears. Based on their experience at Gojolibady, the missionaries realised that in order to convert the Kondhs they had to become one of them and had to prove that the missionaries were their friends. Despite some threats and intimidation, the missionaries were not disturbed because they received the support of some of the leading members of the community. In fact, establishing a friendly rapport with the village or tribal chiefs was important for the progress of the mission. In order to obtain this useful rapport some of the missionaries did not hesitate to grant them monetary benefits whenever possible.[17] Both the 'Rules for the Conduct of Missionaries in Orissa' and the 'Synod of Visakhapatnam', exhorted the missionaries to establish good relations with the local officials, village chiefs, *Panches*, etc. However, extending monetary benefits to the village chiefs and other important persons created some unexpected tensions in the missions. The missionaries were also friendly with the Indian *baboos*, lower officials in the government.[18]

Socio-cultural Projects

Living close to nature, Kondhs and Panos are influenced by the rhythms of nature, which often play an important role in their culture and tradition. They revere their culture and tradition as well as the memory of their ancestors. Having noticed this interdependence, the MSFS sought to incorporate it into the life of the church.

Adaptation/Inculturation

Inspired by the work of Fr. Robert de Nobili, the missionaries were convinced that the conversion of a good number of Brahmin families would help them in the conversion of inferior castes and would also remove the stigma attached to Christianity as a religion for people of lower origin. Therefore, in the hope of converting the higher castes, the missionaries adapted the way of life of the Brahmin *Sanyasis*. Though one could admire the flexibility and openness of the missionaries to change their life style and approach, they were too quick to throw out a method that did not produce the desired results. This gives the impression that they wanted immediate responses and they thought it would be rather easy to convert an orthodox group like the Brahmins.[19]

Three to four years of living out the method was, by any standard, a relatively short period of time. They also applied the method of Fr. de Nobili without considering the background of the people they were interested in converting. They went ahead with it without really contemplating whether such a method was suitable for the particular situation. The abrupt departure of Fr. Seigneur from the mission also gives the impression that depth was lacking in the entire project. One must remember that Fr. de Nobili took a lifetime to convert the Brahmins of

Madurai and Tiruchirappally. In spite of all his dedication and sacrifices, the conversions obtained were not in big numbers. It was not just a change of eating habits, dress and study of Hindu scriptures that made the method relevant and effective, but a constant conversion of self, of adaptation and of understanding the ethos of the people.

The question of the Malabar Rites Controversy was still under discussion, and the Holy See was still demanding an oath from the missionaries working in Madurai, Mysore and the Carnatic region, when the MSFS in Ganjam opted for trying the method in Orissa. Only on April 9, 1940, were the missionaries (working in the above-mentioned region) finally released from the oath relating to the Malabar rites.[20]

It is no exaggeration to state that the MSFS found some values in the feasts and cultural practices of Panos and Kondhs. Possibly influenced by the Jesuits and their adaptation method, the MSFS were of the opinion that the mission should adapt to the feasts and customs that are not contrary to Christian doctrine. In fact, they were interested in Christianising some of the feasts. However, this option never became a reality.[21]

Itinerant Monks

Like the Protestant missionaries, some MSFS felt the urge to proclaim God's Word directly, i. e., as itinerant preachers. They would preach the gospel in the market and in other places where people gathered. They were convinced by Matt 10:14 that the duty of the messenger of God was to proclaim God's Word without any hesitation, whether the people received it or not. Here the missionary does not bother with conversion, because he believes that conversion is God's work.[22] The number of missionaries adhering to this method was small, and the method itself was not acceptable to most of the missionaries. Thus, it never had any lasting impact on the mission.

Music and Processions

The MSFS readily adapted local practices involving music and processions. The people of Orissa are generally fond of processions and religious gatherings. They make it a point to take part in celebrations which they called *Jatras*. Having understood this interest of the people, the missionaries organised processions on special occasions.[23] A band usually accompanied the procession. The music and crowds attracted people, who came from far and wide to witness the event. Sometimes even the Hindus took part in such processions, though not out of religious conviction.

On certain occasions the Christians organised procession with the statue of our Lady, which they believed would stop cholera in some villages. Other processions were held to pray for rain or for protection from other epidemics. Sometimes the Hindus invited the procession to pass through their street.[24] These were some of the rare occasions when the Hindus had the chance to observe the faith of the people and to listen to the preaching of the missionaries. Some of them even came forward to receive baptism when the processions were over.

The children from the orphanage were also allowed to take part in such processions, with the hope that they would learn some of the melodies. They regularly participated in the procession on Sunday after vespers. Fr. Avrillon was especially fond of organising such processions. Though he tolerated the use of some Hindu melodies, Fr. Avrillon composed Christian verses for them and made sure that the choir sang those hymns during the processions. In order to encourage the neophytes and depending on the availability of funds, Fr. Dupont organised feasts, which included community meals. He used such occasions to give religious instructions.[25]

Local Languages and Culture

The MSFS were the first group of Catholic missionaries who worked with the Oriya-speaking people of Orissa, and therefore it fell to them to provide some literature. Besides producing linguistic tools such as dictionaries and grammars, the missionaries tried to compose hymns using European tunes.[26]

Though Fr. Seigneur's proficiency in Oriya and Sanskrit was readily acknowledged by his confreres, especially his skills in composing poetry, his talents are yet to be acknowledged by non-Christian Oriya scholars. *Catholic Bhagavata* was not a translation but an earnest effort to explain the mystery of Christianity in poetry. I. Soreng, who made a study of the Christian contribution to Oriya literature, states that it could not have been the composition of Fr. Seigneur. Though Fr. Seigneur was known for his understanding of Oriya and of the Hindu scriptures, it is doubtful that he could have reached such a level of composition within so short a span of time in Surada. It is possible that he instructed the Brahmin convert, Arato Misro, who, basing his composition on *Hindu Bhagavata*, may have composed the *Catholic Bhagavata*. Fr. Soreng also notes a similarity of the epic with the work of Dante's *The Divine Comedy*.[27]

Some missionaries attempted to translate some French works into *Kui* and *Oriya*. Fr. Balmand claimed to have translated the *Rosary of Mercy* into Tamil for the use of the community in Berhampur. The Catholics who participated in the evening prayers there recited it.[28] Initially the missionaries were ignorant of the culture and language of the people. Therefore, even the occasional references made to their superiors in France were gathered from what they read in the expedition reports of the British troops. Fr. Domenge made some references to the culture of the people in *La Mission de Vizagapatam*, but his account of the Meriah sacrifices was almost a copy of what the British authorities wrote on the infamous practice.

While Fr. J.M. Descombes was convalescing in Cuttack (1898), he used the time to translate the catechism into *Kui*. According to him, that was the first Catholic book printed in *Kui*. Since the Baptists had already published the Gospel of Mark in *Kui*, the catechism became the second book in that language.[29] Fr. Jules Rey was busy with the composition of Oriya Christian hymns in Dantholinghy and with the translation of the lives of the saints into Oriya.[30] Fr. Pétrus Descombes requested a press for printing books in Oriya, since the missionaries had already finished the translations of the lives of the saints, the catechism, and a small catechism used by children for their first communion. They were working on the history of the Church.[31] Msgr. Rossillon wrote several works on the people of Orissa.[32]

Impact of the Missionaries

One can hardly separate the missionary's methods from their lives. Their simplicity and readiness to help people in need produced the most lasting impact on the Kondhs and Panos. Facing the rigours of mountain and jungle, they made of every opportunity to win people for Christ.

Catechists

The MSFS readily recognised the important role played by the catechists in the founding and progress of the mission. Though they received only a small remuneration for their services, their contribution to the progress of the mission was essential.[33] Since the people had certain reservations about Europeans, the catechists were the chief means of contacting them.[34] Except for their initial contact with the people of Montacallau, the missionaries sought the help of catechists to lay the foundations of the church. In the absence of a training centre, the missionaries provided formation at the mission station itself. The catechists received guidelines and instructions in Christian teachings when they came to the mission for their monthly meetings.

The catechists were the first ones to be sent to a promising village, and they spoke with the people about the advantages of listening to the missionaries. Then the missionaries visited those villages which seemed open to Christianity. Afterwards the missionaries sent the catechists again to prepare them for baptism and other sacraments. This was the general pattern in the Ganjam mission. It goes without saying that if the missionaries had contacted the villages without the intervention of catechists, the people would have refused to meet them.[35] Catechists often functioned as village chiefs and interpreters and useful councillors to the priests regarding the culture and tradition of the people.[36]

However, the missionaries were unhappy with a number of catechists, as they lacked goodwill and dedication to their work. Without dedicated catechists the missionaries could not properly respond to the invitation of the people.[37]

Hardships

The climate was harsh, and the missionaries often fell victims to malaria.[38] One reason why some MSFS left the mission was that they were not sufficiently prepared to live in such a feverish country. It is said, with a bit of exaggeration, that the missionaries spent half of their precious time recovering from various illnesses they contracted in the Ganjam Mountains.[39] 1875 was a trying time for the mission of Surada, as most of the missionaries were ill. Fr. J.M. Tissot wrote:

> After the sudden death of Fr. Perissin, Fr. Muffat has fallen dangerously ill, I made him to go to Vizagapatam for treatment. Fr. Décarre who was sent to help Fr. Dupont is also down with fever. He fell ill immediately after he arrived. Fr. Souchon is also in the same condition. Their condition makes me restless. Fr. Souchon is in Surada. Fr. Décarre is in Vizagapatam. Fr. Muffat is in Surada. The Sisters who take care of the orphanage are also sick. It looks as if Surada is a hospital.[40]

Besides their missionary spirit, what kept the missionaries in this feverish country was their concern for both confreres and the people they ministered to. The Synod of Visakhapatnam of 1888 exhorted the missionaries to inform their superiors of the difficulties and hardships which they experienced -- even difficulties with confreres. The hope was that shared experiences might help others to imitate the good work accomplished, to avoid the mistakes committed, and to seek the counsel of experienced missionaries.[41]

Due to limited funds, the missionaries often postponed projects, such as the construction of village chapels. They were well aware of the difficulties of continuing their work if there was no money. They pooled the available resources in order to help the people in need. The MSFS in France and the French people responded generously to the pleas of the missionaries. Uncertain of the regularity of donations from France, the missionaries decided to acquire farmland for the support of centres like the orphanages.

Most of the Christians in the mountains in Ganjam were Kondhs and Panos. Reaching them could be difficult, as Fr. Descombes reported:

> We have in the mission of Surada almost 3,000 Christians, scattered in about 30 villages. These are often separated by long distances, connected to each other by steep mountain paths (which are generally daredevils). Furthermore, during the monsoon, from June to November, it would be imprudent for a young missionary who is not acclimatised to the deadly climate to venture into the mountains, true abode of malaria. That leaves us with only eight months to visit the numerous catechumens and to explore the pagan villages around.[42]

It was not practical for the missionaries to visit the villages during certain times of the year. The decision to embrace Christianity was taken during evening meetings when the elders freely discussed the benefits and difficulties involved. If they decided to ask the missionary to visit them, they would send him a request, formally written by a teacher from the neighbouring school and properly signed by an elder.[43]

Material Inducements and Use of Money?

One of the traditional accusations levelled against the missionaries was that they obtained conversions through the lure of money. That Christianity in India found favour among the people of lower caste, some claim, was due to the material benefits they received from the missionaries. Therefore, they were 'Rice Christians' or 'Wheat Christians'. Although material inducements cannot be absolutely ruled out in all conversions, one also cannot categorically affirm that entry into and perseverance in the Christian religion was due largely to the material help converts received. Otherwise they would have defected once the material benefits ceased or were reduced. The reality is that, except for a tiny minority, most of the converts remained faithful to their new religion.

One of the consistent features of the Ganjam mission was the response of the missionaries in times of need. Whenever there was a crop failure, the missionaries were the first to extend their help. They took special care of the orphans and widows. The missionaries could expect some conversions after a crop failure.[44] The missionaries tried to put their limited funds to good use. Sometimes their generosity was appreciated but on other occasions an imprudent use of money could create problems.

Fr. Ambroise Muffat reported how he solemnly celebrated the first communion of the children of Dantholinghy: "After having prepared their souls, I did not forget their body. I bought each of them a beautiful cloth. There was distribution of sweets after the Mass. One loves them here as well. They were very happy and came with tambourines and cymbals to thank me."[45]

In his article 'L'œuvre de Msgr. Rossillon', Bishop Joseph Baud commented that Fr. Payraud, who did heroic work in the Padangui and Parlakimidi areas, used to give money to the neophytes on the pretext of compensating for a day's work on Sunday when they attended church services. In due time this became a regular practice and the people started to demand it. Once they even threatened to quit the mission if they did not get their due.[46] Some of village chiefs who threatened and intimidated the neophytes became friendlier after receiving presents.[47] Fr. Descombes claimed that in 1897, when he spent two days in Gojolibady, he noticed the misery of the people and so distributed rice after Mass. Such generosity might have solved an immediate problem and may have brought respect for the missionaries; it also created dependence on them.[48]

The Panos described their misery as labourers when the missionary visited them. Sometimes he not only comforted them but also gave them alms, especially to satisfy their immediate needs. In the following account, Fr. Muffat described how the missionaries gathered the people for instruction or prayers in the villages:

> That evening, at sundown, the missionary and his catechist call the people for prayers. Gradually people come and form a group around them. They do it very slowly: in this country nobody is in a hurry [because one cannot be hard on them in this place]. Finally, all are gathered. The priest, sitting on a stone, makes them repeat the prayers. Those who remember the prayers are rare. They will learn them again. Time and again, a goat or a pig comes to interrupt the gathering, but nobody is disturbed, and the prayers continue. After 15 days of instruction, all make their confession and those who learned the instructions well receive communion. To crown the feast, the Father gives a few rupees, with which they kill an old cow for the feast of the villagers.[49]

Though such practices fostered a friendly rapport with the people, soon it became obligatory for the missionaries to provide food whenever the people came together for a celebration. The missionaries were expected to pay for the feast. In one of his letters, Msgr. Tissot wrote that if the Kondhs were to be converted, the mission was obliged to provide them with better clothes, so that they could enter the chapel with dignity.[50] Despite the fact that some priests distributed money during times of need, it does not follow that the missionaries in general maintained the mission through the lure of money. The missionaries' funds were usually too limited to meet all of their own needs.

Negative Influences

Though they readily acknowledged the simplicity and friendliness of the Kondhs, the missionaries were not free of feelings of superiority, which most Europeans had in that era. They were convinced of their mission to civilise the natives and that coloured every step they took. Remarks like, 'their colour is not only black but also their souls', and 'half Negroes who live in the world of fables' represent the prejudices of the time.[51] Even though these comments were uttered in isolation, they were representative of the age. Although this attitude did not block the expansion of the church, it did raise some barriers between the missionaries and the Panos and Kondhs of Ganjam.

Comfort of the Missionaries

The missionaries had renounced all 'comforts and conveniences' for the sake of God's kingdom, yet they found it impossible to live this out literally during their stay in the mountains. Sometimes they were reluctant to go to the interior, even where there were greater possibilities for conversions.[52] The missionaries never travelled alone but in a caravan.[53] Sometimes they were carried on a palanquin or else rode on horseback. Due to the large caravan that accompanied them on their expeditions, they were seen as '*Sahibs*' or lords, and the people had a reverential fear of them. Though they claimed to eat simple meals of rice and *charu* (a Telugu word for curry) the food of the poor, they usually took along a cook and provisions for their expedition. When they were in the mountains, their servants returned to Surada to procure provisions.

Gangpur Mission

As mentioned earlier, the Chotanagpur mission experienced a *Mouvement de la Grâce* as it spread to the neighbouring semi-independent states of Gangpur and Jashpur. Certain factors contributed to the expansion.

a. Similarity of Lives

The expansion towards Gangpur was natural for the Jesuits, particularly when they realised that the inhabitants of the state belonged to the same tribes and were even related to the people of Chotanagpur. When the people of Gangpur heard about the progress of their relatives across the border, they too wanted to avail themselves of the help of the missionaries. This prompted them to send deputations to the nearest station across the border. When the missionaries established the first station at Kesramal, they did not spend much time studying the economic and cultural conditions of the people in order to adopt a suitable missionary method. They just applied the same method that was used across the border.[54] Unlike some missions, where the missionaries went out looking for adherents, the Tribals in Gangpur came to the missionaries and asked them to visit their villages. The missionaries simply responded to their requests.

b. Exploitation: An Immediate Cause

The immediate cause for the mass movement among the Chotanagpur tribals was their exploitation by the landlords, moneylenders and petty officials of the government -- especially the encroachment upon their tenancy rights and the demand for excessive *bethbegari* (free labour). Land alienation and incessant harassment by their powerful neighbours forced them to align themselves together for protection. Since they felt helpless, they were ready to follow anyone who could liberate them from their situation. The missionaries came at the right time and were willing to champion their cause.

At the same time tribals, who believed in malign spirits and held that they were tormented by them. It was their belief that, in order to obtain peace, they had to appease the malign spirits with certain prescribed sacrifices. Fr. S. Fuchs, a leading cultural anthropologist, commented on the plight of tribals in India in this way: "Ignorant of the true laws of nature and the cosmic order, the tribals are strongly convinced that all happenings in the world and in their own lives are controlled by deities and spirits. Especially in times of distress, sickness and misfortune, the latter have to be invoked, propitiated and urged to bring relief."[55] Thus fear and helplessness in both the spiritual and material worlds forced the tribals to seek the protection of the missionaries. They needed a superior power to liberate them from rapacious spirits and from *Dikus* (foreigners or outsiders). Christianity with its monotheistic doctrine of a loving God who is ever-ready to forgive wrongdoers was a welcome relief to them.

In those areas where oppression by the zamindars was intense and the rapacity of the moneylenders most cruel, people were quick to accept Christianity. In their conversion to Christianity, they gained not only the courage to pursue justice for themselves but also the active support of the missionaries. The influence of the European missionaries with the government was a further impetus for conversion. With their newly-found faith and backed by dedicated and competent European missionaries, the tribals became reluctant to pay any extra or illegal taxes in support of temples, rites and ceremonies. They even threatened to expose such practices to the proper authorities.

c. Conversion as Social Change

Conversion to Catholicism meant a social change, what the tribals called a change of *Samaj* or society. This was tantamount to losing one's identity as a tribal person. As mentioned earlier, the identity of the tribal person was woven into society, and ostracism was a death sentence. Having realised this innate principle of tribal solidarity, Fr. Lievens and the missionaries who followed him received the people in groups and even discouraged individual conversions. Probably this was one of the reasons for the initial hesitation among the tribals to accept Catholicism. As one of the missionaries stated:

> What prevents the Hindus and Protestants to come over to Catholicism is just that conversion to Catholicism means a change of social status, a passage from one *Samaj* to another. So, when they get an opportunity to leave their *Samaj*, or when providence in some way or other forces them to abandon their group, they take up the Catholic faith as they had been waiting for it.[56]

Thus, the people's hesitation to enter the church was not due to the religious demands of Catholicism but to tribal solidarity. In fact, the defections among the *Kisans* or *Berga Oraons* was a result of such solidarity. The *Kisans* had been unable to find suitable marriage partners from their tribal community within the Catholic Church. As a result, many of them left the faith.[57] Such solidarity required a village *Panchayat* before making a decision to call the missionary.

Mission Assistants Introduced by Fr. Lievens

In the hope of reaching out to more people and of supervising those already baptised (especially their external practice of religion, such as daily prayers and preparation for the sacraments), Fr. Lievens instituted two important offices in the Chotanagpur mission: the catechists and the *chaprasis*. The first was a traditional office in the church, while the second was typical of Chotanagpur.

a. Catechists

Catechists or *Pracharaks* were (and still are) primary assistants of the missionaries. They acted as intermediaries between them and the people. Each catechist had his *Ilakha* or circle, which he had to supervise. Besides leading the daily prayers, he had to conduct the Sunday liturgy in those chapels where the priest was unable to come for the Mass. He presided at village meetings (especially *Panchayat*) and reported on the progress of the village when the catechists gathered for their monthly meeting or *Tarikh*.[58] They were also to instruct the *Chaprasis* on to how to conduct the Sunday prayers in the village. Concerned with the growth of Catholics in faith, they saw to it that the children went to school and prepared them for the sacraments.

b. *Chaprasis*

The *Chaprasis*[59] were secondary assistants in the Chotanagpur mission. They were, in fact, the local guardians of Christian villages. They were generally influential persons in the village who looked after its religious activities. The *Chaprasis* were placed in all the important villages. They supervised the life of the neophytes, e.g., with regard to Sunday prayers and rest. They guarded against all superstitious practices, like sacrifices and sorcery. They reported the progress of the community to the priest in charge of the village. Although it was not a full-time job, it was an effective means of establishing contact with the villagers. Even in trivial disputes a local man could more easily settle the affair, since most of the inhabitants of the village were related to each other.[60] By 1914 the catechists grew in number, but the mass conversions that required additional workers came to a halt, and the financial constraints of World War I forced the missionaries to put an end to role of the *Chaprasis*. Though their pay was modest, the suppression of the *Chaprasis* brought financial relief to the mission.

Educational and Socio-economic Projects

The missionaries thought that liberation from socio-economic misery would lead to conversions. But they were also aware that economic progress without education would contribute little to the development of a tribal society. However, they did not introduce anything new in Gangpur but simply repeated what had been done in Chotanagpur.[61]

Catholic Schools

Like other Christian missions in India, the Jesuits attached great importance to the education of Catholic children, which they believed would change the face of the tribal society.[62] Therefore the establishment of schools was pivotal for realising such aims. Though the Jesuits followed the traditional system of education, they excelled in the organisation of schools. They established a network of schools that were supervised by a priest who resided at the centre. The missionaries themselves were involved in the apostolate of education, which had long-term effects in the overall development of the tribal populace. In their curriculum the Catholic schools were not different from the schools run by the state, except for the teaching of religion and morals.

The schools of Chotanagpur and Gangpur were coordinated under a diocesan Director of Schools, appointed by the Archbishop of Calcutta. The director had the following responsibilities: (1) periodic visits to the village schools; (2) checking the regularity of the teachers and examining their skills in teaching; (3) providing a uniform syllabus for all the schools in the mission, especially for catechism; and (4) conducting a central examination of the students, whose answer papers were later sent to Ranchi for evaluation.[63] Illustrating the work of the director, Fr. Vermeire wrote: "His [Director's] periodical visits and checking of registers, his examination of the boys and talks with the parents, etc., show to the people of the village that some importance is attached to the work of the school, and gradually the people themselves will be more in earnest about the school of their village."[64] The Daughters of the Cross were called from Chaibasa to look after the education of women in Gangpur.

Village Schools and their Impact

The high rate of illiteracy in Gangpur urged the missionaries to establish schools even in the interior villages. Besides educating the Catholic children in the villages, the schools were expected to train the Christians in the faith. Fr. L. van Hoeck, as the Inspector of Schools, wrote:

> There can, however, be no doubt that in several instances these schools have been the means of saving villages that were growing lukewarm; that in villages where one of our schools exists, some time is devoted every day to religious instruction; and the missionaries in whose districts the schools are working well, will agree that they have been a help to raise the tone of the whole Catholic Community.[65]

The multiplication of village schools was intended to provide education to as many children as possible, who otherwise would have to go to boarding schools, which were expensive. In order to promote education among Catholic boys in the interior, the missionaries introduced scholarships for meritorious students. Some of them were taken from the village schools and were sent to central schools, where the missionaries accompanied them.[66] Besides giving secular lessons, the teachers were expected to impart religious education to the children. In order to pay the teachers and to maintain the school, the missionaries (wherever possible) introduced a system of local support.[67]

In their quest to raise the standard of the schools run by the mission, the missionaries invited all the primary school teachers for an annual gathering during which teaching methods were taught.[68] As in Chotanagpur, the schools were primarily meant for Catholics and others were admitted only when there was enough room. Hence, they were not primarily used as a means for conversion. At the same time, one cannot rule out the possibility that some non-Catholic students were influenced by the missionaries and sought baptism.[69]

The Catholic Cooperative Bank

The Catholic Cooperative Bank of Chotanagpur, the brainchild of Fr. John Baptist Hoffmann, produced positive results in Chotanagpur. Seeing its success, Fr. Sylvain Grosjean requested Msgr. Meuleman to grant permission to start one in Kesramal as well.[70] In his letter dated October 18, 1912, the Archbishop granted the permission on condition that the money deposited would not be put to the personal use of the missionaries.[71] Immediately Fr. Alary wrote a charter on that of the Catholic Cooperative Bank of Chotanagpur. The objectives of the bank were: (1) "to impart to the members of the Roman Catholic Mission the moral and economic training which will in course of time enable them to constitute themselves into a system of federated autonomous cooperative credit societies with their central bank in Ranchi and (2) to offer them the full advantages of cooperation during this period of training."[72]

The British government stipulated that the permission of the raja should be sought before starting a cooperative society in any semi-independent state. Accordingly, a petition to start a cooperative bank in his territory was sent to the Raja of Gangpur in 1910. But the raja did not approve the new enterprise, and so the missionaries had to run the bank with their own resources. They began it with a modest deposit, which later was increased when each member deposited the amount of 5 francs.[73] On November 12, 1912, Fr. Hoffmann was in Gangpur to explain the aims and the operations of the Catholic Cooperative Bank.[74] In 1917 the bank counted 400 members and assets of 4,000 francs. By 1920 there were 1,200 members with assets of Rs. 5,400.[75]

Initially the bank functioned well and enjoyed the cooperation of its members. However, it soon encountered difficulties when some of the members purposely failed to pay back the loans. Yet the bank was able to rescue some of the tribals from the exploitation of usurious moneylenders. The bank lent money to the tribals so that they could begin a trade, which was usually controlled by either the Hindus or the Muslims.[76] Membership was restricted to Catholics and catechumens. The catechumens could not avail themselves of the benefits of loans, if they failed to receive baptism.[77]

One of the basic reasons for the failure of the Adivasis' business ventures was their soft heart for others. They could not say no to borrowers, particularly if they happened to be close relatives – and everyone considered himself a close relative to one who was economically well off.[78]

Nisha Sangat, the Temperance Society

The missionaries realised that the drunkenness of tribals was one of the root causes of their backwardness, and they tried to remedy the situation with some concrete steps. Alcoholism not only was ruining the tribal economy but also led to immoral behaviour of its members. Since tribal solidarity was an essential feature of their culture, the missionaries realised that an association to liberate the people from drunkenness would be acceptable. This idea led to the formation of the *Nisha Sangat*. The missionaries required subscription to *Nisha Sangat* in order to obtain membership in the cooperative societies. The missionaries understood that without any pressure the tribals might not adhere to the scheme. It was also felt that to forbid drinking among the tribals would be too high a sacrifice on their part. Therefore, the missionaries tolerated the use of *Hanria* or rice beer, but they warned that certain limits should not be exceeded.

Nisha Sangat, or Temperance Society was started in Gangpur in 1912.[79] Fr. Alary spent much time drafting the rules of the organisation, based on similar rules adopted in Biru (Ranchi District). Fr. Clement Beck, a veteran SVD missionary, later commented on the relevance of the Jesuit initiative: "After several meetings with the people, the Fathers convinced many of the evils of drink and persuaded them to sign a pledge abstaining from liquor. In many villages, these societies worked well."[80] There were two approaches: (1) those who took a simple oath for one year (*chhota karar*), the visible sign of which was a leather bracelet; and (2) those who took a solemn oath for several years, the visible sign of which was a cross tattooed on the wrist (*bara karar*).

The promise to abstain from *Daru* or country liquor was occasionally required from those applying for loans from the cooperative bank.[81] In spite of such stringent measures, there were some renegades. They fined those who were caught, and the proceeds of the collected fines were used for school purposes. In order to enforce the regulations regarding the prohibition of alcohol, the missionaries sought the help of *Panches* (village councillors).

However, nothing was said about the eradication of drunkenness in the *Litterae Annuae* of 1915.[82] The people had their way of taking to drink once they were back in the villages. The drinking habits of tribal Catholics were so widespread that their crusade against it was regularly discussed in missionary meetings between 1915 and 1925 in Ranchi.[83] In spite of the stringent measures proposed during such meetings, the missionaries could not completely eradicate the habit of drinking. Fr. Vermeire mentioned that in 1915, in spite of the enforcement of Temperance Society in Kesramal, alcoholism was still high among the tribal Christians of Gangpur.[84] The *Nisha Sangat* created an awareness of the problem among the people, but only with the undeterred cooperation of all could this longstanding evil be extirpated from tribal society.

Dhan Gola, the Granary

The *Dhan Gola* or granary[85] was another organization meant to enable the tribals to become independent at the most critical time of the year economically: during the monsoon and the summer, when they borrowed money from the landlords or moneylenders, who normally charged exorbitant interest. Like the cooperative bank, this organisation ran entirely on the investments of the tribals. "The people at the time of harvest could deposit grain for safe-keeping and could draw from it when they felt the need in the difficult summer days ahead when grain was scarce."[86]

It was the responsibility of the catechist to collect paddy and store it in a common *Dhan Gola* (a storeroom). Later, at the beginning of the sowing season, it was sold at a modest price.[87] Each family contributed according to its ability, and the village elders (or a committee selected by the people) would later distribute the grain to those in need. At the time of the harvest, the elders collected the amount given out plus a nominal interest, which was used both for organisational expenses and for the education of children.[88] The people were taught to save for difficult times. However, in case of an emergency, they were advised to borrow from the community rather than from a *Sahu* or merchant.[89] As a rule the accounts of the *Dhan Gola* were kept with the catechist and were checked periodically by the missionary. In July 1917 there were about 26,000 kilograms of rice in the villages of Gangpur. Though modest, it was a good beginning. However, the *Dhan Gola* did not succeed, since the participants failed to return the amount on time. As more members defaulted, the organisation was gradually shut down.[90]

Fr. Hoffmann claimed that the *Dhan Gola* required no investment from the mission, since the people provided the capital. The mission's responsibility was to store the grain on mission property.[91]

Response to Natural Calamities

The missionaries took every effort to be the first ones to help the victims of natural calamities. Immediately after the founding of the parish of Kesramal a famine struck Gangpur. The missionaries responded to it with charity. The Archbishop made great sacrifices in order to take care of the famine-stricken people.[92] Added to this tragedy was an outbreak of cholera during and after the monsoon. This was again followed by smallpox. The missionaries made use of the opportunity to practice their charity, which gained the confidence of people.[93]

Enforcing Factors for the *Mouvement de la Grâce*

In their efforts to evangelise the tribals, the missionaries made use of some tribal organisations and customs. Since these organisations were operative in all the mission centres, the missionaries found it easy to animate them.

Panchayat

Panchayat is one of the ancient political structures of the tribals. It is the highest legislative, executive and judicial authority in a tribal village. All society matters were decided in the *Panchayat*, which was composed of the elders of the village, who had the authority to settle all issues except murder. The aborigines love gatherings and public discussions where one can express his opinion freely. Since the *Panchayat* had a lasting impact on the life of the aborigines, the missionaries did not want to eliminate it. Rather, they adopted a similar system, naming it the *Catholic Sabha*.[94]

The *Catholic Sabha* did not have any legislative, executive and judicial authority. Its competence was limited to recommendations to the *Panchayat* for its execution.[95] Contrary to the *Unnati Samaj* of the Lutherans (GEL), the *Catholic Sabha* was purely religious and Catholic in nature. Its constitution declared that the *Catholic Sabha* was to be guided by Catholic principles and the teaching of the magisterium -- both the universal magisterium of the Pope and the local magisterium of the bishop. Therefore, there were no appeals to the bishop's decisions. An Executive Committee was set up to prepare the agenda for the meetings, but the honorary president (who as a rule was the missionary of the village) had the power to veto unnecessary issues such as purely political issues.[96]

Among other things, the assembly regulated the use of rice beer during feasts and other important occasions in the village. It forbade the members from taking part in pagan dances. It requested the *Panches* (a council of five in a village *Panchayat*) to mete out punishment to delinquents when the latter broke the law. Though the people's participation in such assemblies was high, religious issues were always left to the missionary. Though there was a *Panchayat* in all the villages, the guiding power of the Christians was always the missionary. The *Panchayati* system suffered a setback when the zamindars settled in the village. They did not want to see the traditional village tribunal working independently of their authority.

Cultural Adaptation

Right from the beginning of the Chotanagpur mission, the Jesuits adopted a cautious policy regarding the adaptation of certain feasts into the liturgy. Knowing well that the tribal feasts were pivotal to tribal identity, the missionaries chose those which were very important, and which could be accommodated to the Catholic faith. In christianising the tribal feasts, the missionaries insisted on using the solar calendar. This often resulted in a double celebration, as the tribals preferred to use the lunar calendar. The tribals loved their dances, which had a strong communal character. The tribal dances expressed their joy and happiness. They performed dances for various occasions, such as birth, marriage, harvest, etc. Accompanied by the beat of drums called *Mandar*, the tribals sang songs of joy and happiness -- and sometimes of sorrow. Fr. Lievens and the first generation of missionaries approved the dances, if they were performed in their villages.[97]

Annual Retreats

Annual retreats were an effective way to impart knowledge about Christianity. The missionaries used to gather the Christians in two groups, men and women separately, for three days at the centre.[98] Sometimes they were fed, but when the mission experienced financial problems, the candidates were asked to bring along some uncooked rice and lentils. Such gatherings were very helpful for the missionaries who otherwise found it difficult to go to all the villages. If they did go to the villages, they often did not have enough time for spiritual activities other than the administering of sacraments. Much of the time was spent on *Panchayat*.[99] The missionaries also organised what they called '*Dharma Schools*', where young and old would gather together for instruction. Commenting on such schools, P. Tete observed: "Father organised *Dharma Schools* where besides intensive religious instructions and prayers, they witnessed Christian life."[100]

Missionary Meetings

From the beginning the Chotanagpur mission organised annual missionary meetings which all missionaries were expected to attend. In these meetings the missionaries, together with the bishop and the superior regular of the Bengal Mission, evaluated their work and planned for the future.

Christianity and Social Change

The Jesuits – as well as the Fransalians – often appealed to the courts and the zamindars in order to help the tribals to regain their lost rights over land.[101] Unlike the zamindars and usurious moneylenders, the missionaries looked at the tribals as persons deserving dignity and respect. The mission schools, hospitals and other institutions not only provided service but also helped their tribal converts to find meaningful employment. They became teachers, preachers, cooks, nurses, *Chaprasis* (peons) and *Malis* (gardeners).[102]

The missionaries also encouraged the tribals to confide in them and to contribute towards the maintenance of their catechists and pastors, which helped them in the long run to be self-reliant. The traditional beliefs and customs certainly underwent a radical change -- and is still in the process of transformation. The leap from *Sarna* or sacred grove[103] to *Girja* or church, from *Sal* tree to educational institutions, from traditional to modern and from old to new, necessarily involved sacrifice. The changes were sometimes painful and led to misunderstandings and misgivings about the missionaries. Only time could solve such tensions.[104]

Christianity acknowledged and adapted tribal structures such as the *Panchayat* and other assemblies. Hence, the tribals did not feel that everything was totally new. However, Christianity gave them a new sense of belonging and identity. Before the arrival of the missionaries, agriculture was the only option, and it depended on rain. The more productive lands were in the hands of usurious zamindars. Besides providing employment to the tribals in a cooperative bank, schools, hospitals and other institutions, the missionaries promoted the idea of self-respect and basic rights to the land.[105] The various welfare programmes of the missionaries developed not only the people's confidence and creativity but also their capacity to be a tribal church.

Negative Aspects

The missionaries were not perfect. They also had a "shadow" side, which however did not stop the spread of the gospel, even if it occasionally set up obstacles to it.

Mixed Motives

Not all the people who entered the church came with spiritual motives. Some became Catholics to obtain protection from oppressive elements. Others joined because their relatives were already in the church. Some entered the church because the missionaries were charitable, particularly when the tribals and dalits were ill and hungry. Hence, their motives were mixed. Fr. de Gryse commented: "In my opinion the *Bergas* of Latalaga are people who want to be under the protection of the *Sahib* [missionaries] and nothing more."[106]

Identity as Europeans

The European identity of the missionaries was advantageous to the mission. Besides having easy access to authorities, the missionaries felt confident that government officials would be neutral, if not ardently sympathetic to missionary efforts in Orissa, and would grant their requests and be favourable towards the neophytes. Without the good services of Mr. Christian, dewan of Gangpur, it would have been difficult for the missionaries to procure a plot of land in Kesramal. He also protected them from the calumnious attacks of zamindars and others. British officials were not against the conversion of tribals and dalits, but they expected the missionaries to respect the rules of public preaching (e.g., not to preach in the market as some Protestant pastors did). Neither were the British officials averse to establishing vernacular schools (e.g., Hindi schools), provided the mission did not seek grants-in-aid from the government.

To some extent, the British occupation of India helped in the planting of Christianity. However, sometimes it was also a stumbling block. For the most part, the missionaries were not aided by the British government but were quite independent of it.[107]

The Missionaries' View of the Catechists

One of the recurring complaints of the Catholic missionaries was the inefficiency and lack of dedication of the catechists. Though the Catholic missionaries heavily relied on the catechists in their work with the tribals, they were not always satisfied with them. Missionaries like Fr. van Robays praised the work of the catechists, but others like Fr. de Gryse were rather tough on them. He wrote: "We work here with quite inferior material. The least one should expect from catechists is that they be somewhat honest. I am not afraid to say that with a few exceptions; my catechists are a set of drunkards and deceivers."[108]

Initially the catechists' training was left to the missionary, who gave them instruction when he was free. In the absence of a centralised training programme, it was impossible to know the candidates well. Fr. Alary wrote: "The majority of our catechists are not masters of the situation. Therefore, our results are less shining."[109] Interestingly enough, the diaries and reports of the missionaries are almost silent about the work of the catechists!

The following sentences of S. Neill convey the general attitude of the missionaries towards Indian Christians. He wrote:

> It is plain from the records that the primary concern of almost all the missionaries was well-being of the people whom they had come to serve. But human motives are never entirely pure and unmixed. All too often the missionary held that he could judge better of the real interests of his people than they could themselves; his objectivity was blurred by a certain patronizing, and sometimes even contemptuous attitude towards men whom he could never quite persuade himself to regard as grown up.[110]

Christianity and Other Religions

For the Catholic missionaries, Roman Catholicism was the only true religion. Despite such absolutist or exclusive outlook, they refrained from attacking other religions seriously. However, there are occasional remarks about the sacrifices to Thakurani and religious piety in Jagannath Puri. Fr. Décarre explained the necessity of constructing a church in Puri, which could serve the people. They criticised the horrendous Meriah sacrifice and some other oppressive practices.[111]

But, except for a few missionaries, like Fr. Joseph Seigneur, very few of them took the trouble to learn about the Hindus of Orissa. However, Msgr. Rossillon expressed the need to view Hinduism with openness. He said: "The system hitherto followed by many in refuting Hinduism, viz, to try to show that in Hinduism everything is wrong, irritates the cultured Hindus and it is not therefore conducive to good results. There are things in Hinduism, which are indifferent and even good and need not to be given up by Hindus whey they become Christians."[112]

Catholics and Non-Catholic Missionaries

The Catholic missionaries competed with the Baptists in the Ganjam mission and the Gossner Evangelical Lutherans (GEL) in Gangpur. The Baptists residing in Berhampur seem to be genuinely hostile towards the MSFS in Ganjam. But except for the gratitude expressed at their generous contribution towards the construction of a chapel in Berhampur, no kind word about them ever came from the mouths of the Catholic missionaries. Fr. Bonaventure called them 'the enemies of the Catholic Church' who seemed to have obtained conversions through the lure of money.[113] The mentality of the era dictated that the work of the Protestants had to be combated, and Catholics were exhorted to avoid being contaminated by their doctrine.[114]

From the beginning there was competition among the different Christian denominations working in Gangpur and Chotanagpur. In fact, it was the spread of Lutheranism in Gangpur that motivated the missionaries to expand their own efforts. The pious Jesuits of the Chotanagpur mission braved all obstacles in order to meet the needs of Catholics across the border. Discussing the vulnerability of the Catholics in Gangpur, Fr. Cardon warned that the Catholics might fall into the hands of the Lutherans, who are 'our arch-enemies'.[115] In his letter to Fr. General, Fr. Alary wrote: "Before our arrival [in Gangpur], Lutherans had practically conquered the country. They had established themselves in Gangpur with schools, houses, etc. Then we could not but make rare visits. The majority of our

Christians come from them. But it is impossible or near to impossible to conquer them as they are absolutely attached to their mission."[116]

World War I

World War I had a devastating effect on the progress of the mission. It could not count on reinforcements to take care of even the existing stations. Even before the war began, the MSFS lacked personnel. Jean Rey recorded that between 1908 and 1914 Fr. Bouvard, superior general of the MSFS, could send no more missionaries to India apart from Fr. Larrivaz and the ten scholastics who did their studies at St. Charles Seminary in Nagpur.[117]

World War I also devastated the mission's finances. The missionaries were asked to cut their expenses, even if it meant they had to reduce the number of *Chaprasis*.[118] The catechumenate had to be closed, and it was not reopened until 1921.[119] The missionaries were forced during the war to increase local contributions. Previously the catechumens were fed during the catechumenate, but now the missionaries insisted that the catechumens bring sufficient cooked food or rice and lentils for themselves during their stay in the parish. This requirement proved useful even later.[120]

The Problem of Language

The MSFS had to battle with different languages, which definitely consumed quite a bit of their energy, particularly when they had to learn a language like *Kui* without an organised method. Except for a few missionaries (such as Frs. Dupont and Descombes), most remained in the Ganjam mission for a short period of time. Short assignments and frequent transfers certainly would not have encouraged the missionaries to learn the local language. In Gangpur, besides the tribal languages, the people spoke Oriya, the language of the state. Most of the people did not understand Hindi. Therefore, the missionaries found it difficult to instruct them in the faith.[121]

Other Shadowy Aspects of the Mission

The neophytes tended to take the European missionaries as models, and thus they were prone to adopting Western customs and attitudes. This was evident in their food, clothing, use of names, manners and attitude. Though the missionaries discouraged them from adopting Western dress and habits, the converts did so anyway. They probably gave the Christians a new identity and new security in Indian society. They could then boast that the 'white man' protected them, and they considered themselves superior to the rest of the villagers (that is, to non-Christians).[122]

Catholic missionaries also tended to tolerate the use of alcoholic drinks such as *Hanria* (rice beer) and *Kallu* (palm wine). Though these concessions attracted Protestants, many Catholics were marked by excessive drinking.[123]

Finally, although the missionaries envisaged a self-reliant church in both personnel and finances, the church in Orissa continued to look to the West for both.

Conclusion

The methods and problems discussed in this chapter should not to be taken in isolation. All the missionaries who worked in Orissa were possessed by the desire to proclaim God's love to the people. In order to realise this goal, the missionaries resorted to various methods, which they considered just and suitable for their particular situation. Though these methods to some extent produced the desired results in the Ganjam mission, they did not always promote continuity. The approaches were modified when a new missionary took charge, which often baffled the people. This lack of continuity did not destroy the mission, but it sometimes created problems.

The Belgian Jesuits in Gangpur continued to use the same methods that were operative in Chotanagpur, which produced good results. The great distances between the villages, the scarcity of personnel and the shortage of funds put limitations on their activities. However, the enthusiasm and response of the people encouraged the missionaries to face difficulties and to challenge oppressive situations.

The Belgian Jesuits of the Chotanagpur mission and the French Fransalians of the Ganjam mission were not left alone in their work. One could say that the people of Belgium and France, who contributed spiritually and materially to the mission, helped to make the church in Orissa what it is today.

Endnotes

[1] DEWI MORGEN, "Christian Expansion Since 1900", in S. NEILL (ed.), Twentieth Century Christianity, London 1961, p. 245.

[2] A letter of Fr. Bonaventure portrays the mentality of the epoch and the sense of urgency which the missionaries felt: "Dans l'Inde le missionnaire a sous les

yeux un carnaval perpétuel, chaque indien est un masque en réalité. Son âme est en la possession du démon; son visage tatoué, caricature en cent façons diverses, porte les détestables empreintes de la bête; et cette vue continuelle dégoûte bientôt les plus entichés des mascarades du carnaval." Bonaventure to his uncle, Surada, February 21, 1882, AMSFS 5H5-2/2.

[3] S. NEILL, A History of Christianity in India 1707 – 1858, vol. II, Cambridge 1985, p. 394.

[4] Fr. Avrillon wrote: "Vous serez étonnés de voir une procession le soir de la fête des rois. Ici de la part des supérieurs autorisés, même les missionnaires ont la permission de faire ce que demandent les circonstances et le bien des âmes." Avrillon to Superior, Palcondah, (no date and month) 1867, AMSFS 5H5-2/1.

[5] Recording the positive influence of the catechumenate in the mission, Fr. Tissot wrote: "Ils perderaient leurs habitudes sauvages . . . et se formaient facilement aux habitudes religieuses". J.M. Tissot to Monsieur Mermier, Surada, June 30, 1859, AMSFS 5H5-2/1; Descombes to J. Tissot, Surada, May 8, 1883, AMSFS 5H5-2/2. Some of the missionaries considered the behaviour of the people to be 'half-savage'. But through fervent prayers and other spiritual activities the missionaries saw a change in the neophytes. Cf. Msgr. Clerc to a priest in France, Visakhapatnam, April 9, 1913, AMSFS 5H5-2/4.

[6] As a sign of their baptism, the Christians were given a medal to wear that usually aroused the curiosity of their non-Christian neighbours. Cf. Descombes to Tissot, Katingia, August 9, 1888, AMSFS 5H5-2/2.

[7] Although it is not clear as to what the 'thorough spiritual formation' consisted of, the missionary claimed to have given it to the catechumens. It might have been the daily recitation of prayers and attendance at Mass and obviously a protection from 'superstitious and pagan beliefs'. F. Moget, Early Days of Visakhapatnam Mission 1846 – 1920, p. 251.

[8] Bonaventure to the Superior General, Fr. J. Tissot, Surada, October 30, 1881, AMSFS; Bonaventure to his uncle, Surada, February 21, 1882, AMSFS 5H5-2/2. Fr. Cyrille thought that a similar method would be useful for Surada. He wrote: "Achetez des terres ayez beaucoup de riziéres et établissez les catechumenats." Cyrille to Superior General, Surada, December 15, 1915, AMSFS 5H5-2/4. The documents in the General Archives are silent about the results such a method produced, except that at a later date some of the families settled in the property of the mission sold the land and went to work in the tea gardens of Assam; In his report to the Sacred Congregation Msgr. Neyret wrote about the usefulness of the method for the Ganjam mission. Cf. Msgr. Neyret, "Recit Succint de l'état de la Mission de Vizagapatam. Depuis son origine, le 16 mars, jusqu'à sa division en deux Diocèses de Vizagapatam et de Nagpur le 29 juillet 1887", Vizagapatam, April 11, 1888, APF Indie Orientali: Scritture Riferite nei Congressi, vol. 33, f. 282.

[9] While the Jesuits in Gangpur insisted on the contribution of the participants for their maintenance during the retreat, it is not clear whether the MSFS insisted on it. In all likelihood, they may have provided for the stay.

[10] B.M. BOAL, "The Church in the Kond Hills", in V.E.W. HAYWARD (ed.), The Church as Christian Community. Three Studies of North Indian States, London 1966, p. 308.

[11] Bonaventure to his uncle, Surada, December 5, 1881, AMSFS 5H5-2/2. In a similar way the servants of the missionaries had condemned the culpable to the strokes of a cane. Cf. Anthony Nidhi to Suiffet, Didrobady, July 1909, AMSFS 5H5-2/3.

[12] The resentment of the residents to the paternalistic approach of the missionaries led to a fundamental question: was the approach adopted by the missionaries right, or did they fail to understand the people they were dealing with? Descombes, Surada, May 1889, AMSFS 5H5-2/2.

[13] Fr. Descombes illustrated how the neophytes attracted their relatives: "Ils ont dit 'vous nous connaissez, nous sommes de votre caste et nous sommes chrétiens, faites comme nous, les diables ne nous font jamais souffrir, sommes nous malades, le père vient nous voir, il nous donne des médecines et il nous guérit, quand il y a des querelles entre nous il nous réconcilie, avons-nous des tracasseris de la part d'autrui, le père nous protége et prend notre cause en mains'." Descombes to Tissot, Katingia, August 9, 1888, AMSFS 5H5-2/2.

[14] Fr. Descombes wrote that the people prayed in front of the statue of Our Lady: "Mahaprabou moté bolo coro: habeo me sanum". Ibid.

[15] Msgr. Tissot wrote: "Il est à remarquer que les écoles sont un grand moyen d'avoir accès auprés des Indiens, d'acquérir sur eux de l'influence, de diminuer leur préjugés et de leur communiquer les vérités chrétiennes." Msgr. Tissot, Copie du Compte-rendu général de l'établissement du progrès, et de l'état actuel du vicariat apostolique de Vizagapatam. Envoyé à Msgr. Agliardi, Délégat Apostolique dans l'Inde, APF Indie Orientali: Scritture Riferite nei Congressi, vol. 26 (1886), f. 661.

[16] Cf. Tissot to Gaiddon, Yanaon, November 21, 1859, AMSFS 5H5-2/1.

[17] It is interesting to note the comments of Fr. Marolliat in one of the letters to his brother: "Grâce a Dieu, ils ne peuvent pas me faire beaucoup de mal, car j'ai les deux chefs de caste les plus influents de mon côté, et je les tiens solidement attachés mon char grâce à des prêts d'argent que je leur ai faits." MAROLLIAT, "Informations Diverses: Vizagapatam (Hindoustan)", in LMC 46 (1914), p. 171.

[18] Rey to the Director, Cuttack, August 6, 1884, AMSFS 5H5-2/2.

[19] The frustration of the missionaries and their superiors is clear in the letter of Msgr. Neyret. He wrote: "Donc si toutes les tentatives de nos pères à convertir les païens de caste . . . nous prouvant qu'il n'y a absolument rien a espérer de cette race". Neyret to Monsieur Mermier, Visakhapatnam, August 20, 1860, AMSFS 5H5-2/1.

[20] V. CRONIN, "Malabar Rites Controversy", in The New Catholic Encyclopaedia, vol. IX, p. 98.

[21] M. Domenge wrote: "Il faudra christianiser leurs fêtes et leurs coutumes, leur accorder, sans trop de restrictions, tous les divertissements que la religion ne condamne pas, quelque étranges qu'ils paraissent à nos yeux, et savoir se taire sur bien des choses jusqu'à ce qu'on ait assez d'empire sur eux pour les persuader de mieux agir. Si le missionnaire sait se faire comme l'un d'eux, vivre avec eux, prendre part à leurs joies et à leurs peines, arranger leurs querelles, les assister dans leurs besoins et les élever peu à peu à son propre niveau, en s'abaissant jusqu'à eux, sans cependant jamais s'avilir, peut-être ne sera-t-il pas impossible de voir un jour refleurir chez ces peuples quelques-unes des merveilles du Paraguay." M. DOMENGE, "Au Pays des Khondes", in LMC 25 (1883), p. 484.

[22] Descombes to J. Tissot, Surada, January 8, 1883, AMSFS 5H5-2/2.

[23] Fr. Descombes described the solemn procession he conducted in Surada on Easter Sunday. Cf. Descombes to J. Tissot, Surada, May 8, 1883, AMSFS 5H5-2/2.

[24] Avrillon to Msgr. Clerc, Berhampur, July 7, 1897, AMSFS 5H5-2/3.

[25] M. DOMENGE, La Mission de Vizagapatam, p. 355.

[26] Fr. Descombes thought that the prayers composed by the missionaries were influenced by Sanskrit, with the result that they were not understood. Cf. Descombes to Tissot, Katingia, August 9, 1888, AMSFS 5H5-2/2.

[27] For a detailed study on Catholic Bhagavata see, I. SORENG, Odishare o Odiya Sahithyare Khristodharmo (Oriya) (Christianity in Orissa and in Oriya Literature), Berhampur 1998, pp. 324 – 340.

[28] Balmand to Monsignor, Berhampur, December 25, 1853, AMSFS 5H5-2/1.

[29] Descombes wrote : "Ce le premier livre catholique imprimé en cette langue et le second livre chrétien puisque les Baptistes avaient déjà publié une traduction Konde de l'Evangile Saint Marc." Descombes, "Informations Diverses: Vizagapatam (Hindoustan)", in LMC 31 (1899), pp. 555 – 556.

[30] Descombes to Superior General, Surada, March 29, 1911, AMSFS 5H5-2/4.

[31] J. REY, Les Missionnaires de Saint-François de Sales d'Annecy, p. 445.

[32] Here are some of Msgr. Rossillon's important works : Sous les Palmiers du Coromandel, Chambery 1926 ; Les Drames de la Vie Indienne, Direction du Missionnaire Indien et Libraire Saint-Paul, Chambéry et Paris, 1932 ; Les Moissonneuses du Coromandel, Direction du Missionnaire Indien et Libraire Saint-Paul, Chambéry et Paris, 1933 and a number of articles.

[33] When the missionaries were free or had to wait for an expedition, they concentrated on the formation of catechists. Fr. Tissot thought that without their formation it would be difficult to evangelise the poor people. Cf. Tissot to Gaiddon, Yanaon, November 21, 1858, AMSFS 5H5-2/1.

[34] Descombes to J. Tissot, Surada, May 8, 1883, AMSFS 5H5-2/2; J. J. Vuillez to the Superior General, Ranchi, September 18, 1910, AMSFS 5H5-2/4.

[35] Descombes to Tissot, Katingia, August 9, 1888, AMSFS 5H5-2/2.

[36] Dupont to Clavel, Surada, February 7, 1857, AMSFS 5H5-2/1.

[37] Decombes to the Superior General, Surada, June 6, 1906, AMSFS 5H5-2/3.

[38] At the death of Fr. Ambroise Muffat-Meridol on October 18, 1907, Fr. Petitjean wrote that "at the prime age fell the flower". He was 32. Fr. Henri Petitjean himself went to join Fr. Suiffet in Dighy and fell victim to the dreaded mountain fever. He was 28. Fr. Julien Vulliez died on July 21, 1921. He was 45. Fr. François Fleury died on November 29, 1921. He was 39. Cf. J. REY, Les Missionnaires de Saint-François de Sales d'Annecy, pp. 441-442, and 447; F. Moget, MSFS Obituary, pp. 69, 81, 89 and 100.

[39] Rossillon to the Director, Visakhapatnam, February 26, 1920, AMSFS 5H5-2/5.

[40] Tissot to Petitjean, Nagpur, April 3, 1875, AMSFS 5H5-2/2.

[41] Though this resolution was adopted in the Synod, there is no mention in the letters of the missionaries of how it was executed. The correspondence of the missionaries with their superiors seldom refers to it.

[42] Fr. J.M. Descombes wrote: "Nous avons dans la mission de Sourada près de trois mille chrétiens disseminés dans une trentaine de villages. Ceux-ci sont situés à des distances très respectables les uns des autres et reliés entre eux par des sentiers qui ne sont généralment que de continuels casse-cou. En outre, pendant la mousson, qui dure de juin en novembre, il serait par trop imprudent pour un jeune missionnaire qui n'est point encore accoutumé à ce climat meurtier, de s'aventurer dans les montagnes, véritables foyers de malaria. Il ne nous reste donc que huit mois pour rendre visite à nos nombreux catéchumènes et explorer les villages païens des environs." P. DESCOMBES, "Diocèse de Vizagapatam: Lettre du R.P. Petrus Descombes", in Annales de la Propagation de la Foi 72 (1900), p. 107.

[43] Fr. Descombes narrated the confidence of the Kondhs in the missionaries: "Désormais, disent-ils, nous serons à toi; tu seras notre père et nous serons tes enfants. Si tu nous frappes, tu nous frapperas; si tu nous bats, tu nous battras." Ibid., p. 113.

[44] Fr. Bonaventure wrote: "La failure (manque) du riz lui donne de grandes espérances de conversion. Il compte sur 200 baptêmes l'an prochain." Bonaventure to his uncle, Surada, November 19, 1881, AMSFS 5H5-2/2.

[45] Jean Rey, Les Missionnaires de Saint-François de Sales d'Annecy, p. 440.

[46] Bishop Joseph Baud writes : "d'autres donnaient de l'argent à ceux qui venaient à l'église, sous prétexte de les dédommager pour le temps et le salaire perdus en assistant à la messe du Dimanche. Consequences: les vieillards moururent, et quand on commença à supprimer la 'compensation' en argent les soit-disants chrétiens nous quitterènt en grande majorité". Joseph Baud, L'œuvre de Msgr. Rossillon, Vizagapatam, May 5, 1947, AMSFS.

[47] Tissot to Clavel, Yanon, September 6, 1857, AMSFS 5H5-2/1.

[48] Descombes to Msgr. Clerc, Merycott, (no date and month) 1897, AMSFS 5H5-2/3.

[49] Fr. Muffat wrote: "Le soir, à la tombée de la nuit, le missionnaire et son catéchiste appellent à la prière: petit à petit, un gruppe se forme autour d'eux, mais lentement, car on n'est jamais pressé en ce pays. Enfin, les voilà à peu près tous réunis. Le Père, assis sur une pierre, fait répéter les prières; ceux qui se les rappellent sont rares, eh bien! On les réapprendra. De temps en temps, une chèvre ou même un cochon vient troubler la séance, mais on ne s'inquiète pas pour si peu, et les prières vont leur train. Après quinze jours, les confessions se font et les mieux instruits communient. Pour couronner la fête, le Père donne quelques roupies; on tué un vieux bœuf bien maigre et tout le village est en liesse." MUFFAT, "Lettre de Muffat", in Echos Salésiens 1/2 (1908), p. 28; J. REY, Les Missionnaires de Saint-François de Sales d'Annecy, p. 441.

[50] Tissot to one of the MSFS, Surada, March 1888, AMSFS 5H5-2/2.

[51] Gojon to Ducret, April 10, 1891, AMSFS 5H5-2/3; Gojon to Ducret, October 26, 1891, AMSFS 5H5-2/3.

[52] When a bullock cart was unable to reach a place, or it was too difficult to obtain fruit, eggs, milk, sugar, etc., there, the missionaries normally did not start a station. Cf. Descombes to J. Tissot, Surada, December (no date), 1892, AMSFS 5H5-2/3.

[53] Muffat wrote : "Le lendemain, depart pour un autre village : cinque à six porteurs, chacun une boîte sur la tête, ouvrent la marche, puis le cuisinier, le catéchiste et, enfin, votre serviteur. J'oubliais une petite chèvre qui me suivit fidèlement, donnant juste assez de lait pour blanchir mon café le matin; ici tout est maigre!" J. REY, Les Missionnaires de Saint-François de Sales d'Annecy, p. 441.

[54] M. Vermeire wrote: "In all the villages of Gangpur one hears the same complaint; burdens imposed by the police and quarrels about lands with the Raja's people. In general, one may say that the people of Gangpur are the same as ours in Biru." M. VERMEIRE, Biru Mission History: Kurdeg 1904 - 1940, vol. IV, APBS India 1 – Box 4, p. 22.

[55] S. FUCHS, "Priests and Magicians in Aboriginal India", in Studia Missionalia 22 (1973), p. 205.

[56] Our Field 9/4 (1933) p. 89.

[57] In a letter dated May 3, 1920, Fr. Floor illustrated some of the possible reasons for the defections of Catholics in Gangpur. Cf. M. Vermeire, Gangpur Mission History, vol. I, pp. 181-184.

[58] M. Vermeire, Biru Mission History: Common Subjects, vol. I, Part II, APBS India 1 – Box 4, p. 92.

[59] Chaprasi is a Hindi word, which means a servant or unskilled labourer who is appointed to help an officer or an influential person whenever the latter wants him.

[60] M. VERMEIRE, Biru Mission History: Common Subjects, vol. I, Part II, APBS India 1 – Box 4, p. 92.

[61] Fr. Lievens and the pioneers in Chotanagpur adopted a method that helped them to preach the gospel as well as to protect the tribals from land alienation and from moneylenders. The missionaries also helped the people to free themselves from evil spirits. In finding a suitable method for Chotanagpur, Fr. Lievens considered "the experience of the Lutheran, Anglican and Catholic missionaries, his own experience and knowledge, the prevailing religious, social and economic conditions were all factors that helped him to determine the method he would adopt to achieve his end. This end was to win souls for Christ". A. TIRKEY, "Evangelization among the Uraons", in IMR 19/2 (1997), p. 9.

[62] The Jesuits had a clear objective in establishing their schools. "Our boys have many defects and our chief work is to correct these defects, - the best if not the only suitable time for their systematic correction is the time when the boys are at school, - if all the defects can not be eradicated, much can be done in a quiet way to diminish them." Proceedings of the Conference held at Ranchi on October 17, 18, 1917, ARSI Calcut. 1005 – IX, 2.

[63] H. JOSSON, Un Chef de Mission aux Indes, p. 373.

[64] M. VERMEIRE, Biru Mission History: Common Subjects, vol. I, Part II, APBS India 1 – Box 4, p. 86.

[65] L. VAN HOECK, A Report on the Working of the Catholic Primary Schools in Chota Nagpore, during the year 1912, ARSI, Beng. 4 – IX, 14, p. 12.

[66] The Jesuits in general accompanied some of the good students through the university. Nirmal Minz, one of the leading church leaders in Chotanagpur confirmed: "The formal schooling of children and youth in mission schools and later on in colleges and universities aided by the church has changed the social outlook of the tribal people both positively and negatively." N. MINZ, "Transforming Effects of Christianity on the Tribals of Chotanagpur", in P. DASH SHARMA (ed.), The Passing Scene in Chotanagpur. Sarat Chandra Roy Commemorative Volume, Ranchi 1980, p. 76.

[67] Fr. L. van Hoeck, who was the Diocesan Inspector of Schools and who coordinated the school apostolate in Ranchi, writes in his annual report of 1912: "Whenever possible the people, not excepting the Catholics, should be urged to contribute for the maintenance of the school either by the payment of a monthly or a yearly fee or by voluntary contributions. The amount of fees to be paid, the exceptions to be made etc., should be settled locally." L. VAN HOECK, A Note on Village - Schools, ARSI, Beng. 4 – IX, 14, p. 4.

[68] Ibid. The monthly gatherings were generally held at the bungalow (a term used for the presbytery). Mahto wrote: "Refresher courses in pedagogy were arranged for eight days in a year. Every village had a school. The Panches tried to persuade the ignorant and truant guardians to send their words [sic wards] to the schools. Failing such persuasive measures, some kind of gentle coercion too was applied at

times. For the deliberate absence of the child from the school, a nominal fine was debarred from the membership of the Bank, as a result of which he was refused loans in times of need." S. MAHTO, Hundred Years of Christian Missions of Chotanagpur Since 1845, Patna 1994, p. 197.

[69] Though exaggerated, Sahay's claims had some foundation. He wrote: "It has been reported by some non-Christian informants, that by reading in Mission Schools, at times, the student himself feels attracted towards Christianity. Sometimes the teachers or the Christian class-fellows insisted that he become a Christian." K.N. SAHAY, Under the Shadow of the Cross. A Study of the Nature and Processes of Christianisation among the Uraon of Central India, Calcutta 1976, p. 69.

[70] M. VERMEIRE, Gangpur Mission History, vol. I, p. 69.

[71] Ibid., p. 70.

[72] Byelaws of the Chotanagpur Catholic Cooperative Credit Society Ranchi with Amendments up to 9th March 1933, Registered 17th April 1934, APBS India 2 53/4, p.3.

[73] Alary to Superior General, Kesramal, July 14, 1917, ARSI, Calcutta 1005-XIII, 23.

[74] On November 12, 1912, Fr. Hoffmann addressed a few people in Kesramal on the subject of opening the bank, the school and the Dhan Gola, the granary. He said: "We may hope that by the end of this year our Bank shall have a legal standing in Gangpur. The Political Agent, having received a letter from the top, is to see the Raja on the subject some time towards Christmas." He suggested how the people could save money: "by drinking less, by gathering in some Dhan at the harvest time, from where the villages could help themselves at the sowing time". M. VERMEIRE, Gangpur Mission History, vol. I, op. cit., p. 73.

[75] H. JOSSON, La Mission du Bengal Occidental, vol. II, p. 408.

[76] In order to register themselves as members each one had to pay 5 francs. Cf. Alary to Superior General, Kesramal, July 14, 1917, ARSI Calcutta 1005 – XIII, 23, 2-3.

[77] Concerning the membership of the cooperative bank, one of the rules clearly indicates: "He must be a bona fide Roman Catholic, scl. Baptised or catechumen, not apostatised nor excommunicated. He must be of good character." Bye-laws of the Chotanagpur Catholic Cooperative Credit Society Ranchi with Amendments up to 9th March 1933, Registered 17th April 1934, APBS India 2 53/4, p. 3; S. MAHTO, Hundred Years of Christian Missions of Chotanagpur Since 1845, p. 199.

[78] H. LUTZ and R.D. MUNDA, "Tribal Change and Development in India", in P. DASH SHARMA (ed.), The Passing Scene in Chotanagpur, p.111.

[79] Relating to the beginning of Nisha Sangat, Fr. Alary wrote: "Today (27.10.1912) after the Mass in Jogorpur, there was a big meeting of the men who are willing to sign the pledge of leaving daru, arrack, altogether, and of those who sympathise with the movement, though not yet ready to sign. This Sangat comprises the whole of Girja ilakha (the hamlets around the Church)." Ibid., p. 70.

[80] C. BECK, "Three Great Missionaries of Chotanagpur", in C. SRAMBICAL (ed.), Lead me to Light. Divine Word Missionaries 1875-1975, (1975), p. 91.

[81] M. VERMEIRE, Biru Mission History: Common Subjects, vol. I, Part II, APBS India 1 – Box 4, p. 63.

[82] The following types of oaths were taken: (1) the oath of the chhota karar consisted in touching the Bible before the person received holy communion; and (2) bara karar was an oath taken before holy communion before the assembly with due solemnity. There were to be at least five witnesses. Cf. M. VERMEIRE, Biru Mission History: Biru Common, vol. I, Part II, APBS India Lievens. Ser. B. Box. 4, p. 68-69.

[83] Ibid., p. 68.

[84] Ibid.

[85] The Rules of the Dhan Gola or the Granary were drafted by Fr. Floor and they were adapted for Gangpur by the same missionary. Ibid., pp. 197 - 198.

[86] C. BECK, "Three Great Missionaries of Chotanagpur", p. 92.

[87] M. VERMEIRE, Biru Mission History: Samtoli 1904-1940, vol. III, Section II, ARSI, Beng. 2006, p. 75.

[88] H. FLOOR, "The Dhan Golas (Rice-Banks) and Education", in The Chotanagpur Mission Letter 2/8 (1931), pp. 179 – 181.

[89] M. VERMEIRE, Biru Mission History: Biru Common, Part II Common Subjects, vol. I, APBS India Lievens. Ser. B. Box. 4, p. 70.

[90] Alary to Superior General, Kesramal, July 11, 1916, ARSI, Calcut. 1005-XIII, 8, 3-4.

[91] Hoffmann to Superior General, Bruder-Krankenhaus, Dortmund, October 6, 1919, ARSI Calcut. 1006 – I, 52.

[92] Fr. Vermeire commented: "That year 1908, this [Gangpur] region suffered very much from famine, but thanks to His Grace's munificence, the missionaries were greatly helped, and the poor people enabled to buy seeds. This charity produced about 2000 new catechumens for the Catholic Church among whom some 700 from Lutheranism." M. VERMEIRE, Gangpur Mission History, vol. I, p. 43.

[93] Perier to Superior General, Calcutta, March 8, 1919, ARSI Calcutta 1006 – I, 6; M. VERMEIRE, Gangpur Mission History, vol. I, p. 43.

[94] Commenting on the importance of the Catholic Sabha, Fr. Dumoulin wrote: "L'aborigène aime les réunions, les discussions publiques, où chacun a son mot à dire et peut librement exprimer son opinion: les fameux panchayats, sorte de conseil communal, sont une manifestation très ancienne de cet attrait pour les palabres, comme diraient les congolais." DUMULIN, L'action Catholique au Chota Nagpore, APBS India 2 – 53/2.

[95] Fr. Dumoulin explained: "la Catholic Sabha n'a pas de pouvoir, ni législatif, ni exécutif, ni coercitif. Elle peut tout au plus exhorter ses members à suivre ses

directives, par exemple de s'abstenir de boissons enivrantes; d'aider le missionnaire dans les villages éloignés comme catéchistes volontaires; de contribuer à la construction d'une chapelle – habitation dans des postes auxiliaries, où le missionnaire pourra venir loger un mois ou deux; d'envoyer les enfants à l'école; de célébrer avec pompe telle ou telle fête". Ibid.

[96] Ibid.

[97] From the diary of Fr. de Smet, in M. VERMEIRE, Biru Mission History: Samtoli 1904 –1940, vol. III, APBS India 1 – Box. 4.

[98] Alary wrote : "Alors aussi nous assemblions, une fois par an, un certain nombre d'hommes et de femmes, pour leur donner, ce qu'on pourrait appeler une retraite. On leur rappelait les grandes vérités, on leur faisait faire une bonne confession et communion." Alary to General, Kesramal, July 14, 1917, ARSI Calcutta 1005 – XIII, 23.

[99] Alary to Superior General, Kesramal, July 11, 1916, ARSI, Calcutta 1005-XIII, 8.

[100] P. TETE, "Fr. Louis Cardon , S.J. (1857-1946). The Founder of the Biru Mission", p. 75.

[101] N. MINZ, "Transforming Effects of Christianity on the Tribals", p. 74.

[102] Ibid., p. 77.

[103] Sarna refers to grove of Sal trees where the tribes of Chotanagpur (Munda, Kharia and Oraon) venerate their gods and their spirits. It is therefore called a sacred grove. However, in the absence of a specific term to denote the religion of these tribes, the term Sarna religion is used. Cf. P. BARJO, "The Religious Life of the Sarna Tribes", in IMR 19/2 (1997), p. 41.

[104] Ibid., p. 78.

[105] Ibid., p. 76.

[106] Berga Oraons were from Gangpur state. Cf. M. VERMEIRE, Biru Mission History: Kurdeg 1904- 1940, Vol. IV, APBS India Lievens. Ser. B. Box. 4, p. 22.

[107] K.S. LATOURETTE, op. cit., p. 211. F. A. Plattner remarked that "one must admit that individual officials, especially in the second half of the period, helped the missionaries because of their excellent social work. They sanctioned their projects and expedited their business transactions, like the acquisition of property and so on. So, on the whole one can speak of a favourable situation for the missions, but not of any actual favouritism." F.A. PLATTNER, The Catholic Church in India: Yesterday and Today, St. Paul's Publications, Bombay 1964, p. 25.

[108] M. VERMEIRE, Biru Mission History: Biru Mission History: Kurdeg 1904-1940, Vol. IV, APBS India Lievens. Ser. B. Box. 4, p. 22.

[109] Alary to Superior General, Kesramal, July 11, 1916, ARSI, Calcutta 1005-XIII, 8.

[110] S. NEILL, Colonialism and Christian Missions, p. 413.

[111] Descombes to Tissot, Katingia, August 9, 1888, AMSFS 5H5-2/2.

[112] P. ROSSILLON, Proceedings of the Episcopal Conference of India – January 1921, APF Rubrica, vol. 696, ff. 166-167.

[113] E. BONAVENTURE, "Information Diverses: Vizagapatam (Hindoustan)", in LMC 15 (1883) p. 183.

[114] Msgr. Tissot wrote: "La Sacré Congregation nous avait particulierment recommandé ces populations encore à demi sauvages, parce que d'abord elles offrent moin d'opposition à la predication de l'Evangile, et aussi parce que les missionnaires protestants n'avaient pas encore semé parmi eux leur zizania." Msgr. Tissot, Recit Succint de l'etat de la Mission de Vizagapatam. Depuis son origine, le 16 mars, jusqu'à sa division en deux Diocese de Vizagapatam et de Nagpur le 29 juillet 1887, Vizagapatam, April 11, 1888, APF, Indie Orientali: Scritture Riferite nei Congressi, vol. 33, f. 282.

[115] The incident took place after or during the famine of 1907 – 1908 when the Government was seeking ways to supply seeds through the mission. Cf. M. VERMEIRE, Biru Mission History: Samtoli 1904-1940, vol. III, APBS, India 1 – Box 4, pp. 41 – 44.

[116] Fr. Alary wrote: "Les Luthériens avaient pratiquement conquis le pays avant notre arrivée. Ils étaient parfaitement établis au Gangpur (maisons, écoles, etc.) alors que nous ne pouvions y faire que de rares visites. La plupart de nos chrétiens viennent de chez eux; mais impossible ou presqu'impossible d'attaquer ceux qui leur restent, ils sont absolument attachés à leur mission." Alary to General, Kesramal, July 14, 1917, ARSI Calcutta 1005-XIII, 23.

[117] J. REY, Les Missionnaires de Saint-François de Sales d'Annecy, p. 447.

[118] M. VERMEIRE, Biru Mission History: Common Subjects, vol. I, Part II, APBS India 1 – Box 4, p. 84.

[119] Ibid., p. 87.

[120] The boys and girls of the Girja Ilakha (church circle) were asked to gather at the parish hall for catechism classes after their meals. They were expected to continue this practice till they were ready for their First Communion. It generally lasted for a month. For the adults in the village the catechist taught them the prayers. When they were sufficiently ready, they were brought to the centre for three days of intense preparation. The people brought along their own food for the stay in the centre. Cf. Ibid., p. 90.

[121] J. BRESSERS, The Chotanagpur Mission Letter 1/8 (1930), pp. 121 – 122.

[122] S. BARA, Aboriginals and Missionaries. A Rejoinder to Verrier Elwin, APBS India 2, General 15/9, p. 3; K. N. SAHAY, Under the Shadow of the Cross, p. 56.

[123] Ibid.

Conclusion

The present is better understood in the light of the past. The lessons of the past and the experiences of the present should help in planning for a meaningful future. This is precisely the role of history and historical studies. The historian's task is to bring to light the relevant past to help the present generation face the future. In the preceding pages an attempt was made to recognise those issues and events, which shaped the Catholic Church in Orissa. Therefore, the history recounted was an encounter of the dalits and tribals of Orissa with Christianity. It attempted to describe the circumstances in which the Catholic missionaries proclaimed God's Word, the means they employed to make it understandable and acceptable and, finally, the response of the people. The Catholic Church in Orissa grew as a result of the inadequacy of the old religions to liberate the dalits and tribals from the clutches of the world of spirits that seemed to control human destiny. The missionaries' alertness and their promptness in responding to the outrages of a powerful minority against a powerless majority produced positive results. British colonial rule and their neutrality in matters of religion made it possible for the Church to extend its activity over the entire Indian sub-continent.

When the dalits and tribals of Orissa were hard-pressed by their powerful neighbours, the missionaries shared with them a religion which gave them hope. To the missionaries these 'primitive' peoples held a special value as God's children. They felt it their duty to do something to alleviate their suffering. The dalits and tribals longed for liberation, respect and dignity. The missionaries offered a faith which satisfied those longings.

The missionaries did not do anything extraordinary to attract the attention of the dalits and tribals. All they did was to sympathise with the oppressed and to plead for justice on their behalf. Some of the missionaries successfully identified with the dalits and the tribals by adopting their language, customs and life-style as their own. In this way they became genuine ambassadors, communicating their cultural richness to the non-tribal and non-dalit world. All this the missionaries did in obedience to their master's command of love.

The Inspirational Source

In their activities, the Jesuits and the Missionaries of St. Francis de Sales fulfilled the church's missionary mandate. Pope John Paul II's *Redemptoris Missio* declares that, "the Church is called to bear witness to Christ by taking courageous and prophetic stands in the face of corruption of political or economic power by not seeking her own glory and material wealth; by using her resources to serve the poorest of the poor and by imitating Christ's own simplicity of life".[1]

The critics of Christianity claim that the history of Christianity among the dalits and tribals was one of aggression and forcible transplantation of a European church. In the preceding pages it was made clear that the dalits and tribals accepted Christianity on their own. The village delegations could prove such claims. However, the mission work was not without obstacles and difficulties. The initial response of the people in Ganjam was so negative that the missionaries had to re-examine their work in the area. In their frustration, they even called the territory a 'cursed land'. But this situation changed in 1866 because of the Orissa famine. The missionaries dedicated themselves to the service of the poor and orphans. Henceforth, the missionaries did not have to hunt for conversions; seeing the goodness of the missionaries, the people sent delegations to invite them to their villages.

The dalits and tribals of Orissa, who knew nothing else but estrangement and oppression, experienced a renewed dignity and hope for the future in the presence and activities of the missionaries. To the simple and peace-loving dalits and tribals, this was the good news that the new religion proclaimed. For the missionaries' religion understood the longings of the tribals and dalits and attempted to liberate them from the clutches of slavery and any kind of oppression that degrades the human person, who is made in the image of God.

Liberative Mission

In their efforts to preach the love of God, the missionaries struck at the root of evil by struggling with the oppressed to seek justice. The one fact that was indelibly etched in the memory of the Mundas, Oraons and Kharias was that they were descendants of the original settlers. For them, the one who cleared the forest and settled on the land was its owner. They were willing to sacrifice anything, even their religion, in order to live at peace with their ancestors who had cleared the forest tracts and cultivated them. The Belgian Jesuits not only understood this basic principle but also made efforts to help reclaim their property. They even induced the British government to enact laws in favour of the tribals.

It is true that initially the Kondhs and Panos focused on the material advantages of the presence of the missionary and his work. But it does not follow that this continued to be their motivation. Dick Kooiman has pointed out that,

> the change of religion as a strategy for survival is not a one-way solution, people may turn to Christianity, but there is also the return option: when people try to ward off the dangers threatening their existence they may give priority to ancestral beliefs and practices. Secondly, a close reading of the missionary sources reveals that famines and other cases of emergency merely create a kind of rush hour in already existing religious boundary traffic. Whether the main stream is away from or back to the religion of origin is to a large extent determined by an assessment of the alternative options available to the people concerned.[2]

Had the tribals and dalits considered only material benefits, two possible effects would have happened in the Kondh Mountains: there would have been either a mass conversion to Christianity or an exodus back to their traditional religion once the expected gains failed to reach them. But neither occurred. The poor, illiterate and ignorant people of the mountains were initially hesitant and analysed every action of the missionary before they finally accepted baptism. Once baptised, they remained faithful -- at least the vast majority of them.

Without doubt the tribals of Chotanagpur were first drawn into the orbit of the Catholic Church by social and economic motives. Their very existence and human dignity were at stake. It was the hope of legal protection that first drew them towards the church. However, the missionaries made no secret of the fact that the law alone could not save them. They brought moral and spiritual forces to bear upon the people. They made up for the rather sketchy initial instruction of the people at first by training them more systematically in the faith. Mission stations sprung up at strategic points among the Christian villages. Parishes were laid out with an eye to the future. Although the churches were usually not big enough to contain their entire congregations on Sundays and feast days, every centre had a presbytery, convent, school, dispensary and all the other institutions of a well-ordered parish.[3] The mission stations became the centres of the life of the tribals.

Another important factor for success among the tribals of Gangpur was the missionary adaptation of certain cultural features: the missionary methods: village *Panchayats*, confederation of village *Panchayats*, traditional local leadership, the promotion of tribal unity, etc.[4] It certainly must have been painful for these traditional and peace-loving people to give up the religion of their ancestors with its sacrifices to the spirits and its joyful dances. But they were able to give it up because Christianity did not deprive them of their religiosity but gave it new meaning. Sacrifices to the spirits (especially to evil spirits) were replaced by devotion to the Blessed Virgin Mary, to saints and the guardian angels. The intensity of their traditional religious life was changed to intensity in their Christian lives.[5] This spirit of cultural adaptation paved the way to the ever-increasing missionary expansion and allowed evangelisation to be successful.

Christianity also brought a transformation to society, giving it a new face, a new look. Its horizons widened, and its behaviour changed. The social, economic, intellectual, moral and spiritual progress of Christians -- in short, their complete transformation -- is the most convincing proof of their acceptance of a new faith. The Christianity in Gangpur is vibrant, like that visualised by Fr. Lievens. From the beginning the Jesuits promoted leadership among the laity. The Church has produced excellent leaders, both lay and religious.[6]

Christianity and the People of Lower Origin

The critics of the Christian missions often ask: why does Christianity flourish among the tribals and dalits in India?[7] They have adopted Christian faith, precisely because Christ, its founder, preached that all are brothers and sisters and that the exploitation and enslavement of others is a sin crying to heaven.[8] Some people have questioned the tribals' acceptance of the Christian faith *en masse*, since they say, it was not based purely on religious motives. Yet Jesus himself was not satisfied with prayers and sacrifices. He condemned social injustice and economic exploitation, he insisted that all human beings are equal before God and have basic rights which no power on earth can deprive them of.[9] People follow Jesus' example when they demand justice and oppose social exploitation and degradation.[10] This is exactly what the missionaries in Orissa did. The dalits and tribals of Orissa soon discovered that the Catholic missionaries were deeply interested in their welfare. Once they were convinced of this, they came to the missionaries in large numbers. They may have come first for advice in their land disputes and legal matters. But later they came asking to be received into the Church.

After having witnessed the struggles of the dalits and tribals, the missionaries were convinced that the work of evangelisation had to be accompanied by a struggle for human justice. Had they simply carried on social work among the dalits and tribals by opening free dispensaries and schools, they might have succeeded in calming the unrest among the people. But ultimately this would have benefited the exploiters more than the exploited. Though illiterate, the dalits and tribals still retained their sense of human dignity and their fond memory of being descendants of the original settlers of the soil. They were neither willing to be enslaved nor to be reduced to the state of receiving alms. The missionaries sought genuine remedies for the problems of the dalits and tribals, and nothing short of that would satisfy them.

The Tribal converts began to show a spirit of independence and resistance to the illegal exactions of the landlords. At the same time, rumours of converts' winning court cases strengthened the belief that it was easier to win cases if one became a convert, which encouraged people to seek baptism. Generally, the tribals came to church in groups, retaining their traditional clan affiliations. Inspired and aided by the missionaries, the tribals began to seek their rights through legal means and refused to comply with the traditional free labour.[11] Not all those seeking justice were actually Christians, since many had not been baptised nor even had begun taking instructions.[12]

The Christian missionaries established schools, colleges, hospitals, dispensaries, orphanages and institutions for the maimed and handicapped. They gave unheard-of opportunities to members of the neglected classes, some of whom had important positions in the institutions they ran. Their emphasis on education, including teacher-training and offers of free education, has attracted many people. Others have been drawn by the colourful forms of worship and by the fact that the Roman Catholic community has demanded fewer changes in traditional customs. For these and other reasons, even some Protestants have joined the Roman Catholic community.[13]

The Fransalians and the Jesuits

Both Fransalians and Jesuits worked with people of lower origin who were neglected by both Hindus and civil authorities. The dalits and tribals lived in the forest and were often deprived of basic amenities. Though they attributed their misery to the rapacity of evil spirits, they hoped that one day they would have plenty. Their social cohesiveness worked in favour of conversions.

The Fransalian and Jesuit missions, however, were not identical. There were some differences. The growth in Ganjam mission of the MSFS was never consistent. The missionaries were often frustrated by the lukewarmness and indifference of the people. Their lack of response almost prompted the Fransalians to give up their mission. Nevertheless, natural calamities and tragedies forced them to continue with mission work. The Fransalians, as they are called in India, would have done much better if they had restricted themselves to a small portion of their gigantic mission. But it is useless to philosophise about what should have been done one hundred and fifty years ago. In any case the intrepid Savoyards boldly faced their daunting task. They struggled with a harsh climate, diverse languages, and long distances. But since they were only a handful of missionaries, they could not concentrate on the consolidation of the neophytes.

The Belgian Jesuits in Gangpur were better situated. Many aspects worked in their favour: Gangpur was an extension of the mission of Chotanagpur; the missionaries did not have to begin with basics like language, culture, etc.; there was no long period of preparation between the first contact and the establishment of Kesramal, the first parish in Gangpur; and above all, the missionaries encountered the relatives of the people living in the Chotanagpur mission. However, the Jesuits also faced difficulties: the hostile attitude of the raja; the distance from Ranchi, which limited them to attending only important meetings; and the poor resources to support the mission.

Every missionary has limitations and weaknesses. It would be naïve to presume that as soon as they stepped on foreign soil they automatically became saints. They had their share of scandals, prejudices, disappointments and failures. Some of the missionaries appeared as benevolent zamindars who went about their own way. Sometimes there were conflicts between the messengers of the gospel. But on the whole, through their simplicity and dedication, they have won the respect of the dalits and tribals of Orissa.

This study obviously is not the last word on the subject. If it helps to throw light on the history of the Catholic Church in Orissa, it will have served its purpose. In accepting the new faith, the simple people in the mountains realised that they did not lose their traditions: their culture, their dances, their songs, etc. On every festive occasion the old drums still roll, and the feet still move. Whoever has met the dalits and tribals of Orissa cannot help wishing them a happy future.

Endnotes

[1] JOHN PAUL II, *Encyclical Letter 'Redemptoris Missio'*, 43.

[2] D. KOOIMAN, "Mass Movement, Famine and Epidemic. A study in interrelationship", in *ICHR* 22/2 (1988) p. 128.

[3] F. A. PLATTNER, *The Catholic India. Yesterday and Today*, Bombay 1964, p. 89.

[4] B. TIRKEY, "The Adivasi and the Inculturated Theology", in *IMR* 7/2 (1985) p. 157.

[5] F. DE SA, *Crisis in Chota Nagpur*, p. 336.

[6] A. TIRKEY, "Father Constant Lievens, S.J. The Missionary", in *IMR* 7/2 (1985) p. 142.

[7] Plattner comments: "Many Hindus claim that such conversions are due to the poverty and ignorance of the backward classes. They accuse the missionaries of offering these illiterate people loans, gifts and all sorts of alms in order to convert them to Christianity." F. A. PLATTNER, *The Catholic Church in India*, op. cit., p. 147.

[8] S. FUCHS, "A new Mission Method for India", in *Verbum* SVD 13/3 (1972) p. 231.

[9] Ibid., p. 223.

[10] Ibid., p. 234.

[11] F. DE SA, *Crisis in Chota Nagpur*, p. xv.

[12] Ibid., p. 328.

[13] B. M. BOAL, "The church in the Kond hills," p. 273.

Bibliography

A. Unpublished Sources

1. Rome: Archivium Romanum Societatis Iesu (ARSI)

The archives contain letters of the missionaries and Superiors Regular of the Bengal Mission of the Belgian Jesuits to the Superior General of the Society of Jesus. Gangpur and Chotanagpur were under the Bengal Mission. The following documents are found under the title *Bengal Calcuttensis*.

Beng. 1003 Provinciae Belgicae, 1882-1902.

Beng. 1004 Provinciae Belgicae, 1902-1913.

Beng. 1005 Provinciae Belgicae, 1913-1918.

Beng. 1006 Provinciae Belgicae, 1918-1921.

Provincia Belgica Septemtrionalis, *Historia Domus*, 1889 – 1923.

i) Unpublished Works of Medard Vermeire

The unpublished works of Fr. Medard Vermeire are a very important documentary source for the history of Chotanagpur and Gangpur. Those, which provide some information on Gangpur, were consulted.

VERMEIRE M., *Biru Mission History:Common History to the whole Mission*, vol.I, Part II.
________, *Mission History: Rengarih 1904-1940*, vol.II. Sec.I.
________, *Biru Mission History: Samtoli 1904-1940*, vol.III.Sec.II.
________, *Biru Mission History: Kurdeg 1904-1940*, vol.IV. Sec.III.

ii) Memoirs of Fr. John Baptist Hoffmann

Beng. 2008 contains the Memoir of Father John Baptist Hoffmann. The Memoir is in seven fascicles. Fascicles I and II are missing. The others: Fasciculus III "Initia missionis Catholicae in Regione Chota-Nagpurensi". Fasciculus IV «Mission Patris Lievens, i.e. Successum apparentium et ruinae causae».

Fasciculus V "De Processu reconciliationis officialium anglorum eiusque effectibus bonis pro missione».

Fasciculus VI «De emendatione legum in favourem Aboriginum et de periculis novis missioni instantibus».

Fasciculus VII «De ultimis servitis, quae Aboriginibus preastare potui et de necessitate ominimoda operum socialum".

2. Rome: Archivum Congregationis de Propaganda Fide (APF)

The documents available in the Archives of the Sacred Congregation of the Propagation of Faith are up to 1922. They were found in the following categories.

i) Indie Orientali: Scritture Riferite nei Congressi

vol. 10 (1845-1846)	vol. 11 (1847-1848)	vol. 13 (1851-1852)
vol. 14 (1853-1854)	vol. 15 (1855-1856)	vol. 16 (1857-1858)
vol. 17 (1859-1861)	vol. 18 (1862-1864))	vol. 19 (1865-1867)
vol. 20 (1868-1874)	vol. 21 (1875-1878))	vol. 22 (1879-1881)
vol. 23 (1881-1882)	vol. 24 (1883))	vol. 25 (1884-1885)
vol. 26 (1885-1886)	vol. 32 (1887))	vol. 33 (1888)
vol. 34 (1889))	vol. 35 (1890)	vol. 36 (1891)
vol. 37 (1892)	vol. 40 (Relazioni)	

ii) Rubrica

vol. 71 (1895)	vol. 95 (1896)	vol.197 (1900)
vol. 261 (1903)	vol. 292 (1904)	vol.326 (1905)
vol. 356/357 (1906)	vol. 403 (1907)	vol. 452A (1908)

vol. 476 (1909)	vol. 488 (1910)	vol. 502 (1911)
vol. 517 (1912)	vol. 533 (1913)	vol. 546 (1914)
vol. 577 (1916)	vol. 593 (1917)	vol. 631 (1919)
vol. 660 (1920)	vol. 695 (1921)	

iii) Lettere

vol. 348 (1857)	vol. 349 (1858)	vol. 352 (1861)
vol. 353 (1862)	vol. 354 (1863)	vol. 357 (1866)
vol. 358 (1867)	vol. 376 (1880)	vol. 377 (1881)
vol. 379 (1883)	vol. 381 (1885)	vol. 383 (1887)
vol. 386 (1890)	vol. 387 (1891)	vol. 388 (1892)

3. Heverlée, Belgium: Archivum Provincae Belgiae Septemtionalis (APBS)

The APBS is one of the important sources for the history of the Catholic Church in Gangpur. The archives contain letters of the missionaries and letters and reports of the superiors of the Bengal mission of the Belgian province of the Society of Jesus. The archives also possess copies of letters that the missionaries wrote to the superiors and missionaries in Calcutta and Ranchi. Some of the important letters, which the missionaries wrote to their family members, are also conserved in the archives.

India 1 – 4: Series B: Vermeire Documents

Biru Mission History: 1889 – 1840.

Vol. I. Part 1: Common History (1889 - 1840)

Vol. II. Part 2: Common Subjects

Vol. III. Samtoli 1904 – 1940

Vol. IV. Kurdeg 1904 – 1940

India 1 – 4: Series C: Josson Documents and Documents of van der Schueren, Cardon,

Dehon and Scheys.

4/3: An address on the Jesuit Missions in Bengal: July 1914.

4/4: Luis Cardon: On Oraon Tribes and the Kharias and their Customs

India 1 – 7: Series D: Old Diaries

7/2: Diary of Kurdeg

India 1 – 11: Superiors Regular of the Mission

India 1 – 13: Superior Regular: S. Grosjean – Papers and Letters.

India 1 – 14: Series E: Letters of Missionaries (Alphabetical Collection)

14/1: Luis Cardon

14/2: De Cock, Dehon

14/3: De Smet

14/4: Fierens Jean

India 1 – 16: Series G: Hoffmann letters

India 2 – 1: Ranchi General Sources – Bibliography and History

India 2 – 18: Series A and B: Official letters

India 2 – 22: Official letters of Superiors Regular of the Mission

Box. 22: Bankaert Julien, Waelkens Hippolyte

Box. 23: Perier Fernand, Maurice Veys

Box. 24: Maurice Veys

India 2: Series D: Consulters

Box. 29: Ranchi - Consulters from 1908 to 1930 (1: 1908-1912; 2:1918-1920;

3:1921; 4: 1922; 5: 1923; 6: 1924).

India 2: Series E: Non-official letters

Box. 34: Josson list.

34/1: *La malle des Indes*

34/3: Collection of letters according to the names

Boxes 35, 36 & 37: Individual letters.

4. Annecy, France: General Archives of the Missionaries of St. Francis de Sales (AMSFS)

In the absence of a provincial archive and diocesan archive, the General Archives of the Missionaries of St. Francis de Sales, Annecy is the only source for the History of the Catholic Church in Orissa. The archives contain letters addressed to the superior general. Besides a narration of their journeys, the missionaries' letters of 'self-evaluation' of their work as missionaries, and life as religious are also conserved. The archives conserve some of the letters and reports of the bishops and superiors of the mission.

i) Letters relating to Mission in India are found under 5H

5H1:   Foundation of the Mission

The Visakhapatnam Mission: Mission Register from 1845.

The territory (Maps)

The Visakhapatnam Mission (Anonymous)

R. Cugnet, "Notice sur la mission de Vizag" (1856)

Maurice Clavel "Notice sur la mission de Vizagapatam" (1866)

Histoire de la Mission (1846 - 1853): Original text of Msgr. Neyret.

Domenge : "Un voyage de vacances dans l'Inde" (1880)

5H2:   Notes on certain stations (1866 - 1910)

Letters from Surada (1881 -1889)

Cuttack (1882 - 1884)

Berhampur (1882 - 1883)

The Kondhs (1891)

Gopalpur (1891 - 1892)

Katingia: Notes of Fr. Descombes (1888)

5H3:   The Missionaries: Biography

Life of Msgr. Neyret by Fr. Deborne (1862)

Report of the journey: Guillermin 1853; Bonaventure 1877;

Rossillon 1909.

5H4:   History of the Mission

5H5-2 Letters of the missionaries

5H5-2/1:   1848 – 1868

5H5-2/2:   1870 – 1889

5H5-2/3:   1890 – 1909

5H5-2/4:   1910 – 1919

5H5-2/5:   1920 – 1952

82 Visakhapatnam Mission. (Extracts of the official register)

ii) Correspondence of the Bishops

7 5H5 –2:   Correspondence of Theophilius Neyret

9H1   Our Bishops : Theophilius Neyret, Jean Marie Tissot,

Alexius Riccaz & Jean Marie Clerc

9H4a &b Pierre Rossillon

9H2 6 François Philippe

GAL, Stéphane, *Conversions et Christianisation en Inde au XIXe Siècle: la Fondation de la Mission Savoyarde de Vizagapatam. Vers 1845- Vers 1890*, Jean Moulin : Université de Lyon III, 1991 (Unpublished work).

5. Annecy, France: General Archives of the Sisters of St. Joseph of Annecy

Information regarding the mission under study is found both in the Annals of the congregation of the mission and in the individual letters of the sisters who worked in Surada and Cuttack to the Superior General. The archives also contain some letters of the bishops and the missionaries to the Superior General of the Congregation.

The individual letters are categorized as per the year

2H, J3. A	:1847 – 1867
2H, J3. B	:1868 – 1882
2H, J4. A	:1883 – 1895
2H, J4. B	:1896 – 1905
2H, J4. C	:1906 – 1818

6. Rome: General Archives of the Congregation of the Mission (ACGR)

The documents sought in the archives are precise and limited. The documents concerning the transfer of the mission are found in the following categories.

--Province de Madrid : Superieur de la Mission Cuttack Indes (1922 – 1926/1927)

--Procès Verbaux des Conseils - Tome IX et X (1917 - 1923)

7. Diocesan Archives, Bishop's House, Rourkela, Orissa

VERMEIRE Medard, Gangpur Mission History I & II **(1904-1948),** Unpublished manuscripts

These two volumes are a collection of documents from the early evangelisation of Gangpur up to the arrival of the SVD missionaries (Society of the Divine Word) in 1948. The collection consists of diaries of the first parishes and of the individual missionaries and the official letters relating to the establishment of the mission stations. Though uncritical and more often the translation from French into English is defective, the collection is one of the most important sources for a history of the Gangpur Mission.

8. Vincent Urbaneja, C. M.'s Collections, Gopalpur-on-Sea, India

V. URBANEJA, *Notes on the History of Christianity in Orissa,* A collection of Unpublished documents, Gopalpur-on-Sea.

V. URBANEJA, *El Padre Guemes al Descubìerto. Cincuenta Añnos de su vida. Dia a Dia su diario el Diario de una mision, 1921-1978,* St. Vincent's, Gopalpur-on-Sea, Unpublished manuscript, pp. 3-4.

This is a collection of documents related to the history of the Catholic Church in Orissa.

B. Published Sources

1. Mission Journals

Some of the Mission Journals that published the letters of the missionaries and news from the mission are the following:

i) Les Missions Catholiques (LMC)

Vol. 3 (1870)	Vol. 5 (1873)	Vol. 6 (1874)
Vol. 14 (1882)	Vol. 15 (1883)	Vol. 16 (1884)
Vol. 18 (1886)	Vol. 19 (1887)	Vol. 20 (1888)
Vol. 21 (1889)	Vol. 22 (1890)	Vol. 23 (1891)
Vol. 24 (1892)	Vol. 25 (1893)	Vol. 28 (1896)
Vol. 29 (1897)	Vol. 30 (1898)	Vol. 31 (1899)
Vol. 32 (1900)	Vol. 39 (1907)	Vol. 40 (1908)
Vol. 41 (1909)	Vol. 43 (1911)	Vol. 44 (1912)
Vol. 46 (1914)	Vol. 47 (1915)	Vol. 48 (1916)
Vol. 49 (1917)	Vol. 50 (1918)	Vol. 51 (1919)
Vol. 52 (1920)	Vol. 53 (1921)	Vol. 55 (1923)
Vol. 56 (1924)		

ii) Annales de la Propagation de la Foi

Vol. 27 (1855)	Vol. 48 (1876)	Vol. 52 (1880)
Vol. 55 (1883)	Vol. 56 (1884)	Vol. 63 (1891)
Vol. 71 (1899)	Vol. 72 (1900)	Vol. 73 (1901)
Vol. 86 (1914)	Vol. 88 (1916)	Vol. 89 (1917)
Vol. 90 (1918)	Vol. 91 (1919)	Vol. 93 (1921)

iii) Missions Belges de la Compagnie de Jésus, Bruxelles (MB)

1900	1901	1902
1903	1904	1905
1907	1909	1910
1911	1913	1914-19

1920-21

2. DOMENGE Maurice, La Mission de Vizagapatam, Annecy

The work of Fr. Maurice Domenge is an invaluable contribution for the history of the Visakhapatnam mission. Though the author did not want to reveal his name, the *Les Missions Catholiques* has published that the author is M. Domenge. See LMC 22 (1890), p. 552. Hence the following reference is used in this work: M. DOMENGE, *La Mission de Vizagapatam*, Annecy 1890.

3. Litterae Annuae

Litterae Annuae Provinciae Belgicae Societatis Iesu, 1900-1912, Typis Polleunis & Ceuterick.

Litterae Annuae Provinciae Belgicae Societatis Iesu, 1912-1919, Typis Iulii de Meester & Filii, Wetteren Flandrorum.

Litterae Annuae Provinciae Belgicae Societatis Iesu, Missiones Beng. Occidentalis,1915-1928 (MSS).

4. Gazetteers and Government Records

BEHURIA, Nurusinha Charan (ed.), *Orissa State Gazetteer: Orissa State*, vol. I, Gazetteers Unit, Department of Revenue, Government of Orissa, Cuttack 1990.

__________, *Orissa State Gazetteer: Orissa State*, vol. II, Gazetteers Unit, Department of Revenue, Government of Orissa, Cuttack 1991.

__________, *Orissa State Gazetteer: Orissa State*, vol. III, Gazetteers Unit, Department of Revenue, Government of Orissa, Cuttack 1992.

Bihar and Orissa: Report of the Administration of the Territories now included in the Province of Bihar and Orissa 1911 – 1912, Printed at the Bihar and Orissa Government Press, Patna 1913.

Feudatory States of Bihar and Orissa: List of the Ruling Chiefs and Leading Personages, Government of India Central Publication Branch, Calcutta 1924.

History of the Rise and Progress of the Operations for the Suppression of Human Sacrifice and Female Infanticide in the Hill Tracts of Orissa, Bengal Military Orphan Press, Calcutta 1954.

HOFFMANN, John et al., *Encyclopaedia Mundarica*, vols. I-XI (1930-1937); Vols. XII-XIII (1950), Superintendent, Government Printing, Bihar and Orissa, Patna.

MALTBY, T.J., *The Ganjam District Manual*, G.D. LEMAN (ed.), The Lawrence Asylum Press, Madras 1882.

MOLONY, J. Charters and CHATTERTON Alfred, *Census of India, 1911: Madras: Report*, Vol. XII/I, Government of India, Madras 1912.

Report of the Commissioners Appointed to Enquire into the Famine in Bengal and Orissa in 1866, 2 vols., Office of Superintendent Government Printing, Calcutta 1867.

SENAPATI, Nilamani (ed.), *Orissa District Gazetteers: Sambalpur*, Department of Revenue, Government of Orissa, Cuttack 1992.

__________, *Orissa District Gazetteers: Sundargarh*, Department of Revenue, Government of Orissa, Cuttack 1992.

Society for Evaluation Studies, Social Services, Research and Training and National Institute of Social Work and Social Sciences, *The Panos: A Study of a Scheduled Caste Community in Orissa*, Ministry of Welfare, Government of India, Delhi and Bhubaneswar 1995 – 1996.

STUART, H.A. (ed.), *The Report of the Census: Census of India 1891:* Madras, vol. XIII, Superintendent of Census Operation, Madras 1893

TAYLOR, H.D. (ed), *Memoir on the Ganjam Maliahs in the Madras Presidency*, Orissa settlement reports series, Vol. 46, Revenue Department, Government of Orissa 1969.

The Imperial Gazetteer of India. Provincial Series: Bengal, vol. II, Superintendent of Government Printing, Calcutta 1909.

The Imperial Gazetteer of India, vol. IX, Clarendon Press, Oxford 1909.

C. Books and Articles

ALBERT, S. Vasantharaj, *Orissa: Church and People Groups*, Survey series, Madras: Church Growth Association of India and India Missions Association, 1992.

ALONSO, C., "Agustinos en la India, Relacionse y listas se religiosos inèditas (1624 - 1642)", *Extractum ex Analecta Augustiniana* 37 (1974) 241 – 296.

AMALADASS, Anand (ed), *Jesuit Presence in India: Commemorative volume on the occasion of the 150th Anniversary of the new Madurai Mission 1838-1988*, Anand: Gujarat Sahitya Prakash, 1988.

AMALADOSS, M., "Theologizing in a tribal context", in *Sevartham* 9 (1984), 3-10.

__________, "The Gospel, Community and Culture", in *ZMRW* 80 (1996) 243 - 254

AMBRUZZI, Luigi, *L'India Religiosa: Nella Terra dei Bramini*, Venezia: Le Mission della Compagnia di Gesù, 1925.

ANCHUKANDAM, Thomas, *The First Synod of Pondicherry 1844. A Study based on Archival Sources*, Bangalore: Khristu Jyoti Publications, 1994.

__________, "General Division of the Indian Missions into Vicariates Apostolic: Luquet's role and subsequent controversies", in *ICHR* 32/2 (1998) 77 – 94.

ANDERSON, H. Gerald et al. (eds.), *Biographical Dictionary of Christian Missions*, Michigan: William B. Eerdmans, 1999.

Anonymous, *Notices Biographiques sur M. Pierre Mermier Fondateur et Premier Superieur des Missionnaires de Saint-François de Sales d'Annecy et sur Monseigneur Neyret, évêque d'Olene, Vicaire Apostolique de Vizagapatam*, Annecy 1863.

__________, *Notices sur la Mission de Vizagapatam*, Annecy 1866.

__________, "An Evaluation", in *IMR* 7/1 (1985) 74 - 80.

AUBERT, Roger (ed.), *The Christian Centuries: The Church in a Secularised Society*, vol. V, London: Darton, 1979.

BACHELOR, O.R., *Hinduism and Christianity in Orissa. Containing a brief Description of the Country, Religion, Manners of the Hindus and An Account of the operations of the American Freewill Baptist Mission in Northern Orissa*, Boston: Charles Waite, 1853.

BAHADUR, K. P., *Caste, Tribe and Culture of India Bengal, Bihar and Orissa*, vol. III, Delhi: Ess Ess Publications, 1977.

BAILEY, Frederick Charles, *Caste and the Economic Frontier: A Village in Highland Orissa*, Manchester: Manchester University Press, 1959.

__________, Tribe, Caste, and Nation: *A Study of Political Activity and Political Change in Highland Orissa*, Manchester: Manchester University Press, 1960.

BALASUNDARAM, Franklyn J., "Gandhi's attitude towards Christianity", in *ICHR* 28/1 (1994) 51 –64.

BASHAM, A.L. (ed.), *A Cultural History of India*, Delhi: Oxford University Press, 1996.

BAVINCK, J. H., *An Introduction to the Science of Missions*, trans. David H. Freeman, Philadelphia: The Presbyterian and Reformed Publishing Co., 1960.

BECK, Clement, "Three Great Missionaries of Chotanagpur", in C. SRAMBICAL (ed.), *Lead me to Light, Divine Word Missionaries 1875-1975*, Divine Word Missionaries, Indore 1975, 89-94.

BECKER, C., *History of the Catholic Mission in Northeast India*, trans. & eds. G. STADLER and S. KAROTEMPREL, Calcutta: Firma KLM, 1980.

BEDNARZ, Julian, "Missionstätigkeit der Salvatorianer in Assam", in KIEBELE A. et al (eds.), *Die Salvatorianer in Geschichte und Gegenwart 1881 – 1981*, Rome: Generalate der Salvatorianer, 1981.

BEHERA, Deepak Kumar, *Ethnicity and Christianity: Christians divided by Caste and Tribe in Western Orissa*, Delhi: ISPCK, 1989.

BEHERA, Mohan, *The Jayantira Pano. A Scheduled Caste Community of Orissa*, K.K. MOHANTY (ed.), Bhubaneswar: Tribal and Harijan Research cum Training Institute, 1991.

BLESSES, C., "Father J. B. Hoffmann S.J: The Man and His Works", in *Our Field* 22/1 (1946) 1-5.

BOAL, M. Barbara, *Fire is Easy. The Tribal Christian and his Traditional Culture*, Manila-Bangalore: Christian Institute for Ethnic Studies in Asia and the Christian Institute for the Study of Religion and Society, 1973.

__________, *The Kondhs: Human Sacrifice and Religious Change*. Tribal Studies of India Series T 180, New Delhi: Inter-India Publications, 1993.

__________, "The Church in the Kond Hills: An Encounter with Animism", in Victor E. W. HAYWARD (ed.), *The Church as Christian Community. Three Studies of North Indian Studies*, Lutterworth Press, London 1966, 221 – 343.

BODSON, F., "Dhan Golas in Chota Nagpur", in *Our Field* 11/6 (1935) 199-205.

BOEL, Jozef, *Christian Missions in India: A Sociological Analysis*, Amsterdam: Academische Pers, 1975.

BONK, J. Jonathan, *Missions and Money: Affluence as Western Missionary Problem*, New York: Orbis, 1991.

BOSE, Nirmal Kumar, *Culture and Society in India*, London: Asia Publishing House, 1967.

BOSE, S.R., *A Statistical Survey of Food Grain Prices in Bihar and Orissa 1861 – 1934*, Patna: Patna College, 1939.

BOWEN, J. Francis, *Father Constant Lievens SJ: The Apostle of Chota Nagpur*, London, 1936.

BURGES, James, *The Chronology of Modern India: For Four Hundred Years from the Close of the Fifteen Century 1494 – 1894*, Edinburgh: John Grant, 1913.

CAMPBELL, John C.B., *Narrative by Major General John Campbell C.B. in the hill tracts of Orissa for the suppression of human sacrifices and female infanticide*, London: Hurst and Blacktt, 1861.

CAMPION, E., "Uraon Customs", in *The Chota Nagpur Mission Letter* 9 (1935) 118-121; 151-155.

CAMPOS, J.J.A., *History of the Portuguese in Bengal, With Maps and Illustrations*, Calcutta: Medical Publishers, 1919.

CARBERY, S., "The T.C.T.S: Rules for the Trained Catechists", in *Our Field* 5/2 (1929) 27 –31.

CARDON, L., *The Kharias and their Customs*, Louvain 1923.

__________, *On the Oraon tribe in General*, Louvain.

__________, "Reminiscences", in *Our Field* 11 (August 1935) 262-265, 348-351.

CHANDRA, Rath Ganesh, "Impact of European Companies on the Foreign Trade of Orissa during the Mughal era", in *Indica* 36/1 (1999) 1- 12.

CHATTERJEE, B. K., "The Social and Religious Institutions of the Kharias", in *Journal and Proceedings of the Asiatic Society of Bengal* 27 (1931) 225 – 229.

CHATTERJI, S. K., *The People, Language and Culture of Orissa*, Bhubaneswar, 1966.

CHAUDHURI, Nirad C., "Conversion and Christianity. A well known Indian's perception of the problem", in *VJTR* 63 (1999) 167 – 169.

CHEENATH, Raphael, "The Beginning of a New Chapter", in C. SRAMBICAL (ed.), *Lead me to Light, Divine Word Missionaries 1875-1975*, Divine Word Missionaries, Indore 1975, 95-100.

CHERUPALLIKAT, Xavier, "The Vicissitudes of the Local Clergy in India", in Native clergy in the young churches and the pontifical work of St. Peter the Apostle, Pontifical Missionary Union, Rome 1979, 63 – 68.

CHIRAPPANATH, A. K., "Gandhiji's Great Challenge", in *IMR* 1/1 (1979) 44 – 57.

CLARYSSE, L., *Father Constant Lievens, S.J.*, Ranchi: Satya Bharati, 1984.

_______, "Lievens and the Zemindari System", in *Sevartham* 10 (1985) 5-17.

_______, "Lievens the Missionary", in *IMR* (1985) 18-31.

COMBY, Jean, *How to Understand the History of Christian Mission*, trans. John Bowden, London: SCM Press Ltd., 1996.

CORREIA-AFONSO, John, "The Seventieth Anniversary of the Indian Hierarchy", in *World Mission* VII/4 (Winter, 1956) 408 – 502.

CROHAN, F. X., "Our Jubilarians. Rev. Fr. L. Cardon S.J 1884-193", in *Our Field* 10/8 (1934) 189-192.

DALTON, E. T., *Descriptive Ethnology of Bengal: Tribal History of Eastern India*, Calcutta: Office of the Superintendent of Government Printing, 1872.

DANVERS, F. C., *The Portuguese in India. Being a history of the rise and decline of their Eastern Empire*, 2 vols., London: W. H. Allen, 1894.

DAS, Bhaskar, *Social and Economic Life of Southern Orissa*, Calcutta: Punthi Pustak, 1985.

DA SILVA, José Carlos Gomes, *Orissa: Antropologia e Literatura de Viagens*, Ministero da Educação. Lisboa: Instituto de Investigacao Cientifica Tropical, (no year)

DEHON, P., "Religion and Customs of the Uraons", in *Memoirs of the Royal Asiatic Society of Bengal* 1/9 (1906) 121 – 181.

DELACROIX, *Histoire Universelle des Missions Catholiques*, vol. III, Paris : Grund, 1958.

DE MELO, C. M., *The Recruitment and Formation of the Native Clergy in India (16th – 19th century): An Historico Canonical Study*, Lisboa 1955.

DE MEULDER, E., *The Tribal India Speaks*, Poona: Indian Institute of Social Order, 1975.

DE ROSA, Giuseppe, "Un Saverio in minore. Costantino Lievens (1865-1893)", in *Le Missioni della Compagnia di Gesù* 29 (1943) 191-194.

DE SA, Fedelis, *Crisis in Chota Nagpur. With special reference to the juridical conflict between Jesuit Missionaries and British Government Officials, November 1889-March 1890*, Bangalore: A Redemptorist Publication, 1975.

DEWOLF, Lotan Harold, *Trends and Frontiers of Religious Thought*, Nashville: National Methodist Student Movement, 1955.

DHALL, Manjusri, *The British Rule: Missionary Activities in Orissa (1822 - 1947)*, New Delhi: Har-Anand Publications, 1997.

DHAN O. Rekha, "The Problems of the Tana Bhagats of Ranchi District", in *Bulletin of the Bihar Tribal Research Institute* 2/1 (1960) 136 – 186.

DOONGDOONG, Anthony, "The Kharias - Where do they come from?" in *Sevartham* 6 (1981) 100 - 110.

DORR, Donal, *Mission in Today's World*, New York: Orbis, 2000.

D'PENNA, B., "The SVD in Sambalpur then and now", in C. SRAMBICAL (ed.), *Lead me to Light, Divine Word Missionaries 1875-1975*, Divine Word Missionaries, Indore 1975, 69-75.

D'SA, Manoel Francis Xavier, *History of the Catholic Church in India*, 2 vols., Bombay: Furtado, 1910-1924.

D'SOUZA, Herman, "Caste Outcast", in *World Mission* 9/2 (1958) 78 – 92.

DULLARD, M., "Ignatian Spirituality and Chota Nagpur Mission", in *IMR* 7/1 (1985) 6-17.

DUVAL, Adrien, *Monsieur Mermier: 1790 – 1862*, Bangalore : S.F.S Publications, 1982.

EKKA, Alexius, "Hundred Years of the Christian Missions in Chotanagpur", in *ICHR* 33/2 (1999) 78 – 117.

EKKA, P., "Messianic movements among the Chota Nagpur Tribes", in *Sevartham* 4 (1979) 21-33.

EKKEN, E., "Il Padre Costante Lievens S.I.", in *Le Missioni della Compagnia di Gesù* 16 (1930) 333-334.

ESTBORN, Sigfrid, *The Church among Tamils and Telugus*, Nagpur 1961.

FAUSTO, Gregorio, *Cristo en Orissa*, Madrid: Editorial la Milagrosa, 1973.

FERNANDES, Walter et al., *Forests, Environment and Marginalisation in Orissa*, Tribes of India Series 2, New Delhi: Indian Social Institute, 1988.

FLEMING, Anthony, "Memories are made of these", in C. SRAMBICAL (ed.), *Lead me to Light, Divine Word Missionaries 1875-1975*, Divine Word Missionaries, Indore 1975, 76-79.

FUCHS, Stephen, *Rebellious Prophets: A Study of the Messianic movements in Indian Religions*, Bombay 1965.

__________, *The Aboriginal Tribes of India*, Inter-India Publications, New Delhi 1973.

__________, "Christian Mission in Tribal India", in *India Missionary Bulletin* 2/2 (1954) 71-77.

__________, "A New Mission Method for India", in *Verbum SVD* 13/3 (1972) 225-235.

__________, "The Concept of Salvation in Tribal Religions", in *IMR* 4/4 (1982) 361 – 372.

__________, "Priests and Magicians in Aboriginal India", in *Studia Missionalia* 22 (1973) 201–236.

__________, "Messianic and Chiliastic Movements among Indian Aboriginals", in *Studia Missionalia* 12 (1963) 85–103.

__________, "Die Evangelierung der Urstaemme Vorderindiens", in *ZFMR* 72 (1988) 187 –204.

__________, "The Conversion of the Tribals", in *IMR* 8 (1986) 102 – 114.

________, "The Importance of Anthropology for Evangelisation", in *IMR* 12/1 (1990) 5 – 16.

GENSE, James H., *The Church at the gateway of India, 1720 – 1960*, Bombay: St. Xavier's College, 1960.

GÓMEZ, Felipe, "Method in Mission: Lessons from the History of the Church", in *IMR* 11/1 (1989) 15 – 53.

GOUX, Lucien (ed.) "Il y a Cent Ans les Jésuites Belges sont arrivés à Calcutta", in Missi, (1960), Revue Missionnaire, Bruxelles. 1960.

GOREUX, P., *Conquérant d'Ames (Le P. Constant Lievens 1856-1893)*, Serie Indes NO. 14, Louvain : Xaveriana, 1930.

GRIGNARD, F.A., "The Oraons and Mundas. From the time of their settlement in India", in *Anthropos* 4 (1909) 1-19.

GRIGNARD, H., "A Few Suggestions", in *Our Field* 1/5 (1925) 53 –56.

HALY, George Thomas, *Appeal for the Sufferers by the Present Famine in Orissa*, London: Smith, Elder and Co., 1866.

HARTMANN, A., "The Augustinian Mission of Bengal (1599 – 1834)", in *AA* 41 (1978) 159 – 214.

HENKEL, Willi, *The Native Priesthood*, Aachen: Opus Vocationum, 1989.

HERAS, H., "Two Missionary Methods in the Nations of Ancient Civilization", in *Studia Missionalia* 4 (1950 - 51) 181 – 198.

HOFFMANN, J. B., *37 Jahre Missionär in Indien, tröstliche Erfahrungen beim Naturvolk der Mundas; der Misserfolg in der Missionierung höherer Kasten und seine Ursachen*, Innsbruck 1923.

________, "Principles of Succession and Inheritance among the Mundas", in *Man in India* 41/4 (1961) 324 – 338.

HOTA, Nihar Ranjan, "Human Sacrifices among the Khonds of Orissa", in *The Orissa Historical Research Journal* 8/3&4 (1959 –1960) 158 – 163.

HOUGH, James, *The Christianity in India from the commencement of the Christian era*, London: Church Missionary House, 1860.

HOUPERT, J.C., *Christianity in India Today*, Trichinopoly: The Catholic Truth Society of India, 1938.

HULL, E.R., *Bombay Mission History with a special study of the Padroado question*, 2 vols., Bombay: Examiner Press, 1927.

HUNTER, William Wilson, *Orissa*, 2 vols, London, 1872.

HUNTER, William Wilson, *A Statistical Account of Bengal, Singhbhum District, Tributary States of Chutia Nagpur and Manbhum*, vol. XVII, London: Trubner and Co., 1877.

JENA, K.C., *History of Modern Orissa. Orissa Studies Project No: 22*, Calcutta: Punthi Pustak, 1985.

JHA, Jagdish Chandra, *The Kol Insurrection of Chota-Nagpur*, Patna: Thacker, Spink and Co., 1964.

JOSSON, H., *La Mission du Bengale Occidental ou Archidiocése de Calcutta*, 2 vols., Bruges : Saint-Catherine, 1921.

_________, *Un Chef de Mission aux Indes. Le Père Sylvain Grosjean de la Compagne de Jesus*, Louvain : Museum Lessianum Section, Missiologique No. 22, 1935.

K.J., John (ed.), *Christian Heritage of Kerala*, Cochin: Fr. George Veliparambil on behalf of L.M. Pylee Felicitation Committee, 1981.

KANAKARAYAN, Paul, "How Missions Denationalize Indians", in *International Missiological Review* 8 (1919) 510 – 521.

KANJAMALA Augustine, *Religion and Modernization of India. A Case Study of Northern Orissa*, Indore: Satprakashan, 1981.

— (ed.), *Integral Dynamics. An Interdisciplinary Study of the Catholic Church in India*, New Delhi: Intercultural Publications, 1996.

_________, "Emerging Trends in Evangelization in India", in *IMR* 11/1 (1989) 61 – 78.

_________, "Divine Word Missionaries in Orissa", in *IMR* 10/2 (1988) 152 – 165.

KAROTEMPREL, Sebastian, "Trends in Evangelization in Asia", in *IMR* 11/1 (1988) 5 – 14.

KIERKELS, P. Leo, *To commemorate the sixtieth anniversary of the Catholic hierarchy in India and Ceylon: some hitherto unpublished and other relevant documents*, Bangalore: Good Shepherd Convent Press, 1946.

_________, *Golden Jubilee of the Apostolic Delegation in the East Indies (1884-1934): Retrospect and Prospects*, Bangalore: Belmont, 1934.

KOLLENCHERRY, Antony and MOOKENTHOTTAM, Antony (eds.), *150 Years. Missionaries of St. Francis de Sales*, Bangalore: SFS Publications, 1998.

KOOIMAN Dick, "Mass Movement, Famine and Epidemic. A study in interrelationship", in ICHR 22/ 2 (1988) 109 – 131.

KOONATHAN, V.P., "Certain Implication of Evangelisation in the Context of Tribal Religions", in *IMR* 15/3 (1993) 37 – 45.

_________, "The Religious Worldview of the Oraons", in *Sevartham* 19 (1994) 101 – 120.

KOWALSKY, N., "Die Errichtung des Apostolichen Vikariates Kalkutta nach den Akten des Propagangaarchivs", in *ZMRW* 36 (1952) 117 – 127, 187 – 201; 37 (1953) 209 – 228.

_________, "Die Errichtung des Apostolichen Vikariates Madras nach den Akten des Propagandaarchivs", in *NZM* 8 (1952) 36 – 48; 119 – 126; 193 – 210.

KOYAL, Sivaji, "A Critique of the Missionary Movement in Chotanagpur", in *ICHR* 19/2 (1985) 1845 – 1900.

KULLU, P., Tribal Culture-Religion in Practice, in *Sevartham* 19 (1994) 49-72.

KUZHUPIL, Devasia (ed.), *Souvenir. Installation of Rt. Rev. Dr. Kagitapu Mariadas MSFS, Bishop of Visakhapatnam*, Visakhapatnam: SFS Printing School, 1983.

KUZHUPIL, Devasia (ed.), *Visakhapatnam Province: Souvenir of the Silver Jubilee of the Province 1965 – 1990*, Bangalore: SFS Publications, 1990.

LAKRA, Christopher, "Ranchi Jesuit Mission: Evangelization among the Tribals", in Sevartham 23 (1998) 83-92.

LAKRA, John, "The Genesis of Man. The Uraon Myth", in *Sevartham* 9 (1984) 33-55.

__________, "Are Tribals Hindus?", in *Sevartham* 24 (1999) 5-18.

LATOURETTE, K.S., *The Great Century in Northern Africa and Asia. A.D. 1800 – A. D. 1914*, vol. 6, London: Harper and Brothers, 1944.

LOPEZ-GAY, Jesús, "The young Churches require an indigenous Religious Life", in Native Clergy in the young churches and the pontifical work of St. Peter the Apostle, Pontifical Missionary Union, Rome 1979, 18 – 20.

LOTAN, Harold DeWolf, *Trends and Frontiers of Religious Thought*, Nashville: National Methodist Student Movement, 1955.

MACPHERSON, S. Chaters, *An Account of the Religion of the Khonds*, London: William Clows and Sons, 1852.

MAHAPATRA, Sitakant, "The Meria Sloka: Songs of the Kondh accompanying the rite of Human Sacrifice", in *Man in India* 54/1 (1974) 73 – 82.

MANICKAM, S., "Grants-In-Aid and Christian Missions in the Madras Presidency, 1854 – 1947", in *ICHR* 13/2 (1979) 123 - 145.

MARTINA, Giacomo, *Pio IX (1851 - 1866)*, Roma: Editrice Pontificia Università Gregoriana, 1986.

MASSON, J., *Une Mission Belge au Cœur de l'Inde*, Bruxelles : Office de Publicité, 1946.

MATHIS, Michael A., *Modern Missions in India: A comprehensive study of the Apostolate in India and its difficulties past and present*, New York: The America Press, 1947.

MATTHIJS, F., "The Contribution of Chota Nagpur Church and its Impact", in *IMR* 7/1 (1985) 55-63.

MAYHEW, A., *Christianity and the Government of India*, London: Faber, 1920.

MEERSMAN, Achilles, "Can we speak of Indigenisation of the Catholic Church in India during the 19th Century? Padroado and Propaganda Compared", in *ICHR* 7/2 (1973) 75 – 82.

MENAMPARAMBIL, Thomas, "Emerging Priorities and new perspectives of Evangelization in Asia", in *IMR* 11/1 (1989) 54 – 60.

MENDIZÁBAL, Rufo (ed.), *Catalogus Defunctorum in renata Societate Iesu ab a. 1814 ad a. 1970*, Roma: Curia Generalizia S. I., 1972.

METZLER, Josef, "Foundation of the Congregation "de Propaganda Fide" by Gregory XV", in Sacrae Congregationis de Propaganda Fide Memoria Rerum. 350 Years in the Service of the Missions 1622 – 1972, vol. I/1 1622 – 1700, Rom: Herder, 1971, 79 – 111.

MINJ, M., "The Catholic Cooperative Society", in *IMR* 7/1 (1985) 42-54.

MIOTK, Andrzej, *Das Missionsverständnis in Historischen Wandel am Beispiel der Enzyklika 'Maximum Illud'*, Nettetal: Steyler Verlag, 1999

MIRANDA, J., *On the Formation of a National Indian Clergy*, Trichinopoly: The Catholic Truth Society of India, 1920.

MITRA, S.K., "Some Aspects of Social Transformation of the Tribals of Chota Nagpur in the 19th Century", in *ICHR* 17/2 (1983) 113 – 124.

MOGET, Francis, *Vagabonds for God. A Story of the Catholic Church in Central India 1846 - 1907*, Bangalore: SFS Publications, 1990.

————, *Shepherds for Christ*. A Story of the Catholic Church in Central India 1907 – 1960, Bangalore: IIS Publications, 1994.

————, *Early Days of the Visakhapatnam Mission: 1846 – 1920*, Bangalore: IIS Publications, 1997.

————, *MSFS Obituary*, Uchgaon: Fransalian Ashram, 1999.

MOHANDOSS, T., "Das Kastenwesen und die Kirche in Indien", in *ZMRW* 80 (1996) 255 – 264.

MOHAPATRA, B.N. and BHATTACHARYA, D., "Tribal-Dalit Conflict. Electoral Politics in Phulbani", in *Economic and Political Weekly* 31/2-3 (1996) 160-164.

MUKHERJEE, Prabhat, "Chakra Bisoyee: The great leader of the Kondhs", in *The Orissa Historical Research Journal* 7/3&4 (1958 -1959) 140 – 148; 8/3&4 (1959 –1960) 164 - 167.

MÜLLER, Karl, *Mission Theology: An Introduction*, Sudia Instituti Missionlogici SVD St. Augustin, No. 39, Nettertal: Steyler Verlag – Wort und Werk, 1987.

MUNDADAN, A. Mathias, *History of Christianity in India: From the Beginning Up to Middle of the Sixteenth Century (up to 1542)*, vol. I, Bangalore: Theological Publications in India, 1984.

MURRAY, J., *A Handbook for Travelers in India*, London: Thacker, Spink and Co., 1929.

NADER, Anthony, *The Ignatian land*, Calcutta: A. B. Cusack, 1925.

NARCHISON, J. Rosario, "Missionaries in India – An appraisal of Arun Shourie's Book", in *ICHR* 30/1 (1996) 45 – 72.

NAYAK, Ganeswar, "Transport and Communication system in Orissa (1866 - 1936)", *The Orissa Historical Research Journal* 39/1-4 (1994) 19 - 34.

NAYAK, Radhakant and SORENG, Nabor, *Kondhs: A Handbook for Development*, New Delhi: Indian Social Institute, 1990.

NEILL, Stephen, *A History of Christian Mission*. London: *The Penguin History of the Church 6*, 1990.

————, *A History of Christianity in India: The Beginning to AD 1707*, Cambridge: Cambridge University Press, 1984.

————, *A History of Christianity in India: 1707 - 1858*, Cambridge: Cambridge University Press, 1985.

————, *Colonialism and Christian Missions: Foundations of the Christian Mission*, London: Lutterworth Press, 1966.

————, *The Story of the Christian Church in India and Pakistan*, Michigan: Erdmans, 1970.

NEUNER, Josef, "Um die Bildung des Indischen Klerus", in *NZM* 14 (1958) 208 – 211.

OREA, M. R. and VAN EXEM, A., "The Gutigara Panchayat", in *Sevartham* 19 (1994) 19 –36.

PADEL, Felix, *The Sacrifice of Human Being. British Rule and the Konds of Orissa*, Delhi: Oxford University Press, 1995.

PADINJAREKUTTU, Isaac, *The Missionary Movement of the 19ᵗʰ and 20ᵗʰ centuries and its encounter with India. A historico - theological investigation with three case studies*, Frankfurt: Lang, 1995.

PATHY, Jaganath, "Colonial Ethnography of the Kandha. 'White Man's Burden' or Political Expediency?", in *Economic and Political Weekly* 30/4 (1995) 220-228.

PATON, William, "Relationship between Indian and Europeans", in *International Missiological Review* 8 (1919) 522 – 530.

PATRA, Kishori Mohan and DEVI, Bandita, *An Advanced History of Orissa (Modern Period)*, New Delhi: Kalyani Publishers, 1983.

PEREIRA, J. E. Friend, "Reminiscences", in St. Xavier's Magazine 2 (1930) 97-102.

PICKETT, Waskom J., *Christ's way to India's Heart*, Lucknow: Lucknow Publishing House, 1960.

________, *Christian Mass Movements in India*, Cincinnati: The Abingdon Press, 1933.

PLATTNER, F.A., *The Catholic Church in India: Yesterday and Today*, Bombay: St. Paul's Publications, 1964.

PONETTE, P. (ed.), *The Munda World: Hoffmann Commemoration Volume*, Ranchi: Catholic Press, 1978.

________, "Ranchi Mission: Before and After Lievens", in *IMR* (1985) 32-41.

________, "The Ethics of the Mundas", in *Sevartham* 4 (1979) 112-134.

________, "The Evolution of the Munda Tribe", in *Sevartham* 7 (1982) 3-24.

POOLE, Stafford, *A History of the Congregation of the Mission: 1625-1843*, California: St. Mary's Seminary, 1972.

PORUTHUR, Anto, "Mission in India", in *IMR* 10/2 (1988) 136 – 151.

PRADHAN, A.C., *A Study of History of Orissa*, Bhubaneswar: Panchasila, 1988.

RADAELLI, G., "Le Missioni Cattoliche di Mogol, Golconda e Idalcan alla meta del Secolo XVII", in *II Pensiero Missionario* 13 (1941).

RAJAMANICKAM, S., *The First Oriental Scholar*, Tirunelveli: De Nobili Research Institute, 1972.

REY, J., *Les Missionnaires de Saint Francois de Sales d'Annecy*, Thono-Les-Baines : SIPE, 1956.

ROSNER, Victor, *Ranchi Archdiocese*, Ranchi: Catholic Press, 1979.

________, "Pahan, Cult-Priest of Munda", in *Sevartham* 4 (1979) 57-72.

ROSSILLON, Pierre, *Sous les Palmiers du Coromandel*, Chambery : Direction du Missionnaire Indien, 1926.

________, *La Croisade pour la Conversion du Monde. Les Missionnaires de S. François de Sales dans l'Hindoustan*, Chambery : Direction du Missionnaire Indien, 1926.

__________, *Les Drammes de la Vie Indienne*, Chambéry et Paris : Direction du Missionnaire Indien et Libraire Saint-Paul, 1932.

__________, *Les Moissonneuses du Coromandel*, Chambéry et Paris : Direction du Missionnaire Indien et Libraire Saint-Paul, 1933.

__________, "Moeurs et Coutumes du People Kui, Indes Anglaises", in *Anthropos* VI (1911) 994 – 1009 ; in Anthropos VII (1912) 95 – 104, 649 – 662.

ROUSSEL, René Chanoine, *Un Précurseur : Monseigneur Luquet 1810 – 1858 des Missions Etrangères de Paris*, Langers : Société Historique et Archéologique, 1960.

ROY, Sarat Chandra, *The Mundas and their Country*, Calcutta: Jogendra Nath Sarkar, 1912.

__________, *The Oraons of Chota Nagpur: Their History, Economic Life and Social Organisation*, Ranchi: The Brahmo Mission Press, 1915.

__________, *Oraon Religion and Customs*, Calcutta: K.M. Banerjee, 1928.

__________, "Ethnography in Old Official Records", *Man in India* 2 (1922) 66 - 81.

__________, "The 'Gods' of the Oraons", *Man in India* 2/3 (1922) 123 – 140.

__________, "A new Religious Movement among the Oraons", in *Man in India* 1/4 (1921) 266 – 321.

__________, "The Administrative History and Land Tenures of the Ranchi District under British Rule", in *Man in India* 41/4 (1961) 276 – 323.

__________, "Magic and Witchcraft on the Chota Nagpur Plateau", in *Journal and Proceedings of the Asiatic Society of Bengal* 10 (1914) 349 – 353.

RUSSEL, R.V., *The Tribes and Castes of the Central Provinces of India*, 3 vols., London: Macmillan 1916.

RYAN, John, *A Padre Sahib on the Ranchi Hills. Fr. Constant Lievens SJ (1856-1893)*, Trichinopoly: The Catholic Truth Society of India, 1928.

SABAT, Kalpana Rani and DASH, Nirmal Chandra, "Socio-Economic and Demographic Profile of a Kandh village of Eastern Ghats", in *Man in India*, 76/2 (1996) 127 – 140.

SACHIDANANDA, "Culture Change in Tribal Bihar: Mundas and Oraons", in *Bulletin of the Bihar Tribal Research Institute* 2/1 (1960) 1- 135.

SAHAY, Keshari N., *Under the Shadow of the Cross: A Study of the Nature and Processes of Christianisation among the Uraon of Central India*, Calcutta: Institute of Social Research and Applied Anthropology, 1976.

__________, *Christianity and Cultural Change in India*, New Delhi: Inter-India Publications, 1986.

SAHU, N.K. et al., *History of Orissa*, Cuttack: Nalanda, 1980.

SALDANHA, Julian, *Patterns of Evangelization in Mission History*, Bombay: St. Paul Publications, 1988.

__________, "Conversion without Change of Community", in *IMR* 8/4 (1986) 242 – 252.

__________, "Documents Illustrative of Christianity in British India", in *IMR* 15/2 (1993) 59 – 63.

SAMAL, J.K., *History of Modern Orissa*, Calcutta: Firma KLM Private Limited, 1989.

SAULIÈRE, A., "Father Robert de Nobili", in *Clergy Monthly* 3 (1956 - 1958) 3 – 17.

SCHAFFER, G. M., "L'Apsotolo di Chota-Nagpore", in *Le Missioni della Compagnia di Gesù* 1 (1915) 291-293.

SCHREITER, J. Robert (ed.), *Mission in the Third Millennium*, New York: Orbis, 2001.

SCHUEREN VAN DER, T., *The Belgian Mission of Bengal. Among the Aboriginal Tribes of Chota Nagpur*, 3 vols., Calcutta: Thacker, Spink & Co., 1922 - 1925.

————, *Moral and Intellectual Uplift of the Aboriginal Races of Chota Nagpur, India:(A paper read before the East India Association, with discussion)*, London: East and West, 1900.

SENART, Emile, *Caste in India. The Facts and the System* (Trsl. Sir E. Denison Ross), London: Methuen & Co. Ltd., 1930.

SEUMOIS, André, "Local Clergy and Inculturation of the Church", in *Native Clergy in the young churches and the pontifical work of St. Peter the Apostle*, Pontifical Missionary Union, Rome 1979, 21 – 25.

SHARMA, P. DASH (ed.), *The Passing Scene in Chotanagpur. Sarat Chandra Roy commemorative Volume*, Ranchi: Maitryee Publications, 1980.

SHERRING, M.A., *The History of Protestant Missions in India: From their Commencement in 1706 to 1881*, London: Religious Tract Society, 1884.

SMITH, Vincent A., *The Oxford History of India. From the Earliest Times to the end of 1911*, Oxford: Clarendon Press, 1928.

SODERINI, Edoardo, *L'instituzione della Gerarchia Episcopale nelle Indie Orientali*, Roma: Tipografia A. Befani, 1886.

SORENG, Ignatius, *Odishare o Odiya Sahithyore Khristodharmo* (Oriya) (Christianity in Orissa and in Oriya Literature), Berhampur: Deepti Prasarini, 1998.

SPALLA, A., "Le Missioni Teatine nelle Indie Orientali nel Secolo XVIII e le cause della loro fine", in *Regnum Dei* 27/97 (1971) 1-76.

————, "Le Missioni Teatine nelle Indie Orientali ne Secolo XVIII e le cause della loro fine", in *Regnum Dei* 28/97 (1972) 265-305.

STANISLAUS, L., *The Liberative Mission of the Church among Dalit Christians*, Delhi: ISPCK, 1999

STERLING, Andrew, *Orissa: Its Geography, Statistics, History, Religion and Antiquities*, London: John Snow, 1846.

————, "An Account, Geographical, Statistical and Historical of Orissa proper or Cuttack", in *Asiatic Researches* 15 (1822) 163 – 338.

STREIT, Robert et al., *Bibliotheca Missionum*, vol. VIII, Aachen : Franziskus Xavierus Missionsverein, 1934.

SUYS, Antoine, "Un Vétéran du Chota-Nagpur. Le Père Cardon, S.J.", in *Revue Missionnaire des Jesuites Belges* 10 (1936) 17-20.

————, "Le jubilee d'or de Rév. Père L. Cardon Apôtre du Biru (1884 - 1935)", in *Revue Missionnaire des Jesuites Belges* 11 (1936) 118-121.

SWARO, Dasarathi, *The Christian Missionaries in Orissa: Their Impact on Nineteenth Century Society*, Calcutta: Punthi Pusktak, 1990.

TABOADA, Jesús, *En las Selvas del Ganjam: Los Padres Paules en el Indostan (1922-1947)*, Madrid: Editorial 'Pro Fide', 1948.

————, "The Catholic Church in present day India", in *World Mission* 7/4 (1956) 395 – 417.

TETE, Peter, *A Missionary Social Worker in India: J. B. Hoffmann, The Chota Nagpur Tenancy Act and the Catholic Co-operatives 1893-1928*, Documenta Missionalia18, Roma: Università Gregorian Editrice, 1984.

————, *The Kharias and the History of the Catholic Church in Biru*, Ranchi: St. Albert's College, 1990.

————, (ed.), *To Chota Nagpur with love and service: Pioneers in the Ranchi Jesuit Province. Ignatian commemorative volume*, Ranchi: Catholic Press, 1991.

————, (ed.), *They still speak to us: Pioneer in the Ranchi Jesuit Province*, Ranchi: Catholic Press, 1993.

————, "History of the Mission of Chotanagpur: Facts and Challenges today", in *Sevartham* 21 (1996) 47-67.

THANUGUNDLA, Solomon, *Structures of the Church in Andhra Pradesh. An Historico – Juridical Study*, Rome: PUU, 1976.

THEKKEDATH, Joseph, *History of Christianity in India: From the Middle of the Sixteenth to the End of the Seventeenth Century (1542-1700)*, Vol. II, Bangalore: Theological Publications in India, 1982.

THÉRÈSE, "La Mission des Filles de la Croix de Liége à Kesramal (CN)", in *Autour de Problème de l'adaptation, compte rendu de la Quartième semaine de Missiologie de Louvain, Museum Lessianum no. 6, Editiones et Publications*, Louvain 1926, 102 – 113.

O. M., Thomas, *Bishop Sevrin S. J. Great Benefactor of the Tribals and Champion of Freedom of Conscience*, Allahabad: The Christian Agency, 1963.

TIGGA, Leo, "Consideration on the Population of Chotanagpur", in *Studia Missionalia* 12, (1963) 182 – 187.

TIMMERMAN, C., "Ranchi Mission", in *In Xavier's Footsteps. A Jubilee Souvenir of the 4th Centenary of the Society of Jesus*, (1939) 102-110.

TIRKEY, A., *Evangelization among the Uraons*, in *IMR* 19/2 (1997) 5 - 14.

————, "Father Constant Lievens, S.J.: The Missionary", in *IMR* 7/2 (1985) 109-144.

————, "The Mission of the Jesuits in Chotanagpur today", in *Sevartham* 22 (1997) 35-42.

TIRKEY, Boniface, "Oraon approaches to God and Spirits", in *Sevartham* 7 (1982) 25.

————, "Oraon Ethical Values", in *Sevartham* 9 (1984) 57-68.

————, "The Adivasi and an Inculturated Theology", in *IMR* 7/2 (1985) 152-170.

TOPNO, Martin, "Spirits in the Life and Belief of the Mundas", in *Sevartham* 3 (1978) 5-26.

VADAKKEKARA, Benedict, *Origin of India's St. Thomas Christians: A Historiographical Critique*, Delhi: Media House, 1995.

VANDEN BOGAERT, Michael, "Social Transformation of a Tribal Society. Fall-out of Evangelization in Chota Nagpur", in *Sevartham* 11 (1986) 19-35.

VAN EXEM, A., *The Religious System of the Munda Tribe: An Essay on Religious Anthropology*, St. Augustin: Collectana Instituti Anthropos Vol.28, 1982.

_______, "Creation and Fall in Sarna Religion: A theological interpretation", in *Sevartham* 9 (1984) 3-10.

_______, "The Tribe, A Link with Singbonga", in *Sevartham* 4 (1979) 90-111.

_______, "The World and the World Beyond", in *Sevartham* 6 (1981) 51 – 83.

_______, "Evangelization in Chota Nagpur: Past, Present and Future", in *IMR* 7/1 (1985) 64-73.

_______, "Cultural Liquidation of the Tribe... and therefore Need of Inculturation", in *Sevartham* 15 (1990) 57-63.

_______, "Tribal Religions at the Crossroads", in *IMR* 3/2 (1981) 84 – 102.

VANHOUTTE, C., "The Future of Chota Nagpur", in *Our Field* 12 (1936) 273-284.

VERMEIRE, M., "Village Missions. Further Lights from Experience", in *Clergy Monthly Supplement* (1957) 334 – 339.

VIOLA, Roberta, "Lo Scisma di Goa al tempo di Gregorio XVI (1831 - 1846)", in *Clio* 37/2 (2001) 233 – 256.

WALLS, F. Andrew, *The Missionary Movement in Christian History*, New York: Orbis, 1996.

WALSH, E. James, "De Nobili, Classic Example of Accommodation", in *World Mission* 9/2 (1958) 93 – 107.

YILMAZ, Levent, "How history should be written; or, should it be written at all?", in *Storia della Storiagrafia* 38 (2000) 139 – 145.

ZALESKI, W., *The Martyrs of India*, Mangalore: Codialbail Press, 1913.

ZUPANOV, G. Ines, *Disputed Missions. Jesuit Experiments and Brahmanical Knowledge in Seventeenth-century India*, New Delhi: Oxford University Press, 1999.

Maps

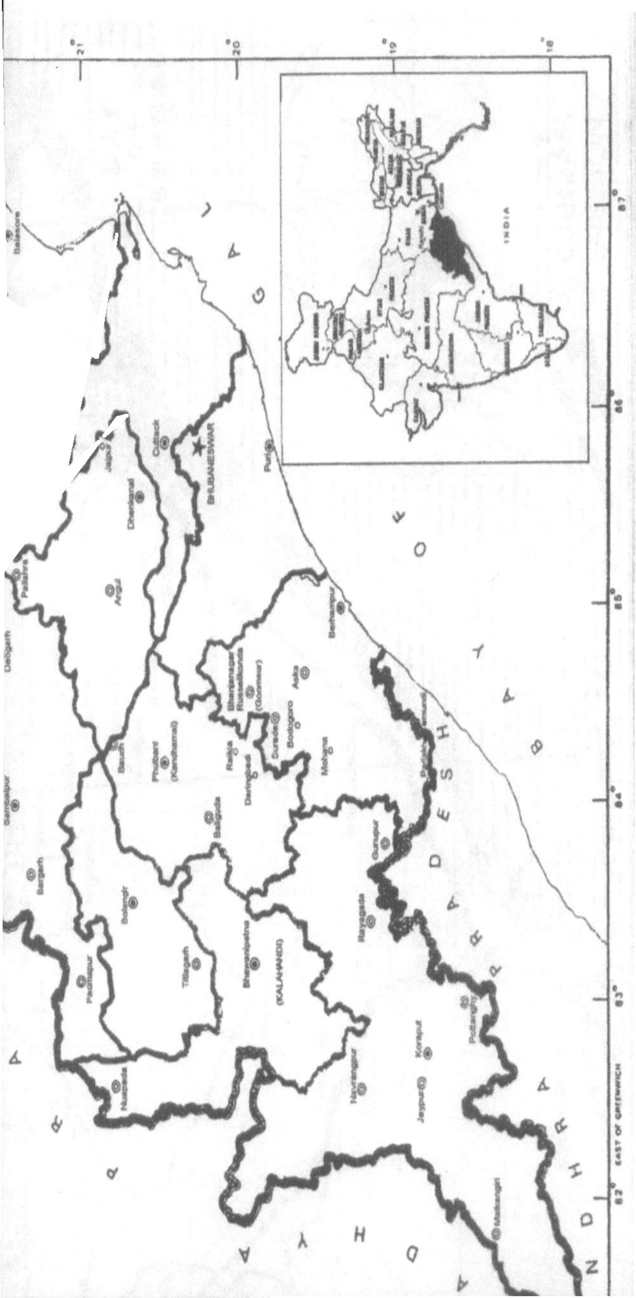

Balasore
Jajpur
Cuttack
BHUBANESWAR
Puri
Dhenkanal
Angul
Pallahara
Deogarh
Berhampur
Aska
Sambalpur
Bargarh
Boudh
Phulbani
(Kandhamal)
Baliguda
Mohana
Gunupur
Rayagada
Bolangir
Padmapur
Titlagarh
Bhawanipatna
(KALAHANDI)
Nuapada
Nawarangpur
Koraput
Jeypur
Pottangi
Malkangiri
INDIA
EAST OF GREENWICH

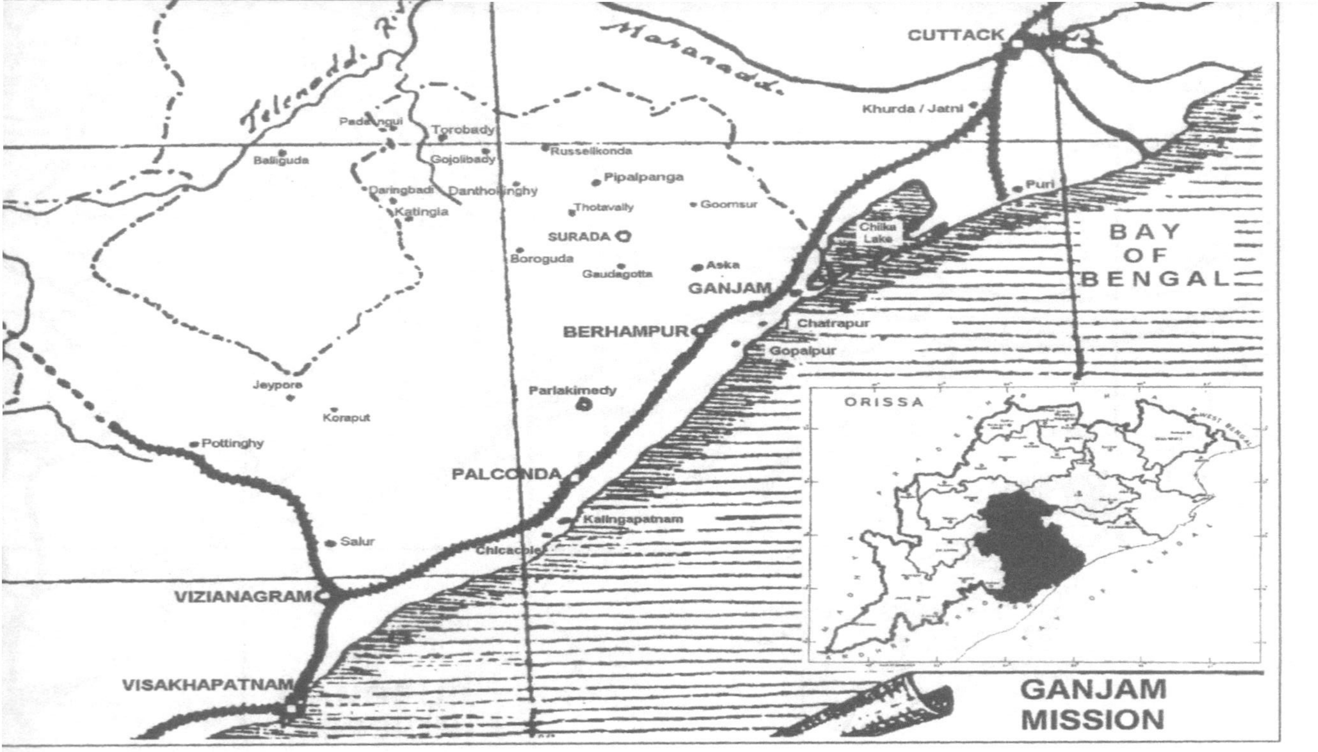
Mahanadi
Telengadi R.
CUTTACK
Khurda / Jatni
Puri
Chilka Lake
BAY OF BENGAL
Padangui
Torobady
Baliguda
Gojolibady
Russelkonda
Pipalpanga
Daringbadi
Danthollinghy
Katingia
Thotavally
Goomsur
SURADA
Boroguda
Gaudagotta
Aska
GANJAM
BERHAMPUR
Chatrapur
Gopalpur
ORISSA
WEST BENGAL
Jeypore
Parlakimedy
Koraput
Pottinghy
PALCONDA
Kalingapatnam
Salur
Chicacole
VIZIANAGRAM
VISAKHAPATNAM
GANJAM MISSION

GANGPUR MISSION
ORISSA
WEST BENGAL
Rourkela
Bisra
(Hamirpur)
Jorobahar
Kulunga
Gobira
Gaghari
Jaldega
Jharbera
Sarum
Gyempoli
Kumarkela
Talmundra
Garpas
Nuagaon
Kedopani
Kahapani
Pochara
Borokata
Sumbarmu
Kusumdegi
Tirma
Sahejbahal
Mundagaon
Barra
Betrenbasa
Palosura
Keano
Rengarbahar
Saigor
Degaon
Saumamara
Gaibira
Koraikela
Koira

www.ingramcontent.com/pod-product-compliance
Lightning Source LLC
Chambersburg PA
CBHW030648120726
47905CB00001B/117